MAGNIFICENT PRAISE FOR

HARRIETTE ARNOW'S
HUNTER'S HORN

from *The New York Times*:

"The truest feat of the imagination in fiction is to create and people a private world, which is what the good novel always does. To accomplish this with no apparent effort, so that the reader simply loses sight of how the thing is done in his enjoyment of what it is, may very well be called *the supreme test of the maker of fiction.*

"*It is a test Mrs. Arnow passes with flying colors.* She writes . . . as effortlessly as a bird sings, and the warmth, the beauty, the sadness and the ache of life itself are not even once absent from her pages. . . .

"A RICH PIECE OF FICTION . . . A CLASSIC."

HUNTER'S HORN

BY HARRIETTE ARNOW

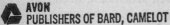
AVON
PUBLISHERS OF BARD, CAMELOT AND DISCUS BOOKS

AVON BOOKS
A division of
The Hearst Corporation
959 Eighth Avenue
New York, New York 10019
Copyright © 1949, 1976 by Harriette Simpson Arnow
Published by arrangement with the author.
Library of Congress Catalog Card Number: 78-67251
ISBN: 0-380-42283-2

First Avon Printing, April, 1979

AVON TRADEMARK REG. U.S. PAT. OFF. AND IN
OTHER COUNTRIES, MARCA REGISTRADA, HECHO EN
U.S.A.

Printed in the U.S.A.

HUNTER'S HORN

Chapter One

NUNNELY BALLEW ROLLED HIS QUID of tobacco from one thin cheek to the other and read slowly, following each word with a knotty brown finger, the printing on the can of dog food in his hand. Finished with the reading, he lifted grave, deep-socketed brown eyes. "Recken it's got a heap a salt in it?"

The grocery clerk shook his head. "It's not salted much, I guess; maybe not at all. How about some oranges? They'd be good for your family."

A quick faint smile like a ray of light brightened the sober eyes. "You ought to see my youngens. Four a liven and there ain't never been a doctor in th house." His eyes were wistful again, studying the dog food. "I recken this here ud be mighty fine fer a old hound when his teeth ain't so good."

"It's very highly advertised. You might try a can: ten cents."

"The sign says three fer a quarter."

"Oh, yes, if you're sure you want a quarter's worth," and the clerk's eyes wandered again to the bundle Nunn had left on the counter. He saw overalls and dress goods and small shoes, children's clothing bought against the fall. And he sniffed again with a wrinkling to his nose, and this time was certain that what he smelled was whisky on Nunn's breath; it was hard to tell through the screen of tobacco, but moonshine it would be; there was no legal liquor in the county.

"I recken three fer a quarter be $1 a dozen an $2 would be two dozen."

1

"Y-e-s. You sure you want two dozen cans? Why don't you try one can and then get more?"

"I need it right away. It'll soon be fine fox-hunten weather, an anyhow I mightn't git in town agin fore spring."

"I see. Anything else you need? There's a sale on dried beans."

Nunn shook his head. "Milly most generally raises enough to run us."

"If you buy two twenty-five-pound bags of sugar instead of the three ten-pound sacks you've already bought, you'll save fifteen cents on the fifty pounds."

Nunn rubbed one hollow cheek and considered the bags of sugar stacked by the lard and flour he had bought, then fingered the money in a hip pocket of his clean starched overalls. "I hate to trouble you," he said after a moment, "but I guess I'd better just take two bags a sugar stead a th three like I aimed. I first aimed to buy a dollar's worth a this dog feed, but seen as how I'm gitten two dollars' worth I ain't got enough left fer all this sugar."

The clerk totaled the purchases on a paper bag. "Eleven-thirty," he said, and silently took the $12 Nunn handed him. He did not go immediately to the cash register but waited while Nunn studied the candy counter.

"Throw in a quarter's worth a that all mixed up—don't fergit a stick a peppermint er so fer th baby, an plenty a them yaller an white things, an a heap a th red. An then I want some chewen tobacco—that with them blue shiny stars I think's th kind."

"That's a little sweetish."

"Milly, she likes it that away—make it about a quarter's worth." He reached in his hip pocket again, brought out a nickel. "Now if I'm figgeren right with this nickel, I've still got a quarter left—make it three more cans a th dog feed."

"Sometimes," the clerk said as he went for the other cans, "on a large order like this we make it thirteen cans to the dollar—that, would make twenty-nine in all."

"Now you are obligen," Nunn said, and smiled straight into the clerk's eyes, and when he smiled like that his eyes, which seemed an even, pure brown in repose, were brightened by the same red lights that shone at times in his brown, closely cropped hair. "I ain't never tried boughten dog feed before, but Lister Tucker—he's got a pretty good hound name a Sourvine—he likes it mighty well."

The clerk smiled back and for some reason his glance happened on the meat counter, deserted for the time by the lunching butcher. "Recken that hound would like a present of some nice fresh bones?"

Nunn's eyes glowed and widened. "Zing, he'd love you like a brother," he said, then went on more soberly, as if confessing a sin, "I've been aimen fer a long time to buy him some good beef bones—but you know how it is with a family an all."

"I know," the clerk said, and as he wrapped and tied the bones, the choicest he could find, he felt a friendly curiosity toward the man.

Yes, he came from the far end of the county; he had a place at the mouth of Little Smokey Creek on the Big South Fork of the Cumberland. Yes, he farmed some—not as much as he'd like. His old place, it had come down from his great-great-grandfather, had gone pretty much to brush and gullies, but there was still some good land left; besides more than a hundred acres of hillsides in cut-over timber there was a fair-sized piece, maybe sixty acres, of rolling almost level land set below the hills in a high creek valley—and a strip of river bottom too.

Oh, no, he hadn't been so lucky as to heir it; he'd lived there as a boy, but he'd gone away and worked in the coal mines and saved his money and bought it. No, he didn't like to work in the mines, but the pay was good. Yes, farming was all right; there wasn't hardly any fence on the old place now, so mostly he kept sheep. Yes, sheep were handy things to have; he had forty-four ewes and ewe lambs, and most of the year they could range in the government forest; that was mostly what there was around his place, timber land owned by the Federal government. Yes, late lambs sold pretty good this year. He'd had thirteen late ones to sell; that was why he was in town. Jaw Buster Anderson had brought the lambs in on his logging truck.

Yes, he fox-hunted considerable, his old Zing was about

the best hound in the country. N-o-o, fox-hunting wasn't
so much fun. Oh, some might hunt for fun, and a sweet-
mouthed hound was a pretty thing to hear, but lots of
times he got sick and tired of the business. Why, he
hunted to catch a fox, a big red fox; he'd hunted him a
long while but he was pretty certain he'd get him this
fall; and when he spoke of his hunting and the fox he
would catch, the easy talkative turn of a man who had
had a few drinks left him, the clerk did not doubt again
that he was cold sober.

Did the clerk mind if he stood in the door and looked
for Jaw Buster? Jaw Buster could get his truck to within
two miles of his house when the weather was dry.

The late summer twilight lay like a thin blue dust at
the bottom of the creek valleys before Nunn had
stored most of his load at Jaw Buster's house and started
home with the bones, a can of dog food, candy, tobacco,
and dry goods loaded in a grass sack over his shoulder.

He hurried, almost running down the steep rocky path
that twisted through spruce-pine trees and ivy bush over
the ridge side. When he came to the footlog over Little
Smokey Creek, he stopped and shifted the weight of the
sack and listened, and smiled his faint slow smile when
from somewere on the bench of rolling land on the other
side, children's voices in some kind of singing game
drifted down to him.

Out of the creek hollow the sunlight lay low and red
across a brushy weed-grown pasture where a bony, long-
legged cow, spotted and streaked in shades of red and
brown, bawled and move slowly up the path toward the
answering bawl from a calf. Nunn followed the path
through clumps of golden-flowered breast-high stickweed
and by giant ironweeds that trailed their nodding purple
heads across his hatbrim. He passed through a grove of
slender yellowing poplar trees that made a screen about a
little roof-sagging ramshackle building, in the days of his
grandfather a grist mill powered by the spring branch that
still flowed past its door.

The old mill, a barn now, fronted on a rutted wagon
road made of limestone blocks, hewn and fitted solidly
and evenly into the earth. The cow crossed the road and
stopped to drink from a moss-grown hollowed-out log
set under a trickle of spring water. Nunn stopped too, and

stooping with the sack on his shoulder, drank long and heavily from the upper end of the log. He broke a sprig of peppermint from the masses growing there, crushed it, sniffed it, spat out his tobacco, put in the peppermint, and drank again. Wiping his mouth with the back of his hand, he looked up and across an old wire fence patched with boards and twists of brush to the rusty tin roof of his house rising above the feathery foliage to a grove of black locust bushes. It was a big old gray house, built in the days of cheap labor and cheaper lumber, with seven great barnlike rooms, two wide stone chimneys, and double porches front and back. But the porch floors were mostly rotted now, and the late sun streamed through the broken-out windows of the empty upstairs rooms.

He laid down his load, for the heavy wooden gate on its one twisted hinge needed his two hands for the opening. The gate creaked and clattered, falling a little sideways, and at the sound a hound dog from somewhere behind the house began a deep joyful baying bark, and children set up a treble screaming, "Pop's got back. Pop's got back."

The big black and tan hound reached him first, a great gaunt ugly beast with a ribby chest and knotted legs and a sad scarred face framed by long hanging tattered ears. He came frisking like a pup, licking Nunn's wrists and his hands, sniffing his shoes, then leaping away and runing madly around him. "Aye, Zing you're not so old," Nunn said, then had eyes for nothing but the children as they came running down the gullied littered yard: Suse, the brown-eyed oldest, with Deb, the least one, on her hip; Lee Roy, all blue-green eyes and freckles and bones in his outgrown overalls; and Lucy, the least girl, a little yellow-headed six-year-old, not much bigger than a baby.

They all flung themselves upon him, hugging his knees, his arms, swinging onto his elbows, Zing running between their legs to lick his shoes and his hands again. "Zing caught possum, Pop. He come walken with it right at daylight after you left an laid it in th kitchen door. Did you git us any shoes? Did you sell th lambs fer a heap a money? Rosie rooted out a her pen. Mom finished cutten th corn in th little swag. We found some hicker nuts. Did you git some dog food fer Zing like you aimed? Did you bring any candy? Did you git Mom's sugar? Lucy stubbed her toe an it bleeded"; and Suse, rummaging in his jumper pocket, cried, "Did you git a paper, Pop?"

He did not try to respond to their chatter but hugged them all, then asked with something like disappointment, "Where's your mom?"

A woman's voice, light and breathless and touched with the same gaiety that filled the children's, called from above the house, "Law, honey, I never thought about you gitten back fore dark. They's a old hen—that old dominecker, th one th hawk pulled her tail feathers out—she hid her nest out an has hatched eleven diddles right here, nearly September; frost'll git 'em fer true fore they feather out, an I've been tryen to git em an put her in a coop, but they're all as wild as quail. Did you honesly git some canned stuff fer Zing like you aimed?"

"Hell, no. I sold Zing to a man in town," Nunn said and winked at the children.

"He's a lyen, Mom," Lee Roy called, squatting on his heels over the grass sack. "He's got somethen here in a can. I'll bet it's that dog feed."

"Zing's a goen to have somethen better'n dog feed tonight," Nunn said, and picked up the sack, one corner of which Zing was already sniffing with eager eyes and a watery mouth.

"Now what you got there?" Milly wanted to know, swooping down for the last flustered chicken and then dropping it with its beeping, yipping brothers into her tucked-up apron.

Nunn drew a bundle from the sack. "Bones, real fresh beef bones. The grocery clerk where I done my traden in town give em to me particular fer Zing."

She came and touched and sniffed the soggy bundle and smiled, "It's beef all right. I recollect th smell," she said, and went on to know if Nunn recollected that spring before Tom was born and Zing wasn't hardly a full-grown pup and Nunn brought home some beef late one evening, way after dark, and the weather was so hot it wouldn't keep till morning and they had set half the night eating beef, and how Zing went half crazy with the smell while it was cooking and they fed him one slice after another and he eat it fit to kill, and look, he recollects now.

Nunn nodded and his eyes slipped over his wife, from her forehead with the little wispy curls that always came when she worked in the field and sweated, down her thin child's body in a ragged faded dress and feed-sack apron to her bare brown feet. He hesitated, his eyes on her feet. Then he lifted the bundle out of reach of Zing's quivering nose. "Thet grocery clerk said these bones—they got a sight a meat on em—was clean an good enough to bile fer soup. Whyn't you cook em first, make you some soup with dumplens, an then give em to Zing?"

"Lord, I've already got a God's plenty fer supper with th possum an all, an the bones would maybe ruin fore mornen, an anyhow they'd be better fer Zing raw. He ain't eat nothen all day—Now, ain't you youngens shamed, eaten away on that candy an never a bite fer Deb. Pore little feller, did you git him any sticks, Nunn?"

Deb, who wouldn't be two till October, turned down the corners of his mouth and began a broken-hearted howling, waving his hands toward Nunn. "Lordy mercy, sugar tit, your ole pop ain't plum fergot his babe. Milly, hold these bones away frum Zing an let me take my Deb. You been a good man, Deb, an helped your mom cut corn?" Deb laughed and clapped his hands on Nunn's cheeks, then grabbed for a stick of pink candy Suse held up to him.

This was the first store-bought candy they had had since spring, when the wool was sold, and Deb's memory did not go back so far, and they all had to watch while he studied the stick and then took his first critical taste. They laughed at his look of pleased surprise, then set up a chorus of "It's good, Deb. It's good. Suck it hard an you'll see."

A little red calf with a white splotched face came down the yard and set up a bawling for the cow, who bawled in return and licked it through a hole in the fence. Milly looked uneasily at the cow, "Betsey, you'll be a teachen it in a day or two to suck you through th fence like you done th one last year, if'n I let you fool around together. Lee Roy, take this apron full a diddles an put em under a tub; the old hen'ull stay around till we can git time to catch her, an then come back quick with a milk bucket. . . . Suse, don't be a looken at them shoes an piece goods now; take em into th house. Lucy, go on now, take your shoes on inside, they've got to run you till spring."

Halfway up the yard, Suse whirled back toward her father, "Oh, Pop, ain't th speckled yard goods fer me an the yaller fer Lucy?—Oh, Lordy. Look, Pop, Zing's a tryen to

eat this." She snatched the flying length of cloth from
Zing only to have him seize a bundle of gray outing flannel that fell from her overflowing arms. "Make him quit,
Pop. Zing, you'll tear it up. Make him quit, Pop. It'll all be
ruined."

Milly giggled. "I ain't seen Zing so lively in a long time.
He's a sayen he wants that outen flannel fer him a shirt,"
she called, and handed the bones back to Nunn, took an
eight-pound lard bucket from Lee Roy, then opened the
gate to let the impatiently waiting calf to the cow.

Nunn strode up the yard. "Now, Suse, go put that piece
goods away; put it in th back room, with th doors shut so
th little youngens an th chickens won't git to it. Lucy's the
least, she ought to have first choice. Lee Roy, rustle
around now an git your kindlen wood. You all ought to
pull some weeds an pick up some apples fer Rosie. Rosie
was hungry, that's why she rooted out a her pen."

Twelve-year-old Suse came skipping through the
kitchen, folded lengths of the flowerdy goods floating from
her shoulders.

"Now, Suse, put that away before I speckle you; an if
your mom ain't got the table set fer supper, you pitch in
an help; she's tired cutten all that corn. Lee Roy, go on
now, git some kindlen wood; an Lucy, you start packen up
the night water; hurry, an then go pick up apples fer Rosie.
Lee Roy, leave be that can a dog feed. Now Zing, you
ain't a gitten these bones fer a while."

Holding the bones high above Zing's nose and stepping
carefully on the sound boards in the porch floor, he hurried into the long barlike room that served as kitchen
and dining room. He laid the bones on the high shelf
that held his fox horn, carbide light, pistol, Bible, and
other things the children should not have, then asked of
Suse, "Where's Maude? Funny she didn't come up to
her colt with Betsey."

Suse set a cracked plate on the table in hasty clatter.
"Lord, mercy, I plum fergot. Mom turned her in th garden to git some good picken, and I'll bet she's cleaned it
up, late corn, cabbage, beans, an all."

Nunn hurried out the door, Deb jouncing on his shoulder as he sprang from loose board to loose board. With
Zing sniffing at his heels, he hurried behind the house
where in the high grass and weeds under the black-

limbed twisted apple trees little red short-core apples
crunched under his feet and sent up a warm sweet cidery
smell. He looked uneasily out toward the stack of oats he
had put in the garden patch because the barn roof was
leaky, and began a kind of loud, friendly talking. "Hey
Maudie, where you gone to? Better git in now, and git
a bite a corn. We've got to go up th hill an bring down a
load a flour an slack coal in th mornen, Sunday or no Sunday, an if you're out there a eaten on one a them
oat stacks you'll git a whippen stead a feed."

From the crab-grass-covered garden patch set on a bit
of flat land above the house, a full-bodied, dark bay mare
with hairy fetlocks, long unclipped mane and tail, lifted
her head from between the cabbage rows and whinnied,
then came down to him. Nunn scratched her under one
ear. "Now ain't that nice, you a eaten away on that crab
grass an never a touchen Milly's late cabbage; but you'll
have to teach Jude to stay out a th sweet-tater patch."

Deb laughed and yelled and held out his candy
smeared hands, and Zing was playful as a pup frisking
about her heels; the long-legged colt shambled up and
began an impatient nuzzling of her bag, but the mare
gave notice only to Nunn. She rubbed his shoulders and
chest with her forehead, then nosed in his jumper pockets for the nubbins of corn she sometimes found there. "I
ain't got no corn now, Maudie, but come on down to th
little barn an I'll give you a little," and holding her forelock, he led her down to the road gate, turned her out,
and fed her three nubbins, using the rocks in the old road
for a feedbox.

When he got back to the kitchen, Milly had finished
dishing up supper and was standing by the table with a
sassafras fly switch in one hand and the can of dog food
in the other, and was trying to read, in the dim green
light that filtered through the hopvines over the broken
windows, the writing on the label. Lucy, with her mouth
and hands full of candy, pulled at her mother's apron
and wanted to know if Zing couldn't have a bone now.

"I'm hungry," Nunn said, and let Deb slide to the floor
and turned to the wash shelf.

"We've got a good supper," Milly said. "That possum
sure was fat, and I've got some sweet taters I dug about a
week ago an let lay in th sun till they're good an waxy."

Nunn slung his wash water into the yard and sat down at the head of the long narrow plank table covered with what had once been a red oilcloth, but now peeled in spots and faded pink from Milly's many scrubbings with strong lye soap. "An green beans with corn biled on top like I like, an okra, an tomaters, an gingerbread," he said, his eyes warm with their faint smiles. "Lucy, quit gommen around with that candy. You'll be haven another spell a worms. Th rest a you youngens leave that stuff in th back room alone an come on an eat."

Milly took Zing's bones from the high shelf and put them in the middle of the table, out of reach of the children who crowded around her with plates and lard-bucket lids. Deb and Lucy took their food and went to sit on the woodbox by the stove. Suse sat on an upturned fifty-pound lard can by her father and Lee Roy stood by his mother's chair, with Zing sitting in quiet dignity just behind him. Nunn alone ate heartily, giving full attention to Milly's food. The children ate candy, fed their suppers to Zing and Flonnie the cat, and looked eagerly and often toward the bones.

Lucy left her lard-bucket lid full of possum and sweet potatoes under the stove with Flonnie and came up to her father, pulling at his sleeve. "Zing wants a bone now, Pop," she begged.

"Aw, Pop, he's a setten there a looken so hungrylike. He knows them bones is fer him. Don't make him wait till we'uns is finished eaten like you allus do," Lee Roy scolded.

"Please, Pop, don't make him wait no longer," Suse begged, and rising quickly from her lard-can seat she grabbed the bones, and whirled and dangled them above Zing's nose. "Lookee, Zing, what Pop brung you."

The old hound leaped for them, balanced on his hind legs, and stood with his paws about the bones. The children screamed with laughter, and Milly, watching with a half smile on her tired sweat-stained face, wished the two in the graveyard could be here to eat candy and watch Zing eat his bones. Angie Mime was most too little to understand the taste of candy, but by now she would have been three going on four; and Tom, who would have been eight now, only two years younger than Lee Roy, had loved Zing like a brother. Children in heaven had fun of course, but somehow—it was a sin to feel that way, she knew—heaven sounded like it was full of the kind of people who wouldn't want youngens to have any silly fun, like kissing Zing the way Tom used to do.

Zing went under the table with the bones. The children followed and sat in a circle about him. Now and again one of them would pull Milly's apron or Nunn's overall leg. "You ought to see him. He knows it's beef all right. Lookee, he's a holden it like Rosie holds a big year a corn. He's a licken it, Pop, and his mouth's a drippen water."

Under the table there was a moment of silence and then a chorus of disappointed cries. "Aw, Zing, go on, eat it. It's better'n any hog meat. It come all th way frum town. It'll make you run faster. Eat it an then you can git that ole King Devil of a fox. Aw, Zing, you ole fool."

Zing slunk from under the table and went and lay down behind the stove, head down on his outstretched paws. His tail lay lank and sad and his ears drooped at the reproach and disappointment in the children's voices. When Lucy came after him with the discarded bones, he gave them a few halfhearted licks, then turned his head away and curled himself up, as if trying in his disgrace to be as small as possible. Suse stamped her foot at him. "Zing, you're th biggest fool hound in th country not to eat beef when you've got it."

"Shut up, Suse," Milly said in the low flat voice that even Suse minded. "An not another word out a th rest a you youngens. Zing cain't help it if he's old an not able to chew, an he never was much of a hand fer raw meat anyhow; if he had a been you all wouldn't be eaten possum tonight. We'll cook em, Zing, an it'll be fine."

She went over and picked up the bones and laid them back on the high shelf, and patted Zing. The old hound uncurled himself, opened his mouth in a big smile, and thumped his tail. When the children came swarming over him with cries of, "Good ole Zing, you're no heathen to eat raw meat," his tail thumped harder and he licked their faces turn by turn.

It was Suse who started it with a command of, "Give him the canned goods now, Pop. He's still hungry."

Children and Zing came on Nunn together, pulling at

his clothing and calling for dog food. Even Zing was young again, standing with his paws on the table and smiling at first one and then the other. Nunn held a glass of butter-milk in one hand and a wedge of molasses bread in the other and considered. "I aimed them bones fer his supper, an that dog food's to do him when hunten gits good this fall an King Devil runs agin."

Lucy began to cry. "I want to see th dog feed."

Milly picked up Deb where he had fallen asleep, face downward, with one of his new shoes in one hand and a stick of peppermint candy in the other, and took him to the fireplace room. When she came back she carried a lamp with a broken chimney mended with the gummed flap of an envelope. "They's a little coal oil left," she said, holding the lamp up to the light. "It'll burn long enough fer you to see to feed him. They've hurt his feelens so, an I guess he's hurt his teeth so a tryen to chew that bone that he'll never eat that plain corn pone I baked him fer his supper."

She lighted the lamp, took the can of dog food, and set it before Nunn and waited, holding the smoking lamp carefully, so that the brightest bit of light fell on the ta-ble directly in front of him, but Nunn hesitated.

"Please, Pop, please. I'm a dyen to see what it looks like," Suse begged.

"Is it pink an round like them wienie things in cans you bought up at Preacher Samuel's fer me when Deb was a baby?" Milly wanted to know.

"Pop, maybe Zing won't like it, an if'n he don't you'll have to take it back to town in th mornen."

Milly nodded. "Lee Roy's right. Zing, he ain't like them cur dogs in town. Maybe he's like Sue Annie an th rest a them that gits th give-away; they say people in town pays good money fer brown flour an grapefruits like they git, but Sue Annie said a bite a brown flour ud choke her to death. Well, maybe Zing's the same way."

Nunn smiled. "Oh, hell," he said and reached for his long-bladed pocket knife. Zing and Milly and the chil-dren watched over his shoulders and arms while he made two slashes at right angles across the top of the can, then folded the triangular pieces of tin outward.

"It's pink," Suse exclaimed, and Lee Roy stuck in a quick finger for tasting.

Nunn slapped his hand away. "None a that now. It's part made out a horse meat so they say."

"All th same it looks plum good," Milly said and bent nearer and sniffed the food. "Look at Zing. He knows it's fer him an he's a liken th smell."

Suse ran for Zing's pan, and Nunn put half the food into it and set it on the floor. Zing sniffed, lifted his head and looked questioningly at Nunn, then, while Milly and the children anxiously watched, began a silent, wolfish, gulping of the food.

Milly sighed with relief. "He's a sayen it's better'n eggs," she said, and after a glance at the height of the oil lamp, turned away to clear up the dishes.

When Zing had finished, Nunn went to the hand of dark tabacco hanging on the wall, stripped the midrib from a leaf, stuck the folded half of the leaf in his mouth, and went to sit by the kitchen door, where he could spit outside. Lucy came to sit in his lap. He leaned the bark-bottomed chair against the doorframe and watched Zing, who was still licking his long-since-empty pan, pushing it around Milly's feet as she stood by the stove, washing dishes.

"It's good to be home," he said, then glanced reproachfully at Lee Roy and Suse coming in from the back room. Lee Roy held his new overalls against his chest to measure their size, and Suse, with her new shoes on her stockingless feet, twisted her head first this way and then that, trying to see how the speckled yard goods looked over her back and around her shoulders. "Now, Suse, go put that away fore I beat th liven daylights out a you. Your mom's tired; go help her with th dishes; an Lee Roy, go clean th ashes out a th stove an lay your kindlen so th fire'ull be all ready to start."

Lucy nodded in his arms, her sleepy head pausing long and longer at each downward nod, until there came a nod when it stayed on his shoulder. When he carried her to one of the big beds in the fireplace room, he went, as was his custom on summer evenings, to sit on a great square of stone under the yellow horse-apple trees that grew in two wide-spaced rows straight out from what had once been the front of the house; there had been a flower-bordered walkway between, but potatoes grew there now, with grass left only along the edges. The rows

of trees faced west down the valley where the hills
opened more widely, forming far away an opening for
the lower sky shaped like a trough, where through the
summer months the sun set, and Nunn liked to sit and
watch the light fade and predict the next day's weather.

Not long after, Milly joined him and sat nearby on a
similar stone. Once, the square stones had been a part of
his great-grandfather's root house, but the root house had
caved in long ago and now the stones were handy things
to sit on. He reached in a hip pocket and brought out the
square of chewing tobacco set with blue shiny stars. "I'll
bet you thought I'd fergot," he said, "or run out a money
like I done this spring when I sold th wool."

"Aw, Nunn," she said, "I hadn't thought a thing about
it," but she took a chew and handed it back to him, "You
take some now. I don't feel right a chewen store bought
an you with nothen but short red."

He waved it aside. "You know I don't like th stuff. You
chew it all."

She insisted and they argued a little and at last Nunn
won, and Milly put the tobacco in her apron pocket with
a sigh. "You just pretend not to like it so I'll have it all."

They chewed and spat a time in silence. The red sunset light faded and fell lower in the west, merging with
the slowly rising river fog; one big star stood pale above
the Cow's Horn, a low long ridge of land that lay like a
bar across the end of the valley; the Cow's Horn was
across the Big South Fork over in Alcorn, but the river
was deeply hidden in a fold of hills, so that in the twilight
the Cow's Horn, with Willie Cooksey's barn silhouetted
against the red sunset, seemed near, and they could
hear the singing of the Cooksey children, a hymn long-
drawn and sad; the Cookseys were religious people and
their children knew nothing but hymns.

Over the fireplace chimney the last of the home-
coming chimney swifts circled and cried with sharp anxious twitterings. Under the apple trees the twilight was
deepening into darkness, and Nunn moved nearer
Milly. "Copperheads'ull be a crawlen. You'd better put
your feet on mine," he said, and Milly placed her bare
feet on his crossed-over brogans.

"Well, I'd better git at the sewen right away; it'll rustle
me some to git new dresses fer Suse and Lucy an a new

shirt fer Lee Roy to wear to th vaccinations up at Deer
Lick Church when county health comes," Milly said, and
went on after a time of silence, during which both
chewed and spat: "Nunn—reckon we could spare some—
jist a little—a that fifty pounds a sugar fer jelly; I been
wanten to make me some jelly—wild grape I think I'd
ruther have—fer th longest time."

Nunn stirred restlessly on the square of stone. "I hate
to tell you, Milly, but there ain't no fifty pounds a sugar."

Milly drew a deep, disappointed sigh. "Didn't—didn't
you git none atall, Nunn, after we kind a figgered it
out a th money, an sold that little black faced yoe lamb you
meant to keep?"

"Twenty pounds—I'm aimen to make some crossties
this fall an winter, an we'll buy a lot a sugar with some
a th money. I would a had money enough, but looks
like everything's gitten sky-high, an by th time I paid
Jaw Buster's haul bill, an th taxes, an bought ship stuff fer
th lamben yoes next spring—they have to have a little
ship stuff er I'd run out a corn, less'n I starved em, an a
body cain't handy starve a lamben yoe; an seemed like
shoes an dry goods cost more'n common, but I guess buyen
so much canned stuff fer Zing was where th sugar money
went. I hate it; I know you an th youngens git sick a
nothen but lasses an honey sweetenen."

She was silent a moment, then laughed her low breathless laugh. "Lord, don't feel so bad, Nunn. Maken jelly
over a hot cookstove would a been a lot a work anyhow,
an while I was a thinken an a plannen on it I couldn't figger out what I'd put th jelly in; ever last jar I've got is
full, an right now I could fill a hundred more with tumaters
an apples. Zing, he needs that store feed a lot worse'n
we need sugar. I git worried about him sometimes; he's so
old acten."

"He is old," Nunn said, "but come fall an cold weather,
he'll be all right. Somethen tells me we'll git King Devil
this fall."

Milly said nothing to that and both were silent while
they listened, smiling, to a young whippoorwill, trying
hard but never succeeding in getting farther than the
"Whip," though his father kept up a patient tutoring of
"Whip-poor-will, whip-poor-will."

There was a sudden scurrying behind them, and Zing

came with Suse at his heels. "I thought I heared a plane," Suse said, and jumped on a square of stone and stood searching the northern side of the sky.

Milly and Nunn listened, too, and heard a faint drone; somewhere up in the hill across the creek it sounded. Then Suse was jumping up and down and pointing. "There it comes; see it, like a star a walken, only redder, ever minnit it looks like it was goen to bump into th stars, only a body knows they're lots higher," and oblivious to Nunn's warning of copperheads in the grass and Milly's admonition to get to bed, Suse kept her eyes on the sky until even the drone of the plane was lost behind the fog.

She ran back to the house then without answering her mothers' advice to quit wasting coal oil and go to bed; the paper Nunn had brought from town would keep till morning. Nunn shook his head and smiled. "She is th readenest youngen," he said, with more of pride in his voice than complaint.

Chapter Two

━━

AFTER THE HARD, active work of summer crop making and canning, easy sitting-down work like sewing made Milly sleepy. On hot days like this she put the machine in the open door where she could look out across the fields to the Cow's Horn and feel the western breeze that drew up the valley. But still she wished the sewing were over and it was molasses-making time. It seemed like she'd been sewing forever on the gray outing flannel Nunn had bought for the children's underclothes.

Outside, the mid-September sun of early afternoon sent all but lizards and snakes into the shade, but inside the log-walled and weather-boarded house it was cool. The windows were covered with ancient vines—Virginia creeper, honeysuckle, hopvine, and ice vine; so that save through the doors the fierce white light of the summer sun never came fully, but was broken and reflected by the many moving leaves into a green-tinged shadowless light like that of some cave half buried in the sea, but scented at times with flowers and with dew lingering in the house shadow until long past noon.

Milly's foot moved sleepily up and down on the treadle of the machine that made a busy, bustling racket out of all proportion to the slowness of its motion. She glanced out between the rows of apple trees and wished Lureenie Cramer, her closest neighbor, would come and sit awhile and talk. She looked down at her work, stared a moment sleepily before she realized that she had sewed six inches on the seam of Suse's gray outing flannel petticoat with the bobbin empty.

She yawned, took her foot from the treadle, and for an

instant after the noise of the machine, the house and the sunflooded valley seemed still. Then one by one, but swiftly, the accustomed sounds of her world slipped into the back of her mind, where they made a little pattern, a pattern she noticed only when some part of it was changed around or missing. The ticking of the clock was loudest and most regular, and over all and under there was the buzzing of flies, and softer, the hum of bees and yellow jackets working over the mellowed quince and apples just beyond the yard. Somewhere in the upper garden a hen clucked to young diddles that answered with soft birdlike twitterings, and she thought sleepily that she must go chase the hen away before she got in the tomato patch and taught all her diddles to peck tomatoes.

She heard the half-grown guineas in the nearer corn swag, and from the big stone chimney in the fireplace room there was a murmuring and a whispering of wings and rustle of young bird bodies as the almost fullgrown chimney swifts stirred restlessly against the dark soot-covered stones of the chimney walls and looked up to the square of sky above and gave their imperative hungry cries. A third nesting of wrens twittered high up under the rotten eaves; the trickle of the spring branch came faintly from below the yard, and all around the valley sounded the bells of cows, grazing now again in the lengthening afternoon as the hill shadow crept downward.

She leaned forward, hands motionless over the bobbin slot, listening; she heard Sue Annie Tiller's big brindly Bess high up across the creek, and from up the valley a mile away, John Ballew's two iron-belled Jerseys; then down from the bench of sagegrass land above the garden dropped faintly the *clunk, clunk* of Betsey's bell, and after a moment the quick tinkle of the pretty bell she had bought for Lizzie, the black heifer, with egg money back in the spring, after Nunn said she could keep Lizzie and two cows. She smiled a little, taking out the bobbin and thinking on the black heifer; she'd always wanted two milk cows like the Hulls had, and never run out of milk and butter.

She stiffened with listening, mouth open, but relaxed soon, and went on with the bobbin. What she had thought was a sheep bell dangerous close to the corn was that new tinkly tin bell over in the Cow's Horn the Cookseys had bought for their mule when they turned him out after crop-making time. If the sheep came close, she'd have to send Suse and Lee Roy quick after school to run them back toward Bear Creek, or they'd be through the old brush and wire fence and into the cane and corn.

She sprang up, fully awake, the scissors crashing from her apron to the floor. She hadn't heard the little snoring kind of noise Deb made when he breathed, even when he was sitting still. She must have dozed off. It seemed only a minute ago that she had heard him in the fireplace room, talking to himself as he played in the ashes.

A dozen disasters rushed through her head as she ran to the fireplace room: snakes, the sinkhole in the nearer corn swag, the steep creek bluff, tempting now with wild grapes and clusters of bursting bittersweet. One of his new shoes, half filled with ashes, lay on the hearth near a cracked fruit jar he had been filling, using the shoe as a scoop. She whirled and ran back through the house and out the kitchen door, remembering she should have gone first to the spring. Lucy had almost drowned herself in the deep cool pool when she was about Deb's size, and would have if Zing hadn't noticed and pulled her out. But Zing was gone to school now with the older children.

She was halfway down the steep spring path, thinking fearfully of rattlers coiled for Deb in the tangles of brush and high flowering goldenrod, when his clear call of "Titty, Mom," came to her from somewhere on the other side of the road gate.

Heedless of snakes and her bare feet, she tucked up her apron and ran through the brush to the gate, calling all the while. He did not answer, but as she climbed the gate she heard his hard puffing breath from somewhere overhead. She found him soon in a close-limbed and brushy but high cedar tree on a limestone ledge above the water trough.

She drew a deep breath of relief and stood wiping her sweaty face on her apron, looking up at him. She saw that he had pulled off his overalls again and wore nothing but his shirt. Somebody might happen along and tell all over the country that Milly Ballew let her youngens run around disgraceful indecent. He was dangerous high from the ground, but when she coaxed him to come down he did not so much as look at her, but shook his head and said "Zing." He had found a place where he could sit on a fair-sized limb and peep between the thick branches and see the path to school, like a long brown twisting line laid in the sagegrass and little scrub pine of Nunn's pasture field.

"It ain't time fer Zing to git in yet, honey," she told him, and started up the tree, pride in his feat of climbing so high when he wasn't yet two pushing away her vexation at his lost breeches. In an instant she had him by one down-hanging foot and felt easier in her mind, and slapped him playfully on his bare bottom and said, "When a body's big enough to climb a tree, they're big enough to keep on their britches an quit th titty, th ole dirty titty."

But Deb smiled slyly and began trying to undo her dress, and Milly settled herself on one big limb with another at her shoulders and let him nurse. She took a chew of tobacco from a little tight roll of home grown in her apron pocket, for the store bought was gone now, and amused herself by spitting at a lizard on a rock and running one hand lightly through Deb's damp curling hair. It was the pale, almost silvery color of weather-wintered sagegrass under a weak spring sun, she often thought, but with a little of the same red that tinged Nunn's hair and Suse's and bloomed like a just opened poppy in Lee Roy.

People said Nunn's mother had been a real redhead when she was a girl. She had come into the valley from away, a smiling, redheaded, gray-eyed schoolteacher to board with Aunt Martha Jane; and before her school was half over she had fallen in love with and married Nunn's father, who had been down near the youngest of Aunt Martha Jane's thirteen children, and was no older than she—eighteen. He had died of typhoid fever not three months after his wedding day; but his wife, at Aunt Marthie's urging, had not gone back to her people but stayed on, living with the old folks until her baby was born, and when Nunn was only a few months old she had taken up teaching again; Aunt Marthie and Preacher Jim hadn't wanted her to, but maybe she had felt in the way and useless, because she couldn't so much as nurse her little sickly baby. Sue Annie always said that without his grandmother by to raise him, Nunn would have died before he sat alone; and when his mother married again

and went off to Missouri, Aunt Marthie and Preacher
Jim made her leave Nunn with them. They had raised
him, but he had never called them either Papa and
Mama or Granpa and Granma, but Aunt Marthie and
Preacher Jim, like the rest of the country.

Deb snorted and gasped for breath as he nursed, got
tired, and pushed the breast away and squirmed around
to look at the school path and whimper for Zing. Milly,
too, glanced up the valley and listened. The school had
been uncommon quiet all day. Old Andrew, poor fellow,
was getting so old that sometimes he never got there till
the day was half over, or he went to sleep at morning
recess and the whole school ran away to the woods and
stayed till time to turn out books.

She forgot the school in watching and listening to Deb
when he tried to nurse again; seemed like his tizic was
worse today. She thought of Tom and Angie Mime and
squeezed him with a hard convulsive movement; they
had both gone in the winter, and winter was coming on.
All the pleasantness of the cedar tree, cool and shaded
as it was by the big sycamore above the spring, was
gone. She had tried so many cures, but maybe it was like
Sue Annie said: he'd never get well without the white
oak remedy.

She sighed, thinking of all the work and materials the
cure required, and the day so hot; but she had put if off
too long already, and it was as good a time as she would
have. Nunn didn't think much of Sue Annie's cures, even
if she was the midwife—witchcraftery he might say—and
he was gone now to cut the river-bottom corn; if she hurried she could do it before he or the children got home.

Back at the house she quickly washed her face and
combed her hair, put on a clean starched dress, a new
feed-sack apron bound with a bit of the flowerdy dress
goods, and her seldom-worn visiting bonnet with the
stiffly starched pink brim and white-sprigged crown. She
washed and dressed Deb, hunted a large nail which, with
the scissors and her tobacco, she put into her apron
pocket, and carrying the Sunday patent-leather shoes that
Nunn had bought with the lamb money, she set out.

She had meant to take the school path as far as the
creek, for it would be shaded and shorter, but Deb ran
ahead of her into Preacher Jim's road, with its limestone

squares that were hot as fire even to her toughened feet.
She caught up with the child and ran carrying him across
the rolling field. The storehouse field it was always called,
because standing all alone, with high foundation posts
like legs in back and the front flush with a leveled-out
space in the hillside, was the good-sized, sound-roofed,
weatherboarded building that had once been Ballew Post
Office.

It was the newest and the best building on the place,
for not long before Aunt Marthie died she had had the
old log store and post office that had stood for nigh onto
a hundred years weatherboarded and roofed with tin and
two side rooms added. But after the old people died and
Nunn went away to work in the mines, Ballew Post Office had gone to Preacher Hull up the hill; and first one
and then another had rented the farm, for none of
Preacher Jim's children had wanted to come back to the
valley, though the old people had prospered there and
raised thirteen children with never the need for a bite of
store-bought meat or bread.

The strangers who came after had plowed up land for
corn, even the steep hillsides that Aunt Marthie had kept
in pasture, then hauled the corn away, and never gave
anything back, not even a fence rail or shovelful of manure; gullies came to the rolling fields and rocks, to show
like bones that come up under the skin of a suddenly sick
and starved cow, so that at last when Nunn had saved
to buy it, the land was hardly worth the buying.

Now, in what had once been a bluegrass and clover-
pasture field, smooth enough for a mowing machine,
scrub pine and sumac bush grew as high as the high foundation posts at the back of the old post office; but in front
there was a smooth and grassy place, shaded by three
silver maple trees people said Aunt Martha Jane had set
on her wedding day. Milly reached the shade of the trees,
the underside of their leaves showing white in the breeze,
and let Deb down to play in the short smooth grass under
them, for this bit of grass in front of the old post office,
where Maude and Betsey liked to graze at twilight, was
the only place on the farm where there were no weeds
and brush to hide a snake.

She dropped to rest on the white-clovered grass, but
Deb was up almost at once, pounding on the big white-

oak door with its pattern of nailhead stars. But the door was locked, the only door on the place with a lock and key that worked; and even when it was empty, Nunn kept it clocked. Milly held Deb up to quiet his screaming, and peeped with him through a big front window, glass broken, but guarded still with heavy iron bars wrought by Preacher Jim in the blacksmith shop that used to be about where the water trough was now.

Overhead the big tin sign creaked in the breeze and Milly looked up at the unaccustomed sound, then paused to read, as she had read many times, letters forming dimly through a coat of rust the words, "Ballew Post Office, General Store"; and in smaller letters, faint and faded, "Buy eggs—ginseng—hides."

She looked back again into the dusky, cobwebby interior of the store, where wisps of last year's corn fodder for the sheep clung to the worn poplar counter of the mail window and lay along the dry-goods shelves. And it seemed to her that in spite of the five winters Nunn had kept corn and fodder in the store, and even lambing ewes at times, there was still about the place a faint odor of cheese and sweet chewing tobacco and the fresh, starchy smell of new-dyed cloth.

The sharp smell of tansy came to her, and Deb held up a full-blown yellow tansy flower and three bruised leaves. Milly took it and sniffed; and it seemed like Aunt Marthie might stop her work in the store and come out and say something like, "My tansy has flowered uncommon fine this year. Could I give you a bundle to carry home to dry?"

Milly continued to sniff the tansy with half-closed eyes, and saw a big woman with wide-palmed, kind warm hands squatting down to set another tansy bed on some misty April twilight before the silver maple flowers had shed, and the stiffly starched bonnet she always wore would slide back from her head and little scattering curls of gray mist-dampened hair would bob about her cheeks and ears. Like as not the spring's first hatching of hidden-out diddles would be beeping in her tucked-up apron, and near her spreading skirts and petticoats a dominecker hen would be clucking and quarreling, not mean pecking quarreling, but contented-like, as if she knew Aunt Marthie, in spite of her full-handed life, always found time to be kind to everything, from the plants and animals under her care to a neighbor's sickly baby.

Milly glanced about for Deb and soon saw his silver head moving down Preacher Jim's road, for the road, wide as two wagons and smooth enough for a fine low car—if a car could have got to it—went on past the big barn, then curved down like a broad ribbon into the trees and brush of the creek crossing. The part across the creek and up the hill had long since been washed away, so that in muddy weather Maude could hardly make it with a sled; but here in the open field, the road still held a new fine look, and about it there was a waiting expectant air, as if a wagonload of mail or company of people might at any moment come out of the trees by the creek crossing and stop at the post office.

It was cool by the creek, and Deb wanted to stop and play in the water and look for minnows in the deep pool below the road, but Milly carried him firmly across in spite of his screaming, and reminded him that he must stay clean and pretty if he wanted to go to his Uncle John Ballew's and get the brace and bit so that she could bore a hole in a white oak tree and cure that old tizic.

Old John Ballew was not an uncle really, though she and half the country called him that. His father and Preacher Jim had been brothers, so that he was only Nunn's second cousin; but in kinship he seemed more like uncle than cousin, for he was old, nigh onto seventy, though his youngest boy, Silas, was not much older than Lee Roy, for he had married somewhat late in life a woman much younger than he.

In the days of Preacher Jim's grandfather, the Ballews had owned miles and miles of land along the Big South Fork and back to the headwaters of Little Smokey and Bear and Brush creeks, but John and Nunn were all that were left of the name of Ballew in the whole country; as far back as before the Civil War, the Ballews had started going west or into Texas. All of Preacher Jim's children had gone, and all of John's except the two youngest.

It seemed a pity that none of John's grown children had stayed, for he had almost a thousand acres of land, more than five times as much as Nunn, and in it were hundreds of acres of pine and poplar timber that people said were worth a fortune. He farmed a long level stretch

of land in the creek valley, and made money from sheep
and cattle that he let run most of the year on the forest
range, and now and then he could be persuaded to part
with a little timber, so that nobody knew how much
money he had; but now, even in his old age, he was always wanting to make more; and days in spring when the
old man's legs ached and good workhands were high and
hard to find, he would go into long quarrelings about how
his children were gone from the land and he was too old
to farm.

Milly hurried along the road that followed the windings
of the creek through the cool green twilight of a beech
and oak woods. But when she came to the place where
the creek valley widened and she could see Old John's
valley fields and houses and outhouses all neat and
straight and shining in the sun, she walked more slowly,
looking. John had always been the same careful kind of
manager that Aunt Marthie had been, and was held to
be the best farmer in the country, so that Milly was more
than proud that he was kin of Nunn.

The yard to his big two-storied house, built from his
own lumber, was neatly fenced and bordered with flowers, and even his beehives were set in rows, not scattered
all over like the ones at home. His fences were dead
chestnut rail, with no brush in the rows and no holes; all
his gates worked and none of his roofs leaked; nobody
had ever heard of his haymow being empty any more
than his corn crib.

After making certain that no one watched, Milly went
down to the creek and washed her dusty feet, and after
drying them with a handful of green maple leaves she
put on her patent-leather shoes and went on. She walked
a few steps, then stopped and stood with Deb on her hip
when from the big three-storied barn by the road she
heard John's shrill old-man's quarreling; she was always
borrowing things from him and never liked the job, and
especially hated it when he was in an ill humor. A hen
with ruffled feathers ran squawking around the barnyard
and Milly glanced up, wondering if a hawk had tried to
catch her, she was making such a commotion.

Instead of a hawk she saw John; he leaned from the
window of the third haymow with a pitchfork in his hand
and watched the hen and quarreled; he saw Milly and

smiled at her, a secret conniving sort of smile, like that
of a child up to some pleasant trick of meanness.

He motioned with the pitchfork for her to come up to
him. She went to the end of the long barn hall, climbed
a step flight of ladderlike stairs, turned, and started up
again with Deb in her arms, but stopped when she overtook a hen three steps above her on the second stair. She
was one of John's wife Nancy's fat, yellow-legged White
Rocks, and she went hopping up, pausing briefly at each
step, looking around and talking to herself with a soft
craaking and clucking, like a hen on her way to her nest.
A slight movement overhead caused Milly to look up.
She saw John standing motionless by the stair hole, holding his pitchfork and watching the hen.

He saw Milly, smiled the pleased sly smile with which
he had greeted her, and though he was a tall, spare-
fleshed, bleak-faced old man with gray whiskers and an
old man's thin gray hair, he looked young for an instant,
younger than Nunn. The hen hopped at last to the haymow floor, and as she stood there, squatting a little, debating aloud whether to walk or fly to her soft nest in
the hay, John shoved the hayfork under her so deftly
that her legs went between the prongs, and with the
squawking hen so trapped he lifted her, and moving
quickly as a young man, turned and pitched her through
the window. She fluttered squawking to the ground, and
after circling the barnyard in an addled sort of way, ran
up the lane toward the house, as if seeking the protection
of Nancy.

"Nancy's gone to her sick sister's fer th day," John
called after the hen as he leaned from the window and
watched with satisfaction; after sending a stream of tobacco juice in the hen's direction, he turned to Milly with
a gay pleased smile, "That'll larn her—makes eight I've
took off this mornen." He chucked Deb under the chin.
"I'll be a teachen you meanness, but I cain't hep it; I
wouldn't a cried if I'd a killed her."

He saw a curl of chicken manure contaminating a wisp
of hay at the foot of a mountainous pile filling half the
mow, and as he flung it through the window he went into
a long quarreling, telling Milly a thing that she and the
whole country well knew: his hatred of all hens in general and of Nancy's in particular; her hens seemed pos-

sessed of the devil; they ate up his corn, scratched in his meadows in the spring when young grass and clover were coming up, worried his bees, ruined the cider apples; but Nancy got all the chicken and egg money, and he didn't like chickens to eat in any shape or fashion, neither their dumplings nor their eggs. Now they had taken to laying in his third haymow, where he kept his best hay. He nodded viciously toward a split basket hung on a peg above the stair; every egg he found in his mow went into that basket and up to Samuel's store, and he gave the money to the church.

Milly listened while he quarreled on, her thoughts more taken up with his wealth of hay than his words. She stroked a wisp as she might have touched velvet. He noticed and his gray eyes lightened as he carried a forkful to the window so that she could the better see its perfection. "It's mighty nigh th prettiest greenest lespedeza hay I ever made," he said. "Hardly a leaf shattered—allus try to make green hay; stock does better on th green—but it took me twenty years to learn that." He looked at her. "You all ought to clean up some a them fields an make you some hay. They's more'n sixty acres there that Preacher Jim used to mow."

Milly said nothing to that; she was suddenly afraid he might ask her how much dog feed Nunn had bought with his lamb money; he wouldn't like his buying any; he thought Nunn ought to farm more and hunt less. She was silent, looking up the valley toward the creek gap where the folded hills broke apart, leaving a V-shaped opening against the sky. The folded hills, like the fields leading up to the creek gap, belonged to John; and men said that what he had there would ten times buy the rest of his farm, for the loose, black, never plowed soil of the upper creek held an almost pure stand of yellow poplar, a stand so pure that now in September, before many of the other trees had colored up, the poplar hills were like golden mountains against the deep blue sky.

"Them's pretty, ain't they," Milly said, nodding toward the poplar groves.

Old John looked up the valley, searching out his trees. He smiled on them, a more tender smile than he would have given any of his children. The smile died and his eyes were old, dwelling on his trees. "An when I'm gone

an my youngens git my land, ever last one a them poplars'ull be cut down an sold; they'll plow up th land on
them hillsides, an my place'ull go to brush an gullies like
your place now." He spoke slowly, with no anger, but with
a sad resignation, an infinite sorrow, as if this thought
were always inside him, under all his angers and his old
man's jokes and even the prayers he prayed in Deer Lick
Church, where he was a deacon.

Milly wanted to comfort him but could think of nothing
to say that was right for him. *Lay not up for yourselves
treasures on earth where*—came into her head, but she
did not say it. John didn't mind to part with his money,
but he wanted his trees to live on, a kind of everlasting
life for himself on earth; and now that he was old and
ready to die, it was for the first time sinking in on him that
he couldn't have what he wanted. It was a sin to want so
much and him a church member; he ought to give himself
to Jesus and learn to lean on Him.

"Maybe," she said, looking up into his face but speaking
without much conviction, "one a your two least ones'ull
love farmen like you do." John's boys, like Preacher Jim's,
had turned against the land as soon as they were old
enough to go away. "Or maybe," she went on, "that if'n
it does git run down, somebody'ull come along that loves
it, an fix it back like Nunn's allus aimen to fix back our
place fine as it was when—"

He looked down at her, and there was such scorn in
his glance that she stopped confused. "Nunn," he said,
and said it again with a kind of pity, "Nunn."

She mumbled something about having come to borrow
his brace and bit, and vowed she'd never ask him for another thing as long as he lived. But he was kind, giving it
to her with no show of hesitation, though he had to leave
his hen watching and go and unlock the tool house where,
in addition to his forge and tools, were many other things
he wanted kept under lock and key: today, a great pile of
juicy, well ripened little sugar pears. He pressed an apronful upon her in the silent surly way he had of giving things,
explaining, when she tried to thank him, that he'd rather
see them rot than have Nancy spend any more on sugar
and jars for canning; she had all her jars full and had
canned stuff now that was three years old.

Milly made a little silent Thank you to Jesus when

John did not ask her why she wanted the brace and bit. She promised to take good care of it and return it soon, and after exchanging the usual parting words of, "Better come an go along home with me," for his, "Whyn't you come in an eat a bite an stay all night," she hurried down the road home.

At the creek crossing she took off her Sunday shoes and sat a moment on a shaded sloping rock and wriggled her thin brown toes in the cool creek water, for already they smarted and ached from the unaccustomed confinement of the Sunday shoes. Then, leaving John's gift of pears by the shoes, she picked up Deb and the brace and bit and climbed up the steep creek bank, over limestone ledges and through tangles of underbrush and grapevine, until she came to a little bench of rolling, almost level ground thick with beech and maple trees and a scattering of smaller white oaks.

It was a secluded place, hemmed by the steep creek banks below and a brush-grown limestone ledge above. She put Deb down and studied first one and then another of the little white oak trees. At last, after much walking about, she selected one that seemed straighter and stronger than the others. Then, shading her eyes with her hand, she squinted down the creek toward the sun, then across, and then up the valley. "I recken this is about th south side now, Debbie," she said. "Sue Annie says it's got to be on th south side if'n th cure works," and she stood him straight against the tree and took the nail from her apron pocket and scratched a line on the bark even with the top of his head.

Deb watched with round wondering eyes while she fitted the bit into the brace and bored a hole in the middle of the scratched line. When she had bored through the bark and tiny chips of white wet wood had begun to come out, she stopped and with the scissors she had brought cut a fair-sized lock of Deb's hair. This she pushed into the hole with the nail, then drove the nail in deeply with a stone.

She stepped back and looked at the driven nail and the lock of hair with satisfaction. "I ought to ha done that a long time ago," she said, to the child, "fer soon as that little tree grows an lifts that lock a your hair higher than you are, that ole tizic'ull leave you sure as shooten."

She cut a fresh chew of tobacco, picked up the brace

and bit, and took Deb by the hand to lead him down the
creek bank, when all her motions stopped and she stood
stone-still, her hand clutching Deb's fingers with a hard
excited grip that more than words meant, "Be still."

She had heard nothing, had seen nothing she could
name; but some sound so faint she heard it without knowing, or something glimpsed briefly as a picture remembered from a half-forgotten dream made her know that
some live thing was near. Automatically she dropped the
brace and bit, picked Deb up, and looked all around for
snakes. During the summer she had killed many copperheads, and in huckleberry-picking time had killed a big
rattler on this very hillside.

Her swift survey of the ground was done in an instant
and her glance swept higher and wider, through the beech
and maple trees on the hillside, past a stunted cedar, then
on to the limestone ledge above. She stared at the ledge
and gave a low excited gasp, her eyes excited and fumbling, trying to see this thing both as a whole and piece
by piece.

The sun was low in the sky and a little behind her; its
rays fell slantwise of the ledge and made a fiery brilliance
of sweet gum and scarlet dogwood leaves and the red and
gold of maple brush growing in the rock. In one place the
leaves on the ledge seemed richer, redder, like the flaming
bush that appeared to Moses in the Bible. But the thing
was not leaves but a great red fox, brightened by the sun.
As if eager for her to see him, he stood still among the
red leaves, head turned toward her, fiery-tipped brush
lifted, mouth open, happily, pleasantly, like a dog.

He looked at her and she at him; he was so close she
could see the hairs in his eyebrows, the teeth shining in
his half-open mouth, and the green fire in his coolly appraising eyes; with the red sunlight playing on his lifted
tail, his back and shoulders, his pointed ears, he looked
big, big as a half-grown cow; she looked more closely and
saw the nicked left ear. King Devil it was, the fox Nunn
had chased in hatred and in anger for the last five years;
he had stolen from every family in the country, led many
hounds to their death; every hunter was sworn to kill him;
many had seen him long enough to learn his mark, but
never had he stood so still and close as this. With a last

cool glance, he dropped his head and picked up a hen, one of Nancy's White Rocks, fresh-dead and limber.

She wanted Deb to see. She looked down to see if he did see, but Deb was watching her, looking straight up into her face. She pointed to the ledge and Deb looked at it in perplexity. There was nothing there to see but a lot of pretty red and yellow leaves. She stared a moment stupidly, then climbed up on the ledge and parted the bushes with her hands and looked at the damp mossy earth above the stone; she could see nothing. That was like King Devil, to go without sign or sound. He might be below her or above in the woods watching her, or miles away, gone to his den that no foxhound had ever been able to find. He might have stood and watched her all the while she bored the hole. She picked up Deb and the brace and bit and hurried down the creek bank as she would have hurried from a haunted house. Not a dozen feet from the rock on which she had sat to pull off her shoes she found a single white feather. She shivered and hurried faster, eager to be away from the creek that lay now in the long blue evening shadow of the hill.

Chapter Three

MOLASSES-MAKING TIME was hard, but Milly liked all parts of it. She liked to strip the long broad blades from the shining silvery stalks, tie the blades into bundles, and think of Lizzie, the black heifer, feasting on cane fodder with the little black calf that was to be working hard on two teats while she milked the other two. She liked to stand on tiptoe, reaching for a head of cane, golden-brown and shining, she and the cane head alone an instant together against the blue-silk sky; then she was pulling it down, cutting it off, and feeling a second's sadness at the emptiness of the sky; but the sadness was forgotten in reaching for another and knowing that up and down the cane rows grew a mounting pile of chicken feed—and Milly in her mind's eye would see fat hens pecking at the cane heads on a snowy day.

Lucy and Deb put the cane heads into piles; Nunn came behind with Maude and the sled; he cut two rows at once, threw the stalks onto the sled, and hauled them away to the molasses mill, where Suse and Lee Roy helped Sue Annie and Blare Tiller feed and grind and cook and keep the blindfolded old mule borrowed from John going round and round. Blare and Sue Annie took their pay in molasses; making to pay for the loan of the mill and the mule and the cooker.

Two solid weeks of fine clear molasses-making weather and they were almost through. Milly wished it could go on forever; molasses-making weather was no good for fox hunting, and Nunn was never gone from home at night and never ill turned by day, as he often was when he'd

32

been out half the night or maybe till sunrise and came home with nothing but a sleepy head and a tired Zing.

But one night about the middle of the week, while they were eating in the early twilight, Jaw Buster Anderson's horn call came floating down from near Preacher Samuel's. Soon the Tiller horns were answering. Rans Cramer blew almost immediately after, and there was a talking back and forth of horns, with Rans's young unmarried brother Mark joining in from across the river and holding for them to come to the Cow's Horn—a joke on a fox horn—for there'd never been a fox in the Cow's Horn.

Zing ran to the road gate and whined, following the different horns with turnings of his head, then he loped back to the kitchen and stood whining behind Nunn's chair, and when Nunn gave him no answer he ran to the high shelf and stood with his paws on the wall under it, reaching and reaching until his eyes were level with the shelf. He scolded the silent horn there with shrill sharp barks, then turned and looked over his shoulder at Nunn and scolded some more.

The children laughed and Nunn swore and scolded the old dog, but hardly were the quarrelsome words out of his mouth before he was up, taking the horn from the high shelf. He stood in the kitchen door and blew, the long crying call of the yellowed silver-banded horn echoing and reechoing through the twilight.

The others answered and it was agreed they should all come by Nunn's place. If the hounds found a good scent, the men would go up to the Pilot Rock to listen. Nunn sat in the kitchen door with Deb on his lap and took his after-supper chew of tobacco and lowed Zing might run a little, but he'd be pretty certain to do his listening from the yard. Mostly, he reckoned, Jaw Buster wanted to see how Rans's pup would do in a race, and that fool Rans had been plaguing them all to have a hunt for his pup in spite of the dry weather.

There couldn't be much of a race; the night was no good for hunting. An almost full moon, red-stained with autumn, was already showing above the pines at the head of the creek. Worse yet, a warm wind out of the southwest dipped at times into the valley, and it would take a rare good hound, after a fresh strong scent, for any race to last long through the dry blowing leaves.

Rans Cramer came first, whistling as he walked the short-cut path he had made through Milly's upper garden. His young hound came frisking ahead like a playful friendly child. He ran to Nunn in the kitchen door, jumped on his knees, licked Deb's face, and then, his tail waving like a triumphant flag, frolicked into the kitchen. The eating table was not completely cleared of supper, and much to the delight of the children, Del—short for Delano— leaped into the middle of it and began eating wolfishly from a bowl of fried sweet potatoes rich with lard and honey.

Rans, running up behind, swore at the pup; the children screamed at Del to hurry up and help himself, and Nunn jumped up and jerked the bowl away and roared at Milly, "What th hell, woman, a standen a letten him eat that stuff—he'll kill hisself a runnen full a that greasy grub."

Milly took her hands from the dishwater and wiped them on her apron. "Aw, Nunn, cain't he have somethen? He acts so hungrylike," and she came over and stood with the others and studied the young hound in the dim yellow light from the lamp on the high shelf. She scratched his throat. "He's a sight like Zing used to be when he was young. Recollect?"

And the old hound, hearing his name spoken by Milly, came from his listening post in the kitchen door and put his paws on the table and studied his son with a lifting of his grizzled brows. The young hound, after making certain there was no more food on the table, wagged his tail at Zing, barked a little, and rubbed him with one paw like a playful kitten.

Zing twisted his head away and growled. Milly patted him. "You're jealous, Zing, a thinken on how you used to be young an pretty like that, with no gray hairs an no scars."

Rans cursed the pup again. "They'll be a fighten in a minnit if I don't watch out. He don't know how to act. I have to keep him chained up all the time."

"Why?" Nunn asked.

"Th damn fool ud be off a chasen rabbits, an I ain't hardly had him long enough to know what he'd do."

Nunn shook his head in pity over the pup and felt like picking a quarrel with Rans. It was hard to have any man but himself cursing around his womenfolks under his own roof, and especially Rans, who with his big blue eyes and black waving hair thought he was too good-looking to abide by the rules that held other men. "Th pup's got to learn about things," he said after a moment. "Leave him chase rabbits. Zing allus has when th notion struck him an there was nothen else to chase—if'n it ain't in a hound dog to leave everything fer fox scent when he finds it, you cain't put it in."

He looked into Del's eyes, big and brown, full of something a man couldn't name; not sense exactly, more than sense, something Rans and a lot of people didn't have. A hound could have a deep chest and strong straight legs and a fox foot and a cold nose, but if he didn't have that other thing he wasn't any good.

Milly smoothed Del's ear; Zing had been like that once, clear black and tan and yellow, and smooth as silk all over, not streaked and grizzled and scarred like he was now. Nunn never seemed to recollect it now, but Zing had been hers. One night after work Nunn had stood in the kitchen door of the mining shanty, with that warm kindling light in his eyes that had used to come often, and said, "Here, Milly; I've brung you a contraption guaranteed to keep all the varmints away frum that garden an them chickens you're a goen to have soon's we git back to th Old Place."

Zing had wriggled under his jumper then and she had understood his gift and been so tickled she'd squealed out loud as Suse and Lee Roy. She'd been plaguing him for a dog for a long time. It was before Tom was born and when Lee Roy was two, and that night he'd cried to sleep with Zing. She caught her breath with sharp realization; that was eight years ago; eight years was old for a hound that had hunted hard.

She looked at him for reassurance and fell into a long musing as she stared at him. Among the bigger scars in his ragged left ear, there was a little whitish thickened place where the hair was thin. One rainy day, when she was washing in the kitchen, she'd heard Zing cry out from the middle room like death was upon him; she had gone running and found Angie Mime, hardly able to stand alone good, but with plenty of teeth, hanging onto Zing's ear like a turtle; she recollected she'd come near slapping Angie Mime, and had cooked a big piece of fresh pork shoulder specially for Zing. And once Tom had set fire to his tail; there was a little scar near the end a body could find if they looked hard.

"I wouldn't let him git wind a King Devil yit fer awhile," Nunn was saying. "If he's real good, he'd keep up close to Zing an run hissef to death; and if'n he's jist middlen, he'll git so plum disheartened a tryen to unravel th scent he'll quit."

"If he quits I'll kill him," Rans said.

Del looked up at Nunn and laughed at his owner's threats.

Nunn picked up one pinkish and uncalloused paw and squeezed it gently. "Rans, he's big, but he's still a baby; he ain't through growen; he'll mebbe be bigger'n Zing. I don't think I'd let him run atall with other hounds in a race—mebbe not fore spring—treat him good, buy him some dog feed, an you'll have a rare good hound," he advised, his dislike of Rans forgotten, his eyes kind and warm over Del.

Rans smiled slyly. "Mebbe he'll run so good tonight I can double my money thout keepen him till spring—they's one wants him mighty bad. An anyhow he'll jist have a little fun tonight. I heared you say a comen through th garden th race couldn't last long."

Nunn shook his head. "Fox-hunten ain't never fun to a serious-minded hound. A body cain't never tell—King Devil might come out; he could ruin a pup like this, break his wind in one race, er kill him even."

Rans laughed with a flashing of his big white teeth. "Nunn, you've tried so long to git King Devil, an no luck, you're a thinken he's bewitched. You're afeared this pup'-ull git him and put Zing to shame."

"I wisht to God he could; but he won't," Nunn said.

Zing had left the group around the table and gone back to the door and resumed his listening, ears lifted, great eyes following the sounds that came to him from across the creek. Lister Tucker with his Sourvine and Jaw Buster Anderson with his Speed—the only two hounds in the country that could begin to match him in either wind or nose—were coming over the hill. He heard the men stop at Sue Annie Tiller's gate and call for the Tillers—Blare and Joe C.—each with two worthless hounds, mostly mouth. They came on, the men walking the post-office path, the six hounds talking a little, now scattering, now together, sniffing, circling, hunting.

He glanced back at Nunn and whined impatiently for him to come on, but Nunn was smiling at some trick of Del's. A sound faint, but full of music, like a bow drawn once across the muted D string of a violin, came to him smothered and low from John Ballew's high-growing poplar timber up the creek.

He leaped through the door, lifting his own clear bell-like voice in his hunting call. Sourvine was telling him he'd found fox scent, not a straight trail, but scent that might be unraveled.

At Zing's call Del lifted his head and looked through the open door. He stood for a second on the table, the laughter gone from his eyes, a wonder coming there, and then an eagerness. Nunn glanced over his shoulder at the empty door, then at Rans with a question in his face. He flung out his arm to grab the pup, but Rans's hand came between. Del shook his head like a child rousing from sleep, looked up into Rans's face, and realized he was un-chained and that foxhounds were calling, and with a mighty bound that took him over Lucy's head and half across the kitchen was gone into the darkness.

He never noticed Milly running after him and crying, "Come back, Del; oh, come back, Del; come on, puppy."

In a moment his unformed puppy's hunting cry was mingling with the others racing toward Sourvine's call, but Milly, turning from the door, was crying now to Rans, "Don't let him go. Please, don't let him go."

And Rans laughed at Milly, his eyes like blue marbles in the lamp-light. "Hell, he's a foxhound. I tell you, you're all skeered to death he'll git King Devil."

Lee Roy said, "Damn," and followed Nunn and Rans outside.

Milly went back to dishwashing. "He was a pretty pup," she said, "jist fer th world like Zing."

And Lucy asked, "Ain't he comen back, Mom?"

"I wouldn't lay money on it."

"Is it King Devil he's a chasen?"

"I recken so."

Suse stopped with a dish half dried and studied her mother sharply. "You sound like you knowed somethen, Mom."

Milly took her hand from the dishwater and pushed her hair back with her wrist, and tried hard to look like a woman who'd just been talking—maybe she ought to have told Nunn about King Devil by the creek, not half a mile from where Sourvine had found the scent tonight. She stared down into the dishwater, remembering: so big he had looked, his whole body red and glowing somehow, like hickory embers; the green fire of his eyes when they looked at her, the easy sassy way in which he had picked up the big dominecker hen and vanished; just vanished like a red devil's ghost; and now it would be about like him to run on a windy, witchery moonlight night like this, when a young and untrained pup was in the race.

She heard the men start up the hill toward the Pilot Rock. Lee Roy went up the outside stairway, and from the upstairs room over the kitchen climbed into the attic, where by leaning out the gable window he could hear almost as well as the men up the hillside. As soon as the dishes were finished, Suse followed him. Milly would have liked to have gone too, but Deb was whining by her knees, and ahead of her was another hard molasses-making day, so that her conscience would hardly let her lose sleep in such idle foolishness as fox hunting.

She blew out the lamp to save the oil and rocked Deb to sleep in the moonlight-brightened fireplace room, but now and again she broke off her song and held the rocker still to listen; and often she heard the hounds, first near and then far, with Zing, as always, in the lead; mad happy he sounded, as if the scent was hot like a fire under his nose. Once she thought she caught the wild eager note that came into his voice only when King Devil ran, and holding the drowsy Deb in her arms she went to stand in the door for better listening; but he had swung low into Brush Creek Valley that lay behind the Pilot Rock, and she could hear nothing but the clamorous haroufing of Drum and Blunder and Lead and Drive, the four Tiller hounds still on this side of the mountain.

She sighed and thought of the young pup, Del—back awhile she had heard him, his happy puppy's broken barking, clear though with the promises of a deep sweet-toned bay when he was a full-grown hound.

Deb went to sleep at last; and though it was past her bedtime, Milly felt too restless to sleep, and remembered with something like joy that the churning was ready to do, a job that would give her an excuse to sit outside and listen.

She carried the big red cedar churn to the chopping block under the walnut tree, and sat in the pattern of moon shadow the leafless branches made, and churned, but absent-mindedly, with long pauses between strokes of the dasher. For more and more in the snatches of cry she heard from Zing, she understood that King Devil ran, or maybe she only imagined it—she was too low in the valley for good hearing, and the gusty wind at times drowned out all other sounds, even the big-mouthed Tiller hounds, who instead of following the scent around the mountain like Zing and the other honest, hard-working hunters, even young Del, waited or possum-hunted while the leaders made a complete lap, and then cut to the sound of Zing's voice and thus put themselves in the lead with a great saving of breath and time.

The gable window by which Suse and Lee Roy listened was just above Milly, and when the Tiller hounds cut, Lee Roy called down to her, "Them damned Tiller potlickers, they'll be th ones to git King Devil if he's ever got; some day they'll cut in so fer ahead a Zing they'll turn around an grab King Devil by th nose when he sails by."

"Do you recken it is King Devil?" Milly asked in a calling whisper.

"Zing's a sayen it is," Lee Roy said, and added worriedly, "I'm afeared this'ull go hard with Zing. It's too hot fer a long run—an he ain't run enough yet to be in good shape. Little Del's a killen hissef already—he's a fallen behind."

"They'll be all right," Milly comforted. "Mebbe it ain't King Devil—an enyhow, whatever it is, them hounds cain't hold th scent on a high windy ridge."

"King Devil knows they's a young pup a runnen an he'll swing him around th hillside till he's dead," Lee Roy said.

"He was a pretty pup," Milly said, and sat with lifted dasher, listening. The hounds were on the side of the mountain, running high under the cliffs that led up to the Pilot Rock. Then, on the flank of the mountain back of Lureenie's, where the lowlands of Smokey Creek ended and the long sweep of Pilot Rock Mountain rolled downward to the river bluff, Zing's voice told they were coming down, down in a long straight sweep that for an untrained pup on King Devil scent could mean only one thing.

Lee Roy was jumping up and down and crying, "He's a headen fer th roll over, but he cain't fool Zing. Del's ahead. Golly! He'll go over," and Lee Roy, unable to sit still, scrambled out of the attic and down the stairs.

Milly herself ran up to the upper garden, but could hear nothing except men's voices on the hillside; loudest was Rans's bragging, "Del got ahead; Del got ahead."

She heard Nunn's voice and Blare's; they came to her in a low murmuring, and she did not hear Rans again; the fool, somebody had to tell him what had happened. She worried a moment for Zing, but that was foolish; he had been in the lead that night, not two years back, when King Devil had led Lister's Nannie Belle, a seasoned bitch and smart, but tired that night, to her death on Kelly's Point.

She stared out across the moonlight-flooded valley into the black shadowed hills, listening. She heard nothing but the wind in the ridge pines, the muted voices of the men, and after a moment hurried back to the churning. She made a few more licks, then carried the churn into the kitchen and sat in the square of moonlight falling through the open door and churned until the butter gathered. She wasn't afraid outside in the moonlight, but she kept seeing in her mind's eyes the red laughing fox; he had smiled at Del, given him a happy time around the mountain, then had laughed and run down the mountain, taking his time on the steep hillside. He had taken short little steps to make the scent strong, and gone clean to the bluff edge, and most likely right on the edge he'd set himself down and reached over and patted the underside of the overhanging rock with his paw; then he'd turned sharp and gone along the very edge, so close that mostly the wind held him up. Or maybe he had back-tracked and sat and watched and grinned as little Del leaped to his death on the rocks below.

She listened, but could hear nothing except Lee Roy climbing the outside stairs, grumbling because Nunn would not let him go to help hunt Del. She had finished the churning and started to the spring for a bucket of cold spring water to wash the butter when she heard Zing on Schoolhouse Point, an angry, baffled, disgusted Zing, circling, crisscrossing, sniffing, fighting to unravel a tangle of scent laid in the dry windy leaves. Zing, poor fool, didn't know, while he worked so hard at unraveling, that as far as catching King Devil this night, the race was over.

Milly washed the butter by moonlight and went to bed, but Suse and Lee Roy continued to listen by the attic window. After a long while they heard Zing find a fresh, straight trail, and then the running of all the hounds until they were far away, somewhere past the creek gap. They waited, but did not hear again.

Lee Roy went to his bed in the middle room, but Suse watched and listened by the window a long time. She liked to watch the round moon fight its way through the thin scraps of cloud flying from the west, and feel the warm wind on her hair, hear its broken thunder in the pines. It would be fun to run and run forever, like King Devil through the windy, silvery night, to be held by nothing, worried by nothing, not even God and the neighbors.

The wind flung leaves through the windows and now and then brought a strong smell of honeysuckle flowers, for all around the tumbledown root house the honeysuckle Aunt Marthie had set was blooming as if it had mistaken the warm fall weather for a second spring.

After a while she heard Mark Cramer's horn—the race had been so short that he had never crossed the river—not calling a hound but blowing a tune; Mark's horn had a singing, restless, stirring kind of call that somehow matched the moonlight and the restless southwest wind and the loose blowing leaves. Mark was like that; wild, wilder they said than Rans or any of his brothers; and his horn seemed to say that he wouldn't stay in the Cow's Horn forever, working on his father's farm, going round and round and getting nowhere like a blindfolded mule in a molasses mill. Maybe he wasn't going home now, but to a dance somewhere; people said he danced well, but not often; at most dances he played the banjo or the fiddle for the others; it would be fun to dance to Mark's banjo music, even if it was a sin.

She heard men's voices on the Cow's Horn road, and listened carefully, her body tense as Nunn's when he listened for Zing. After a moment she relaxed and hurriedly tiptoed downstairs to bed. Nunn was coming home sober; they were all sober, sad sober, and Del was dead, broken on the rocks below the bluff.

She heard the kitchen door squeak and knew it was Nunn and tried to breathe as if she were asleep. It seemed a long time that she had been waking at Nunn's home-comings, even as far back as the nights in the tar-paper shack above the mines, when they all slept in one room and Nunn worked a night shift. He would come home and stand washing by the fire, and the lamplight from the one lamp in the kitchen, where Milly would be gone to fix him a snack, would lay a square of yellow light through the door; and he would stand there sometimes, washing his pale white body with its ropy muscles, or by the cracked stove with the broken door that let streaks and squares of red light fall over him; and sometimes she would have to tuck her head under the bedclothes, for she could not re-member when she hadn't known from Milly's teaching that it was wicked for a little girl to look at a naked man per-son.

And after a while, from under the dirt, Nunn's face would come out gray-looking and tired, and Milly would move about him, taking away dirty clothes, warming clean ones by the fire, soaping his back sometimes, listening to what talk he had, saying little herself, except always to re-mind him when he was in a black bitter way of feeling, as he often was, that this work in the mines wouldn't last for-ever; soon there would be enough saved to buy the farm. The Old Place they called it then; and gradually Nunn would get into a better humor and they would talk on of how fine the Old Place would be and how they would fix it up until Aunt Marthie Jane, looking down from heaven, would smile to see what her grandson had done with her farm that others had sent to rack and ruin. And talking so, they had not seemed to Suse like her father and mother of the daytime, but two children, Nunn and Milly, hardly stronger than herself, two timid children playing house in some secret place where the bigger, rougher children would not find it and tear it down.

But tonight there was no nighttime Nunn; only her fa-ther, home from the hunt, sober and tired, tiptoeing gently, so as not to awaken Milly and the children.

The setting moon was low and pale over the long swell of the Cow's Horn before Zing came home, walking slowly and stiffly down Preacher Jim's road like a tired, defeated old man. His tail drooped and he took long, stiff, carefully chosen strides, as if each step hurt. He stopped at the water trough and took a few slow laps and stood a moment looking up toward the black silent house, silhouetted against the pale west, as if uncertain whether to go on to it or let his tiredness lay him down by the water trough.

After a while he went on, up the yard path and through the kitchen door, always left ajar for him. He took his place under the eating table and lay down slowly and carefully, like a rheumaticky old man getting into bed. He lay on his side with his neck and his head and his legs on the floor. Flonnie the cat came from under the stove and lay down between his outstretched legs, snuggling in against his belly. Ordinarily he would lift a paw and touch her, or by bending his legs draw her close to him, for they had slept much together, but tonight he did not move.

The bed in the middle room squeaked and in a moment Lee Roy came feeling his way through the dark to the eating table. He got down on his knees and reached until he touched the old hound, and whispered, "Are you all right, Zing?"

Zing gave one slow feeble flop of his outstretched tail and sighed a long sigh of utter weariness and dejection. Lee Roy patted him. "Don't feel bad, Zing. It looks like King Devil wuz made to be chased—never caught," and added, "You allus watch out, Zing. Look at what happened to pore little Del tonight."

Milly came soundlessly in her bare feet. She knelt by the child and the hound and put a hand on each and whispered, "Lee Roy, it's a good while fore daylight. You git on back to bed. You'll be a waken your pop—an he needs his sleep."

Lee Roy rubbed Zing's forehead. "He's a feelen awful bad, Mom; too wore out to lick hissef."

"Sh-h-h, he'll be all right. I'm a goen to warm him some milk."

Lee Roy went reluctantly back to bed. Milly lighted the lamp and noiselessly built a fire in the cookstove. Then, holding the lamp carefully so that the light did not shine directly onto his face, she went over Zing's head and body for possible cuts and bruises, and picked up each hard calloused paw and looked at it, and in his left hind foot there was a gravel bedded deeply down between the toes. She worked it out gently, talking to him in whispers all the while, and once he opened his swollen bloodshot eyes and looked at her and flapped his tail.

She threw a shovelful of coal on the kindling wood and went down to the spring for the night's milk kept cooling there. Mostly she warmed milk for Zing only in rainy weather when after a long run he came home stiff and wet and cold, but he seemed so tired tonight.

When she had lifted the bucket of milk from the spring, she stopped and looked up at the sky. It was the time she liked best, the black time after moonset and before dawn, when for a little space she was alone and the world belonged to her alone, for it was the time when all things slept; even the children were quiet and asleep, and all the work and the thousand worries that hounded her through the day seemed sleeping too, and she would feel young and strong and fresh, like all the years had never passed and she was a child again, looking up in wonder at the stars with their mystery come back again, and all the mystery of the world that belonged with childhood—the scrape of a windblown leaf against a stone, the black hills against the stars, the creek fog seen dimly, like a milk-white river rolling slowly past the little barn; the black east with the morning star, and in front of her, like it was stuck into the hill across the creek, the Big Dipper riding straight upon its handle.

She remembered that her new-started fire would burn out if she didn't hurry, and turned up the path, but at the kitchen door she paused and looked once more at the Big Dipper; fall rains and winter would come soon, and for whole weeks together she wouldn't see the stars; the stars would be covered with mist and fog even when the days were clear.

And Nunn would hunt and hunt some more; all his heart would go out to the hunting of the great red fox.

Chapter Four

LATE NOVEMBER'S GENTLE misty rains made a fog across the hills and brought a grayness and a stillness to the bright noisy leaves. The good hunting weather, the dog food, eggs, fresh milk, and scraps of meat from a just killed pig all gave new life to Zing. This fall, as on other falls, he was the pride and the wonder of Little Smokey Creek country.

Stretched on boards on the middle room upstairs were one red and two gray fox skins; and no man, not even Blare Tiller who was forever claiming an injustice done him or somebody else, disputed Zing's right to them. Always the first to give tongue and be off among a dozen hounds clamoring in anger and bewilderment over a puzzle of crosses and backtracks in a half-cold scent, he was likewise the first to hole the fox or bring it down.

On nights when there was no fox hunting, he would sometimes slip away, and hours later Milly would awaken to his soft whine. She would get out of bed and go to the chopping block were Nunn skinned all the game Zing caught. Once in two weeks' time there was a fat possum, and twice a big coon, dead but never much mangled, with the skin good enough to save and the meat good enough to eat. Lee Roy would come too, and no matter how wet or cold it might be, the two of them would skin the animal by lantern light and praise Zing for his smart ways and thank him for the meat.

Both Milly and Lee Roy liked better the nights when Zing was a tree dog than when he was a foxhound. On fox-hunting nights Nunn would come home, cursing Zing and every other hound in the country with ugly bitter oaths that made Milly pull the covers over her head and hope that Aunt Marthie Jane wasn't listening. Night after night and never a scent of King Devil. He was still in the country. One of the Townsends on the other side of Bear Creek had seen him walking down the road past his barn, walking along and taking his time like somebody going to church, the Townsend had said; and big as a full-grown sheep he had looked to be.

And every day for almost a month something had taken one of Nancy Ballew's big fat White Rock hens. They'd hear one short, smothered-down squawk, sometimes not even any cackling from the others; he slipped up so slyly nothing saw him, not even the hen he killed. Nancy and John and the two boys and the white feist dog would go running but never find a thing, often not so much as a feather. Sometimes the hen squawked in the woods above the house and sometimes down by the barn, and once right in the yard, not fifty feet from where the feist dog was sleeping; and sometimes she never squawked at all. Nancy would count her hens, and there'd be another missing—even the guineas were going.

It was enough to make a body believe that red fox was kin of the witches, John said one day while he and his neighbors squatted by the road in front of Samuel's store and waited for the mail.

"He'd never come that close to Zing," Nunn said with pride.

John watched a long shaving curl up from the piece of yellow poplar he was whittling and shook his head. "But Zing'ull never git him, though. He's like me; he's gitten old. It'll take a young hound to git King Devil—if he's ever got."

Jaw Buster Anderson eased his back against an apple tree. "But take a young hound now; why, he'd be old fore he could begin to learn all King Devil's tricks, an Zing, he knows em."

Willie Cooksey, who disliked Nunn—mostly people said because Preacher Jim had never thought much of the Cooksey generation—nodded and grinned. "But looks like it's taken perfessor fox hunter here a right smart spell to live up to his brags. It's goen on five year now, ain't it, Nunn, since you run that first race on King Devil, an you was goen to have that red fox hide come Christmas?"

"I ain't fergitten," Nunn said slowly and evenly. "Less'n

that red fox is a witch er a devil a flyen though th air, I'll
be gitten his hide one a these days. Zing's jist now a
learnen how he runs."

"Aye, Lord, Nunn," John spoke kindly, "everbody
makes brags that sooner er later he has to swaller. I recollect onct—was fore I jined th church an settled down
more'n forty year ago—I bragged that a team of mine
could pull a heapen wagonload a coal up Little Smokey
Creek hill in muddy weather, an I tore my wagon up an
beat my mules an made em pull till blood run frum in under their tails—an I never got that coal hauled till nigh on
spring when th hill dried up. That King Devil'ull never
be took by normal hound to my mind, an you'd better be
at your farmen."

"Oh, I recken I can fox-hunt a little an still keep frum
starven out," Nunn answered shortly, and remembered he
had meant to start that very afternoon making shakes to
mend the big barn roof that was leaking on the corn and
fodder, and that Milly had been quarreling fit to kill because there was a puddle big enough to swim a hog in
Betsey's stall in the old grist mill. John, now, wouldn't tol-
erate a leaky roof. He always kept a stack of seasoned
shakes handy in case a wind blew off one or he found a
leaky spot.

"Aye, Lord, I used to think they was nothen so pretty as
good hound-dog music," the old man said, and added almost defiantly, "If'n th weather ain't too bad, I'm a comen
with you all this comen Saturday night. I ain't been on a
good fox race in a long spell."

"It's a goen to be a shindig, all right," Jaw Buster promised. "You'll hear some real runnen, an I'll bet you a
drink a J. D. Duffey's last run that old King Devil comes
out."

But four nights later, when the hounds with Zing in the
lead swung hour after hour with long joyful bays down
through the valleys and around the ridges, nobody remembered the bet. King Devil ran. The men squatted in tense
silence on the Pilot Rock about a burned-out fire that nobody bothered to replenish, not even old John, whose
rheumaticky bones ached in the damp cold.

All of the Little Smokey Valley men except Preacher
Samuel were there, and others besides. Willie Cooksey
with his one old wornout hound that looked to be half cur;
and Rans with none; and Newt Taylor from the other side

of Bear Creek, with his two fine spotted July hounds; and
Ernest Coffee from the valley, who had come to the end of
the gravel in a new Chevrolet with two hounds—Trigs they
were—he'd made his brags about before the race began,
for he had paid a good $100 of railroad-section-gang
money for them in London Town last spring.

But for hours now Ernest had said no more than Willie
Cooksey. His hounds were back somewhere with the
others, while Zing, followed close by Sourvine and Speed,
took the lead and held it. Nunn squatted a little apart from
the others, with his back sheltered from the wind by a
scraggeldy pine, and listened with that strange wild
pounding hope in his heart that always came when King
Devil ran and Zing cried that his scent was hot. Maybe
this time, this once, Zing would catch him—and it would
be the end. Zing gave tongue, his bell-like cry rising up
from near the head of Anderson Fork of Little Smokey,
and echoing and reechoing through the valley.

Nunn could feel the anger and the eagerness in his call.
King Devil would be close; Zing never gave tongue like
that except when the scent was clear and hot. King Devil
was an animal, flesh and blood and bone like Zing; press
him hard enough and he could take no time for the devilish traps of backtracks and jumps and water runs he laid
that would hold Zing up for minutes together while the red
devil sat resting and laughing as he listened to the troubled
hounds.

Zing's voice and Sourvine's voice, with Speed's occasional bay just a little behind, grew fainter and fainter until
they seemed no more than a fainter note of the thin whisperings of the wind in the stunted pines on the Pilot Rock.
After a little space Nunn knew it was only the wind he
heard. King Devil had taken the hard steep road up Caney
Fork going north from Little Smokey Creek, and Zing, in
the narrow gulch of the valley, could not be heard. But
when the hounds had topped Casseye Ridge and King
Devil had headed back toward the river, as he would,
Nunn could hear Zing again.

He heard the Taylor hounds, followed soon by Lead and
Drive, come up the creek, and after a while most of the
others; but they were the stragglers and did not count, and
he did not bother to unravel the tangle of sounds and learn

whose hounds were still in the race and whose had slunk home or gone possum-hunting, but looked overhead at the sky, ragged with patches of stars and of cloud. At sunset it had looked like rain, but it was clearing now, with maybe frost by morning. The Big Dipper lay low in the northwest now, and when Zing first got scent of King Devil it had been well up in the sky; and now the bottommost stars of it would fall behind the hills and swing free again before the race would end.

So many nights like this he had watched the Big Dipper and the Little Dipper and the Seven Stars and the evening stars go down, and the morning stars brighten and then pale in the sky, and he had stared at the unblinking, unmoving North Star until he knew the patterns of the stars from the Pilot Rock at all hours of the night and in all seasons as well as, maybe better than, he knew the fields and boundaries of his own land. Maybe this would be the last night; he was tired of the stars and the wind and the sitting in the dark—but the thought was old and familiar as the stars, and he got up and walked restlessly about the cliff edge.

"Don't be a walken in your sleep an a fallen off, man," Old John warned.

"Hell, I know this cliff better'n my own bed," Nunn answered shortly, and wished Zing would come within hearing soon.

Willie Cooksey and Ernest Coffee, whose hounds had not been heard for hours, were talking of going home. Willie lowed his old Bogle had swum the Big South Fork with a rabbit in his mouth, and was now sound asleep in the kitchen at home, and Ann Liz would be up waiting for him with the poker and the quilting frames, for whenever Willie got drunk, Bogle always went on home; but this was one night he was cold sober and away from Bogle. But Ernest was worried over his hundred-dollar hounds, and wondered and reckoned on their being lost; though Blare told him not to worry, for he'd heard them hole a possum and dig it out, and then start that new Chevrolet coupé for going back to London Town. John, in some exasperation, told them either to go home or be quiet, so a man could listen; he wanted to hear Zing come in.

But Nunn, as always, heard him first; to the other listeners it was only another noise of the wind, but Nunn knew, and bowed his head and shut his eyes and held his breath for better listening. King Devil had skirted the sloping side of Casseye Ridge where the running was hard in the rocky side-hill ground, a grown-over field thick with saw briars and sumac brush. Zing's voice came faintly, too faintly for Nunn to understand much of what he said; the fox scent, he could tell, was still hot and strong; he could hear that much, but how close he was he could not say.

Maybe close, one leap, two leaps; the running through the briars and sumac brush would be hard for the big long haired fox, harder than for Zing. Maybe there on Casseye Ridge Zing would get him, now, this night, this very minute. He heard Jaw Buster's short excited breathing, and the sound seemed like thunder, drowning out Zing's voice.

He gripped his hands angrily, impatiently, as if he would tear away and destroy all the sounds between him and Zing's voice out there in the darkness. Jaw Buster's breathing, the wind that had sunk to a moaning sigh in the pines, the rattle of the river over the shoals, and far away and faint, a train blowing for a tunnel past the Cumberland. It was uncommon for King Devil to run a straight race with no tricks and no foolery for so long. Maybe Zing was pressing him so hard he couldn't backtrack, for not once in the long running had Zing boogled or fumbled or given anything except the happy anger of his warcry when on the scent of the big red fox.

Nunn stood for a long while straining his ears, but when he heard Zing give tongue again he was on Kelly's Point at the end of Casseye Ridge, too far away and smothered by trees and rocks and wind for Nunn to hear much of what he said, whether the scent lay hot like fire in his nose or if King Devil were slipping ahead and the scent growing cold.

He squatted again and eased his back against the pine. All about him he heard the low talk and movement of men, but gave them little heed, his ears remembering still Zing's last call, his mind working it over, trying to read it like the writing on a piece of paper half washed away by rain.

He heard Jaw Buster cut a fresh chew of tobacco and John stomp his feet against the cold and Blare Tiller go on with one of his endless lying tales about how much money he had won and gambled away again on a slot machine in

Newcastle, Indiana, when he had made big money working for Chrysler. He saw Lister's big catlike body, a black shape on the edge of the Pilot Rock, moving lightly between him and the stars.

"You'd ought to be a gitten on in home, Lister," Old John called out in his cross old man's way. "Ain't Babe expecten any minnit?"

Lister's head bobbed across a star. "Any minnit's right. I thought I seed a light at Sue Annie's, but I recken I didn't. They'll know I won't git in fore Sourvine. When he kills a fox er runs it to th end he jist allus goes on in home."

"But Sue Annie can't hold th younguen back till you make up your mind to git home," John quarreled.

"Sue Annie ain't bringen no baby er she'd a left a light at home like she allus does, an Dave can't sleep when they's a light a burnen an he'd be up a fiddlen fit to kill. I recollect th night Ivan come, Old Dave must a played 'Sourwood Mountain' a thousand times," Lister went on, coming away from the edge and squatting down by Nunn. "I been married twelve year an I've got five younguens an I've allus been on hand for ever one an I ain't never missed a big fox race yet."

John shook his head. "It's no way to do; stayen away from a woman in that shape. You ought—"

Nunn and Lister rose soundlessly to their feet like twin springs and stood listening, breath hushed, teeth clamped tight on tobacco; but Blare Tiller was now telling about how he had shot down and rolled eleven ton of coal out of Uncle Ansel Anderson's mine in one day, and by the time Jaw Buster, straining his ears for Speed, had shut him up with a whispered curse, a gust of wind thundered through the pines and they could hear nothing.

But Nunn squatted again, satisfied if a little puzzled, smiling softly to himself. On a long race Zing and Sourvine were almost never right together like that, but that didn't have to mean that Zing was slowing up; in a straight race where there wasn't much nose work, like tonight, Sourvine could come on as fast as Zing; there were even those who said, or at least hinted, that Sourvine had been known to use Zing's nose.

"Zing's a pressen him hard tonight," Nunn explained to John, who hadn't been able to hear. "This is one race when

King Devil can't take no time for tricks; they're a comen straight down th ridge, a taken that old loggen road. An when King Devil runs a road he's in a hurry."

"They'll be comen down Deer Lick Ridge in full hearen pretty soon," Lister whispered excitedly. "An man, oh, man! they're a pressen him hard."

Even Blare was silent now and listened like the others for the hounds to top the ridge. Nunn watched a little patch of ragged cloud come up behind the Cow's Horn and move on above Sue Annie's house on the hill above the river; he saw it, like an unmarked hourglass marking unmeasured time, creep across one end of the Big Dipper; and he wondered if it would get high enough to cross the North Star and how long it would take.

But before a corner of the cloud had touched the North Star, the deep wild bay of a coarse-mouthed hound broke over the ridge crest across the valley, as loud and clear as if it had been on the Pilot Rock. Nunn sprang to his feet and stood openmouthed, staring through the darkness toward the sound. Rans Cramer called in jeering laughter, "Hell, ain't that Speed? An Nunn allus a braggen that old Zing can outrun any hound in th country. Where's he now?"

Nunn turned slowly, stiffly, suddenly tired, with the heat all gone from his body. "Zing, he's dead, you fool."

"Aw, Nunn," Jaw Buster comforted, "mebbe Zing got hurt; mebbe he's took sick sudden; listen—mebbe we'll hear him."

"There ain't no rattlesnakes now an nothen could hurt him a comen down a straight loggen road, an he ain't no fool to run over a bluff like Del." Nunn spoke over his shoulder, for he was already striding through the darkness toward the first jumpover ledge down the path from the Pilot Rock. "I tell you, man, he's dead. In all these years a their runnen together, him an Speed an Sourvine was never far apart; but Zing never missed a time, never one, a bein in th lead."

Lister hardly stopped to listen to his Sourvine singing on the ridge crest. "But somethen different could a happened tonight—Sourvine's jist now a comen in an a little while ago he was ahead a Speed—mebbe Speed jist got uncommon fast," he said, following him, his talk loud, but with no heartiness and no belief in it.

Blare, who was afraid to take a step in any direction until he had a light, was yelling for them to wait until he could get a carbide filled and lighted; they'd break their necks jumping over in the dark. If a body did happen to miss the path by a foot on either side, he'd land on rocks a hundred feet below, but Nunn crammed his old felt hat into his pocket and sprang down with no more need of a light that King Devil himself.

Jaw Buster, with Lister at his heels, came behind him, and together they went down through the woods and brush of Nunn's fields, crossed the creek, and took a short cut through the woods to Honeysuckle Point, above the schoolhouse, where Zing had last been heard. They walked swiftly, soundlessly, as they always walked in the dark, never groping or stumbling or worrying over the path, but swinging their feet as if it had been daylight, though under the spruce pine in the creek canyon it was black as a coal mine and a man could not see his hands before his face.

Among the wind-battered sweet gum and scrub oak on the far side of the ridge, the gloom was not so deep, but Nunn stopped and called to Blare, who came crackling and crashing through the brush, to hurry on with a carbide. "Th last time I heared him he was right about here," Nunn said, "an Sourvine sounded right beside him, so I figger he was about done then."

Willie Cooksey, who could never see in the dark and had worn his miner's carbide for crossing the river, walked behind while Blare and others walked ahead with his light. But in the unaccustomed brightness the night woods were unfamiliar to Nunn and he kept stumbling and grasping at shadows, hurrying from one side of the road to the other, only to find that the bit of brownness he had thought was Zing was a sandrock or a pile of watersoaked leaves or nothing at all.

It was Jaw Buster who found Zing. He lay in the middle of the old logging road with his legs outspread as he had used to lie at home by the hearth fire, but his wide-open eyes remained fixed and unwinking in the blue carbine light, and his mouth was open wide, with the worn teeth shining the way they did when he laughed with the children.

The men came up in silence and in silence squatted about him in a close circle and looked at him. "Funny,"

Blare said after a time, "he seemed well as could be, frisken around like a cur-dog pup, fore th race started."

"He was," Lister said.

Blare glanced uneasily into the wall of blackness past the carbide lights. "What killed him then? A hound don't up an die like that."

"That damned red fox run him to death," Nunn said, finding it strangely hard to speak at all.

Lister shook his head and sighed. "An I thought all th time Zing was a pressen him so hard he couldn't take time to play any of his devil's tricks—an mebbe him with his head set all th time on runnen Zing to death."

"He knowed Zing was old," Joe C. Tiller said.

Old John watched the whiskers by Zing's mouth move in the light breeze. "That red fox ain't so smart as all that, man. He's a fox like any other fox."

Blare cut a chew of tobacco. "Now, how many times have any a you even seen King Devil's sign?" he asked suddenly, and in a voice loud enough to make Willie Cooksey jump.

"You know nobody ain't ever seen it," Nunn said, still staring down at Zing. "But that ain't a sayen he's a witch er some sinner's haint that cain't rest easy in his grave an has to run over these hills. He's jist uncommon smart, that's all."

Jaw Buster nodded. "I'll bet he could be spotlighted same as a rabbit or a fish."

"He ain't no rabbit an he ain't no fish," Willie Cooksey giggled. "But it ud be right good pastime to see you all try. Nunn, you're reckoned one a the best shots in th country."

"Listen, men," John spoke up eagerly as a boy. "If'n you all kill him this night I'll give you $10. He'll kill five times that in lambs fer me this comen spring."

Nunn seemed not to have heard, and the others were silent while he stripped off his overall jumper and laid it over Zing. Lister looked down at the old dog and after a moment said with a little sigh: "He was th best foxhound, I recken, that's ever been in these parts, an thout him my Sourvine ain't worth a damn; he's th runninest fool that ever was, but I've allus thought that in a tight spot he used Zing's nose. Now no hound'ull ever unravel th scent an King Devil'ull never be took."

Ernest Coffee took a chew of tobacco, then stopped with his mouth open, listening into the darkness. "He's still a runnen, an I'm a thinken a goen after my rifle; I brung it along jist in case, an I want to see if them two good-fer-nothen potlickers a mine had sense enough to go to th car. An with my rifle I'll git $10 an King Devil this very night. Recken you'd help me, Nunn?"

Nunn rolled Zing into the jumper and buttoned it up. Rans Cramer snorted. "He ain't no man to be a covern up his face that away."

Nunn listened to Sourvine, headed now for Cedar Thicket Holler, before he answered. "Zing was a damned sight more deserven a th name a man than many a one that walks on two legs. He never lied to me or any man, nor swore, nor used his teeth on anything but a varmint I wanted him to kill. Many's th time I've seen him stand an cry while th little youngens, fore they was big enough to know better, would pull his tongue. In all his life he never stole so much as one egg, an he never was afraid."

Jaw Buster nodded. "We seed him kill a wildcat once, an there's th scar still on his nose."

"Once for me he found a newborn lamb th old yoe wouldn't claim," John said.

"He was allus killen copperheads for they had a chance to kill th youngens up at school," Joe C. Tiller said.

Willie Cooksey squatted over him and rolled a cigarette; grains of tobacco fell on the jumper and Nunn flicked them away. Willie blew out a breath of smoke and smiled at Nunn. "Well, he never got drunk and he never made his brags, like some I could name, about how quick he'd git King Devil; but a hound's a hound; I've lost a many a one; they's no use a carryen on so."

Nunn studied the man, moving nothing but his eyes. "Look, you; it's none a your business if'n I lay $10 gold pieces on his eyes an bury him in a walnut coffin lined with lamb's wool an wrapped in silk."

Jaw Buster got up and looked down at the Cooksey while he talked. "Aw, Nunn, nobody wants you to leave him here fer th buzzards. I'll help you carry him home. You're fergetten, I recken, how you helped me dig a grave fer my little Bonnie that night she died a chasen this same red bastard an got bit by a rattlesnake, I recken it was."

"I'll help, too, soon's I git my rifle out a my car an see about them potlickers a mine," Ernest offered. "You're a good shot, Nunn; whyn't you help me kill that fox when he swings around this ridge agin an into a spotlight? I'll split th money."

"Do you honestly think a body could kill him by shooten?" Newt Taylor asked in a low surprised voice.

"Mebbe he's jist part fox an has got claws like a wild-cat an will stop an climb a tree when he sees that spot-light," Blare suggested only half jokingly.

"Did you all ever think that mebbe—mebbe th scent stops an somethen else a hound dog won't foller—er nothen a tall begins?" Joe C. asked with an uneasy glance out into the dark woods.

"Good God, man, but you talk like a half-crazy woman in th family way," Nunn said, rising disgustedly to his feet. "Sometime somebody'ull come along with a hound that'll press him so hard he cain't jump a bluff into th Big South Fork or do whatever it is he does do when he gits tired a runnen—Listen. Recken Sourvine's a chasen a haint; for all you know he's after Bill Weaver's haint back frum hell an a tryen to find some liquor."

Old John listened to the lone hound a moment, then shook his head reproachfully at Nunn. "When you're as old as I am, man, an if'n you've still not give your heart to God, you won't be a talken so easy an offlike about hell an them that's dead an cain't hep theirselves. An anyhow, accorden to th Bible, angels can come down to earth an th dead can show theirselves."

Nunn said nothing but continued to listen to Sourvine. "They're a swingen around Pilot Rock Hill right now, like they done about three hours ago; an mark my word, King Devil'ull go right back where he's already been, an he'll cross th creek an swing back this away agin fore mornen. I'd lay good money on it. An, Blare, you an Willie can take a carbide an find out if'n it's a haint Sourvine's a chasen."

"Not me," Blare spoke quickly.

"Nunn," Old John spoke with urgent earnestness. "Whyn't you git a gun an wait by th road and help Ernest kill him? It ud be worth money to ever farmer in the country to be shet of that red fox, an you're about th best shot around."

Nunn said nothing.

"Aw, come on, Nunn, help me kill him. Look at th hounds he's caused to die an mebbe mine lost now fer good. No hound'ull ever git him. I'm afraid a missen by myself," Ernest begged.

Jaw Buster turned wearily away from listening for his lazy-mouthed Speed. "Aw, go on, Nunn, spotlight him. Without Zing we'll never git him."

John nodded. "Zing, he was th likeliest chance, an he's gone; an none a you men an none a your hounds ain't never goen to git him; an in th last five year he's killed enough little lambs fer me to buy a dozen foxhounds."

"Whyn't you kill him, John? You're so certain he can be killed," Blare said.

"Ain't I tried? Traps, hunten, watchen my yoes an their lambs night after night last spring, with my little white feist dog an a cocked shotgun, till me an th boys was drunk fer sleep; an never seen nothen, never hearen nothen but a little lamb a cryen fer a minnit, an sometimes not that, an one time not a hundred feet from me." He shook his head in remembering, then looked hopefully at Nunn.

Nunn picked up Zing and held him cradled in his arms, but continued to squat on the ground and stare out into the dark and listen. After a while he looked overhead at the stars. About three o'clock it must be, and he was tired. Tomorrow, while he walked miles rounding up his sheep and salting them, his usual Sunday job, he would be tired, with his body crying for sleep; and he was tired of being sleepy and tired of always hoping and tired of remembering the brags he had made five years ago. And what if he had made his brags? He didn't even have a hound now and no good pup in sight and no money to buy one. He cleared his throat, but the words he knew he ought to say would not come, and when he did speak he spoke to the stars: "I allus aimed to take him fair an true with a hound, an I'd mebbe shoot him if I had a gun, but I ain't aimen to walk four miles back home fer one."

Lister, who had been standing a little apart from the others, straining his ears for Sourvine, came into the shaft of light from the carbides. "I been kind a worried about Babe; from here I couldn't see to tell whether Sue Annie's light was burnen or not. What about me a goen home an seen about her an gitten my gun? You know it, an a truer-shooten rifle was never made, but I never was no hand at spotlighten; I'd be sure to miss him an kill Sourvine."

Nunn shook his head, as if flies buzzed about his ears, and said nothing.

Blare shivered. "It could be that fox is bewitched; he could come runnen up to a man an tear out his throat or make a gun shoot backards."

Nunn's voice rose angrily. "Fool! He's flesh an blood like any other fox. Give me that carbide an a rifle an I'll kill him, spotlight an bust him right between th eyes, jist as easy as killen a frog. He ain't Bill Weaver's ghost an he ain't no haint an he ain't no Jesus Christ he ain't th Holy Ghost, but I wish to God I had a drink."

Ernest Coffee pulled a pint Mason jar out of his overall bib. "I been a saven this to help my feelens when I cain't find them hounds a mine, but you're welcome; they's a little more in my car anyhow. It's awful tasten, made a lasses stid a sugar, but it's got plenty a burn."

Nunn glanced at it in the carbide light, hardly more than a third full but enough to warm a man's heart and put warm blood in his hands. He swallowed it all without taking his lips from the jar, gagging a little as the stuff went down.

The others watched, some with envy, some with disapproval. "Don't go gitten on one a your roaren, hellraisen sprees," John warned. "I'm gitten old an not wanten to git mixed in any trouble."

"Hell, that wasn't enough to puke a baby," Nunn answered, walked a few steps away from the glare of the lights, and squatted with his back to a tree, waiting for Lister and Ernest to go for the guns. He heard Sourvine give tongue—tired and worried he sounded—up toward the mouth of Caney Fork again. King Devil would swing back this way sometime before morning. He was having his fun tonight, making that fool hound think he could catch him.

Blare came and squatted by him and shivered and glanced up at the stars, and spoke in a low voice as if afraid of being overheard. "You know, lots a times I know King Devil ain't a red fox like other foxes."

Willie Cooksey shivered too, and thought they'd better

build a fire; the night was growing colder, he said. But the others decided against it; King Devil might see it miles away and shift his course.

The Big Dipper turned lower toward the west, the wind died, and by the time Ernest and Lister got back with the guns, frost had begun to glitter on the withered leaves. The men moved quietly about, talking little, and then in low voices, like men at a funeral, and stamping their feet against the cold.

Nunn continued to sit apart from the others, silent, looking sometimes at the stars, or now and again sighting down the barrel of Lister's gun. It had a big buck sight, fine for hunting. Shooting King Devil as he ran confused and befuddled into a blinding flash of carbide light would be easy.

He heard Speed, and an instant later Sourvine, loud and clear, rounding the head of Neeley's Creek. King Devil had doubled, a longer double than the last; and he might double again before he got here, but come back this way he would.

He could not sit still, but got up, clutching the rifle in his sweaty hands. The good Lord God in heaven could damn his soul to hell if he didn't make an end of that red-tailed bastard tonight; and he, Nunnely Ballew, could be a man again, working his land and raising his family, instead of a piece of pore white trash getting drunk under the stars, and cursing the coming of daylight because every bone in his body ached for sleep. To hell with his loud brags and all the fine things he had said back yonder five years ago when Zing first got scent of King Devil. He'd thought then it was a red fox he had to catch, not a red devil.

Ernest touched him on the elbow and he jumped as from the touch of a ghost and swore for no reason at all. "How you aimen to do it, Nunn?" Ernest asked, too excited to notice that Nunn had called him a dirty name.

"Right between th eyes, God willen."

"I mean where you goen to wait, an where'd I better stand?"

Nunn considered a moment and then, without answering, moved away through the darkness to the knot of men about the carbide lights who now stood tense and silent, listening, whispering when they talked at all. Nunn whis-

pered, too. King Devil could not have heard, but whispers
went well with his tongue; it lay dry and numb in his
mouth, and he kept trying to work up a stream of tobacco
juice and could not.

He commanded them to fill the lamps with fresh carbide and water, then directed Blare to give Ernest his
lamp, while he took John's for himself, miner's cap and
all. He then had the lights put out, and with the others
following he went down the old logging road. Now and
then he called to them in whispered curses to be silent,
for Blare and the Cramers, without lights, sounded like
a herd of cattle crashing through the brush.

Sourvine gave tongue again, no farther away than the
upper end of the ridge, and Nunn hurried, almost running
toward what he was hunting, and found soon, with no
groping, a great moss-grown pine trunk, uprooted in some
unremembered storm, thick enough so that a man on his
knees could be hidden from anything on the other side.

In a high whisper he told Ernest to come on and get
behind the log with him. He heard Sourvine again, no
more than two miles away it seemed, straight up the
ridge, already turned into the old logging road. He cursed
the hound in whispers for his noise. King Devil might
come at any minute now, and if he were made of blood
and bone like any other animal, he would, no matter how
soundless his coming, make a noise that Nunn could hear.

He fumbled for a match and it seemed hours that his
sweaty hands were fumbling to light it. The big brass in-
laid buttons on his jumper, so good for striking matches,
were on his jumper still, but the jumper was on Zing; his
overall buckles wouldn't do. He grabbed Ernest and
scratched the match on his belt buckle, and it went out as
he struck it.

"That's bad luck," Ernest whispered, staring down at
the glowing but flameless match.

"Granny woman," Nunn said, and struck another
match, and lighted his lamp and Ernest's and listened for
King Devil's coming. Faint it would be, like the Big South
Fork's whispering on a rising tide or the noise of a copperhead's coiling, but it would be a sound that he could hear.

They held their lights low behind the log, the flames
so small they barely lived, and shielded by their hands
and arms. "I'll give you th first three shots," Nunn whis-

pered, and his words sounded as loud as Samuel's radio when the batteries were new, "an if they stop him, John's $10 is your'n. Me, I ain't a wanten th money. An lift yer head an shine th light when I say 'Ready.' "

The carbide light in his miner's cap, encircled by his lifted arms, made a little world of brightness behind the log, and Nunn leaned above it, listening. His stomach no longer lay heavy and dead, like a cold anvil under his ribs; he felt lighthearted and happy. It would soon be over; King Devil would be dead, and he could sleep easy in his bed, like other men, not out staring at the stars, or sitting under a rock house for shelter from a cold drizzly rain and listening, always listening and hoping and thinking.

Tomorrow, when he rounded up his sheep, it would be fine walking over the hills warmed by the knowing that King Devil was dead, and that he could farm and bring the Old Place back to what it had once been, raise sheep and corn so fine that men would forget he had spotlighted and shot the fox he had bragged to catch.

He caught a whiff of Ernest's breath and realized the man must have taken a long drink when he went to his car, and that killing King Devil would be a job for Nunnely Ballew alone; he had only meant to help. It seemed a long time ago that he had promised. Something like regret stirred the far corners of his mind where lay the thoughts and things remembered that he kept pushed from out the center of his life.

Not twenty yards away a dry leaf rattled faintly, and Nunn whispered, "That's him. Ready." Both men turned toward the sound, lifting their heads and clicking the carbides on full blast.

Nunn saw the green fire of two eyes—big as a man's eyes they looked, and somehow like a man's eyes they were, too. The eyes were looking past him, coming straight on, not turning away or blinking; blinded and scared, they looked to be no more than a man's eyes in the light. Ernest's bullets sang, and he heard the *pop, pop* of the rifle. Above him in the woods men were screaming, "Shoot, Nunn, you fool, shoot. Ernest ain't a stoppen him. Shoot, damn it, shoot!"

He heard Jaw Buster yell something about recollecting that Speed might be right behind, for on a hot race old

Speed never said much; Lister was yelling to look out for
Sourvine, and mixed through it all were John's curses.
And his mind, somehow loose and unhung, like a feather
floating from a striking hawk, thought that the old man
ought to be turned out of church for such black talk; but
mostly it thought that here was King Devil, point-blank
at the end of a loaded rifle, and his eyes didn't look the
way he had thought they would look; it wasn't a bit like
shooting a rabbit or a skunk.

When he'd worked in the company mines, a coal car
had broken loose from the engine and run backward; he'd
heard the man scream somewhere in the dark and he had
gone with his miner's cap on his head like this and spotlighted the man's eyes—wide open they were and they had
looked like this just for a second, and then they were not
man's eyes, but only something glittering like glass or ice
or a bit of jack.

He automatically turned his head, keeping the oncom-
ing eyes full in the glare of the light, expecting them to
swerve aside or stop suddenly like a rabbit's eyes under
the spotlight, and all the while he could hear the men behind him yelling and cursing him with black bitter oaths,
and Ernest's bullets still singing and the *pops* of the semi-
automatic rifle that seemed minutes apart instead of seconds.

The popping stopped and Ernest was yelling, "If you
ain't gonna shoot, gimme that gun. This 'uns empty."

Like a man in his sleep he rolled the gun over his
forearm and handed it to Ernest, but even as he did so
the eyes disappeared, like stars swallowed in a cloud.
"He's jumped over the ridge or run behind a tree," Ernest yelled, and sprang over the log and ran toward the
ridge bluff.

"You'll break your fool neck. It's high there and
straight down," John called to Ernest, and his voice
sounded old and tired and disgusted. "You couldn't find
him anyhow. Whyn't you kill him, Nunn?"

Nunn leaned motionless against the pine log and stared
off into the darkness. "I wisht I had a drink," he said.

"You've had drink enough," John told him. "You'd
better be getten back to your woman an youngens."

"That little swaller's dead in me already," Nunn said,
and added softly, "Don't be gitten mad at me, old man,

an don't be tellen me what to do. Nobody can tell me
what to do. The good Lord God in heaven cain't tell me
what to do. But I can tell you what I'll do. I'll ketch that
big red fox for you, take him fair an true with a foxhound."

He got up and shook his fist over the ridge side. "I
hope th good Lord God in heaven sends me to brile in
hell through eternity without end if I ever stop chasen
that fox till I git him. I'll git him if I have to sell ever last
sheep I've got to buy me a hound an sell my mare an my
cow to feed him. I'll chase him till I'm crippled an blind
an bald an . . ." He got up and went back toward Zing.

John shook his head more in sorrow than anger. "Put's
me in mind a th time his grandad Jim got th call to
preach. We was cutten pine timber to saw for a new barn,
an that barn never got built till his oldest boy got up big
enough to do it hisself."

Chapter Five

SUSE AWAKENED AND SAT up in bed, listening, shaking her hair out of her eyes, wondering why she awoke. That it was nearly daybreak she judged by the burned-out look of the fire; she remembered there was a big race on and Nunn was gone, but it was not a hound's crying or the blowing of a fox horn that had awakened her. Then it came again: a snatch of laughter and burst of loud man song, clearly from across the creek.

She sighed like a tired old woman and got out of bed; Nunn was coming home drunk, and the Cookseys and Tillers and maybe a lot more were with him.

Milly awakened while Suse was building up the fire. She lighted the lamp, then she and Suse tiptoed to the kitchen and set about building a fire in the cookstove. Nunn would need coffee, and Zing warm milk, for the race had been long and the night was cold. They stood in the kitchen door and listened, shivering, but more from the cold than fear. There were a lot of men but they didn't sound bad drunk.

Milly's heart leaped suddenly with hope. She whispered to Suse, "Maybe they've caught King Devil. Somethen's made em leave th Pilot Rock an cross th creek since we went to bed."

Suse shook her head. "Another hound killed most like."

Long tongues of light from the carbides pushed up from the creek crossing and flickered soon around the little barn and by the gate. But once through the gate the men lingered in the road in a sudden queer silence, with no talk and no laughter, and in a moment Nunn's voice came clearly, "I'll take him now, Jaw Buster," and Nunn came

64

on, his feet striking the rocks in hard uneven steps, like a man carrying a heavy burden.

There was a heavy burden cradled in his arms; Milly saw him lay it by the chopping block when he came into the light from the kitchen door. She rushed down the steps to meet him, and Suse came behind her with the lamp, the flame burning straight in the still night like a lamp in a room, and in its light Milly saw Nunn's eyes and forgot to wonder what it was he carried home, for there was a look in his eyes she had seen before, a look he couldn't live with, and so must try to lose in a long drunk. She laid her hand on his shoulder and saw he wore only his shirt and wondered if he wasn't cold; she began a low urgent pleading, "Come in, Nunn; please come in, honey."

Down on the Cow's Horn road Willie Cooksey tittered, and she knew it was no good. Nunn was never much to mind her anyhow, and never when other men were listening. Suse held out the lamp for her to take, then stooped by the load Nunn had carried. She pulled the jumper away, then held it up to him asking, "Pop, is Zing bad hurt?"

Nunn took the jumper and said, "He's dead," and turned away to the waiting men.

Milly watched the lights move along the Cow's Horn road until they disappeared in the corn swag, but Suse was kneeling by Zing and shivering, sobbing, angry at the grief that hurt her so. "I never knowed I thought so much a him," and remembering suddenly, said, "Pore Lee Roy."

Milly turned away from the lights and knelt by Suse, and for the first time the full realization of Zing's death came to her, and it was not like losing an animal but a long piece out of her life; he was something her dead children had loved and touched, and his going made them seem far away. "We'd better put him down in th little barn, Mom," Suse said, "so's Lee Roy an th rest won't see him fer a while."

The front of the grist mill had once been used as a storage place for grain, and Nunn used it now as a corn crib and a place in which to keep Maude's harness and his few farming tools. Feeling their way in the dark, they carried Zing there and covered him with shucks. Suse squatted a moment by the pile of shucks and said in a low hard voice, "Mom—if Pop don't come in pretty soon—I'll think up some nice way a tellen Lee Roy," and added in embarrassment, "An, Mom, I wouldn't worry about Pop; he'll be all right; he allus has been."

Neither went back to bed, but sat by the kitchen fire so as not to awaken the younger children. The windows grayed slowly in the coming dawn, and Milly was restless, listening for Nunn's footsteps, or going often to stand in the kitchen door to watch for sign of sunrise. When it was hardly light enough to see, she left the house on pretext of feeding Rosie. "Why, Mom, it's awful early, an me er Lee Roy allus—" Suse began and stopped, flushed with too much understanding.

Milly went away, forgetting to take the slop pail. She hurried up the garden path and stopped among the old bean rows, staring out across the valley, but the dawn was full of cold crawling fog and frost and gray clouds smothering the sunrise. She could hear no drunken singing, see no smoke from a fire the sober might have built for the drunken, and after a little while went on over to the graveyard knoll that stood higher and gave a wider view.

She stood a long while by the graveyard fence, listening, looking in first one direction and then the other, but could see little except the sky, like a roof across the hills, and the fog rising from the river. But she continued to stand, shivering in the misty cold, hoping against her reason now that she could see or hear some sign of Nunn. Most likely there had been little liquor left in the party and they had all gone off, maybe miles, to hunt some more.

At last her eyes reached for what they had been careful not to notice since she had first come to the graveyard fence: two small graves marked with slabs of wood and decorated with shells from the river and bits of colored glass. She hesitated a moment, then climbed the fence quickly and went to the graves and smoothed the smaller with her hand, and sat so, squatting on her heels and trying not to cry. Trouble was a funny thing; no matter how much of it a body had, new trouble never lessened the old. It was silly for a woman with two children dead to feel such a hard choking hurt over a dead dog— or maybe the hurt was because Nunn was gone. But Zing had been so kind.

She heard steps across the frozen ground and sprang up guiltily, wiping her eyes on her apron. She saw that it was Lureenie coming across the graveyard field with an eight-pound lard bucket swinging empty in her hand. She knew Lureenie had seen her crying there and she felt naked and ashamed; the whole world would be knowing that she, an old married woman nearing thirty, was out looking for her man and crying for a dead hound—and especially did she hate to have Lureenie, with her proud ways and pretty looks, see her so.

But when she went up to Lureenie she knew by that thin-faced big-eyed look of a woman who hasn't slept a wink all night that Lureenie had her troubles too. Her smile was pitiful, coming from Lureenie, begging somehow, saying things that could never come past her tongue; pleased she was almost to crying to meet Milly walking about in the frosty dawn. "I didn't know but what you might still be sleepen," she said, "but I come early like this while th youngens was still asleep; the fire went out and I hid th matches, an while it's so cold they won't be into any meanness. I hate to leave em but I wanted to borry a little flour. It's Sunday mornen an I hated not to have biscuit bread for breakfast, an Rans, he fergot to git me any at Samuel's." The words rushed out while she stood stiff and still, looking into Milly's eyes and smiling her proud but beseeching smile.

Milly patted her on the shoulder. "Lord, Lureenie, if'n it takes fergetten flour to make you come an see me, I'm wishen you'd be out a flour half th time. Whyn't you come around an stay all day an bring th youngens," she invited heartily. In spite of all her own troubles, she felt sorry for Lureenie; her proudness and her prettiness were breaking; her face looked gray and pinchd for a woman not yet twenty-one, and even her curling red-gold hair was dull, and her big eyes, deep blue under the long dark lashes that had somehow always made Milly think of the wild iris by the creek, looked hard now, with the glittering look of eyes that had shed so many angry tears they had learned the pain of going dry.

"I recken Nunn's gone, too," Lureenie said as they walked along. Her voice rose in shrill anger. "Rans went a fox-hunten with th others, and him with nary a hound, an I heared em a comen and I went to th door and he

stopped jist long enough to tell me he wasn't comen in.
Aimen to foller that gigglen fool of a Willie Cooksey
over th river to J. D. Duffey's still; that's where they was
a goen." She added bitterly, "An in all this cold an th
youngens all croupy an not but two sticks a wood for th
fireplace, an th ax so dull I cain't make it cut, an him
spenden money for that foxhound, and then liquor an
hardly a bite to eat in th—" She stopped and bit her lip
and walked quickly ahead.

"Law, now, Lureenie, everthing allus seems worse
when you first wake up in th mornen," Milly comforted.
"Pears like some men has to go git drunk, and seen as
how they do, you'd better be glad they've gone to J. D.'s
stid of around the Brush Creek road to old man Gib-
son's; if they got drunk there they'd mebbe keep on a
goen till they got out on th highway, an there th law ud
git em fer true."

"But I'd about as soon Rans was in jail as over at
J. D.'s; he'll spend ever cent on him fer whisky, and be a
dancen his dances an a maken his eyes at that old whore
of an Ethel that hangs around there. She'll flop on her
back fer a cigarette frum any man."

"You're just imaginen things," Milly said. "Nunn, he's
mebbe a cutten his capers fit to kill, but th only time him
or any other man would look at a slut like Ethel would be
when he's liquored up so's he couldn't do nothen nohow,
and they say she's got th bad disease," she went on, and
for the first time in hours the chew of tobacco in her
mouth tasted like something better than a dirty dishrag.

Nothing would happen to Nunn at J. D.'s; Jaw Buster
and Blare would take care of him if he got too drunk; and
the law never came to J. D.'s—his house was over in
Alcorn, too far from the highway for a sheriff to come,
and that gun-carrying fool of a Lonzo Cramer, Ran's
brother that shot a hole in Jaw Buster's leg last Decoration Day and had got run out of the county on a whisky
charge, wouldn't be there; and Mark Cramer who wasn't
so mean, just wild, would most likely be gone off to a music party, seeing as how it was Saturday night.

Suse, plainly glad to see Lureenie, met them at the
kitchen door and commanded them to sit down and have
a cup of coffee. Lureenie sat by the eating table and
drank the coffee gratefully, and after only a little urging

took a second cup and more than once glanced at a pone of molasses bread Milly had left on the table as a late snack for Nunn. Suse pushed the bread toward her. "Have a piece. I'll bet you're hungry walken so far before breakfast."

"Aw, Suse, ain't you ashamed, offeren anybody that old lasses bread. Jist give me a minnit an I'll have hot biscuit with butter an sausage an sausage gravy fer Lureenie—we killed our first pig about two weeks back an the sausage is jist gitten good," Milly said, and got up and began hunting the butcher knife so that she could go upstairs to the cold middle room where the sausages were hung.

Lureenie broke off a fair-sized piece of molasses bread, bit into it, and spoke with her mouth full. "Lord, I jist come to borry a little speck a flour, not fer breakfast . . . but say what you please, this bread is real good."

Milly sighed as she looked under the wash shelf for the butcher knife. "I've baked lasses-sweetened bread so much I could make it in my sleep an never draw a deep breath—seems like there's allus somethin else to buy before we git to sugar, so we never git to sugar. . . . You're lucky you don't have to use nothen but sugar fer sweetenen."

Lureenie broke off another piece of the bread and stared down at Milly's faded oilcloth as she chewed. "We don't allus git sugar either, an we don't have no lard cans a molasses an crocks a honey to fall back on like you all have, an that $40 a month Rans makes on WPA don't allus stretch over Rans's liquor an lots a groceries too." She reached for another piece of the stale bread and chewed on, still staring down, a red flush creeping into her face, and both angry and embarrassed she seemed, as if all she said and did were against her will.

Suse looked at her mother with a puzzled, troubled air; she had never seen Lureenie, the one to boast and dream, acting like a broken-down woman. Milly by now had found the butcher knife and turned around as if she didn't want to hear any more, and much to Suse's relief Lucy awakened in the fireplace room and began a whimpering for her daddy. "Your pop's gone off on a long fox hunt an we've got company," Suse called out.

As she dressed Lucy, she raised her voice loud enough

for Milly, upstairs, to hear. "Mom, don't you think it'd be fun fer me to run an git Lureenie's youngens an have em all visit all day? I'll bet Rans has gone on that long fox hunt too."

Milly came into the kitchen with her hands piled high with sausage meat and a jar of her huckleberry jam sweetened with honey under one arm, and thought Suse's suggestion a fine one. Lureenie got up hastily and made a great show of having to go back; she had a good Sunday dinner all ready to cook; the baby might get croupy from bringing it out into the cold, or Rans might come home and find her gone, but all the while she made her hasty, halfhearted excuses her eyes kept snatching at the rounds of sausage meat Milly was rolling in flour and laying into a skillet.

"Aw, hush such talk; it'ud tickle all th youngens to visit together," Milly urged. "They can pop em some corn an make em some cracker-jacks an lasses candy, too. An anyhow, you'll all have to come fer breakfast. I've cut enough sausage meat fer Coxey's Army."

Lee Roy, who had stayed up so late listening to the race that he was just now awakening, rushed barefooted into the kitchen, and after a quick glance at Zing's empty place behind the stove, ran to the door and had it open, looking outside, before Milly could push back the choking in her throat enough to say, "Zing ain't back yit, Lee Roy. Why don't you git your duds on an run help Suse pack Lureenie's youngens; they's two ain't big enough to walk."

He looked at her; his eyes narrowed a moment with suspicion, then he ran away to put on his shoes. She wondered if, when he knew, he'd hold the little lie against her; but it was easier to wait till Nunn got home.

Still, the lie hurt, especially when she realized he believed her; it was after breakfast, and Lureenie's two oldest had made a great gome of sausage meat and gravy and biscuit on their plates, and Lureenie was quarreling at them for wasting so much food, but Lee Roy smiled and said, "Zing'ull thank em for that mess when he comes in cold an tired."

Suse, who had just been pecking at her food, took Lureenie's baby and hurried off to the fireplace room and began rocking it and singing "Good-Bye, My Lover, Good-Bye" in a sad, lonesome voice.

Lee Roy looked suspicious again and sat a moment with his chin lifted, like a person thinking hard or listening, but he never asked her about Zing again; and sometimes through the day she would discover he was missing, and after a while he would slip in again and sit a time by the fire, looking into it when she looked at him, but more than once, when she was thinking of other things, she would be conscious of Lee Roy's hot brown eyes searching her face.

She was glad Lureenie and her children were there; the talk and laughter and whindling of the babies was like a blanket between her and her troubles. About midmorning, before the sickly yellow sun had half melted the heavy frost, a cold wind smothered the sky with clouds from the northwest, and by noon a sleety snow was rattling on the old tin roof.

Now and again Milly glanced outside and hoped that if Nunn were dead drunk some place he was safe and warm from the snow, with some sober man by to tend a fire and keep him from rolling into it; it wasn't so many years back that Sue Annie's oldest boy had lain drunk with his feet in the fire. His feet went all rotten before spring and he suffered a sight before he died in the summer, she'd heard people say.

After the good breakfast Lureenie was her old self again; as she sat by the hearth helping Suse and Lucy pick out walnuts for molasses candy, she was like a pretty, happy child who has never known trouble. She had borrowed the comb and combed her hair, and it shone now in the firelight like copper-colored silk, soft and fine as a child's hair, and her lips and her eyes were soft and full of smiles as she talked in a soft dreamy voice about the woven-wire fence Rans was going to buy and put up and the garden she would have—she'd already picked out the seed—flowers and all kinds of vegetables—from her old seed catalogue.

Milly rocked the baby and listened absentmindedly to her prattle. Lureenie had lived around in the old Ledbetter cabin going on five years, long enough to get three children and that was all; but still it was good to see her her old, proud, bragging, planning self again.

Suse, as always, was drawn into the magic of Lureenie's plans. One spring, three years back, Suse had gone around to see Lureenie real often, for Lureenie was in the family way with her second one and always lonesome, and Suse could take Angie Mime and Lucy and tend to them there as well as at home. Suse and Lureenie had worked themselves half to death traipsing in the woods hunting log dirt—Lureenie was going to have a flower garden like her mother used to have. She even spent some of Rans's WPA money on flower seed ordered out of a catalogue. Sue Annie heard about the flower garden and nearly laughed herself to death—Lureenie had better worry about a tater patch before flowers and have fence before she bought her seed; but Suse would come home talking about Lureenie's flower garden until a body could almost smell marigolds— and Suse had cried and cried when Old John's hogs came one night and rooted in the pansy bed, and two or three days later Nunn's sheep nibbled off everything above the ground. Lureenie and Suse had piled brush around a little place and planted some more flowers, but by then the weather was dry, and Suse had to stay home and help hoe corn, and Lureenie was so big in the family way she couldn't carry water and Rans wouldn't, and the flowers had never got big enough to bud.

Then Lureenie was going to have a pretty house, as if that old log cabin with the little bit of broken-down secondhand house plunder she and Rans had been able to get together could ever be pretty; first, she'd tried papering; but a hard windy thunderstorm had come, and the cabin leaked so in both roof and walls that the paper fell off, and it hadn't stuck very well anyway on the log walls; then she'd tried whitewashing, and the rain had blown in again and the clay chinking had washed down into the whitewash, until Hattie Tiller, who went around to see it, declared the walls were pied as a copperhead.

But now Suse was listening, a cracked walnut held forgotten in her hand, as if all Lureenie's plans had come to something and she lived in a white-painted weatherboarded house set in a flower-filled picket-fenced yard. Lureenie was nodding and smiling, her red curls trembling, "Cincinnati wouldn't be a bad place to live in—that is if a body could live out a little piece, an have a house with electricity an a yard so's th youngens can play. Rans

declares he's a goen one a these days, an I don't see why
he cain't; one of his cousins over in Alcorn is got a good
job in a radio-maken place; th pay's fifty cents an hour."

Suse gasped at so much money, and Lureenie said that
after a while the men in this factory made even more than
that. She and Rans could save up enough to buy their furniture and make a down payment on a little farm like
Rans's cousin said they had out from Cincinnati; just
four or five acres, but big enough for a big garden and
chickens and a cow; she could tend to all that easy while
Rans worked, for even the farms around Cincinnati had
running water and the electric, but the first thing she'd
buy would be a radio: "Then all th day long, while I'm
goen around worken, I'll have pretty music, dance music if I want it, an I'll never be lonesome."

Milly shifted Lureenie's baby to the other arm; Lureenie made her feel old. Long ago she had outgrown the
foolishness of dreams, learned to be satisfied with holly-
hocks and chrysanthemums and other flowers Aunt
Marthie Jane had set and a grazing cow wouldn't eat. But
Lureenie would plan on and on, until Milly would interrupt to ask about local news and gossip.

And Lureenie would a little regretfully leave her farm
out from Cincinnati and Suse would go back to the molasses candy in the kitchen while Milly learned something of
affairs in the Cow's Horn, where Lureenie had visited
Rans's father, Keg Head, not two weeks back.

Milly shifted the baby to her other arm, spat into the
fire, looked past Lureenie at the snow outside, and fell
into a long wondering worry over Nunn. And Lureenie's
bubbling childish talk came through the wall of Milly's
troubles, as when she described old Keg Head Cramer,
whom she hated: "Him with the scripture verses rollen
off his tongue like molasses off a biscuit, and never taken a
bite to eat—that is, when anybody was around—without
a blessen long as your arm, and prayen so loud in church
he waked the little youngens, and never taken a drop
when anybody offered him a dram, and ready to have
anybody turned out of the church that so much as drove a
nail or cut a stick of wood on Sunday or thought about
saying 'Damn'; well, that old psalm-singing sinner—"

Milly nodded absentmindedly and stared into the fire.
She was thinking now of Suse, busily bossing the candy

and cracker-jack making in the kitchen. Aye, Lord, it would be better never to have a girl child; they saw nothing but pain and trouble and work, and so many went wrong, or else married some good-for-nothing little feist when they were too little to know that kisses come easier than victuals and that a houseful of youngens comes easiest of all.

Thank God, Nunn owned his own land and wasn't afraid of work; but Suse mightn't find a man like her daddy, and Suse, poor soul, didn't have much looks to help her in the hunting. It wasn't safe to let a girl get too old before she married; she was certain to go wrong then. That Beulah Ashcraft was old, going on twenty. Lord God, but there was a lot of trouble in the world; look at Lureenie. Rans would never have a steady job or a foot of land to call his own, nothing but youngens and more youngens.

Lureenie did not go home until dusty dark, and still Nunn had not come. The weather had made up its mind and settled down to dropping a thick-flaked snow out of a low gray sky; and with the snow and Nunn gone, trouble was real, like the ghost of Aunt Marthie you could hear walking but never see. Nunn had been meaning to sled down some more slack coal from the old pile on the hill across the creek, but had never got around to it, and now they were out, and no wood. Lee Roy could split wood or chop kindling, but when he tried to chop a sugar tree log with Nunn's big double-bitted ax, his head flopped forward so that it looked as if he would knock out his brains.

"Lemme at it," Milly commanded, and took the ax. The chips flew, but Lee Roy watched with a mounting distaste. It wasn't two weeks back since Silas Ballew and Alben W. Barkley Tiller had jibed him with his lazy foxhunting father who hadn't cut a stick of wood since he was married. It was a lie, of course, but Milly did have to cut a lot of wood.

So Lee Roy went hunting the cross-cut saw. Nunn had sharpened it up and put it away with strict instructions for nobody to touch it, for he planned to use it in his crosstie timber on the river hill. But Lee Roy went after the saw just the same; it was down in a corner of the crib part of the grist mill barn.

And Zing was there, too, half covered with shucks, as Milly and Suse had left him. Lee Roy did not jump or scream when he saw the old dog. He knew death. He had at funerals seen many people dead, and he remembered Angie Mime, and more faintly Tom; he had sat by the hearth and watched him die across his mother's knees. He smoothed Zing's ears and laid him more evenly on his side, and then, his eyes filling slowly and against his will, he aimlessly, blindly ran his fingers through the graying hairs on Zing's thin ribbed sides. "Aw, Lee Roy, don't be a letten Mom see you cry," Suse begged, coming suddenly into the barn.

"Hell, I ain't a cryen, an go leave me alone." He dropped his face into Zing's hair and lay as he had lain so many nights by the fire.

Suse pulled him gently by the shoulder. "Aw, git up, Lee Roy. Mom's all worried about Nunn still off fox-hunten."

"You mean he's still off drunk, mebbe a whoren after that old bitch that hangs around J. D. Duffey's er a puken his damned guts out in some rock house." He got up, a hot brightness in his eyes drying the tears. "Pop's th reason fer Zing's death. He's run him too hard all fall—I wisht I was a bastard so's Nunn Ballew could be no kin a mine."

"Lee Roy, you'll go to hell a holden sich talk—don't —don't feel so bad. Mebbe Pop ain't drunk, at least not awful drunk." She glanced down at Zing, choked up, looked quickly back at Lee Roy, and spoke with a stiff fixed smile. "Maybe Zing can go to heaven. I'll bet he's already there. Angie Mime, she'll be tickled to see him, an I'll bet th angels'ull feed him a raw egg ever day an all the dog feed he can hold; you know he allus liked it."

Lee Roy shook her words away like drops of rain. "Zing he was good an—" He choked and pushed his hands hard into his eyes.

Suse pulled him toward the door. "Aw, Lee Roy, he's already off up in heaven—maybe on a big hunt right this minute."

Lee Roy jerked away and turned back to Zing. "Aw, hell, this God-damned world's made all wrong. If'n a hound goes anyplace, he goes to hell. Ain't you heared Preacher Samuel say lots a times that less'n anybody

jines th church an gits baptized they go straight to everlasten damnation an hell-fire?"

Suse sighed. "Well, mebbe Zing he'd ruther go where
Pop goes anyhow—but this comen Monday ask old Andrew. He's smarter'n a lot a preachers. I'll bet he'll tell
you Zing went to heaven an that if'n you're good you'll
see him sometime."

But Lee Roy leaned his head against the stable wall;
Suse saw the stain of his tears spread against the wood and
went away.

More than once that night, as Milly sat by the fire, she
thought she heard smothered sobs; but each time she
made the rounds of the children there was only dead silence in Lee Roy's bed and only the little sounds of the
others in their sleep, soft sounds that made her feel alone
in her wakefulness and filled her head with thoughts of
death and trouble.

It might have been midnight or later, when the fire was
low and cold and snow a blurry band of whiteness on the
dark windowpanes, that Milly heard, or thought she
heard, the steady but soft pacing of feet upstairs. She listened, then relaxed somewhat from her rigid crouching by
the fire, and after a time took a chew of tobacco for company. Aunt Marthie Jane was watching with her; she had
walked like that last winter when Lucy had been so sick
with what Sue Annie said was pneumonia fever; and one
night, when Nunn was off fox-hunting, and she had
thought the child was going to die, Aunt Marthie had
hovered around. Once she came downstairs, and Milly
heard the rustle of her full gingham dress and stiff
starched apron in the middle room where Lee Roy slept.
Milly had listened that night with fear like a wedge in her
throat; if Aunt Marthie walked outside, especially toward the graveyard, Lucy would die; for when Aunt
Marthie left the house, trouble always came. But she
had stayed and Lucy got well.

And tonight, as long as she didn't go outside, Nunn
would be all right.

Oh, God, there was a deal of trouble in the world and
Aunt Marthie had had her share; sometimes it had
pressed her so hard she had gone walking over her fields
in the dark; she never had time in daylight. Her troubles,
they said, came thickest when she was old and Preacher

Jim had thought for nothing but God and she was left alone to worry over her children, the boys wild after drink and women, the girls marrying and having babies, and all moving so far away they forgot home and almost never wrote.

Oh, dear Lord God in heaven, why do you send trouble thick as the falling snow on a woman? Did you have a spite against us when you created us from Adam's rib? Oh, God, it's hard to be a woman. And Milly unconsciously lapsed into prayer. God, Jesus, and Aunt Marthie Jane were by her, listening, and to them she poured out her troubles and her fears.

Chapter Six

J. D. Duffey's sixty-three years lay on him light as thistledown as his feet tapped out the tune that Nunnely played on a borrowed fiddle, for J. D. had done a thing he almost never did—he had drunk himself his own sorghum liquor, and now with his old feet full of undanced tunes and his heart soft with the love of his fellow man, he gave away the moonshine he should have sold, while his third wife, just turned seventeen and with a sleepy baby on her hip, stood in the black shadow of a carbide light and watched with hard, scornful eyes.

Somehow, like the slow scattering of pollen from a cedar tree on a still day in March, word had drifted over the hills from midnight Saturday till sundown Sunday that a music party with liquor and dancing was going on at Duffey's, and now, by Sunday full dark, the house and porches had long since overflowed; men and half-grown boys stood close-packed by the windows and doors; cries and whoops and curses came from the barn, while half a dozen slack coal fires lighted the legs and arms and faces and sometimes the sodden shapeless bodies of men dead drunk and oblivious to the snowy cold.

Less than a dozen women seasoned the great gathering of men. There was young Mrs. Veda Duffey, who did not count; she was only there because she would not carry her baby away from the warm house into the cold. There was old puckered-faced, bleary-eyed Ethel Simpson, the woman the whole country called worthless, a kindly soul whose body was well known to men so old their own wives slept with them as if they were sapless as babies, and boys so young they had hardly given over sleeping with their mothers or older sisters, and all men in between who had need of a woman, for Ethel had a price no more than water has a price. For years while old J. D. lived alone as a widower, she had kept house for him and helped in the liquor sales, both as a sort of added attraction like a free lunch, and as a helper in the liquor business, where she was of great value, for she never drank.

She danced now with Rans and now and then glanced worriedly at Idie Sexton. Idie was going on seventeen and had two bastards by two different men, and from her goings on with Willie Cooksey seemed ready to get herself bigged with a third. She was a great rawboned creature with fine strong teeth, wheat-colored hair, and wide pale-blue eyes, untroubled and empty as a child's. Willie had three children older than she and eight younger, but some unaccustomed energy had sent him out into the snow after Idie and her two babies, now sleeping on Mrs. Duffey's clean feather bed in the back room.

There was little Zadie Coffin, who had been turned out of the church for using swear words and now went into the brush with the boys, and Annie Mae Cooler, who'd gone off to work in a factory in Cincinnati and came back with the bad disease, and Lena Lawton, that people said drank a bottle of turpentine every month and so never got caught.

They danced with twice their number of men a square dance on one side of J. D.'s big fireplace room, with Blare Tiller trying to call the sets as he had heard Billy Buckskin call them over the radio, while Mark Cramer and Uncle Dave Tiller drew squeaking, twanging shrieks and cries from a fiddle and a banjo.

In a far corner of the room Nunn squatted in the half dark and played still another tune on the borrowed fiddle. He looked no higher than J. D.'s flying heels, his half-closed eyes warm with their faint smiles: contented he was and warm, not just his body, but warm clear down to his heart, the world immeasurably fine, immeasurably pleasant, the tobacco smoke and the dust billowing up from the swaying creaking floor boards; and the fumes of liquor and carbide and sweating bodies and gusts of coal smoke from the open fire and the smell of the snow-soaked hounds and cur dogs asleep on the hearth—all these were fine, not so much in themselves, but because they were a part of the enchanted, untroubled world to which he, Nunnely Ballew, belonged. The hatred of the red fox and the long nights of hunting him were gone from his heart; in its place there was only pity that such a fine beast must die soon and sorrow that good hunting such as he had might soon be ended.

Aye, God, but he, Nunn, would raise up a pair of fox-hounds the likes of which had never been seen in the county. He didn't know just where he would go, but he'd find them somewhere; one hundred good dollars apiece he would pay, if that was their price. Money—he spat contemptuously on the floor. Lizzie, the black heifer, was worth $75 any Saturday in the stockyards. There was the money he had saved back to pay taxes—taxes could wait and so could a man's craving for pork—one pig was enough for one winter, he would sell the other two. Milly had raised lots of beans—and if all that wasn't enough, he would sell Rosie, the brood sow. What did a man need with a brood sow anyhow? Just something to feed corn to; and if a man didn't have to feed corn, he wouldn't have to grow it and waste time out from training his hound pups and then chasing King Devil till he bust his heart just like he had busted Zing's.

Lord, but it was a sweet world, with no corn crop to work a man's guts out on and no more worry about hog-killing weather, worrying if the moon was right and if there'd come a warm spell before the hams took salt.

"It's a funeral song I recken you're a playen, Nunn." Willie Cooksey had left off dancing with Idie Sexton and now stood unsteadily a few steps away, looking down at Nunn, his face loose and ugly, full of aimless wrinkles, like a tub of cold hog's guts, the half cunning, half stupid smile natural to the man when he was either drunk or sober flickering across his pale eyes. "It's a funeral song fer pore ole Zing, the best foxhound you'll ever have," he repeated with a hoarse giggle.

"More like a wedden," Nunn answered good-naturedly, not looking up, "a wedden fer you and Idie."

Willie shook his head and giggled again. "If'n a man could use a team a women like a team a mules, I'd take her now, but I got one pretty fair woman and no fireplace room fer another'n . . . I'm a goen to have to build me a heaten stove; there jist ain't room fer all my youngens around th fireplace. . . . Pore I am, like you, Nunn. Me, I'm youngen pore, an you, you're youngen pore an land pore both."

Nunn was listening carefully now, looking straight up at Willie, old Dave's fiddle silent and forgotten in his hands. "Man, I ain't pore," he said placatingly, as he might have spoken to a mistaken child. "I can lay my hands on a right good heap a money."

Willie giggled and shook his head. "You'll never git rich a farmen er a fox-hunten neither." He squatted by Nunn, laid his hand on his knee and spoke in a confidential whisper, but loud enough for any in the room sober enough to listen to hear: "I feel sorry fer you, man, a losen that good ole hound, an no money to buy so much as a little white feist dog . . . an maybe nothen to feed one if'n you had him." He stopped and glanced across the room to where Idie Sexton was listening; she tittered drunkenly, then smiled her encouragement to keep up the play.

"An seen as how I feel sorry fer a man in your fix, an seen as how we're good friends, Nunn, an seen as how we're both pore, I'll tell you what I'll do, Nunn. I'll loan you my hound if'n you'll give him his board an keep an not send him home to me to feed after he's run all night."

Nunn laid the fiddle on the floor and got up, sliding Willie's hands from his knee as he did so. "Listen, you Cooksey from th Cow's Horn, I ain't a needen one bit a yer hound. . . . He ain't worth a dust a meal a month . . . Part rabbit-hunten cur he is, I'd say, like th man that owns him. Don't you be a worryen. . . . Wait an see. I'll git King Devil fore I die. But I've figgered it all out," and he spoke deliberately, like a sober man. "It'll take two good hounds, good an better than Zing was . . . so I'm buyen me a pair of young pups, an damn good they've got to be, no pore white trash raised."

Willie giggled again and lowed it would take somebody else to raise them besides Nunn; and one of the Sextons, another Alcorn County man and kin of the Cookseys, listening with his back to the fire, broke into loud laughter. "You'll never git that red devil of a fox; you might as well hunt a March wind aimen to make a fart."

"What's it to you, my gitten King Devil," Nunn wanted to know, and something about his voice made the Sexton, who was more sober than drunk, turn abruptly around

and stare straight into the fire, as if he had lost all interest
in foxes or hunting.

Willie smiled and patted Nunn on the shoulder. "Now
don't be a gitten riled. You cain't blame people. That
brag a your'n about gitten King Devil is so old it's full a
skippers. Recollect bout six years back when you first
come back to this country how you was a goen to have
that red fox's hide a warmen your woman's feet fore th
weather got cold." He giggled and wiped his upper lip with
the back of his hand, waiting for laughter.

Idie Sexton laughed tipsily and came across the room to
enjoy the fun, and J. D., who had been dancing for some
time with no tune save the clapping of his own hands,
stopped suddenly and broke into loud braying heehaws,
bending nearly double with the violence of his mirth.
"Pore lil woman in a pore lone bed; her footsies is cold a
waiten fer a fox skin, an her backsides is cold a waiten fer
her man."

The more drunken, lounging in the corners and pressed
against the windows, roared in laughter, but the more sober began a sudden, silent slipping away, like birds taking
cover from an approaching storm.

Nunn was silent, looking first at the giggling Willie and
then at old J. D., who now squatted on his heels, head
swaying between his knees as he struggled with an uncontrollable fit of senseless, drunken mirth. The old man's
laughter held some uninhibited infectious quality that
gathered and swelled the scattered laughs and chuckles
into a bawling uproar that awoke the babies in the back
room and brought those men sober enough running in
from the barn and yard to see the goings on.

Calls and cries of, "You said it, J. D. . . . Come on,
Nunn, bring in that red fox hide, your woman's cold all
over. . . . Let's go hunten an git him now, so's th pore lil
woman won't have to wait no longer. . . . Yippeee! Sic
em, hounds. . . . I'll bet any man a liven a salt barrel full
a gold that that red fox'ull never be took; he's bewitched,
he is." Half-witted, bird-tongued Rufus Cramer broke
into a shrill yodel of "Aye, le oh ladee, he hee hee hee,
oh ladee," and old Uncle Dave Tiller laid down the banjo
and began a tremulous, drunken calling concerning the
whereabouts of his fiddle, while Blare, who never drank,
began calling his father to come home.

The hounds sleeping on the hearth and under the floor woke and set up a furious barking and howling, and two of the Anderson boys, Rayme and Paul, the best tenors in Deer Lick Choir, broke into the wailing strains of "There's a Glad Day Coming By and By."

Nunn picked up old Dave's fiddle and went across the room and laid it carefully on the mantel. Men called to him; some in drunken, good-natured, but insulting banter, and some hiccoughingly sympathetic: "Don't pay em no mind, Nunn: they ain't got no sense. Nobody minds your brags; git ten Wheeler hounds an a panther. That fox he's th devil incarnate. Nobody'ull ever git him. We know a haint had you by th trigger finger an you couldn't shoot. We know your woman's feet ain't cold, just her front sides. Sic em, Nunn; you don't need no hound; you've eat rabbit till you can run like one."

Nunn paid no attention to any of them. He went from the hearth to the crowd by the door and pushed his way through, walking with his eyes straight ahead, like a man in his sleep, though men pulled at his clothing and wanted to know where he was going or advised him to knock the guts and daylights out of old J. D. and Willie.

It was cold outside, with a thickening scud of snow cloud and a skim of steely round grains underfoot. One of the Widow Martin's little boys, scared and cold and sober, stood just inside the porch roof, his neglected carbide gleaming a cold pale blue. "Turn up that light, boy, an gimme a shine," Nunn commanded.

The boy hesitated. The crowd of curious who had followed Nunn to the porch were laughing and calling, "Don't you do it, boy. He's a goen fer a shotgun. He's a goen fer to git that ole King Devil with his own bare hands."

Nunn put his hand on the boy's shoulder, "Listen, boy, turn up that light, quick."

The boy's hands were cold and they trembled, but he pulled off his miner's cap, and with many frightened stares at Nunn, poured in fresh carbide from the flask in his pocket, then turned up the flame until it burned clear yellow-white, and went docilely forward when Nunn commanded, "Shine me down to th barn an git a move on."

In the barn the light glinted on the upturned steel prongs of a hayfork leaning by the cow's stall, and Nunn

stopped and examined it, but when he saw that the handle
was cracked and loose-fitting in its socket, he went on
through the barn, looking at first one thing and then another. But it was not until the light picked out the dull
glow of oiled iron shining through the cracks in J. D.'s
corn crib that the hunt was over and he went in and found
J. D.'s mining tools. The boy stood still in the open door
and stared, mute terror in his rolled-up eyes, while Nunn
examined first a short-handled, short-pointed miner's pick,
and then a four-foot miner's drill shaped like a giant steel
corkscrew.

The pick would be a handy thing, but so would the
drill; he took them both. He slung the miner's pick, handle
down, under the bib of his overalls; he grasped the long
drill in his two hands, and holding it as a man holds an ax
who would fell a tree at one blow, turned back and
plunged through the crowd. At the porch steps the Martin
boy flung the light, cap and all, from his head and scuttled into the darkness, but Nunn, busy searching the crowd
for a Cramer, paid him no mind.

The Sexton who had stood by the hearth and laughed
at him, gaped at him now an instant in fear and wonder,
then dropped his head and hunched his shoulders so that
Nunn's blow fell on his shoulders, the force of it somer-
saulting him over onto his head, with his legs for an instant upended and treading the air like the legs of a stuck
pig; and then, like a tree falling in a thicket, he brought
two men, already unsteady on their feet, down with him
into a groaning, cursing, whooping tangle of arms and legs.

Nunn studied the squirming pile a moment, debating
the feasibility of quieting it all with one good blow, but
Rans seized the drill from behind and would have jerked
it from him had he not pushed it backward with all his
strength to send the man spinning, blood trickling from a
hole in his shoulder where the drill had bitten into him as
into a vein of coal.

He heard women scream and dogs bark and men curse
and yell: "Put out th lights. Nunn Ballew's went crazy.
Git him, somebody, quick. I'm a comen, Nunn. Hold em,
boy. Git a shotgun an kill him, Rans. Let's kill ever
Cramer in the Cow's Horn. Lay into th dirty bastards,
Nunn." And over it all Blare Tiller's frightened calls of
"Pap, oh, Pap, come git on home, Pap." But Nunn an-

swered nobody, hardly heard, in fact. He wanted Willie
and old J. D., and they didn't seem to be where they had
been.

He heard glass breaking and saw Willie's legs lifting
through a window on the other side of the room. He
hurried, but Willie was already half through and swinging toward the ground, so that try as he would, he couldn't
get him square on the head, and not even a good swing on
his ribs, for the arms and hands wrapped around the
empty window sash got in the way and took most of the
force of the drill, and Willie, blood jumping from his
hands, was pitching down to the ground like a sack of wet
meal.

He heard cloth tear and knew it was his own and knew
that another one of the damned Cookseys or Cramers was
trying to cut his heart out from behind. He whirled and
spun the drill before him as a drummer spins a baton, for
there was no room for a good rousing blow. He saw the
flash of the knife blade, cold blue it was in the carbides,
and young Mark Cramer was at him, strong as a panther
and about as quick. Nunn ducked; the knife blade hissed
over his shoulder, as swift, it seemed, as a knife hurled,
but with it there was a clenched hand grazing his shoulder; Nunn h'isted his shoulders and for an instant he and
Mark swayed together in a tight embrace, each supporting
the other, yet fighting to be free.

Somebody pushed Mark from behind and Nunn swayed
toward the wall, but using the drill as a cripple uses a
crutch, he held it steady in his free hand and pushed
quickly with all his strength, flinging himself forward so
violently that Mark fell sprawling from him into the arms
of a Sexton trying to help him. Once more Nunn had his
two hands free and space enough for the drill.

He swung it over the squirming, struggling Cramer and
Sexton, but there wasn't room enough, and he knew from
the feel of the blow that he hadn't bashed in their heads
and smeared the lard in their skulls that passed for brains
over the floor as he had wanted to do.

Nobody came at him for an instant, and he stood gasping, swaying a little, supporting himself with the drill.
Mark was struggling to his knees, shaking his bloody head
like a hound with the sidehead, but the Sexton didn't
move. Then, from the corner of his eye, Nunn saw Rans

gather himself like a cat crouching for a bird, brass-knucks gleaming on his clenched hand. He spread his feet and lifted the drill, but a hard blow on the back of his head from something in the window behind sent him staggering toward bloody Mark, the long blade of his frog sticker poised like a dagger.

But Mark let out a yowling curse, his face and neck muscles suddenly corded and twisted as Jaw Buster, who had come up, stood on his foot and jerked the hand holding the knife straight upward with his two hands, and as Jaw Buster was heavier by thirty pounds than Mark and stronger, Mark was for an instant no better than a piece of tough beef between two hungry hounds. Jaw Buster took Mark's hand and knife in his big left fist and with his right knocked all pain from him. He then lifted one big brogan and kicked the Sexton hard in the groin. Just then a rock whizzed over the heads of the other men and caught Jaw Buster above the ear.

He sat down like a man going off balance on ice. Rans, with blood on his face and an ugly look in his eyes, grabbed the knife from Mark's limp hand and jumped on Jaw Buster. But Paul Anderson, who with Lister had quieted the rock thrower in the window, jumped on Rans, and the three in their struggles came down on Jaw Buster together.

Other Little Smokey Creek men came swarming through the window, armed with rocks, oak planks, and knives; with Joe C., who had somehow got his hands on a gooseneck hoe, shrieking in a drunken singsong, "I'm a goen to chop me a liver out a ever Cramer frum th Cow's Horn."

Nunn, suddenly tired and unsteady on his feet, with his head roaring like a settling swarm of bees, lifted the minter's screw to strike, but deliberated on which man to kill. Around him there was a tangle of violently agitated arms and legs and backs and shoulders, but none of them semed interested in him. Jaw Buster had half a dozen men struggling on top of him, each either trying to save him or make an end of him, and all kicking, hitting, knifing.

Somebody gave Nunn a violent shove from behind. The screw clattered to the floor and Nunn followed. He fell with his face on the shoes of some Cramer who forthwith tried to stomp out his brains. Nunn clawed with his

hands, something cracked above him, sharp in the roar of
curses and cries and groans, and the shoes were still, with
ankles limber like the legs of a fresh-killed ram. Nunn remembered the miner's pick in his belt and struggled to get
on his hands and knees, but the owner of the shoes sank
gently but heavily onto his head. He tried to turn over
and had half succeeded when somebody, apparently trying
to run, stumbled over his outstretched legs and fell on top
of him.

The man who had tried to stomp out his brains settled
heavily on his head and shoulders, like a wet feather bed,
and somebody else jumped or fell on the man who had
stumbled over him. The weight on him pushed him
down, and like weakened timbers under a heavy load of
slate, his body caved slowly down until he lay with his face
pushed hard into the floor, but half protected by his
cupped-up hands.

Somewhere a shotgun roared, followed by a woman's
wild screaming, then silence broken soon by two pistol
shots, right on top of him they sounded. He lifted his head.
He knew his eyes were free and open, but nothing came
to him but black darkness, blacker than any he had ever
known in an unlighted mine or the dark of the moon on a
cloudy night.

He realized he could hear nothing, not a curse or a
moan; the blackness was death and so was the stillness.
He gave one violent superhuman struggle and shrieked,
"Git me home, boys. I'm a dead man." Then he was silent, saving his strength. He wanted to see Milly. Good
Lord God, please let him see Milly again, just once before
he died—if the kind sweet Jesus would let him live he'd
never touch another drop, and join the church. He
groaned; Hell was close; there was no time for deathbed
repentance; worse, there was in his soul no desire for it.
He couldn't promise God he would quit chasing that red
devil of a fox; the worst part about Hell yawning up for
him was that he couldn't chase him there. It was the
damned fox that was sending him now to eternal damnation and hell-fire everlasting with liquor in his belly and
not one sin prayed from his soul.

He heard screaming again: "Nunn Ballew's a dyen.
Git him out, somebody. They've shot Nunn Ballew. Oh,
Lord, pull him out, somebody," but still he couldn't see.

There was a pain like fire in his stomach; shot in the guts he was, like he'd ought to have shot that fox; only the fox was bewitched and wouldn't let himself be shot; he had to chase him through all Hell. A greater weight was grinding him down, smothering him until he had no breath, until there was nothing but stars and rainbows, with the long hunt going on and on and under.

There was a crack of light by his eyes, and he lay a long time considering, wondering, trying to remember, remembering a little, enough to make him afraid to try to move or open his eyes. Then somebody was shaking him, yelling in an impatient, disgusted voice, "Fer Christ's sake, Nunn, wake up. You aimen to sleep forever? It's Monday mornen an broad daylight."

Nunn groaned and opened his eyes and met the cold yellow of a clear frosty smile just touching the mouth of the Juber Dan rock house across the river from Brush Creek. Somebody shook him again, and pain like red-hot pokers played across his eyeballs and his back and thighs. "Careful, man," he begged hoarsely. "You'll make me start bleeden agin."

"Bleeden, hell, you're th onliest one a th whole caboodle that ain't got a scratch. Me, I was cold sober an my head's got a bloody lump big as a four-pound lard bucket, an I thought Pap was a sure goner fore I could git him out. It was so bad that pore old J. D. Duffey, that has run frum th law an fit it all his days, was a beggen fer somebody to go git th law fore it was over. Ann Liz Cooksey in the Cow's Horn heard th ruckus an got skeered might nigh to death an is about to miscarry, Mom said when she sent Hattie an Flonnie a hunten us all."

Blare stopped for breath and then rushed on. "God, you ought to a seen them women—mad; Rans Cramer's mebbe bled to death by now, an Jaw Buster said he thought he had a fractured skull; it shore to God looked like it, an—Lord, Lord, wake up, Nunn, you've slept this blessed night like a baby. An I've set, when I'd ought to a been home with Flonnie, a watchen you an a thinken mebbe yer insides was squashed somehow, when Veda Duffey—she was cold sober an skeered jist like me, pore girl—shot out the lights in th hopes a quieten th fracas, an everbody that wasn't already on top a you fell on. Then they got more lights an th fighten it got worse, but you passed out, leastways yer head wasn't worken by then."

Nunn opened his eyes again and held them open, making a mighty effort not to wince with pain. It was Blare Tiller all right; not St. Peter at the judgment day with a trumpet in his hand. He rolled over slowly, clenching his teeth so as not to groan, and sat up. Then slowly, very slowly he got to his feet.

The earth swayed and rocked under him, and he teetered on his heels, waiting for it to subside. Then he passed his hands carefully over his body, pausing longest on his stomach. Blare watched in disgust. "It's a wonder yer guts ain't strung from here to J. D.'s, a layen th way you was, all squashed down on that miner's pick. What if'n it had a been turned pickenwise, an all them men on top a you."

"It might a been a good thing," Nunn said, and shook his head to drown the buzzing in his ears. He set his hat on straight and started home. If he hurried, he could hew ten crossties before nightfall.

He stopped still in the road, frowning. The wonder that had hounded him for hours was back; why hadn't he killing King Devil? He shook his head; but unlike the buzzing, the hound of this thought would not go away.

Chapter Seven

As soon as Nunn had gone away to work in the crosstie timber, Milly and the children shrouded Zing in one of the new feed-sack aprons, laid him on two wide planks, and carried him up to the old graveyard above the garden patch. Lee Roy had dug the grave alone; he had come to Milly in the dawn before Nunn was home and asked if he could dig it there. The old graveyard was a pretty place set on a high bench of land below the Pilot Rock, with three big black oak trees and a poplar, about the biggest trees on the farm, for the graveyard had been old when Preacher Jim was a boy, and no one knew who lay under the unlettered, moss-encrusted stones; some said Indians, and some said white men killed by Indians. But nobody had ever plowed the land or cut the trees.

It had been hard work carrying Zing so high up the hillside through the snow, but when his grave was neatly mounded and stacked with stones, Milly was glad they had taken the trouble—it was a sin to think on a hound like a human, but he was better here in a place with people—and he had liked the spot when he was alive. In huckleberry-picking time she would leave him and the least ones in the shade of the trees and go up the hill, and Zing would lie there with one eye for the children and the other for the valley opened wide before him.

Milly squeezed her eyes hard; she wouldn't cry before the children. Far below her she could see Lee Roy's red-brown head moving through the scrub pine and sagegrass; running he was, in long lopes, like a little wild animal running from scorching fire. She wished she could help him; he was too little to know that a body could never run away

90

from pain and trouble. She watched as he turned into the school path, the first time in his life he had ever gone to school without Zing—maybe old Andrew could make him feel better: he was a wise old man. But nobody could help a body much till they learned to lean on Jesus—and sometimes even He seemed far away. Below her the valley looked cold and desolate, with snow on the last year's corn patches and brush showing ragged black and ugly; far below she could see one spot of river water, like a lake shut off by the curving bluffs, and it was gray-looking and cold like the sky; and her own heart too, seemed like.

That morning in school Lee Roy had five words in spelling and missed three, but old Andrew only pulled his spectacles down and looked at the boy's red-rimmed eyes and said nothing. Lee Roy went back to his seat and after a while laid his book in the door and went off to be excused in spite of the fact that Paul Ballew's book was already in the door, and it was against the rules for two books to be in the door at once.

Lee Roy sat a long time halfway up a big beech tree not far from the schoolhouse and took a chew of long red. He would have stayed longer, but the tobacco was dry in his mouth and the wind in the pines above made him sad, and he knew if he didn't move on he would start crying again.

Old Andrew never even seemed to notice when he finally did come back.

After a while one of Old John's mules stuck his head through a broken-out window, as he often did in search of a biscuit or a little scratching from one of the children. Lee Roy hit him squarely in the eye with a hickory nut so that he reared and came near jerking out the rest of the window frame.

But Andrew, instead of telling Lee Roy to stay in at recess as he ordinarily would have done, only stopped with his finger under the word that Bernice Dean Tiller was trying to read and said, "Boy, you know better than to hurt a poor dumb beast that's not hurten you."

Lee Roy sank dejectedly back into his seat. Without wanting to, he glanced at the two Tiller hounds asleep by the stove with the worn spot on the floor between them— that had been Zing's place. And to keep his eyes away from it he fell to staring at a knothole in the floor near his seat. It was a big knothole, so big that he could look down and see a low ray of the early winter's sun streaking across Tillys nose as she lay suckling her eight pigs down in the warm dust under the schoolhouse.

After a while Lee Roy pulled a piece of binder twine from an overall pocket, took the big safety pin out of the back to Ruby Tiller's dress, took it so gently that Ruby, busily matching her name with Andy Hull's, never noticed. He tied the safety pin to the twine, then went back to the water bucket. He walked quietly and sipped a long while at a dipper of water, watching Andrew as he sipped.

When Andrew bent his old bald head to make a row of ABC's on Lucy's tablet, Lee Roy seized his four-pound lard-can dinner bucket and rushed soundlessly back to his seat. Silas Ballew watched him wonderingly, but hunched his head and shoulders over his end of the desk so that Andrew might not notice the dinner bucket.

After some consideration Lee Roy selected a baked sweet potato from the assortment of food in his bucket. He wrapped and pinned it well in the twine, then pushed it through the knothole and watched and waited. Tilly wriggled her nose with sniffing, then lifted her big ears and looked interested, and at last stretched out her neck. Lee Roy flipped the sweet potato still nearer. Tilly rolled over, scattering her pigs with an uproar of angry squealing, while with a gentle grateful oinking she reached for the potato.

The pleased oinking changed to a fearful squealing as the potato leaped out of her reach. Tilly charged after it, but the knothole was out of nose reach, and Tilly, agile razorback though she was, couldn't get to it without a prop for her front feet, and she had no prop. She squealed and oinked and cursed, and the pigs, outraged at being disturbed in the middle of their meal, squealed and cursed too. Tilly reared on her hind legs like a frightened mule, and it looked like she was going to make it. Silas leaned over Lee Roy's shoulder and Alben W. Barkley Tiller crouched over the knothole.

Ruby got up on her knees in her seat to see the goings on and her safety-pinless dress fell down her shoulders, and what children were not already tittering and whispering over Tilly set up a wild choked, hissing laughter to see

Ruby with her dress falling down and her purple outing underbody showing.

The drowsing hounds awoke, and half asleep, ran first to the window, barking like cur dogs, and seeing no strangers, circled the room until they came to the knothole and there they stopped and bayed as if they had treed a coon.

Andrew threw a piece of chalk at Lee Roy to make him pay attention, "Boy, what are you a doen to that hog?"

Lee Roy sat stiffly in his seat, staring straight before him, "Who? Me?"

Andrew sighed, pulled his glasses straight on his nose, and glanced at the slant of the sun through a window, "Th rest a you all can have recess now but Lee Roy, an he has to set in an maybe take a whippen. . . . You little youngens put on your sweaters an jumpers; it's cold out; an don't set on th ground or go off an eat wet walnuts . . . you'll be sick. . . . An when you bigger ones play fox an hounds, don't run clear out a th country, like you done yesterday, and not git back till evenen recess."

He sat and waited while the fourteen pupils followed by the hounds, ran noisily to the row of lard buckets on the water shelf, pried off the lids with a great clattering, seized biscuits and baked sweet potatoes, and then, with their hands full, ran screaming and whooping into the yard.

Andrew hitched his chair nearer the stove, opened it, and spat his old chew into the fire, then pulled a plug of tobacco from his pocket and cut a fresh chew. When he had returned knife and tobacco to his pocket, he glanced over his glasses at Lee Roy, absentmindedly deepening a set of initials on his desk with the blade of his pocket knife. "Boy, what ails you anyhow? Don't cut them initials that away. Your pop done that mighty nigh thirty years ago; I recollect a thinken he was awful smart to know how to cut initials when he was so little. . . . Now leave em be, an come set by th stove."

Lee Roy slowly folded up his jackknife and just as slowly came and sat near Andrew on an upturned powder keg. "Boy, what ails you anyhow? You wanten a whippen? I could wear out a hickory limb big as my wrist on you and it wouldn't be half enough for all th meanness you've been into lately."

"Aw, hell, Andrew, I ain't done nothen much mean . . .

not mean enough fer a whippen. Jist let me set in an I'll do better."

Andrew opened the stove door and spat in a mouthful of tobacco juice, then, using both hands, pulled his glasses all the way down to the end of his nose, crossed his legs, and considered Lee Roy. After a while he sighed. "Well, whatever you do you can't do much worse, less'n you pull th schoolhouse down an put it on the roof. If your pop knowed how you was misbehaven, he'd wear you out; he was a good boy in school an got his lessons."

"An growed up to be a drunkard."

"Aw, Lee Roy, you mustn't talk like that; he's not what you'd call an out-an-out drunkard like a lot a men."

"He would be if he wasn't too lazy to work out th money to buy whisky."

"Now, Lee Roy, if he wanted to be real bad, he could make his own or mortgage his place to buy drink, like Absolem Tiller. You're mad about somethen or you wouldn't be talken this away. He give you a hard whippen fer some meanness you been up to?"

Lee Roy swallowed and stared at the stove with hard bright eyes. "He run Zing to death. . . . I'd a lot d'ruther he'd a beat all th skin off my back."

Andrew shook his head. "Nunn didn't kill Zing. He was old; he run himself to death like any good hound ought when he's old enough to die."

"If'n Pop hadn't a been so dead set on catchen King Devil, he'd never a let Zing run so much. I've heard Mom beg him many a night not to let Zing run, that he was getten too old to hunt so much, an Pop, he'd jist fly up an tell her to mind her own business an take him anyhow, maybe not git in sometimes till after we'd all had breakfast.

"Now, Lee Roy, you've been letten your mind run too much on Zing. You had to lose him sometime. I recollect he was middle-agedlike when he started comen to school with you in th primer . . . an now you're ten. And he'd be gitten old fer a hard runnen hound."

Lee Roy frowned down at his overall knees. "Mebbe so," he said, and after a time of staring at the stove in silence, he hitched his nail keg nearer Andrew's chair, glanced swiftly about to see if any one was listening, swallowed, then went on in a low choked voice: "Tell me,

Andrew, they's somethen I want to ask you—does hounds
—good hounds like Zing, I mean—do they ever git to
heaven? I hate—I hate to think that Zing ain't nothen
now," he finished in a faltering whisper.

Andrew smiled and spat another stream of tobacco
juice into the stove. "Is that all that's a worryen you?
Heaven's chuck full a hounds, an all other kinds a dogs,
but especially hounds. Why, I'll bet Zing's a chasen a fox
right now—a smart red fox like you don't hardly ever
find outside a heaven—that'll give him a run fer
his money. Only Zing's not old any more. He's young now
with spring in his legs an wind enough to run three days an
four nights an never stop given tongue."

A little of the trouble left Lee Roy's eyes, but he shook
his head unbelievingly. "I've heared Preacher Samuel say
that man is th onliest crittur that has got a soul, an if you
ain't got no soul you cain't git yer sins prayed away an git
saved an git to heaven."

Andrew pulled off his glasses, held them in one hand,
and smiled with a superior, knowing air. "Just between
you an me, Preacher Samuel's a good man, but he didn't
write th Bible. Some dogs, hounds in particular, have got
bigger souls than a heap a men; they don't have no sins to
begin with. Take you an Zing, for instance; many an
many's th whippens I've give you, but I hardly ever had to
so much as speak to Zing, not like them Tiller hounds that
are allus under my feet or a chasen Old John's pigs. Zing
never bothered nothen nor nobody."

He spat again, then leaned forward with his hands on
his knees, and looked into Lee Roy's thirsty eyes. "An
hunten's might good in heaven, better than any your pop
has ever seen, an thats a sayen a whole heap. Heaven's
just a way a liven right on; ever man an ever hound lives
th way he liked th best on earth. Don't it say God sees
th little sparrow fall? Well, it stands to reason that He'd
notice Zing a lot more'n he would a sparrow, an have a
place ready prepared fer him when he comes."

Lee Roy smiled. "Recken that's all so, Andrew?"

Andrew looked disgusted, then waved his specs to em-
phasize his words. "Well, if you don't want to believe me,
don't, an don't be a asken me, ask all the preachers an all
th smart men. I recollect a hearen County Judge Saunders
say once that he was certain an old mare of his had gone

to heaven, an many's th smart man I've heard say th same thing about some hound. Look at Job; I've always figgered that patient like he was, he would like fox hunten; he's maybe hunten now with Zing."

He spat out his recess chew of tobacco and cut a small fresh chew to keep him through books until dinnertime. He glanced up, met Lee Roy's eyes, happier, but troubled still, and handed him the tobacco. "Here, boy, have a chew; it's better'n that long red you've been a chewen. Go on out fer a while an fergit about Zing. He'll be all right till you git to heaven—but if you don't change your ways, you'll never go there."

Lee Roy grinned and reached for the tobacco. "Gimme time, Andrew. Pop ain't got religion yit, an I've heared say that Preacher Jim never got it till he got his oldest boys raised up big enough to help Aunt Marthie Jane with th farmen."

He ran out the door and around the house corner and bumped hard into Ruby, who had been peeping and listening by a broken window. She fell sprawling but had wind enough left to call him a little patched-britch son of a bitch.

Lee Roy smiled and heisted his overalls. "But I don't eat give-away grub—cow feed. Your Mom makes bread out a that brown flour they give to Joe C. and them other WPA workers, an it ain't nothen but cow feed—cow-feed eater," he taunted.

Ruby smiled and tossed her permanent wave at a taunt that ordinarily made her curse. "Leastways I ain't a goen around a cryen over a old hound—cry baby, cry baby. An my pop works; he don't let his family go half naked an live on rabbit an poke shoots cause he's too lazy to do nothen but fox-hunt."

Lee Roy nodded and smiled. It was a weakness to deny a taunt. The idea was to fling back a better one. "Rabbit an poke shoots is good fer a body's brains, though. Look at Suse, younger'n you an ready fer th eighth grade. But look at you," he went on, hanging his head low on his shoulders and rolling his eyes over Ruby's large hips. "You've not got sense enough to spell 'fart,' but Lord, when it comes to letten one, you've got a behind big enough to blow over a haystack if you let all th wind out a that big belly at one time."

Ruby cursed and sprang for his hair. He sidestepped, then tripped her. She got up, her pale eyes glassy with anger; but from experience she knew that chasing him did her more harm than him, and that hitting him with a rock was harder than hitting a squirrel. "Jist you wait, Lee Roy Ballew. I'll fix you, an ol Andrew, too, him a tellen you that animals has got souls; that's a goen agin th Bible, th old, ol—idolator. I seed him give you a chaw a tubaccer, too, an that's agin the law," and she strode away, nodding her permanent wave, calling over her shoulder, "Jist wait'll I tell Mom an Granma an you'll git th hide whaled off'n you."

But two mail-day evenings later, when Nunn came home from the post office and told Milly, sorting dried applies for cooking in the fireplace room, what Sue Annie had told him, he showed an unconcern that surprised Lee Roy and Suse, who were listening by a broken window; but then Nunn had been strange-turned and absent in his ways since his last big drunk when Zing died; he was like a man with his mind gone off on a long hunt.

Nunn went away to the sheepfold and Milly sighed after his tired, slumped-downlike back; he'd been working so hard in his crosstie timber that she almost wished he had a hound to take him from his work. She wondered if he ever thought what she thought sometimes—that the Tillers made fun of Suse and Lee Roy and caused all this fracasing and fighting; maybe that was why he'd been working from daylight till dark in the tie timber—to buy things for his family. Suse was telling her the other day, not complaining, just telling, about Ruby's red raincoat and blue overshoes, and how all the rest of the Tillers and, of course, the Hulls, too, had overshoes; and Milly had understood, without asking, that her youngens were the only ones without such things.

All through supper-getting, Milly thought of schemes for raising the money for overshoes for Suse, but during supper she forgot both Tillers and overshoes in watching Nunn. He'd never seemed right since Zing died, but tonight he seemed more like a man gone daft than ever; instead of eating he sat squeezing a piece of corn bread and staring at the lamp flame; and after supper, when Suse and Lee Roy started a fight right under his nose over whose turn it was to carry the night's slop to Rosie, he only, in a kind of addled, sleepy-headed way, caught Suse by the dress tail and held her on his knee. Suse sat there with the dishrag in her hand, afraid to speak, afraid to move, for ordinarily Nunn wouldn't stand for a quarrel amongst the youngens, much less fighting.

Lee Roy dashed off to slop the hogs and the little youngens tiptoed off to the fireplace room; but Nunn still sat, staring like what he saw was inside his head, while Milly fiddled around the stove and watched from the corners of her eyes.

All at once he jumped up with a big oath and wanted to know what in hell was the matter with that damned smoky lamp. He had a letter to write and it didn't make enough light for a man to see to spit by. He jumped so suddenly that Suse, sitting tense and stiff-legged on his lap, sprawled head over onto the floor, but was up in an instant, dashing for the lantern to set by the lamp, while Milly took off the hot lamp chimney and polished it on a corner of her apron. Suse shined up the lantern and hurriedly freshened the fire in the cookstove so that he might keep warm, and Milly took the ink pen and ink and an ink tablet from the high shelf and put them on the table. After a hissing whisper to Lee Roy, she and Suse tiptoed off to the fireplace room and there, with a deal of shushing and dire threats of peach tree limbs, quieted the little youngens, who had set up a wrangling over who should have the two powder kegs and who should sit on the hearth.

Nunn was left alone with a blank shiny ink tablet staring up at him. He stared back at it for a long while, got up, got a drink, walked restlessly around the kitchen, put more coal on the fire, finally remembered to take his long overdue after-dinner chew of tobacco, and then sat down again. After much head scratching, cursing, and ruined sheets, the letter was written:

Jonathon Wheeler
Apple Reach, Ky.

DEAR SIR: I don't guess you know me. I live on Little Smokey Creek at Ballew, Ky., and I fox hunt some. A while back my old hound died while he was running a red fox. I mean to catch that fox fair and

squar before I die. Folks have told you raised foxhounds to sell and I want to buy me a pair of pups,
and I want same young and not trained and I would
like same as cheap as you can make them. But I
want good pups that has got long wind and good
nose. This red fox I been chasing for nigh on six year
can't be hunted with nothing but a good hound. I'd
be obliged if you could please let me know if you
have any of same to sell and how much same pups
will cost.

Yours Truly,
N. D. BALLEW

It was almost two weeks before the answer to the letter
came, all printed like, on white paper with no lines on it.
Nunn carried it unopened out of the post office, but
stopped halfway down the hill and stood behind a big
poplar and read it. Yes, he had some pups; they could be
weaned in two weeks' time; and he'd sell one for $40 or a
pair for $75, cash down.

"The business could be done by mail," the letter read,
"but it would be better for you to come and see before
you buy. You understand that raising and training one or
two young foxhound pups is a risky business. It would be
safer and a lot less trouble to buy one of my young trained
and guaranteed hounds, priced $90 and up, depending on
performance and pedigree—"

The gray winter twilight was crawling up from the
creek valley before Nunn came walking slowly up the
path, with his head bowed like a man tired or old or sunk
in troubled thought. Milly was milking in the old grist mill
and heard his feet on the rocks and called, "Any mail,
Nunn?"

"Nothen much," he answered shortly after a moment's
pause. He came on and stood in the stable door and
looked at her and Betsey and then at Betsey's calf in the
little pen that Milly had knocked up for it in one corner of
the stable. Nunn studied the pen—he'd always meant to
fix a place for the calf, but Milly hadn't wanted Betsey to
stay out in the sleety rain, and certainly not the calf, and
so had made the pen herself before he got around to it.
He could, even in the half dark, see the big rusty nails
she'd tried to drive and bent every which way, and the

old boards and half-rotten rails she'd used because she couldn't go to the woods and cut good oak poles as he had meant to do.

He cleared his throat and waited, hoping that Milly would turn and look at him, say something, do something, that would make it hard, so hard he'd never do what he planned to do—or else easier. But Milly milked on, stripping now, patiently determined to get the last drop from each flabby teat.

"Milly—are you given Betsey's calf any corn? It looks kind a porely."

She sighed and shook her head. "Jist fodder an shucks like you said, an jist a little bit a milk, enough to make Betsey come to it. Pore thing, it begs me so with its eyes. It's all I can do to keep frum given it a little corn anyhow."

"Give it some nubbins frum now on."

Milly got up from the milking and looked at him in some perplexity, then reminded him that back last fall he had said there mightn't be corn to run them through crop-making time.

Nunn met her wondering glance and hastily put his eyes on the spotted calf and kept them there. "I'm wanten that calf in good shape. I'm aimen to sell her—th last Saturday fore Christmas I recken it'll be."

Milly's troubled "Oh" was more like a weary sigh than a word. "It's got th maken's uv a pretty cow," she said, then added quickly, as if afraid of hurting his feelings, "but then I've allus said if we could have two cows, one to milk while t'other was dry, I'd be satisfied—an Lizzie's due in February."

"I'm a taken her to th stockyards when I take th calf—she'd mebbe go as a beef heifer." He spoke quickly, looking past her at the calf pen.

Milly looked at him, no anger but a piteous disbelief, a kind of tortured hope in her wide brown eyes, like the eyes of a child about to be whipped, who after he has felt the first few blows keeps hoping against his belief that there will be no more. "Nunn, you don't aim to sell her fore she's had her calf—they—they might kill her fer beef." She looked at him, and when he only turned sharply away with no answer, two tears slid down her face.

That night, when the children were asleep and Nunn

and Milly sat by the fire taking their after-supper chew of tobacco, as was their custom, Milly sat silent, chin on hand, staring into the fire. At last, when Nunn had pulled off his shoes, spat out his quid, and was banking the fire for the night, she turned to him and spoke in a low halting voice, like a child delivering a memorized speech before an unfriendly and critical audience.

"Nunn—I know we're awful short a money—it takes a lot fer me an th youngens—but, Nunn, I'll do without anything, everthing, if'n you can jist keep Lizzie till her calf comes. We'll need th milk so this spring, an anyhow I hate to see her killed fer beef. I've raised her all by hand frum jist a little calf. Old Uncle Ansel Anderson's big black cow died a bornen Lizzie, an he didn't want to fool with th calf, an you was up there with a turn a corn to grind, an brung it home to me; recollect?"

"Lizzie'ull git a good home," he said, and added in harsh bitterness, "An as fer you a doen without, you do without everthing under heaven now." He turned his back on her and went to bed. Tomorrow maybe he could tell her that Lizzie and Betsey's calf were not the only things he'd have to sell.

Sometime in the night something awoke him, and he lifted himself on one elbow and stared in first one direction and then another, but could see nothing in the black silent room except the faint glow of the coals in the fireplace, could hear nothing but the thin whisper of the wind in the pines on the ridges and Deb's croupy breathing. He lay back down and felt it again, the gentle, almost imperceptible shaking of the bed. He fidgeted a time, turning from first one side to the other, but even so he felt, or thought he felt, the smothered quiverings of the bed, and at last he could stand it no longer. Milly was crying there in the dark with a pillow pulled over her head so as not to awaken him. "Shut up, Milly, you're keepen me awake."

The shuck mattress on the old sagging springs rattled again, more violently than before, then silence. He listened but could hear nothing—she had the pillow jammed hard into her mouth, he guessed, half smothering herself to death so he wouldn't hear her cry. He lay with his fingers interlaced under his head, as he had often lain on the Pilot Rock on warm nights when King Devil ran, but now instead of the stars there was only the thick blackness of the room.

He stared into it, and all the troubled doubts and anger and pity of the days since he had failed to shoot King Devil settled on him like vicious hungry flies, and he could not sleep. He got out of bed and went to sit by the fire, and while he sat wondering, torn within himself about selling the heifer, the calf, the two remaining fattened pigs, and some ewes to raise $150 to buy pups and dog feed and pay the cost of the trip he must make, he heard high up toward the old graveyard the bark of a fox. He hurried outside barefooted and in his underwear and listened.

It came again soon, clearly King Devil it was; no other fox would bark like that in the dead of night close to a man's house. Milly would have a hen gone tomorrow. King Devil it was, daring somebody to catch him, making his brags tonight—the red son of a bitch; hateful bastard devil—but let him—come two years from this night, he'd have his hide on the wall.

There were other nights like that, when he doubted and questioned and cursed, but always he knew he would do this thing; and so he made arrangements with Jaw Buster to haul his stock on the Saturday before Christmas.

On the morning of his going Milly was up long before day, and by the time he awakened she had breakfast ready and Suse and Lee Roy up and getting ready to go with him to help in the driving, for not even Jaw Buster's truck could make it through the half-frozen mud of the hill.

Nunn ate breakfast quickly, hardly knowing what he chewed, putting bites into his mouth and swallowing with the hasty guilty air of a man eating stolen food.

Milly was silent, moving between the table and the stove as she brought him biscuit hot from the oven, poured fresh coffee, or sat on the nail keg by the stove, her accustomed seat when he took meals at odd hours like this. Their glances were continually meeting, but they seemed the glances of strangers each too timid to speak to the other. He would see the sorrow and the troubled wonder in her eyes and think he must tell her why he sold Lizzie and their winter's meat, but when he tried to find words for the telling, the thing he did seemed yet more nightmarish and unreal, the act of a man gone crazy—taking food out of his children's mouths he was.

Then Lee Roy was looking out the door and saying, "It's light enough to see, now, Pop," and Suse was bringing his wool-lined jumper. Milly picked up the coffeepot and started to bring him more coffee, saw he was pushing back his chair, and stood still, holding the coffeepot, watching him with a drawn, gray face, like an old woman's face.

He was taking his hat from the high shelf before she asked hesitantly, "Nunn—try to find a man that wants a good milk cow—Lizzie mightn't behave so good—she ain't been used to menfolks."

He nodded, and she followed him to the door and asked all in a breath, her sad eyes searching his, "Nunn, you ain't took a mortgage on th place—er got in some kind a bad trouble where you have to have money quick?"

"Aw, hell, Milly," he began, trying hard to put an assurance that all was well into his voice, "it ain't nothen like that," and he was out the door and hurrying down the yard.

Milly sat a long time on the nail keg, staring at the stove top

Chapter Eight

THE BELL in the courthouse steeple chimed for half past ten as Jaw Buster drove over the hill toward the stockyards. Nunn felt suddenly nervous and ashamed to be coming among all the rich farmers in fine big trucks and trucks full of fine fat cattle, with his handful of mud-streaked scrubs in Jaw Buster's converted coal truck, windowless, doorless on one side, battered all over and given to innumerable coughs and rattles.

A short distance from the stockyards they were hailed by two men. Jaw Buster stopped and the men climbed up a side of the truck and hung on the slats and looked at Nunn's stock. "Whose'n?" asked an older man in a gray store suit and white shirt with white, short-cropped, upstanding hair.

"His'n," Jaw Buster said, lifting a thumb from the steering wheel in Nunn's direction.

"Want a sell?" the man asked, looking at Lizzie.

Nunn said nothing. He never could make up his mind to deal with penhookers like these or sell it in the auction ring. Everybody said that either way a man was liable to get cheated out of his eyeteeth. John dealt with the hookers, but Preacher Samuel never would.

"Well, how much?" the man asked, running one hand along Lizzie's ribs.

"I don't know."

"What a you mean, you don't know? What'll you take for th calf an heifer?"

"I dunno how things are sellen."

The whiteheaded man shook his head and his face was long, "I can tell you, boy. It's my business. Things is sellen bad, mighty bad; cattle's off, way off; you ain't goen to git much, but I'll give you more'n anybody else," and he gave all the things in the truck a swift but calculating survey.

Nunn shook his head, Jaw Buster gunned his motor a little, the man gave his shoulders a slight shrug that seemed to say he was losing little by not buying and jumped down with his companion, a youngish man who had shown no interest at all.

They drove into a wide enclosure crowded with trucks and men. A man with a white-painted cane dashed from a nearby truck, jumped onto the running board, and stuck his face in almost against Jaw Buster's. "His'n," Jaw Buster said.

"How much?"

More penhookers swarmed over the truck and shouts of "How much?" crossed each other in the air, but over the voices of the penhookers there rose the steady bawl, the moaning cry of unhappy cattle, the squealing and oinking of pigs, long, somehow sobbing brays of mules, while somewhere a horse whinnied excitedly and a bull bellowed with an angry roar. And over the smell of gasoline, Nunn smelled fresh sawdust, hay, cow sweat and cow manure, and stronger than anything in the cold, the smell of fresh urine. "Looks like they'll have to have their say," said Jaw Buster, nodding toward the penhookers.

He killed the motor, and more men, most carrying small canes, closed on the truck. Some were in manure-splattered overalls, some in high boots and lumberjacks like the foresters wore, a few wore store suits with ties, and one even had a long-tailed overcoat. They poked Lizzie, felt her belly for the kick of a calf, thumped Betsey's calf, kicked up the pigs, but showed little interest in the sheep.

"Name your price, boy," grinned one hooker, big bellied, big jowled, "an I'll pay it. I got it an I'll let it go. I don't mind," and he pulled out a great roll of bills and started to peel them off. "How much fer th heifer?"

"I dunno."

"Name your price, boy. I gotta know so's I can pay you."

"I don't trade much," Nunn muttered, embarrassed, trying not to look at the money.

"Hell, boy, this ain't traden. All you have to do is set a price."

Nunn shook his head. The penhooker waited a moment, bills in either hand, then, with a lifting of his shoulders walked away.

Following the law of the penhooker's trade, never to bid against each other for fear of raising the price, one never tried until another had finished. The next to try was a tall, thin, shock-haired boy, no more than twenty. "You oughter name a price, mister," he said. "You'll do a heap better with me than in th pen. Things is sellen way off."

"I heared that."

"You'll hear it again. Everything's off. Now me, I got feed at home an nothen to feed it to. How much fer that heifer?"

"Well—$70."

The boy looked pained and surprised, as though Nunn, for no reason at all, had kicked him. "Oh, mister, you can't git $70 fer that heifer, nowhere. I couldn't give you half that."

Nunn nodded. "Well, what'll you give me fer th sheep?"

"I dunno." He went away, and another came, demanding a price on the pigs.

"Well—$50," Nunn said with a doubt he couldn't quite keep out of his voice.

"Now, now, boy," the man said with an exaggerated look of surprise, "why they won't weigh more'n a hundred an fifty."

"Recken so," Nunn said, his insides tight with anger at the insolent ways of the hookers.

The hooker leaned back from the truck and squinted. "They might make a hundred an sixty, but they won't bring tops—mebbe eight cents a pound—I tell you, make it $25 fer th couple—you'll git $20, mebbe less, in th pen. Fore I sell em, I'll take em home an pop th corn to em."

Nunn shook his head and Jaw Buster backed into one of the three unloading chutes. Unloading was easy, except for Lizzie, terrified into madness by so many men, but even she soon left the truck and ran down the chute under the hard blows of a friendly penhooker's cane.

Jaw Buster drove away and Nunn found himself alone

with his stock in a little pen that seemed entirely made of gates, each leading in a different direction. All were closed and Nunn, not knowing what to do, waited in some embarrassment. After a while another truck wanted to unload, and the driver shouted to Nunn to get an attendant and move out his stock. So he walked down a lane between rows of pens, his feet sinking deep into sawdust and manure, past clusters of men talking and arguing and dickering amid good-natured laughter, until he found a tall, stoop-shouldered, one-armed fellow, expertly cracking a leather bullwhip, with the sound of pistol shots, after four fat shoats. Somebody opened the gate to a pen, men dashed to keep those already in from getting out, and the four shoats, grunting, oinking, and cursing, joined twenty of their fellows—fat hogs with sleek, round bodies that make Nunn realize how poor his own were.

Nunn led the way, liking the one-armed man; he was not like the penhookers with their bargaining smiles, and there was something good about his eyes. With a speed that left Nunn bewildered, he had each animal where it belonged—the pigs with a bunch no better-looking than they, Lizzie with others of her kind. Betsey's calf in a pen of thin, many-colored calves like herself, and the six ewes in a pen all alone, everything weighed, numbered, and ticketed.

The sheep were last, and Nunn turned to the attendant in some trouble. "Mister, I ain't seen no other sheep this time a year?"

"Hell, nobody wants to buy nothen they can't git rich on," the attendant said. "Not much doen in sheep in the late fall an winter, but they'll be sheep men along a looken. Stay by your sheep, an if I see any sheep buyers, I'll send em over."

Not long after there came a big, red-faced man who, after nodding to Nunn, went into the pen with the ewes. He sneaked up on a ewe and grabbed her by the wool on her neck so gently that Nunn knew here was a man who had handled lots of sheep. He felt her back, then her udder, while asking, "Them piney-woods ewes? Where'd they come from? Had any trouble with worms?"

Nunn pulled out a plug of tobacco and cut a chew before answering. It was plain the man wanted the ewes. "I ain't never had no trouble with worms—them sheep was raised on beggar-lice and sweet fern; they ain't hardly ever smelt a barn."

The fat man examined another udder. "Bred to lamb late, I recken."

Nunn spat out a slow stream of tobacco juice, then squatted, and with his hands on his knees, gazed disinterestedly at the sheep's belly, as if seeing it for the first time. "Oh, I dunno—they've been with some rams up around Bear Creek all last fall—they could lamb early."

"What kind a ram?"

"I dunno; belonged to th Tuckers—fancy purebred rams; got em off their country agent."

"How much for these ewes?"

"Oh, I dunno. I figure to sell em at auction."

The fat man was silent, his head hidden under the sheep's bellies while he examined their udders and felt for the kick of a live lamb. "Ever have twins?"

"Ye-es, off an on. Last year they just about all had twins."

"Well, how much?" The fat man was looking in their mouths to see how old they were.

Nunn shook his head slowly and turned his wide deep brown eyes full upon the man. "I dunno. I ain't never sold ewes before they lambed before."

"Fifty-five dollars for th bunch."

Nunn gulped and came near swallowing his tobacco; the most he had ever got for a ewe from the traders who drove through the backwoods in the fall was $8. He shook his head slowly. "Oh, I dunno. Them's a good young ewes, an a body could count on at least seven, eight lambs from th five, mebbe ten, an it's not long till pasture's in."

"Fifty-seven dollars—an that's a good price. Save waiten around till dark to put em through th pen, an mebbe nobody'ull be here that wants em."

Nunn shook his head. "I figure them ewes is worth $70 anyhow. They's $10 or $12 worth a wool on em."

"Fifty-eight, an that's more'n you'll get in th pen."

Nunn shook his head and they bargained a time; in the end the fat farmer got the sheep for $59.50 and agreed to pay the sales fee of twenty-five cents a head. He wrote a check for the amount and handed it to Nunn with a crinkly frown across his weather-stained forehead. "That's more'n I've ever paid for any kind a ewes, excepten registered ones. . . . But they are pretty," and his eyes looking on the huddle of ewes, kindled warm and kind.

Nunn was glad this man had bought his sheep. "Well, if'n any one a them ewes don't have at least one good strong lamb, send me word an I'll bring you anothern."

"An to where would I send word?" the fat man asked, as if he didn't much expect to need the word, and still looking at the ewes.

"Nunnely Ballew, at Ballew Post Office."

The fat man looked at him with more interest. "Any kin of old Jim Ballew that used to own all of that holler? I recollect goen down there with my dad to buy sheep—aye, Lord—must a been forty years ago. He had a grist mill an a post office as a great drove a sheep an a big family."

"He was my granddad," Nunn said with a mingling of shame and pride—pride in his grandfather and the farm he had had, shame for the place now and his treatment of it.

"You live on th old place?"

"Part of it—tween a hundred an fifty an two hundred acres I recken—"

"It was a pretty place—some good-looken land an timber on th hillside, too, I recollect," the man said with a faint sigh.

He might have talked more, but Nunn mumbled something about having to sell the rest of his stuff and moved away. He wished he could know the man better, but in that case the man might get to know him better—he'd hate to have him see the brush and gullies the place had come to now.

He sold the pigs to a penhooker, a buck-toothed one with straight-up hair. The two of them weighed 412 pounds, and after a deal of haggling, during which Nunn lied about their age and said they were younger than they were—all of which turned his stomach—he got eight cents a pound, this time in cash.

There was over $90 in his pocket now; the most cash he had had at one time since, after paying for his farm, he had taken the last of his savings and bought Maude and Betsey. But the money seemed little in his pocket, no more than a handful of change as he wandered about, waiting for the auction to begin. Everywhere there were farmers, men with money in the bank and good farms behind them, men who had never had the bitter taste of doing another man's bidding as he had done through the years when he worked in the coal mines. Nobody had ever bossed these men but maybe their wives and the weather.

Few dressed any better than he, most were in overalls, some clean, a few dirty, many patched and faded; here and there a short leather coat, once an overcoat, but mostly jumpers; and their faces were weather-stained and wrinkled, and their hands, bare almost to a man in spite of the cold, were the big, tough, wide-palmed hands of men who worked.

It wasn't the way they looked or the way they acted, for they were friendly enough, that made him feel nobody but a poor stranger among them, but their talk and something solid and substantial in their lives that his seemed to lack. They strolled singly or in two's and three's among the pens, now and then stopping to study some animal with a negligent and indifferent air, as if it didn't matter whether they bought or sold; the world would roll on and they with it.

Little groups of men, generally in the same place, but continually depleted and renewed, like a spot of foam in a quiet eddy which at each slow turn drops a little and takes a little, were gathered here and there. Nunn lingered a time on the fringe of a group by the weighing-pen chute, and listened to a great chunk of a man in new overalls and an old jumper tell of selling forty-three black steers at the Stanford yards for $4,400—all grade, not one purebred in the lot.

The red-faced man who had bought Nunn's ewes grunted and opined there was more money in sheep—quick money—wasn't his steers about twenty-six months old at least. Now take that much hay and feed and time and turn it into lambs; look at himself; he had never kept more than 200 ewes and last June he had marketed 227 fat lambs that averaged $13, then 44 late lambs that brought close to $11 apiece, besides wool—about $2 worth from each ewe—and the cull ewes into the bargain—and the whole hadn't eaten as much as 44 cattle nor taken half the time, and he still had the pick of the ewes.

The chunky man made a lazy belittling gesture with one big hand. "I let the county agent once get me into th sheep business, an I wouldn't be worried with th things agin for th finest farm in the bluegrass. It was the coldest January an February you ever saw, an I spent most of it—an by most of it I mean night an day, night an day—with them damned ewes a lamben in ever direction. About twenty lambs died on me, their blamed noses an ears froze while they was in th bornen, an th old woman nearly come down with pneumonia from bean out a worken an a foolen with th things, an sometimes we had th brooder house an th kitchen full.

"Two ewes died on me an left twin lambs, an some a th ewes wouldn't claim their lambs, an th youngens took it into their heads to raise them orphan lambs in th house; an th dern things blatted an cried night an day, night an day, an kept us awake, an we just had two cows a given milk, an be danged if I didn't have to buy another'n for them orphan lambs.

"An then ever last sheep on th place got worms an ever last 426 a them had to be dosed an drenched, not once, but three times before I finally got shet a th lot. The dogs was always getten in—I killed three. One belonged to a neighbor woman, th peacefulest, quietest dog; he wouldn't so much as bark at a snake. I shot him down dead one white moonlight night a chasen th sheep, an I'm still expecten to be killed or lawed any day by that woman—she never got over it—and fence, nothen outside a five-foot wove wire an two strands a bob wire would hold em."

"But I bet you didn't lose nothen on em," the fat man said.

The big man looked somewhat sheepish. "Well, th lambs come early, an I had plenty a pasture, an early fat lambs was scarce that year, so's they averaged $14 a head, an wool was a good price, too. An the ewes—they was young, brought in from Texas—I got rid of to a neighbor fool enough to pay me $1 more a head than I paid."

"If you'd a stuck to sheep, Elias, you'd a been rich by now," the fat farmer said reprovingly.

"Rich, hell, I'd been crazy or dead."

Everybody laughed, and Nunn wandered away feeling poorer than ever. He sat for a time on the side of a pen holding a young unbroken mule that, judging from its actions, had never known stable or pen. Time after time it tried to jump out, but would end always with no more than its head and knees over the eight-foot stout oak plank wall of the pen; and when it seemed it must strangle and choke itself to death through hanging on, it would give way and stand panting in the center of the pen, then scream and bray and cry with a rolling of its eyes and pawing of the earth.

Nunn sat on the top plank with his feet inside the pen and fell to talking to it in the same persuasive gentle fashion he talked to a terrified, half-wild ewe that had run in the forest and not smelled a man for months. The beast lunged at his knees, white teeth shining, ears laid back, but Nunn did not move; the mule changed his mind and tried to jump out on the other side, but after a time he grew quieter and listened to Nunn, and after a long time came and sniffed his hand, shyly, standing far away with outstretched neck, like a crow.

"You wouldn't want to buy that mule, I recken. He's come close to you of his own free will, an that's more'n he's ever done for me."

Nunn shook his head, without turning to look at the speaker. "I got a mare an a colt an that does me."

"Aye, God, nothen'll send a man to th porehouse quicker than a lot a horse an mule stock. Kill yourself raisen hay an corn in the summer so's they can stand in th barn all winter an craunch, craunch, craunch away."

"How you doen, Sam? Ain't that wild zebra somethen you've raised?"

"Headed straight for th porehouse. Let me sell you a good piece a mule stock—sired by th devil in th dark a th moon when th sign's in th left hind leg, guaranteed to kick your head off, bray all night an eat all day."

The mule, as if to give weight to its master's words, screamed, slashed out against the wall with its unshod hind feet, then dashed, mouth open, at the man named Sam, who hit it between the eyes with a bullwhip. The other chuckled. "Better stick to tobacco, Sam. From what I been a hearen you'll be able to buy th porehouse when you get there."

"What a you been hearen?" Sam asked, trying to hold back a note of pride.

"I heard you sold a shade over four thousand pounds a tobacco that averaged thirty-eight cents, an off'n less'n a two-acre base."

"One an seven-eighths, it was; an it ought to be three. I

been to that danged AAA office fifty times, a tellen them danged blockheads that for years back I never raised less'n three acres, but it don't do no good. They're all fools."

The other agreed but with reservations, for it seemed he was an AAA committeeman and knew when the next carload of superphosphate would be in, and where the tobacco grower could buy some clean lespedeza sericea seed. Other men drifted up and a cluster of heads grew around Nunn's feet, for he had turned around and now sat on the pen with his back to the mule.

The talk went on about the AAA, superphosphate, and tobacco quotas, with a little spurt of argument about the good of nitrate of soda—was it worth the cost and trouble? —and how many times to spray with Bordeaux and the merits of Judy's Pride tobacco seed.

Nunn, with a last friendly glance at the unbroken mule, let his feet down and stole away. He had never grown tobacco except for his own chewing, nor seen the county agent or the AAA. Last year a bright young AAA fellow had come down to Old John's. The old man had quickly sent him on his way; he'd be blowed if he'd have anyone telling him how to run his farm or take fertilizer free from the government; it was a sin for the government to be wasting money in any such fashion, so Old John said, and before he'd have anything to do with such he'd quit raising tobacco. Preacher Samuel, too, had never had anything to do with the AAA; he agreed with John in many matters, especially politics and religion.

Nunn wandered on to a nearby pen to stand among a little knot of men gazing at a great black bull, a huge, black-tongued, short-legged, heavy-behinded monster tied to a post with a rope through a brass ring in its nose, standing with an air of quiet scorn, not deigning to look at the men, but past them, as if seeing lush deep pastures full of fat cows all eager to be bred.

He wondered how it would feel to own a bull like that, and thought he'd better take a last look at Lizzie, and passed down an alley of pens filled mostly with scrubby milk cows. One cow, an ugly, big-hipped, hammer-headed thing, all scraggeldy hide and bone, with mud to her knees, and streaked and spotted in divers shades of red and brown and black, lifted her head and bawled so loudly and mournfully that Nunn stopped for a closer study. A tall stoop-shouldered man in ragged overalls splashed with mud the same color as that on the cow uncoiled himself from the fence and asked timidly, in a disheartened way, as if he had asked the same question so many times he already knew the answer but must ask anyway: "Want a buy a good cow for $50, mister?"

Nunn shook his head but continued to look at the cow.

"She's a good milker an'ull be fresh in April, an young, too," the man went on in his timid urgent voice.

Nunn warmed to the man; he made him feel, if not exactly rich, at least less poor than the others did. "She don't look so good now," the tall man said, "but we started out walken yesterday even fore th ground froze. . . . A trucker won't come to my place." He spoke in a low mumbling tone, as if it didn't much matter whether or not Nunn heard what he said, the important thing was for him to say it.

"When I left home with her anybody'd a give me $50. Th old woman, she said to me, 'Well, take th cow but be sure to bring back th boy,' an now I'm thinken that for me to get th $50 I'd ought to have brung th calf too . . . but it was a heifer well growed an weaned . . . an me an th old woman figured we could keep it an have another cow in less'n two years. It's hard to raise a big family without a bit a milk."

Nunn nodded, pity and curiosity mingling in his head. "Well, I hope you get your boy back," he said, trying to keep the question out of his voice but not quite succeeding and ashamed to be poking into the man's business like a piece of fool white trash, but he listened while the man went on to tell how his boy had done just a little thing—when a body was low on meat a pheasant was a sweet-tasting thing—but a game warden had found him with the pheasant and taken him to jail, and after awhile the judge had fined the boy $50 for shooting a pheasant and resisting the law, for he had tried to run—so the old woman had sent him to sell the cow and get the boy out of jail.

A little splintery sort of man, who had listened with the others, shook his head in sympathy. "Lord, God, down my way on Caney Fork, it's gitten so's a body can't step out to shit thout runnen into a game warden or a fire guard for that Cumberland National Forest or a gov'ment surveyor measuren off more land or a bunch a AAA boys."

"Times is changen fast," an old man with a mustache said.

After looking at Lizzie, Nunn went outside to see some great hairy-footed horses, so big they'd make Maude look small. They had come from Indiana, a man said; up in Indiana everybody was selling his team and buying a tractor; pretty soon it would be so that a body would never see a horse except in a circus.

Nunn smiled. "I'd hate to see a tractor try to get over my land."

The man gave him a sharp, almost belligerent, glance. "Can you plow it with anything—mules, horses, oxen?"

"One old mare."

"Then you can tractor it, by God. I tell you, man, they're a maken them things now so's they can do anything, go anyplace, from picken corn to driven billy goats."

Nunn thought that the man, who was a trucker, was lying, but listened while he talked of Indiana farms and Iowa wheat and tractors and irrigated land in California where an acre of alfalfa was worth more than ten acres of corn in this country.

As he turned down a long alley, he heard above the lowing of cattle and squealing of pigs and the other sounds a mighty bellow of, "Who'll make it $8. Who'll make it $8? Eight, do I hear, boys? Come on, you men that wants a good stocker calf cheap. I'm a given this steer away; just a little more hay an you can turn him on pasture, browse him on brush, an he'll gain 400 pounds an sell at $10 this fall. Come on boys, it's goen. It's a giveaway. Do I hear $8? Goen . . . goen . . . gone at $7.95."

The veals were already sold and the stockers going quickly, so that Nunn was hardly settled on one of the planks in a tier that formed three sides of the ring before Betsey's calf danced bewildered and bawling under the bullwhip of a yard boy into the sawdust ring.

"Here, boys, is just what some a you need; a good browser, tough and healthy. She'll fatten on persimmon shoots and saw briars; an it'll take hardly a dime's worth a feed to bring her through till spring. What do I hear for this little heifer, 220 pounds? Who'll start at $8 for this nice thin stocker? Somebody say $8; come on, boys, we can't wait until dark. This heifer's cheap at $10. She'll really grow on grass."

"Six-fifty," somebody said.

The auctioneer wiped his neck and looked over the crowd. The red-faced farmer who had sold the forty-four steers nodded his head for a nickel more and the auctioneer boomed: "What do you think you're buyen, a cutter cow? This heifer's got all her life and growth before her."

"An all her feed bill, too," somebody said from down near the right. There was laughter but no bids, and Nunn felt a hot shame not unmixed with anger. Let them laugh at his scrub calf—some day before he died, and when he had caught King Devil, he would drive into this yard with a truckload of fat black cattle that would make every farmer here hot with envy.

But the laughter was good-natured. The price rose by nickels on the hundred, as was the custom, a nod or lifted hand meaning another nickel, until Nunn, watching, was afraid to move for fear the quick-eyed auctioneer would sell him his own calf or catch him as a bye-bidder. The price rose to $7.80 and stopped.

Nunn figured the amount in his head to be better than $25; now if Lizzie would bring $50 he'd have money enough for the pups, feed for some months, his trip, and a bit left over for spring expenses. He relaxed somewhat and watched the men around him; some talking in low voices, others sitting with hands on outspread knees, sitting with the easy quietness of men unafraid of what the next hour or the next ten years would bring, bidding at times in an easy, careless kind of way, as if they and money were well acquainted. Traders, he guessed, or buyers for a packing house; farmers wouldn't be apt to have that much money, for here it was all cash in hand.

Finally came the mixed stuff, old cows and bred heifers, not good enough to go as stockers or beef. Lizzie came after it seemed that half the cattle in the county had been sold, for Nunn was getting restless now; the fears and forebodings and hopes that had pushed his mind in countless directions since he first wrote to Wheeler grew stronger until he seemed to himself no better than a half-grown fox torn piecemeal by a pack of hungry, hot-mad hounds.

It was cold in the auction ring, the puddles of urine

seeping out of the sawdust were already skimmed a little with ice, but when he saw Lizzie walk quietly past the auctioneer's stand, he took out the blue handkerchief Milly had given him freshly ironed that morning and wiped his sweaty forehead. He wiped it again when somebody bid $3.25 with the lazy careless sound of some big farmer who didn't care whether he bought her or not.

The auctioneer exhorted, got tired, and went off into one of his chants that sounded to Nunn as if he were trying to yodel and imitate a pack of coarse-mouthed hounds at the same time. Nunn strained like a man pushing against a crushing weight, while nobody but himself and the auctioneer seemed to know that Lizzie was being sold. A few of the men joked and talked and cut fresh chews of tobacco, but most sat staring vacantly, like men in church, waiting for the sermon to end.

The auctioneer came out of his yodel with a red face and husky voice. He cleared his throat and asked in a conversational tone: "Do any a you all want this heifer? She'll drop her calf—I've already seen it kicken—an it'll be a yearlen before you all make up your minds—if you're too lazy to open your mouths, nod your heads, lift a hand—well, blink an eye—I'll see it. Do I hear $3.40? . . . You, did you say forty or did you just wake up and shake your head? No? Come on, boys, $3.35. Let me hear forty. Forty, do I hear forty? This is a pretty heifer to throw away for less'n $30. Her calf'll be worth more'n that come fall."

In his agitation Nunn almost slipped from the plank seat, and he stared so hard that a very clean old man with faded blue eyes sitting next to him said, "That's your heifer, I bet."

Nunn did not answer, he hardly heard. "These danged traders an rich farmers won't bid agin each other. If she was my heifer, I'd take her home," the man said, but Nunn sat tense, waiting for the $3.40 on the hundred that never came.

He sat a few minutes longer, and watched dazedly while a Jersey heifer, no bigger than Lizzie, but registered, sold for $80, then he went out and got his money from the cashier in a little cubbyhole near the weighing pen. He counted the money, added it to the check and the cash he had; there was enough to buy what he had to buy with a little left over.

Chapter Nine

THE BIG NIGHT BUS that went all the way from Cincinnati to Chattanooga, Tennessee, stopped in the ankle-deep snow. The driver opened the door, looked out into the darkness, then up at Nunn, who waited expectantly in the aisle with a split basket on his arm. "Are you sure, buddy, this is where you want off? There's nothen here, no light, nothen."

"It's th beginnen a th graded graveled, an I recken I know my own way home," Nunn answered shortly. The driver, he guessed, thought he was drunk. And he'd had only that funny little long-necked bottle of wine and the beers in Lexington and just the half of the little pint of bottled in bond; the rest he was saving for Milly's camphor spirits. "It ain't more'n ten, twelve miles to where I live, and they's a road—most a th way—so's I'll git in by daylight," he went on, angrily conscious of the driver's sober speculative gaze.

The driver gave a low whistle and let the door clang together behind him. He stood and watched the bus lights like a big bright sickle slice through the thickly falling snow, then the bus had rounded the curve, and he was alone with the pups in their basket and the muffled whisper of the high pines in the snowy dark.

For the first time since Milly got him out of bed yesterday morning, he felt he was himself, sober, and in his right mind. Looking back on the day that seemed to have its roots in some time so far away it was but half remembered, he felt as if through it all he had been drunk, just drunk enough to know he was drunk, with sense enough to act as if he were sober. Maybe he had been drunk—or

118

crazy; he'd come away with a truckload of stock; he was coming home with a basket of pups and little money between . . . two little just-weaned things that could die before they ever smelled a fox.

He lifted the basket level with his ear but could hear nothing. A sudden terror swept him. He'd heard about people dying in tight shut-up cars, and the bus air was bad and pups like these could die easy. He hesitated, frightened but unwilling to undo the wrappings of the basket here in the dark and risk their getting dampened with the wet snow.

He squatted suddenly on his heels, and teetering a little, set the basket on his upthrust knees. Impatient with the wrappings he could not see, he jerked them away. A startled yelp came from the basket. He plunged his hand in and felt the two warm, sleep-soaked bodies, smooth and firm-fleshed under the short hair. Curving his back like a half-moon to shield them from the snow, he felt with gentle anxious fingers until he found both noses, cold but not wet. Then with much fumbling in the dark, he covered them up again, sitting flat bottomed, with his legs outstretched under the basket to protect it from the snow.

He felt warm and pleasant and happy with the clean air that smelled of pine in his nose, the warm pups on his knees, and his bottom in the good warm snow. It was good to be home in his own country. Just to think over all the places he had been and the people he had seen and the people he had had to talk to made his head swim so that he was glad to sit awhile.

His mouth felt dry and hot from all the dirty air he had breathed in the bus. He needed a chew, but the tobacco was down in a hip pocket and he couldn't get to it unless he moved and if he moved he'd have to set the basket in the snow. He didn't want to do that; he bowed his head on the basket handle and thought it over for a while. Was a chew of tobacco worth risking the lives of the pups? Maybe the pups wouldn't mind; of course they had a good kind turn like that of the man away off in the bluegrass who had raised them. And they had papers to their names; no whores and no bastards in their line clean back to Adam, and that was more than could be said for a lot of men.

He sighed, his head slipping lower down the basket handle; snow fell on the back of his neck and sifted down his jumper collar. Slowly he became aware of a cold wetness down his spine; and his bottom in the snow from feeling warm grew wet and cold as a sleet-caked lamb. He stirred and lifted his face and looked toward the sky, but could see nothing; black, pure black it was, spitting snow into his eyes when he tried to look into it.

The good warmth and joy at coming home sober were gone and he knew himself for what he was; cold and wet and tired, a fool and a coward, afraid to go home and say, "Milly, here's two pups I bought fer $70, an you without a decent shoe to your name—an th youngens half naked an our winter's meat sold fer these pedigreed pups." No, he wouldn't say "pedigreed"; nobody between the Big South Fork and the Cumberland had ever heard of a pedigree.

Every man around would laugh at him for a fool, say he had been drinking and let somebody cheat him out of his money and give him two half-weaned pups not worth a dime apiece. It would be easier to throw the damn things over the ridge side, basket and all, and go home and say he had got drunk and lost the money. Better to be pitied for a drunkard than laughed at for a fool.

An angry whine came from the basket; it jiggled as if the pups were trying to get out. He lifted his head and listened, tried to look behind him, then pushing hard in the snow with one hand and holding the basket in the other, he got his weight on his feet. He squatted a moment, teetering on his heels and squinting his bloodshot eyes first this way and that into the darkness.

He tried to see squarely behind him, and failing, he sprang upright with one swift unfolding motion. He turned in his tracks so that he stood with his face in the direction opposite to which it had been. He thrust his chin out and glared straight before him. "It's you, is it?" he asked in a whisper.

He knew King Devil stood there less than twenty feet away; it was the smell of him that had made the pups whine, and then he, Nunn, as he had sat with his head bowed, had felt first his green eyes boring into his back, and then his breath hot on his shoulder, but by now he had moved away and stood out there in the dark, looking him over, laughing at him, weighing the worth of the pups.

He shivered but stood, still staring before him. Aye, God, let him laugh, let the whole God-damned world laugh; Old John and Samuel and Lister and the others; they laughed because he was fool enough to waste his life and starve his family for a fox that could never be caught. King Devil laughed because he knew Nunn had to chase him—had to—had to—had to. The damned red fox had put a wall between him and the rest of the world; other men did what they pleased; he chased a fox because he had to; King Devil ran because he had to—he couldn't stop—he had to run; he was bewitched; Nunn was bewitched; they couldn't die, they couldn't stop; they lived in some God-damned bewitched world that other people didn't know about. King Devil had to run, and he had to follow—had to—had to—had to—

He strode off along the gravel road, his head bowed a little and the basket carried on his forearm, hugged inward against his belly so that it might be sheltered from the cold. He'd never walked in the dark on level gravel road before that his feet could remember, and sometimes when he put his foot down it was like waking out of a deep sleep into nightmarish dozing, and he would think for an instant that he was lost in the bluegrass or walking the streets of town. Then he would feel the basket on his arm and know that everything was all right—he was walking home on the gravel.

The road followed the windings of a ridge and for a time was fairly sheltered from the keen wind by the high pines on either side, but a sharp turning brought it square into the northwest, and the wind poured down the road like flooded river water racing through a narrow gorge. He felt the bite of it through his jumper, and bent his head yet lower and walked faster, but his hand above the basket, usually insensible to all weathers, first grew cold, with pains in the fingers, and then numb.

The pups worried him; with the wind in his face he could no longer use his body to shield them from the weather. Many times he had felt it, but still was uncertain about the cover. Maybe snow was sifting in and the pups were getting damp and cold—pneumonia they would have and be dead in a day or two—John and Milly and the others would pity him for an unlucky fool, but King

Devil would laugh—he'd sit on the Pilot Rock and laugh like a damned hyena all winter.

Nunn stopped, turned his back square to the wind, hunched his shoulders, and once more went through the business of uncovering the basket to see if the pups were all right. But by now his hands were so numb he couldn't tell if the pups were hot or cold—a harder, heavier wave of wind-flung snow rattled over him, sending flakes down his neck and making the seat of his underwear like cold sheet iron against his skin. Aye, Lord, the good Lord God in heaven had sent a blizzard against him and his evil ways to freeze the pups to death, or more like, the devil working with King Devil; well, he'd fooled the devil once today by coming home sober and he'd fool him again before the night was out.

He peered out into the darkness. Many was the bitter night he'd spent on a fox hunt behind a fallen tree trunk or in a close-growing thicket of young pines. If he could find something like that now, he could hole up till daylight and warm the pups with his body—but once, a few years back, one of John's boys had holed up on a cold wild night, and when they finally found him curled around a little low-limbed cedar tree, they'd had to cut his clothes off his back and cut others to put on; right funny he had looked and comfortable, curled in his coffin like a possum in its hole; but then the boy had been drunk and he was cold sober. He laughed, thinking it all out; he couldn't find much shelter in this dark; King Devil had sent the thought to his head; he wanted him to freeze to death, and once he was cold and dead curled round his tree, King Devil would come, the dirty bastard, and eat up the pups just as he'd eat a couple of lambs.

The best thing to do was to get the pups home to Milly; and he'd get them to her with never a chill wind to touch them. Cursing his numb hands and working slowly, he held the basket in one hand, pulled his other hand and arm out of his jumper sleeve, using his teeth to help, then shifted the basket and pulled out the other arm, and tied the jumper over the basket, knotting the empty sleeves firmly around the bottom.

He walked then, with no looking or stopping or shifting from the wind—walked until the sweat seeped out of his underwear onto his shirt and froze across his back. After a while he hardly felt the cold. The snow was not deep enough to bother much about walking, not a man like himself who had sheep-hunted for days together in eight-inch snow.

As he passed the church house he could see the roof of it, an indistinct square of blacker blackness against the black sky toward the east, and he knew daylight was on the way and he felt so good he sang, stepping swiftly to the tune:

"I watched the boat go round th bend,
Good-bye, my lover, good-bye;
'Twas loaded down with railroad men,
Good-bye, my lover, good-bye."

There was a light in Preacher Samuel's house, a pale blob of yellow with snow cutting across it, and he knew there would be a light at home. Aye, Lord, have pity on all men out in the snow and the dark who had no light of their own to go to; it was worth all this head-swimming trip just to come back to Milly's light.

He turned down the short-cut path home, and across the valley he saw Milly's light, faint as a fog-smothered star, and though it was black as an unlighted coal mine, he hurried on, slipping and sliding down the snowy ledges.

At the creek he didn't bother to hunt the stepping-stones. A freshly frozen pool bore his weight for a few steps then slowly broke; he struggled to stand upright, but falling, half fell and half sat in the shallow, muddy-bottomed pool, careful through it all that the basket should get no jar. For the first time since the beginning of his walk, he remembered the half pint of whisky in his hip pocket. Maybe it was broken. He sat still in the creek water, and felt. The bottle was whole; he shook it by his ear and it gave a sweet warm gurgling.

He thought of telling Milly and the children the cost of the pups and wanted a drink. After a moment he let the bottle slip back into his pocket and got up. Milly would have her spirits of camphor. She'd been wanting some good safe whisky spirits to doctor Deb's croup. By God, she'd have it; a Christmas present; at least he'd give her that much.

When he had climbed out of the creek canyon, he saw

her light again and went on looking at it so intently that
he almost bumped into Milly hurrying down the path to
meet him. She caught his arm as if to steady him, and
stood breathing hard and gulping like a child afraid to cry.
There was no anger, no scolding in her voice, nothing but
glad relief when she said in a low caressing whisper,
"Nunn, oh, Nunn, you're all right. I thought it was you I
heared a comen over th rocks."

He patted her shoulder, saw the snow on her bare head
and coatless shoulders, and only then remembered that in
all his tormented doubts yesterday morning he had forgotten to tell her he was going to take a bus in town and
go to a far place in the bluegrass.

She looked at the snow-encrusted jumper bundled over
the basket, at his overall legs wet to the knees, and at his
frozen shirt sleeves with a troubled but knowing air and
said nothing. She only put her arm under his elbow as if
afraid he would fall. He slapped his hat over her hair then
took her arm. "What th hell, Milly, do you mean a runnen
out bareheaded—you're liable to catch your death a
pneumonie fever."

"I was in sich a hurry to see you, I fergot, I reckon.
You're th one that's liable to come down with th fever—
out all day an night in—"

"Lord God, woman, who's been out all night? You
think I'm drunk, I recken. Why, I ain't hardly touched a
drop since bout dark yesterday, an that wasn't enough to
puke a baby."

She stepped behind him a little and looked at the seat
of his pants coated with creek mud and ice. "Law, Nunn,
honey. I know you ain't had a drop an are cold sober; I
didn't mean nothen, but come on in and git some good
hot coffee fore you go to bed."

"Go to bed, th devil," he began, then stopped with a
windy sigh. Milly had made up her mind he was drunk,
and right now he was too tired to try to change it. He
almost wished he'd bought a quart in Lexington and was
coming home in a happy haze, too drunk to mind telling
her about the pups. He felt sorry for himself as he walked
on in silence, with Milly still holding his elbow and guiding
him over the snowy rocks with solicitous care. Then he
comforted himself with the thought that she would know

he was cold sober when he gave her the half pint of bottled in bond.

After the long walk in the cold dark, the lamplit kitchen, with a roaring fire in the step stove and smells of fresh coffee and boiling dried peaches, seemed even finer than the promise of its light. The children were just waking when he went in. Suse heard him first and came rushing in from the fireplace room with her dress unbuttoned and her shoes and stockings in her hands. The rest came running behind her, down to Deb, carrying one shoe and dressed only in the undershirt in which he had slept.

It seemed like a year since he'd seen all his children; he took two quick steps toward Suse. She looked from the snow water trickling down his shirt sleeves to his jumper on the basket; instead of springing into his arms she made a quick backward movement that put the eating table between them. The three younger ones followed their sister, and all stood and gaped at him with the disheveled, half-witted, terrified air of children suddenly awakened by some nightmarish specter.

Their huddling there behind the table had happened so quickly he never realized the trouble and took a quick step toward Deb. He wanted to scoop him up in his arms; it was good to see him all red-cheeked and healthy-looking. Deb squeaked like a frightened half-grown guinea and rolled under the table. Nunn saw the terror in the child's eyes and stopped in mid-motion, with his hands outspread. He straightened and looked at Suse and Lee Roy and Lucy; even in the dim light he could see fear in their eyes, but, unlike Milly's eyes, there was open defiance with the fear. Suse was clutching her shoe, holding it like it might be a rock she was ready to throw.

Instead of anger he felt a warm wave of pride. Aye, Lord, he had children; no white-trash youngens to take and take, then lie and cry and whine behind a man's back. He wondered though, as he slowly unknotted the jumper from the basket, how much did he or any man know about his family. What did Lee Roy, standing there with the red sparks big in his eyes, think of him? What had Suse thought and said the last time he came home drunk?

Conscious of Deb's hard breathing from under the table and the three pairs of appraising, waiting eyes, he drew the jumper from the basket, shook it a little, and went and

hung it on its accustomed nail under the high shelf. He did
not open the basket at once, but looked first at the children and then at Milly, who had poured him a cup of
coffee and now stood looking at him and holding it as if
unable to make up her mind whether to offer it or not.

He felt sweat pop out on the palms of his hands and a
hotness creep up the back of his neck, but he looked
straight into the children's eyes, cleared his throat, and
began. "Youngens, I didn't bring you no candy or nothen
—I spent most a th money frum th stock I sold, an it was
over $100, on what you'll see here in the basket."

Suse's eyes opened wide at the enormity of the sum,
and Nunn, looking into them, forgot what he had meant
to say and stood silent and confused, his eyes beseeching
his children, hoping they would understand.

The children, terrified more by his strange sober manner than they would have been by his usual drunken
dancing and preaching, stared at the basket, but made
no move to crowd around it.

He pulled away the cover, looked down into it, then
back at his children. "A long time ago I made my brags
about ketchen King Devil—well, Zing, he died a tryen.
After Zing died I made my brags that I'd raise me up a
pair a pups, fine pups that ud git King Devil."

He fidgeted with the basket handle, but looked straight
at his children while he talked: "I couldn't go back on my
word, could I? White trash does that; so yesterday, soon's
I sold the stuff, I took me a bus out a town an went to a
place in th bluegrass, where I'd heared it said a man raises
th finest foxhounds in th whole world—he let me have my
pick a two litters—most too young they was to sell
—but—"

A soft crooning "Oh," came from the children, and
they all rushed to the basket. A pink-nosed pup with one
brown and one white ear and a brown splotched face had
put two cream-colored paws on the basket side and sat so,
looking at the children.

"This is th little boy hound," Nunn said, "an you all—"

Lucy had seized the brown-eared pup just as the basket
turned over and the other pup rolled out. Milly was setting the coffee down and exclaiming, "Now ain't that th
prettiest thing; why didn't you tell us, Nunn, honey? It's
been so lonesome thout no hound atall," and she caught

up the second pup, while Deb came out from under the
table so fast he bumped his head, and then stood on his
father's shoes the better to see. "White?" he said, staring
up into his mother's arms.

"Th onliest white hound in th country," Lee Roy said,
and shook his head in wonder, for the she pup Milly held
was pure white, with a faint sprinkling of gold on the top
of her head, as if someone had held a sifter of golden
dust above her and given it a little shake.

Milly was holding up her face, looking down into her
eyes. "Ain't she blackeyed, Nunn? Th onliest black-eyed
hound in the country."

Nunn rescued the boy pup, the perplexed center of a
fight between Deb and Lucy as to who should hold him,
before considering the little bitch's eyes. "We was talken
about that when I bought her—she's mighty nigh black-
eyed, an her a been white like that makes em look
blacker." Lucy tried to grab her from Milly, and Nunn
pushed her hands away with gentle sternness.

He put both pups on the table and turned to the children. "Now these ain't to be played with—leastways not
while they're little; an I don't want a see a one a you a
tryen to feed em one bit a anything; they'll git a little
milk at first, an I've spent a sight a money fer special pup
feed—it's a comen in th mails. An listen to me an bear
this in mind," and he shook his finger into the ring of
solemn eyes. "They ain't like Zing; he could ketch foxes
an he could git rabbits an he was a tree dog, too. But
these have got to grow up into foxhounds pure an true.
If'n I ketch any one a you ever a tryen to make em chase
anything—a rat er a rabbit—er anything, it'll be too bad.
You could ruin em. An I'd ruin you."

Suse studied the pups, a little frown of concentrated
effort to remember something puckered on her forehead.
"Pop, are them pups . . . pedi—pedi—pedigreed?" she
finished triumphantly.

Nunn came near dropping a pup. "Sure they're pedigreed—an registered. I've got their papers right here in
my pocket. But what a you know about such things?"

Suse never answered her father's question, but whirled
on her toes until her dress tail swirled out level with her
waist, crying, "Can't I put it over on old Paul now, him
an his brags," and only stopped at Milly's twice-repeated

command of, "Suse, quit that—a great big girl like you showen your underclothes any sich away."

Suse flushed, saw her father was not angry, and standing carefully still, but giggling happily, told how she knew all about pedigrees—she'd read the agriculture book in school through three times—and then how Paul Ballew had been bragging at school about his uncle on the other side of Tuckerville in MacLellan County—his mother's brother—who had a registered bull, all pedigreed, and Paul had said it was "th onliest bull—"

"Suse," Milly's voice cut in low and level and angry, "quit talken that a way, a usen that word—if'n I ever hear a you a sayen that name fer a brute up at school fore th boys I'll beat you half to death."

Suse gave her mother an impatient glance. "I allus say 'brute' at school in class, but Paul, he says 'bu—,' the other word, not 'brute,' an th agriculture book it says 'bull.' "

"Suse—" Milly began.

"Fer God's sake, Milly, let th youngen talk. Them blue-grass women says 'bull,' I bet. I know I heared one say 'bitch' an mean no harm; she was a talken about our little girl pup—now go on, Suse."

"Well, Paul, he's been braggen away about his uncle's registered pedigreed brute, a sayen it cost $250 an that it was th onliest piece of registered stock in th whole country—"

Nunn shook his head in disgust. "Just a lot a talk—they's registered stuff all around, an in th bluegrass, oh, my Lord, they ain't hardly nothen else; an who knows? We might have a registered bull uv our own some day an people bringen their cows frum miles—"

"Shit-fire, Nunn, I can't stand it. Quit talken that away; you'll have Lucy talken dirty up at school," Milly scolded.

But everybody, including Nunn, was too happy over Nunn's feat of coming home sober with two pups to mind Milly's scolding, not even Milly, who suddenly remembered that Nunn oughtn't to be standing around in wet pants. She dashed off for dry overalls, sent Lee Roy to freshen up the fire in the fireplace, sent Suse for fresh spring water, sent Lucy to run look under the floor for eggs, shooed Deb after Lee Roy so that Nunn could

change his overalls, then stoked the step stove and set a
fresh pot of coffee to boil.

Nunn had not wanted to bring out Milly's gift of
whisky while the children were around; Lucy would tell
up at school that he had brought home whisky, and by
the time the news got to the post office, word would be
out that Nunnely Ballew had got roaring drunk on bottled
in bond and brought six quart bottles of the stuff home.
He had changed his clothing and was ready to give the
bottle to Milly when Lucy came in with two eggs.

Then Milly was calling for Lee Roy to come slop Rosie
while she milked, telling Suse to keep the fire good and hot
and get her dad some fresh hot coffee right away, and
then to go upstairs and get a can of apple preserves for
breakfast, while in between times she repeated over and
over to Nunn that he must go quick and warm good by
the fire before he caught his death of cold. She went off to
milk and left Nunn still holding his wet pants, uncertain
of what to do with the whisky hidden in a deep hind
pocket. In the end he left the bottle in the pants and
hung them up, bottle-side against the wall.

Suse screamed at him to hurry to the fire, she was pouring his coffee; Deb and Lucy ran to push him up a chair
close to the fire, so close that he had to get up while they
pushed it back again. While Deb and Lucy each took off
one of his shoes, he drank two cups of the good hot black
bitter coffee that only Milly could brew exactly to his
taste, then tilted back his chair and sat with his legs
stretched to the fire. Deb and Lucy each rode one leg and
laughed up into his face and patted his hands. They were
not just exactly certain what it was he had done over and
above coming home sober; that in itself was joy enough,
especially to Lucy, who had, following her mother's ex-
ample, cried half the night with thinking he was either
dead or down drunk someplace in the cold.

Milly called to the children that their dad was too tired
to be bothered and that they must come away; Nunn protested, then remembered the whisky and hoped Milly
would come to the fire and they could be alone long
enough for him to tell her about it.

The firelight in his eyes made him drowsy, and filled
with the good coffee and the good thought that at least his
wife and children were proud of him, he grew pleasantly

warm and sleepy. He was aroused suddenly by Milly's tapping him on the shoulder and whispering in an urgent way, "Here, Nunn, take this; it'll break up any cold that's a gatheren," and the powerful fragrance of bottled in bond heated to boiling, with plenty of dried peppermint and a little water and sugar, leaped up his nose and surged down his chest until he came wide awake with a coughing fit.

"You're already a comen down," Milly said, shifting the hot cup to her other hand. "Wake up an drink this quick fore the youngens gits in. I sent em all to look fer eggs in th little barn; I don't want em knowen you brung liquor into th house. I found it in your pants pocket where you'd fergot it."

"Jesus Christ, woman, a body couldn't fergit liquor, not bottled in bond. It was fer you—bout th best I could buy —I drunk half to give me heart to stand that bus trip home, an saved the rest fer you to make some spirits a camphor like you've allus wanted—an now look what you've gone an done. God damn it."

"Aw, Nunn, honey, don't be so cross an us all so happy you're home alive. Drink this quick; you need it now a lot worse'n I'll ever need spirits a camphor—drink it now; there's still more on th stove. I'll bet it's real good; I used that sugar I been a saven fer coffee sweetenen when we have company. Hurry up now, an then you'll feel good enough to eat some breakfast. I'm cooken th last a th sausage meat. Hurry up now, fore the youngens gits in an smells it."

"They'll smell me," he said, cursing again, but when he saw she looked ready to cry, he drank it all, even the other cupful, in hot hasty gulps that set his throat on fire and brought water to his eyes.

When Milly had gone back to the kitchen, he cursed her, the whisky, the pups, and himself in whispered but black oaths. His stomach was empty, he wasn't used to drinking before sunup, so that Milly's tea was doing for him what the other half of the bottle in bond, the beers, and the wine had failed to do; the fire had too many flames, and the chimney walls were bowing in and bending out like the legs of a bowlegged drunken man.

Some sober spot in his rapidly befuddling mind recalled to him that only a little while ago he had told Milly he was hungry. If he didn't eat she'd declare he was either drunk or coming down with pneumonia fever, and give him a dose of feverweed tea; and if he fell while trying to get to the table, she'd go off and cry.

Suse came in and sniffed her nose and looked at him with a knowing in her eyes, but with none of the angry contempt that had been in them, the pride in having anything so fine as the pups filled her for the moment with a gay forgiveness and she giggled as she advised, "Pop, you'd better go to bed, you smell worse'n J. D. Duffey's kitchen when he's maken a run."

Nunn tried to lay a stern look on his face, but his eyes felt big as baked apples and it was all he could do to keep her head, that wavered like the chimney walls, in range of his vision. "Now, how could a little girl like you know th smell a whisky?"

Suse reached for the comb on the mantelpiece and began combing his hair. "Lord God, Pop, where do you think my nose has been all these years you've come home a puken like a foundered dog? Last time it made Mom so sick to her stomach, me an Lee Roy had to clean it up, wash th bedclothes an all." She called kitchenward, "We'll be in in a minute, Mom. I'm a comben Pop's hair."

She combed his forelock and twirled it round her finger. "An please, Pop, try not to let on fore Mom. She's so tickled—she's like I was—we both thought you was sober —an got a good breakfast, an you'll have to eat some a it." She wrinkled her nose, bent her head over his face and sniffed with a critical wrinkling of her nose. "That bluegrass whisky don't smell like old J. D.'s—smells sort a like horehound er somethen."

"Pep'mint," he said, and explained in a low sorrowful, blurry voice about the half pint he had saved for Milly's camphor spirits and how she had doctored him with it all —"An my stomach was empty," he finished, and Suse thought he was going to cry.

She hugged his neck backward and whispered, "Don't feel so bad, Pop. Just hang onto my shoulder when you go in to breakfast an set still an don't talk none, cept to say you're tired an sleepy an go to bed soon's you can —but please, Pop, don't let pore Mom know. She'd feel so bad."

Nunn did as Suse directed and got to the table in pretty good fashion, and even ate, though he did spill his coffee, took two helpings of dried peaches, each time thinking he had sausage, and only found out after he had covered them with gravy, but Milly never noticed, for she was hovering over the roaring stove, determined to have another fresh-baked biscuit ready for him as soon as he finished one.

After breakfast, while Milly and the children watched the pups drink milk, he slipped out and walked up the hill into a thicket of scrub pine, and there vomited up his breakfast and part of the tea, he hoped, and then staggered in to bed.

When he awoke he found Suse and Lee Roy had been on a long sheep hunt; they had started off in the direction of Lureenie's, made a great circle over into MacClellan County, across Bear Creek and through Tuckerville, where they had stopped at the homes of half a dozen Tuckers, and then come home through the creek gap past John's, where they had also stopped. And with all their long walk, twelve or fifteen miles at least, they said nothing of having heard bells or seen sheep sign, and after a little stray talk with them at supper he realized that they had not really hunted sheep at all, but had gone to spread the word that he had bought two pups with pedigrees.

Chapter Ten

EVEN THE DEEP SNOW did not keep people away; Sue Annie came at Sunday sundown, Blare and Joe C. on Monday, and Jaw Buster and Lister came at Monday dark. As many people, Milly said with pride, to see the pups as ever came to see a newborn baby.

And many were the exclamations and the head shakes and the questions, the most usual being, "God, a white she hound," and, "Did them little things cost more'n $100?"

If Nunn were not about, Milly would nod triumphantly. It was too much trouble to explain that Nunn had paid only $70 for both pups and that the rest of the money had gone for expenses connected with them, such as feed and Nunn's trip.

By midweek and Christmas Eve word had gone to the far end of the Cow's Horn, where Keg Head Cramer, Rans's father, lived. Though he was a religious old farmer like John, with one white feist dog and no use for a hound, he had heard that Nunnely Ballew had two hound pups that had come registered, collect on delivery, parcel post, air mail to the post office, and that Nunn had laid fifteen $20 bills on the mail window in order to get the pups, and so he had waded the deep snow to see. On the way he had stopped at Willie Cooksey's house, and all Willie's family had set up such a howling to see the pups that he and ten of his children had come along, leaving only his wife and baby at home; with all of her own family and eleven Cookseys and Keg Head, Milly had dinner in four shifts that day and opened half a dozen half-gallon jars of canned goods.

When the company had gone in the snowy twilight, Nunn realized with a start that it was Christmas Eve and he had nothing for Santa Claus, not even a stick of peppermint candy for Deb. But after supper Milly made everybody, even Nunn, hang a stocking above the fireplace. Then as soon as the two least ones were in bed, she lighted the lantern and she and Suse went upstairs with a mysterious air. They came back soon, loaded down with things for the stockings, popcorn balls and molasses-pull candy they had made on the sly, the nicest of the little short-core and rusty-coat apples saved from the fall, a dozen or more of the big late pears, yellow mellow now, and as a final triumph a dozen nickel sticks of peppermint candy and a big square of Nunn's favorite chewing tobacco.

And Nunn remembered with a hard choking hurt how he had noticed once or twice at breakfast lately that Milly and Suse never ate fried eggs with their lard gravy, each saying she was tired of eggs; there was no meat now, and no fried chicken, nothing but a few eggs—and they had done without eggs and sold them at Samuel's for Christmas candy.

While Milly was filling the stockings, the pups came whining around her feet for their fourth and last meal of the day, and she leaned over and sh-sh'd them, smiling, telling them in soft whispers to be quiet or Deb and Lucy would wake up and learn there was no Santa Claus. And the little she pup put her paws on Milly's shoe and wagged her tail as she looked up, puzzled by the stockings; and her eyes in the firelight were like Zing's eyes, different in their deeper darkness, but full of that same something a man could never name. And Milly, her hands busy pushing things into the stockings, whispering again, "Be quiet now, like a good girl an I'll hurry; the milk's got to warm, you know," was plainly pleased with the pup and the whole world.

And Nunn, watching her, wondered. It was his turn now to bring out his part of the Christmas, a package he had got in the mail two weeks ago and kept hidden in the corn pile—the yearly package from his mother in Missouri. Suse seized it with a whooping cry of joyful anticipation, and in spite of Milly's entreaties not to tear the pretty paper, tore the wrappings away, even the fancy ones filled with pictured Christmas trees. And, as always, there were books for all the children, story books with many colored pictures for the younger ones, a book of wild animals pictured with their tracks for Lee Roy, and a whole long story—a novel, Milly was afraid it was—for Suse, called *Lorna Doone*. Suse sighed with pleasure, Milly sighed with disappointment—always she hoped for hair ribbons or fancy mittens—and Nunn smiled with pleasure at the books; he would have hated it had his mother sent them clothes or such; when she sent books he knew she didn't think them poor and needy.

It was a good Christmas; the best, Milly declared, she had ever had; the youngens were all well, and though she never said so, it was one of the few Christmases when Nunn had neither hunted all the night before nor went off and got drunk during the day—and she wasn't in the family way.

Long before dinnertime the Tiller men were tearing up the country; repeated blasts from their shotguns made the valley roar, and in between blasts Rans Cramer could be heard singing "Nine of the Bent Two Over the Bow" to the tune of Old Dave's fiddle. Milly had visions of Lureenie and her youngens sitting out Christmas Day at home, maybe with no stove wood and no groceries, and sent Suse and Lee Roy around to her place with instructions not to come back without her if she were home alone. And sure enough Suse and Lee Roy were back directly, each with a little youngen and Lureenie with the least one, but laughing like a child as she dodged a snowball from Suse.

Milly was glad to have her for Christmas dinner; she'd killed two big fat hens and had a mountain of light fluffy dumplings, yellow with chicken fat. In spite of Rans off drunk, Lureenie was all smiles and happy talk. Rans had lost so much time from his WPA road work because of the rainy weather that he had made up his mind for true he was going off to Cincinnati to get work come spring. While he was gone she would have a garden and fill a lot of jars and be all ready to go back with him in the fall. And as soon as the hens started to set, she wanted to buy a setting hen and eggs from Milly and raise her some big dominecker fryers; there was nothing so good as a big fat yellow dominecker, she said, as she let Milly help her to another plateful of chicken and dumplings.

While they were eating, the pups, who had already had their noon meal, came sniffing around the woodbox where Lucy and Lureenie's oldest one, Bill, sat, each with a plate of food. Milly, busy feeding Deb and waiting on table and listening to Lureenie, paid the little youngens no mind.

But all at once Nunn, who had happened to glance in their direction, let out a roar like a wounded boar, jumping up from the table so fast to get to Lucy that his chair fell over backward. Lucy let out a squeal and sprang up, spilling her plate of chicken and dumplings onto the floor. Lureenie's Bill, scared by Nunn, set his tin pan of food on the woodbox and ran to his mother. The little boy pup grabbed a chicken thigh out of Bill's pan and the little girl pup took a big mouthful of the dumplings Lucy had spilled.

Nunn grabbed the girl pup, but the boy pup, his big ears flopping and his brown eyes black with meanness, galloped off to the fireplace room with the chicken thigh, Milly had to laugh, he looked so funny; but Nunn, with the girl pup tucked under his arm, let out a big oath and ran after him. The dog with the chicken thigh ran under Aunt Marthie Jane's big four-poster bed in the corner, and everybody got down on his hands and knees and began begging the boy hound to come out.

Nunn was too big to get under and yelled to Lee Roy to go after him quick, he was eating the chicken thigh, bone and all. But Milly's canned fruit was stacked under the bed, and Lee Roy couldn't seem to get started; and by this time the pup was so far back under the bed they couldn't see any of him except his eyes that sparkled out like lights as he glanced at them between bites.

"That stuff'll kill him," Nunn roared and ran to the foot of the bed and tried to jerk it away from the wall. With Milly helping he had managed to move it a little, when Lucy gave an awful squeal, "You're killen me; I'm been squashed to death behind th canned stuff."

Everybody had forgotten Lucy. Nunn's nose turned blue with anger as he got down on his knees and glared under the bed. "Why in hell didn't you speak up an git that pup out? Come out of there right this minute an bring that pup—I'm a goen to beat you haf to death anyhow. I seed you give him a chicken bone—hell-fire —Deb knows better'n that. I told you all never to give em a bite a nothen—not one bite, then you give him a chicken bone—hell-fire—chicken bones—th very worstest things fer pups—Lee Roy, run git me a hickory limb."

Milly breathed more easily. The closest hickory tree was half a mile away. If he'd meant business, he'd have gone for his razor strop.

The boy pup came out licking his chops and wagging his tail, but now everybody was busy on his knees again begging Lucy to come out before her pop took all the hide off her back with a hickory limb long as two crossties. But Lucy continued to take turns sobbing and screaming and arguing: Zing had always had chicken bones and candy when they had it, and it was Christmas and they'd all got candy and a big dinner, but the pups never got one thing —she hadn't thought one little bone would hurt the boy pup—it was his Christmas present; and anyhow chicken bones never hurt Zing.

"But Zing didn't have no pedigree," Suse explained; "when you've got a pedigree, you don't git chicken bones; when you ain't got a pedigree, chicken bones won't hurt you."

Milly was racking her brains for a Christmas present for the pups, when Lureenie bent up like a crazy woman with laughter, snatched off her hair bows and held them under the bed for Lucy to see. "Lookee, Lucy, lookee? I'll give them pups my hair bows—they're long enough to tie pretty around their necks," and she took the girl pup from under Nunn's arm and began tying the pink ribbon about her neck.

Then Nunn, who wanted to get back to his dinner, for he did love chicken and dumplings, had the best thought of all. "We'll give em a name fer Christmas, that's what we'll do—now shut up that bawlen an crawl out, an start thinken."

Lucy stuck her head from under the bed and lay on her stomach and watched Lureenie's slim, quick fingers fix the ribbon on the little girl pup's neck.

Nunn suddenly jumped up. "Jesus God," he said, and ran to the kitchen. "Jesus, God damn," he said again when he got there, but he didn't sound so mad any more, more like he was worn out.

They all ran behind him; Milly saw at once that things were bad, but she couldn't help but laugh; poor Nunn, she felt sorry for him, but the pup did look so funny. He had jumped on Nunn's chair, and it was a long stretch for him, but by keeping his hind legs on the edge of the chair and his paws on the table he could just reach Nunn's plate. Right in the middle of a big gulp he turned around and peeped at Nunn, sideways from under his big ears, for all the world like a child with its face gomed up with yellow chicken dumplings, and a smear of sweet potato on one eyebrow.

"From now on," Nunn said in a quiet resigned voice as he picked up the pup, "you youngens are a goen to stay right around th table and do your eaten, an these pups are a goen to stay out in th fireplace room with the door shut—this day's business could make this'un bad sick."

The boy pup's pink-bottomed belly was stretched out like a balloon and Milly, as she emptied Nunn's plate into the slop and then washed it, suggested that maybe Nunn ought to give him a dose of Deb's medicine, but Nunn declared he didn't want his pups taking any old strong patent medicine; it might kill them; and, anyway, he looked so lively it was hard to think he could be sick.

They started Christmas dinner all over again, and after much discussion it was decided to name the pups Samuel and Vineria; the girl pup's name was Lucy's choice, after ter Granma, she said, because she had red on her head like Granma; and Suse and Lee Roy, proud of their books and proud of their grandmother, whom they had never seen, agreed at once. The Samuel was for Preacher Samuel. Suse had suggested that. There was something sober and settled about the big-shouldered boy pup, in spite of his meanness, that made her think of a preacher.

Lee Roy shamed her; Suse was naming the pups after her future father-in-law, Lee Roy said, but she needn't think that when she married Andy she could keep a hound —he'd be like his daddy, too religious.

Nunn glanced at Suse over his coffee cup and set it down quickly with a little sloshing of the coffee. "Shut up, Lee Roy," he said, and felt for an instant off balance and unsettled, like a man walking through his own plowed field run into something unexpected like a bear or a panther, for Suse was blushing red, her eyes bright like she might be ready to run off and cry. She had always been a brash-turned youngen, nothing had ever plagued her; now she was coloring up over a boy like a timid grown girl, like Milly in their courtship days; he felt still more unsettled when after a little counting in his head he realized that Suse was twelve going on thirteen; not much more than two years younger than Milly was when he started courting her—Suse was smart, she must have an education like his mother—she could be a teacher like his mother.

Not long after dinner John and his two boys came, bringing as a gift a great round of souse meat of Nancy's making, but so eager were they to see the pups and so eager were the children to show them that the basket was left on the kitchen table unopened and forgotten until time to go home.

After admiring Sam and Vinie in their pink ribbons and telling Nunn with his peculiarly sly but kind smile that if a body had to buy hounds it was better to get good ones and maybe raise pups and sell them, John sat by the fire and he and Nunn talked of farming in general and sheep and weather in particular. John in his usual dour fashion when his mind went on sheep, for he hated sheep, predicted a warm wet winter when the ewes would catch cold from getting their wool wet in cold rains, with maybe one hard cold spell along about lambing time that would freeze the lambs in the borning—and, as always in the winter, he thought come spring he'd sell his sheep. The country was changing—come all these new graveled roads, people with cars and cur dogs would be coming in and the back-hill range wouldn't be safe for sheep.

He spat into the fire and shook his head and sighed, and as the children had been hoping, launched into a long story of a wild-turkey hunt he had gone on sixty years ago. Nunn listened with but half a mind to John's tale of the wild turkeys, for Preacher Jim had been along and used to tell it to him when he was about Lee Roy's size. He glanced sometimes into the fire and sometimes through the open door that faced west across his fields; and under the deep layer of snow there was no red earth of wide-split gullies or sagegrass or loose gray rocks to torment him with their crying out that he was a no-good

lazy farmer; and sitting so, he fell gradually into the pleasant dreaming state of mind in which, when he worked in
the coal mines and saved to buy the farm, he had often
spent whole days together. But of late years the dreams
and the plans had come less often, and now for months on
end they never came at all. Each day was futureless, a
time to do some work because the work could wait no
longer, a space of light bound on each end by darkness
and sleep, broken by eating, all dimmed and dulled by
the long shadow of King Devil.

And now mixed with his determination to get King
Devil was a relief that he couldn't hunt him again until
the pups were a year old. He would keep on making
crossties when it was too wet or snowy to farm. In good
weather he would clear the brush from the sandfield and
put it in corn next year—it ought to make a good corn.
He would pick up the rocks in the graveyard field and the
three corn swags where he had had corn for the last four
years, sow them to grass and lespedeza the way John did,
rent a mowing machine from Samuel or John, and save
enough hay for his ewes so that he could bring them in
early from the range and keep them home till after sheep-
shearing time in the spring, and not have to waste so
much time sheep-hunting. He had in the last five years,
he guessed, spent enough time hunting sheep to build
ten miles of rail fence or twenty of cedar posts and wire
—but wire, woven wire that would hold sheep, cost
money.

He thought of the wire the pups would have bought
and looked quickly at John and put his mind on the
story.

When John had gone, Milly reminded Nunn of the old
man's prediction of a cold snap, and once more urged
him to fix the broken windows in the middle room where
Lee Roy and the pups slept; the pups, she declared,
would catch their deaths of pneumonia fever. She had
wanted them to sleep in the fireplace room in the first
place, but Nunn had said a heated room would ruin their
noses; then she'd wanted to make them a little feather
bed, but Nunn wouldn't hear to that either; they'd be better off outside, he said. But she had held out for at least
a shuck mattress in the middle room; he grumbled some
but consented; they'd be ruined by a raising like that of

a city cur dog, he said, but Milly had pointed out that the middle room was about as cold and airy as the out-doors anyway, and Lee Roy said it was colder.

John's hard cold spell never came, the pups throve, and Nunn never fixed the windows, but Lee Roy com-plained less of sleeping alone in a cold room and even gave up sleeping in his socks. One day Milly found one of his socks with the toe chewed out, and surmised it had happened while the sock was on Lee Roy's foot in bed, but she never said anything. It looked like the pups would chew up everything in the house anyway. She couldn't keep a stocking on Deb. He'd run and they'd run after him and grab one of his always hanging-down stockings, or if the stockings were up they'd grab his overall leg; he'd fall and they'd play with him like kittens playing with a ball.

It was a good winter; it was hard to do without meat, and Betsey didn't give much milk and there were not many eggs, but Milly had plenty of beans and potatoes and canned stuff, and best of all there came in January a long spell of clear frosty weather, like a second fall, people said, and as fine a spell of sheep and crosstie-making weather as Nunn had ever seen. No damp snows or cold rains to sicken the ewes just before lambing time, and from the way their sacks were hardening up, it looked as if several would lamb anyway by the 1st of February.

After a hard day in the crossties Nunn liked to take the lantern and go out to the sheepfold under the store-house. Lee Roy would have fed them their shelled corn and fodder when he came from school, but Nunn wanted to count them himself, for some, like old Bossie Jean, a bell ewe, who usually dropped two big early lambs, had the bad habit of slipping away at lambing time.

He would hang the lantern on one of the foundation posts and sit a time squatting on the ground, taking his after-supper chew of tobacco; and gradually the ewes that had been wild as deer on the range in the late fall would come up to him, shy-eyed and hesitant still, but not afraid, cautiously sniffing his hands and his jumper pock-ets and his old felt hat. He would sit perfectly still until one came that seemed bolder than the others, and then with a carefully unconcerned slowness, as if he were not much interested in the ewe, he would reach out and scratch behind her ears and under her tail, and usually she would stand for him until he could feel her teats, her eyes in the lantern light still wild, but trusting. The other ewes would be quiet, looking at him, their great luminous eyes full of gentle wonder, each eye carrying the cross Aunt Marthie Jean had used to show him as a child.

Gentling his ewes, he was, for lambing time and sheep shearing, the way Aunt Marthie had gentled hers. She had had a wonderful hand with any animal; she could bridle a half-broken colt none of her boys could touch, and drive a yearling bull a hired hand couldn't handle. John now, whose sheep were wild, springing up like startled rabbits when he walked among them, envied Nunn his hand with sheep and often said so, but Nunn took no credit for the business; unlike John, he had had Aunt Marthie Jane for a grandmother.

He liked to sit among his ewes with their good warm sheep smell, a smell he had loved since childhood, sharp in his nose, and listen to the northeast wind scream high above in the pines, pleasantly conscious that no breath of it hit the sheepfold, for all of the back and part of the two sides were dug out of the hillside, and with the storehouse above crammed with fodder, it was warm and secure as any cave. And listening so to the wind, Nunn would have the same feeling of security and peace he had had as a child when he sat with Aunt Marthie Jane among her ewes at lambing time, a piece of knitting in her hands or maybe the Bible; for the gentling of her ewes was one of the few jobs at which she could sit still, and he would dream at times of how some day he would have a hundred ewes, registered maybe, and a real sheep barn and wove-wire fence to keep them always home.

But one night before he had hung up his lantern or started to count, he knew something was missing, a sound; there were six sheep bells and one was not there; in a moment he knew it was Bossie Jean's bell.

She had run away to lamb; he cursed her and counted the others; she was the only one missing. He took the lantern and went outside; the night was like the others of the past week, cold, with a northeast wind and a scud of cloud across the stars; a new-dropped lamb could freeze even in the shelter of one of the rock houses below the Pilot Rock, the most likely place for Bossie Jean to have gone. He circled up the hill toward a spring in a little cove where in cold weather the ewes went to drink because the water never froze. But there was no sound of the bell near the spring, and he went on, zigzagging back and forth across the hill, cursing the foolish ewe and the hard cold.

It was a long time before he heard her bell, one tinkle and then silence far around on the side of the hill toward John's end of the valley, a place where the sheep had never gone. He did not hear the bell again, and in spite of the cold he sweated as he tore through the brush and briars; the one tinkle could mean that Bossie Jean had moved her head in her sleep, but she could be down, straining hard, and never moving her head, or she could be sick. Early in the evening as it was, the other ewes still chewed their cuds with a constant jingle jangle of their bells.

The lamb's head and front feet were out when he got there and poor Bossie Jean was straining to get its shoulders through. He set the lantern on a ledge of stone, and without frightening her into unnecessary movement, he looked at the half-born lamb and shook his head. The lamb's nose had a blue dead look, its ears were whitening with frost, and the ringlets of wool on its forehead were studded with tiny icicles. Bossie Jean looked up at him and there was no fear in her eyes; more like she was glad to see him.

He glanced around the little rock house, a poor place she had chosen, facing east up the valley and shallow, so little protected from the wind and with no droppings or other sign of her having been there for more than a few minutes that it made him think she had just run in there to have her lamb; she had not even tried to make a bed.

He got as far back as he could from the freezing wind, jerked off his jumper, then his shirt; and after stuffing it in a tight bundle under his underwear next to his body where it would be ready to receive the newborn lamb, he put on his jumper again and stood waiting, talking to her in a voice he tried to make soft and calm in spite of his teeth chattering from the cold. "Hurry up, now, Bossie Jean. Your pore little lamb's goen to freeze. Be a good girl an I'll give you a good warm feed a ship stuff I been a saven just for this."

Bossie Jean got up and walked around and sniffed the ground and blatted, then sniffed again and stood a moment in the front of the rock house, waiting, listening, then giving the low tender mother bleat of a ewe for a new-born lamb.

"Come on now, Bossie Jean, you're all addled—you've been so long in th bornen you think it's come already. Come on now." He waited, shivering, afraid to walk over-much or stamp his feet or clasp his hands; addled as she seemed to be, one quick, noisy movement might stampede her and her half-dead lamb into the brush.

She came and sniffed his hands and blatted as if there was something she would say; he talked again, begged her to put her mind on her business or the lamb would be dead, and gradually she grew quieter, began to strain harder and faster and the lamb was born.

The moment Bossie Jean bit the navel cord he jerked the warm shirt from his bosom and went to work on the lamb, a little ewe, limber lifeless, with its ears frozen and its nose frosted. He rubbed the wet wool quickly but gently, and at short regular intervals squeezed its ribs and moved its forelegs, blowing now and then into its mouth until he was out of breath and sweat stood on his forehead. He almost never lost a lamb in the bornen and somehow, for the moment, reviving this weak worthless thing seemed important, more important than saving a whole flock of full-grown ewes from a sleet storm.

Bossie Jean watched him quietly, showing little interest in her lamb; at times he spoke to her, urged her to hurry and bring the other one, for this one was so little it was bound to be a twin lamb and she most always had twins. It seemed he had been working an hour when as he bent up the limber forelegs they did not fall down but remained for an instant pulled up against its chest.

An elation like God at the creation quickened his heart and he rubbed the still damp wool again, saw the hind legs jerk, the eyeballs move, and suddenly the lamb was a live, breathing thing. Once more he ran a forefinger across its tongue to clear away the mucus; now the lips came to life and pulled on his finger with a weak sucking. And the wonder of life, the lamb a perfect living thing, complete with suckling lips and tongue and small sharp teeth that would in a few days' time be nibbling, came over him like some grand all-pervading wave of water or wind or sound that for an instant blots out all things but the man himself.

He squatted a moment, smiling while the lamb's lips pulled harder on his finger, then he pulled his finger away and the lamb gave a weak birdlike cry.

Bossie Jean came and sniffed the lamb, at first disinterestedly, then with more and more eagerness. The lamb struggled to its knees, its head wobbling still with weakness, but sensing hunger, hunting the teats. Nunn took his pocket knife and clipped the soiled, matted wool from Bossie Jean's udder, then the three of them struggled together for a time, each with the goal of getting warm milk in the lamb, but no one seemed to know exactly how to go about the business. Bossie Jean wouldn't stand still, and the lamb, still too weak to stand upright, would let its head fall sideways just when Bossie Jean's milk-swollen teats were over its nose, and though it would suck Nunn's finger it seemed to have no notion of what a teat was for; but at last the thing was accomplished and Nunn slung the sweat from his forehead and smiled at the lamb, now able to stand, though its legs wobbled still.

The lamb had finished nursing when Bossie Jean strained down again, but instead of another lamb came the afterbirth only. Nunn stared at Bossie Jean in puzzled disappointment—one lamb only and it so little. Bossie Jean was getting old.

But all the same, he sang as he hurried, almost running, over the hill. He had left the lamb warm and dry and fed, where only a little while ago it was like the dead.

Next morning, as soon as it was light, he started after Bossie Jean and the lamb. She should have water and a warm ship-stuff mash, and it was easier to carry the lamb home than to take feed to Bossie Jean. The pups were having their early-morning run outside, and when he was halfway up the hill he realized with disgust that they were following him.

The weather had been so bad and they were so young that he had never let them follow any of the family on any long trip into the woods or rough brush. They were such lively nosey things that he was already afraid they might pick up some fox scent, King Devil's even, and be off and lost before a man could turn around.

He swore at them to go back, called Milly; but Milly, busy getting breakfast, never heard. He rounded the hillside above the barn spring and forgot the pups, following somewhere in the brush behind, when he heard Bossie Jean. She was where he had left her but her bell was jangling as if she were pacing the rock house, and every few moments she gave the mother bleat of a ewe for her new lamb, and there was no answering blat. It had died, he guessed, and hurried on. But there was no lamb, dead or alive, in the rock house.

He stood a moment staring at Bossie Jean before he understood—something had carried the lamb away while it lay sleeping warm and full of milk by Bossie Jean—done it so stealthily that Bossie Jean had never wakened.

An insane anger surged over him—King Devil had done that—he alone could steal so silently—any other fox or a wildcat would have wakened Bossie Jean.

He stood a long time, his shoulders slumped, staring at the ewe; red light from the rising sun touched the rock house, and he realized that he was cold and had had no breakfast. Bossie Jean did not want to leave the rock house and turned sorrowful puzzled eyes on him when he cursed her in a loud voice and did a thing he almost never did to any of his animals—hit her with a heavy hunk of brush.

He understood it all now—her blatting for a lamb last night before the lamb was born, the one lamb only, the poor shelter she had chosen, the slow birth. Somewhere in a good warm shelter she had borne her first lamb; King Devil had stolen that; he had maybe shown himself to her —for he was never one to hide himself—and scared her in the birthing of the second; she had run away to the first rock house she found; he had followed her there, and stolen the second, but poor worn-out Bossie Jean had neither seen nor heard him.

He had forgotten the pups and might have gone home without them had he not heard a troubled whining down by the barn spring and more yapping from the woods around the hill. He ran to the spring and found Sam, shivering and crying, as he clawed round and round in the deep pool of water just below the spring. The edges were caked with ice, and these had maybe saved him from drowning when he got chilled, but they had also prevented his clawing his way out.

Nunn jerked him out, clapped him under his jumper, and though the pup whined and shivered still, he ran on into the woods after Vinie. She was running up and down and yapping by a long high dead chestnut log.

Fox scent she had found—King Devil scent—he had jumped a log too high for her to climb across.

Nunn left Bossie Jean and strode angrily home. King Devil—King Devil. He killed two lambs in one night but never harmed the pups—somewhere on a back hill he sat and laughed and planned things for them as he had planned for Zing.

Chapter Eleven

IT WASN'T LONG after Sam's icy bath, a morning early in February, that Milly shook Nunn into wakefulness, and her voice was full of the terror and despair that only a bad sick child could give. She was thrusting a clean shirt into his hands and saying over and over, with a tremulous sobbing, "Git up, Nunn. Hurry. You'll have to go to Town."

He'd hewed crossties all the day before and had slept like a log and known nothing all night. His first thought was that one of the children had got a bad burn or some other accident, but when he rubbed his eyes hard he saw all the children, even Deb, with the corners of his mouth turned down and trying hard to cry, at the foot of the bed.

Suse rushed up with his shoes, clean and freshly rubbed with mutton tallow, and Lee Roy came with his other pair of socks, dolorously declaring he couldn't find the needle so Milly could sew up a hole.

Milly took the socks, shook him again. "Wake up, Nunn, honey; you've got to go to town and take Sam—he looks like he'll die with ever breath, but the veterinarian Samuel had onct with his cow could maybe save him." Didn't Nunn recollect Samuel's cow that couldn't have her calf last fall, and Sue Annie had give her up to die and the veterinarian had saved her? If Nunn left early enough he could catch Jaw Buster before he went off to haul anything, and they could catch the veterinarian before he went off to doctor a sick cow. She had tried giving Sam some feverweed tea and a drop of turpentine, but there wasn't any sugar to put with it and it hadn't done any

148

good. Green cockleburs boiled in sweet milk might save him, but she couldn't get any green cockleburs, not now in February, and please, for pity's sake, put his socks on—he'd have to hurry; it was almost daylight.

Suse put a cup of boiling hot coffee under his nose just as he bent his head to find his feet. The collision with the coffee, some of which sloshed between his unbuttoned underwear around his navel, wakened him enough so that he got into his clothes.

But even after he had crossed the creek and started up the hill, black still under the trees, he felt like a man walking in his sleep. Milly, for the first time in their married life, had sent him off with no breakfast and only one cup of coffee. Lee Roy came behind, carrying Vinie, kicking Nunn's heels with his toes at every other step, and saying when he could spare breath from the steady climbing, "Hurry, Pop, hurry; it'll mebbe be too late."

Nunn reached back for a chew of tobacco, found he had none, and cursed and remembered that in all the tumult he had put nothing into his pockets but a handkerchief and the bit of money he always tried to save back to see him through spring planting. The wanting of a chew of tobacco awakened him completely; he glanced down at Sam cradled on one arm and cursed himself for a fool. Since the morning King Devil had led him into the water, Milly had been declaring he didn't act right—but Milly was forever doctoring on something—and now the pup was sick, bad sick, his nose hot and swollen, his eyes swollen shut and seamed with yellow pus; but worst of all was his panting, gasping, irregular breath, and up against his jumper he could feel his heart race like a watch wheel.

He could die before he ever got to Town—the veterinarian might be good, but he wasn't Jesus Christ to bring back the dead—and it would cost a lot of money. John and Samuel would call him seven times a fool for running away from his work and spending good money to take a sick pup to the doctor; Jaw Buster had all the hauling he could do and wouldn't want to be bothered with taking a sick pup to the doctor, certainly not one so sick it looked as if it would die before he could get it there. He stopped dead in his tracks, thinking it over, and Lee Roy's toe came hard on his heel.

"You gitten tired, Pop? Look, why'n't you carry
Vinie, er let her walk; there ain't nothen th matter with
her nohow. Mom jist sent her along fer good measure, I
recken—an Suse said if'n it was th distemper, she might
take it, too, an ought to get doctered up. Anyhow, I think
I'll run on an tell Jaw Buster fore he gits away."

"They's no use in acten like a fool over a sick hound
—th whole family carryen on worse'n if it was a baby."

"But who ever heared of a baby costen $35 an haven
papers an a pedigree?" Lee Roy wanted to know as he
went running away up the hill.

Nunn sighed and picked up Vinie, who was sniffing the
road dust, and walked on with a pup on each arm. He
was fully awake now and no longer able to feel like a man
who on first awakening continues to hope he is still sleeping, troubled by a nightmare instead of the real thing. The
full meaning of Sam's very possible death came to him:
the lost money, the lost time, the lost hope—or would the
hope of catching King Devil be lost? He felt old and stiff
and tired.

He walked on, taking his time, expecting to meet Lee
Roy coming back to tell him Jaw Buster had a load of
coal or crossties on his truck and couldn't go. Instead,
Blare came down the post-office road at a fast walk and
he looked as if he had been running. He took Vinie,
glanced at Sam, and frowned at Nunn, "Cain't you
come on a little faster? That pup'ull die."

Nunn, nettled at being told what to do, especially by
Blare, yawned and reckoned there was no hurry. Jaw
Buster might not be able to take him. Blare was certain he
would. He, Blare, had started to shoot down some coal in
Uncle Ansel Anderson's mine, and had met Lee Roy on
the road. He had run back home to tell Flonnie he was
going to town, and hurried back before Flonnie had time
to iron him a clean shirt.

They topped the ridge side and heard Jaw Buster's
truck roaring around the bend by the church house. Lister
was with him. They all rode in the cab; Blare and Nunn
held the pups, Lister held the horn down, and Jaw Buster drove, roaring around the blind curves of the ridge
road, flying up and down its dips until even Blare, who
liked fast motion, forgot to chew his tobacco. And Nunn

was glad when they had to stop to fix a flat just this side of the highway.

Blare hinted to Jaw Buster that he thought they were going too fast for safety; they'd skidded sixty feet when the tire blew. Jaw Buster grunted and lowed they were safe enough from everything but the highway patrol. Nunn had heard vaguely of the State Highway Patrol but had never seen it and had supposed when he thought about it at all that it stayed mostly around Town. Blare rattled on about how everybody had better be good; a patrol of four of the toughest-looking men he'd ever seen, with forty-fives in holsters and big guns in the back of the car, went up and down the highway all the time, looking for trouble; the other day they'd come clean out to Samuel's store and nobody had ever found out what they were after, just drove up and turned around—it was the truth, Blare said; his mom, Sue Annie, had gone to the store for a four-pound bucket of lard and two squares of chewing tobacco and had seen them with her own eyes, and Ruth Hull had too.

Lister opined they were just looking around, that was their job, looking around for trouble, and when the graded graveled road was finished, a body would have to go clean to Alcorn before it would be safe to take a drink.

Nunn had borrowed a chew of tobacco from Blare and felt better, and as he screwed a nut on the wheel asked what kind of trouble the patrol looked for. Blare said any kind, but mostly traffic-law breaking, like going too fast on the wrong side of the road, and liquor trouble. It sure wasn't safe to fool with liquor any more; that is, selling or hauling on a road—the patrol would get you for true— and Lister said that unless they had better luck finding it than he did, they'd never make any arrests. He'd hardly had a drink since that night at J. D.'s, and J. D. hadn't been able to make any since—he'd started some, unbeknowningst to his wife, he thought, and she had fed the mash to the hogs, bucketful by bucketful, unbeknowingst to him, so that when he went to see if it had started to glug, the mash barrel was empty. He hadn't said anything, because he wasn't certain, but his hogs had been growing a sight; and then next day there was the barrel catching rainwater by the kitchen door, and he asked Veda how it come there, and she said, "Not by cryen or prayen,

J. D.," and kept on rocking the baby. J. D. left it there, so
Sue Annie said; he was getting old and an old man
couldn't hold a young wife on a tight rein.

And Lister shook his head and said if J. D. didn't look
out, Veda would be cuckolding him one of these days—
but he wished to God somebody would make some good
whisky; he was afraid of that stuff they made over in
Alcorn; one of the Crabtree boys in the Long Bend had
taken one drink and had spit up one tonsil and swallowed the other. Jaw Buster said that if he was Nunn,
with plenty of corn and no real close neighbors, he'd
make him a run of good safe whisky, the kind they use
to doctor babies; whatever he had left over he could sell.

Nunn laughed and didn't think that from the way he
felt he'd have any left over, and said no more of moonshining. A thought had hit him like a falling log, and he
was silent, thinking how much he needed money, how
easy it would be to make a little whisky and sell it.

He forgot about whisky when they got back in the cab.
Sam seemed so nearly dead; he was twitching and shaking like a child with a convulsion. Blare looked at the pup
and said he thought they might as well turn around, but
Lister said keep right on going; when Sourvine was a pup
he had been almost that bad with something like the fever,
but Babe had pulled him through with hot onion poultices.

They were down the long curves into the Valley and
over the Cumberland and up again and across the pretty
high-rolling farming country that lay around Town before
Nunn had got all the good from his borrowed chew of
tobacco.

The sun was up, at least high enough to touch the
courthouse steeple, but the streets were still and the courthouse porch benches empty and they saw only one farm
wagon, the *clop-clop* of its mules' shoes echoing in the
courthouse square. Jaw Buster stopped at a hamburger
place always open across from Purdice's big flour mill
where a sleepy-eyed girl didn't know anything about vet-
erinarians but looked Dr. Hibbetts up in the telephone di-
rectory, hunting down the page with a long purple-painted
nail. She told them how to get there.

Jaw Buster drove a little out of town, past a gray stone
church and into a wide silent street where the roots of
wide-spreading sycamores and maples had wrinkled the
pattern of worn faded bricks in the sidewalk; and stopped

by a wide lawn, green with bluegrass that sloped up to a
big, fine old brick house. The likeness of a little colored
boy done in iron stood near the wrought-iron gate and
held out a brass hitching ring.

It seemed a funny street for a horse doctor but there it
was, "Dr. J. W. Hibbetts, Veterinarian," in a small iron
sign above the gate. Nunn picked up Sam and Blare
took Vinie. Over and over Milly had warned that Sam
must not get chilled on the breezy ride and had wrapped
him in a shapeless child's red fur-cloth coat, handed all the
way down from Suse and cast off at last by Deb. Nunn
left the coat, but as Sam just at the moment was having
a hard fit of the shivering shakes he put him under his
jumper and went up the walk with Blare at his heels. It
seemed to him his feet rang loud enough across the porch
to wake the town, but when he knocked on the door nobody came. They waited and looked at the door. Nunn
felt Sam's shakes give way to one hard, convulsive shud-
der and then he was rigid under his arm—dead, he
guessed, and felt dull and heavy and dead inside.

Then Blare pushed a button by the door. "It's a door-
bell," he whispered as he held his finger to it. "I've seen
people push em in th movies up in Indiana."

The door was jerked open by a fat shiny-faced Negress,
wrapped in a red kimono. Blare jerked his finger from
the button.

"Nobody's deaf," the Negress said, and added wrath-
fully, "You'll wake up the doctor."

"What a you recken we're tryen to do?" Blare asked.
"We got a bad sick animal."

"The doctor can't make no calls this time a day," the
Negress said. "It ain't even time for him to get up. Telephone him about nine o'clock an see if he can come," she
said, and looked past them to Jaw Buster's battered truck
by the front gate, and her eyes said plainly that she didn't
think the doctor could come to the likes of them.

"He couldn't come . . . not to my place," Nunn said,
and added, his wide brown eyes full of the same sorrow
and lostness that hurt his throat and tightened his stomach:
"I'm sorry we bothered you. . . . I don't think th doctor
could do no good, not now." And he let Sam, stiff,
with his eyes rolled back, slide from under his jumper.

The Negress pushed the door wide open and took a

long close look at Sam. "Whyn't you say you had a bad
sick hound? Real foxhound, ain't he?"

"Pedigreed," Nunn said.

"He ain't dead," she said. "Dr. Hibbetts is a wonderful
fine doctor an he's crazy fer hounds. You wait and
let me see if I can't git him up . . . . He was up late with
a case of milk fever, but he'll maybe come down for a
pedigree hound." She giggled and went running up the
wide curved stairs, as light-footed as if her big body was
cut out of nothing heavier than soapsuds.

She was back soon to say the doctor would be right
down, and led them to the stairs above his office in the
basement. Nunn was glad to be out of the hall, with its
rugs and furniture and doors leading into rooms that
looked too fine to live in. He wondered if the doctor who
lived in such a place wouldn't be a hard-turned man to
deal with, but when he came, an old man with a
shock of white hair, Nunn liked him at once; and from the
way he went about his business, he had been handling
and doctoring sick animals all his life.

He laid Sam out on a little steel table, and he looked
so much like he was dead that Nunn wondered if he didn't
waste his time—still, little Ezekial Cooksey was stretched
out stiff like that and Sue Annie and Milly had pulled him
through—but Sam wasn't a Cooksey.

The old man took a thing like a hose, put the end pieces
in his ears, and stuck the rest of it against Sam's chest,
listening here and yonder. Then, with the thing dangling
around his neck, he went into drawers and desks, taking
out a long shooting needle like the county health nurses
used to use to shoot typhoid into the children, a little bottle of
medicine, pills, and a piece of cotton.

He swabbed a spot under Sam's leg where the skin and
hair were thin, using something that looked and smelled
like moonshine; then he took the needle, dipped it into
the little bottle, and shot it into Sam. Blare shut his eyes
and winced, but Nunn looked on, and as the old man
lifted his head he met Nunn's troubled, inquiring eyes.

"He's pretty sick, but I think he'll pull through—that is,
if he responds to drugs—once in a great while they don't
—but his heart's in good shape. He's not been bad like
this long, has he?" he asked.

Nunn shook his head, and told about how he'd got wet

in the frozen spring branch about a week ago; he'd seemed puny, sniffling around and not eating so good, but he'd never got bad sick until last night when he took with something like distemper, but what his wife said was just like pneumonia in a baby.

The doctor smiled, wrinkles coming up around his eyes, and said that was about what it was, pneumonia, only you didn't call it that in a hound. He dropped sixteen pills with a slit across the top into an envelope. "Give him one every four hours until they're gone," he said, and handed the envelope to Nunn, then turned to Vinie with a kind of eager quickness, as if he had been anxious to look at her all along.

His eyes brightened and he shook his head slowly. "That's a pretty thing, now," he said, "a pure white, pure-blooded hound—don't know as I ever saw one before."

"She's got a little dusten a red," Nunn said, trying to act unconcerned about Vinie's beauty, but Vinie understood at once that here was a man who knew what a pedigree was, and so went into her prettiest poses. She sniffed the floor just enough to show she knew there was no fox around, but long enough to show how pretty she was with her nose down and her white ears dangling by her black eyes; then she tossed back her ears like a child pushing hair out of her eyes, and looked at him and showed her fine face and the dainty way she had of standing lifted on her toes, as if she spurned the ground, and when he said, "Fox-footed," she understood his admiration, and all unafraid began to investigate the stethoscope with one paw and her teeth.

But he had a way with hounds, and after a minute she stood for him, only twisting her head a little to see what was going on. She had some cold, he said, nothing to worry about, but Nunn must be careful and let neither pup get too hot nor too cold nor wet; and they both ought to have some cod-liver oil; get a quart at any drugstore and give each about a teaspoon a day at feeding time. Also, Nunn should be careful of letting them go among other dogs—in six weeks or so, when Sam was strong again, they ought to be inoculated against distemper and maybe rabies, too; and they oughtn't to be around wormy animals.

The last worried Nunn, and though he hated to bother

the doctor so much, especially before breakfast, he asked about worms in his sheep. He kept his ewes on the range most of the time, but every winter he had to bed them down in the same place, and lately he'd found a few worms in their droppings—he knew he ought to change them about, but he didn't have the barn room.

The doctor wrote the name of a drug—phenothiazine—on a piece of paper and told Nunn he could buy it at any drugstore, and then asked him if he knew how to drench a sheep without strangling it—a lot of people didn't and caused their ewes to take pneumonia. And Nunn must go over to the county agent's office and get their bulletins on sheep; there was a new one on worms that was very good and maybe they had some bulletins on dogs.

Nunn thanked him for his trouble, paid the $2 fee—he had expected it would be more—and started to pick up Sam. He was breathing easier already and had had no more fits, but the doctor suggested that he leave him there until he was ready to go home. The old man seemed so interested in the pups that Nunn lingered a moment longer to ask if he thought the spell of sickness had hurt Sam's nose.

The doctor considered and said he didn't think so, but it would be hard to tell. Some hounds had better noses than others and maybe when training time came Sam's nose would show up fine as the rest of him, and again it might not; the bitch was apt to have the better nose and maybe the prettier mouth, but she mightn't hold up so well. And he wanted to know about their sires and grandsires and if Nunn planned to train them himself or sell them when they were a little older.

Blare couldn't be quiet any longer; he had to let the doctor know the pups were already hunting; they didn't have to be trained. They were both chasing foxes with never a sniff for anything else, not even a rabbit when it ran under their noses.

Nunn had never seen a rabbit run under their noses, but he sat silent and listened with the doctor. The old man pulled off his already slipped down glasses and sat and held them and listened with the interested but incredulous air of a man hearing an exciting, well told lie. Blare as usual made the truth a little bigger than it was, but the pups had chased King Devil, and when Nunn explained about how Sam got his wetting in the spring, the doctor looked surprised, but he didn't look as if he still thought it was a lie.

Outside in the truck again, the men discovered they were all hungry, and as Lister and Jaw Buster had got into an argument about the color of the fingernails on the girl in the hamburger stand, they went back there, and while Lister convinced Jaw Buster in whispers that the fingernails were purple and not black, as Jaw Buster had claimed, they breakfasted on hamburgers and coffee, all except Vinie. She had one soft fried egg, a raw hamburger with a piece of hard toast and a glass of milk, all of which she ate from a clean white saucepan the girl with the purple-painted fingernails furnished after Blare explained that she was a pedigreed foxhound and couldn't go without breakfast.

Jaw Buster wanted to try to find a secondhand muffler for his truck; Lister had to buy some things for his wife and swore he wouldn't leave town anyway until he had found a drink, and as Blare was never in a hurry and Uncle Ansel's coal could wait, they all gladly agreed to wait until Nunn went to the county agent's office for his book on sheep worms and bought the drugs and other things he needed. Blare said he'd like to take care of Vinie as he had nothing else to do. Nunn was grateful; he didn't want to carry a hound pup all over town, even if she was pretty with papers and a pedigree.

Chapter Twelve

NUNN HAD HEARD a lot about the AAA from Samuel and John; it was sinful to begin with, corrupting the voters by giving fertilizer away, and worse yet, it told a farmer how to run his business. The county agent, whom he supposed to be a part of the AAA, he had always thought was a man; now it turned out to be three women, pretty young women with friendly faces, nice friendly, and all of them looked up when he went in. He hesitated; it seemed funny to ask one of these girls to give him a book on sheep worms; if it was a store, now, and they were clerks and a man was buying it, it would be different, but just to walk into a place and ask somebody to give you something—the doctor had said they were free.

Then one of the girls, the tallest and the prettiest, in a thin white blouse, got up from a desk behind a rail with a telephone on it and said, "Something I can do for you?"

"I've got a place down in th south end a th county," he began, for it had seemed more polite to work gradually up to the sheep and worms—he had given over all thought about a dog book—"nigh onto two hundred acres an—"

The girl smiled relievedly, "Oh, and you've come to get your AAA fertilizer."

He shook his head.

"You have your fertilizer?" she asked, and he could almost hear the interested listening of the other two girls.

"Nom'm—I don't belong to the AAA."

"You don't!"

"No—o m'm. I bought—"

"Oh," and she smiled and forgave him and turned and pulled a card and some papers out of a desk drawer, and picked up a fountain pen.

"The former owner, I suppose he belonged," she said.

Nunn swallowed and blushed. "I've had th place goen on six year, Mam."

"Oh!" She held the fountain pen ready above the paper. "Name, please."

Nunn drew a deep breath. He did want the book about sheep, certainly after all this trouble, but he didn't want to have to join the AAA to get it. Preacher Samuel and John would take him for a turncoat; then he thought of the fat farmers in the stockyards—and joining would please Suse. "Nunnely D. Ballew," he said and hoped he didn't have to drag out the Danforth.

He didn't. The girl hurried on. "Post office?"

"Ballew."

"School district?"

"Ballew."

She frowned in concentration. "Are you that last farm in the southeastern corner of the county, on the Big South Fork along Little Smokey Creek—John Ballew on the east—Hull on the north—a government boundary and an abandoned farm on the south, I believe—"

"Yes'm," Nunn said, startled that she knew so much.

"We'll look it over," she said. "I don't know that section so well. Nobody in your school district belongs to the AAA." She got up and led the way to a little room, all of one side of which was taken up with cases of big pictures, three or four feet square they looked to be.

"That would be, I think, in Square 19," she said, and started leafing through the pictures.

Nunn looked over her shoulders, mystified, struggling to make head and tail of the business without asking too many questions. They were pictures of land; he could make out houses and barns and fenced fields, but often there looked to be nothing but trees and brush.

She came to one that looked all wilderness, with only fields here and yonder and a river; then clearly, as if he had been a hawk hunting chickens, he saw with one sweep of his eyes all his farm; he could stand in Sue Annie's yard and see the lower half on the far side of the creek, but never all like this.

"That's it," he said, and thrust his hand over her shoulder, then hesitated to point it out. They had leafed through a lot of pretty well fenced fields and now he must point out a boundary of brush and gullies. The girl put her finger on the storehouse, for the storehouse field showed fairly clear, with only the corners blurred by brush; here and yonder he could even make out a bit of fence in the brush. "This is your house, I guess," the girl said.

Nunn explained that he used that for a sheep barn and put his finger on the house, or what little of the roof could be seen through the locust and black walnut trees and the honeysuckle around it; it didn't look like much of anything but a smudge in the brush.

The girl apologized for getting his houses mixed and told him how the maps were made; a photographer in a low-flying airplane had taken pictures of the whole county; together they made a picture so big it would more than cover the walls of the room; that was why it was cut in squares and numbered. Now, they could take a thing like a magnifying glass, only more complicated, look at a pictured farm through it, measure the slopes of the hills and bluffs, and compute the acreage of any field just as accurately as a surveyor could.

Nunn forgot his shame and his dislike of asking questions in listening to her talk. It was fun to see the place take shape when he marked out the boundaries; for the river, the creek, John's rail fence, and other boundary lines showed clearly.

"That's a lot of land," the girl said, and added with a respectful air, laying her finger in Cedar Thicket Hollow, "It looks as if you had quite a bit of timber."

"Cut over," Nunn said.

She wanted to know then if he ever cut hay or used much permanent pasture.

He shook his head sheepishly, and said mostly he raised a garden patch, a few oats, sorghum cane, and corn.

She nodded as if she understood. "I suppose you have a family and the family has to eat and you have to grow corn to feed the chickens and hogs and stock, even if the corn growing does take all your time and is bad for the land." She pointed to the brush-grown hillsides above the garden and around the old graveyard. "This is pasture, I suppose?"

He nodded and told her about the land that he wanted to put down in grass this spring and how he planned to pick rocks off the graveyard field and make it smooth enough to mow.

They made out a thing called a "farm program" then; garden patch of one half acre, potato patch, an acre of sorghum cane, two acres oats, twelve acres of corn counting the river bottom, maybe fifteen acres of hay, and, well, maybe fifty-six acres for pasture. He wasn't certain about the pasture; it was, to be truthful, mostly brush and sagegrass—and it needed fence, but his cow and sheep did graze it.

She was sympathetic and thought the land could be counted as pasture; after all, it had been crop land and wasn't outside—she figured up the fertilizer—he would be allowed 3,600 pounds of 40 per cent superphosphate to be spread at the rate of 400 pounds to the acre—this fertilizer was twice as rich as ordinary phosphate, she warned, and he didn't need to use as much for his soil-building program. And, let's see, that would be enough for twelve acres, which then would have to be sowed to grass and clover; the least seed he could sow of lespedeza would be ten pounds to the acre and two pounds of grass. "But to get a good stand you ought to use twice as much," she added.

So, for twelve acres he ought to buy at least 120 pounds of lespedeza and twenty-four pounds of grass seed—try to get the lespedeza without dodder in it—dodder causes an awful lot of trouble after two or three years—the seed got into the manure and when the manure was scattered on the garden, it got all over little things like lettuce and would be an aggravation to his wife.

"Dodder doesn't hurt so much on pasture," she said, "because the cows will eat it. But it will ruin your hay. It cuts your crop and sometimes tangles the stems so bad you can't mow it at all."

Nunn reckoned to himself, of course, that his wife would be a lot more aggravated if she could hear him talking to a young pretty town woman about manure, than over lovevine in the lettuce bed, but after the way she talked about manure he didn't mind so much to ask her about getting a book on sheep worms, though at times it seemed he never would get around to it. First, she had to tell him about soil-building units—most anything that helped the soil and kept it from washing away—was called a soil-building unit; putting rock dams in gullies, sowing corn lands to grass and clover, planting trees on gullied slopes too steep for pasture, burning lime and spreading it—his land, at least some of it, maybe needed lime. A man could do these things and get paid something, but most farmers preferred to take it out in government fertilizer—if Nunn wanted fertilizer, there were three carloads down on a stockyards siding waiting to be unloaded —it was a good plowing day, and after so many wet ones the farmers were all so far behind with their spring work they didn't want to take a day off to come for their fertilizer and it had to be unloaded.

He saw that she expected and wanted him to take the fertilizer. And he said he would, but one question troubled him—would a man get into bad trouble if he took the fertilizer and then didn't sow enough grass and clover seed to earn all his soil-building units—would he go to the penitentiary?

The girl said no. The price of his fertilizer would be charged against him and he couldn't get any more government fertilizer or get paid for future soil-building units until he paid for the fertilizer he had used the year before.

That sounded all right to Nunn and so he signed his name to the farm program, got a paper authorizing the man down at the fertilizer cars to give him thirty-six sacks of fertilizer, and then asked if she had any bulletins on sicknesses of sheep or anything about raising pups.

They went back to the main office, half full of men now, apparently waiting to take up some business or ask a question. The big farmer whom he had heard tell of his troubles with sheep in the stockyards, in the same old jumper with nails sticking through its pockets, was wanting to know where in thunder he could get a tractor part— he had looked all over town, while another, with many gestures and motions, was describing how he had castrated a lamb and it bled to death and now what could he do— would there be a demonstration of lamb castration any time soon.

"Maybe it bled to death from the docking," one of the young women, walking swiftly with papers, said from behind the counter. As her heels tap-tapped away, a young man with shiny black eyes and teeth shining from between a week's growth of black whiskers said, with a derisive grin:

"If you wasn't so blamed particular an used your teeth like you're supposed to, they wouldn't be bleeden to death on you."

The farmer glared. "I ain't taken no sheep's balls in my mouth for all a you an them. I'd sooner let 'em die first, filthy things. A man can start with little lambs' balls an no tellen whose balls he'll have in his teeth fore he's done." The group broke into laughter.

Sudden silence fell as the young girl who had talked to Nunn came back hunting him. Guiltily he hurried after, leaving the silent, slyly grinning men.

The girl showed him where the bulletins were, told him to take any he wanted, but right now there wasn't anything in the office on dogs. Since he had several different kinds of stock, maybe he would be interested in a new government book called *Keeping Livestock Healthy*. He could drop a note to his congressman and ask for it—it was free to farmers.

Nunn was feeling guilty about taking up so much of her time while others were waiting; he thanked her for all her trouble, promised to get his fertilizer that very morning, thanked her again when she shoved into his hands a garden bulletin, a bulletin on the castration of sheep and the docking of their tails, and bulletins on worms of sheep, of hogs, and of horses and told him once more if he saw anything else he liked, to take it.

Suse was always begging Milly to let her bake a real honest-to-goodness sugar cake with frosting, and so he took a bulletin on homemade cakes and pies and another on plain baking.

He was hunting Jaw Buster in the square when he saw a good-sized crowd clustered around one of the Civil War cannon that always pointed toward the courthouse. He went by, then heard a familiar voice, slow and soft-spoken and persuasive.

"It's th truth I'm tellen you—an she wasn't much more'n full weaned, just walked off in th woods an hunted her a fox an th place lined, just literally lined with rabbits an possums an polecats—but she never paid em no mind—went right on a runnen that fox—a big red thing thet could a turned around an kilt her—till he got skeered an clumb a big log, too big fer her to git up, an so she—" It was Blare, and after one glance to make certain that Vinie, squatting on Blare's arm with her paws on his shoulder and greatly enjoying the attention of the crowd, was all right, Nunn backed away.

He found Lister and Jaw Buster in the junk yard, where they had found a muffler and radiator cap and an uncracked windshield, all of which would fit the truck.

Nunn told him about the fertilizer, and since the roads were dry, Jaw Buster agreed to take the fertilizer all the way to Nunn's storehouse for $4. Nunn paid him and found that the money he had expected to stretch over grass and clover seed was almost gone; he had wanted to buy a slab of side meat for Milly—she was funny that way, missing things more in the cooking than the eating. He sighed and cut a chew of tobacco, and was so silent, ruminating and cogitating, that Jaw Buster comforted him with the assurance that Sam would be all right—Nunn hadn't thought about Sam since he got tangled up in the AAA; right now he was thinking of a way he could make money if he would, but then maybe moonshining went against the grain of most men who did it—it was no sin like stealing, just something against the law.

Jaw Buster took him to the yards where they loaded the fertilizer, and as they drove along they saw Blare again; this time on a bench in the courthouse porch, with Vinie across his knees, or at least Nunn supposed it was Vinie; there was such a crowd around he couldn't see, but Blare was still talking, and his audience now included three bad women—or at least Lister, who knew about such things, said they were bad women—and one tired hill woman with a baby on her left arm and a knee-high child clutched in her right hand, and they were all listening with interested believing eyes.

Lister wanted to stop and listen some more; two hours ago he had heard Blare tell that the old woman of the man who owned Vinie never had to piece a quilt or send wool away to have a blanket wove—she bedded all her family down under red-fox skins—and that when the owner got a little low on money all he had to do was show the pups the place in the Sears Roebuck catalogue where it said they paid money for fox skins and away the pups would go and never come back till they brought a good,

big, full-furred red fox apiece, the skin in fine shape, because they were always careful to drive a fox into one end
of a hollered-out log and smother it to death or else ham-
string it; and once this same man—"you, Nunn"—had a
tree dog that—

Jaw Buster, who had driven twice slowly around the
courthouse square, studying every one he saw with his
slow, thorough glance, punched Lister in the ribs. "Ain't
that two little onion sets over on that apple cart—one red
an one yaller?"

Lister leaned far out in order to see around the cracked,
discolored windshield, "Why, hell, yes; an I looked all
around a while ago." He looked around but no State
Highway Patrolmen or either of the two members of the
town police force was in sight. "We'd all better go—it'd
look more natural—an buy some apples."

"I'll buy some apples an go my share, but not too
much, boys," Nunn said, and wished they hadn't seen the
little red onion and the little white onion.

"It's mostly fer you, Nunn, I want to buy it," Lister
told him. "You need a drink with your pup sick an all."

Lister bought a gallon of apples and handed the man
—a long-headed, thin-featured, worried-looking sort of
person who looked as if he had never done anything all
his life but struggle to raise a big family on a rocky hill
farm—two $1 bills. "We want some onion sets, too."

The man shook his head. "I'm all out. I jist happened
to have them two left over."

Lister put his hands on his hips and leaned very close
to the man. "Listen, Brother Amen, I ain't no fool—them
sets wasn't there fifteen minutes ago. Recollect last winter
when you was sellen pears, an it took too much talken to
make you recollect you wasn't out—recollect?"

The man sighed, put a little more distance between his
face and Lister's. "I'm recollecten an that's why I'm fergitten now. You an him"—he nodded to Jaw Buster—
"planted yer onions too soon. I was certain you'd git took
up fore you got out a town, an would ha been, but it jist
happened the police was both in on a big crap game."

Nunn stepped forward, a small sad-eyed man between
two big ones. "It's fer me, mister," he said. "I got a bad
sick hound. I won't let th boys do no meanness fore we
git out a town."

"She don't look sick," the man said, glancing around toward Blare on the courthouse porch.

"It's th other'n," Nunn said, and he showed the package of medicine with Dr. Hibbetts's name on it and the directions.

"He'll be all right," the man said. "Hounds can git awful sick. I had one—a old red-bone, down fer a week an me a given it everthing, an my wife made tea an cooked him everthing—she biled a guinea hen fer that hound, I recollect—anyhow he never got no better till I started a given it whisky." He had picked up the money and returned a quarter and a paper bag of apples. "But you'd jist better take th whisky—whisky an doctor's medicine mightn't mix so good. Drive up over past th new bus station and you'll see a man peddlen Irish taters an fat hens —say to him, 'I paid Joe fer a pint a yaller onion sets, them early sprouten kind,' say that an nothen else, an then git out a town; but fer God's sake, mister, don't tell that man with yer pup. He talks too much. An give Joe this card so's he'll know you paid."

He took from a vest pocket a shiny yellowish card with the likeness of a large-eared man on one side above a paragraph of print. He underlined some words with a pencil before handing the card to Nunn, who glanced at it and asked, "That new jailer turn out to be obligen like he promised?"

The onion seller nodded. "He had them cards left over frum his election an give em to me. I jist happen to be usen em today." He sighed and added, "Every day different words or a different card. They's dishonest men in this county."

Nunn grunted and Lister read in solemn slowness the words of the day: *sweet smelling as a girl.* The jailer had, among other things, promised the wives and girls of the county to take good care of their men: the jail would serve good food, the bedclothing be abundant and bugless, there would be a religious atmosphere with grace and prayers, and the whole—jailhouse, jailers, and inmates—would be sweet smelling as a girl on her way to Sunday school.

They drove away eating apples and got the pint fruit jar, packaged neatly in a paper sack with onion sets. It wasn't good as a first run of J. D.'s but not so sickly tasting and bad smelling as that from across the Big South Fork. Nunn wondered if the apple man or the potato man had made it, but Lister thought somebody else did, or maybe they all took turns; it would be hard and risky for one man to do it all.

"Whoever makes it knows what to do with th carbide," Jaw Buster said. "They's plenty a carbide an mebbe lye in it, too," he added after a critical shake of the bottle, "but it don't knock you like some carbide liquor does."

Nunn pushed his hat back and reckoned it all brought early death, and Jaw Buster said he wished they'd bought a quart, Nunn still seemed so worried and sad. But Nunn said the whisky was working backward in him today—it was the wrong time of the moon, he guessed, and they'd better get over to the seed and feed store and let him buy his little jag of seed.

The store was a large place, specializing in farmers' supplies, with tractors and brooder heaters scattered among fifty-pound stands of lard, bull-tongue plows, egg-laying mash, piles of horse collars, and rolls of barbed wire. Nunn was looking at a roll of four-point hog wire and wondering if he could buy just one roll—one roll would fence off the garden, at least enough to keep out the stock—he could keep Rosie and her pigs up all summer the way he usually did—when the same big sheep-hating farmer in dirty overalls whom he had just seen in the county agent's office came out of the back end of the store, followed by a clerk wheeling three one-hundred-pound sacks of what looked to be clover seed.

The man was still quarreling about tractor parts; the clerk, who also seemed to be the owner, was urging him to buy a new tractor. The man said he was too poor right now to keep a tractor in grease, let alone buy another, and anyhow he had to build a new tobacco barn; last fall he had had to hang in everything from the dwelling house to the dairy barn—and was he going to have his throat cut when he went to buy tin roofing. He came abreast of Nunn, smiled, put out his hand, and said, "My name's Elias Higginbottom. Ain't you Nunnely Ballew, th man with that pair of pedigreed foxhound pups? I saw you in th AAA."

"Pleased to meet you," Nunn said, and added as he took the ham-shaped, red-haired hand, "I don't know if'n

I've got a pair of pups—one was about dead th last time I seen it."

"Aw, that pup'll live to catch many a red fox," Higginbottom said, his round blue eyes brightening up like twin fires in his brick-colored face. "Doc Hibbetts showed him to me when I went to see about haven my cattle inoculated for th blackleg—you wouldn't sell th pair, I recken. I saw th bitch down in Roy's fillen station."

Nunn shook his head. "I've got too much time an trouble an money worriation in th things ever to git out what I've put in."

"Raisen any kind a pure-blood animal is a hard job. I've got a herd of pure-blood Angus, Red Cap strain—" and his big eyes flamed up again. "An they've give me more trouble, allus somethen. Them pups, they come straight frum Wheeler's, Doc Hibbetts said. That right?"

"Yeah."

"They're already part trained, ain't they? I didn't know a pup that age could take any kind a trainen."

"They ain't been trained at all."

"But th doc said you said they'd been runnen, an to hear that other man talk they can catch a fox, skin it, an do just about everything but sew on the buttons after they finish maken a fur coat out a th hides."

Nunn sat down on a roll of barbed wire and looked up at the man; he never liked to stand and look up at a man, and since he had to look up, even standing, it was pleasanter to sit down. "I figger it's like this," he said. "A hound pup's like a man—he is er he ain't—you cain't train out an you cain't train in. They've got noses er they ain't got noses—they'll stick by th fox er they'll run rabbits er coons. These pups has practiced a little on a old red fox that th devil with a witch fer a hound couldn't git —they ain't tried to run no rabbits, but that ain't a sayen they won't, an it ain't a sayen they'll live to stay two nights an a day by a red fox an unravel his scent ever half hour like a hound I had once."

"I'd be willen to chance it," the farmer said, and sat down on a hundred-pound sack of sugar across from Nunn. The manager of the store rolled his load to the door, then came back and sat down on a pile of horse collars a few feet away.

"Whyn't you go an buy a pair of full-grown trained hounds or weaned pups like I done?" Nunn suggested.

"Trained hounds'd mebbe be burned out, an if I got young pups I'd be certain to pick two rabbit chasers—an I've been wanten two good hounds a long while." A sigh quivered across his big belly, up and out his mouth. "Farmen, just farmen, never nothen but worriation an work an trouble, is a goen to drive me to drink."

Nunn pulled his tobacco from his pocket. "Fox hunten, never nothen but fox hunten, has driv me to drink."

"Quit it then an sell me th pups fer $150—or I'll trade you a team a mules, four-year-olds fifteen an a half hands high, an harness to boot."

Nunn put the tobacco into his mouth. "A hundred and fifty dollars is too much fer a pair a pups an one half dead."

The farmer reached for his tobacco. "Well, sean as how you paid $100 not so long ago, fore you knowed they'd chase a fox, I think it's mighty little."

"I paid $70. You been listenen to Blare Tiller. He can't help it. . . . He just naturally makes th truth too big."

The farmer pulled out a long hook-bladed pruning knife and cut his tobacco. "I guess he was just adden in your time an trouble in buyen em an feeden em an trainen em. Better sell; I'm goen into th fox-hunten business. I had a champion hound once . . . or he was th champ at th fox-hunt meet at Crab Orchard . . . but by then I'd already sold him; needed th money to buy me a registered boar, an I'll always be sorry. I hate hogs."

"There's money in em . . . sometimes, though," observed Nunn when he had worked his tobacco over a couple of times.

"There's money in hounds, too . . . sometimes," the farmer said.

Nunn turned his wide solemn eyes full on the farmer. "I wish to God I could sell th pups . . . but there's a fox I've got to ketch. I can talk sellen when I've got him. Soon's school's out an my youngens are handy to watch an listen, I'm aimen to start letten these pups run."

"What th hell. Ain't your school out?"

"No. Half th time it's not out fore April, the old teacher we got misses so many days. He's old Andrew Haynes, been teachen Ballew School fer more'n thirty years—wore out by now, I recken, leastways he ain't no good."

"Whyn't you git another'n?"

Nunn shook his head. "Been aimen to try to—but I don't know th superintendent, an since they done away with trustees, John Ballew—he was allus th trustee after my grandaddy died—he don't seem to take so much interest any more."

"Ever district's got to have a teacher that comes ever day—I'll see to that next board meeten—I'm a member a th county board a education," he said, and asked quickly as if to get away from a boresome subject, "Big red fox you're a chasen, I recken?"

Nunn nodded.

"You'll burn em out catchen him, an they'll be no good, cept th bitch fer breeden."

Nunn shook his head. "They ain't th burnen-out kind —a good hound don't burn out—he dies. Th best hound I ever had, an him part tree dog, too, died a runnen an him in th lead."

"Busted his head on a black gum tree, I allus said." Blare had come in with Vinie.

Mr. Higginbottom got up and looked at Vinie, looked into her eyes, down her ears, into her mouth, felt the beginnings of hard steel-tough muscles in her legs, ran his hands over her deep wide chest, then stepped back and with his head on one side studied the total effect with a pleased smile. "God damn, but she is a pretty thing. I'll make it two bred, full-stock Angus heifers worth $100 apiece."

Nunn shook his head, his eyes sorrowful. "They's nothen I'd like better than to take you up on it—but I dasn't—not till I git that red fox."

The board member nodded and sighed in understanding, his glance still on Vinie. "It's too bad. You'd like to sell an I'd like to buy. Catchen a smart red fox fair an true's no easy thing, an when an if you ever do git him it'll be like everything else in this world—you'll be sorry—if you ain't dead."

"Not me," Nunn said, and wished the farmer would go away. He had seen something he wanted to buy, but he wished to God Blare hadn't come into the store.

However, after a good deal of talk about foxes and foxhounds in general and the pups in particular, and a last injunction to Nunn to let him know if he ever changed his mind, Higginbottom finished his trading and went away; Blare took Vinie and went to hunt Jaw Buster and Lister.

The manager himself came to wait on Nunn, who, wary of showing too great an interest in the fifty-pound lard can with the tight-fitting cover, asked first about lespedeza and grass seed. The seed with some dodder in it was $1 cheaper on the hundred, but mindful of the warning words of the AAA girl, he bought two hundred pounds of seed with a tag on it saying it was free of dodder for $9 a hundred. By the time he bought the lard can, which he still wasn't certain he would use, there would be almost no money for grass seed, and already the storekeeper was trying hard to sell him hybrid yellow corn seed and certified Irish potato seed—and, oh, Lord, how he wished he could buy some, and he had his heart set on a roll of barbed wire and he had to have some dog feed.

"You'll more than make your money back on certified seed," the storekeeper was saying. "Not many farmers plant their own corn and potato seed any more. Now up at th experiment station—" he began, and Nunn, bitter and weary with the fox chase that wouldn't let him buy seed, interrupted:

"I know, but I tell you, man, I ain't got cash, not right now. I'll mebbe have to mortgage my place to feed them pups."

"You mean to say you ain't got a mortgage?"

"I don't owe nobody nothen."

"You're behind th times, mister. How much land you got?"

"Two hundred acres more or less, but it ain't worth much—down on th Big South Fork."

"Any river bottom?"

"A little, no more'n four acres."

"Timber?"

"Some."

"Coal?"

"Yeah, a whole heap—but it's doen me no good down in th ground."

"Stock?"

"Mare, filly, cow, sow, young pigs, thirty-eight ewes, not done lamben."

"Road?"

"Graded gravel a comen closer an closer."

"Don't sound bad."

Nunn sighed. "Could be worse, if'n I don't have to sell th sheep to feed the pups."

"No need in doen that long as your credit's good," the storekeeper said, looking about for the dog feed. "I've helped raise half a th stock in th county, I recken, on credit. Let me sell you a nice bill a goods—unless some uncommon bad trouble overtakes you, you ought to be able to pay it back in six months. That's my regular time to any kind a farmer."

Nunn pushed his hat back and looked at the lard can. "Why, I don't hardly know. I can see my way clear to payen for any stuff I buy now on credit, but some very uncommon bad trouble could overtake me."

The storekeeper didn't think it would, and in the end Nunn came away with seed, dog feed, two rolls of barbed wire instead of one, a hundred pounds of certified Irish Cobbler potato seed, and two pecks of yellow hybrid corn seed, all on credit except $10.

Going home, Blare remembered it was give-away day at the Valley—WPA on the graded gravel had been shut down for weeks but the give-away still came. Today, however, it wasn't much, mostly butter, eggs, and cheese. Blare complained that the little give-away the WPA got every month wouldn't keep wind in a rabbit, and half the time a body couldn't eat the stuff; why didn't they give em lard instead of butter; last time it was a lot of grapefruits and whole-wheat flour; the cow would eat the whole-wheat flour but there wasn't a thing on the place that would eat the grapefruits, not even after Flonnie wasted a lot of good lard frying some.

Lister, who had a good job working on the railroad section gang five days a week most of the time, wanted to know why a body couldn't make wine out of grapefruit juice and use the whole-wheat flour instead of cow feed for the capping on whisky; Blare said he'd thought about it, but Flonnie wouldn't let him try it.

Nunn listened and said nothing; he'd never worked on WPA and he'd never signed up for any of their give-away, but he might do the other, and he began to wonder how he could hide the lard can from Milly and the youngens.

But the whole family was so completely overcome by the sight of a truck coming over the hill and Nunn on it, all the way from Town and back and it hardly dinnertime, that while they all stood jabbering around the cab trying to see everything at once, he jerked sacks of fertilizer over the lard can, and when Milly came asking him about the mountain of fertilizer and sacks of seed and what ailed Sam, he told her to take the pups quick to the house; they might get chilled, and not let any of the youngens around while they were putting the stuff in the storehouse as the fertilizer was powerful stuff and the fumes might give them the fever.

It was a pretty afternoon for work, dry enough to plow the garden, but Nunn didn't get much done. After the excitement of the truck's coming, Maude was skittish and mean, forever getting her feet out of the trace chains, pretending to be scared to plow closer than six feet to the apple trees in the garden, and calling Jude up every five minutes to see if she were calming down from the truck.

Milly was not much better, and the youngens worse. Every half minute one would come running with another question about something he had done or seen or bought in Town.

"Did Sam cry when th doctor stuck th needle in him? You goen to make us eat yaller bread frum yaller corn you'll grow frum that yaller seed, Pop?"

"Nunn—reckon it'd be awful bad wrong fer me to sneak out a little a that gov'ment fertilizer an use it in th garden?"

"Pop, did people think Sam an Vinie was pretty?"

"Pop, are we goen to have a honest-to-goodness bob-wire fence?"

Milly threatened Suse with a peach-tree limb if she didn't quit leaving her work of digging up an early lettuce bed to run look at the government bulletins and the newspaper every five minutes, and then Milly would forget her aggravation while listening to Suse read a cake recipe or tell about the war across the waters, or on thinking up a pretty way to make up the pattern of blue, rose-sprigged dress goods Nunn had bought for Suse.

Suse was twisting around with the goods draped round her waist when Lee Roy came up with a load of hen manure for the lettuce bed and jeered at her, saying you

couldn't hang flowers on a freckled bean pole and make a
sweet petunia out of it. Suse called him a little buck-
toothed jackass, Lee Roy threw a handful of hen manure
in her hair, and Suse leaped out of the flowerdy goods
and caught him by the shoulders and they went down in a
half fighting, half teasing tussle.

Nunn, resting Maude at the end of a garden furrow
near the house, roared out at them, but Milly only folded
the flowerdy goods, laid it in the crotch of the quince tree,
picked up the manure and came on. She glanced back at
the struggling pair with something like satisfaction. "Aw,
let em alone, Nunn. It's good to see em act like theirselves
—this mornen it was awful; they thought Sam ud be dead
an you'd come home—feelen bad, an they set around an
cried."

Chapter Thirteen

SAM WAS WELL, able to chew up one of Nunn's old hats before the split-top pills were gone, and the terror of his bad sickness was soon forgotten, though Nunn's adventures in town made pleasant conversation for many days. Keg Head Cramer had to make another trip from the Cow's Horn to learn if it were true that a member of the county school board had offered Nunn $500 and a registered bull for Vinie.

Nunn shook his head and smiled at the tale and wondered idly if Elias Higginbottom were really a member of the board of education; and wished he hadn't talked so about old Andrew—he was always a loose-tongued fool after a drink—then he forgot the whole business.

But early one morning two or three weeks later, a breathless Sue Annie was calling at the back door, "Is anybody home?"

Milly felt a sharp sorrow in remembering Zing's watchful ways, mixed with an exasperation she always felt when somebody came right up to the house and took her unawares. Still she called out gladly enough, "Yes, I'm home, a patchen a patch that's patched a patch."

Sue Annie stuck her head in and whispered, panting and with an excited rolling of her eyes, "Is Nunn in?" then rushed in and dropped on the first nail keg handy while Milly was saying he had made an early start to the tie-timber woods.

"Milly," she began, "can you start Suse to th schoolhouse right away to start a fire? I sent word fer Ruby to go but Dave's so slow . . ." She paused, gasping for breath, and above her loud excited breathing came the ticking of a clock, which from the sound seemed to be somewhere hidden in her tucked-up apron.

At hearing her call, the children came bounding in, Lee Roy in his shirt and underwear and Lucy without her shoes, and all, with Milly, stood gaping at Sue Annie and listened wonderingly to the clock while she sat gasping, her swiftly darting black eyes speaking of some never-before-heard-of disaster, something already bad but liable to worsen fast. She glanced at Milly, saw her startled almost terrified face, and spoke with trembling reassurance.

"Don't be scared, Milly. I've run all th way down an I can't talk. Nobody's dead or hurt; just th super—in—ten—dent is on his way to visit th school."

Suse alone knew what a school superintendent was. She had never seen one, but she'd heard enough about them to know.

"Mom," she said, "where's my speckled dress? You said last night you had it clean an ironed an was saven it for me to wear to th post office or some night meeten. An where's th broom? The school-house ain't been swept for God knows how long. Lucy an that good-fer-nothin Bernice Dean carried it off to their playhouse away last fall an I recken Old John's mules eat it up." She saw the dress hanging on a nail under the high shelf and ran, stripping off her ragged everyday dress as she went. Milly rushed up to help with the buttons on the back, then thought she'd better hunt the broom and ran to the fireplace room, then outside and up the stairs when she remembered Deb and the pups had been playing horse up there with it.

Suse met her at the house corner with matches in one hand and pine kindling in the other, seized the broom, and dashed down the yard, but stopped as she was climbing the gate to call back for Milly to hunt her up two pink Sunday hair ribbons off the high shelf and send them on by Lee Roy. She leaped the spring branch, ran a few steps, then whirled back, calling something about sending all the cups and glasses. Milly could catch nothing except her excited cry of, "It's th law. It's th law," and started down to the gate, but Suse would not wait and ran on, waving the broom. Then the kitchen door was jerked violently open and Sue Annie screamed out something to the fast disappearing Suse and waved the clock, but Suse, whose ears were often bad when she was in a hurry, ran on.

"I meant for her to take this clock an plumb fergot," Sue Annie explained, sitting down again. "I think it's th law fer ever schoolteacher to have a timepiece a some sort, an that old superin—tendent will git Andrew when he finds out he ain't got one. Oh-h, them dirty devils," and Sue Annie took a chew of tobacco with the vicious jerk of a hound tearing into a fox. "Is there any coffee in that pot? I ain't been so plumb give out since last spring when I fit fire till everything turned black."

She stopped, poured out a saucer of coffee and blew on it slowly, staring at the oilcloth in sad reflection. "You know, Milly, it's hard when a body gits old like me an Andrew. They's many a woman a sayen now that I'm gitten too old to bring babies any more, just like they's many a one . . ." she looked darkly at Milly, "an Nunn's amongst em, that says pore old Andrew's too old an no good to teach school. An I recken somebody's went to th super—intend—ent a complainen so he said he'd be down. An down he is—that is, part way."

"Nobody could git from Town down here this quick, less'n they left in th night," Milly said.

"Lord God, Milly, don't you know they've laid gravel right nigh to th top a th Deep Holler, an then when th ground's froze hard anybody can roll clean to Samuel's in any kind a car in no time at all?" She giggled.

"I recken whoever told th superintendent said he could git close to th school on a cold mornen . . . so he picks this mornen, an it ain't cold enough an his car gits stuck in a right deep chug hole bout a mile yon side a th church house, an Rildy New's youngens seen him, an it don't take em long to learn who he is an where he's a headen.

"They tell him they'll git him a team a mules an they run straight off to Samuel's . . . that's th closest team; but Samuel's off to a funeral over around Crackerneck an they tell Ruth an she's awful busy in th store an Silas is there, bringen some letters to mail, an he says him an Andy—he's th one that wants to go to high school but he's a goodhearted boy—they'll take th mules an pull th super —intend—ent out.

"Ruth, she gives em a funny look—Flonnie's there a mailen a letter to Spiegel May an seen it all—an tells em

to go on but don't hurry the mules an don't press em too
hard, pullen out th car. An then she says, 'I wonder does
old Andrew know th superin—tendent is comen, pore old
soul; he'd want to be in a clean shirt an pants; th youngens
say he goes kind a ragged sometimes.' And she says in a
low voice with a look at Flonnie, 'I wish'd I could git
away from th store, but I dasn't when Samuel's gone.'"

"An Flonnie, she answers back, 'Well, I got to git on
home an stay with th little youngens so's th big ones can
go to school, but Sue Annie, now, she can sort a tend to
things,'" and Sue Annie giggled again and got up, for
nothing rested her like a good cup of strong hot coffee and
a little talk. "An here's Sue Annie a tenden to things. An
with Silas an Andy a helpen him, I don't guess that old
sup—erin—tendent will be here much afore dinner . . .
an . . ."

Lee Roy came flying in to know if wasn't his other shirt
clean, and couldn't he have a piece of flour sack for a
handkerchief—the health book said all children were supposed to bring a handkerchief to school—and could he
have some lard to slick his hair and make it took nice.

Milly said yes to everything and wished to God he
didn't have to wear patched britches, but Lee Roy, seeing
her frowning gaze fixed on the new patches, said patches
on his knees didn't matter, he'd keep his legs behind a
desk and the superintendent wouldn't see them; and Sue
Annie told him nobody would notice how he looked for
they couldn't see anything for that red hair, and to hurry
and get up there and see if all the scholars had come, and
if they hadn't to run off to their houses and get them
quick.

There came a pounding at the door and it was two of
the little Hulls and two of Sue Annie's grandchildren, asking for all of Milly's cups and glasses. "Suse said th law
says all us have to have somethen to drink out of sides th
dipper, an that if we didn't have, the superintendent
would send us all to jail. An she wants soap an rags to
scrub some a th bad words off'n th wall," the biggest Hull
explained.

Milly packed her two cracked cups and four little
glasses that had come in boxes of oatmeal, and apologized
for not having more, but the little Hulls said that would
be plenty—Paul had slipped back to his house and was

stealing out some of his mother's—and could Lucy come back with them now.

Lucy, who had been staring at them with her finger in her mouth, let out a sudden shriek and dashed for the fireplace room. If Sue Annie had brought word that the devil, horns, tail, fiery breath and all, was on his way to the school, Lucy could have shown no more terror. Followed into the fireplace room, she dashed barefooted outside, then upstairs, where she tried to hide among the sweet potatoes in the chimney cubbyhole.

Milly and Sue Annie, with little Deb and the wide-eyed Hulls trailing at their heels, found her there. Milly threatened her with a peach tree limb as long as a bed, threatened to send word for Nunn, threatened to send word to the superintendent and have him come and get her, but Lucy only squatted on her knees and knocked her head against the sweet potatoes and screamed and squealed.

Sue Annie, who after an admiring whisper of "She's such a quiet-turned little thing, a body'd never know she had it in her," offered her a nickel for candy, told her Andrew would lose his job if she didn't go, offered to let her wear one of her big celluloid hairpins back between her braids, and shamed her for being a baby. Lucy screamed and held her breath until she began to turn from purple-red to blue, and Milly looked ready to faint. "Poor little thing, let's leave her be. But, honey, th superintendent won't whip you. It's just old Andrew he's after."

Lucy held her head still in the sweet potatoes and pounded her bare feet against the wall and screamed until Sue Annie said, "I declare, if she was mine I think I'd take a switch to her," and Milly looked down at her, torn between pity for the child and determination to do her duty by Andrew. The little Hulls, trained in obedience from birth, drew near and peeped at her wonderingly; and little Rebecca whispered, "She's like th woman in th Bible fore Jesus cast out th devil."

And little Sarah, the least one, sighed over her in sorrow, for she and Lucy sat together in school. "She won't get no red polish on her fingernails like we'uns is a getten from Ruby cause th superin—tendent's a comen."

Lucy checked her breath in mid-scream and lay with her cheek on a big sweet potato and looked at Sarah. "Ruby goen to paint yer fingernails?"

The little Hulls nodded and Sarah explained. "Ruby is a
goen to fix ever girl there, soon's we get th house
cleaned up."

Lucy got up from the sweet-potato pile, tossed back her
tangled, unbraided hair. "Mom, can I go to school?"

But before Milly had her ready to go, freshly washed,
with Sue Annie's nickel in her pocket and the fancy celluloid hairpin and Suse's bows on her braids, there came
another wild pounding on the door. It was Paul saying
that Suse had said that if them Hull youngens didn't get
on with the soap and rags she'd make them wash the wall
with their noses when they did come, and that she wanted
some black shoe blacking, all they could get, but at least
enough for old Andrew, and couldn't they borrow Nunn's
good clothes—they would come nearer fitting him than
anybody else's.

Sue Annie giggled. "Lord, such youngens, a thinken a
everything. . . . Just run on with your shoe blacken an
leave Andrew to me."

The little Hulls, lacking Lucy's imagination, were more
afraid of Suse than the superintendent, and ran after Paul;
Lucy ran screaming for them to wait for her, Deb began
a howling to go, too, and Sue Annie stood in the door and
outscreamed them all until Paul came back. After many
threats and warnings of what would happen if he dropped
it, he was allowed to take the clock, and further, ordered
to go down to his father, Old John—the only man in the
country who carried a watch and kept it wound—and get
the right time and set the clock, but just ask for the time
easy and offlike and not let his father know about the
superintendent, for he might get notions and might even
come up to school.

When he had gone, Sue Annie glanced outside at the
house shadow and reckoned it was time to get on. The
youngens were right, she said: if the superintendent saw
Andrew dirty the way he came, he'd fire him on the spot,
and Nunn's clothes were the best fit she could think of.
And none of the black-hearted devils that had wanted the
old man fired would ever hear a breath about the clothes
—she, Sue Annie, would swallow her tongue and her teeth
into the bargain before she'd ever breathe a word. She
meant to wait for the old soul where the path crossed the
creek and tell him everything and make him spit out his

tobacco and slip into John's little hog house and change clothes.

Milly got Nunn's good clothes, the overalls she kept clean and starched in case he wanted to go to church or somebody died and he had to go to a funeral, a clean blue shirt, and his suit coat—remains of the only real suit he had ever had, one he had bought when he was courting her.

Sue Annie had hardly gone before Paul came galloping back. Suse had sent him for pen and ink—every teacher was supposed to have pen and ink—and to borrow the comb. Andrew never carried a comb, and half the time he came with his hair and mustache tangled like a sheep's tail. After promising Milly he wouldn't lose the comb or waste the pen and ink to write his initials on the rocks, he hurried back.

When Paul returned, all the scholars were present and Suse made them sit down. She took stock of them and the situation together. She had scrubbed and Ruby had scrubbed and Rachel Hull had scrubbed until their arms ached, but still all the bad words had not come off the walls, and so she directed Paul, who was naturally of a saving disposition, to go around and dab a little shoe blacking over them. Since everything else had been scrubbed, including desks and blackboard, she let Ruby start polishing fingernails, while Rachel was to attend to hair that needed combing.

When Paul had finished the walls, Suse took the shoe blacking to the stove, gray and potbellied. She painted the crack that went clear around the firepot—Blare Tiller, back twenty years ago, they said, had put a big snowball into a raging fire to see how fast a snowball would melt in hell—and painted the door, but had to save the rest for Andrew's shoes.

Little Alben W. Barkley Tiller's hair just wouldn't stay down and there wasn't any grease for it until Rachel remembered she had brought fried sausage to school and that it was pretty fat, so she rubbed a sausage over his hair and it lay down fine and combed out smooth.

It was Rachel also who remembered that they all ought to know their lessons so that the superintendent would think Andrew was a good teacher; but since Andrew didn't hardly ever give them lessons to study until he got

there of mornings, nobody knew what to study until Suse
took their books and gave them reading and copying and
spelling and arithmetic and set Rachel to helping the little
ones with some reading and numbers. She was good in her
lessons anyhow.

The fire needed new coal, and as Suse started to pick
up the powder-keg bucket she stepped on the tail of
Ruby's dad's old hound and he jumped and let out the
yelping howl he always did when somebody stepped on
his tail, and old Lead, the other hound, jumped up wide
awake and ran barking to the windows the way he always
did when he woke up suddenly.

Suse, after a moment's consideration of the offending
beasts, called to Ruby, "You gotta do somethen with
em. . . . Hounds ain't supposed to be in a schoolhouse an
that superintendent'll do somethen to Andrew."

Ruby held up Sarah Hull's right hand and studied its
freshly painted nails critically and considered, but Paul
had the happy thought of stealing out some plowlines from
his dad's barn and tying the hounds to a tree way off from
the schoolhouse.

At that moment Lee Roy, who was then the lookout in
the poplar tree, saw old Andrew hurrying up the hill and
sang out for all the school to hear. They rushed out and
ran down to meet him with cries of:

"Andrew, do you know who's a comen?"

"Why, Andrew, ye're all cleaned up."

"We got th schoolhouse all clean."

"Ruby polished our fingernails."

The little ones grabbed his legs and coattails, the bigger
ones dancing around him, screaming at him to hurry one
minute, then begging him to stand still the next and let
them see how pretty he looked in his nice clean clothes.

Once inside, Suse pushed him into his chair while Ruby
fell to combing his hair and Rachel and Opal Tiller
cleaned and polished his cracked brogans. Suse made all
the little ones start studying again and sent the bigger boys
to rock John's mules and hogs clean to the other side of
the field, telling them to be careful and not let John see
them. Paul came tearing back with rope for the hounds
and a red tie for Andrew that had belonged to his older
brother, Aaron—he had used it when he went courting in
the Cow's Horn for a Cramer girl who had liked red, and

after he married, his wife would never let him wear red, so Aaron had left it at home.

Old Andrew was silent, smiling on the tie, peering at it over his spectacles with his dim old eyes just as he had studied Lucy's red fingernails and little Alben W. Barkley's slicked-down hair. Rachel tied the tie, a beautiful smooth knot like she always tied for Samuel when he wore one to preach in.

It was like having a tooth pulled; the string was tied and you knew it was coming, but somehow it was a surprise when it came so soon. Lee Roy rushed into the room and cried, "I seen 'em a comen. Oh, golly, it won't be long now," and he dashed to his seat and opened the first book his hand fell upon—a geography.

Suse reached two seats down and punched him hard. "Take off that hat, you little fool, and study your arithmetic."

Rachel Hull rushed to distribute the fifteen new tablets and fifteen penny pencils sent down by her mother, Ruth.

Little Bernice Dean Tiller began a troubled whimpering and made a dash for Ruby's seat, while Lucy implored Suse with her eyes to let her come sit with her and Rachel; and old Andrew stood by his three-legged chair with sweat on his forehead and a trembling in his hands and seemed to see only the blackboard. Suse dashed up to him, pushed him into his chair.

"Be a setten easy an offlike when they come in, Andrew," she said, "not a standen like a man waiten to be hung. An you, primer class, go an start writen th numbers to a hundred. Rachel, you put 'em on the blackboard fer them to copy real prettylike. Lee Roy, you an Ruby git up to this here recitation bench; bring your arithmetic an tablets an pencils. Now, Ruby, soon's th door opens you stand up an start sayen th fives—th fives is the only thing you do know an you better say 'em all th way if you know what's good . . ."

"They're a comen. Oh, Jesus, God, they're a comen. I hear 'em," and Alben W. Barkley Tiller, who had gone back to get a drink to wet his dry tongue, dropped the untasted dipper of water into the bucket and rushed back to his seat.

Lee Roy and Ruby sat stiff and straight on the recitation bench, staring at the door; the three least ones at the blackboard and all the others in their seats turned and stared at the door, waiting; only Andrew, sitting unnaturally straight, with his knees uncrossed and a hand on each, did not look at the door.

The voices drew near, paused, then silence save for the sound of feet being cleaned on the big rock that took the place of the long-missing step. Then the ramshackle sagging door began a slow grinding push into the room.

Old Andrew got up, put his glasses straight on his nose, and looked around. Ruby turned white, swallowed, looked at her red fingernails, shook her permanent wave into place, then slowly, with all the animation of a wooden doll, got up and began in a shrill breathless singsong: "Ought times five is ought. One times five is five. Two times five is ten. Three times five is fifteen." And she whirled on, gathering speed as Andrew, after a time of staring straight before him, turned slowly to be greeted by the visitors.

Swift glances, like the flying darts of little birds, flew from all parts of the room, leaped back to settle unseeing on blackboard or open book.

Instead of one man there were three, all in store-bought suits, with hats in their hands and overcoats on their arms. One, in a brown suit, was tall, with big glasses and hardly any hair; one was big and red-faced, with hair almost as pale as cream in winter; and one was short and whey-faced, with black hair and dark-rimmed glasses. And all of them seemed very happy about something, smiling widely and showing many teeth.

"And twelve times five is sixty," Ruby sang out exultantly, breathlessly; there had been a bad moment back in the thirties when she wasn't sure she would come out at sixty. She waited, staring straight ahead; the room seemed suddenly filled with the ticking of the clock. Ruby drew a long breath and began again, "Ought times five is five." But at three times five she suddenly changed her mind and collapsed on the recitation bench. She pushed Lee Roy up with a hoarse whisper of, "It's your turn now."

Lee Roy arose, but first he looked at the tall man in the brown suit and smiled. The tall man smiled back and sank with a tired air into the seat with Andy and Alben W. Barkley, while Lee Roy, determined to do his best for Andrew, began in the two's, galloped through the three's, and on and on, swinging his arms and smiling a little at the dark-haired buck-toothed man, who continued to smile back even when Lee Roy fumbled and came to a dead halt at nine times eight, then recollected himself and dashed on, hardly pausing for breath, until he reached, "Twelve times twelve is one hundred and forty-four," and sank into his seat, breathing hard.

"I see we've interrupted an arithmetic lesson. That boy certainly knows his multiplication tables," the short man said, nodding toward Lee Roy. He glanced at Andrew, who still stood with the air of an uninvited visitor, uncertain of whether to sit down or stand. "Now, Mr. Haynes, you go right on with your classes just as if we weren't here."

Andrew sank gingerly into his three-legged chair before Lee Roy and Ruby. Lee Roy remembered to shove the problems Rachel had worked for him while he was in the tree under the old man's nose, and Ruby gave him the problems she had tried to work the day before; he took them all and corrected them and handed them back, and after reaching in his pocket for a chew of tobacco, then remembering and jerking his hand away as if coals were there, he said, "Class dismissed," He sat and glanced uneasily about the silent room, his round cheeks red as if he had been running, and his glasses falling almost to the end of his nose without his ever noticing it.

Suse got up, looked back at Andy sitting unconcerned and unafraid in the same seat with one of the men, took courage, and walked up to the recitation bench with her arithmetic and tablet and pencil. After a moment Andy followed. "Here's my problems, Andr—Mr. Haynes." She handed him two sheets of paper, but only the bottom contained problems. On the top sheet was written in a large bold hand:

Send me and Andy to the bord and let us work them silo problums, page 271. Then have Rachel's arithmetic, page 167. She's got it real good then have the third grade they've got problums in taking away then have me and Andy up in history, tell us to go to the bord and draw a map of the US and show when each part got here. We do that real good.

There was a bad moment while the old man stared over
the tops of his glasses, first at Suse, then at the paper,
fumbling, trying to find her problems, and the clock ticked
loudly again, but Suse—she could feel the eyes of the
three men right between her shoulder blades—spread the
sheet of paper open before him and said loudly into the
waiting stillness, "There's my arithmetic problems; did I
work 'em right?"

Andrew adjusted his glasses, looked long enough to read,
then lifted his head and smiled on Suse. After that classes
came up to the recitation bench, brought pages of problems as proof of their industry, went to the board and
worked other problems, answered questions, went back to
their seats and worked industriously, all in perfect decorum and dead silence, broken only by Andrew's gentle
quavering voice or the low frightened murmur of a child
answering a question, though somewhere upon the ridge
side above the schoolhouse a fox hunt seemed to be in
progress. Hounds howled and yelped and bayed as if in
distress; but as the hounds seemed always in the same
place, the visitor judged the fox had been brought to hole.

The taller of the men drew out his watch after the last
arithmetic lesson; but Suse and Andy were already on the
way to the recitation bench with their history, and they
looked so eager to recite and old Andrew looked so eager
to hear them that the visitor leaned back and watched and
listened while they answered questions with their books
shut and then upon Andrew's bidding went to the board
and drew maps from memory.

As soon as they had finished, the short man got up and
with a wide wonder and puzzlement in his mild brown eyes
told Andrew that it was a real fine school. Then his smile
grew even wider and he beamed on the childern and
praised them mightily and asked questions like did they
like to come to school and they, following Suse's lead,
chorused, "Yes." And he said that was fine, and it was fine,
too, that every child had a tablet and a pencil, because in
a lot of the schools he visited some of the children didn't
have them and had to interrupt classes to borrow them,
and he said that every child had a clean face and clean
hands and such nicely combed hair, and smiled specially
on little Alben W. with his hair shiny smooth with sausage
grease.

Then he told them a story about a little train that
thought it couldn't pull and showed them how to play a
crazy game where you weren't supposed to do what he told
you to but what he did. And then he introduced Mr.
Simpson, the supervisor, and Mr. Counts, the attendance
officer. Mr. Counts smiled a lot too, and asked them if
they always got to school on time, and they all said yes,
this time without waiting for Suse. Then he asked them if
they came every day, and they all said yes again; and then
he asked them if they got good grades on their report
cards, and after a moment's silence they chorused yes
again; then he wanted to know if anybody had ever thought
of going to high school, and they all said yes again, though
to most of them high school seemed as far away and unreal as a ship at sea.

He seemed a little surprised to hear that—nobody, he
said, had ever gone from Ballew School but—and he
smiled specially at Andy—Andy had said as they were
walking down that he would like to go and from the way
he was learning his lessons he would certainly get there;
and the little girl in the same class, wasn't she going too—
and he smiled at Suse. "You know, there'll be a high-
school bus when the gravel road is finished," he said.

Suse, suddenly bashful and overwhelmed at just the
thought of high school, let alone speaking out to the great
man, turned first white and then red, and couldn't say a
word and wouldn't have been heard if she had.

There had come a dreadful howling and whining and
yelping at the door and paws clawing on wood. Ruby,
who had always been of a bold brash turn and had never
used to cry when she was a baby and a stranger came,
tittered and then yelled above the uproar, "That fool
hound must be a thinken they's a fox here."

Mr. Counts began again, but old Lead howled like a
gravedigger-painter by a fresh-made grave, for it was past
dinnertime and he thought the children were inside eating,
giving their scraps to some strange hound. Andrew sat at
his desk and looked at Mr. Counts as if he were listening
to him instead of the hound; finally the superintendent
himself got up and opened the door and old Lead ran in
between his legs with a little bark of pure happiness and
ran waving his tail and his ears, sniffing up and down the
room until he came to little Alben with the sausage grease

on his hair and there he stopped. And the whole school
first tittered and then roared as old Lead, with the chewed-
up plowline trailing behind him, sniffed and sniffed at little Alben's hair and then licked it.

Alben slapped Lead's nose. Mr. Counts sat down. The
superintendent told Andrew he might dismiss for dinner
recess. The children did not rush for their lard pails as
they usually did, but continued to sit in their seats and
watch, with all their laughter scared out of them. The visitors had asked to see old Andrew's daily schedule. Whatever it was, he didn't have it. Then they asked for his
record book. The children knew about that: Andrew always got it down from the high shelf in the corner once a
month and sent either Silas or Lee Roy home for pen and
ink and then put down marks in the book and made out a
thing called a monthly report. Andrew got it down now
and handed it to Mr. Counts, who looked at it and said,
not in the pleasy-mealy voice he had used on the children,
"But there's no record here for the last three weeks."

Andrew said, "Oh, I can recollect. There's not so many
an they're mighty good to come."

Mr. Counts looked some more, thumbing pages back to
the beginning. "Where are the grades? What if a child lost
a report card?"

And Andrew said, "Oh, I'll put the grades down when
I turn it in at the end of school."

And the superintendent, who had been watching, said,
"Let's see the report cards."

And old Andrew stood still and twisted his neck, for he
wasn't used to a shirt with the top buttoned, let alone a
tie, and Suse, watching him, wanted to cry out, "Lie, you
old fool, lie. . . . Say we've just took 'em home," but Andrew wasn't any good at lying. He just reached over to the
high shelf again, and his hand pawed around aimlessly
while he told the superintendent, "They've always been
so bad to lose their report cards, I just make 'em out an
give 'em out at th end of school," and he handed the
superintendent a handful of report cards blank and new-
looking the way they had been last summer when he had
got them at the board of education.

The visitors did not touch the blank cards, and the short
man with the slicked-down hair said in a sour scolding
kind of way, "You mean that at the end of school you just

fill up all the blanks with grades, no monthly tests or anything?"

And old Andrew looked at the floor and said, "Yes, sir," in a low voice, and after that the children knew it was no good. Then the visitors were gone and little Sarah Hull began first a sniffling and then a howling—when her pop got home from his funeral he might whip her half to death for having nail polish on her fingers, for it was a sin like paint on your lips, but Rachel said, "Shah," it would come off with a little turpentine. Paul was pulling the chewed-up plowlines off the hounds and thinking with shivers about his old dad when he found it out.

But old Andrew sat at his desk and stared at the closed door and noticed nothing. After a while he reached for a chew of tobacco, and finding none in the borrowed clothes, got up slowly and went away.

Chapter Fourteen

THE SOUTHWEST WIND blew and made a thunder through the pines and laid a piece of March in February. Nunn whistled as he half-soled the sled runners with stout oak planks from the storehouse. All winter he'd meant to build a new sled for picking up rock and hauling manure, and had found, after a deal of hunting in the woods, two crooked white oaks of the proper shape for runners; but what with his crosstie making and winter weather dry enough for plowing he'd never got the sled built.

But new sled or no, he would do a thing he'd meant to do for years—pick up rocks and get a piece of ground ready for his grass and clover seed—the weather was dry and mild, with no hard-frozen earth, and school was out so the youngens could all help. Old Andrew had never missed another day after the visit of the superintendent, and Nunn, thinking on the matter, stopped his whistling; he hoped his bit of loose talk hadn't caused the old man to lose his job; then he whistled again; not even Elias Higginbottom would be able to find another teacher for the school.

Next morning the nearer corn swag was still a blue hollow in the pale clear sunlight when they all went to work on it. The work went swiftly, with Deb picking up pebbles and Nunn sweating over the crowbar under the big tight rocks. Above them on the graveyard knoll the headstones glistened in the springlike sunshine, and the cedar trees between Tom and Angie Mime whistled in the wind with a gay light note different from the angry roar or sad murmur to the pines.

Each time Nunn went to unload a sledload of rock in

the gully between the garden and the corn swag and turned the sled and looked up, he saw the gleaming angel head on Aunt Marthie Jane and felt a peace close to contented happiness—the old woman would be pleased to know what he was doing. In her day there had never been a gully, and no loose rock on the fields, and a mowing machine could go any place in the valley fields. Most of the land had been kept as meadows or pastures, and never corned to death, but when she died and year after year it was plowed up with no rye in the winter or grass in the summer, the rocks had come up one by one.

The feeling of peace and joy in doing a long-needed bit of work communicated itself to Milly and the children and even the pups and Maude. The children worked quietly and quickly, picking up rocks and flinging them into the sled with no quarreling; Maude seemed lost in a long pleasant dream, moving only when Nunn told her and with no touch from the lines, and stopping close to the gully for unloading like a lady, never rearing back and jumping around in pretended fright. Deb never whined once all morning, and when he had trotted after the sled until he was tired, he went to sleep on the sunny, wind-protected side of a log.

By noon they had finished the corn swag and most of the gentle slope past the big sinkhole up to the graveyard, and not even Lee Roy, with his sharp critical eyes, could find a rock. Milly, as she started away to get dinner, smiled down on the field, tired but dreamy-eyed, and wondered aloud to Nunn if he really would sow lespedeza and grass seed like John, and if John would really come with a mowing machine and they could save enough hay so there would be some for Betsey, enough so that she would give gallons of milk, with lots of butter all winter.

But at dinner her dream of hay all winter seemed far away when she looked at Nunn hunched over his plate, shut up in himself, hardly eating his fodder beans. He didn't like fodder beans much anyhow, and when he did eat them he wanted plenty of meat seasoning, but she couldn't help it if they were out of meat and almost out of the lard he had bought in Town. The chickens ought to start laying in March and she could buy lard, but she didn't know how she could better the bread. The corn pone was a dirty-looking gray with a rough dry crust; he liked corn-

bread made with buttermilk and eggs and smeared so
thick with butter that melted butter dripped out the bottom, and there wasn't a bit of butter.

Betsey must be getting old; she'd never known her to
start drying up so soon—she wouldn't come in before June
—still, they wouldn't starve on bread and potatoes and
canned goods with what lard she could buy, or maybe the
egg money would have to go for dog feed; Sam and Vinie
had to be fed right.

Nunn, she thought, was maybe so hungry he was thinking about the same thing. She felt so sorry for him she
could have cried. He had finished a little plate of beans
and was sitting, holding his knife, looking about for the
butter. She kept waiting for him to say, "Milly, what th
hell, have you lost th butter?" but after a while of looking
he kind of ducked his head and started eating the hard,
water corn pone with plain molasses. He glanced up, met
her eyes, and looked away. Maybe he thought about the
black heifer that would be fresh now; he didn't look mad,
more like he felt guilty and ashamed. She didn't hold it
against him.

She fed the pups, as usual, a little milk with their feed
as directed, and Nunn, resting with his chair against the
wall, watched her frowningly and frowned more yet when
Lucy, who had always been a fool for milk, came whining
up for some and there wasn't any. He didn't say anything,
but there was a long, hard set look about his face, like a
mule making up its mind to kick or bite or even run away.
After a while he got up and stood looking around the
kitchen with a hunting look in his eyes until his glance fell
on a brown paper sack half full of pumpkin seed, and he
asked how much sugar cost a pound.

"Tween six an seven cents up at Samuel's," she said,
and added quickly, "Honey, soon's th hens start layen, I'll
buy a little sugar along an have somethin fit to eat. I know
you're tired a lasses sweetenen."

"Aw, hell, I git plenty to eat. I jist happened to think
about sugar. We've still got plenty a lasses, ain't we?"

Milly nodded. "Th youngens don't eat hardly none
when they's no butter, an with not much lard I ain't baked
as much gingerbread as common."

"It's a good thing. Th yoes are looken kind a porely, an
I'll mebbe need to feed it all out fore spring's over." Milly

said nothing; on other springs Nunn had only fed molasses when the ewes looked sickly or didn't have much appetite, never to them all. She had thought she might sell a few gallons of molasses; Mrs. Hull had sent word by Suse to know if Nunn would have any to sell, and she had sent word back that she thought they could spare at least five gallons; and at seventy-five cents a gallon that would have been $3.75.

She had meant to buy lard and sugar with the money or dress goods, and maybe two blue cups; just cups oughtn't to cost much. She still had three saucers but now only one cup and that the one with the big nick and the crack; Nunn cursed every time he noticed the crack and said he had the old cracked cup again. He never seemed to know there was just one cup and that she drank her coffee from the pot and a saucer.

Maybe the molasses money would had to have gone for something ugly like ship stuff for the ewes, but it was nice to think about buying something all of her own choosing. She would not give up without a struggle; two blue cups and some sugar and the rest in that blue-checked gingham, Preacher Samuel, she could hear herself saying. "Nunn," she began hesitantly, "couldn't— couldn't th yoes eat honey?" and she went on to tell about all the honey there was left, maybe as much as twenty gallons; didn't Nunn recollect how back in the summer the youngens had left the lid off the biggest crock and the yellow jackets and waspers got in it, and after that everytime she put any on the table out of the good crocks with no waspers, the youngens always said she was trying to feed them hornets and wouldn't eat a bite.

Nunn pushed his hat back and appeared to consider, and Milly rattled on, hoping he'd spare her the molasses. "Looks to me like honey would be good fer a yoe same as lasses, an it's there a wasten; th onliest thing I can do with it is make vinegar."

"Vinegar?"

Milly nodded. "Sue Annie told me once how she made some real good vinegar out a honey; just thinned it with water an stirred it up good, an set it away with a cloth tied over it; she never did make but one batch because Uncle Dave was so bad to skip off an drink it while it

was souren; once, she said, he got down dead drunk on it
an—"

"Soured honey's that strong," Nunn said, as if he were
thinking out loud.

"It makes mighty fine vinegar, Sue Annie says; but
I've already got more apple vinegar now that I've got jugs
fer, an anyhow, who wants soured hornets?"

Nunn pushed his hat yet further back, until it seemed
standing on his jumper collar, and a soft pleased look
came into his face, "Honey would be good fer Rosie's
pigs, an maybe Maude, too; she's awful foolish over anything sweet." He started off to get Maude, but he hadn't
had time to get around the house corner before he was
back in the kitchen door yelling for her, "You awful
busy?"

"Why, I'm a aimen fer us all to come help in th rocks
like this mornen."

"Hell, I don't need so much help. I want you all to
shell me a turn a corn, a big turn."

She reminded him they still had plenty of meal from
his last trip to mill.

"I'm a aimen to take Maude an th sled up th hill this
comen Friday, so you all might as well shell a turn: I'm a
goen to start feeden th pigs meal."

Milly sighed. First honey for the pigs and now meal.
She didn't want to stay inside to shell a turn of corn in all
this pretty weather. It was mean of her, she knew, but as
they were going back to the field she told Suse and Lee
Roy they'd have to shell bread corn in the morning, a
job they, like herself, hated.

Through all the afternoon they worked at picking up
rocks in the high level graveyard field. Behind them, their
upper edges fringed with glistening pine, the steep sagegrass field rose up to the Pilot Rock, and straight across
the rolling field below them stood the dark pine- and
cedar-covered slopes of the nearer hills.

Deb and the pups went to sleep again, and even Jude,
the filly, grew tired of running and kicking her heels, but
the others worked on, emptying sledload after sledload of
rock in the big gully. Lee Roy and Nunn thought they
could finish the field by dark, but Milly wasn't so certain;
maybe they could if there was coal oil enough so that she
could cook supper by lantern light.

The sun rolled behind the shoulder of Pilot Rock hill and blue lakes of twilight filled first the creek and river valley and then the lower fields. The graveyard field, still touched by long low bars of sunlight, was like a golden island in the sea of twilight. Their shadows and Maude's shadow, already long, grew longer until dimly they could see their heads, giantlike and strange, on the walls of pine across the creek. Lucy danced and waved her hands to her head on the hill, but for an instant only; shadows crept up Sue Annie's hill and a young moon began to show dimly halfway up the sky. The wind stilled and the night air made a tingling on their cheeks. From down by the house, Betsey bawled for Milly and her night's feed, and Maude nickered back to her impatiently, as if to show the lazy cow that she, Maude, worked still. And Nunn comforted her with kind words, telling her it was the last load and that she would have a good feed, for if the weather held it would be dry enough to plow by tomorrow morning.

Milly studied the sunset, clear, blue-green washed with red, and thought the weather would hold, at least long enough for him to turn the garden and the potato ground.

The last rock was out. Nunn loaded them all into the sled, with Milly holding the pups, and they rode down the graveyard hill home, and Nunn sang with the others joining in:

> "Go build me a castle forty feet high,
> So I can see Lulu as she passes by."

In spite of the lateness, Nunn did a job he had long been planning to do. Tonight, instead of following the Cow's Horn road straight to the little barn, he drove through a place where the garden fence was down right up to the house, so he could let all his family out at their own front door in style, he said.

While Milly seemed fully occupied with Deb and the pups and giving the others their directions about the night work, Nunn went over, and in what he hoped was an offhand manner, picked up Milly's rain barrel and started rolling it toward the sled. Milly stopped in the middle of feeling Sam's nose and telling Suse to go get a cabbage out of the hole for supper, to know what in the world he meant by taking off her rain-water barrel. She couldn't get along without it.

Nunn tried to look surprised and managed to wiggle a slightly loosened stave. "Hell-fire, woman, what ails you? It's no good to you anymore. Look, it won't hold water—an I need it over in the storehouse to—put my grass seed in."

"Shit-fire, Nunn, honey, are you daft? They ain't a thing wrong with it—th youngens turned it over last washday, an it's got a little loose frum bean dry; it'll be watertight soon's it stands a little in th rain—it gits loose if'n I don't watch it ever time we have a little dry spell."

He continued to assure her it was no good as he rolled it onto the sled. He drove away as fast as Maude would go downhill. Milly quit quarreling and he thought she was crying; he hated like hell to do it, but he had to have a good sixty-gallon barrel. She could have it back when he got the smell out.

Next morning by daylight they were all ready to start picking up rock, when Nunn remembered the turn of corn that must be shelled. Milly had to threaten the youngens with Nunn's razor strop before they'd go, and then they went grumbling and quarreling at having to stay inside while Nunn and Milly went to the field.

Deb and Lucy and Sam and Vinie went to sleep on a shuck pile, and Lee Roy, ill humored over a stubborn ear, looked at the sleeping pups with something close to contempt. "They ain't nothen near th hound Zing was, an Zing didn't cost nothen."

"They ain't three months old, an that's too little to tell," Suse said defensively. "An allus recollect they've got a pedigree."

Lee Roy spat at a dead fly in a dusty spider web, knocking it out of the web. "Pedigreed fer rabbit-chasen to my mind—if they'll chase anything. I ain't never seen em look at nothen, cepten somethen to chew. We could all git burned up alive and murdered an they wouldn't so much as snore."

"They follered King Devil once," Suse said, "an they're a saven up fer him."

Lee Roy threw a cob at Vinie's nose. "Could ha been a rabbit. King Devil'll never be took. He's a haint like

Aunt Marthie. Pop'll never git him, an them pups ain't worth a dime."

"You're mad cause you have to shell corn, an you've been a listenen to them Tillers, but you'll live to eat them words," Suse said blackly.

"They couldn't tell a fox smell frum a mule's foot," he said.

Suse hit him with a tossed corn cob. Lee Roy called her a dirty name and threw a handful of corn in her face, and Suse, who was sitting flat-bottomed on a shuck pile with her lap full of shelled corn, ducked and fell backward; her legs flew up and the corn spilled into the shucks.

Lee Roy jumped on top of her but Suse lay lax and still. Lee Roy tapped her once with his fist on the head, and she did not move and he got up and stood looking down at her in frightened concern. The fracas aroused Lucy and she, half awake, began screaming that Suse was dead. Suse rolled over and shook her fist at her. "Be quiet you little fool. I was just a thinken; I'm gitten mad, but I don't want to waste corn fighten an mebbe kill Lee Roy, an Milly would blame me with it all—Lee Roy, let's let th pups settle it. They're big enough to run thout it killen em."

"Rabbits," Lee Roy said.

"Pop said we'd mebbe start grubben out th sandfield fer a corn crop today after dinner; if'n we do, you put their noses in a rabbit hole an see what happens. If they chase a rabbit, I'll slop th hogs an split all th kindlen ever night fer two weeks."

That afternoon, while Sam and Vinie and Deb slept on a sunny bed of pine boughs and everybody else, even Lucy, piled brush or cut or grubbed out the roots, Lee Roy, in grubbing out a long-rooted sumac, found a rabbit hole. The little rabbits hadn't come yet, but the nest was ready for them, lined with hair from the old rabbits.

Lee Roy rested on his grubbing hoe and looked cautiously around. Milly, who would be quicker to notice than Nunn, was on the other side of the patch piling brush, a good piece from him, but not far from the sleeping pups. Nunn was cutting down a band of small pines, a good piece from the pups but close to Lee Roy and the rabbit hole.

Lee Roy laid his hoe on his shoulder and strolled in the direction of the pups as if he were just looking for better grubbing. He walked slowly and gave Milly time to glance at Deb and the pups, as she did about every two minutes. When she had turned her back, satisfied they were all right, he hurried soundlessly over, dropped his hoe, scooped Sam and Vinie into his arms and ran, staggering a little under their burden, back to the rabbit hole.

He dropped them down by the hole, took a bit of the hair lining and rubbed some on each nose. Sam lifted his head and looked up surprised, like Chicken Little when the sky fell on his head. Vinie sneezed. Nunn heard the sneeze and stopped, ax lifted, looking over the field. He saw Lee Roy and the pups, and though the distance was great, he seemed to see the hair on Sam's nose and know it for rabbit hair. He roared and came running, seizing a scrub white oak limb on the way.

Lee Roy blinked his eyes and ducked as the limb, poorly aimed and too brushy anyhow, struck him once across the shoulders. Nunn flung it away and grabbed the pups. Cursing black breathless oaths, he rubbed each nose hard with the palm of his hand, then blew where the hairs had been, then squinted at each to see if there were rabbit hairs yet clinging, then got enough breath to blow again.

Milly came running up with the lard pail of drinking water and washed their noses with a wetted corner of her apron, trying to help Nunn in the blowing and soothe him at the same time. "Don't take on so, honey—one smell a rabbit won't ruin em—they'll be all right."

"But their first smell, their very first smell; they was too little when they got that scent a King Devil by the spring to recollect," and he cursed again and his voice shook, and Lucy thought he was going to cry and cried herself with a heartbroken howling. Deb awakened, and finding nothing about him but pine needles and sky, screamed, too; Lee Roy, unable to bear the sudden consciousness of the full awfulness of the thing he had done, unashamedly gave over to blubbering.

Suse alone was calmly derisive. "One little rabbit smell ain't a goen to scare th pedigree out a them. Zing knowed a rabbit frum a fox an a possum frum a coon an King Devil frum anybody, an they ought to be better'n him."

Nunn cursed some more and set them on the ground and studied first one and then the other, as if trying to decide how much harm the one smell of rabbit had done.

Vinie went over to Deb and after a moment's exploratory sniffing began chewing the shredded remains of one stocking. "Look, Vinie ain't hurt," Suse comforted. "She don't know she's smelled a rabbit. I'll bet if you let her smell a fox right now she'd go after it."

"I seed a fox track down there in th woods under a ledge when I was hunten mushrooms," Lee Roy said with a speculative glance at Nunn.

"They's no use a talken a fox tracks," Nunn said. "If Sam an Vinie's any good, they'd run theirselves to death."

"I could keep up pretty close with em, little as they are," Lee Roy said, glancing sideways at Sam sniffing in the direction of the rabbit hole. "An anyhow, th tracks I seed had two toes missen on th front right foot, an to my mind it's that old gray fox Sue Annie an Uncle Dave had th fight over. Recollect? She trapped a gray fox, a old she, that was stealen her chickens, an Uncle Dave made her turn it loose cause th fur wasn't no good."

Milly looked eager but spoke hesitatingly. "Nunn, mebbe they could chase a old she like that—I don't guess she'd run much—her den's most likely in th bluff someplace."

Suse looked at her mother's face and that was enough. She threw her arms around Nunn's neck and began "Please, Pop, please," adding argument to argument; the gray fox was old, she was crippled and couldn't run fast; she wouldn't run far enough to tire the pups; the scent was already most likely cold anyhow; she and the rest would scatter out and watch and listen, and if a wildcat or anything else came along to hurt the pups they'd scare it off; they needed a smell of fox to make them forget the rabbit—"An anyhow, they might lose th scent after ten feet."

Milly came up with Deb on her hip and chided Suse for saying Sam and Vinie might not run, and in the next breath assured Nunn they wouldn't run much—they'd run all right, she knew, "but they're most too little to do much good, but honey," she finished hesitantly, "it would be nice to hear a hound agin, our own hounds, I mean."

Lee Roy stood apart from the others and watched Sam and Vinie, whom everybody else had forgotten. Vinie had been annoyed when Milly picked up Deb and took the stocking out of reach. She had tried to follow it by standing on Milly's shoe, but Deb lifted his legs and draped them around Milly's thin waist, and after a disappointed but hopeful sniff or so in the direction of the stocking, she dropped her paws and trotted away; after circling about and sniffing the air and the ground, she trotted back to the rabbit hole, and Sam trotted after her.

Lee Roy watched and waited until there came a lull in the clamor about Nunn and then said with loud unconcern: "There ain't no use in talken. Them pups could eat with a fox an never know th difference. It's a pair a natural-born rabbit chasers you've got—look!"

Nunn whirled and sprang toward the pups sniffing industriously in the dug-out rabbit hole. "Jesus God, you little devil, why in hell didn't you take em away, stead a standen there yappen?"

Lee Roy stood silent until his father had picked up the pups and was once more rubbing their noses, so angrily it looked as if he would raise a blister. "Jesus God yourself. You'd a beat me to death this time a sayen I put em in th hole like you done awhile ago. I'm afeared to git close to em; can I hep it if that Vinie can smell a rabbit a mile away?"

Nunn and Milly reached Lee Roy at the same time, and his shirt tail tore under their anxious fingers. "There ain't no marks on him," Milly said relievedly, and then her relief changed to disgust when she saw that he had, against all her laws, stripped off his heavy underwear here in the last of February. But Lee Roy was saved from a good scolding when Nunn found a long switch mark on his bare arm in the tender part between his elbow and high-rolled sleeve.

Nunn picked up the arm and looked at it intently, then sighed and dropped it. "Lee Roy, when I think a th whippens you need an never git, an then I give you one lick that leaves a scar fer nothen."

Lee Roy tossed his red forelock out of his eyes and smiled. "Aw, don't feel so bad, Pop. Th next time you break a limb fer me, recollect I'm one whippen ahead."

Milly was once more wiping the pups' noses on her wetted apron. "Nunn, I don't like to butt in on your business, but don't you think maybe you ought to let em have a little smell a fox. If'n you don't they'll allus be a thinken on rabbit."

Nunn's troubled glance went first to Lee Roy's switch mark and then on the pups. "Hell, Milly, I aint goen to start trainen em now. They're too young; an they could git another scent a King Devil; recollect what happened to Rans's pup; an it ud be th ruination uv em to make em quit fore they holed him or lost th scent."

"But that's a old crippled gray fox, I tell you," Lee Roy said, and rubbed his switch mark.

"Oh, hell, I don't know," Nunn said and pushed his hat back.

"They'll be all right," Suse said, and ran up and over a low sagegrass knoll and down to the edge of the steep wooded banks and ledges that lay above the river. The others came running behind her with Sam and Vinie snatching at Lucy's tattered stockings. They had all known suddenly from Nunn's resigned face and voice that he was going to let Sam and Vinie smell the gray-fox track. Only Nunn glanced back once at the clearing with his ax blade and the grubbing hoe shining in the sun. Then he heard the children crashing through the woods and roared out that they mustn't run over the fox tracks; he didn't aim to train a pair of bloodhounds.

Even in February the river-bluff woods were a pleasant place: deep banks of winter-softened leaves below dripping limestone rocks where fern and walink and moss were green all winter and where in spring the foam flowers came with their white spires of delicate bloom. Overhead were the big trees, black walnut and old scarred sugar maples and beech and oak, never logged out because the river when in flood made a slow eddy below them that would drift the logs into the creek mouth instead of pulling them down the river. The ledge with the fox tracks in the dark dusty soil under it was halfway down the hill. Below, lay the flat strip of black silt-covered bottom corn land and past that the blue river, fringed with alder bush and red river birch and white-limbed sycamore.

The children and Milly lay on the ledge, chins over,

looking down while Nunn swung himself down, careful
not to step too near the tracks. Milly handed down first
Sam and then Vinie, and the silence was like a frozen
thing while they waited. Sam shook his brown ears and
looked around with his usual calm manner that, though
never vulgarly inquisitive or overly enthusiastic, was yet
without timidity or fear.

So now it was Vinie, forever inquisitive, who first gave
an exploratory sniff under the ledge, a mildly interested
little sniffing, the same as she gave to the rabbit hole or
the strainer cloth or Nunn's socks or any other thing she
thought might be good to chew. But now, instead of
lifting her head and thinking about it, her nose went lower
yet, until it seemed as if she would eat the very dirt; and
the dirt was interesting, more interesting than anything
she had ever had, even food when she was hungry. Her
nose moved quickly back and forth over the ground, not
jumping up and down but staying low, with the white
silky flaps of her ears almost touching the dirt. Her body
quivered; she was like one who has found something un-
believably fine and good, better than anything known or
dreamed, and yet familiar, some wonderfully precious
thing long lost and now found. Her pushing nose went
on and on; she forgot to move her legs and it looked as
if she would topple in the dust. Then she moved her
legs with a clumsy running and at the same time let out a
little yipping cry.

Sam turned from his calm inspection of the river and
ran up to Vinie, who by now had sniffed her way to the
end of the rock dust and was going over a steep bank of
leaves. The bank was too steep for her untrained legs;
she slipped, rolled over on her back, then in her struggles to get up turned over again. Sam had reached the
bank of leaves; until now it had been hard to say
whether he followed Vinie or the fox; unlike Vinie, he
paused at the leaves and got his legs in hand and then
went on slowly and carefully, like a man in a dangerous
business.

Milly ran around the ledge to Vinie's help, but Nunn
waved her back. "She's got to learn," he said.

The children left the ledge and ran along the bluff side
a few feet above Sam. With a fierce switching gesture,
Nunn brought them to a standstill, but all his fierce face

could not silence Lucy. "Sam's ahead a Vinie now. An she found it. It ain't fair, Pop. Lemme run an git her."

"She's got to learn to run on a sidehill if she's ever ketchen King Devil," Nunn said, and Lucy tearfully watched Vinie's struggles to claw her way up the steep slippery leaf bank and paid no attention to Sam's steady going up and around a big sugar tree, then up to a fair-sized dead chestnut log fallen slantwise of the bluff side.

By the log he yipped, but whether it was meant to be a hunting bay of triumph or a yelp of bewilderment it was hard to say. It must have been a hunting bay, for after a moment he sniffed his way up and around the log. By now Vinie had clawed herself up the leaf bank and was hunting the scent again. She paid no attention to Sam's voice or to anything, not even her legs, except the smell. She found it and went on as though the world were empty except for her nose and the smell under it.

Nunn, who had been squatting rigidly by the fox tracks, got up and stretched himself like a man awakened from a deep sleep. His whole family had forgot him, forgot everything but the pups. He looked around, down to the river and up at the sky laced with beech and maple twigs, and smiled a soft triumphant smile.

He went up the hill until he caught sight of Milly anxiously watching Sam trail along a sloping rock. He called to tell her that he was certain it was an old gray fox: a young lively animal would have jumped the log instead of going around it, and the pups would most likely bring it to hole or lose the scent if it did jump over a ledge, and so he thought he would run home and get his hunting horn and teach them to come to his call.

Milly protested mightily—couldn't Lee Roy or Suse go after the horn. She was afraid to be left with the pups. "What if they go on around an git right above th river an roll off . . . or fall in?"

Nunn yelled back that if they couldn't swim out, they'd do better to drown anyhow, and walked quickly away. When he had climbed the river bluff and was well out of sight of his family, he ran. But remembering Sue Annie's curiosity and old Dave's long-visioned eyes, he cursed and ducked into the heavy fringe of brush on the edge of the old fields above the creek and ran until he came to the

Cow's Horn Road. There he walked again with long impatient strides until he reached the old gristmill.

He glanced around to see that nobody was coming from the direction of Old John's, then slipped into his own outbuilding as if he were a thief, went over to a side wall and standing on tiptoe, he found a tightly woven grass sack and an old trace chain.

He went to the house, got the hunting horn, stuffed it into his overall bosom, and then went to the freshly shelled sack of corn and put about a peck and a half into his sack. Holding the string that had tied the corn sack, he mused a moment, then put the string in his pocket and pushed the sack with his foot until it fell with a slow lazy motion and lay, corn flowing out from its top like victuals from Aunt Marthie's speckled horn of plenty.

At the kitchen door he stopped, his sack on his shoulder, and looked first up the valley and then down, and after flinging an oath up to Sue Annie's cabin, dashed from the kitchen door straight down and across the Cow's Horn Road to the creek bluff, then worked his way down the sheer ledges and steep brush-tangled banks to the bottom of the canyon, and walked along the edge of the swiftly flowing water until he came to the Blue Hole.

This was a deep still pool at the foot of a low waterfall, perpetually shaded by the tall hemlocks on either side and shut away by the sheer cliffs that rose up and up to Nunn's fields on one side and to old Dave's tilted farm on the other. Not even a goat could come straight over the hill to it from either side, and though Sue Annie might have pitched a rock into it from her lower cow pasture, she could reach it only by coming around to Nunn's side of the creek; and at no time, winter or summer, could she look down through the hemlocks and ivy bush to see what went on there.

Nunn tied an end of the trace chain firmly around the top of the sack of corn, then holding the free end of the chain, flung the sack out into the water. He pushed his hat back and stood a moment, holding the chain, smiling a little as he watched the sack with its weight of corn sink lower and lower in the water.

He fastened the chain on a hemlock root that grew under the water, then straightened himself and smiled up at the steep bluff that lay on the Tiller side of the creek.

"Sue Annie, Sue Annie, what wouldn't you give to know that I'm a sprouten me some corn to dry an grind fer malt fer to make me some moonshine to bootleg."

He hurried away, for he had to follow the creek almost to the river bluff before he could find a break in the wall of rocks he could climb. If he went on down to the creek mouth and came up the river hill, Milly would want to know what in the world he had been doing down on the river when he had no fish basket or trotline out. He reminded himself to recollect to tell her that she must never leave a turn of corn untied; the rats had already been in it and spilled it and gomed it around.

Once on top of the creek bluff he could hear Sam and Vinie yipping and crying like angry children; they must have holed the old gray fox. He smiled and lifted the horn and blew loudly and long. The neighbors would all know he was out wasting time on his fox hunting when he ought to be grubbing on a corn patch. And King Devil would know he was after him again—but nobody would know just how he aimed to feed his pups and his youngens at the same time.

Chapter Fifteen

EARLY IN MARCH there came a deep wet snow and Nunn borrowed John's hand seeder and sowed his grass and clover seed; the melting snow carried the seed down and laid it firmly against the damp earth. Thus it was that Aunt Marthie had sown her seed and always she had had a good stand. As he listened to the whispering patter of the seed on the snow, he smiled a warm-eyed, dreaming smile—aye, Lord, but he would have hay this year—for six springs he had meant to do this thing and he was doing it at last. King Devil and fox-hunting troubles were far away; the real thing was his rolling fields giving out their strong earth smell under the wet snow, already quickening, sending up all manner of wild grass and clover and shoots and sprouts of things—but some day there wouldn't be a weed, only grass and clover.

There was more seed than he had land clear of rocks and brush, and so when the snow was gone he and Milly and the children set sagegrass fires on still afternoons near twilight and burned off a great sweep of land between the graveyard and the sandfield. All through the hills farmers were setting their sagegrass fires; at twilight the soft springlike air would be dusty blue and sweet-smelling with smoke, and sometimes on the farther hills crowns of flame, pale red through the smoke, would creep slowly upward until nearly midnight; and the fire-warden's helper was busy going on foot from farm to farm, handing out brush-burning cards and counseling people on the danger of fire.

Then the wild March winds came. They and the over-full creek filled the valley with thunderous song, stirring

as a brass band, full-blown and playing a swift tune. The
sun was hot and higher in the sky, and all Nunn's
household went mad and crazy with the breaking up of
winter and coming of the spring. The ewes ran away to
the back hills; Betsey forgot she was an old heavy-with-
calf cow and ran away, kicking her heels with a jingle-
jangling of her bell to the cane brakes by the river. All
day long the hens sang and cackled as if each had laid
ten eggs, and one day Nunn threatened to beat Maude
and the youngens all to death if they didn't pay more
attention to their work of cleaning out the cow stable and
hauling the manure and putting it on the Irish-potato
patch. Twice Maude tried to run away with the empty
sled; Suse and Lee Roy had a fight with sheep manure,
and Lucy, daring croup and a hard whipping, pulled off
her shoes and went wading in the cold creek water.

Nunn would roar at them all one minute and the next
be forgetful, as he looked off toward the graveyard field
where already he had found the two tiny pale leaves of
a just-sprouted lespedeza seed. Even Milly, scraping up
buckets of hen manure under the floor and putting it in
her cabbage hills, looked away toward the storehouse and
thought she might find a mess of wild greens.

Her good sense told her she wouldn't find wild greens,
not on a dry March day, but she took a milk bucket and
the butcher knife and went hunting, the pups playing with
her wind-tossed apron and stepping on the few thin-leaved
bunches of rabbit lettuce she did find.

Under the hot March winds the earth was soon dry
enough again for plowing, and day after day Maude and
Nunn were out at daylight, dragging first the already
turned potato and garden ground, then turning the oat
ground; lastly would come the corn and cane. Nunn cursed
and was impatient with Maude, wishing often for two
mules like John and Samuel, but every day the patch of
dark-ridged, fresh-turned earth grew larger, while Maude
grew thin and hung her head in weariness at the end of
the day.

The dry weather held, and life for them all was a race
with planting time. The early garden stuff, like sallet
peas and beets and turnips, came first; then, while Nunn
plowed, Milly and the children cut the seed potatoes, carefully, for these were the first store-bought seed potatoes

they had ever had, dusted them with sulphur as Aunt Marthie had always done, and laid them in the deep furrows eye up. In time the dark purplish green shoots pushed above the ground, so rich and rank that Sue Annie and others passing by commented on their fineness.

Milly's conscience troubled her when she looked at the fine potatoes. One afternoon before Nunn dragged the turned ground, it had looked so much like rain that he and the children went off to burn some big brush piles in the sandfield. Milly had found herself alone; even Deb was not around to watch; he was asleep. So she had sneaked out more than half a sack of the government fertilizer and spread it on the potato patch; it was so dark when the others got in that nobody noticed the whiteness on the plowed ground. Milly slept little during the early part of the night; the promised rain was slow in coming, but at last it did come and soaked the fertilizer down so that nobody could see, and saved her from she knew not what—a body could maybe go to Atlanta for years if they used government fertilizer on a garden. Now and then she worried still if Sue Annie, working late in her garden, had looked down and seen her; she was always glad when the leaves got green to make a curtain between her and Sue Annie.

But the hard work outdoors plus her usual chores of cooking and scrubbing and washing and ironing never left much time for worrying about anything. Nights found her dead for sleep and mornings she was tired with an ache in her shoulders and a stiffness in her hands; she pitied Maude and the children—they got even more tired —Maude was carrying a colt and the children were too young to be fully broken to dullsome work. Suse, particularly, chafed sometimes under the slow jobs like setting little onion sets hour after hour. But most wearisome of all turned out to be the spreading of the government fertilizer. While Nunn plowed, Milly and the children went to work with it in the nearer corn swag, even Deb, who walked along with a four-pound lard bucket full, squatting now and then to put down one tiny careful pinch and always sneezing. It was such stinking stuff, and it seemed somehow to go all through a body, deep under the fingernails and up your nose until you could taste it, sour and gritty.

Suse hated it worse than the onions; she would sometimes stand for minutes together with a handful unspread,
the gray stuff falling in a thin trickle unnoticed on her
bare feet, while she stared out over the greening hills as
if she were a bird making up her mind where she would
fly, too lost in her own mind to be either angry or
ashamed when Milly had to tell her to get to work.

Milly never scolded her at such times; poor child, soon
enough would come the time when not just her body was
tied down by work, but her mind, too, with troubles
and worries—it seemed sometimes like God made women
for trouble; she wasn't real certain, but then she never
was certain right away—or maybe she only wouldn't let
herself believe—but it seemed like she was in the family
way again. The thought would check her suddenly in
whatever she happened to be doing, and she would stand
a second openmouthed and staring; this thing had happened to her again. An instant later she would chide her
sinful heart; women were made to have babies, it was a
sin not to want them, and a black, black sin to try to keep
from having them. The thing was to work as long as she
was able.

By the second week in April, Nunn had less than two
acres of the sandfield turned for corn; the plowing was
almost as hard as that in a new ground; overgrown brush
roots and tight rocks were always throwing the plow out
of the ground, and in spite of all the rocks they'd picked
up and the roots they'd grubbed out, there seemed to be
a million more. And Maude pulled the heavy hillside
turning plow less willingly, with less and less spring and
eagerness to be done with the heavy tedious work than
in the first days of plowing. Milly and the children left off
their fertilizer spreading to come and pick up more rock
and grub out more roots.

The pups came, too, and frolicked over the field, seldom getting out of sight of Milly's watchful eyes, but no
longer babies to be watched away from sinkholes and the
river bluff. But one morning Milly stayed behind the others to sprinkle ashes and Paris green on the young cabbages to keep the cutworms off, and when she came and
asked after the pups they could not be found. Nunn, unwilling to leave the plowing, cursed the pups and told the
children to hunt around the fields and over the river bluff.

But when after an hour or so no one had heard either
Sam or Vinie, he unhitched Maude, tied her in the
shade, and went hunting himself. In his opinion they
had followed the old three-toed gray fox around to Brush
Creek and would be back soon. Milly said nothing, only
begged him to go in a hurry; she'd never told him for
fear of throwing him into a fit of bad temper, but something was taking the hens, taking three or four a week so
slyly that she never heard a cackle nor saw blood
or feathers; when Zing was alive such things had never
happened, and now she lived not only in fear for her
hens, but for the pups as well; they could get scent of
King Devil and follow him to their death.

Lee Roy ran for the hunting horn; Nunn took it and
strode away toward the Pilot Rock, angrily conscious of
the steady gees and haws rising up from John's valley
fields, the rows of big and little Cookseys marching over
the sandy knolls of the Cow's Horn as they hurried with
their corn planting, and the silence of Samuel's ridge
fields that told he was already finished; now, farther behind than any, he must lose still another day.

It was past dinnertime before he heard the pups, yipping and yapping like lost children in Brush Creek Canyon, two miles on the other side of the Pilot Rock. He
blew his horn, but they answered with a dolorous yapping
that they could not come.

He found them at last, and with all his anger at the
lost day, there was pride at the way they had held the
scent through all the rough going. King Devil it was, he
was certain, when on the edge of a fifty-foot bluff he
found a bank of moss torn with the pups' toes and claws;
had it been night and they with hounds older and swifter
than themselves, they would have been dead now on the
rocks below. But as it was they had lost neither their
footing nor their heads but kept on, following the scent
around and down on the very edge, jumping down
shoulder-high ledges where, had they fallen, they would
have dropped sixty feet or more to the bottom of the
creek. More than once he shook his head as he worked
his way slowly down to the pups by the creek water; it
was as though King Devil had left him a note that said he
didn't play now; he was out to get the pups.

Vinie saw him first and came running to meet him with

Sam at her heels, both barking wildly in joy that he had come to get them out of a place from which they saw no way out; they couldn't climb up the steep bluffs down which they had come, and they were too inexperienced to know that after only a little wading in the cold swift creek water the valley broadened, and they could follow it to the Brush Creek Road crossing and thence the big road home, the way Zing had learned to manage.

Lureenie in a pink-checked apron and sunbonnet, out spading up what he took to be a flower bed, waved to him and called in the friendly way of a lonely person who sees few people. She asked after Milly and the children and chatted on about the pups as if she'd never heard that he and Rans had tried to kill each other back in the fall. He felt foolish as he walked away; she thought he was out hunting for fun—and his corn land unturned and Maude switching her tail in the shade.

As he cut across by the graveyard he heard a boy's gees and haws, thin-voiced and tired, mixed with a few oaths which, when the boy tried to make them sound loud and strong as a man's, became shrill and faintly piping like a child's. The plow handles were breast-high on Lee Roy, and his sticklike arms were puny things behind the heavy plow and Maude, but his red head rode proudly on his narrow sweat-soaked shoulders. As Nunn watched, the plow hit a rock and jerked out of the ground; Lee Roy's body swayed as he struggled to stop Maude and jerk the plow back to balance, but in an instant the plow point was biting into the earth again, and both Maude and the plow were obedient to his will as they made a straight furrow down the field.

Ahead of him Milly swung the grubbing hoe and Suse and Lucy picked up rocks, while not far behind Lee Roy walked a tall man, his hands clasped behind his back, his shoulders bent a little, as he studied the plowed earth, bending sometimes to examine one of Lee Roy's furrows to see if the land was fully broken or full of streaks of unturned earth covered with dirt from the next furrow.

It was John come up on some business, and finding Nunn gone had stayed, apparently to give Lee Roy a plowing lesson. The pups ran ahead and leaped on Milly; she dropped the grubbing hoe and knelt by them, looking into their faces, going over each body with quick anxious fingers. Lucy and Deb ran up with shrill joyful cries and hugged and kissed first Vinie and then Sam; Suse, bowed a little by the weight of a big sand rock she was carrying to a pile on the lower edge of the field, turned and looked at them, but Lee Roy never slackened his plowing. John, watching Lee Roy with a critical, satisfied air, glanced around for Nunn, saw him coming out of a thicket of scrub pine that bordered the field and called good-humoredly, "No need to come home; you can fox-hunt all through corn planten. You've got a good plow-hand."

Nunn felt himself flushing; anger or shame or disgust or maybe all three boiled up in his insides so that he could hardly speak, and when he did speak he couldn't make his voice sound like that of a man with an easy conscience, a man who is doing what he ought to do.

Lee Roy kept on with his plowing and Nunn put down an impulse, that he knew was mean and childish, to tell him to stop, that his turning was not deep enough, that Maude was overheated, that he had no business wearing out his only pair of shoes.

Milly and the children were respectfully silent, holding back the multitude of questions they wanted to ask about where the pups had been and if they had caught anything, while the men talked. John was through with turning, he said; he had left Paul and a Cooksey boy he'd hired, each with a mule and a drag to break up clods, and had come up to see if Nunn could take time to look at one of his ewes that wouldn't eat and dragged around; he'd tried doctoring her, but he couldn't tell what ailed the dad-blamed thing. He grinned his sly old man's grin. "If'n I'd a knowed you was out fox-hunten, I'd a come early this mornen."

Nunn flushed. "I was pup-hunten, not fox-hunten," he said.

John nodded and studied the pups with narrowed eyes. "I was jist funnen. You couldn't leave em stay lost, sean as how they cost nigh as much as a mule."

Lee Roy had reached the end of the furrow, and Nunn, watching, could not but admire the way he swung the heavy plow around, a weight more than equal to that of himself, and turned Maude, neatly and quickly, so that she was unable to step out of the trace chains. Now he rested a moment, leaning on the plow handles, listening to John and Nunn discuss sheep and how soon they could safely shear. Nunn watched the boy, his mind but half taken up with John's talk, for as Lee Roy listened he slowly, and with no change of face, spat out a long stream of tobacco juice. Not three months ago Nunn had happened upon him chewing on the sly and had threatened to beat him half to death if he took up the filthy habit before he was a man grown—he, himself, had never chewed until he worked in the mines.

He wished Lee Roy would smile and act embarrassed instead of standing there not five feet high and acting like a man grown, so cool in his knowing that now, for some reason that would never come to talk between them, he would go on chewing tobacco, and Nunn would not whip him for it.

He put Maude in motion again and went back down the furrow, and the wind riffled his red hair, so much in need of a cutting it was curling a little, and Nunn thought of his mother, the red-headed woman for whom Aunt Marthie had often prayed because she had not been meek to clothe herself in black and sit out her life in the valley with one baby and memories of her man, dead before they had lived together in a home of their own. His mother could not sit and accept life like a dead tree in a snowstorm; she had gone out and gathered it with her own two hands, even if in the gathering she had to leave her widow's weeds and her baby. Lee Roy, no more than she, would sit with folded hands, accepting—and neither would Suse.

Then Lee Roy was past him and he was seeing the tired child's back and all his thoughts were like a dream hardly remembered. Lee Roy was a little boy, too little to plow. He hurried over and took the plow and praised him for his work and as a rest sent him to the house for the sheep bulletins and the big book on keeping livestock healthy that he had got from Senator Alben W. Barkley.

As he walked away, Nunn saw how ragged were his clothes, and a loose sole flapping on one shoe. The boy, like the others, needed everything, and would need more than the little money he could get from wool and crossties and early lambs would buy. The money that had gone for the pups, their feed, and their medicine by rights belonged to Milly and the children.

Other days would come when he fox-hunted and his family worked in the corn—the pups had to learn the country—they had to learn the tricks of King Devil; today they had learned a thing about ledges that would maybe save their lives in some hard race to come; but he would manage and his family wouldn't suffer.

The sprouted corn long since spread to dry in a windy corner of the storehouse was ready to be ground for malt —the barrel was ready—the half-gallon can of ready-made malt, the twenty pounds of sugar he had bought secretly in town on a chance trip with Jaw Buster in his truck—everything was ready—his hands were slippery wet on the plow handles. He wasn't afraid the law would come and take him away—the law had never been in the valley. It was his neighbors—John was an outspoken old man—he would remind him he was a grandson of Aunt Marthie and Preacher Jim; Samuel's silent disapproval would be worse than John's word thrashing; Samuel might pray for him in church—not by name—but people would know. He was glad he had never given his heart to God and joined the Church; he couldn't do this thing if he had. Worse than anything would be the friendly smirking ways of the trashy Tillers and men like Rans Cramer and J. D. Duffey—you're one of us now, they would say, and always be coming around the place.

Old John was looking at the sky, pure blue, like an autumn sky, and complaining about the weather; the last new moon had been dry, he said; the fall and winter had been wet and now, in his opinion, it would be a bad season—last night the wind had come out of the east and there was most likely a dry spell on the way right now.

The cold spring dew had fallen and the children and pups were asleep when Nunn got back from looking at John's sick ewe—bad wormy, he would say, was what ailed her and he had given her some of his phenothiazine. Milly complained because John had kept him so late when he already had his hands full with the spring plowing. Nunn grunted and took down the lantern. Milly was disgusted; he'd better sleep instead of worrying over his ewes here in April; the few that hadn't lambed wouldn't come to any harm no matter where they dropped their lambs.

"Hell-fire, woman," Nunn said, "it ain't th lambs that ain't borned. It's them that is. Some a th littler fellers cain't chew corn to do no good. I'm aimen to crack em some with your sausage grinder."

As he took the grinder from the shelf behind the stove and went off, Milly was quarreling after him that he would work himself into a sickness and begging to come with him and help. He reminded her that only one could turn the grinder and bade her somewhat harshly to go on to bed with the youngens like a woman ought.

He shook his head and wondered wearily how, if he had this much trouble getting away from her to mix the stuff, he could ever think up enough excuses to stay away long enough to still it—and where would he still it—it had to be close to water.

The water-soaked corn, with its pale yellowish sprouts, had dried until it seemed even harder than just shelled corn; and as he slowly and with much exertion put handful after handful through the dull noisome grinder, it seemed to him that in the night stillness the sound of the grinder was loud as rumbling summer thunder. Samuel, sleeping on the hill, would rouse and stand on his porch to listen, and Sue Annie, with the unconcern for night walks of a log-seasoned midwife, might at any moment come calling shrilly at the door, "What a you a doen, Nunn?"

He wished he had done his grinding during a hard roaring rain or, better yet, when the creek was wild and full of sound. The light worried him; good hard-working people like the Hulls and John's folks were worn out with the spring rush of work and sleeping soundly at home, but there was always the chance that somebody like Blare Tiller, who never worked hard enough to get tired, might be on his way to see about a trotline or fish basket in the river, or come over into his fields to spotlight a rabbit, and he wondered if Rans had passed; often he was late coming home from his WPA work—an enmity had been between them since the night of the big fight, and in a chance passing they spoke only, and that in cold low voices.

Lighted only by the smoky yellow lantern flame, the

storehouse seemed twice as big and full of black shadows, with the far corners like caverns, full of whisperings and rustlings and rattlings each time his grinder was silent. A bat flew through a broken-out gable window and circled above the lantern with confused squeaks and cries. A bat or a bird in the house was a sure sign of bad luck, and as Nunn stood staring up at it a thousand fears that mostly he kept pushed down below the thinking part of his mind swarmed over him like a thousand black bats: death; a child drowning in the river; cur dogs in the sheep; some night when he'd a drop too much he could walk over a cliff or into the Blue Hole; dry weather that wouldn't let him raise a kernel of corn; bad luck with his liquor and months in the jailhouse or Atlanta even; men coming with guns and handcuffs to take him away. The bat with an angry squeak thudded against the ceiling, came low, brushing his hat, and was gone between the bars of a front window.

He stood staring after it, the handle of the grinder upright and motionless in one hand, grains of sprouted corn in the other; cold sweat oozed on his forehead and his feet; he took one quick step toward the door—the storehouse was suddenly like a prison. He saw the lantern on the mail window and stopped, thinking of Aunt Marthie passing letters across the counter. He had never known her to be afraid. Preacher Jim would storm out if one of the children forgot and brought a hoe into the house, and shiver and sweat as he, Nunn, shivered and sweated now if a bird or a bat came into the house—but Aunt Marthie would smile and say, "God's will is God's will. When our time comes to go—we go."

He went back to the grinding and worked for what seemed many hours and was surprised when he went out for water to soak the ground-up malt to find the new moon, that had been low above the Cow's Horn when dark came, just going down. At least the moon was right; many times he had heard J. D. say that a mash barrel would glug only on a new moon.

Next day's plowing went slowly; Maude took advantage of Nunn's sleepy, absent-minded ways, and more than once he was aware of Lee Roy's eyes, critical over his furrows. He quit early that afternoon. Fortunately, Milly's beet rows needed thinning and the weeds were coming in the onion beds. He set all the children to work helping her, then walked through the house, picked up a water bucket, sneaked out three more of Milly's half-gallon fruit jars with rubbers and glass-lined tops to match, and as he went behind the gristmill he cut and peeled a poplar stir pole—years ago he'd heard old Uncle Dave Tiller say that mash had to be stirred together with a peeled poplar pole or it wouldn't come clear in the still-ing.

With a last glance to make certain no one was around, he went into the storehouse, locked the door behind him and set to work. He crumbled up the dry yeast cakes and tossed them into the barrel, and it seemed to him that already it smelled. He dumped in one of the two ten-pound sacks of sugar, but as he opened the other he thought of Milly and poured it slowly in, saving back a pound or more—he would, in a day or so, find a paper sack to put it in and take it to her, saying he had bought it at Samuel's; the sugar was in sacks of fine white cloth and he wished he could give her the sacks without her knowing, but his wish was lost soon in the wonder of what to put in next.

He remembered the can of store-bought malt; he didn't need both store-bought malt and sprouted corn, but since he'd spent his money for the malt he might as well use it; maybe it would make the mess taste better and work faster. He stirred in the malt and debated a time how much honey and molasses to use, and in the end emptied in the whole of a fifty-pound lard can of molasses and a five-gallon crock of the wasper honey filled with dead waspers, hornets, ants, and unhatched bees.

He dumped in the bushel of corn meal and stirred until pains shot through his wrists, but the corn meal lumped in the molasses and the thick hunks of honey in the comb seemed determined to mix with nothing. He wished he had asked Milly sometimes how it was she could stir up cornbread so smooth, and that he dared use a paddle instead of the poplar pole. In the end he took the first loose plank he came across, a part of an old red gum counter, and stirred until the stuff had some semblance of smoothness. Dusty dark had come and under him the ewes in the sheepfold were knocking their heads against the empty mangers, but fortunately Milly's onion rows were weedy

and she worked on as long as she could see and apologized for the lateness of her supper. Nunn only grunted,
wondering if he did right to let the cow-feed capping wait
until tomorrow.

The dry weather held and Nunn picked together a
brushy white oak drag and let the children take turns
riding it behind Maude to break down the clods in the
corn ground. Then he laid off corn rows while Milly and
the children dropped the seed and covered it. Then he
went on turning the rest of the field. He figured it was
better to have one piece only middling late than wait and
plant it all at once and have it all so late it was liable to
have the dry spell, that usually came late in August, catch
it right in the silk. The river bottom could be planted as
late as the last of May and still make good corn; dry
weather never hurt it.

John, as usual, seemed to have been right in his
weather prediction; the wind shifted first due east, then a
shade to the north, and came cold and dry down the valley. Late April that year was blighted, with no hot sun
and no white showers sweeping in from the west; wild
things never bloomed; the mornings were never wet as
after a rain with dew and thick fog, but clear and cold,
even a little skim of frost, enough to hold back the garden
and kill the tender things like peach buds. Milly sighed
over her garden; it never seemed to grow but stood still
for the cutworms and bouncing bugs to eat and the baby
chickens beeped in the cold. Even now, at almost May,
Milly had not yet had a good big mess of cooked wild
greens. She gathered wild sweet-potato vine by the river
and wilted it in hot grease and vinegar and that helped
some, but now and then she looked longingly at the turnip
patch. She was craving cooked greens bad, and if she
didn't get some pretty soon, this child she carried would
be marked with greens and would never in all its life get
enough of them to eat.

Sue Annie came by one day while they were all in the
cornfield, on her way to the river bottom to hunt a mess
of wild sweet-potato vine and crow's-foot sallet. She studied Nunn with a narrowing of her sharp black eyes, and
Nunn, already wondering if she had hunted greens around
the storehouse and had smelled anything, felt uneasy un-

der her sharp glance and turned away to go on with the plowing.

She called after him: "Nunn, you act like you was runnen frum the judgment day. What's yer hurry?"

"I don't want a rain to come fore I finish corn planten," he said.

Sue Annie looked up at the pale-blue, bone-dry sky and made exaggerated squintings and rollings of her eyes, as if searching for a cloud, then giggled and rubbed the back of her hand hard across her nose as she looked again at Nunn. "I can think uv a lot worse things that could happen to a man in yer business, honey, than a spell a dry weather—Milly, you'd better leave th grubben an come green-hunten with me," and she smiled again at Nunn, a pleased smile like that of a woman finished planting a rare seed in fertile soil where she is certain it will grow.

Chapter Sixteen

THE WEATHER CONTINUED bleak and cold and unlike April, and the mash barrel, like the growing things, seemed killed of all its growth and stood lifeless in the cold, then slowly it began to glug and smell, a sour yeasty smell that it seemed to Nunn a body could almost taste. When he mixed it he had hoped for a spell of warm weather that would quickly bring it to full glugging and then the silence that would tell it was ready for stilling, but in the unnaturally cool weather the barrel, as if through sheer perversity, took its time.

By May 1 it seemed as if the mash had been souring since Christmas; each time Nunn laid his ear against it the closest thing to a prayer he ever made was in his heart that the blamed thing would be silent and he could get the business of stilling over with, but always he could hear subdued growls and gluggings, and whistlings that made him think of the insides of a foundered cow. And day by day the smell grew stronger. He wanted so much to be rid of the smell that he was tempted at times to feed the whole mess to Rosie and her pigs.

On days when the sun was hot and the east wind stilled, he would pause at his work in a sweat of cold fear that the wind would change and carry the stink up the valley to John's, and always he expected Milly or one of the children, who he tried to keep out of the storehouse field as much as possible, to ask what it was that smelled so.

At other times it didn't seem to matter; he would feel certain that his family and the neighbors knew. At the post office Samuel's cold blue eyes searched over his face

220

as they searched for sinners in church, and John, who was always cross through the spring rush of work because his old legs ached and he couldn't work as he had used to, seemed surly and short-worded with him, hardly caring to speak.

Late one mail-day afternoon he walked down the hill as far as the Tiller turning with Blare and Joe C. They had been uncommon friendly of late, giving him a mess of fish from their baskets in the river; and one day, when they passed through the sandfield, they lent a hand in the corn planting, for their little half-turned hillside patches were long since planted.

At parting, Blare asked with the sly narrow-eyed smile of his mother, "How's yer business, Nunn?"

"I could use a little rain. Th taters are beginnen to hurt."

"You won't need to worry over a tater patch if yer business turns out all right," Joe C. said, with an emphasis on the word "business."

Blare gave him a slap on the back and said with a laugh, "Man, you don't need rain. A good cold spring's better'n tubs a rain water—you oughta know that."

"This uncommon cold weather's kind a slowed things up," Joe C. said, with no teasing, but seriouslike and friendly. He added with a wink that seemed to say, you're my blood brother. "Now, if'n you need any help, let me know."

Nunn went slowly home. It had come to a pretty pass when the Tillers were giving him advice, and worse than their advice was their brotherly concern.

Supper that night was lard gravy, water corn pone, boiled cowpeas seasoned with lard and fried potatoes; from the size of the slices he knew Milly was about to the bottom of the pile—she always used the big ones first—and the condensed milk and cans of dog feed on the high shelf were almost gone. No need to ask Milly if she was out of canned stuff—she wouldn't set a lean meal like this because she was too lazy to put it on the table.

Suse, who was brown and thin and stringy from the corn planting, stirred up a plateful of cowpea soup with corn bread, took a few small bites and burst out in a kind of tired anger, "I wisht to God we had some meat or somethen."

"Quit that bad talk an be thankful you've got grub to

go in your belly," Milly answered, and added more kindly, "We'll have lettuce and reddishes an greens an new taters pretty soon."

"Meat would be good," Nunn said, and wished for butter or good gravy or something to go with the hard corn pone.

"Kill us a mutton, Pop," Suse said. "You said t'other day that big old fat black-faced ewe wasn't goen to find no lambs that you could tell."

"Th meat frum that big ole thing'd spile fore we'd eat it," Milly said. "I could can it, though—I ain't never had no trouble keepen sausage meat—that is," she went on, "if'n Samuel's got any jar rubbers this time a year. You allus have to have new rubbers to keep stuff like meat an green beans."

"The weather's dry—why don't you slice it thin an try dryen it like it tells about in one of them government bulletins . . . an like th Indians used to dry deer?"

"Shit-fire . . . who ever heared a eaten dried mutton? What ud folks say?" Milly wanted to know.

"Jesus God, Mom," Suse burst out, "you worry more over what that old Sue Annie Tiller thinks than about God."

"God don't go a tellen tales, an anyhow I'll bet th ole bitch sees more'n God," Lee Roy said.

"Shut up that trashy talk, youngens," Nunn roared, as he jumped up from the table, though he had eaten but little. "Suse, I'll limb you fer sassen your mom. . . . Where's that bulletin on mutton-dryen anyhow?"

"Beef," Suse said.

"Aw, Nunn," Milly said, pushing Vinie's nose out of her lap, "if it don't spile, we cain't never eat th stuff."

"It ud make dog feed. Sam an Vinie need to chew on somethen, an we ain't got no bones."

"That ole black-faced ewe'd have plenty a bones an vitamins, too," Suse said as she went off to hunt the bulletin.

But Nunn was not interested in bones and only pretended to read the bulletin; he was thinking of smoke and fire, any excuse for smoke and fire in the storehouse. He had already fixed up the lard-can cooker, cutting a hole in the middle of the tight-fitting cover to receive the piece of copper pipe, and had gathered a good-sized pile of dry hickory wood; for sound, well seasoned hickory made but little smoke. Next day was Saturday, and early he sent Lee Roy and Suse out to get the black-faced ewe and put her under the storehouse, where he would feed her corn and fodder for a few days, he told them. But when he laid his ear against the mash barrel that night, it was almost silent and the capping was going down; he straightened and looked at it and drew a long breath, like a man gathering himself for a leap into icy, dangerous waters.

Next morning the barrel was silent and the beer was still and blue. He hurried back to the house, and assuming a jovial air he did not feel, told Milly to work up a big appetite, for she'd have mutton by dinnertime.

"But it's Sunday, Nunn," she complained. "It's bad luck to work on Sunday. An it's meeten day at church an Samuel ull think hard on us, none a comen to hear him preach an it a pretty Sunday."

Nunn pushed back his hat and considered; a pretty Sunday was a dangerous time to start anything. If Milly and the youngens all went to meeten, Milly would be apt, as usual, to bring anywhere from five to thirty Tillers and Cramers and Cookseys home with her for dinner, as she often did on summer Sundays; on the other hand, there was just a chance she and the youngens might go home for dinner with Sue Annie and stay gossiping till dark—that would be fine—but as he considered the matter he thought there was a still bigger chance that Milly would entice a crowd home on promises of fresh mutton, and that would be bad, especially if Sue Annie happened to be in the crowd: she'd sit all afternoon in the wind from the storehouse, sniffing.

"You'uns can miss meeten day once," he said and went off to butcher the ewe.

The ewe was fine and fat as could be, and when he and Lee Roy carried Milly the liver and back bones and a hind quarter for cooking fresh, she was pleased as a child with candy at Christmas; he realized for the first time that she had been craving meat bad, and felt almost lighthearted as he went about his work. If things worked out all right, she wouldn't crave meat any more; he'd have money for side meat and fresh beef even.

After a good dinner of fried mutton and gravy, he began the tedious work of cutting the still warm meat into thin slices for drying. He had hoped Milly and the young-ens would stay at the house, but when the dishes were washed they came in a body. Fortunately, he was on the eastern side of the storehouse in the shade—and leeward of the smell—but once Milly stopped stringing the thin slices on a piece of trotline and wrinkled her nose, sniffing toward the storehouse. "Nunn, I've been aimen to ask you, what is that a stinken so? Two, three times I've noticed it . . . an didn't know where it was comen from, an it's th storehouse. Ain't you noticed?" and she got up as if to go see.

Nunn's mind jumped frantically for some excuse to send her home and keep her there. "I hadn't noticed," he said. "It's mebbe that government fertilizer. . . . It's funny stuff, allus stinken. An I had some meal fer th little lambs under th winder an th rain blowed it an it got wet. . . . Mebbe it's spiled."

"Aw, Nunn, a letten good meal spile. . . . Spread it in th sun an it could mebbe be saved fer hog feed; lemme see," and she laid down the string of mutton.

Lee Roy, washing meat in cold spring water, looked up. "Mom, last night when I took this black-faced ewe some corn I seed a chicken snake, long as a fence rail an thick as my head, hangen all in loops on one a them crosspieces in under the store; it's mebbe up above now, an it'd skeer you to death," and Lee Roy looked up at his mother, his eyes solemn, almost sad, the concerned eyes of a worried man.

Milly flushed and sat down quickly as she asked, "Whyn't you kill it, Son?"

"They's nothen better to git rats," he said.

Milly said nothing, but glanced furtively at Suse; her two oldest knew she was in the family way even before she was far enough along to show; she wondered what they thought and how they felt about a new one in the family —and how they knew. A body didn't want their youngens knowing; it made them feel ashamed somehow.

Nunn, too, glanced at Lee Roy with an uneasy glance; Lee Roy was quick to notice things like Suse, but never once had he or Suse mentioned the smell—maybe they knew what was inside the storehouse and never let on. Aye, God, once let him out of this tricky mess and he'd never try again.

He made the vow all over again when dark came and he was alone with his stilling. Milly, who was deathly afraid of fire, had consented to his staying; but in spite of Lee Roy's chicken snake she had wanted to come back after supper and keep him company and help. But she had already helped more than she knew. He had long worried about water, cold water for cooling the worm, and knew that through the night he would have to carry many bucketfuls. But at milking time here came Suse and Lee Roy with the washtubs and water buckets. Mom had been afraid the storehouse would catch fire and had told them to fill the tubs and set them by the door. Nunn thought the tubs ought to be inside, and let the children hand him buckets of cold spring water which he poured into the tubs, though the place was by now so full of smoke a body could see or smell little.

When the children had gone, he began dipping the thick stinking beer, pouring it through a feed-sack-strainer cloth into the cooker until it was three-fourths full. He set it on the iron framework, blew up the fire, and threw on some of his seasoned hickory. While the beer was heating he put on the lid, shoved the bent end of the copper pipe into the hole, wrapped the connection round and round with rags, then chinked the whole with clay so that no steam could escape; he arranged his two tubs so that a bend of the copper pipe fell into each, then set a half-gallon fruit jar under the down-hanging end of the pipe and squatted, waiting, curiosity as to just what the contraption would do overpowering at times his ever present fears of being seen by some of the neighbors or that the thing wouldn't work at all.

A drop of hottish grease hit the back of his neck and he sprang up with an oath; he had forgotten the drying mutton, and with the dry hickory in full blast the stuff was frying instead of drying. He untied the trotlines and was hanging them on a rafter further from the fire, when a furious glugging and hissing made him look around He dropped the mutton and sprang to the cooker. The fire had got too hot, steam and liquor were spurting up around the connection, more was escaping around the edges of the lid, which seemed ready to blow off at any minute, and instead of a thin clear trickle, yellowish, bubbling beer was foaming into the jar at the end of the worm. Worse yet, where the wild stuff touched the fire, there was only a faint hiss, then a blue flame leaped up. Nunn stared a second stupidly and thought that if the stuff would burn like that, what would it do to a man's insides; then, as the blue flames leaped almost to the top of the lard can, he threw water from the cooling tubs onto the fire. Steam flew up and nigh scalded him, and for a little while the storehouse was such a fog of steam and wet smoke he had to open the door for his very breath.

Impatient as he was to get through, it seemed hours before the cooker had cooled enough to take the top off and pour back the half-stilled stuff that had run into the fruit jar. In the meantime he rearranged the meat, dipped the water out of the tubs, and made trips to the spring for fresher, cooler water.

He was at last able to put the cooker on again, and this time he kept the fire low and was soon rewarded with quick drops which at times amounted to a trickle of liquor clear as the clearest spring water; had it been ever so faintly yellowish or milky, he would have had to still all over again, for he and his neighbors would drink nothing but clear moonshine. Even a faint trace of color could mean dangerous bad doctoring.

He wished to God he had a thump keg, but Andy Hollars over in Alcorn had never had a thump keg, and Nunn did as he had always done. He filled each jar half full; the first half jar was so strong that even a cautious sniff burned his nose and made his eyes water, but in spite of his troubles, he pushed his hat back and smiled in gratification when he tasted the beginnings of the fifth half jar of the first cooking; it had plenty of burn yet, but with it there was a smoothness and a kindness to the tongue not to be found in any of the sugar moon he had bought lately. He thought the goodness came partly from the wasp-stuffed honey and partly from the good homemade sprouted corn malt he had used.

The last and eighth half jar from the boiler was weak as toddy water for a colicky baby, and he pondered a moment, wondering if he had stilled too low; and sure enough, when he took the boiler off for emptying, washing, and refilling, there was only a little thickish settlings in the bottom—but then he had heard some say that old J. D. stilled until his boiler puckered at the seams from dryness.

He strained out more beer and refilled the cooker and felt a little less worried about the whole mess when he saw that when this second cooking was finished he would be half through, for most of the stuff left now in the barrel was a thick sediment of meal, cowfeed, and honeycomb. He would get what he was supposed to get, sixteen half-gallon jars of liquor from a barrel of mash; it was only the dishonest who weakened with water, then strengthened with carbide, ivy juice, or lye, who got more.

The second lard can full cooked off with little difficulty; he had learned that it took only a little fire to bring off the first strong stuff, but as it gradually grew weaker the fire must be hotter, until the last weak half jar needed a fire almost hot enough to boil water. This time he put the weak half jar of the first cooking under first and filled it, so that it was half the weakest and half the strongest, then on up the line, so that the first strong half should get the last weak half. But the jars filled slowly, like watching a sugar tree fill a bucket with sap, and if he tried to hurry the work and built the fire up even a little, the cooker would start sputtering around the pipe and along the edges of the lid, and he would have to stuff more rags down with the tip of his pocket knife, his eyes smarting with smoke, blisters popping out on his hands, and his face hot and prickly from the steaming it had got when the boiler overflowed.

Now and then he looked at the mutton, and it was drying nicely, curling up and turning a grayish brown like a weather-seasoned oak shingle and about as hard.

The little stars above the creek gap were dimming out and fading as if to give the morning star full room in the sky when he had filled the eighth jar and set the cooker off to cool. He looked off toward the house, but it was black and silent in the gray valley; after another glance at the east, he rinsed out the cooker, filled it again, and saw with a kind of tired delight that there would be only one more cooking. God willing, he would be done by dinnertime that day.

Before the third batch was finished, Milly sent Lee Roy with a cup of hot coffee and word to let his fire die down and come eat breakfast. As soon as it was light, Nunn had locked the door as a precaution against the children, but much to his relief Lee Roy knocked without trying the latch and did not try to look through the windows and made no comment when Nunn sent back word to Milly that he didn't want any breakfast, only to send him a little more coffee. He put green hickory twigs around the edges of the fire and made a great smoke, so that if anybody should come looking through the windows, they would see nothing but smoke.

It might have been ten o'clock; the sun was high and the dew dried and his last cooking was just going on the fire when there came a subdued and breathless calling at the door, "Nunn, Nunn, lemme in—hurry up."

He recognized Sue Annie's voice and with a whispered oath hurried to the door and opened it part way. "You cain't git in fer all this meat smoke an enyhow Milly's at th—"

She darted under his arm, pushed the door shut behind her, and leaned against it panting. He stared at her: corn and pumpkin seed with beans mixed in her tucked-up apron, her white head rag, always so smooth and low on her brow, jerked back at a crooked tipsy angle, showing streaks of sweat-soaked hair; she was bare-footed and a long briar scratch across one ankle was bleeding.

After his first addled surprise he began trying to open the door and at the same time keep between her and the cooker. "Sue Annie, I've got sich a meat-dryen smoke, you'll smother—git outside," he begged.

She drew a long quivering breath and her black eyes were soft with a troubled sorrow that usually came only when she watched over a bad sick child or with a woman in the last hellish hours of a slow childbirth. She shook her head and leaned against the door for support and said without looking at him, "Nunn—honey, everbody in th country knows what you're up to—an th law it knows, too—an it's come."

She heard his sharply indrawn breath, but when he said nothing, only looked into her face, searching for her eyes that he could not find, she went on in a beseeching but breathless whine, "Three of 'em—somebody's told—but, Nunn, honey, I'd swear it on a stack a Bibles high as th veneer-mill chimneys, it wasn't me."

"No, all you done was tell it all over so's somebody else could tell th law," he said, and drew a deep breath, surprised that the thing he had sweated and shivered over and lost sleep on had come and that he felt less terror than the night he had ground the sprouted corn; more than fear was his anger, an anger like a boil in his insides that wanted to burst but could not and so would burst him; he had done no wrong; he had neither stolen nor coveted nor fornicated; he had broken none of the Ten Commandments—but he could be locked up in the Federal penitentiary for God knows how many years.

Sue Annie was wiping the sweat from her forehead, straightening her head rag, and getting back her breath. Soon her tongue was its nimble self again as words poured out in an unbroken stream. She'd been out planting a roasting ear and cornfield bean patch when here came Andy Hull loping one of his dad's mules as it had never been loped in its life, riding it hames, collar, trace chains, and all.

Her first thought was that his mother was taken with a miscarriage, and when he swung into her road gate, near knocking it off its hinges, she dropped the hoe and ran to meet him, bare feet, seed corn, and beans.

She paused to wipe her sweaty forehead and adjust her headcloth a shade before going on with the story. Andy had been plowing corn close to the house when he saw what he thought was a government truck drive up to the post office; three men dressed like national-forest men in boots and khaki clothes got out; first they knocked on the post-office door, and when nobody answered, they went knocking at the front house door. Andy went for the water bucket on the porch; he drank slow and he listened when the men spoke to his mother, for his father had gone to a wedding in Alcorn—God, but preachers had it easy.

Where, they said, did Nunnely D. Ballew live, and could a body drive a car down; government business, it was, they said; he lived on the Big South Fork, they knew, but they didn't know just how to get there. A young tall man did the talking, but it was another one that stood still and didn't say a word; the sun flashed on the badge he wore and on the leather, polished like a looking-glass, of his two pistol holders and on the pistol handles, steel and blue—he was a middling-to-little man with hat pulled down on his eyes.

Ruth Hull couldn't do a thing for a minute but look at that man's badge and his pistol handles, like a bird at a snake's eyes. She looked at Andy and her face was pure white and she swallowed and she said in a low voice, her hands all shaking, "It's a fair piece," she says, "over th hill an around; you could drive in but not handy out," she says. "Go on down th big road, an you'll see a gate past a big old slack pile by a old mine mouth," she says, "that's th Tiller place, an they'll point th rest a th way out," she says.

And Ruth looked at the man's badge, and she looked into Andy's eyes over the dipper rim and she didn't say a word—but Andy never finished that dipper a water; he went back to his mule and plowed his furrow to the back of the field, laid down the rail fence and galloped to her—she stopped for breath and looked at Nunn like a person just awakening from the trance of her own story. "Shit-fire, man, what a you a standen here fer? Git on, honey, git on into Alcorn—break the lock on Joe C.'s boat an go—they may find yer still but they cain't find you."

"An leave em go to Milly an skeer her to death—she's in no shape to be skeered."

Sue Annie's professional interest in Milly's condition, of which she had not known, only suspected, for an instant outweighed her concern for Nunn. "Jesus God, it's liable to make her miscarry." She shook her head darkly. "Th law a comen into this valley where it ain't never been before's a goin to be bad—them that's got little babies ull be so skeered their milk'ull cause colic, an them in th family way'll miscarry over fretten on marken their youngens—I hope to God pore Ruth ain't in th family way."

She remembered the cause of the possible miscarriage and caught Nunn by the shoulder. "Git, honey, git before it's everlastenly too late; I left Dave a setten by th gate—he'll direct em th long way round by th big road—you'll have plenty a time to git clean into Alcorn."

Nunn pulled her hands from his shoulders. "Listen, I ain't no Lonzo Cramer to be a runnen frum th law. Let em come. Somebody told, an th first time I come back home they'd tell agin."

"That good-fer-nothen tale-bearer Rans Cramer it was," Sue Annie said, and begged him again to go. "Let Milly talk to em. She could talk good, fer she's th onliest one in th whole country that don't know."

Nunn shook his head, staring through the barred windows; the sunlight fell through and the shadows of the bars fell across his body, and he felt them cold and hard and heavy on his heart.

Sue Annie saw it was no good and sighed heavily and looked outside at Aunt Marthie's maple trees. "I was on hand at your bornen, Nunn, an a hard time your mammy had—an when I was a little slip of a girl my mammy borned your daddy an sent me on th riverbanks to hunt walink fer him—an, Nunn, you've been like my own born youngen to me—an you're a standen there now a thinken I told an I didn't—everbody knowed." Her old eyes begged him hard. "Oh, Nunn, I cain't stand an see you tuck away by th law. Aunt Marthie Jane ud turn over in her grave," and Sue Annie's face was old and sad and her hard black eyes were soft and gray with tears, like limestone rocks in a spring rain.

Nunn grunted; it would serve the loose-tongued old devil right if she had to stand and see him shot. "Aunt Marthie, pore soul . . . has already turned so much she's wore th corners off her grave an a little more turnen won't hurt her."

"Oh, God, Nunn," Sue Annie said and walked over to the cooker, already beginning to hiss again. "Well," she said, "you're a smoken mutton so you'd better be a smoken mutton. . . . Hep me lift this contraption off'n th fire an we'll put on a lot a wet wood an build up sich a smoke they can't see their hands afore their faces. . . ."

He helped her, not much caring what she did; it didn't matter.

"If it was jist cold," she lamented, "we could hide ever last thing. Nunn, honey, when you stillen you ought to keep a passel a hogs handy. . . . In a pinch they can eat ever last bite." She peered into the mash barrel. "These squeezens now, we could feed'em right to Rosie an her pigs if they was handy, an liquor . . . it can be easy hid."

"I need a drink," he said and picked up the middle jar of the first eight half gallons he had stilled and took a long slow swallow.

"They'll smell it, Nunn," Sue Annie said, sniffing inquisitively at the jar.

"I'll stand an blow my breath in their faces an they'll fergit to look in th storehouse," Nunn said.

"Mind if I take a little sip, Nunn? It smells right good," Sue Annie said.

"Help yourself," he said.

Sue Annie took a slow but long swallow, and when she had finished she stood holding the half-gallon jar in her two hands appraising it with tilted head and a little smile. "Why, Nunn, fer th first try you've done good, real good. How'd you make it, honey?"

"By th special Nunnely D. Ballew recipe . . . secret," he said.

"A body can tell it's strong, powerful strong," Sue Annie said, "but it's smooth, curious smooth. . . . And it's like I told Dave," she went on after a little pause, "he's been wanten some whisky to steep poke root in fer his rheumatism; it'll be safe, I said. No carbide er ivy . . . a body could give it to a newborn baby er a woman when she's bornen her baby." She took another sip, slow but somewhat longish and set the jar down, but continued to look at it, rubbing her nose reflectively with the back of her hand. "Nunn, honey, don't you think it ud be a pity fer all this to git broke up . . . Raiders allus break ever jar they can find."

Nunn, busy in the back of the storehouse throwing shreds of last winter's corn fodder over the cooker, stopped and looked in her direction with a sly, almost gay look. "Sue Annie, I bet you come a thinken I'd let you carry it all off fer nothen, jist to be shet of it."

Sue Annie unscrewed the lid on a jar and sniffed. "Now Nunn, you know I ain't no person to take advantage of a body when they're in deep trouble like you are. . . . Which is a middle jar, Nunn? I allus think they're th best . . . that is, where a body ain't got no thump keg."

Nunn came over and made a clicking noise with his tongue. "Sue Annie, Sue Annie, a comen to a blind pig in your old age—it's your mammy's turn now to turn over in her grave."

"Aw, Nunn," Sue Annie, said, picking up two half-gallon jars, "I been a wanten some good safe whisky fer my doctoren fer months—I never did trust J. D.'s—an Dave he wants some, too." She set the jars down, reached in the bosom of her dress, and pulled up a tobacco sack, fastened by strings tied to a large safety pin in her underbody. "Lucky thing I allus carry my money with me," and added as she fished out a five-dollar bill, "I recken you'll charge the same as J. D.—$7 a gallon."

"Hell, no—$7 is what he charges fer fifth-run sugar moon—this is so close to genuine bottled in bond it's worth $15—but sean as how I'll mebbe not git to sell it all, I'll make it to you fer $8."

"You ought to be glad to give it away," Sue Annie complained, but slowly brought out three $1 bills.

"If they find that on you a goen home, I'll give you your money back," Nunn said as Sue Annie picked up the jars and started for the door.

She giggled. "I've got plenty a time; city fellers like them, it'll take em more'n a hour to git here a comen around th big road th way Dave'ull direct em." Full realization of Nunn's predicament engulfed her again. "Nunn, honey, you ain't a goen to stand an let em take you—it'll go hard—whisky, mash barrel, squeezens, cooker, an all. Git, fer God's sake, git. Think a Milly."

"That's what I am a thinken on."

"But, Nunn, if'n you run away an git safe into Alcorn, th law cain't go a chasen you ferever."

"That's where you're wrong, Sue Annie," a man's voice said, and John's black felt hat and sweat-soaked shoulders could be seen dimly through the smoke on the other side of the barred front window.

"Ruth Hull must ha sent him word," Sue Annie said, and clasping the jars, one in the crook of either arm, she hurried to open the door.

John's face was red and streaked with sweat and his eyes were troubled, and he had the look of a man, unused to running, who had run a long way. He leaned against Aunt Marthie's dry-goods counter and fanned the smoke away from his face with his hat, squinting through it at Nunn, who had not yet covered the cooker to his satisfaction.

"Listen, Nunn," he spoke quickly between rapidly drawn breaths, "don't run—that's th worstest thing you can do—I'll go your bond—it ain't like you was a hardened criminal—an whatever you do, man, don't try to fight; it's no good—three to your one."

"I ain't a runnin," Nunn said, "an I ain't a fighten—I keep a hopen I can mebbe fool em with all this smoke."

John shook his head. "Aye, Lord, man, cain't hope to

stop a bull with a red bed sheet jist cause he'll run after a red rag." He looked at the row of filled half-gallon jars, "Man—man if you was so hard up it's come to this I could a lent you th money. I don't hold by sich—more'n once since you started th business I've laid off to have my say to you—but it wasn't none a my business."

"That's right," Nunn said.

John's eyes flared with anger. "It's not right. Me an you is th onliest ones left with th name a Ballew in th country. It has allus been a honorable name." He shook his head sadly. "Th first time in th mem'ry a man th law's ever come to th valley an it's come fer a Ballew."

Nunn winced; John spoke the truth; his words, unlike Sue Annie's, could hurt. But before God he wouldn't show it, no more than he would show he was afraid; not before Sue Annie, and have the old rattle-tongue tell, when he was away in the jailhouse, that he'd been scared so bad the law had to drag him away on his knees. His youngens might have a lot of talk thrown in their faces, everything from bare feet and patched rags to a worthless moonshining daddy, but nobody would be able to say, and speak the truth, that he had been afraid. The smoke was getting so thick John was beginning to cough, and his own eyes smarted but he hated to go outside—it was the last thing he might do of his own free will, go outside.

John went over and picked up a jar of whisky. "No need, I recken, to ask if'n it's safe—I know you ain't gone all th way on th road to hell."

"I wouldn't be too certain," Nunn said, and added, "I cain't say it's pure corn like they used to make in th old days—but it ain't pure sugar moon neither. I'd say take it an age it a little while in a white oak keg and it ud be right good."

John unscrewed a jar and sniffed. "Smells all right." He reached down in an overall pocket, brought out his long wallet. "Mary ain't had nothen safe to use fer medicine since our oldest boy brought her a quart a bottled in bond frum Lexington. How much?"

"Eight dollars a gallon, but how'll you git it home? Th law's a comen around th big road; you could run smack into em about th creek crossen."

"They ain't had time," Sue Annie said, but looked a little anxious. "I'd better be a gitten on. I don't want a be seen neither, not barefooted like this."

Nunn tried to draw a deep breath; the smoke was so thick he could hardly breathe or see; it was time to go outside. But John lingered with his jars, looking into his face, as if he would read what he would do. "Listen, Nunn, you act like you was in a fighten humor—feelen like everthing's up an not given a damn—well, don't try to fight. If'n you've got a gun on, take it off. Recollect them," and he nodded toward the house where Suse could be heard singing "Round the Canebrake."

"I'll come into Town an go yer bond, an I'll see that Milly an th youngens don't need fer nothen; an Nunn," he went on, speaking in the slow solemn deacon's voice he used in church, "you make up your mind that when this is all over you're a goen to give your heart to God an settle down—it's th onliest way to live. I never prospered till I learned to live with God."

Nunn drew a long breath, remembering the cause of his troubles; God and King Devil couldn't go together. "I promise," he said, "when I've caught that red fox."

John looked at him with sorrow. "Oh, Nun, that fox'ull never be took—you'll let him lead your soul eternal straight to hell."

"That's what I figger sometimes," Nunn said, and added as he cut a chew of tobacco for his dry mouth, "I've heared say that a lot of men sells their souls to th devil, an if I foller a red fox to hell it won't be so different. An sometimes," he went on, speaking with a seriousness he had not meant to uncover, "I wonder would God have my soul."

Sue Annie, who had listened respectfully but impatiently to the churchlike talk, rushed to the door. "I've got to be a gitten, Nunn; luck to ye," and in a lower voice, "I still think you'd better run."

She went outside and around the storehouse, and headed for the thick growth of brush between the creek and the field, so as to be hidden as quickly as possible.

Nunn held the door open for John, then lingered a moment looking about him. He saw the water bucket and dipper and picked them up; he might take them back to the house or he might go around to the sheep spring; it would be hard to stand still under Aunt Marthie's silver maple trees. He wished John would go; he wanted to

meet the law alone, but the old man was fumbling with the
screw caps on his whisky jars; tightening them hard with
the caution he gave to all things.

Nunn glanced idly toward the big barn and saw, not
walking Preacher Will's road as expected, but in the middle of the field, as if, like Sue Annie, they had cut over the
hill, three men in the knee-deep sagegrass, and on one, the
last, polished pistol holders caught the sun and glittered,
mirrorlike.

Sue Annie's jars as she walked around the storehouse
had caught the sun like that; where was Sue Annie anyhow? While John stood all unknowing by the door, fiddling
with his jar caps, the law was walking up on him, and in a
minute Sue Annie would run into it. He hurried to the corner of the storehouse around which Sue Annie had gone;
she was just leaving the lower corner.

He called to her softly twice before she heard, and
when she finally did turn and look at him she did not
understand, though he pointed to the field and shook his
head. Another step carried her out of the shelter of the
storehouse wall. She stopped then, so suddenly she came
near falling backward with her effort not to go forward.
After an instant of motionless staring, she whirled and ran
back up to him. "Take these quick," she begged, holding
out the jars.

Nunn shook his head. "They ain't mine no more, an
anyhow they ain't time to unlock th storehouse an hide
em."

Sue Annie breathed hard; sweat popped out between
her bare toes and made blobs of wetness on her dusty feet.
"Take em, Nunn, take em," she begged, her arms trembling so that the jars threatened to fall.

"Here," he said, and grabbed the water bucket and put
the two jars into it. John was staring at them in wonder.
Nunn grabbed his jars, too; one he laid in Sue Annie's
tucked-up apron, the other on her arm. "Now git to th
sheep spring," he whispered; "you're a goen fer a bucket a
water."

"They'll see me," she whimpered.

"If'n you hurry an cut acrost in front uv em, they'll see
nothen but your back an th water bucket. Git."

Sue Annie went, her knees shaking, her body twisted
sideways with her effort not to show what she carried. For

a little space the sheep-spring path led almost directly in front of the men, then it turned up the hill and around, and Sue Annie was following it, the men not noticing.

The two in front had turned their backs to the sun and in the shade thus made were unfolding a curious-looking paper; they bent to study it, one man searching with his finger. The man with the badge and the guns had also stopped a few steps behind, but instead of a paper, he searched the hills, his head turning slowly as his eyes went from point to point; and at last it seemed he found the smoke-spouting storehouse most interesting and looked longest in that direction.

Nunn looked at him, then away to the curving shoulders of the hills, pure green now with the pale tender green of middle spring. He would miss the hills; and something of Aunt Marthie came to him, *"I will lift up mine eyes unto the hills, from whence cometh my help."* That wasn't right; maybe for Aunt Marthie but not for him. It was funny not to be afraid—Sue Annie's white-livered terror had seemed funny; he was just mad, mad clean to the bottom of his heart; he had done no wrong; his own corn on his own land.

He wouldn't stand still and wait—he would walk a few steps to meet them as was decent when strangers came. He was walking down Preacher Jim's road, only half conscious of John's calling in a dry whisper, "Don't try to fight em, Nunn."

"Howdy," he called, when he had reached a spot directly above and in front of them.

The man with the pistols was already looking at him and the other two looked up from the paper. "Say, whose place is this?" one of the men asked in a loud friendly kind of voice.

"Nunn Ballew's."

"Nunnely D. Ballew's?"

Nunn nodded—his name spoken like that sounded strange—how did the law know he had a "D" in his name?

"Praise th Lord," the other said and laughed, and Nunn saw they were both young, hardly more than boys. "I'll bet you've been expecting us sooner," the bigger one said, walking on up through the sagegrass.

Nunn was conscious of John's white, fear-tightened face

peering at him, and he tried to put a gay not-give-a-damn
sound in his voice as he answered, "Why, in a way I'd
sooner it had a been later."

The two young men laughed and came, one carrying the
paper still unfolded, but the man with the pistols, who
had not yet spoken, stood still, looking about him. The
other two introduced themselves as Joe Tuttle and Jim Bill
Simpkins, and shook Nunn's hand in quick cordiality and
said they were glad to see him. The one named Joe Tuttle
looked at the big piece of paper and shook his head frowning and Nunn saw it was a map, a curious kind of thing,
with brown wavy lines all over and full of dots and many
little flags of different colors. "Something's all wrong,"
Tuttle said. "This contour map calls for a post office right
about here on your farm; everything lays right by the air
map in the office and it couldn't be wrong. . . . According
to it, this big old barn is right where it belongs."

Nunn nodded with vacant staring eyes and wished he
dared squat down and rest his suddenly water-weak knees
—he didn't know yet about the man with the pistols, but
the two young ones were AAA boys come to measure his
land like he'd heard it said they did, only he'd forgot the
matter.

His tongue seemed numb and stammering while he told
them that if the map were as much as ten years old it
would show a post office: that had been a post office, he
said, pointing; a body could still see the sign around in
front.

They looked at it curiously. "We'd still been on th
way, but we saw smoke through the trees and figured
somebody lived in this direction," Jim Bill, the big one
said, and asked, "Don't you have a shortcut? You don't
go all th way around that wagon road every time you go
to th post office. We had come a good piece down th hill
when we saw an old man—Tiller—an he told us to take
th wagon road. We walked and walked, but by this map
you live straight over th hill—so we cut over."

Nunn shook his head in sympathy. "Uncle Dave Tiller
must be gitten in his second childhood, misdirecten you
so. . . . Why, his wife come down th path not half an
hour ago. I guess, though," he went on with a kindly
tolerance for an old man's lapses, "he thought you all
wanted John Ballew's place. He's kin a mine an lives on

up th valley," and he introduced John, who, unacquainted with the workings of the AAA, came forward with a mystified suspicious air ill becoming a man with almost a thousand acres of land and over a million board feet of timber.

"Him an Miz Tiller," Nunn explained, "smelled my meat-dryen smoke an come to see about buyen some fresh mutton. Did you all ever hear a anybody smoken mutton?" he asked with another quick glance at the man with the pistols, who had not yet said a word, though he was not ten feet from the AAA boys, and listened to the talk with the half-interested air of a chance passerby.

Jim Bill Simpkins showed no surprise at the idea of smoked mutton; his people had used to dry part of a young beef every fall, and in his work he had met a man over in Rockcastle County who dried mutton—cut it in thin strips and dried it until it was like shavings, but the man said it was good.

"I ain't a figgeren on eaten much a this," Nunn said. "I got two young hounds . . . fox hounds . . . an I figgered to try em on it."

"Hounds run good on mutton," the man with the pistols said, and the AAA boys turned and looked at him.

"Why, Pinkney, we forgot all about you. . . . Don't be so timid an scared. This is Pinkney Deegan an he's got a little business down in this country an since he's kind a scary, he come along with us for protection and company," and Joe Tuttle laughed at his own joke.

And grave-eyed Pinkney smiled as he shook hands with Nunn and John. He was a small man, not even as big as Nunn, so that John and the two strapping AAA boys towered above him; but Nunn, looking into his eyes, the even pale blue of a cold March sky, with their small, seeming unnaturally black pupils, knew that here was a man with whom he wanted no quarrel, and it was but seldom he had met a man who gave him such thoughts. He wondered if the slow ever-searching eyes would not read him at a glance and know the meaning of everything —the presence of Sue Annie and John, the smoke from the storehouse, and why the hand he shook was so clammy and cold.

But Pinkney smiled and pushed back his black felt hat, showing hair pale above his tanned forehead, and said

he was sorry to bother Nunn with business that was not
pleasant, but he had wanted to see some law-abiding
farmer with land along the Big South Fork. Had Nunn
ever noticed any blasts that sounded like they might be
dynamite down along the river?

Nunn was so relieved at being certain Pinkney's business did not concern whisky that he almost answered,
"Sure, I've noticed dynamiten lots a times," but then he
remembered that his man was the law; he pushed his hat
back, making a pretense of trying to remember, but trying in reality to read the man, to find out what he was
after: Dynamite shots? The river? The law? Only last
week Lureenie had come carrying Milly a water bucket
of fish and had said in an offhand way that Rans and
one of his young cousins had got a mountain of fish with
just a little dynamite—hell-fire, that was against the law
—he remembered now how he had read in Samuel's
county paper that the law was after fish dynamiters because it was a penitentiary crime; and he had forgot it,
his head was so full of his moonshining trouble. After a
moment he shook his head. "Th river's down in a deep
gulch like, an a body cain't hear nothen goen on down
there less'n they're close to th bluff."

Pinkney nodded, understanding. "I'm a deputy game
warden," he said. "Now, last week a report came to us
through th Alcorn County office that there was dynamiten
in this neighborhood, on this side a th river. . . . Who's
your closest neighbor?"

"John, here, I recken."

"I meant next to th river."

Sue Annie was coming down the spring path, plainly
ashamed of her bare dirty feet, which she was picking up
and putting down in a kind of tiptoeing sideways fashion,
trying to make them as small as possible; and he could
tell by the way she came on, her eyes glued to the men,
her head stuck out like a hungry hen, that though she
was scared, stronger than her shame and her fear was
her curiosity. Sue Annie lived on the river and would
catch on at once that Rans was not to be mentioned.
"Oh, Miz Tiller," he called, lifting his voice a little,
"here's th law wants to have a word with you."

She stiffened, like one struck by a bullet, was stock-still
a moment, then shifted her water bucket to the other

hand, shifted it back again, set it down, and at last, after a moment's troubled smoothing of her apron, picked it up and came on.

"Is that good spring water?" Joe Tuttle asked.

"Oh, Miz Tiller, these men would like a drink . . . a water," Nunn added. Relief made him gay.

"If the good sister's got anything stronger'n water, I'd take it and obliged," Jim Bill Simpkins said.

John gulped and Nunn smiled. "We'd have to wait fer th law here to git on."

Pinkney smiled back. "Mostly deputy raiden's my business, but not today. They're after dynamiters. I'd like to take a fish dynamiter; mean business, dynamiten."

Sue Annie came on with the water and stiffly held out the bucket to Jim Bill. "Where's th dipper, Sue Annie?" Nunn wanted to know.

Sue Annie glanced wildly about, not knowing whether she had lost it in the spring or hidden it with the whisky and seed corn. It was calm Nunn who remembered that she had not taken it at all, and went for it and served his guests with cold spring water, while Sue Annie stood working her bare toes and smoothing her apron, throwing quick apprehensive glances at Pinkney, now at his hat brim, now at his badge, now at his pistol handles. She waited while they all drank, Pinkney taking two full dippers with the slow savoring of a man who loves fresh cold spring water. He wiped his mouth and looked at Sue Annie, searching her face with his flat blue eyes. "You live on th river?"

Sue Annie was visibly relieved. She pointed across the creek toward her cabin. "Not right down on th river, but up on th bluff above."

"Close to the edge?"

"A body could almost throw a rock in frum my garden."

"Do you ever hear any noises . . . like dynamite goen off?"

"Dinnimite?" Sue Annie said, suddenly puzzled and skittish as a horse led into a strange barn in the pitch dark.

Pinkney nodded. "Dynamiten th river fer fish," he said softly, "is a penitentiary offense. . . . Didn't you know that?"

Sue Annie shook her head, staring at him, plainly terrified. John cleared his throat. Nunn fidgeted; he wished to God he hadn't called her—he'd wanted to throw the scent away from Rans, the guilty one, but from the looks of things Sue Annie's Blare and Joe C. were into it, too; maybe even Sue Annie herself. It was plain now that if she said she hadn't heard, Pinkney would take her for a liar, but if she did say—

"I've heared noises," she said, "up th river frum my place . . . could a been dynamiten. . . . I don't know how it sounds, a course. It could a been somebody shooten off a shotgun."

"When?" Pinkney asked.

Sue Annie dropped her head, studying the ground but now and then giving Pinkney swift, terrified glances from under her down-bent brows. "Oh, bout a week ago . . . up around Rans Cramer's."

"Why, Sue Annie, you couldn't hear around th bend," Nunn said.

"Up so high like I am, I could," she said with undue vehemence, and Pinkney, disregarding Nunn's interruption, remarked, "Rans Cramer . . . he was in the country jail fer drinken an disturben th peace about a year back. . . . Where does he live?"

"Around from my house a piece," Nunn said, "right peaceable feller . . . works on the WPA."

"Up th river?" Pinkney asked, and when Nunn nodded, he added in a kind of careless way, as if it didn't matter, but somehow a body felt it did, "They've been doen a lot of blasten on this new WPA road . . . with dynamite."

Nobody said anything and Pinkney was still, chewing a straw and staring past Nunn toward the house. Suddenly his face lighted, his eyes friendly, warm almost. "A blonde," he said, "mighty nigh pure blonde; no wonder Lias Higginbottom—he's my neighbor—wanted her bad."

Nunn looked behind him and there was Vinie, a big girl now, strolling inquisitively in their direction. She stopped when everybody turned and looked at her, but when they all started toward her she did not bark or make any unladylike display of emotion, but stood, tail and head lifted, poised lightly on her toes as if she would fly. The sprinkling of red gold dust on top of her head sparkled in the morning sun.

"She is a pretty thing, now," Pinkney said again.

"Pretty," Nunn said, "but I'm wondering if she'll eat my dried mutton. It's like oak chips," he said and tried not to hurry as he led the men past the old storehouse, their eyes on nothing but Vinie.

"Grind it up an mix it with a little meal," Pinkney said and talked of his own four hounds—not such great hunters—two Trigs and two Julys—but they had the prettiest tongues; he'd rather sit and listen to foxhounds than hear the finest band or choir was ever made. But he got quickly back to business and thought he'd go look along the river and see what he could see. The AAA boys had to be at their work of looking over fields; they wished Mr. Ballew could come along.

Mr. Ballew shook his head and wished again they'd come a little sooner or a little later; he'd like to show them over his place but he couldn't handy leave his meat-smoking fire—dry as it was it would be a dangerous bad thing to do—the AAA boys agreed he ought not to get out of sight of it.

"My boy could go," Nunn said and looked toward the house, and Lee Roy stepped out of some bushes a few feet above the road; his hair was slicked back and he had on his shoes and a clean shirt, but Nunn wished he wouldn't act so solemnlike and bashful, like a little scared rabbit caught in a fence corner and not knowing which way to turn.

Lee Roy and the AAA boys never got back from their tour till well past dinnertime and Pinkney was even later; he had walked up the river a piece, swung around and had come back by Rans's path through the garden; Nunn wondered somewhat uneasily if he had stopped at Rans's place but did not ask.

Milly called dinner right away and at the table the AAA boys talked to Nunn about farming; praised the way his grass and clover even in the burned-over un-plowed ground was coming on and said that though it would take years to build the place back to anything like it had been, it would be worth it; put most of it in pasture and keep sheep and cattle.

They praised Milly for the good table she set, all of

homegrown food; and Milly beamed and wanted to give
thanks to God that they had come at such a lucky time
when there was fresh mutton to fry, still enough Irish
potatoes for a mountain of mashed potatoes with cream
gravy—real gravy. The cans of condensed milk Nunn
had saved back in case the pups got off their feed went
into that gravy. She pulled the first lettuce of the season
for a big bowl of slaw; she put all the youngens to hunting all over the house, under the beds and in all odd
boxes and corners for canned goods, and sure enough,
they found some quince preserves sweetened with honey
that even the silent Pinkney declared were wonderful and
a half-gallon jar of wild strawberries; but the strangest
thing of all was the sugar, about a third of a ten-pound
sack right in front of her on the high self behind th
carbide light—how could anybody overlook sugar like that
—and so she made a strawberry cobbler with egg dip
made from another can of condensed milk.

It was a good dinner, even Sue Annie said so, and the
men ate heartily. It was during dinner that Pinkney recollected the word he was to bring Nunn. "I almost forgot,"
he said. "Lias Higginbottom said tell you he has a new
schoolteacher . . . a nice good girl . . . smart, fresh out
of college."

Nunn looked surprised and Suse, brash and bold as always, in spite of the three strange men, said, "Oh,
goody," and had little sense for the rest of the day.

Chapter Seventeen

THE WEATHER CONTINUED dry through sheep-shearing time, and men began to shake their heads and say it would be a bad crop year. Though the dry weather and the uncommon strangeness of the wind in coming so long from the east would ordinarily have been topics worth full hours of conversation on mail-waiting afternoons, they were now picked up and examined briefly, then dropped as one drops a not too curious stone when there are jewels to be weighed and hefted and looked into.

Nunn's moonshining caused little of the talk; his success or failure at the business had for the past several weeks been the object of much speculation, but there was nothing out of the ordinary in a man making a little run and selling it when he was short of cash. True, the Ballews no more than the Hulls had ever done such things, but Nunn was Nunn, not John; a body could never tell what he would do—he had been a strange one to stick so long in the mines and marry a wife whose grandparents could have been crazy for all he knew—he had never seen them, and it was risky business for a man to take a woman whose grandparents were stranger to his kin; but Nunn was lucky—Milly had turned out all right.

And so had the whisky business—for Nunn. Strange times when the law walks past a man stilling full blast to look at some half-rotten fish killed by a man with no thought for breaking laws or making money. At mention of fish Uncle Ansel Anderson would shake his cane and roar: God made the fish free in that river—true, it wasn't exactly right to dynamite and kill all the baby fish, but Rans had neighbors, the only ones by right con-

cerned—the law had no business to come meddling—
like the AAA and a lot of other foolishness it had come
in on the graded gravel—the first time the law was ever
in the valley and it took the graded gravel to bring it;
the graded gravel was at the bottom of it all—it would
bring nothing but sin and wickedness; and if Nunn Ballew had never joined the AAA the law most like would
never have come—it wouldn't have known who to come
to or how to get there; and Rans Cramer, he wasn't much,
but he was a man; he wouldn't have had to run away to
Cincinnati and leave his wife and family.

But Samuel, who had a hard heart in many matters,
would declare it was a good thing Rans had to leave;
right off he'd got a job, a real job in Cincinnati paying
forty-five cents an hour; none of your WPA charity work,
as Lureenie liked to brag as she came freshly starched
and ironed to the post office for her letters from Rans;
there was not always a letter, but Lureenie would walk
away proudheaded as she came, nobody able to tell
whether she was sad or glad. When she had gone, more
than one would wonder how she made out. Some said
she was better off—Rans's brother Mark came from the
Cow's Horn and cut her some stovewood and sledded
down a load of groceries; for Rans had left so suddenly
he left behind a WPA check due.

There were many, including John, who shook their
heads dourly and declared that Rans could never come
back. Pinkney had found too much evidence: dynamite
caps and part of a burned fuse along the river close to
the path that went up to Rans's house, fish scales and
bones all over the back yard. And when he walked up
the path, blowflies guided him to a pile of fish dumped in
a tangle of brush not far from the house. Pinkney had
examined the half-rotted things; and anybody could tell
a dynamited fish, certainly this Pinkney—a strange one
now, he had told nobody what he found—that was left
for Lureenie.

She had seen him coming; Rans had gone squirrel-
hunting, for it was a Monday about the middle of the
month and he'd had an off day on WPA. Pinkney had
walked up and asked Lureenie where her man was gone,
and she had said, "Squirrel-hunten," before she thought.

And Pinkney had pushed his hat back and looked at

her and said, "Don't he know hunten squirrels out a season is agin th law, too?"

So that some said the warrant Pinkney got for Rans was for dynamiting fish, shooting squirrels out of season, and stealing dynamite from the WPA to dynamite the fish, and that the stealing part was the worst of all; a man could go to Atlanta for a long time, stealing from the Federal government.

Rans hadn't waited to see his warrant; quick as he'd heard about Pinkney's visit, he had gone to his father, Keg Head, in Alcorn to get money to get away on. Some said it was a good thing for Nunn Ballew that Rans had had to leave in a hurry. But Nunn laughed at that and said killing a man took only a minute.

Early next morning, after Rans had gone, Lureenie came to Nunn in the cornfield. She was so mad her eyes glittered green. She's learned from the Tillers that Pinkney had come first to Nunn, and she accused him of being an informer to get the $50 paid for turning up a dynamiter; she threatened to have the law on him for running a still.

Nunn told her to shut up and mind her manners and go see John and listen to his side of the tale—if anybody told, he said, it was Sue Annie, and she hadn't meant to. She was scared so bad she didn't know what she did.

Nunn's words reached Sue Annie; she angrily denied being scared. Of course, she hadn't been like Nunn, knowing all the time what the men were after and never saying a word, but keeping her and John scared to death and in the dark about the real business of the men. She hinted darkly, too, that the two Ballew men, for it was well known that neither had any use for Rans, had told the law all they knew before she got there with the water.

And so the tales flew, racing all the way to the valley and deep into Alcorn.

John got so mad he was like to had a stroke; a tale got out that he was partners with Nunn in the moonshining; and when late in May he went to the valley to sell his wool, a strange woman with paint on her lips and red fingernails smiled at him and beckoned slyly with her hand for him to come out of the store where the wool was being weighed.

The old man thought nobody was watching, but Blare

was: John tripped outside after this Jezebel, his face all
lit up like a full moon, for it was plain he thought she
wanted to sell him something most thought he was too old
to use any more; it flattered him to death—Blare had
tiptoed to a window and watched and listened—but the
woman only wanted to buy ten gallons of good corn
liquor—she'd heard he had some of the real thing—offered him $15 a gallon—she needed it for her place down
the road a piece.

It was all Blare could do to keep from laughing out
loud, so Sue Annie said; John came near swallowing his
tobacco; his nose turned blue and he stood for a minute
with his mouth open, batting his eyes like a frog in a hailstorm. And when he could speak he almost screamed,
"Jezebel, who do you think you're a talken to?" and
stomped back into the store.

Another tale got out that Nunn had cleared $500 from
his liquor; it went so fast. Uncle Ansel Anderson, who
with his gristmill and Spanish-American War pension and
big valley farm always had money, bought three gallons.
Sue Annie, mad as she was, came back and got two more
with a mysterious air—not for herself, she said, but for
somebody so good they wouldn't carry liquor through the
woods. Nunn suspected some good woman, a church
member most likely, who had wanted some to keep for
medicine, the way Milly liked to have it around.

One night at twilight, two days after Pinkney's visit,
J. D. Duffey came, and with a sheepish air, for his
young wife would no longer let him make it, asked to buy
some; the first time in his life since he was big enough to
stir a mash barrel that he'd ever been out, he said; but
Nunn was sold out and planned that night, as soon as
Milly went to bed, to feed the stuff left in the mash barrel to Rosie and her pigs.

"A waste and a sin," J. D. said, and told him to dump
in more sugar and water and a little meal, quick while the
stuff was still alive in the barrel, and make another run; it
wouldn't be so good as the first run but it would be a sight
cheaper; Nunn, though, mustn't sell it for any less; every moonshiner in the country would be down on him
for selling pure first-run liquor for only $8 a gallon. Nunn
could make half a dozen runs from the same barrel, each
cheaper than the last; of course, after the third or fourth

run he'd have to use lye and it would be so hot and head-achy that only a half-drunk customer would buy it.

Still, the second run was always good; it was a shame for Nunn to cheat the country so—the Cooksey boys hadn't had a drop, and lots of men in Alcorn were plagu-ing him for some. Nunn at last agreed to one more run, though much against his heart; it was hard to buy sugar from Samuel with Samuel boring him with his cold blue eyes, knowing what the sugar would sweeten.

It was while Nunn was working on the second run that he found the two loose planks in the storehouse floor, cov-ered with corn fodder, but not so deeply but that a boy of Lee Roy's size could push them up from below enough to get into the storehouse. Nunn looked at the loose planks a long while; they forced him to be certain of a thing he had never wanted to believe—Suse and Lee Roy knew, and maybe Lucy, too. It was they who had taken the leftover sugar to Milly, placing it so that she thought it was just an-other lost thing found.

He could shut his eyes and see Lee Roy darting up from the weeds, his freshly combed hair shining red in the sun, smiling at Pinkney and the other men he thought had come to take his dad, and even as he smiled the shotgun in the weeds still warm from his hands. The gun must have been in the weeds; for two days it was gone from its corner in the fireplace room, and three shells were gone from the high shelf; the shells returned to the high shelf, the shotgun to its corner, rusty, as if it had lain in the dew—and Nunn shut his eyes to the matter and said nothing.

But sometimes at night he awoke in a cold sweat, shiv-ering, thinking that one or the other of his family had blown the top off Pinkney's head.

Then it was daylight and breakfast time with the chil-dren around him, eating, laughing, talking unconcernedly; and Milly, through with the stomach sickness of the first weeks of her pregnancy, eating and laughing, too. Milly alone of all the country never knew. Sue Annie was deathly afraid of miscarriages and spread word thick through all the neighborhood that if Milly Ballew knew what Nunn had done it might be her death. And so the tales flew over her like birds across a pond; she was pleased when Nunn came home with new shoes and dress goods

for the family after selling the wool and the crossties, and
thought he'd made an awful lot of money, but crossties
and wool, like everything else, so Suse said, were worth a
lot more because of the war across the waters.

Bringing Milly the extra groceries and dry goods had
been a pleasant thing; she'd been tickled to death
with the four dozen new half-gallon jars; and the girls
had been pleased with their new clothes—but Lee Roy
was a boy, clothes meant little to him, and Nunn wished
he could buy him something, a thing he wanted that
would maybe help him forget the black thoughts and the
shiverings he must have had while he sat in the brush and
held the shotgun, maybe with a bead drawn on Pinkney.

He was thinking of such things when he came upon
Lee Roy one day in the hall of the big barn as he talked
to and petted the weaned but wild Jude. "Look, Pop,"
he called softly, "I got a halter on her."

Nunn walked up with the careless unconcerned way he
always affected when around a wild or frightened animal,
but even so, Jude reared and rolled her eyes at his coming, and he saw with a twinge of something he didn't want
to think was jealousy that Lee Roy would maybe be a better hand with stock than he had been.

Lee Roy pulled off the halter in one quick gentle
movement and let Jude go, but so tame was she that she
went only outside the barn and stood there looking at
Lee Roy. And Nunn, studying her, thought it was time
she was sold and how Maude would be dropping another
foal in August, and always he had to sell the yearling colt
for $30 or so to get the $10 stud fee that was due when a
living foal was born, and that must be paid to a prosperous farmer over in Alcorn before Maude could be bred
again in late September.

Lee Roy smiled after the colt and said, without looking at his father but with more of wistfulness than he almost ever showed for anything, "Pop, wouldn't it be fine
now to keep her an have a team of mares like I've heared
you say Granma used to have,"

Nunn remembered that this was one year, thanks to his
whisky sales, that he didn't have to worry about cash for
a stud fee. "That's what I was aimen to tell you, Son. I
been aimen to keep a likely looken filly fer a long spell,
an Jude's th one."

"Oh, Pop," Lee Roy whispered, and again, "Oh, Pop." And the love and admiration and knowledge that his father was a fine good man made a redness in his face that matched his hair, and he was once more the little boy who had used to tag after his father in worshipful adoration wherever he went; then, as if his skin would burst with standing still and holding so much happiness, he ran outside and followed Jude in a long race over the storehouse field.

Nunn stood in the shade of the barn hall and watched the two of them run through the bright sunlight, and looking after them, he felt old and tired.

"Nunn, oh, Nunn." It was Milly calling.

He cursed, pretty certain what was the matter, and then, when from the graveyard field he heard the pups, he knew they had found fox scent. Through the spring and early summer he had lost several days from his work while they hunted, and once, rather than leave his plowing again, he sent Suse to the Pilot Rock; but that was the day the pups holed and killed a big gray fox, and the whole family went crazy and nobody got any work done for the rest of the day—hardly six months old and already holing their fox and digging it out like seasoned hounds. And only yesterday they'd run such a long race he'd missed going for the mail.

But today, even though the pups were out of hearing before he reached the road gate, nobody was in the yard listening, and from the house came the clackety whir of Milly's sewing machine, and over it, like the shrill singing of a buzz saw, Sue Annie's tongue. Suse came charging down the spring path with the water bucket. "Oh, Pop, Sue Annie has got word in a pink letter frum th schoolteacher that she's a comen down this comen Friday to see her boarden place an her scholars an bring th books."

"Anybody listizen to them pups?" he asked.

Suse ran on without answering, and as he went into the middle room where Milly sat at the sewing, Sue Annie, though still mad at him over the various tales, held up a pale pink letter and shrilled, "Your pretty gal teacher is a comen down fer one night fore school starts to see can she stand her boarden place." She giggled. "It ain't much but it's th pick a th lot—ain't nobody else got room to board a schoolteacher," and added with a savoring of anticipated pleasure, "She can larn th scholars, an I'll larn her."

"She'll never git along—not a girl teacher," Milly said.

Sue Annie nodded and went into a long résumé of the opinions of the various members of the community as expressed yesterday at the post office: John was certain a slip of a girl could never manage his boys, Preacher Samuel hoped she didn't paint her fingernails or her face, and Joe C. wondered if a town girl wouldn't be uppity and proud-turned. Sue Annie ended by rolling her eyes slyly at Nunn. "You'd ought jist to a been there an heared em talk about your woman teacher," with an emphasis on the "your," and her sly eyes saying that Nunn had stayed away on purpose because he knew the letter would be in the mail. She then lay a doleful sadness on her face and wondered if poor old Andrew wouldn't starve.

She gave him the letter, addressed in a neat round hand to Mrs. Susan Anna Tiller, and told him to read for himself, but already the writing was so smudged by many pushing brown fingers that he could make out little except that she was coming for one night and that she wanted to meet as many of her pupils as possible.

Sue Annie cared nothing for the whole business but she felt it her duty to do right by the girl, and so on Friday night she was having a kind of party: Dave would furnish them with fiddle music, Joe C. and Blare could sing duets, and maybe Ruby a solo. She was warning everybody to leave his hounds at home so there would be no hound fights, and added, with loud emphasis and a sly smile at Milly's busy back, that she just dared any moonshiners to come trying to sell their stuff.

Nunn flushed, Milly sewed on unconscious of what it was all about, Suse tossed her braids and muttered "Damn," but Lee Roy, who had come in to see what the commotion was about, smiled at Sue Annie: "Them that makes good liquor never has to go peddlen it," and wondered in the next breath if the teacher were afraid of snakes.

Nunn said nothing; already he felt uneasy; the new teacher was his doing; if Elias Higginbottom had never seen Vinie—he remembered why he had come to the house and wearily took his horn from the high shelf and went up to the Pilot Rock to listen, and on the way his unpatched fence and rocks still in the hayfields cried to him. Once he hesitated, but with an oath went on; and it seemed to him, as he walked through the hot June sunshine, that King Devil ruled his life as man was never ruled by mortal king.

The race was long and the day hot and there was no water on the Pilot Rock, but he stayed listening till midafternoon, when the pups cried that they had lost the scent in Brush Creek. When he blew his horn after they had cried their bewilderment, they came over the gap in the ridge above John's place, for they were experienced now, learning the short cuts home.

And on Friday the household was in such a dither of preparation for the teacher's visit that even the pups stayed home, hanging around the house, sniffing new shoes, taking exploratory chews of new stockings; and while Suse was washing her hair, grumbling because she had no rain water and nothing but homemade soap, Vinie ran away with the towels, and Suse, with wet hair over her face and soap smarting her eyes, almost got a whipping from Milly for kicking out blindly at Vinie and hitting Sam with her bare foot.

Nunn quit fence patching early to shave, a thing he detested doing anytime except on Sunday mornings, and after a sketchy early supper of leftover cold corn bread and beans, Milly filled the biggest washtub half full of water and began the business of scrubbing up the children, beginning with Deb and working up to Lee Roy, who insisted that he was big enough to bathe himself like Suse. Suse, already dressed in new patent-leather slippers and the new voile dress sprigged with blue flowers that Milly had purposely made with a full skirt so that Suse wouldn't look so much like a bean pole, was twisting and prissing and prancing all over the place, impatient to be off.

She wondered if Andy would be down at Sue Annie's and wished the roses were not all gone—she would put one in her hair; but Aunt Marthie's rose-of-Sharon bushes were blooming out by the tumbledown root house, and Suse broke two sprays of buds and flowers and twined them in her hair and wished she dared undo her braids and let her red-brown hair float down behind her shoulders—she wondered if Andy would notice it.

Vinie pressed a cold moist nose against her knee and

she slapped her angrily away, not so much because she minded Vinie's nose on her knee, but because it was a reminder that her knees were bare, and Ruby Tiller, hardly a year older, had rayon hose so fine her hairs shone through, while she had to wear socks of coarse cotton, like a child.

Up on the ridge, Jaw Buster's Speed cried, a long-drawn hunting call, and Vinie stiffened, listening. "No, no, Vinie; Nunn won't let you run in a race with older hounds after dark, not yet," Suse said and caught her by the scruff of her neck.

Vinie struggled to be off; for up around the schoolhouse Sourvine cried sweetly and the Tiller hounds were answering. Suse dropped to her knees and flung both arms around Vinie, calling meanwhile for Nunn, but nobody heard.

Milly had been taking a bath in the kitchen when the hounds sang out; Sam had been under the walnut tree by the kitchen door. Nunn, all shaven and ready, was in the fireplace room stripping the midribs from a dampened hand of tobacco and rolling a twist of leaves for the night's chewing. Heedless of Milly's naked condition, he ran through the kitchen, hunting the pups with Lee Roy and Lucy at his heels. Milly set up a screeching and a screaming at having her privacy so invaded.

Nunn ran on cursing the hounds and their owners. Lister and Jaw Buster, knowing what a risky business it was to let young and valuable pups run with old hounds at night, had all through the spring gone to Kelly's Point on the other side of Deer Lick for the beginning of their Saturday-night hunts, so that it was but seldom their hounds came into the valley. Deer Lick Ridge was high and wild and steep, and King Devil was about the only fox that cut across it; others who tried it were almost always holed or caught.

But now, before full dark, when it was hardly time for a hunt to begin, all the hounds in the country were running in full cry no further away than the schoolhouse. Sam was answering in an instant, but with his answer there was a call to Vinie to come on. Vinie howled and struggled in Suse's arms; Sam ran to the house corner and stood a second hesitant, with a glance in Vinie's direction. Should he go to his Vinie, who sounded in deep trouble, or to the running hounds? Sourvine let out a hot wild bay that echoed through the valley and Sam was off to the hunt. Nunn was yelling, "Head him off, Lee Roy. . . . Fer God's sake, head him off. I don't want em a chasen King Devil in th night in a race."

Lee Roy was closer to the hole in the fence than Sam and reached it just as he did. Sam was a big thing now, weighing better than thirty pounds, and when Lee Roy tackled him they went down in the dust together, Sam yipping and snorting, snarling and whining, and at last doing a thing he had never done, snapping at Lee Roy. Nunn, as he fell upon the two of them, heard Lee Roy's new overalls tear. He began cursing King Devil with black venomous oaths, but some sense came to him and he realized that all his noise and all the hullabaloo were only exciting the pups. He fell to talking in a soft calm voice, explaining that it was King Devil the old hounds ran, King Devil, the wicked fox who had already killed many pups and grown hounds and had tried to kill him and Vinie twice.

Suse was calling angrily, threatening to let Vinie go if somebody didn't come help; Vinie was ruining her new dress; Milly, half dried and slippery with homemade soap and but scantily draped in Nunn's dirty shirt, the only thing she could lay hands on in a hurry, ran to her help.

Sam had quieted enough so that Nunn had picked him up, when he saw Jaw Buster coming along the school path. "What th hell," he called in some anger, "ain't that King Devil swung over frum th other side a Deer Lick? Sounds like him."

Not far below the schoolhouse the hounds were crying and quarreling and running; no one of them was still; Speed in particular ran and cursed and cried, not because the scent was lost, but because there was so much of the hot stuff in every direction that he couldn't tell which way to go.

"Listen," Jaw Buster called. "Speed ain't a sayen it's King Devil." He listened a moment more and laughed and came on—Jaw Buster no more than Speed ever laughed when King Devil ran. "We was all a comen along peaceful, aimen to see your new schoolteacher, when Speed jumped this scent right yon side a th post office, an it's been one long unravel ever since, craziest thing I ever

seed . . . It ain't King Devil. . . . A young frisky, feisty
red fox, I'd say," he went on, coming up and petting the
angry, whining Sam. "King Devil, when th scent's hot as
this, ud be a jumpen an a breaken ever five minutes."

He picked his cap up, set it further on the back of his
head, and began working on Nunn to let Sam and Vinie
run: they were better than six months old; they were
healthy; they'd already hunted considerable; the night
wasn't real hot like it would be later; running a crazy fox
like this they couldn't get winded—just let them run once
with the other hounds; he and all the others wanted to see
how they'd show up with Speed and Sourvine. Blare Tiller
had been declaring that Nunn was afraid to let them run
with the other hounds.

Lister came and added his urging to Jaw Buster's, and
less gentle than Jaw Buster and less respectful of pedigrees, laughed down all Nunn's fears. Hell, if they were
so feeble-minded as to learn bad habits from the Tiller
hounds now, at their age, and after all the hunting they'd
done, let them and then knock them in the head. Oh, no,
it wasn't King Devil; he'd swear to that; Sourvine said it
wasn't. And, if they had no more sense than to run into a
sinkhole or over the river bluff in the dark, let them.

Nunn's arguments grew feeble and more feeble; he had
long wanted to show off Sam and Vinie, for it had seemed
to him of late that they were getting uncommon fast, both
as to legs and noses, but with no other hounds to run with
it was hard to tell, and as Jaw Buster said, it was a good
night, neither wet nor too hot nor too cold. Still, he hesitated, listening again to the hounds who, after a short
course of straight running, were baffled again low down
by the creek; his hand was slowly loosening on Sam, but
he wondered—King Devil had played so many tricks, had
killed so many hounds, he might, as a new and devilish
trick, change his whole way of running.

Sourvine had unraveled the scent and his voice came
sweetly from along the creek bank; Sam gave a piteous
little moan of pure broken-heartedness. "Aw, Nunn,"
Lister began and was silent.

Nunn had let Sam loose. "Hey, Milly," he called, his
voice shrilling a little with excitement, "let loose a Vinie."

Milly's jaw dropped in disbelief of the command and
she tightened her hold on Vinie. "Nunn . . ."

"Hell-fire, woman, let her go. Sam's gone. . . . It ain't King Devil."

"Could be," Milly said, and her long sigh of relinquishment was like the swish of a bird through the twilight. She glanced down at Vinie's gold-sprinkled head—like sending a little youngen all by itself on its first day of school or putting the old baby to sleep away from your bed when the new one came.

"God damn it, send her on, woman," Nunn roared.

Milly took her hands away. Vinie, first shaking her disarranged hair into place, leaped after Sam.

Suse stood angrily inspecting her new dress and, sure enough, found a place, hidden by the sash, where the skirt was ripped from the waist.

She started to show it to Milly, still staring up the valley after Vinie, her eyes glittering with tears, and for the first time saw what she wore.

"Mom . . . Mom . . . them pups'll be all right, but you'll scandalize us all, out half naked an th yard full a men," she whispered.

Milly glanced at her thighs gleaming sinful white above her brown shins and with a little gasp ran into the house and a few moments later was calling Suse plaintively to come help hunt her new patent-leather shoes.

Suse sighed and looked up toward Sue Annie's; it would soon be dark, even now it wasn't a bit too early to start, and the new schoolteacher there all ready to be seen. She went back into the house. She guessed that the pups had carried off Milly's shoes and they maybe wouldn't find them before full dark, and already Deb was whindling to have his new shoes taken off—his stubbed toe hurt. Milly stopped the hunting of her own shoes to debate in her mind the matter of taking Deb barefooted: if she took his shoes off now to give his feet a little rest, she'd never get them on again. He began screaming, "Off . . . off," and she bent to untie the strings, but Suse, on her knees, looking under the bed for Milly's shoes, called sharply, "Don't, Mom, please. Who wants to have a barefooted youngen . . . trailen along. . . . What'll that schoolteacher think?"

"I can't have poor little Deb a hurten," Milly said and unlaced the shoes.

Suse sighed and went to look under Lee Roy's bed. It would be nice to belong to a family that always wore

shoes like people she'd read about—she hated going barefoot and she hated the feel of mud or hot rocks or sand on
her feet—she dreamed a moment of how it would be to
be so rich that everybody in the family could have two
pairs of shoes—one for every day and one for Sunday.

She pulled her head out from under the bed and there
was Sam, standing in the middle-room door, pulling sand
burs with his teeth from a patch on his shoulder.

"My God, have you caught King Devil so quick?" she
asked, and Sam looked at her, then went back to cleaning
himself.

"Jesus God," Suse said, "this'ull kill Pop. . . . Runnen
away frum a fox race." She ran to the kitchen door calling, "Pop . . . Oh-h, Pop."

The race had crossed the creek and gone into Nunn's
old pasture field on the other side of the big barn. Nunn
and Jaw Buster and Lister were listening hard. They had
heard the eager yipping of the pups as they ran up the
valley and a few more scent-hunting yips when they
joined the hunt, but nothing since.

Susie called three times before Nunn, who never liked
to be yelled at by his womenfolk when he had company
and certainly not when he was listening hard to a fox
race, answered in low-voiced anger, "Shut up. I'm busy."

"I am too," Suse said in a meek, mild-mannered voice,
"an somebody ought to bur Sam, an they's ticks in his
ears, too, I think."

Even in the deepened dusk she could see how Nunn's
eyes blazed and bulged when he whirled and looked at
her. "Sam?" he screamed.

"Yeah," Suse said. "He needs some help with his
burs. . . . He's in th middle room," she explained in pleasant conversational tones and hurried to warn Milly either
to get some clothes on or hide—men might come in.

"Burs," Nunn was roaring, "I'll bur him. . . . Runnen
away frum a fox race," and followed by Jaw Buster and
Lister, he strode stiff-legged through the kitchen into the
middle room, but stopped a few feet from Sam as if afraid
of what he might do to him.

Jaw Buster and Lister looked at Sam in sorrow and
perplexity; Jaw Buster had bragged on the fine pedigreed
pups a neighbor man of his was raising, and the men on
the railroad section gang who worked with Lister were

eagerly awaiting some word of the pups' performance in their first real race. Their troubled glances crossed, came to rest on Nunn shaking his fist at Sam, who had left off burring himself and was studying his master in some perplexity.

"You . . . you . . . little rabbit-chasen feist," Nunn hissed, "I ought a throw you in th fire . . . like Josh Sexton done his rabbit chaser."

Sam dropped his tail and whined, and Milly, peeping through a crack in the door of the fireplace room, let out a troubled whimper. Modesty and concern for Sam wrestled within her. She still wore only Nunn's shirt.

"Aw, Nunn," Jaw Buster soothed, "mebbe some a th old hounds chased him home."

"A real hound would ha run if he had to stay a mile behind th others," Nun said, glaring at Sam and moving a little closer to him.

"Mebbe it ain't no fox," Lister said, growing uneasy for Sam's safety.

"I recken your Sourvine has took up rabbit chasen. Mebbe it's a polecat they're hunten," he added in vicious sarcasm.

"Aw, Nunn," Jaw Buster said, trying as unobtrusively as possible to put himself between Nunn and the now thoroughly troubled Sam.

"Aw . . . hell. Where's Vinie; why didn't she come home?"

"She did, Pop." Suse spoke quietly from the middle door.

Nunn whirled just as Vinie strolled through the door. She had either not heard Nunn's outburst or was in no wise perturbed by it. She was apparently hunting Sam and on seeing him stopped and glanced up at the strange men. Just then both Speed and Sourvine bayed right across the creek, long-drawn, singing, sweet and hot with anticipation. Vinie lifted her ears a little, listening, her dark eyes staring through the middle door, then, with a bored indifferent air, she yawned fully and completely, rising on her dainty feet, arching her back like a cat, then lowering it in a long stretching, with the lazy, luxuriant air of a great lady preparing for a good night's sleep.

Lister leaned against the wall, weak with uncontrollable

laughter. "I cain't help it, Nunn," he gasped. "She said plain as words, 'I don't give a damn. I'd ruther sleep.' She's so pretty anyhow you can put her in th movies—it's like they said that Pinkney said, 'Nunn's blonde now—she shore is pretty.' "

"Laugh, I don't blame you," Nunn roared at Lister, then turned back to Vinie. "An you—you—you jist don't give a damn, do ye? You—you bitch." Nunn's eyes were bulging and tobacco juice dribbled on his angry red chin.

The door to the fireplace room was pushed suddenly open, but just as suddenly stopped when the opening was wide enough for Milly's face, shining with soap, to peer through. "Sure, she's a bitch—God didn't mean fer her to be nothen else." And with a dropping of her voice to kindly gentle persuasion, "Git in here, Vinie—you, too, Sam. Come on now."

The pups, with no backward glance for Nunn, scampered through the door, and once they were safe, Milly's voice rose again in wrath. "God made em fer foxhounds, an foxhounds thcy arc. Whatever that varmint is them fool potlickers out there is a chasen, it ain't no fox. You'd better git on—you'll be late—I don't feel like goen," and the door slammed shut.

The three men stared at it, silent, blinking; after a moment Jaw Buster said, with a delicate attempt at diplomacy, "Babe, she's allus like that when she's in th family way."

Nunn scratched his head, still staring at the door. "But Milly, she ain't allus like that."

Suse came running in, her wide skirts swirling out from her slim waist, her eyes brimming with angry tears. "Please, Pop, oh, please, come on. The music's done started playen an somebody's brought a banjo. Please, Pop," and she caught his arm.

Nunn had forgotten his schoolteacher, and for the first time since hearing about her, he was glad she was on earth; he wanted to get away from Sam and Vinie and Lister and Jaw Buster and Milly, too.

He and Suse with Lee Roy and the two men were halfway to the road gate before Suse remembered her mother, and even after Nunn's growled "No," to her question of weren't Milly and the little youngens coming, she raced back to find out what had happened.

Lucy was asleep across the foot of the bed, her new shoes cradled like twin dolls on her arm, and Deb wiggled his bare toes happily in the old ashes on the hearth while Milly sat in the cool north door, taking her after-supper chew of tobacco and combing her hair with the pups at her feet, luxuriating in the twilight coolness as they watched lightning bugs. "Vinie here don't want to go an she don't want to stay home by herself; that's why she hid my shoes," Milly said, and smilingly shook her head to all Suse's pleadings that she come.

"Me an Lee Roy an Lucy'll hunt ever minute tomorrow that Pop's out a th house—you don't want him to know —till we find em," Suse promised, and after a lingering and almost sorrowful last look at her mother, sitting quiet and tired on the doorstep, ran after Nunn, but stopped again, and was respectfully still when Milly called after her, "Now, if they start a playen old dance tunes, honey, you set still till yer pop brings you home."

Chapter Eighteen

‡‡‡‡‡‡‡‡‡‡‡‡‡‡‡‡‡‡‡‡‡‡‡‡‡‡‡‡‡‡‡‡‡‡‡‡

BUT THE MUSIC that came from Sue Annie's bright carbide-lighted fireplace room was not dance music, but the long wailing sorrow of "Sweet Fern," sad as only old Dave could make it on his fiddle.

Jaw Buster cursed when he saw the crowd; men, women, and children packed in the house, spilled over the porches, and into the yard. "We can't hear them hounds nohow, not with all that racket an them people," he said. "We might as well try to git a look at Nunn's schoolteacher an then go back an listen."

Uncle Ansel came up to report on the schoolteacher, and learn how the race was going, and the men and Lee Roy stopped outside, but Suse hurried on until she reached the open door where Sue Annie, smiling proudly and looking strange with no white head rag or apron, but nice and neat in her Sunday voile and patent-leather shoes, greeted everybody with a smile and an outstretched hand. Under cover of the music she explained to Suse that she couldn't stand in the door, as she herself only stood there to keep out hound dogs and men who looked as if they might have liquor, and keep a passageway clear so that a little air could get in.

Some one pulled Suse gently by the sleeve, and there was Andy smiling at her in his Sunday clothes. She could have his place in the windows of the fireplace room where it was not so crowded, and leaned on the low sill and searched the crowded room until she saw in the place of honor by the fiddlers on the hearth a girl-like woman, perfect and pretty as a great wax doll, untouched by human hands.

262

Suse drew her breath in sharply and looked with all her eyes. "Mom an Pop don't like her looks one bit, but she's pretty, ain't she?" Andy whispered.

Suse nodded and a little sigh escaped her, not entirely of envy, but more for all the things gathered in the teacher, things mysterious and unattainable: a college education, hands white and delicate as some curious plant grown in the shade, the color of her nail polish, the way her carefully curled hair of a bright, rich yellow shone in the lamplight and lay around her head; the innumerable mysteries of her dress, a pale pink silk, short-sleeved with big buttons shaped like ships; silver bracelets on one arm, and on the other a wristwatch.

She wished she might get near enough to study the wristwatch; she had never seen a watch except John's and Preacher Samuel's—big ones on chains—and then only remotely.

She must have felt Suse's stare, for she moved her head and their eyes met. Suse smiled, a sheepish but adoring smile, as if to ask forgiveness for staring so, but Miss Betty Catharine Burdine's glance moved on and rested a moment on Jaw Buster Anderson's tall unmarried brother behind Andy. Suse flushed; already the new teacher would take her for a little back-hill fool for staring so—but she at least had seen her eyes, big and blue and less warm than her hair. After a moment she looked her way again, but instead of the teacher's glance she met Mark Cramer's eyes searching around the room as he leaned his head above the fiddle he played; he smiled at her as she looked away, and Andy was whispering, "She's pretty, but reckon she'll be smart enough to git us through th eighth grade. You know," he went on, "people are a sayen th new gravel road'ull soon be finished as far as our place—an that that high-school bus will start runnen this comen fall a year."

Suse shook her head. "We won't be on it, most like."

"Your pop, like mine, believes in education," Andy said.

"Believen an aimen an then doen is different things with Pop," Suse said, with a swift, calculating glance at Andy. Would he really go to high school like he'd been saying ever since the new graveled road was started? Not bragging talk—Andy never bragged—but stray whisperings to her alone when they did their lessons together in the back of the schoolroom. If there should be a school bus and he graduated from the eighth grade and went to high school, she might go too, riding back and forth to town—have half a dozen strange teachers like she'd heard they had, maybe sit next to a girl she'd never seen—her skin prickled with excitement.

Unnoticed she smiled again on Miss Betty Catharine Burdine; she was a piece—a fine though as yet unknown piece—of the outside world come to Suse; that world she had dreamed about since she was big enough to read in the prime about a policeman, and glimpsed vaguely through schoolbooks and the few other books and newspapers and magazines that had come into her hands.

Miss Burdine had had candles on her birthday cake and had eaten from tables set with china and silver on a lace cloth like those in the mail-order catalogue; she had known bathrooms and furnace heat and innerspring mattresses instead of shuck ticks; she knew water that came from a faucet instead of a spring; had ridden in elevators and maybe seen the sea and mountains with snow and rolling plains like those pictured in the geography; she had ridden in many automobiles, seen many movies, been in many strange buildings, had known many strange people; she had maybe, if she were not religious, danced in a long full-skirted dress with flowers in her hair, moving her feet in time to the music of many violins—and Miss Burdine would be her friend and tell her how those things were— and some day she too would be like that—a part of the outside world.

The banjos were silent and old Dave and Mark Cramer carried the music alone and the sad wailing of the violins became as one with Suse's thoughts—their wordless yearning cry of hunger, not for food alone or clothes, or shelter —a hunger like a hurt, an ache for things mysterious and unseen, nay, undreamed.

She realized that Miss Betty was looking at her sharply and that she was staring worse than a hill child from deep behind the Cow's Horn who had never heard a train blow. She flushed and looked away and saw on Sue Annie's wash bench, packed tightly in the scant space and perspiring from the heat, a row of the neighbor women, school mothers Sue Annie had put near the hearth in a place of honor, for most of the company were standing or sitting on the beds—the chairs were taken up entirely by the music makers and the teacher.

Suse studied them, then shivered and looked away; she would never be like that, dull and dead and uncaring; she thought of Milly sleeping at home; she would fit well with the others on the bench. Had she or any of them ever heard the trains blow far away and sad, calling you to come away, calling so clearly you wanted to cry? Or had they ever wanted to run and run through the woods on a windy moonlight night in spite of what God would think and the neighbors say? How could they sit so quietly now? How?

Andy was whispering. "Lookee, Suse, did you see what she brought with her? He's comen in now—must a been chasen a rabbit. She's never been in th woods an she was afraid."

"Afraid," Suse said, staring at the great yellow-brown long-haired cur dog that had apparently been standing in the door for some time, searching out the teacher, for after a moment it walked across the room to her. The children made way for it with subdued squeals and frightened glances; even many of the women and some of the men drew aside with looks of fear, for few in the Little Smokey Creek country had ever seen such a big fierce-looking cur dog.

"He's a long-haired collie," Andy explained, "town raised, like she is, an broken frum barken even when he's rabbit chasen."

The music stopped amid a great stomping of feet and calling for more, but Sue Annie held up her hand and said the music players must rest, and ordered all parents and scholars who had not met the teacher to come forward.

"She ain't seen Perfessor Fox Hunter yet," Willie Cook-sey, lounging by a window, called loud enough for half the company to hear.

Suse flushed in anger and embarrassment and thought of the pups—for an instant she hated them; they'd let Nunn down and shamed him by leaving their first race—and now the whole country would laugh at him and his pedigreed pups. She flipped back the braids that had fallen over her shoulders. Let them laugh. . . . Some day she'd be so far away their laughter wouldn't matter.

Nunn strode through the door, his head high, and mindful of his manners, he held his hat in his hand. She wished

for an instant that her father was a big man, tall and
handsome like some of the Cramer men, and that he had
a suit of store clothes with a white shirt and tie, like
Preacher Samuel, instead of the starched overall pants and
the blue work shirt, the top button unbuttoned, that he
wore with a kind of proud carelessness, as if he didn't give
a damn.

Here among so many bigger men he looked small, childish somehow, with his slicked-down hair parted on the
side, his face thin and eyes big the way they always got
after a long spell of hot weather, when he worked hard
and sweated.

But he was smiling gaily like a man whose pups have
won a prize when he walked up to the teacher, and his
smile was brighter yet when Willie Cooksey asked with a
great show of interest and a long look on his face, "How's
your pups runnen tonight, Nunn? I heared they'd gone to
their first real race."

"You heared more'n that," Nunn said, smiling now at
the schoolteacher. "Them pups is sound asleep at
home. . . . They run nothen but fox."

"An what's that Speed's a runnen now? I heared him
not a minnit ago," Willie asked, with an elaborate face-
twisting wink toward Joe C. Tiller.

"Go ask him and see," Nunn said and held out his hand
to the schoolteacher. "My name is Nunnely Ballew. I've
got three youngens an two hounds'ull be a comen to
school."

Suse bit her lip in anger. Nunn had been drinking, she
knew; the schoolteacher was pulling away her limp white
hand, staring, not knowing what to say. Sue Annie was
cackling and asking the teacher if she was a good hound-
dog teacher; old Drum and Blunder and Lead and Drive
always went to school, and there'd be John's mules that
liked to graze around the schoolhouse and his sow that
always found her pigs under the schoolhouse floor.

Angry tears flared up in Suse's eyes and even Lee Roy
seemed ashamed of his father and looked up at him a moment with hot disgusted eyes, then his glance went back
to the thing he wanted most to see—the big cur dog.

It was standing behind the teacher's chair with an uncertain, bewildered air, plainly puzzled by the press of people and the loud talk and the music.

Lee Roy, who had followed his father, smoothed its forehead, and the dog seemed to take comfort from his touch and drew near him. The teacher looked at his rough warty hands on the dog's silken head and said, a little sharply, "He's not used to strange children; he might bite."

Lee Roy pulled a tick from the animal's ear while it held still in silent gratitude. "He won't bite me," he said, and added in slow, carefully chosen defiance, for his father and the others listening, "I like cur dogs. . . . I think they're pretty."

"Cur dogs like that make mean sheep killers," Mark Cramer, who seemed unimpressed by the teacher, said.

"He's as fine a looken cur dog, though, as I ever seed an—"

Miss Burdine interrupted Blare and her voice was sharp, "He's no cur dog. . . . He's a thoroughbred collie."

Lee Roy smiled kindly at her stupidity. "He is a cur . . ."

Miss Burdine's cheek trembled. "He is not a cur dog. . . . Why, he's pedigreed on one side."

"Sire or dam?" Nunn asked.

And Lee Roy, who continued to look at the teacher in patient pity, said, "But a cur's a cur. He could be pedigreed on both sides, but he ain't no hound."

"Nunn, here, now; he's got two hound pups pedigreed long as . . ." Blare was saying, talking fast and loud with the hope of being heard in spite of Sue Annie, who was uring the music makers to strike up again; she wanted Blare and Joe C. and Ruby to sing "Sweet Beulah Land" for the teacher; she'd noticed Frankie Cramer on the porch, and he was the best bass in the county, so they ought to sing a quartet while there was a good bass handy.

But just as the quartet was assembling, Lister stuck his head through a window and bellowed for Nunn—he must come listen to a race after the craziest-running fox that ever ran. "Th nose work is so plum bewilderen . . . Most a th time my Sourvine, stead a Speed, is ahead. Hurry on if'n you want to hear good; they're runnen just over th hill, kind a worken thisaway."

Suse gripped the window sill. Shame and anger like a fire burned inside her when Nunn turned his back on the teacher and strode away; half a dozen others left the room

to listen, and Sue Annie rubbed her nose with her knuckles
in disgust at their ignorant uncivilized ways.

Ruby stood up with her father and uncle and the
Cramer man, blushing furiously and plucking at her skirt
with her fingers. Suse, watching her, felt an envy she didn't
like to own; Ruby was a Tiller and dumb; she was older
than Suse but lower in her schoolbooks than Lee Roy—
but she could sing like a bird and had a way with the boys.
She was singing, "I've reached the land of corn and wine,"
when her glance happened on Andy and she smiled boldly
as she sang on, "And all its riches freely mine."

Suse, glancing sideways at Andy, saw with disgust that
he smiled back, straight into Rubys' eyes, as if her glance
were sugar candy and he was hungry. She glanced away
and realized with confusion that Mark Cramer was looking
at her again. Old Dave was carrying the tune alone and
Mark had given his chair to two of Blare's little girls who
fidgeted and breathed hard in the presence of the teacher.
He lounged against the mantelpiece, his restless dark blue
eyes wandering over the room and through the windows,
as if searching for something.

And Suse in quick glances, when he was not looking her
way, noticed for the first time how tall he was, not heavy
tall like Jaw Buster, but slender in his waist and hips, with
wide shoulders. And she wished Andy had eyes like his—
blue in a dark tanned face under dark thick brows—he
was looking at her again; she flushed and looked quickly
away, but not before their glances met and he had smiled
again; a smile bold as Ruby's but somehow secret, as if
they played a game of glances all alone in the crowded
room.

Frankie Cramer stood with his eyes closed and patting
his foot, his throat red and swollen like a frog's, as he intoned in a bass uncommon deep and throbbing because of
the teacher, "Sweet Beulah Land, sweet Beulah Land,
sweet Beulah Land."

Then somewhere out by the road gate a hound sang
out, a wild triumphant song louder than "Beulah Land."

There was a stir among the men and boys near the
doors and windows and a drawing off of those on the
porch as they ran toward the gate to see Speed get his
fox—for his cry told plainly that the fox was not many
feet away.

Sourvine joined Speed and they bayed together, closer than before, like great bugles wafting sound over the company. Frankie Cramer opened his eyes in the middle of a "Beulah Land," craned his head and squinted an instant through the door, but seeing nothing, closed his eyes and intoned another "Sweet Beulah Land."

Blare, the alto, opened his mouth to sing, but no sound came out as he listened hard for Drum and Blunder.

The teacher fidgeted in her chair, staring uneasily toward the sounds, plainly strange to her. Sue Annie stood in the door, alternately smiling reassuringly at the teacher listening to the race, then frowning at the company for silence.

Speed and Sourvine circled the house, their bays triumphant and long-drawn. Drum and Blunder and Lead and Drive topped the hill and lingered a moment, baying and snarling and barking as if they would tear Sue Annie's gate to pieces because it stood in their way; then Drum, with a triumphant cry, found the hole in the fence he always used anyway and came on with the other Tiller hounds in full tongue at his heels.

Sourvine and Speed ran under the kitchen porch, where they gave short, unsatisfied but still hopeful bays; the teacher crossed and uncrossed her legs as if she would rather stand up than sit still.

When his hounds topped the hill, Blare had started again to sing, but his listening made him absent-minded and he sang the fourth stanza while Ruby in shrill soprano went on with the third. Drum bayed on the doorstep. Blare stood an instant silent, then with a cry of "Jesus God, where is thet fox?" ran from the room, almost tripping over his mother's outstretched foot and giving no mind at all to her hissed command of "Shit-fire, boy; mind your manners."

Joe C. followed Blare, and Frankie Cramer opened his eyes, saw the alto and tenor were gone, stopped on a growled "Sweet—" and hurried after them. Ruby, smiling straight ahead at nothing with all her eyes, sang on alone.

Nobody heard. Drum and Blunder were baying on the front-porch steps; Sourvine was still quarreling under the floor, and Speed bayed on the back porch near Suse and Andy.

An instant later he leaped through the door. Amid a

bawling and squealing of just awakened babies and aggravated women crying "Shoo," and slapping at him with their
hands, he began a furious circling of the room, his nose
sniffling and snuffling as if he would eat the very flowers
off Sue Annie's linoleum. Speed bayed, telling all the other
hounds he had found fresh scent on Sue Annie's linoleum.
Sourvine leaped after him into the room, and in spite of
Sue Annie's spreading both her arms and her legs wide and
calling loudly for help, the four Tiller hounds charged
through the front door; Drum went under her legs and as
she staggered, clutching the doorsill, the others went over
her shoulders and between her arms.

The teacher jumped up and looked wildly about as if
hunting a hiding place; her cur dog pressed against her
knees, his troubled eyes following the rough wild hounds
as they bayed and sniffed and snapped in the space they
had cleared for themselves in the center of the room.
Town bred, he did not bark or try to join in the fun as a
country cur might have done, but whined softly.

Through all the tumult, Drum, of whom it was often
said that he hunted by ear, heard the whine. He stood a
moment motionless behind the bench of women before he
placed the sound. He leaped, knocking Mrs. Hull's hat
askew and bringing an angry "Jesus God," from Hattie
Tiller. The others followed, some running round the bench,
some leaping over.

The cur dog dashed for the door and as quickly dashed
away when he ran against the press of people. Whining,
whimpering, with his tail between his legs, he began a fren-
zied circle of the room; the company made way for the
strange dog, of which they were afraid, and closed again
before the harmless hounds.

Speed, never afraid but always wary, leaped at him,
bringing blood to his shoulder, then as quickly leaped
away. He circled, seeking the throat, fighting as he would
have fought a razorback or wildcat. But the collie was
neither. He dropped on his haunches and wriggled under
the bed just as Sourvine raked his flank. Speed and Sourvine, old and forever cautious, now certain of their quarry,
stood barking, debating on how best to tackle this creature.

Preacher Samuel, who had walked off to the kitchen for
buckets of water when Speed leaped through the door,
was calling in his most commanding preacher's voice for

the company to make way so that he could scatter the hounds with water. The teacher was standing on her chair, screaming and crying, begging them not to let her dog be killed.

Blunder, less wary than his wiser brothers, ran under the bed. A yipping cry from the cur dog told the others it was the thing to do. They followed.

Sue Annie, with her side combs falling out of her hair, screamed to Jaw Buster and Lister, "Move th bed. Move it . . . fore they kill him. Let him jump out th back side."

Old Dave hobbled up, calling, "Don't move thet bed. . . . It'll fall to pieces. . . . It's my granma's."

But six strong men had already swung it away from the wall; the cur dog, bleeding from a dozen wounds, sprang up on the back side, and the men swung the bed back just in time to catch Drum's head between the bed and wall.

Through the many-voiced uproar the teacher's screams could be heard, "Don't let them kill my dog!"

Speed leaped into the middle of the bed, high with two feather ticks and a shuck mattress, but Jaw Buster leaped too, falling on top of him. At that moment Samuel came up with the buckets of water, flinging a bucket over Jaw Buster and the cur dog. None touched Speed, for he was under Jaw Buster. Sue Annie in high anger screamed, "Damn you, man, you'll ruin my featherbeds; they're worth more'n any cur dog."

Blunder and Sourvine and Lead and Drive came out from under the bed and jumped on Jaw Buster, apparently thinking in the confusion that the cur dog was under him; there was much baying and barking but none of the hounds could keep their footing among the deep feathers. In spite of Sue Annie's curses, Samuel threw on the other bucket of water, though it was hardly necessary. Nunn had caught the wet, shivering, and completely dazed cur dog firmly around the nose with one hand and by a hind leg with the other and swung him through an open window. Mark Cramer ran up on the outside and following Nunn's direction to lock him in the kitchen, took him and carried him there.

The kitchen door was fastened with a latch, and when Mark, with no hand free for the opening, called for help, no one came; he saw Suse standing by the window and called her by name twice before she noticed that someone was calling. Mark was laughing when he shoved the dog, small-looking now, with its hair plastered down and its tail between its legs, into the kitchen, but Suse, hardly conscious of him, stood listening to the noise that came from the fireplace room—Sue Annie's shrill quarreling; the tumult of the hounds; the laughter and loud talk of the men trying but halfheartedly to get them out; the just awakened bawling babies—with bright hot angry eyes. What would the schoolteacher think? "Th damned hounds, allus th God-damned hounds."

"You're too pretty to cuss like that."

It was Mark looking down at her and smiling. She flushed, realizing she had spoken aloud and he had heard. "I won't tell," he said, and added, "It'll teach that fool teacher a lesson—bringen a strange cur dog to a place where they's nothen but hounds, then a screamen an a carryen on—whyn't she grab her dog?"

Suse tossed her head and went back to stand by the window; Mark followed and stood with her, and together they looked into the room. Most of the men were gathered about Nunn; even Willie Cooksey looked respectful, and Preacher Samuel interested. Blare was slapping Nunn on the back, the congratulatory slaps peculiar to him that almost knocked a man down, and Joe C. was repeating over and over, "But how in th hell, man, did them pups know it was a cur dog stid uv a fox?"

Lister shook his head in wonder. "One little sniff an they knowed."

Nunn stood with his hat pushed back, pleased, but with the air of a man not too surprised by the outcome of things. "They knowed it wasn't no fox," he said, "an mebbe back in the bluegrass where they were born they was around cur dogs a sight an recollected. An, anyhow, this cur dog was a chasen rabbits—mebbe they got a smell a rabbit right off an come home," and he smiled at Willie Cooksey in generous forgiveness of all his jibes.

Nunn and the crowd about him drifted outside. The party was over. Women were gathering up babies and bundles of diapers and hunting their men and older children with callings that it was time to go home. Sue Annie and some of the more sympathetic of the neighbor women were inspecting the damage done to her featherbeds and the white counterpane the hounds had jumped on. Everybody seemed to have forgotten the teacher; she stood by the mantel and busied herself with a little silvered compact that glittered in the light. Suse watched with fascination while she powdered her nose and straightened her lipstick and so removed all traces of her tears and fright and anger.

"Look at her," Mark said with disgust. "I wonder, now, does any of her belong to her by rights."

"I guess she thinks we're all fools," Suse said.

"Who cares what she thinks—raised in town an been off to school an putten on her airs. Times are gitten good —soon's th corn's laid by I'm a goen to Cincinnati an mebbe on to Deetroit."

"Deetroit," Suse whispered, turning and looking at him.

Mark nodded. "I got two cousins there; they say if a body can endure th place, th pay's good."

"Endure?"

"Yeah—they don't like it." His dark blue eyes glowed. "But me, I would."

"I'd love it—better'n anything on earth," she whispered, looking up at him, her thin face ecstatic almost, like the face of a worshiper glimpsing the dim outline of a distant shrine.

"You're too little now," he said, "to go so far away," and added like a careless afterthought, "but you're big enough to let me take you home."

Suse flushed. "I don't know you," she said, "That is, nothen but your horn."

"Oh, you listen for my fox horn," he said, pleased. "I'll play you a tune this comen Saturday night."

Suse giggled at his silly thinking she listened just for him. "I don't listen for it—a body couldn't help but hear it."

"Hey, Suse. What's goen on here? Time to go home." It was Nunn hunting her and plainly displeased at having found her on a dark corner of the back porch with one of the Cramers and the wildest one at that. "Evenen, Mark," he said curtly, took Suse by the hand and led her away, but not before Suse looked back and smiled a glowing smile that transformed her face; and Nunn saw, with a sharp twinge like a foreboding, that lots of people might

think her beautiful. He couldn't know that the smile was
for Detroit.

Aye, Lord, women were like horses; a dumb lazy filly
with foal was the easiest broke to plow of all; it was the
smart pretty ones that made trouble. He'd never much
liked pretty women; if Milly had been any prettier he'd
never have married her—but his mother was pretty—he
shook his head, perplexed by his crisscross thoughts.
He didn't want his Suse broke to the plow, but everybody
had to be—Lee Roy was in a way—too much so, maybe.

"Suse," he said, interrupting her flow of wonders and
comment on the new teacher when they were going over
the hill, "don't be gitten sparken an walken with th boys
in yer head. You ain't a goen to do it."

She whirled round in the path three times, then
stopped, facing him, her face like a young witch's in the
carbide light. "Law, Pop, I ain't never walked with a
boy. Mark was a tellen me he was a goen to Deetroit—
an anyhow," she went on, seizing his arm and holding it
with both hands and skipping beside him down the path,
"you an Mom was sparken, when she wasn't but fourteen
—an recollect I'm goen on fourteen. Mom wasn't much
more'n fifteen when she married," she giggled. "That
means I've got not much more'n a year to pick me a man
an spark in."

"I'll spark you," he said with a playful slap on her bottom, and added in what he hoped was a dignified father's
voice, "But I was old with money saved—an your mom,
recollect she hadn't no home."

Suse said nothing to that, but ran ahead of him, heedless of his command to wait for the light; dry as the
woods were, all the copperheads and rattlers in the country would be down by the creek. He shook his head as
he heard her light feet tap over the footlog, unafraid of
snakes or losing her footing in the dark; he had money to
live on for a spell, his pups had shown themselves this
night the smartest hounds in the country—and now it was
his womenfolks.

He stopped, wondering if Milly wouldn't rub it
in about the cur dog. How could she have been certain it
was no fox when she yelled it was no fox? But now she
had the right to act as if she had been certain.

When he went into the fireplace room, she was sitting

propped up in bed, indulging in an extra after-supper chew of tobacco, while she listened, smiling, to Suse and Lee Roy tell about the party, describing with much laughter and many gestures the antics of the cur dog when the hounds rushed in. Sam and Vinie, lying under the bed, listened with mild interest and with the others looked up at Nunn as he paused in the doorway.

Milly smiled more widely, reached over the bedside, and patted Vinie's head as she said, "Me an th pups now, we'uns ain't no fools."

Chapter Nineteen

BETS TO THE CONTRARY, Miss Betty Catharine Burdine did come back, but the big cur dog stayed in town, and Sue Annie's grandchildren took his place, walking with the teacher through the woods to and from school. But even so she cried much and was afraid; she was lonesome, she said; nights at Sue Annie's the screech owls troubled her: days she was restless with fleas from John's hogs under the floor, and seed ticks that seemed uncommon plentiful that year.

Still, nobody could deny but that Miss Burdine did all the law required; a car brought her early on Monday morning to Samuel's store and came for her on Frday afternoon; through the week she came on time and never left early much, complaining even if the children missed a day or came late or left at afternoon recess during blackberry picking and corn-laying-by time; she worked in her record book every day, the children said, and filled out all kinds and colors of cards.

One afternoon in early August the children had come proudly home each with a report card, which Nunn signed and returned, though John and the Tillers sent her word to keep the reports till the end of school—the youngens would only lose or dirty them. John in particular grumbled at such new-fangled notions—a youngens learning was in its head; it would in time show good or poor, and what in tarnation had a piece of paper to do with it.

However, the teacher was discussed less than she might have been. The hot dry summer took men's minds from most things except their failing crops. Keg Head

276

Cramer held the weather was an act of God, punishing His stiff-necked people, for most of the older men had seen dryer years, but few when the little rain that did fall came when it was needed least. They watched the Irish potatoes and early garden stuff like sallet peas and cabbage turn brown and die before they had hardly made back their seed, then hard-beating rains and thunderstorms rolled in from the west and the parched earth was flooded in one night. The dry dusty soil of the rolling sandfield and countless other hillside cornfields was carried away by the water and the roots of the young corn lay bare in the next day's hot sun.

Corn on level land and sweet potatoes and tomatoes and peanuts and all late things revived; the sorghum cane seed, dry in the ground for weeks, pushed pale tender spears above the ground, and Nunn's hayfields were green again; grass that had looked dead revived, and in the low rich swags the lespedeza seemed to have grown three inches in one night.

Then no more rains fell. Hot winds came steadily in from the southwest and the plowed earth of the fields was like hot metal, glittering under shimmering heat waves. Men watched the yellow rise in their corn, leaf by leaf, and the tender silks come out, not long and luxuriant, as in good years, but only a few, halfheartedly peeping from the withered shoots as if they knew the hot winds would bring death before they could catch a grain of pollen and give life to the waiting seed shapes below.

After the silks died and the tassels were brown as October fodder, men looked no more at their corn, save the lucky few, like John, with acres of deep moist creek bottom; even Nunn was lucky because he had a little strip of river bottom that might yet make some corn. There was still hope of sorghum cane and hay and sweet potatoes and late garden truck; but John was dour and full of forebodings of a hard winter, when food for both man and beast would be short. Springs that had never been dry in the memory of man went dry, and great cracks divided earth that ordinarily lay under ponds or pools of spring water.

At times Nunn cursed bitterly when he looked at his dying corn or walked through the woods where the beggar-lice and wild grasses and clovers that had flour-

ished and fattened his sheep in other years, were like his
upland corn—dead before they made their seed; and the
sheep, particularly the late lambs, were thin, grazing
along the creeks and even in the river cane brakes. Nunn
would think ahead to the winter; he had some cash left
from his sales in the early summer, and there would be
more, but not much: his lambs were too thin to bring
good prices, and in spite of poor feed prospects he still
planned to keep back enough of the better-looking ewe
lambs to make a flock of fifty. He wondered uneasily sometimes how he would manage through the winter; for
the first time since coming to the valley he would have
to buy corn, maybe even bread corn, and something for
his family to eat to take the place of the Irish potatoes
and other food he had always raised; from the looks of
things he wouldn't even have sorghum.

He tried to put on a good face around Milly. She sor-
rowed enough as it was; more than once he caught her
looking sadly at the four dozen new jars still stacked
empty in their boxes in a corner of the kitchen. It had
been her proud boast, like that of the neighbor women,
that she'd never gone into the winter with an empty jar;
now hardly half were full and two hundred half gallons
of canned stuff, with the children eating and growing the
way they were, wouldn't run them much past Christmas.

August that year, for Milly, was a miserable time, with
the world seemed turned all wrong. She missed the roaring canning fires, sometimes outside, sometimes in,
when she boiled green beans four hours in the jars
to make certain they would keep, or stirred molasses-
sweetened apple butter endlessly, or peeled tomatoes by
the dishpanful—there were hardly enough green beans
and tomatoes to get a mess a day—but more than anything she missed the apples; at least the weather was good
for apple drying, and it was strange to have none spread
on sheets to dry in the sun, no exciting rushes to get the
apples in when a sudden thunderstorm swooped down
into the valley.

It was a sin to think such things, but sometimes, instead
of good kind Jesus smiling over them all from somewhere
behind the sky, there was a grinning red-eyed devil, hot-
breathing and hard as the cracked earth, but cold in his
heart as the late frosts of the blighted spring that had

taken the apples. And when Milly thought of the
devil, she would think of King Devil, who had appeared
to her last fall, green-eyed and smiling, and the devil in
the sky would, without her will, take his face; and day
after day in August, while the earth cracks widened and
the corn died and even the heat-loving rattlers came
down from the dry timbered ridges and made a pestilence along the creeks, dry save for a few scum-covered
pools, this King Devil of the sky grinned down on them
all.

It had always seemed to Milly that when she was in
the family way she minded the heat more, and now, with
nothing to do, not even sewing, for that was long since
done, she brooded often on the birth of her child that
was to be in the early winter, recalling to mind all the
gruesome details of every hard, unnatural birth Sue Annie
had ever described or she had ever witnessed.

At times she was afraid, waking at night in a
cold sweat of fear, memories of the long agonies of other
births vivid as fresh-dreamed dreams; at other times she
was filled with a hot hate and an anger against the dry
heat, her weary body, and even the children. But mostly
she was resigned and sorrowful: she put her trust in Jesus; He would take her and look out for her children,
and nothing else mattered; at such times she would go
about with her clothing so slipshod that Suse, studying
her with a mingling of pity and vexation, would be thankful Miss Burdine never came down to visit as she had at
first hoped she would.

And in the coolness of the twilight, when Uncle Dave
Tiller fiddled and the Cookseys in the Cow's Horn sang,
Milly would sing, too; doleful things like, "Shall we
gather at the river, the beautiful river that flows by the
throne of God?" in a sad, tired, yearning voice, as if she
would rather be by the throne of God instead of where
she was.

Nunn, listening, would move restlessly about, though
it was the time of day in which he ordinarily sat
and watched the sunset and rested from the heat and
work of the day; his dying crops needed no help, but
through the heat he worked hard, mostly at clearing
brush and rocks from the storehouse field where he
planned to sow grass and lespedeza next spring. Milly

turned his thoughts to death and trouble, and trouble now meant starvation; anxious thoughts that had never used to come to him would swarm over him like black spiders sucking his blood in a nightmare. He had never doubted himself. When he went to the mines, he had known that sooner or later he would save money enough to buy a bit of land—Aunt Marthie's if it got cheap enough; when he married he had been certain he could care for Milly and raise a family and prosper in the valley as Aunt Marthie and Preacher Jim had done; but now, listening to Milly sing, he doubted his worth as a man and felt a failure in all things, from farming to catching King Devil.

Milly's religious resignation troubled him so that he was almost glad when she would take a quarrelsome, ill-turned spell, slapping the children, even Suse, who was kind and patient with Milly as some wise old woman, though sharp and critical of all other things and people about her, including Nunn.

Susie and the older ones could get away to school, but Deb had no school and no work to take him away, and life at times was hard and puzzling. At one time Milly would only sigh resignedly when he came in without his breeches though he was a big boy going on three; the next time she would give him three hard slaps across his bare bottom and shame him so that he cried more with a hurt heart than a hurt bottom.

The pups, almost as tall as he, were equally troubled and went about with drooping tails and sad eyes. Nunn might roar at them, Lee Roy curse, and Suse kick at them with her bare feet and they would frolic away untroubled; but if Milly scolded when they got under her feet or put their noses in her lap, they were instantly all shame and sorrow; for even more than Zing they were Milly's own. She had worried for days before the opening of school for fear they would go to school as Zing had done, and start running with the trashy rabbit-chasing Tiller hounds before they were old enough to be set in their ways, but on the first day of school they had stood contentedly with Milly in the kitchen door and watched the children go.

And now through the fierce dry heat they never wandered far, but seemed to know in Milly there was safety.

Nunn wanted to chain them up, afraid that King Devil might come within range of their wanderings and lead them away to the high dry ridges where a running hound could die for lack of water, or down to the creek or the river where a terrible death could wait from a rattler coiled in the coolness. There were mad dogs, too, over the country, or at least fearful tales of frothing, red-eyed beasts; and one of a cow that gave bloody milk and bit a little girl.

But Milly wouldn't hear to having the pups tied; at night they slept on the hearthstones, the coolest spot in the house, and by day they lived up to what Milly said of them. "They've got might nigh human sense, Nunn; they know when it's no time to go away."

They took over the care of Deb, much as Zing had done Lee Roy. They knew snake smell now; Vinie in particular was good to stand and bark until somebody came running with a hoe. The three of them—Deb and Vinie and Sam—took as their favorite refuge against the heat and Milly's scoldings the cool green twilight under the big low-limbed sycamore by the spring. The pups would lie stomach downward in the cool damp earth just above the water; Deb would settle himself in like fashion on the low limestone ledge above the pool and watch the crawfish; sometimes the big bullfrog that Suse called Old Uncle Dave would come out and hop on a square of stone that once had been part of a spring house and croak a song for him.

Birds, all kinds of birds, even big catbirds that could, when they were so minded, make the sound of a young lamb, lived in the sycamore and the tangle of brush. They came to drink and bathe and fight and gossip and educate their young in catching bugs and hunting worms. Snakes, too, came, and sometimes squirrels, and once Deb had seen a polecat.

Tired of watching the life below, he would turn from his stomach to his back and stare upward, peeking at the sky through the sycamore leaves; often the mockingbird that lived in the tree would come, hopping lower and lower, pausing on each downward limb to study the motionless child, and at last on a low white limb would sit and sing, and Deb would forget his game of hide-and-seek with the sky through the leaves and listen to the mockingbird.

At other times, using some of the knives and forks or
his mother's scissors, he would carve out wondrous hills
and valleys and river bottoms in the damp black earth
around the spring. Then after a while Milly's slaps and
scoldings, his wanting of milk, the heat that made him
prickle and itch would go far away and he would fall
asleep.

Milly would come and find him sleeping, see the tear
marks on his face, and stroke his silver hair and berate
herself for being a mean careless mother who let her child
wander off and fall asleep, and know it was a black sin
on her to quarrel and carry on so. Everything would be
all right—she had so much—this spring, now, it was
about the finest in the country. Springs all over the country were dry—some, like Lureenie, had to carry water
from the river—but around her spring the wild asters
and woods goldenrod were blooming as on any other fall.

Then her eyes would chance on the big stone crock in
the spring branch under an outspreading wild hydrangea
bush, and she would think of last fall when it had always
been full to overflowing with tomatoes and cucumbers
and muskmelons kept cooling there for the children to
eat when they came from school; and now, except for a
few scrawny tomatoes and crooked cucumbers, saved
stingily to eat with the beans at supper, it was empty.

And the empty jars and the withered garden and her
tired swollen body that suffered in the heat were torment-
ing, driving her once more to sorrowful tears or angry
scoldings. Deb would look at her in troubled wonder
when she stormed at him—he had only asked for a drink
of milk or a piece of bread and butter. Then hardly
would the angry scolding be done than she was crying
and petting him. But no matter what she said or did,
there was never more than a sip of milk between meals
and no butter to mix with honey.

Deb was too little to understand why his mother
stormed and cried when he asked for milk, but Suse did,
and so never drank any of the little milk that Betsey
gave, and never ate butter; somewhere she had read
that women who were going to have babies needed milk,
and there were times when she hated her father because
there was no milk. He had sold the black heifer; he had
spent money for dog feed that might have gone for cow

feed. Worse yet, he would sit all unnoticing, with a big glass of milk in his hand, holding it up, maybe, while he said something. And Suse would see Milly's eyes, like hungry birds, dart swiftly to it, and then as swiftly dart away. Deb and Lucy would study the glass with unhidden longing when their own small ones were empty, but they never asked, and Nunn, who never touched Betsey or handled her milk except to drink it, never knew.

Suse would think of Lureenie; she didn't have to worry about the weather and soon she wouldn't have to worry over what the neighbors would say, for, much to the surprise of everybody, Rans was sending her money regularly. He planned for her to come to Cincinnati in the late fall; he had written that he would rent a furnished room, and all she had to do was bring herself and the youngens, but first she must get them all some clothes.

Sometimes Lureenie would read aloud some bit of exciting news from Rans: he had been to a movie full of women dancing and big ships in a storm on the ocean, and he couldn't wait to take Lureenie. She had been to two movies in the county-seat town before she was married, but Suse, who had never been to any except the fire-fighting pictures the national-forest men showed up at the church house each fall, trembled with anticipation. She, too, would see such things, and more, before many years were over.

Even better than Rans's letters was the catalogue Lureenie got from Montgomery Ward all new and smelling of ink and filled with real things more exciting than any imagined because they were bought and used by people in the outer world. Suse studied it for hours; Mrs. Hull was the only person in the country who got a catalogue regularly, and Suse had never looked at it for more than a few minutes at a time.

The selection of what clothing and materials Lureenie could buy took no end of time and many consultations with Suse, and Milly, too, who, though she read but slowly and went mostly by the pictures, could with no pattern turn yard goods into a dress pretty as one pictured. When after much discussion Lureenie wrote the order, and Suse was allowed to go at daylight and mail the letter in time for the mail mule that left at eight,

there was the long exciting wait for the order to come
C.O.D.

Supper would be late on the night of its coming, while
Milly neglected her work to caress the material and drape
it this way and that, head tilted, frowning, while she decided just how it should be sewed. Nunn never complained if they had to eat by lantern light. When Lureenie
was around, smiling and nodding and gabbling away,
Milly would forget her troubles and smile and talk and
plan over the fine new cloth, holding no envy that it was
not her own, but sometimes to Nunn there would come
a sharp hurt that he couldn't order stuff like that for
Milly.

At times he was conscious of Suse's wistful eyes as she
listened to Lureenie chatter away about what she would
see and do and buy in Cincinnati. He would feel restless
and uneasy as when he had seen her smile at Mark
Cramer. He worried more, but kept carefully silent when
after a trip in the twilight around to Lureenie's to help
carry children and bundles home, she would speak casu-
ally of having seen Mark Cramer there; he had come to
cut wood for his sister-in-law or ask for news of Rans.
Sometimes Suse quoted Mark, whose father, Keg Head,
took a county paper; times were getting good and jobs
plentiful; it was the war across the waters, people said.
Mark would wait until the river-bottom corn was gathered
and he would go to Cincinnati, maybe when Lureenie
went, so as to help her with the children.

Nunn would look at his withered corn and wonder if
he, too, ought not to go away and hunt a job—and then
he would think of King Devil. He would run again come
fall.

Late in August, when pasture fields were dusty and
most of the corn save that in the river and creek bottoms
was dead, there came a two-week spell of hot rainy
weather that made the creek run again and flooded the
springs. It saved Nunn's river-bottom corn, revived a little of the garden stuff, such as the late roasting-ear patch
and some of the sweet potatoes, but best of all, the
lespedeza and grass in the low and fertile place of what
was to be the hayfield were saved. Nunn would have a
hay crop—not half of what he might have had in a good
season, but some.

John, though somewhat grudgingly, since he was afraid a rock had been left in the fields to break a tooth on his mowing machine, came with mowing machine, hayrake, and team.

The haymaking was like two holidays together; Joe C. and Blare came and their older children and John's two boys, and though Nunn would just as soon he hadn't been there, Mark Cramer came with Lureenie and her youngens. The women and Suse cooked great chicken dinners for the haymakers and even Milly was light-hearted as load after load of the sweet-smelling hay went into the barn; Nunn went around with smiles in his eyes, and Blare said he thought he'd join the AAA and grow lespedeza; even John praised the hay, as good as his, he said; that government fertilizer was the stuff and hay the thing for a dry year.

More than the hay, John praised Lee Roy; a better worker, he said, than either of his last two boys. Lee Roy flushed and ran away, choked up with happiness, to see Maude's fresh-dropped foal, three days old and big and wild, but he succeeded in getting his hand on its shoulder.

Chapter Twenty

SUSE HATED THE HAYMAKING; it made her miss two more days of school, and already because of Milly's condition, she had had to miss more than usual to help with the washing and the floor scrubbing; and Miss Burdine complained and scolded each time a scholar was even late. And now when Suse came back after the haymaking, Miss Burdine was even more sharp, because Andy had gone on in his studies and Suse had missed a lot. They had got into one of the hardest places in the eighth-grade arithmetic, where a body had to build a whole round silo with a round floor and a bottom thicker than the top, reinforced with four-inch pipe, and all of concrete at so much a cubic yard, and figure out how much the whole thing cost, even to the paint.

Suse read the problem three times, and then whispered to Andy, sweating over half a tablet full of figures, "I reckon she explained it all th first day I missed."

"Kind of," Andy answered, "but I somehow couldn't much understand—we worked some a th same kind in water tanks last year, recollect, but not so long. I recken I'm a worken this right, but I keep missen th answer. It allus costs a little too much."

Suse studied the explanations in the book for a time, then worked the problem; her answer was within a few cents of Andy's but was several dollars more than that in the book. Arithmetic class was not far away. "Let's ask her are we on the right road," Suse whispered.

Andy shook his head. "She don't much like to be asked about arithmetic."

"You're bashful," Suse said, and as soon as Miss

Burdine had finished third-grade reading class—John Robison Tiller—she raised her hand and asked if Miss Burdine would please look at their silo problems a minute: she and Andy had worked and worked; their answers were almost exactly alike but different from that in the book, and they couldn't find any mistake they'd made; could the answer in the book be wrong, she asked—once they'd used an arithmetic book and Andrew had found three wrong answers.

Miss Burdine smiled the distant, half pitying, half ridiculing—or so it sometimes seemed to Suse—smile she often gave the children. "Now, Suse, you know the answers in our textbooks are always right. You missed the day I explained the problems and I can't interrupt my work to explain again. . . . Maybe you're copying from Andy and that's the reason you get the wrong answer."

She called fifth-grade reading, Lee Roy and Ruby, and turned away. Andy gaped at her in surprise, but Suse bent her head and stared at her figure-covered tablet page through embarrassed, angry tears. Arithmetic between her and Andy had always been a kind of game— they'd worked much together and copying would have destroyed the game.

Andy was patting her on the back and whispering, "Don't feel bad, Suse. Anyway she didn't explain the silos to me—she read out loud what th book said an told me to start worken. Sometimes," he added worriedly, "I think Mom's right. Th woman ain't smart as old Andrew."

Suse shook her head sadly. "She ain't no fool, but she thinks I am."

"Then she is a fool," Andy said, and shrugged Miss Burdine's no-whispering-please look off his shoulders.

During morning recess they sat under a poplar and worked still, and back in the schoolhouse they figured some more, but when Miss Burdine called their class, their answers were still dollars from the book, but exactly the same; Suse had found a mistake in subtraction. As usual, Miss Burdine asked if they had had any trouble. Until today the answer had always been "No," and she would then have them put the problems on the board, explain how they had been worked, assign some more problems and dismiss. Today she showed displeasure at the answered "Yes," opened the arithmetic, frowned a moment over the problem, then turned to Andy. "Suppose you put the problem on anyway. I'll go over it and find the mistake. You're doing something wrong."

Andy went to the painted strip of wall that served as blackboard and quickly, with no copying from his previous work, put the problem on and got the same answer. Miss Burdine took a piece of chalk and slowly, so that she finished several minutes after Andy, checked as he worked and came out with his answer. "Your figures are right," she said, giving her words a sound of authority.

Andy turned his mild brown eyes on her, and there was also authority in his voice when he said in mild slowness, "No, they ain't no mistakes. Suse checked em."

"Watch your grammar, Andy," Miss Burdine said, flushing a little. "Don't say 'ain't.' "

Suse wriggled on the recitation bench. Why didn't she work the problem as old Andrew would have done? Andy had worked on it two days already, and she was tired of hearing about grammar. " 'Ain't' ain't bad grammar," she said; "it's bad English. . . . You work it for us," she added quickly, before she could be scolded for bad manners. "They's somethen we're doen wrong, some little somethen."

"Yes," Andy said, and laid down his chalk. "You work it. Somewhere we're maken a mistake in th worken, not th figgeren."

Miss Burdine's face looked red and damp the way it looked when seed ticks harassed her. She picked up the opened arithmetic, stared at the problem a moment, then holding one finger on it, leafed backward to the explanation, and read a moment with quick grasping movements of her eyes.

Suse and Andy watched her and behind them the room grew still; even Bernice Dean forgot to wriggle in her seat for watching; why she watched she didn't know, but Lee Roy, with whom she was secretly in love, watched from across the aisle, and his eyes were pleased and knowing.

Slowly, as Miss Burdine reluctantly laid the book down and picked up chalk, Suse's eyes grew knowing, too, but they were not pleased—stricken they were as the eyes of a pilgrim who, traveled far to worship at a golden shrine, finds the shrine made of new veneer overlaid with gilt.

Andy looked stern, like his father when a church member back-slid, but unsurprised. The radius of the bottom was nine and a half feet. Miss Burdine, after some fidgeting through the book, started to multiply by 22/7. "Double th radius to git th diameter an then multiply by 3.1416; we ain't used 22/7 since we was in th seventh grade—th answer would come wrong," Andy said.

Miss Burdine bit her lip and floundered on. Suse stared out the window at John's mules dozing in the shade. Old Andrew on a hot day like this would have had the school outside in the shade. He would be sitting almost lying against the big white oak with his hat pulled over his eyes; he would be ill-turned when she and Andy came to him with an unsolved problem, and say, "You ain't used your heads right, youngens; try again," and most likely go to sleep. They would awaken him when once more the wrong answer turned up. He would spit out his tobacco and say something like, "You're letten it skeer you cause it's round; a silo ain't nothen but a rolled-up wall. Did you figger them iron rods right?"

Old Andrew faded and she thought of the iron pipes going up—she'd forgotten it was to be rolled up when she counted the pipes—they wouldn't stand at either end like posts in a fence. She turned quickly to Andy, frowning over Miss Burdine as she floundered through cement for the wall. "We got one pipe too many, Andy," she whispered.

He understood in a moment how it was and looked at her with awe for her smartness and a shade of envy at not having thought of it himself, but a moment later it was his turn to whisper excitedly, "Suse, them pipes is holler—we didn't take out cement fer them—we worked it like they didn't take up no room."

"I can't concentrate when you're whispering," Miss Burdine complained. "What is the answer again?"

Suse read it, $874.97, and Miss Burdine wrote it in a corner of the blackboard and went on figuring. Andy was busy over his tablet on his knees; it wasn't easy to find the cubic contents of the four-inch pipe. "Now there's the answer," Miss Burdine said, and looked around for the eraser, which had fallen on the floor.

Andy picked it up and held it, studying the blackboard. "You've got a mistake there," he said, "where you

added th cost a th cement an th cost a th pipe an th paint
together."

Miss Burdine flushed and looked hungrily at the
eraser. But she added again and the answer was not the
one in the book, nor the one Suse and Andy had had.

"That's wrong," Suse said. She would never have sworn
to it, but Miss Burdine said something softly, and it
sounded like "Shit." Andy heard it too, and looked at
Suse, then looked quickly away. Miss Burdine was saying with an air of finality, "That's the right answer, I'm
sure. Books can be wrong."

"But me an Andy—" Suse began.

"Andy and I—It's already past time for this class to
be over," and she added as she glanced at her wristwatch, "Class dismissed."

Andy got up from the recitation bench, turned on his
heel, slammed his book on his desk, and clumped out the
door.

Suse sat a moment gaping at Miss Burdine. After a moment she got up, and with head hanging as if she and not
the teacher had done the wrong, went back to her seat
and listened with a grim, uncaring look while Miss Burdine
told Lee Roy to hurry and drive out Drum and Blunder,
who had come in while she had stood with her back to the
door, working on the problem.

None of the Tiller hounds had ever seemed to learn
that school was closed to them this year because the new
teacher both feared and hated all hounds. Suse and Andy
and Rachel, the more conscientious of the pupils, had tried
all school to keep them out of the house and away from
Miss Burdine on the rare times when she came out on the
playground.

But today nobody frowned, and Rachel smiled on Lee
Roy when after a few soft-voiced beseechings more suited
to a flustered, frightened hen with young chickens than a
hardened hound, he sat down with a helpless shrug of his
shoulders. Drum and Blunder remained by the stove, a
favorite spot in hot weather because the square of tin in
front was cool to their bellies. Miss Burdine looked at
Ruby; her father owned two of the hounds. Ruby giggled.
"Pop allus says a woman cain't manage a hound."

"An it's dangerous to try," Silas Ballew said.

Not long after, Lead and Drive came in and took their

places as of old. Miss Burdine looked both frightened and exasperated but said nothing.

The hounds came on to school, and now and then, as in Andrew's day, life was enlivened by a little rabbit-chasing or an occasional gray-fox hunt. Suse or Andy could have stopped it; but since the silo problem, Andy was stern and silent in the presence of Miss Burdine, and Suse was silent, too, gazing at the teacher at times with sad disappointed eyes that made Miss Burdine fidget as under many seed ticks.

The hounds gazed at the teacher, too, all four of them lying by the stove, and there was much of speculation in their looks, or so it might have seemed to a stranger like the teacher. It was as if they said among themselves, "Here is a new and chaseable animal that might run like a rabbit, and if cornered, give no more fight than a possum," and daily they grew more contemptuous of her. Drum, the elder, took to growling when she came near him. She appealed to Ruby to have her father chain him up, but Ruby giggled and said it was dog days and hounds were vigrus then, dangerous to chain; and when Miss Burdine looked about the room, seeking denial of what seemed Ruby's lies, heads nodded soberly to Ruby's words, and eyes agreed.

One morning, not long before recess, Lee Roy, after a deal of whispering with Silas Ballew, who had just come back from a long time of being excused, got up and drove the hounds so far from the schoolhouse that he never got back till recess time. He then came to Miss Burdine and asked her did she want to see some fun—he'd seen a gray fox run down below the schoolhouse and she could, by standing in a safe place above the schoolhouse, see a fox race. He smiled his most engaging smile, and Suse was at once mistrustful, suspecting some trickery with a polecat or worse, but said nothing. Whatever Lee Roy was up to, the Tiller hounds wouldn't hurt the teacher.

They almost never hurt anything, not even a fox, and it was only a few days back that Hattie Tiller had come up from the spring under the river hill—all the upper Tiller springs were dry—hot and worn out from carrying two buckets of cold spring water up the steep path, and found Blare's pigs rooting in the sweet-potato patch, and Drum and Blunder watching from the shade of the house wall;

she'd got so mad she'd thrown one whole bucket of her precious water all over Blunder, for he did hate cold spring water.

Miss Burdine, after many assurances from Lee Roy and the others that she wouldn't be hurt, that the hounds would not even come close to her, consented to sit on the spot Lee Roy pointed out—a hollow log above the schoolhouse. Suse wondered if he had discovered a patch of seed tick there or a snake or what, but kept silent. If she raised a racket, Lucy, who wasn't always too reliable in such matters, might go home and tell that Lee Roy had tried to kill the teacher.

The four Tiller hounds were soon heard baying wildly up on Schoolhouse Point. In a few minutes the trail straightened out and they came on, over the hill and on down to the school spring and hog wallow that lay around the hill from the schoolhouse.

They came hard around the spring path, their voices loud and angry, as if they would eat the very earth under their feet. Miss Burdine began to look apprehensive and started to leave the log to be with the children gathered by the school path. Silas Ballew waved her back. "They'll come closer here," he called, and added gallantly, "If you're skeered I'll come stay by you."

Followed by Lee Roy, he ran to stand on the log, and just then the four hounds, running like one and baying like twenty, came in sight. About fifty feet from the schoolhouse door, and when they were almost opposite Miss Burdine, they left the path, running above the schoolhouse instead of below, and straight toward the log.

Lee Roy and the Tiller boys began screaming, "Run, Miss Burdine, run fer th fence; they're after you," said Silas, on the log, let out what he hoped was a scream of terror and ran up the hill while Lee Roy, with another scream, shinnied up a tree.

The hounds came nearer the log. Miss Burdine stood a second longer, staring wildly about. Lee Roy screamed, "Run fer th fence, Teacher," and John Robison shrieked, "Climb a tree! Oh, my God, climb a tree, Teacher! They'll eat you up alive—they've left fox scent fer *you!*"

Miss Burdine screamed, leaped from the log, and ran toward the fence with the labored, awkward stumbling motion of a woman running through the woods in high-heeled shoes.

The hounds reached the log, ran over it and round and round, investigating it with angry snarls and whines and harroufings. Miss Burdine reached the fence, and heedless of its barbed-wire topping that tore her hose, and snagged her skirt, pulled herself over and stood a second panting, looking back at the hounds on the log with the dazed terror of one narrowly escaped from death. Old Drum leaped from the log toward the fence, and Lee Roy and his Ballew cousins screamed, "Run, Teacher, run! They're a comen fer th fence—run! Oh, my God, run! They've plum fergot th fox an they'll chew you up alive."

Miss Burdine, with an ear-splitting cry, disappeared in the thick woods, the hounds cascaded over the fence, and for minutes longer the children could hear her piercing, panting screams, rising even above the hounds' cries as they ran along the Tiller path.

Suse turned on Lee Roy. "You all ought to be ashamed —you seed a gray fox run around an stop on that log an then go over the fence."

"Watch yer English, dear," Lee Roy said in a shrill treble, but John Robison Tiller was interrupting, " 'Twas me an Silas seed th fox from th schoolhouse winder."

Chapter Twenty-one

So ANDREW CAME BACK on a windy, windy day in mid-October, not walking, but riding a little mule, almost of donkey size, that the children named Andrew's Airplane. Though the county superintendent had talked to him sternly about the importance of keeping records and coming every day, and reminded him that if he didn't do better he'd never get to teach the two more years he must teach in order to be pensioned for life, there was little school for the first week. The children, particularly the Tillers, were always interrupting to tell some just remembered queerness of Miss Burdine's.

Suse, when they talked of Miss Burdine, was silent: even now she could shut her eyes and see Miss Burdine, the fine smart woman from the city hunting for the eraser to wipe out the problem she couldn't work, hear her whispered nasty word, and life, even school, seemed dull and empty at times.

She was glad when on a day of Andrew's first week there was no school: some government business where the three teachers of the voting precinct must meet at Deer Lick School and register all the men in the district. Mark had told her about it one afternoon at Lureenie's—it was because of the war across the waters—the men were not going away to fight, only to train for a year. Mark wished he were twenty-one instead of eighteen; he would go away and train to be a bombardier, but as it was he couldn't even register.

Nunn and the Tiller and Anderson men went in a little body, their hounds trailing at their heels, good-naturedly put out at losing a day for nothing. Single men in their twenties were to take the training, not the married ones; so why should the government make them register—especially old ones like Nunn, thirty-four with four children, or Jaw Buster, who was twenty-seven and had three.

In the schoolhouse there was talk and laughter. Blare said he thought he'd volunteer if they'd take married men: he'd like to get away from Flonnie and the youngens for a change; and Lanie Anderson, wife of one of Jaw Buster's younger brothers, who had walked over with her husband, said if they took Oscar she'd go, too, and Roxie Sexton laughingly agreed that it could be an excuse for all the men to get away from home.

But old Ansel, with his six sons between sixteen and thirty, shook his cane at Roxie. "Laugh, laugh, an then go read Revelations—fore it's over your man'ull mebbe be at war—across th waters—his eyes blind with blood an mud. They took em acrost th waters onct an they'll do it agin."

Roxie's mouth, open with laughter, closed, and she whispered softly, "War," and looked at her tall husband and squeezed the baby.

Silence, like a cloud across the sun, came into the schoolroom, and Andrew could be heard asking Reuben Anderson, "Now when was it you was married, Reubie—last July was a year ago?"

And Reuben looked at his father, Ansel, and grinned, "What was th date, Pop? July 7 I keep a thinken, but seems like that was this July, th day th baby come."

"Th 14th was your wedden day," Ansel said, and stared a moment at his big son, then looked away to the bright leaves outside.

Old Andrew shifted in his chair. "I don't like this," he said. "Puts me in mind a th last war; I registered th boys then; some I never saw agin."

"But this is registration, nothen more fer married men like me," Reuben said. "I cain't leave Corie with a little youngen—who'd cut her wood—she cain't cut wood."

"It's just registration," Roxie Sexton said, speaking slowly and carefully, as if through careful speech she would give truth to the words. "They said th boys won't have to fight; they'll be back in a year, an none a th married ones will have to go."

"They, They," Uncle Ansel repeated, and shook his stick at the still blue sky.

Brief thoughts of the war across the waters stirred in
Nunn as he and the pups walked over the hill together
through the bright rustling leaves, but the bloody mess was
far away as the stars at noontime. When at home Milly
shook her head worriedly over all the government business
and wondered if They would take the boys across the waters, he laughed, but Milly sighed and looked away to the
colored hills and said there was something sad about the
fall; the days were like warnings that such would never
come again, and had he noticed the sunsets? Red they
were, like blood.

"It's th shape you're in, Milly, that makes th world full
a signs an warnens; an you're sad cause you ain't got a
great jag a stuff to put away like you had last fall. It'll rain
one a these days," he comforted.

But through the fall almost no rain fell. Old John grew
stringy-necked and big-eyed from little sleep. The night
wind whispering and tossing the fallen leaves and the
smoky haze over the farther hills, with at times a whiff of
wood-smoke smell borne on the south wind, all reminded
the old man of the ever-increasing threat of fire that lay in
the bright dry leaves; and on the windy moonlit nights he
was restless, looking often around the valley rim, searching out his poplar timber, or walking through his barns
and outhouses.

At dawn the winds would die and smoke gather thinly
on the edges of the sky and blur the outlines of the hills
and lay a redness on the sun, while overhead, day after
day, the valley was ceiled with a low dull sky, not bright
and blue as on other falls, but thick with smoke and dust.
Nunn, like John, was restless in the dry dead weather; he
worried little about the threat of fire, but fall was running
into winter, the harvest moon was in the wane, and King
Devil had left no scent that Sam and Vinie could find.

But one night when the hunter's moon was near the full,
there came a little mist of rain, and next morning, while
Milly was shelling corn for an early mess of hominy, she
heard a train blow sharp and clear, as if it had been up at
Sue Annie's, instead of miles away at the Cumberland
River Bridge.

Deb looked up in surprise at the unremembered sound,
then made a soft woo-wooing with his lips. "That's th be-

ginnen a winter, Deb. Air's a comen frum th north, an now you'll have to start wearen them new shoes."

She got up and went to the kitchen door, the shelled corn still in her apron. At a casual glance the day looked much like yesterday and dozens of other days of fall; the sun was warm above the valley, the oak trees were bronze-red still, and red and yellow leaves still clung to the beech and maple trees. But high on the shoulders of the hills the pines glittered coldly in the sun, and Milly, studying the pattern of light and sound and air, noticed the blackness of the shadow of the leafless walnut by the door. The lines of the farther hills rolling away from the creek gap were no longer softly blurred in an autumn haze, but rose clear and sharp and hard, like rows of blue-steel knife blades laid against the sky. Across the river in Alcorn she could see Willie Cooksey's barn, see it so clearly that she could tell where new shakes had patched the old.

She shivered and hurried back into the kitchen, threw more coal into the cookstove, and though Deb screamed and struggled, for now, as last fall, he thought of his new shoes as playthings only, she got him into his shoes and stockings. Though she had the hominy corn shelled and a batch of clean maple-wood ashes ready, she quit work on it to get ready for winter.

But today there was none of the pleasant bustle of other falls, when every cranny of the house was stuffed with dried things to be protected from mice or canned goods to be covered from the cold. Empty jars would not hurt in the cold, and by noon she had put away her scanty store of canned goods, covered the small pile of thin-rooted sweet potatoes upstairs, and put more dirt on the one small hole of Irish potatoes. Nothing was left but the flowers, the late-blooming marigolds and chrysanthemums and cosmos she had kept alive through the hot dry summer with dishwater; these she would leave for the children when they came from school; they could cut and save a few, but most must be left to die in the coming hard frost.

She never told Suse, singing as she cut the flowers in the sharp still twilight, that this was a job she hated, the cutting of the flowers before the first hard killing frost. It seemed so far away, the time when there would be flowers again; and winter was a hard time. Angie Mime an Tom had both gone in the winter, and—Nunn—and a baby coming—she almost wished Sam and Vinie were pups again, not big enough to hunt.

The children put water in all the cracked fruit jars and empty lard buckets they could find and filled them with flowers; and the sharp spicy odor of the chrysanthemums and marigolds hurt her throat—there'd been chrysanthemums withered and dead on the mantel December when Angie Mime died—and maybe these the children put there now would be smelling still when the baby came, sometime before Christmas, if she figured right. She was glad to leave the house for the milking.

It was deep twilight now, the sun fallen behind the long swell of the graveyard field, leaving the sky a cold blue-green in the west, with one low-hanging star, big and bright and cold, like a star in winter. And Betsey, thin from the scanty autumn, was like a cow in winter, the hairs lifted along her spine and her back humped with the cold. Milly milked a long while but came away with less than half a gallon; Betsey would most likely go dry while she was down with the baby, and they needed milk so; she looked down at the bucket, half lifted it to her lips, then left it to swing in her hand; Nunn and the children craved milk, too; the unborn baby might be marked from her bad wanting milk, but the wanting had gone on so long it was marked already.

The hard frost came that night. At midnight, when Milly was up making the rounds of the children to see that they were warmly covered, she felt the hard cold through the house; and outside, past the black shadow of the house wall, the white frost glittered colder than snow in the moonlight.

Next morning the buckets of water in the kitchen were skimmed with ice, and the young pines above the garden were white to their tops with frost. Milly hurried as much as her clumsy body would allow through the work in the kitchen, for the little step stove warmed the great barnlike room with its worn floor and missing windowpanes no more than the moon warms the sky. Her feet hurt while she got breakfast and waited on Nunn and the children, but by the time she had fixed the dinner buckets and washed the dishes and put a kettle of fodder beans to boil, they were as blocks of wood.

After a while the weak, pale wintry-looking sun got

high enough above the valley rim to melt the frost, and all the leaves except part of the oaks began a limply silent falling. By noon the last of the fall brightness was gone, and the valley seemed bigger, with a bare look, like a room from which the bright hanging curtains have been taken, and the sun dimmed early behind thickening layers of cloud. By dark, a cold, straight-dropping autumn rain was falling.

Milly sat that night and listened to the hiss of the rain down the chimney and thought of the children's leaky shoes and the scant food saved against the winter, but mostly she thought of Nunn, rocking Deb to the tune of a gay song—promise of good hunting made him gay. Through the few races of the dry windy fall, the pups had shown themselves as good as, and sometimes better than, old experienced Speed and Sourvine. Nunn's hopes were high for getting King Devil before spring; she sighed, frowning into the fire—he'd had high hopes last fall and on many other falls.

Though the next night was a Wednesday, which meant he must hunt alone, for most of the other hunters, even the Tillers, could go only on Saturday nights, Nunn and the pups went away into the cold drizzly dark and never got back till the dawn was whitening the tops of the hills. King Devil had not come out, but a smart swift red fox had given Sam and Vinie some good practice, Nunn said, hollow-eyed from his sleepless night in the cold, but gay almost as he drank the steaming coffee Milly made fresh for him; the pups had run well, he said; by Christmas they couldn't be beat.

That was only one of many nights when Nunn hunted alone and came home late and hollow-eyed, for the fall that year was a time of good hunting, with thin, quick-melting snows and mists of rain. More than once King Devil let himself be chased, usually on Saturday nights as if he scorned to be hunted by two hounds only, though by late November Sam and Vinie almost always ran ahead of Speed.

It was in the last days of November, after a good race on King Devil, that the pups had their first birthday, and Milly baked a sugar-sweetened cake for them—the dried-up cane patch had gone for fodder, and now and then Nunn bought five pounds of sugar, for nothing but a little honey-sweetening was hard to get along on. The children made a party of the sugar cake and Suse used two little splinters of fat pine for candles and there was much gay laughter; but when Sam came and put his head on Milly's knee, she looked down into his brown eyes and whispered with something close to sorrow, "Your baby days are over, honey; you're a full-growed hound, an they's many a long hard hunt ahead."

Sam wagged his tail and whined; it was as if he knew he could hunt now with no letup and no holding back. Like Vinie, he had grown into a great tough, long-legged beast weighing close to fifty pounds. Now when they walked to the post office with Nunn, men studied them with more respect and less of the curiosity mingled with contempt they had held for them when they were only costly little pups with pedigrees, and snowy-white Vinie, with her unnaturally dark eyes, was more and more a thing to be admired.

Men were agreed that the way things looked now the pups might get King Devil; their chances were discussed more than the war across the waters coming to this side or the chances of the graded graveled road's coming to Samuel's. Zing had been a good hound, but Sam and Vinie had already shown themselves better. It had taken old Zing months to figure out what happened when King Devil ran a rail fence or in the edge of a swiftly flowing creek, but before the fall was ended Sam and Vinie knew. When the scent disappeared by a rail fence, Vinie would clamber up the fence, sniffing as she went over, and keep it up, back and forth, until she found a trace of scent; the scent once found, she would run along, leaping up and sniffing the top of the fence every few steps; Sam would keep to the other side, leaping and sniffing too; and when the scent hit the ground again, after even the longest of leaps, one or the other would find it. If they lost King Devil by the creek, Sam would cross over, swimming, fighting a swift current if need be, then together they would work the sides of the creek, backward and forward, circling, sniffing until they found the scent.

By December, Milly was slow in all her movements, her days long reaches of time that somehow must be got through, with work done in spite of backache and toothache, puffed feet and hands, and the bigness of her body

that seemed to hinder her in all things, be it sweeping
under the stove or squatting to milk Betsey. But no matter how slowly she might walk to the spring or the milking
or on other outdoor errands, the pups followed at her
heels, matching their swift pace to her slow one, sometimes
running round and round her, but never leaping on her
as from sheer exuberance they sometimes jumped on
Nunn and the children. And she would smile on them
and know they understood how things were with her
better than any of her human family; and with her own
feet slow and heavy, she would joy in their swiftness,
think how good it was that something on this earth could
run light-footed and free, running freest and fastest and
gayest when it did what God had meant it to do—hunt.

She wished she could be certain that catching King Devil
was God's will for Nunn; more and more as he hunted
alone through the fall it seemed as if he went against all
things: his own body that needed sleep, the weather, the
opinion of the neighbors, and God's will. Often in the
black time before dawn, when he was not yet home, she
would sit shivering by the fire, or move from first one window to the other, listening, staring out into the dark or
the cloudy moonlight. Suse would awaken and come to
her and say, "Your back hurten you bad, Mom? Could I
rub it?"

She would shake her head and tell Suse to go back to
bed, but Suse would linger with her by the fire, studying
her sometimes with big sorrowful eyes, full of a pity and
an understanding that Milly would as lief not have had
from her own child. Suse knew it wasn't her back that
drove her to walk the floor in misery.

All the warnings and portents of the year would come
back into her mind: in October a bird flew into an upstairs room, and a bird in the house was a certain sign of
death; last fall, in potato-digging time, Lee Roy had
brought a hoe into the house, and that was a sign of trouble; the last two new moons she had first seen barred by
the leafless branches of the walnut tree, Deb's tizic tree
had done but poorly in the hot dry summer, and now he
was taller than the measure of his head last year—that
could mean he was going to die, outgrowing his tree like
that; worse than anything was the memory of Sue Annie's
face, witchlike and full of mysteries, as she nodded her

white-turbaned head and declared that King Devil would
never be taken until he had had man blood; oh, he
wouldn't kill the man himself; he'd never killed a hound,
but many was the one he'd led to its death, and he'd never
be satisfied till he had led a man to his death.

And Milly, remembering, would shiver and think of
all the ways a man could die: pneumonia fever in the
cold damp weather, the cliffs where a man numb with cold
or not too wide-awake could, with one false step in the
dark, kill himself. On and on her mind would go, until all
the future was a black burden in her heart and on her
head.

And Suse would watch her mother and envy Lureenie,
who was going to a place where men never hunted and
women had doctors in childbirth.

But it was near mid-December before Lureenie came
running home from the mail, laughing and chattering,
her arms spilling packages and a letter from Rans clutched
in one hand. "I can go now," she cried, and her voice was
thin and breaking, as if she were ready to cry. "Rans sent
me a money order big enough to come on, an the
youngens' coats has come."

She was suddenly silent, looking around the kitchen,
the Montgomery Ward package forgotten in her arms; her
glance wandered through the window to the hills across
the creek, their pine- and cedar-covered slopes gray-black
in the dusk. She drew a long sigh and said with a slow
shake of her head, "It's th onliest thing I've ever wanted
that's come to pass—gitten away. I cain't believe it yit.
It's like I was dreamen that in two, three days I'll be in a
place where I can see people, hear em talk; th nights
won't be so still—I hate th pines at dusty dark an on
windy nights, an I'm sick a th hills around th house,
shutten out th sun—an all th light I want at night—it's so
dark in that house, an so still since—"

She stopped, ashamed even now to give herself away,
as if she knew that Milly and others of the neighbor
women had pitied her, off by herself like that, with no
man person on the long dark nights of the fall.

Suse, too, looked out the window at the hillside; she
liked to look at the hill; like the rest of the woods, it was
for her full of more change and excitement than any other
part of her life; it was fun in spring to leave the corn

planting and hunt flowers in the woods or wild greens by the river, and the long grape hunts in the fall—sudden and unreasoning fear of the future filled her for an instant with a painful doubt.

It was hard enough to be a girl shut off from the world. How would it be to be a woman like Lureenie, married with little youngens, but wanting still the outside world, tied down to a house and youngens, with one baby in your arms and another big in your belly like Milly—and always the knowing that you could never get away until you were dead?

She shrugged her shoulders and smiled at the hill as the strong smile at the threats of the weak; she wouldn't be like Milly and she wouldn't be like Lureenie; she'd make her own life; it wouldn't make her.

Lureenie was in a hurry to get herself and the little youngens home: the fire would be out and the house cold; she'd maybe have to cut wood by lantern light; and she had a lot of work to do if she got away by Monday morning; and somehow she'd have to send word to Mark in the Cow's Horn; he'd been working hard to gather his father's river-bottom corn so that he could be ready to leave when she did and so help with the children.

Suse helped her carry the children and bundles home through the cold cloudy twilight, Lureenie hurrying ahead in her eagerness to get some work done before full dark; but when they came within hearing, they heard the ring of an ax, and Lureenie slackened her pace and smiled relieved. "Mark's got th word, too, an we'll git away fer true this comen Monday."

Mark went on with his woodcutting, while Suse, as Milly had directed, stayed to see the package opened and the fit of the new coats on the children. She lingered too long admiring the pretty checkerdy coats, and full dark had fallen in the low places before she knew it. Milly would have a fit, for she had warned Suse repeatedly that people would talk about a girl if she went around alone in the dark. As Suse rushed through the door, Lureenie wanted to know if she wouldn't be afraid and offered the new Montogmery Ward flashlight.

But Suse was afraid she would drop the new flashlight and ran on laughing as she called back, "You know I never was afeared a th dark; it's jist what Sue Annie might tell."

"Nunn won't like it," Lureenie said, "you runnen around in th dark."

But Suse ran on, her feet light and quick over the rocks in the darkening path, her heart full of bubbles, her head in Cincinnati in a world of wonder and glory. She was almost to the graveyard field before she noticed the feet behind her, light and free as her own, and Mark called, "Wait, Suse; Lureenie sent me to see you home."

"You're a scan me, ain't you?" she called over her shoulder, laughing and running on.

He was up with her in an instant, catching her hand, and they ran on together, laughing as he said, winded a little, for he had started later than she, "Nunn'ull hear you a runnen an me a comen behind an think I'm a wildcat a chasen you home an have me blowed in two with a shotgun."

"More like he'll think you're a bear—you're too big fer a wildcat," she said, laughing again for no reason except that it was fun to be alive and run with Mark down the slope of the graveyard field, smooth after the mowing, going faster and faster, the dull red glow of the dead sunset fading, the blackness of the corn swag reaching up for them, fun to pretend the corn swag was a place of deep mystery, unknown and exciting, full of the dark dangers people said city life held for girls.

Then they were down, and as the ground leveled out they stopped and stood facing each other, laughing still, their faces tingling in the frosty cold.

Suse realized that Mark still held her hand and tried to pull it away, but he put his other over it and stood looking down at her. She was conscious of his nearness and the warmth and bigness and hardness of his two hands on her own, and how tall he was, and how when he lifted her face to look at him in the dusk there was that same secret hidden something in his dark blue eyes and black eyebrows that had been on him even under the bright carbides at Sue Annie's the first time she had ever really looked at him.

"Let go," she said, pulling at her hand. "I hate to be held like a horse on a bridle when I don't want to be." She was laughing again, but a quick puzzling anger was hrusting through the laughter, an anger more at herself han Mark, because she didn't feel the way she ought to eel when a man, almost a stranger, held her against her will.

"But most horses, specially mares, learn to like their bridles," he said, and went and kissed her upturned face, quickly on the lips; and then he was running up the hill calling softly, "I'll be a missen you, Suse, but I'll be a sean you."

She stared after him, unmoving and unthinking, her face upturned still as when he had kissed her. Then she was brushing the kiss hard away, blushing, puzzled by this strange new self that was neither ashamed nor sorry.

At home Milly quarreled and scolded, not only because Suse got in after dark, but also because she, generally so good to come home and tell her all about everything, could give only vague descriptions of Lureenie's coats and their fits on the children.

Chapter Twenty-two

ONE DAY NOT LONG after Lureenie left, but a short time before Christmas, Nunn came home from the mail with a card from the deputy sheriff Pinkney Deegan—he had invited Nunn to bring Sam and Vinie and hunt with him the next weekend; if Nunn would come he would meet him with his car at the end of the gravel.

No sooner did they hear the news than Milly and the children started begging Nunn to take Sam and Vinie and let them show themselves among the fine hounds around Town; they'd bet anybody a salt barrel full of gold that Sam and Vinie would outrun them as they outran old Speed and Sourvine. But Nunn glanced at Milly, where her waist had used to be, and said he didn't think he'd go, and they could all see he wanted to go but only stayed because he was worried about Milly and the stock. When the children were in bed, Milly assured him that her time wouldn't be at hand for three or four weeks, and begged him hard to go. She wanted him to go, not only so that Sam and Vinie could test themselves in the wider world, but because for two nights she wouldn't be worried about him; he wouldn't be alone and he wouldn't be with wild drinking men like the Tillers.

So Nunn somewhat against his will, sent Pinkney word to meet him; he wouldn't have gone in any case except that he needed to buy some groceries in Town with the money he had got from the sale of Betsey's calf to Uncle Ansel Anderson two days before, and maybe some feed, too, if the money would stretch so far, and he wanted to see about his AAA fertilizer for the coming spring.

Milly felt right proud after he had gone early on a Fri-

306

day morning; he among all the fox hunters around was the only one who'd ever been asked to bring his pups to run with the big hunters around Town, and invited by a man like Pinkney Deegan—a prosperous farmer, they said, and officer of the law.

However, the children were hardly off to school before Sue Annie came, full of sighs and headshakes and dark hints that Nunn had no right to treat Milly so, going off like that when she was expecting any minute; and she studied Milly's abdomen with a critical tilting of her head and declared she thought the child had dropped already; in that case it might come before night and Milly oughtn't to have let Suse go off to school; and though she said never a word in that direction, she hinted that Nunn had gone off against Milly's will.

And Milly, watching the black eyes roll, had visions of tales buzzing over the country—Nunn Ballew and Milly had had an awful quarrel, and he'd got drunk and then mad and left her right when her time was on hand, and not a stick of wood or bite to eat in the house—her mind shifted away from the last; it was too much like the truth. There hadn't been enough corn to fatten the pigs, and the little meat the second one made was almost gone; there was no canned stuff left except a few jars she was saving for the company that would be around when she got down; the sweet potatoes were already gone, and the few knotty Irish potatoes left wouldn't last a week.

She changed the subject to Lureenie and told in detail of the contents of the two letters she had sent: about how well she liked Cincinnati and the two furnished rooms and how nice it was to have the electric and be able to go to the store every day and have different things to eat, but how Bill, the biggest child, cried to come back home so that he could have some place to play, and how she was going to a movie soon.

But Sue Annie only sniffed and said she lowed the woman had already been to half a dozen movies by now, and further remarked that running to the store every day cost money, and that the first time Rans went on a long drunk and didn't work for a week and the rent came due and they ran out of grub and coal, Lureenie would sing a different tune and wish for her log cabin above the river.

Milly shifted the subject again, this time to Suse, how tickled she was that she and Andy were going to graduate from the eighth grade, and asked—though she knew it was sly meanness—if Joe C. planned to send Ruby on through the eighth grade and into high school—Ruby didn't have sense enough to pass out of the third; it was her big size and not her brains that made Andrew put her up with Lee Roy in the fifth. None of the Tillers had ever finished their schooling like Nunn.

Sue Annie knew it and that was why she sniffed so now when she said what difference would all the diplomas in the world make to girls like Ruby and Suse two or three years from now; it would matter more for them to know how to diaper a baby than to spell diaper; and, anyhow, Suse nor Andy neither mightn't pass their examinations.

Milly silently agreed with Sue Annie about the foolishness of giving girls much schooling, but wouldn't let on, and was glad when, after divers warnings and dour reminders of what could happen to a woman all by herself in such a shape and a last admonition to blow the fox horn in case of need, the old soul went home.

When she had gone, the brave front Milly had put on left her and she sat for a time staring at the fire. A body wanted it over with, but, oh, God, so many things could go wrong. What if it got caught on the crossbones like Vadie Anderson's third one. She suffered for six days until she lost her strength and her nerve and her mind almost, and men had to push her legs down while she chewed her tongue till the blood ran and begged them to kill her, and cursed God and her man and the whole world— and lived, but God punished her with a dead baby and she'd never walked straight since.

What if she died like Maisie Martin? Maisie died with twins—her fourteenth child the second twin would have been—and Maisie was like this, shivering and crying and knowing for weeks she would die, she smothered so. What if she flooded to death, just lay and bled and whispered the room was full of smoke and she couldn't feel her hands and then died after all the trouble and the pain, never knowing it was death and not smoke?

She shivered and got up, wiping her wet palms on her apron—God's will was God's will, but it was not always easy to understand. The comforting thought came that in all her years of midwifery Sue Annie had lost but one woman, the Martin woman with the twins, and weeks before she'd tried to get her to go into Town and get her heart doctored; she'd never had a woman flood to death, and she'd never let a baby stick more than a day or two on the crossbones.

She was suddenly sick of the house and eager for the outdoors; she wanted to see Maude and the ewes and all things on the place; she ought to go comfort Betsey, fastened in the big barn so that she couldn't run away to hunt her calf; it had been weaned for months but Betsey and the calf had continued good friends, and now the poor thing was lonesome, the only piece of cow flesh on the place; she sighed a moment, thinking on Lizzie, then put on Nunn's old jumper and wrapped Deb well against the cold. Her back ached and it was slow walking with her swollen feet in Nunn's castoff shoes, so slow it was hard to keep warm; still, it was pleasant to be out in the bright cold.

Betsey stood in an unaccustomed stall—the only one on the place that would fasten securely—and bawled, sometimes angrily, sometimes with sorrow, looking so long up the hill in the direction of Uncle Ansel's that Milly wondered if she had heard an answering bawl from the calf. Milly pitied her and gave her as a grain of comfort a wisp of the precious hay, then walked on to look at the ewes wandering quietly here and there or standing in the sun and chewing their cuds in calm contentment; and she wished she were as good as they—each heavy with lamb, waiting out her time with no fear and no sinful questioning of God's Will.

She stood in the kitchen door and looked up into the high pale sky where cold-looking little clouds ran like new-hatched chickens before the sun. A body could never know God's will; maybe he willed it that she should die or maybe he willed it that she and the child should thrive and she bear seven more, and have twelve living children like Ann Liz Cooksey in the Cow's Horn—seven more times. She'd better be about her quilt piecing instead of carrying on so over this one time that could be still a month away.

Next morning, though, she was glad that the day was a Saturday and the children would be home. The day was

dreary, cold with broken clouds and a spit of snow on a
keen north wind. Her back had kept her awake most of
the night, and all the time she was getting breakfast sharp
hard pains in her legs almost jerked her down. She sighed,
thinking of the days ahead; sometimes she had pains like
that for a month before, and now they'd been going on
only a week or so.

She felt so poorly that when Lee Roy went to count
and feed the sheep, she told him to drive Betsey over to
the little barn and she would milk her there; afterward
he could water her and drive her back and fasten her up
again, for Nunn had thought that while he was gone Betsey
oughtn't to be let out, for fear she would go hunting her
calf.

Lee Roy drove Betsey up, then went back to the sheep,
but sometime later came back with a worried air to say
that he had counted and counted and always came out
five ewes short, among them Bossie Jean.

Milly looked at the sky and sniffed the wind, soft and
smelling of snow; by this time tomorrow there could be a
deep snow on the ground and the ewes could eat ivy bush
and poison themselves and die. They'd most likely left
for Brush Creek at daylight, but a body couldn't tell. The
thing to do was for Lee Roy and Suse and Lucy all to go
by the Pilot Rock at once and listen hard.

"But, Mom," Suse began with a swift glance at Milly's
body, "you oughtn't—"

"You're gitten sassy as the Tillers," Milly said in some
anger. "I know what I ought and oughtn't to do. You git
on—them ewes'ull be gone and your dad'ull have a fit."

Suse went away, and Milly, looking after her, saw her
lift her hand to her face, as if she brushed away tears.

She had put a kettle of cowpeas to boil and was settling herself by the fire for quilt piecing when she remembered that in all the worry over the gone ewes everybody
had forgotten Betsey. She hurried to the door and heard
Betsey's bell halfway up the hill across the creek toward
Sue Annie's—she'd started to Uncle Ansel's up by the
post office, and if she once got there and saw her calf,
she'd come back only on the end of a rope; and dry as
she was now, she'd not give a drop after missing even one
milking; Deb needed milk and Nunn could hardly get
along without it when they had no meat.

Milly debated a moment. Sue Annie would head her off as she passed her big road gate if she heard her, but she might not hear. She'd have to take Deb, and it might give him the croup to walk so far in the cold, but she'd have to go; heading her off would be easy, for Betsey, unfamiliar with the country, was following the twistings of Preacher Jim's road up the hill, and Milly, by following the short-cut post-office path, could be above her in a few minutes' time.

All her aches and pains but a little smear of backache dropped away as she crossed the creek and started up the hill, which faced south so that the path was sheltered from the stinging wind. The snow was still only a scattering, and Deb ran ahead, laughing, trying to trap a flake on his outstretched tongue.

Milly smiled and told him that the snowflakes didn't want to be eaten alive. It was good to be going up a hill; it seemed so long since she'd been out of the valley. Valleys were nice and hill and ridge tops were wild and windy places, but everybody ought to climb up to one once in awhile—it was good somehow.

Now and then she stopped to listen for Betsey, and on her last stop realized that Betsey was also taking a short cut, and might beat her to the place where the post-office path went into the big road, a little above Sue Annie's gate. She hurried, but soon Betsey's bell sounded above her, then a minute or two later she heard Sue Annie's yell at the cow, "Git home, you fool," then her shrilling to Dave, "Don't let th beans burn—Nunn's gone off fox-hunten an I'll have to take Milly's cow home," and her voice dropping, "pore thing."

Milly suspected the pity was for her. She didn't want that old rattle-tongue's pity—she could mind her own cow; it was none of her business if Nunn went fox-hunting. She had clear visions of Sue Annie at the post office as she told with a rolling of her eyes and smacking of her lips how Nunn Ballew wasn't fit to be hung, going off and leaving Milly while she followed him to the creek crossing, crying and begging him to stay because her time was so close. "Never mind, Sue Annie," she called, raising her voice as much as she was able after the long climb, "I'll take her home."

"God in tarnation," Sue Annie's voice came back.

"What in th name a Jesus are you a doen out in th shape you're in?"

"Gitten Betsey," Milly said, climbing farther up the path as Sue Annie, with an apron full of nubbins and Betsey's head reaching hungrily over her shoulder, came down. On seeing Milly, Sue Annie stopped, all unmindful of Betsey pulling a nubbin from her apron. She studied Milly with the frowning, outraged, almost unbelieving look she would have given a child twice punished for some uncommon bad meanness but into it again.

Milly in turn gave Sue Annie a hard glance. "Law, Sue Annie, a old woman like you's got no business out in this weather—you'll be a comen down with th fever. I'll take her home; pore thing, she's a hunten her calf."

"An you'll be a hunten a youngen," Sue Annie said, untying her apron, her eyes bright with anger. Nothing made Sue Annie madder than to tell her she was old, or to make any remark with reference to her and the weather. She was often angry in the knowing that for many years she had been the butt of countless jokes linking her name and the weather. Used to be when it rained people with a leaky roof would say, "This place leaks might nigh as bad as Sue Annie's kitchen," or when the wind blew hard, "This place is nigh as windy as Sue Annie's."

She now jerked off the apron of nubbins, swung it out of Betsey's reach toward Milly, and said, "Well, sean as how I'm gitten old and weakly an they's a three-foot snow on an you're young an spry, take this cow on back home an if that youngen's marked by a white-faced cow, don't blame me," and added with a windy sigh, as if she washed her hands of the whole business: "An if it comes while you're a tryen to git home, bite th cord like a yoe an take it on—yoe drops their lambs off by theirselves when th ram ain't around, but generally," she went on, sniffing the north wind that came keenly here, "they've at least got sense enough tu pick a rock house."

"Nunn ain't no ram, you—you—" Anger made Milly stutter, and before she could think of a word, plenty bad but not too bad, Betsey was grabbing the nubbins and Sue Annie was striding away with no backward glance.

She put the nubbins in front of her and hurried, determined to make them last until Betsey was in the barn, otherwise Betsey, finding her apron empty, might turn around and go back up the hill. And in spite of her big talk to Sue Annie, she didn't think she could make it up the hill again; her back was killing her and she was beginning to think Sue Annie had been right yesterday when she said the baby had dropped—for seemed like more and more it bothered her about walking.

Betsey butted her shoulder, almost knocking her down a steep place in the path. Milly circled around a tree, hastily fishing out a nubbin, then ran for a few clumsy steps. Betsey ran, too, kicking up her heels like a cow hunting a bull. Deb, now left behind, began a whindling and a whining for her to wait, but she couldn't wait; even by ducking around trees and handing out nubbins with lightninglike thrusts, Betsey was always right behind her, butting her shoulders and threatening to knock her over the hill. There was another reason, too, she thought; seemed like she felt a labor pain—so little and short a body couldn't be certain.

Betsey's head came over her shoulders and her big tongue, in its eagerness to grab a nubbin, curled around Sue Annie's apron. Milly jumped away and jerked the apron, and in so doing lost her balance on the uneven ground and fell forward on her knees and one hand, the other still holding the apron of nubbins. Betsey, craunching one nubbin, reached for another and stepped on her dress tail. Milly smacked her nose away, grabbed a sapling, and jerked herself up, leaving a piece of dress tail under Betsey's foot. The one thing now in her mind was to get herself and Betsey home: her time had come, and if Betsey got away now, she'd be sure to go dry. The main thing was to get her across the creek into the narrow path where she couldn't turn around, beat her with a brush, then toll her into the stall and nail the door.

She slid down a ledge where Betsey couldn't follow, and calling first to Betsey and then to Deb, who was bawling lustily now for her to wait and carry him, ran on, slipping and sliding but catching to trees and never quite falling, taking care to walk not in the path, but in the rough ledgy places where Betsey couldn't run over her.

Betsey made a game of it, tossing her head and kicking her heels like a mettlesome calf, but all the same she followed the nubbins to the creek crossing. There Milly grabbed a sycamore limb broken in some flood, and while

Betsey was finishing the last nubbins broke the brush on
her rump with a hard two-handed blow. Betsey gave her
one startled heartbroken look, then ran up the narrow
path, and feeling thirsty after all the dry corn, stopped
at the water trough for a drink.

Milly came on, panting, gasping, torn by a dry breathless sobbing—she'd almost reached Betsey when a hard
pain caught her; she grabbed a little poplar sapling with
both hands and stood trying not to bear down until it had
passed. Her knees were shaking, and she wondered with
a terror she kept trying to push down if she shook because she was tired or if it was the childbed shakes.

The pain passed in a moment, and hurrying before another could grab her, she pulled open the big road gate,
ran to the little barn for more nubbins, and grabbed an
apronful. Before Betsey could think to run away, Milly
had tolled her into her own stall in the little barn. She had
dragged up a big old fence rail and was propping the door
shut with it, when another pain caught her, nigh jerking
her to the ground before she could get a hold on anything
and then only the old wire fence that sagged and
screeched under her tortured weight.

She heard Deb sobbing on the other side of the creek,
worn out like he sounded, as if he had sat down to rest.
She wondered if he'd go to sleep and maybe catch his
death of pneumonia—but she couldn't go to him.

She hurried to the house, built up the fire in the cookstove, dreading, putting off the moment when she must
blow the horn for Sue Annie—the old fool would cackle
like a just laid hen and tell all over the country that Milly
Ballew had dropped her youngen in the creek.

She got water on to heat; another pain came, and
passed while she sweated, moaning a little as she clung to
a chair.

She reached on the high shelf for Nunn's horn, then
remembered, and pulled away her empty hand. Nunn had
the horn with him. She'd have to fire the shotgun. She got
it from its accustomed corner in the fireplace room, but
had another pain, long and hard, that made her whimper
like a beaten dog before she found the shells. In hiding
them from the youngens, Nunn hadn't told her; and when
she did find them, there were only two. She knelt in the
kitchen door, set the old number-ten gauge on the door-

sill so that it wouldn't knock her down, and pulled the
trigger. The sound roared out enough to bring Aunt
Marthie Jane running from her grave. She fired it again,
then left it lying on the floor; her one goal, that now
seemed far away and insurmountable, was fixing the bed
with the oilcloth Nunn had bought, under the clean sheets
she had laid away just for this.

Between moments of terrified wondering if the baby
was coming right—it could be feet first or breech fore-
most for all she knew—she wondered if Sue Annie would
understand the shotgun, if Deb were all right—he might
be playing on the ice in the creek; some of the holes were
deep, and he could break through and drown or follow
the creek to the Blue Hole.

She wanted to wash her feet and her face, and in trying
made a mistake—she just managed to make it to the bed
and remembered with sorrow, even as the baby cried,
her new nightgown—pink outing flannel she'd briar-
stitched in blue. "Pore little youngen," she said, and her
voice was not doleful but gay; "lay there a minnit, an
don't cry if your old mammy did have you in a dirty
dress."

Terror swooped down on her. She ought to get up and
cut the cord—it could maybe die like that. What if it were
deformed or bad marked or blind—she wanted to get a
good look. Oh, God, how she wanted to see it—but Sue
Annie always said that if a baby was seen first by its
mother, the look gave it nothing but sorrow for the rest
of its life and the life would be short.

Then came the sound of feet on the rocks and Sue
Annie's shrilling. "I'm a comen, honey—blame it on yer
old mammy. Where's th soap, Milly—never mind. I'll use
a little a my Lysol. You got any scissors biled an a clean
white rag ready biled, too—never mind, I'll use a little
Lysol—an scorch it on th stove."

"Hurry," Milly begged; "it could be a dyen."

"You ought to a said thet two hours ago—be still an
quit worryen er I'll have a woman dead on my hands
frum bleeden to death. We'll write to th papers if th
youngen dies; first I ever seed to die a squallen like a catamount." She was rushing in, her sleeves rolled above
her elbows, her freshly scrubbed hands held high and
carefully in front of her, but her big white baby-catching

apron had been put on so hastily the bib flapped unpinned on her stomach.

"Is it marked?" Milly asked anxiously as Sue Annie bent over the bed.

"Marked by Nunn—wearen his hat jist like him," Sue Annie said, working quickly with scissors and twine and a scorched rag. "You wasn't worried, was you?" she went on in a kindly, reassuring tone. "I oughtn't to had sich talk —but, Milly, it was aggravaten—I come down yisterday a meanen to stay, an you was so uppity."

"Th devil in me," Milly said, and reached and patted Sue Annie's head rag. "I oughtn't to a called you old— why, you'll be a bringen this youngen a youngen fore you're through."

And there was peace between them.

Milly's shotgun blasts had roused the country. Nancy Ballew, running ahead of John, got there not far behind Sue Annie, and in time to clean up Milly and get her into the new nightgown.

Hattie Tiller and Flonnie came with Blare, and not long after, Ann Liz Cooksey from the Cow's Horn. The children came in with the sheep; Suse came back with Deb; all admired the new baby, and the three older ones were sent to the river bluff to hunt walink for tea to break out the hives on the baby, though already the smell of catnip steeping on the hearth was pleasant through the house.

Milly was given a strong cup of coffee and a fresh chew of tobacco, but chewed little as she lay warm and painless and peaceful, half listening to the laughter and bustle and woman talk that rustled all around her, gayer than at any time she could remember, because the birth had been quick and easy and nobody was worn out with watching and no shoulders ached from long hours of pulling on her hands. All the fears and doubts seemed foolish now, the terrors and the tears; the easiest time she had ever had, and a fair-sized boy at that.

She had ordered up a good dinner for everybody— there was still some meat from the last little pig, but she had told Hattie and Flonnie, who loved to cook other people's grub, to kill two fat hens. Seemed like she wanted herself a good bait of chicken and dumplings; and, thank the Lord, there was enough lard and flour to run anyhow till Nunn got home, so people wouldn't talk —she hoped Flonnie made the biscuit and dumplings; Hattie had a heavy hand when it came to lard.

Nunn came home late Sunday, the pups running ahead through the snowy twilight. They never stopped till they hunted out Milly propped on pillows in Aunt Marthie's big bed in the fireplace room. Much to Sue Annie's scandalization, they put their paws on Milly's pillows the better to lick her face and bark their greeting. This roused the new baby and Vinie leaped into the middle of the bed to investigate the unfamiliar cry. Sue Annie grabbed the broom to shoo her off, and succeeded, but not before Vinie had given the baby two exploratory licks across the face.

Nunn, coming behind, hurrying a little so as to look at his ewes before dark, had stopped in the little barn to hide a back load of Christmas trinkets he had bought in Town, when he heard Sue Annie's shrill screeching at Vinie. He had met no one on the way, and only now hearing Sue Annie's voice, realized what might be happening. He dropped his load all spilling in the shucks and ran, his heart pounding and rising in his throat.

Somebody heard his feet on the threshold of the kitchen door, and hounds and children and neighbor women poured over him, and their shrill many-voiced crying of the good news was like the chorus to some gay song, with Sue Annie for a moment carrying the lead, laughing and rubbing her nose with the back of one hand while holding a cup of steaming catnip tea with the other, crying, "Easiest time a woman ever had. Whyn't you go off an stay another week, honey?"

He reached Milly's bed with the children clambering over him, and the pups, excited by all the to-do, running round and round him, as if they had left him ten days ago instead of ten minutes. Milly smiled up at him, and through all the hub-bub he heard the baby's cry. In spite of having been told by many different ones that it was here, a boy, strong, with a good grip on life, its voice startled him, and for the first time he realized that here was another being, his child, dependent on him for food and clothes. He drew a long breath; seven they were in the family now: seven mouths to feed—and King Devil still not caught.

"I do believe he's another redhead," Milly was saying as she turned to draw the baby to her.

He nodded, studying her face. He hadn't remembered it so small and thin and brown, with her front teeth showing brown and snaggeldy with rotten spots like those of an old woman, and the skin on her neck red-brown and wrinkling—and such a little while ago she had looked as young as Suse looked now. Pinkney's wife was plump and smooth and fair, with three children all of school age; older than Milly she was, he guessed, but she had a good house with electricity and linoleum on the floors and a radio to listen to while she sat and sewed. She'd worked hard, but not like Milly, and always she had lived in peace and plenty.

His eyes wandered from the child's wizened, red-purplish face to the fireplace and then around the room, and for an instant he saw it with the eyes of a stranger—ugly, bare, but very clean, and there was something pitiful in the wide cracks and worn knotholes in the clean scrubbed floor and mended flour-sack curtains; his fields had for an instant seemed strange, glimpsing them through the trees as he came over the hill, unkempt and ragged with rocks and brush and sagegrass under the thin layer of snow; not like Pinkney's place or the places of the other men he had seen—he would be ashamed to have them see his place or eat at his table; he wondered what Pinkney had thought the day he was here.

Milly was asking if he had had a good time and how the hounds ran, and Suse was wanting to know if he had got a paper, and Deb and Lucy were screaming for candy.

He roused and felt guilty and ashamed of thinking such thoughts.

While the snowfall thickened, he sat in the firelight with the baby across his knees and told Milly about how the pups outran every hound but one, a bitch, older than they and with a pedigree, too, and used to running in that part of the country. As always after a trip away, even a long sheep hunt, he told her all he had seen and done—or almost all. He did not tell her that when he was in Town to see about the AAA fertilizer for the coming spring that he had also visited the store where he had charged a bill last spring; and because he had owed a debt and paid it, the manager was more than willing to let him have feed to run him through the winter on credit and what groceries and seed he would need before he sold his spring lambs. He had thus been able to spend some of the money from Betsey's calf on a few clothes and little things for Christmas.

Better than $50 the debt was now, and winter hardly started. Before he could pay it with lamb money and money from the crossties he planned to make, it would be more—but his lamb and wool crop ought to bring more than they had ever brought; he had more sheep, and prices would be high—people said.

Nor did he tell her that had he wished he could have swapped Sam and Vinie to the board member, Elias Higginbottom, for a mountain of feed, a milk cow, fresh with calf by her side, and two fat hogs.

Chapter Twenty-three

IN SPITE of Sue Annie's dark warnings that Milly would kill herself by going around on the eighth day—as it was well known that everything in a woman dropped back into place on the tenth day after having a baby—Christmas that year was gay with more presents than the children had ever had. Nunn had bought candy and oranges and presents for everybody; there was his mother's gift of books, this time a real dictionary for Suse, a thing she had long wanted, like the pupils she read about in her schoolbooks who were always consulting their dictionaries; but even more than the dictionary, she thought she liked Lureenie's gift of six thin jangling silver bracelets and two women's magazines full of stories and pictures and fashions.

Milly frowned over the bracelets, saying they looked sinful and heathenish, and forbade her to wear them to church. Nunn frowned, too, but for a different reason; a disturbing suspicion was in his mind that Mark, and not Lureenie, had bought the bracelets, and Lureenie's Christmas letter had a suspicious sound: "I am sending you a little Christmas gift of some magazines, and Mark is saying Merrie Xmas too."

But he said nothing, glad that Suse was so taken up with schoolwork, studying nights by the broken-chimneyed lamp or by the firelight when they ran out of coal oil, determined to pass the eighth-grade examinations at the end of school. She never mentioned Mark, and, like the rest of the family, was absorbed in the day-to-day life about her, a life fuller than common, what with

the good Christmas, the triumph of the pups in the outside world, and the new baby.

It was Suse who suggested that the baby be named on
Christmas Day: last year they had named the pups at
Christmas and they had done well, so this year why not
name the baby? Milly, as in the case of the other three
boys, wanted to name him Nunnely Danforth and then
call him Junior, like a family she'd worked for in the
mining town, but Nunn had never liked Danforth and
thought even less of Junior. This year, however, Milly
was more insistent than in other years; Suse had increased in argumentative powers since Deb's birth, so
that in the end the baby was christened William Danforth
after his father and his great-grandfather. In five minutes
he was no longer "it" or "he," but Bill Dan, a person
promising red hair and a high temper and a love of
hounds, for he never cried when Vinie licked his face.

As usual, many neighbors dropped in during the afternoon, more than in other years. Not only was there the
new baby to see, but the exploits of Sam and Vinie must
be heard from Nunn himself. Keg Head Cramer had
heard that Nunn had visited with the high sheriff
and hunted with the county prosecutor, and that Sam had
in the course of a race swum the Cumberland and run
through a railroad tunnel; and that his son Mark had sent
Nunn's oldest girl a twenty-one jewel, solid gold wristwatch for Christmas.

Many carried pumpkin or watermelon seed or a bunch
of dried herbs or handful of green walink or mullen to
make tea for Bill Dan. His bowels had gone loose and
greenish when he was three or four days old and he grew
more and more fretful. Sue Annie said that he would get
no better until she got the hives broke out on him, and
hinted, when she came in the late afternoon with a bottle
of freshly made rattleroot tea, that she was afraid the
hives were working in on him instead of out, or even going into the boll hives.

At mention of the boll hives Milly's eyes widened with
terror; they could kill a young baby, and even plain hives
could be dangerous if they worked in. She watched worriedly while Nancy Ballew held his nose and Sue Annie
poured spoonfuls of the rattleroot tea down him; poor

child, the stuff tasted awful, and he fought it so. Then in fifteen minutes it was all to do over; he'd puked it up.

Nunn came in with a load of wood while the women were struggling to get the second batch of tea down Bill Dan, and watched a moment with a worried, disapproving frown. He laid the wood in the corner, brushed all snow and sawdust from his clothing, warmed himself well, then took the baby, who, much to Sue Annie's disgust and Milly's worry, was vomiting again. "Looks like I'll have to take him in hand to git him well," Nunn said.

"An what a you a aimen to do?" Sue Annie wanted to know with a sarcastic smile.

"Nothen," Nunn said, and rocked the baby gently while he cried with a reddening of his face and pulling up of his knees.

Nancy Ballew went home to her milking, and Sue Annie went off to the kitchen but came back soon with a fresh brewed batch of catnip tea. She bent to give the baby a spoonful; Nunn waved it aside so roughly that the tea sloshed from the spoon. Sue Annie looked ready to throw the tea in his face and Milly looked ready to cry, but Suse, with the dishrag in her hand, watched in the door and nodded approvingly. "Th health book says that too much medicine not give by a doctor is—"

Milly turned on her in an anger fierce and unusual for her. "Shut up an git back to that work in th kitchen where you belong; you're a fine un, disputen with Sue Annie. You're a learnen so much frum books it'll be your ruination."

"Her pappy must ha been a readen, too," Sue Annie said with a pitying smile at Suse's back. "Don't git so mad, Milly; your milk'ull colic th baby; soon's she's got one a her own in a couple a years, she'll fergit all that book larnen—strong doctor's medicine ud kill this baby, any little baby."

Bill Dan vomited some more, his vomit smelling of pumpkin seed, walink, and rattleroot, or so it seemed to Nunn, but gradually he grew quieter, and Nunn was still in the rocking chair while he rested stomach downward across his knees. Sue Annie waited, elbow on the mantle, chewing and spitting into the fire with sharp angry jabs of juice, as if each were a mouthful of words she would like to hurl at Nunn.

Nunn rocked on with slow creaks of his chair and spat in slow contemplative streams, like a man certain of victory. Sometimes he glanced up at Sue Annie and smiled. "Set down, Sue Annie," he would say, and she would answer sharply, "I've got to be a gitten home—it's gitten dark an they's nobody to fix Dave's supper."

Nunn would glance outside; it was so dark he couldn't tell whether the snow still fell or not; he ought to go feed Maude and the ewes and do Milly's job of milking, but the minute he left Sue Annie would be pouring tea into the baby—if she stayed the night he'd sit like this all night—he'd sit her out if it took a week.

A gray snowy darkness had fallen into the valley when Suse and Lee Roy came in, covered with snow but with the proud smiles of people who have done things. Suse swung an eight-pound lard bucket. "Lookee, Mom," she said. "I got more milk frum Betsey than Pop would a got."

And Lee Roy smiled at Sue Annie; he knew nothing of baby doctoring, but there was a battle on between Nunn and Sue Annie, and whatever the merits of the case, Nunn must win. "Th ewes is fine, Pop," he said. "All there. I counted em twict. Maude an her colt an Jude an Rosie, they're all right, too."

Nunn settled more comfortably in his chair, Milly sighed heavily from the bed, and Sue Annie fidgeted with the bowl of paper roses on the mantle. "Nunn, honey," she said after a time, "lemme give that pore little thing jist one more try at rattleroot tea—them hives ull go into th boll hives an kill it—your own born granmammy doctored with rattleroot."

At mention of Aunt Marthie, Nunn stopped chewing a moment, but fresher memories came and dimmed those of the big woman with cups of steaming tea, and after a while, summoning all his nerve and clearing his throat he called Suse from the kitchen. "Recollect that bottle with th rubber nursen nipple I brung home with th pups in case they wouldn't eat so good after their trip—you put it away in Granma's trunk upstairs along with their papers?"

Suse nodded, and the children, crowding behind her, listened to Nunn with big solemn eyes. Milly dragged herself up from the bed and looked at him in terrified wonder, and Sue Annie gaped at him while he directed Suse to get the bottle, boil it and the nipple, then boil some fresh spring water, cool it, and put in a little sugar to keep it all warm, ready for Bill Dan when he awoke.

"Nunn, what in th world?" Milly whimpered, her eyes wandering anxiously over the still sleeping baby.

And Sue Annie frowned on him and asked worriedly, "What's got into you, Nunn?"

"Nothen," he said, and rocked on. Be damned if he would tell them that all he was trying to do was give his little youngen the same careful kind of care he had been told to give the pups if they got off their feed when they were little, or the book on livestock said give a sick lamb when its stomach got upset.

More than once during the fall, when Deb and Lucy were hoarse and croupy or crying with earache and Milly doctored them with teas and poultices and worried over pneumonia while her eyes would grow stricken with terror in thinking of the two in the graveyard, Nunn would think of Dr. Hibbetts and the long needle going into Sam and the big white split-top pills—and Sam had been sick, sick as Tom and Angie Mime, sick as anything he'd ever seen that died.

Bill Dan awoke with a whining cry and Suse came running with the bottle, but Bill Dan would have none of the rubber nipple. Milly begged to let him nurse or have a spoonful of tea, but Nunn gave him only a few drops of sweetened water from the end of a spoon, and after a while he went back to sleep.

Sue Annie, after a last mournful headshake over the baby and a last supplication to Nunn to let her give it some tea, started home, but stopped in the kitchen door to tell Suse that if the baby took a bad turn in the night and the hives went in, she'd come back, even if she wasn't appreciated now.

However, Bill Dan slept peacefully through the night. Once he awakened and cried, and though Milly begged Nunn with tears to let him nurse, Nunn got Suse to fix the bottle of sweetened boiled water again. This time Bill Dan took it, and while he nursed, though it was sometime in the cold black hours of the early morning, all the children, even Deb, got out of bed and hung over Nunn to watch a baby suck a bottle, a thing of which they had hardly heard and never seen. Sam came too, and stood with his paws on the arm of the rocker and watched with a critical lifting of his ears, but Vinie stayed behind and lay whining worriedly under the bed where Milly sobbed and said the nipple would give her baby the thrash—Ann Liz Cooksey had told her once about a baby her cousin had tried to raise on a bottle because its mother had died in the borning, and the rubber nipple on the bottle gave it the thrash and it died.

Nunn shivered and hesitated, half ready to draw the bottle away, but he happened to glance up into Suse's pleased approving eyes as she leaned over the rocker.

Sue Annie came at daylight when all were still sleeping soundly, including Bill Dan, who lay unfrowning, his fists clenched pink and damply warm by his neck. She punched him, poked him, looked him over and said it was like a miracle and shook her head, and later, when Bill Dan's bowels moved, not green but smooth yellow, she gave Nunn a searching, suspicious glance. "No medicine an he's all right?" she said.

"If'n th hives had gone in, his bowels ud be real bad by now," Milly said, happy but puzzled.

"Nunn must a done some prayen," Sue Annie said with a sly roll of her eyes.

Three days later Keg Head Cramer was more than surprised to hear that that drinking, fox-hunting Nunn Ballew had turned faith healer; his young child had been at death's door, and he had thrown all Sue Annie's concoctions and teas into the fire, and scalded the ear of one of his pedigreed hounds in so doing, given the baby nothing but plain water and prayer, and next morning it was well.

In a few days' time Milly was her old self again, Bill Dan sucked and slept and cried and kept a length of diapers drying by the fire or freezing on the line, and gradually took his proper place in the life about him, less the center of attention than in his early, ailing days. Deb came out from under his shadow and took his old place on his father's knees of evenings, though for a long time he cried each time he awakened to find himself sleeping with Lee Roy instead of his mother.

Shortly after Christmas the winter settled down, a bleak dead time with no snow to soften the bitter cold. More snowbirds and sparrows, with the two redbirds that always nested in the walnut tree by the kitchen door, came to the spot in the yard where Suse threw out the dishwater, and pecked hungrily at any tiny scraps of food they found. None of the ewes, not even Bossie Jean, ran away to the scanty pickings in the hard frozen hills, but hungry and heavy with lamb, wandered no farther away than the spring branch, where they went to drink their fill of the warm trickling water, the only thing in the hard cold that seemed to make a sound.

All day long the sinkholes in the valley smoked, until the bordering trees and bushes were spangled with icicles, some delicate and fine as the first spring flowers. In the short days, frost never melted from the northern slopes of the hills. Milly milked in the bitter, big-starred twilights and pitied Betsey and all dumb beasts in the cruel cold, and never quarreled at the big-ribbed, big-hipped thing when one night she went to milk and there was no milk. She turned away and stared a moment up at the big bright stars that seemed hardly higher than Samuel's house on the hill.

Though a slack-coal and wood fired roared in the fireplace all day long and most of the night, the house was never warm; fresh spring water froze in an hour not ten feet from the little step stove; and Deb, too restless to sit by the hearth, whindled and cried from morning till night because his feet hurt so in the cold, and at night whimpered in his sleep with earache. Lucy had such a hoarse croupy cough that Milly never let her out of the house. Milly lived in perpetual fear of some bad winter sickness in all the children, and especially for Bill Dan; but Bill Dan early learned to smile at the howl of the north wind in the ridges, and loved to lie on his sheepskin by the hearth and watch the flames.

Hunting was good: rabbits and pheasants and quail were hungry, hunting in the hard cold for the scant food from the summer, and foxes hunted them, and Nunn hunted the foxes. He caught many and many times he chased King Devil.

With Bill Dan nuzzling at her breast when she awakened to find Nunn's side of the bed empty, Milly worried less about Nunn than in the hunts of the fall. The ending of each day was too much like a victory in the long battle to bring the children through the hard winter into spring on

less food than she had ever had to cook, for her to wrestle
with any trouble until it came. She lived for the spring,
when the least ones wouldn't be sick so much, and
dreamed sometimes at night that she was cooking a great
meal of fried chicken and things fresh from the garden, or
eating hot biscuit and butter.

But spring would come. It was early on a zero morning
during the first days of January that Nunn, putting a fresh
backlog in the fireplace, heard her gay call from the
kitchen, "Come quick, Nunn; spring's come."

He thought he knew what he saw, but went all the
same to find her peeping through a spot on the window-
pane from which she had scraped the frost. "Look, Nunn,
th sun's started back—seems like it's been stuck fer a
month, a comen ever mornen out a this side a that dead
pine halfway to th Pilot Rock."

"You didn't think it was stuck fer good an th world was
a comen to its end, did ye?" he asked teasingly, but
scraped a peephole for himself in the frost and looked with
her at the small red winter's sun, pushing above the pines
far to the southern side of the creek. Sure enough, it had
moved a little, and hung now like some strange red fruit
on a northern limb of the dead pine where three days ago
it had been on the southern side of the trunk.

The older children came and watched, too, as he had
used to watch with Aunt Marthie Jane, but they were less
excited than their mother because the sun had started
northward, for they had little memory of other suns rising
in other places; but Milly, until she came to the valley,
had never lived long enough in one place to get acquainted
with all the paths of the sun through all the seasons. The
sun quickly covered itself with a web of red light that
dyed the frost on the windowpanes red and sent out long
yellow-red rays to sparkle the frost on the walnut tree
and lay the blue-white shadows of the hills across the
school path; then the light changed into brilliant gold, too
bright to watch.

Milly hummed as she got breakfast, even though the
water bucket was frozen so solidly that she gave up trying
to melt it with hot water and set it by the fireplace.

Nunn, too, thought of the spring, not as a victory over
the winter, but as another milestone in his long failure to
get King Devil.

Night after night the hounds ran and night after night
Nunn was out in the cold, sometimes with other men, but
often alone. If it was only a fox that ran, he would build a
low fire in some rock house in a ridge side and listen,
sheltered from the cold. But when King Devil ran, and
he ran a lot that winter, he would climb to the top of the
Pilot Rock and listen for long hours in a zero wind he
never felt.

And sometimes it seemed to Nunn that King Devil ran
like one chased, not taking his will with Sam and Vinie
as he had so often done with Zing. Hope would rise and
pound in his heart—if the pups were good enough to
quicken the red beast's evil heart with danger, he would
let himself be chased until he was caught. He could not
leave the valley as long as Nunn chased him, any more
than Nunn could quit as long as he was there to be chased.

On nights when his hounds chased a fox other than
King Devil, Nunn would sit by his hunting fire, listening
with but half his mind, drowsing sometimes; and in the
half sleeping, many thoughts would come to him, dreamlike and frightening, that never came by day; it was then
that he understood most clearly that the big red fox had to
run—he had to chase him; and this being so, he and the
red beast were tied together with a bond stronger than any
made by God or man, be it the link between a man and
his child or his wife or his land.

He would rouse from the nightmarish thinking, shaking
his head, dreaming King Devil ran, only to find himself
stiff with cold by a burned-out fire and Sam and Vinie
crying their disgust with him because he would not come
to help them dig out a red fox run into a limestone ledge
where their paws were useless; and Nunn would go and
dig out the fox if it took the rest of the night and half the
day. Once he had to get a charge of mining dynamite
from the Tiller men, and half the men in the valley
dropped their work to come help get out the fox, for it was
well known that if a hound, particularly a young one, did
not get his fox after holing him, he might get discouraged
and not try so hard.

And the whole country was agreed in the belief that
Sam and Vinie Ballew ought not to be discouraged. By
late February their voices singing in triumph or snarling
and barking and howling in rage over a lost scent or a

holed fox were known to two hundred square miles of
country. On frozen white moonlight nights when their wild
hunting cry echoed and reechoed over wide spaces of the
hills and Vinie on a hot trail was like a singing banshee,
mothers would quiet the crying of their young children
with a whispered, "Hush, that white she hound's a comen
after you."

People in distant cabins who had had brief glimpses of
Vinie's white body leaping through the moonlight told
fearsome tales of her size and the length of her leaps and
the depth of her song.

More and more as Nunn lost himself in the long hunt,
it was Lee Roy who went after supper to look at the ewes,
and many was the newborn lamb he dried and helped to
its first milk. If he were gone too long, Milly would go,
too, and find him struggling to get a young lamb dried or
to the teat, not with the disgusted, worried impatience of
Suse, but calmly and unhurriedly as if time on a black zero
night could be spent in no pleasanter fashion.

Nunn, when he came home from the hunt, would look
in on the sheep, and often, no matter what the time, dawn
or midnight, he would find Lee Roy there, and at other
times a lamb, dry and warm and well, that had not been
there when he left at sundown. He would feel grateful to
Lee Roy, but at the same time there would come a disturbing sense of loss: only a while ago Lee Roy had been
his child, his little boy, but now at times he seemed more
the man of the house than Nunn did, though he was not
yet twelve years old. Now, when the ground was hard
frozen and the wood pile chanced to run low, Lee Roy,
with no word from anybody, would catch Maude and
snake up logs for half a day.

Then in a night or so Nunn would forget Lee Roy, the
lambs, his lessening pile of store-bought feed that wouldn't
last through March, and all other things because King
Devil ran and the hounds cried that the race was close.
Instead of at dawn, he would come home near noon, red-
eyed and sleepy as the hounds; but unlike them, he could
not curl himself in the winter sun and give himself up to
their heavy dreamlike sleep.

Everywhere work shrieked at him; brush clearing that
would go well in the dry cold weather, crossties that should
be made, barn litter to be spread, the AAA fertilizer that

Jaw Buster had brought down with a lot of feed and which would need spreading soon, and always the fence. Everywhere it was falling down. Whole lengths of it were now nothing more than rows of brush, rotted from the years before. At other times the house with its broken windows, roof and walls in need of paint, and rotten porches cried for his work, galled him like a nail in an old shoe that slowly makes a sore spot, hardly noticeable at first, that breaks one day into flaming pain.

And more and more it hurt his pride to come home after breakfast to find Suse doing her mother's work in the kitchen while Milly and Lee Roy worked outside at hauling and spreading manure, patching fence, or at some other thing that until this winter he had always done alone. He would at times speak sharply to Milly for leaving Bill Dan with Suse, but Milly would only laugh, "Law, Nunn, it's good to git outside fer a change—Suse's plenty old enough to mind th baby an cook a bite," and she would point out that Hattie Tiller and Ann Liz Cramer worked out and let their older girls look after their houses and babies.

In spite of the bitter bleakness of the winter, spring that year for Nunn was like an expected but unprepared-for visitor. It seemed hardly a day after school was out in early February and Suse came running home with the news she had passed her eighth-grade examination that it was a red windy sunrise in early March and Milly was crying, "Look, everbody; look. Spring's come; th cedar tree by th barn's a smoken."

The children ran to the kitchen door and Nunn looked too, and saw, spiraling up and spreading slowly outward in the still morning air, the blue smoke of the cedar tree that Milly had not seen for two springs, for the tree smoked only once in a spring and then for a little time only. Some people lived and died and never saw a smoking cedar tree; they were rare things to begin with. Sue Annie had none and John only a few in all his timber lands, and Milly, when she saw the smoke from her tree, felt as lucky as if she had found a four-leaf clover.

The sun, rising now in the creek gap, lifted higher, and for an instant the blue thin cloud above the tree was touched with the rosy light, then it was gone and the cedar was like other cedars, dark under the shadow of the hill.

Deb stood on the woodbox, wondering, looking first up into his mother's smiling face then down toward the cedar tree. "It's a sign a spring, Deb," she said, picking him up and giving him a hard hug. "Spring's a comen right along —th hens'ull be a cacklen an a layen eggs, an they'll be eggs to eat, an them Georgie onions in th garden, they'll soon git big enough to eat, an we'll have lettuce an wild greens, an then one a these days Betsey'ull start given milk agin—an you can bust yer hide with milk an butter," and she squeezed him again, then sang as she got the breakfast of lard gravy, water biscuit, and fried hominy.

Nunn hurried away to his barn chores; but he was absentminded, thinking that through the winter Milly had been cold and hungry, colder and hungrier than he had known.

Chapter Twenty-four

EVEN JOHN THAT YEAR, with his aching legs, and hired hands asking $1.50 a day instead of $1, praised the goodness of the spring. It fulfilled the long dream that had pulled the old and the weak and the poor through the hard winter. There was a newness and a wonder in it as if through all eternity the world had waited for the glory of this one spring; a time never before and never again, when the air would be so soft and fresh at dawn, the woods so full of flowers and springing mushrooms, the thundershowers of early April so fresh and white and warm, quickening all the life of the earth, people as well as flowers.

Every scraggeldy seedling peach in the valley, like the wild plums, the dogwood, the redbud, and later the old twisted, black-limbed apple trees, the quince, and the pears, made a pinkness and a whiteness everywhere; and on foggy nights and dewy mornings their blending fragrance made Suse restless, and she wished she could, like the sheep, run away to the flowering hills.

Sam and Vinie, grown thin and red-eyed and sleepyheaded from the hard hunts of the winter, slept long hours in the sun, while Nunn gave himself up to the joys of the spring work in the fine soft growing weather. It was pleasant to be out laying off corn ground by daylight, the smell of the earth and of growing things sharp in the dewy stillness, the birds singing as if there was but one morning of their lives in which they could sing, and this the morning; his family, all but Suse, who had to stay in the house to cook and mind Bill Dan, moving down the corn rows, putting seed into the ground; Milly gayer and more gigglesome than any of the children, proud of her garden—

332

she'd beaten Sue Annie on lettuce this year—gay because all around her, in the garden, in the old fruit trees, the black walnuts, among the thousands and thousands of little bells of opening huckleberry flowers, the budding black-berry bushes, Betsey's swelling sides, and the thriving baby chickens, there was a promise of full jars and a well set table.

The hens were laying as they had never laid before, and eggs twenty-two cents a dozen at Samuel's; King Devil and no other varmint had bothered a chicken or a guinea or a young lamb. It was a good time. All the meanness and the treachery hidden in the sky last year when it blackened the fruit with frost and scorched the corn with drouth seemed gone; and Milly, smiling up into its soft blueness, thought of angel's heads and a kind-eyed Jesus looking down over the shoulders of her dead children.

It was on a showery day in late April, when the wild iris and the foam flowers made a blueness and a whiteness by the creek banks and the wild pansies were opening on the ridge tops, that Nunn went walking up the hill for the mail in the early afternoon and soon came walking back again, a circular from the AAA in his hand. Milly, nursing Bill Dan, looked up at him in wonder, returning before midafternoon, but Suse understood and skipped across the kitchen on bare toes, shouting, "Th graded graveled road's finished to Samuel's, an they're a haulen th mail in a auto-mobile."

He nodded slowly, feeling strange still; he had known it was coming, a graveled road clean to the edge of his farm, for the post office was almost on the edge of Samuel's land and his land bordered Samuel's, but the road was like the spring, unprepared for and so unexpected. The world was close in his face: the road would come on, they said, down the hill and up the creek; it would be a handy thing to take things out, but what could take out could bring in—Pinkney and other men to hunt—strangers to see his run-down farm and ragged children. Suse was dancing up and down and asking him for what might have been the doz-enth time, "Did they say anything about a high-school bus a runnen clean to Samuel's, Pop? Oh, I bet it does."

"I dunno," he said, and turned away. He heard lambs calling and the sheep bells. The sheep had come back

from a short wandering in the woods; he must go look at
them.

The lie he had just told Suse pressed heavily on him as
he walked through the springing grass and clover to the
storehouse. Last winter when he went hunting with Pinkney, Elias Higginbottom had told him, in his capacity as a
member of the county board of education, not as gossipy
farmer, that this coming fall there would be a high-school
bus running to the end of the graded gravel, wherever the
end happened to be. There were at least a dozen children
in the three schools of the voting precinct ready and anxious to go to high school but with no way of getting there.

Weeks ago, when the diplomas of Suse and Andy came
in the mail and everybody in the post office had crowded
around to see the impressive, much-signed things, Samuel
had held up Andy's with an indifferent air, trying hard
to hide his pride. "Look agin in four years more," he had
said, "an Andy'ull have a high-school diploma alongside
a this." Mrs. Hull had nodded to her husband's words,
smiling proudly; and the Hulls were not ones to brag.

Nunn had kept silent until several asked if he meant to
send Suse to high school. "Oh, I don't know," he had
said; "Milly cain't see th sense a senden a girl to high
school, an sometimes I don't neither," and had hated himself for hiding behind Milly's opinions, which were not
his own.

Sue Annie had rubbed her nose and smiled at him
slyly. "But, Nunn, I thought that was what all th ruckus
was about. Back a year ago you was a chewen fire cause
Andrew wasn't gitten th youngens through th eighth grade
an you couldn't send Suse to high school an make a
teacher out a her like yer mammy."

He had said nothing and come quickly home. Suse
was watching from the yard as she had watched on many
mail days, and seeing the tube of cardboard he carried
had run to meet him, crying, "It's come. It's come," and
had jerked it out of its wrapping and stood staring at it,
tears in her eyes, smiling and choking.

He had come near choking too, seeing her so: not feeling her rags and her bare feet, though it was a raw March
day, but seeing herself in high school. Milly had wanted
to frame the diploma and hang it above the mantle, but
Suse had said, "No." She would put it in the trunk with

the pups' papers—a body could never tell; some day she might have a high-school or even a college diploma to go with it.

A lamb, too young to be afraid, sniffed at his shoes, a fine fat lamb, but he stared at it unseeing, thinking of Suse. He wished she had another year in common school —maybe by then things would be different. These sheep and one good season would see him out of debt, even though he'd have to buy more corn and lard and flour on credit to run his family and Maude through crop-making time. Maybe in another year he would have caught King Devil; through the winter there had been races that were close and hard; Sam and Vinie were not yet to their full powers; the money he spent on their feed would more than pay Suse's bus fare of fifty cents a week and keep her in high school—but Suse was like the spring; it raced into summer whether a man planted his corn or no.

The long, dusky sweet-smelling April twilight had fallen, and all around him the young lambs played, giving themselves completely to great stiff-legged, straight-up jumps or quick leapings over the sloping field; curiously they played and in silence, as if their borning and all their life were for the one thing only—play in the spring twilight. The ewes, gentler than common from the long hard winter and the much feeding, crowded round him, and gradually his troubles slipped behind the pleasure he took in watching his sheep, the most and finest he had ever had—ninety-seven in all, counting breeding ewes, young lambs, and the yearling ewes he had saved from the year before, not due to lamb until next year.

The hard dry cold of the middle winter had been good for sheep, and he had had hardly any trouble with worms since he started using phenothiazine as the bulletin directed; also the sheep bulletin had been his guide in what feeds to buy, and though the mixture recommended had seemed a curious one, his sheep had done better than in other years when he had little but homegrown feed with no hay.

Bossie Jean had run away to lamb this winter as last, but unlike last winter, no King Devil had come to steal her lambs; in fact, since the middle of the winter, when Sam and Vinie got onto his tricks, King Devil had shown

himself but little in the valley, and not at all since the
deep March snows; and Nunn, thinking on him for the
moment, hoped he would stay away a little space longer
and let the pups rest and give him a chance to finish his
corn planting—but it would be like the evil-hearted thing
to toll the pups away on every good plowing day, as he
had done last spring.

However, King Devil seemed to have taken on something of the goodness of the spring and never once
tempted the hounds away with his scent, so that Nunn's
corn planting in the upper fields was finished before
May 1, and Nunn and his family worked at getting rocks
out of the storehouse field, where already the young grass
and lespedeza made a green carpet on the ground.

As they worked, the winter-gentled sheep came often
among them to nibble the short tame grass, and many
times, as Nunn squatted, heaving at some tight flat rock,
he would grow forgetful as he gazed warm-eyed at a fine
stocky and thick-fleeced lamb. More and more as the
sheep flourished and the weather held its promise of the
early spring, his debt seemed a little thing: he could pay
it with less than half his wool and lamb crop. By next
year, or even this fall, he ought to be able to start building fence, good fence, around the fields he was putting
down to grass and clover that would hold the sheep and
keep them always home. Once fenced and cleared of
rocks and brush, he had enough land on this side of the
creek to pasture a hundred breeding ewes and grow hay
and corn for them, too. And with a hundred ewes he
need never lack for cash.

And he would dream on until Maude grew impatient
with his idle ways and walked away with the sled.

But the spring seemed made for dreams. Dark walls
of warm, flower-scented rain cloud came often to the
valley, lifting the grass and clover almost to a baby's
knees and showing green lines of corn across the rolling
sandfield. Then it was time for Nunn to do the thing he
hated to do—drive the sheep into the far back hills, for
in one hour's time the flock of them could, with their
closely nibbling lips, ruin half the corn in the sandfield.
A cow could bite young corn and it would grow again,
but a sheep sheared it off so closely that the growing
heart of the leaves was ruined; and with the woods full

of tender wild things, there was no need to take chances.

Nunn, with Milly and Lee Roy and Lucy and the pups, leisurely drove the not unwilling sheep far back into the deserted fields of the government forest land on the other side of Brush Creek. Some of the Tucker sheep were grazing there, for food was plentiful and all plants tender in the quick spring weather. In other years Nunn had never taken the trouble to drive them so far away before shearing time, but not until this year had they ever known the luxurious taste of tame grass as they had found it in the graveyard field, and he was afraid that if not driven far they would be back.

Though Milly complained that if she didn't hurry back to Bill Dan her breasts would burst and he would cry himself to death, Nunn lingered a time, watching his sheep spread out and disappear. He sighed as he turned away; they represented a lot of money for a poor man to leave wandering in the woods.

It was a Monday morning less than a week later that Milly, standing a moment in the kitchen door to sniff the fine spring air and watch for sign of sunrise while the cookstove heated, stiffened suddenly with listening, then ran around the house corner the better to hear—two sheep bells close to the graveyard field.

Nunn was out by the chopping block, washing his face in fresh cold spring water with such a blowing and splashing that he heard nothing until she called, vexation in her voice, "Th sheep's a comen home."

He swore and came running, water dripping from his hair and eyebrows. He listened a minute, then hurried on, though Milly begged him to wait at least until the coffee boiled and she could get the youngens out of bed to help.

"I'll be back by full sunrise," he promised. "If'n they git any more a that lespedeza or one taste a corn, they'll never stay in th woods," and he ran on in the gray light, cursing his lack of fence and wondering worriedly if some without bells were already in the corn.

He had crossed the graveyard field and was hurrying through the low rocky wooded swag between his place and where Lureenie had lived, not looking about for sheep, since they wouldn't be apt to stop in the woods with fine pasture a short distance away, when he heard above the noise of his feet and his own breath the gasping tattered breath of a winded ewe.

He stopped, fear rising in choking waves inside him, his eyes jumping frantically around to find her. She stood a few feet from the path, head down, legs planted wide apart to keep from falling, and about her there was the look of a thing that, unable to go further, had stopped to die.

She never showed any sign of life except a spasmodic quivering of her eyes when he felt her udder, hot and hard with too much milk: milk her twin lambs should have been taking now. Where were the lambs? He listened—somewhere ahead a ewe blatted with short, tired cries, but no lambs answered; and for the first time he realized that he had heard two bells only. Where were the others?

He left the half-dead ewe and ran toward the sound of the bells, and hardly paused over another ewe, still breathing, but lying on her side with outstretched feet by the side of the road.

It could be poison, but more likely cur dogs—cur dogs —he hadn't worried much about them since he first came to the valley; he had worried a little the first year his sheep were on the range, but as nobody's sheep were ever bothered, he forgot about cur dogs. There hadn't been any in the country since they got into Aunt Marthie's sheep when he was a boy; Preacher Jim and his sons, with John and his bigger boys, had gone over the country killing every cur dog on sight.

Even against his reason his mind fought to believe it was something else—poison, but what poison would they eat now—nothing; maybe somebody had cut a wild cherry and they had eaten it wilted; maybe they'd got into some sprouting buckeyes; maybe something not a cur dog had only scared a few—he would find the others all grazing peacefully—but where were the lambs?

He asked the question again when he came upon the two belled ewes, not run to death, but plainly tired, scared until they were addled, with no thought for their missing lambs. A little further on he found two lambs— one stood spraddle-legged in the road not far from Lureenie's door; the other lay, as if dying, by a clump of flowering blackberry briars.

He was almost to the mouth of Brush Creek before he came upon the first dead ewe—one of the big yearlings he had saved from the year before. She lay with her throat cut, blood matted on her white wool, her head turned toward home. There was no smell of death about her, no sign of a long hard run; something had leaped out of the dark early this morning, cut her throat while she grazed in a bed of fern—and something that had been briefly in his head came back again and would not go away—"maybe something not a cur dog—"

The path twisted down and around the high bluff above Brush Creek, and as he followed it, he found dead lambs, some dead with cut throats, some dead with no mark upon them but sign of a long hard run, some dying; and once, far below, near the creek water, he heard the piteous cry of a lost, frightened lamb.

He tried to count the dead he found, then forgot the number in the creeping misery and the growing fear that the only ones left alive were those half dead on the way home.

Brush Creek Canyon lay foggy blue and smelling of flowers in the spring sunrise, but on the ridge tops above, the light fell, slanting yellow-red and warm; and higher than the ridge, circling slowly into the light above the canyon, a buzzard came, and then another, and another high and slowly sweeping. He watched as their circles narrowed, grew lower until they were black ugly things wheeling within the shadow of the canyon walls up the creek.

He, too, went up the creek, and soon the smell of death was stronger than the smell of flowers. He found Bossie Jean under a flowering mountain laurel, knowing her only by her bell; the buzzards had been at her, sometime the day before, he guessed.

He walked on up between the narrowing canyon walls, and in a spot where there was a bit of level land by the creek, hemmed all around by bluffs and broken waterfalls, the buzzards flew up, slowly and heavily, lifting their gorged bodies out of the narrow space with a loud, awkward flapping of black wings.

Something had driven a great band of sheep into the trap where there was no turning up or out and killed them all. He stood a moment, slump-shouldered and staring, then turned to a lamb with its nose in the creek water, looked for the mark and found it—his own—and went on counting and looking; at twelve he stopped and leaned against a tree and retched and retched, his empty stomach writhing and twisting his whole body. Hemmed as he was with the smell of rotten flesh, he gagged and vomited so often that he no longer stopped for an attack but worked on, though he trembled in his legs and water dripped from his mouth and his eyes.

At last he had counted all he could see and that was forty-two—three had John's mark and two the mark of Jeremiah Tucker. The rest were his own.

The sun was higher, striking deeper into the canyon; and in the rising warmth the rotten death smell was like a gag forced up his nose and down his mouth.

He was halfway up to the creek mouth when a big, rough, spotted hound came loping through the brush, followed quickly by two others. Then, breaking through the hemlock and ivy bush, he saw two of the Tuckers, big men with red beefy faces, sweat-glistening now with worry and quick walking.

They stopped and looked at him, and each spoke a slow "Howdy," not cordial as was their custom, but filled with worried wonder as to what he had found up the creek.

"Just two was your'n, Jeremiah—three was John's—th rest was mine—thirty-seven."

Their big faces grew strained and puckered with sympathy, but they stood silent, ashamed of and trying not to show the relief they felt that the thirty-seven were not their own. After a minute Jeremiah said, "We never seed any buzzards till nigh sundown yisterday, and then it was too dark to come."

"It was cur dogs; but them hounds a our'n they'll chase em down an kill em like foxes," Hiram said.

And his brother asked, "Them pedigreed hounds a your'n now—I've heard they won't chase a cur dog?"

"They won't," Nunn said, and added as he started walking again down the creek course: "No hound'ull git a scent a anything up there but rotten sheep. They've been dead three—four days—but by th path I come, they's fresh dead, mebbe done a little fore daylight this mornen."

Jeremiah cleared his throat and said, without looking at Nunn, "Up on th ridge now, on our side a th creek, they's fresh dead, too—we come past em onct, but without th hounds—we never thought at first to bring em. Hiram he went back an got em, but we come a short cut to th buzzards—we never thought till we found that first batch a dead this mornen but what it was a hog er a stray calf fell over th bluff th buzzards was after."

"How many you find dead on yon side?" Nunn asked, his head bowed and walking on.

"Nine, we seed."

"My mark?"

"Five—three a Hiram's an one a John Ballew's."

"I seed one a you'n as I come along—fresh dead."

"An your'n?"

"Eight, I recken."

"Throats cut?"

"Yeah—some jist run to death; last night was hot fer early May."

"It was cur dogs all right," Hiram said again.

"They ain't none in this country," Nunn said.

"What else?" Jeremiah asked. "They ain't a hound that'd tetch a sheep."

"An nobody's seen a wolf since Pap was a boy," Hiram said.

"See any cur-dog tracks?" Nunn asked.

Hiram shook his head.

The hounds came back, tails trailing from the dead-sheep scent, and hurried ahead, walking sometimes in the creek water, as if they would cleanse their bodies of the foul smell. The men had almost reached the creak mouth when high overhead, near the bluff edge, Nunn heard first Sam and then Vinie in long-drawn eager hunting cries; happy they were in the fresh spring morning, because they were hot on the trail of a thing they hated.

Nunn lifted his head and listened a moment, staring toward the sound with vacant, unsurprised eyes. He raised his clenched fist as it he would strike something, then dropped it as he remembered he was not alone, for Hiram was asking, "Them's your hounds, ain't they?"

"Yeah, they've found fox scent."

Jeremiah was a religious man, a church member, but now he said "Damn," as the three Tucker hounds ran down the creek and around, their rough cur-doggish voices echoing and reechoing in the narrow canyon. He flushed, realizing what he had said, but went on with some disgust, "Your hounds now, they've picked up fox scent somewheres, an mine, they'll foller them an never try to hunt th cur dogs."

"Yeah, they'll foller fox scent," Nunn said.

At the mouth of the creek above the river, Milly sat with humped shoulders and hanging head on a big water-rounded sand rock near the running water. She saw the men and got up, waiting, smoothing her apron, trying to smile. "I thought you might be up that away," she said to Nunn, and added, "I seed th buzzards?" her voice rising so that the last was a question asking how many sheep the buzzards hunted.

"They pick up that scent by them fresh-killed sheep along the path?" Nunn asked her, then looked away toward the sound of the hounds' voices, faintening in the distance.

She nodded, but her glance, as if she knew what he could be thinking, refused to meet his, and wandered away and fixed at last up the creek, where the buzzards were circling again.

"I thought them hounds a your'n wouldn't chase a cur dog," Jeremiah said.

"They won't," Nunn said.

"It's a fox; they sound like it was King Devil," Lee Roy called, and never noticed the swift, angry "Shut-up" glance his mother gave him. He and Lucy had started with Milly, but Lucy had been unable to keep up with Milly, blown along as she was by a mounting dread, a fear to learn and at the same time an unbearable need of knowing how bad things were. The children were silent, Lucy staring at her father, he looked so strange; but Lee Roy glared straight ahead. He wished he could go off and cry; the dead sheep—the ewes he had fed and the lambs he had helped to their first milk—hurt, but worse was the one look he had taken at the defeated face of his father.

Nunn listened to the Tucker pack pick up the scent and go in the direction Sam and Vinie had taken, then he started across the creek. "Might as well go see what else we can find," he said.

The others followed, more silent than people at a funeral. They had come upon six sheep, not far from the road and about two days dead, when John came riding hard on one mule, his two boys on another. After Milly left, Suse had taken Deb and Bill Dan and gone to tell John there was trouble in the sheep on the range; John had only around sixty and his were not as fine as Nunn's.

"You ain't lost a dozen, John," Jeremiah said when he saw the tired, harassed face of the old man.

"What a you call loss, man?" John began in a high shrill angry voice, but changing to look into Nunn's beaten eyes, he asked with a sudden change to gentle concern, "How many you lost, Nunn?"

"Somewhere's around sixty," he said, and walked away to find the mark on a just noticed lamb—the mark was his.

John and the Tuckers said nothing more of their losses, but put their children to work with Lee Roy to scour the country for sheep, dead or alive.

Nunn sent Milly and Lucy back home with directions to send Suse with all the grass sacks she could find; the wool on the dead sheep was worth something and could be pulled from the rotten flesh.

Milly begged Nunn to come home and at least drink some coffee, and the Tuckers, who lived less than two miles away, each begged him to come to his house for a snack, but Nunn would go to neither.

Word of sheep-killing dogs in the hills spread quickly, and by ten o'clock more than a dozen hounds had come, but all had picked up the scent at the top of the bluff and gone after Sam and Vinie into the rough forest lands. Jaw Buster heard and left his truck loaded with crossties and came with Speed, who, it was known, would follow cur-dog scent. Lister was gone to his work on the railroad section gang, but his wife, Babe, sent Sourvine with her oldest boy; the Tiller hounds came, likewise the Sextons and Bogle Cooksey from the Cow's Horn.

All day Nunn walked red-eyed through the woods, sometimes hunting for sheep, sometimes listening for sheep bells or the bleat of a lost lamb, but most often for Sam and Vinie, unheard for hours, and always as he walked, trying, like a wounded beast fearful its own kind will send it to its death, to keep alone. He was conscious

of neither tiredness nor hunger, nor the scratches and
bruises from his swift heedless walking that marked his
hands and his face and his body. His thoughts were like
swift hounds, chasing him as hounds chase a tired, holeless
fox. When Sam and Vinie had found King Devil scent
by the fresh-killed sheep, all sense of loss had left him,
and in its place came insane anger. Worse than the anger
was the helplessness.

Night came but not one of the hounds came home except Bogle Cooksey and Drum Tiller on the trail of a
rabbit.

Nunn and John with their children came in at dusty
dark, driving a band of sheep—forty-seven were John's
and twenty-three were Nunn's; the twenty-three and the
six that had lived after the hard run home were left of the
flock of ninety-seven. John had fenced pasture lands that
would, with a little more barbed wire, hold sheep. Though
the pasture was none too good and needed for his mules
and milk cows, he offered to keep what was left of Nunn's
flock until he could decide either to sell them or build
fence, for sheep-killing dogs in a country were worse than
fire or flood or drouth; sooner or later such things were
finished; a man could know when and then begin where
they had ended, but nobody could tell about sheep-killing
dogs; there might be only two and there might be a dozen;
they might live quiet and peaceful at home as far away as
the valley, keeping their meanness carefully hidden from
their owners; and, worst of all, nobody could be certain
when the last one was dead.

The old man talked on as they walked homeward behind the weary sheep, and his opinions were much like
those of the other men Nunn had heard during the day.
It was a shame Sam and Vinie had to pick up fox scent by
the dead sheep; the hounds like Speed that would follow
a cur dog if left to themselves might have found the right
trail if Sam and Vinie hadn't found the other first. Now,
no hound would be likely to pick it up until the cur dogs
came in for a fresh kill, and following them would never
be easy; most likely they'd come in either on the graded
graveled road to Samuel's or the one that ran from the
valley to Tuckerville, and if they ran in the track of a
rubber tire the hounds couldn't follow them. The cur dogs
might come again tonight or not till next fall, or it could

have been the dogs of men camping somewhere along the river or in the forest that would never again be in the country.

But John was taking no chances; he would fatten his sheep a little on hay and corn from last year and sell them not long after shearing time; there was, he said, no money in sheep if a man had to keep them home all the time, and Nunn ought to sell his; they wouldn't be safe again on the range, and sheep fence would cost a mint of money.

Nunn said nothing; almost the only cash he ever saw came from sheep—and by God, who was he to let that red-haired, green-eyed devil force him out of the sheep business? His credit was good and he had land he could mortgage to buy fence. He wished John would hush his silly talk; a cur dog wouldn't have sense enough to drive the sheep into the trap of Brush Creek Canyon any more than a cur dog would have sense enough to run in a tire track like a fox.

Most of the night he walked restlessly back and forth across the little table of stone that formed the top of the Pilot Rock, listening for hounds he never heard.

Dawn came and Milly sent for him. He came reluctantly home and drank coffee, and because he could think of nothing else to do he began plowing the young corn; there was something he had meant to do on Monday—yesterday, when his sheep were alive and before this red madness that would not let him rest had come into his soul.

At noon, while he sat and made a pretense of eating, Sam and Vinie came home. They walked slowly and soundlessly, tails drooping in defeat as Zing's had after a long King Devil chase. Their eyes were red slits between the swollen lids, and as they breathed in short tired gasps, their ribs showed big and bony, like the ribs of old hounds too cruelly worn to be of much use in the hunt again.

Milly sighed over them as they lay under the walnut tree and wished she had some milk to give them; but Nunn, after a short glance at each, started back to his plowing. Milly called after him, reminding him that it was Tuesday, a mail day, and if he didn't hurry all the men would be gone home and he would see nobody—they all

stayed such a little time since the mail started coming in
a car.

He stared across the creek. He didn't want to go to the
post office and sit and listen to a lot of foolish jabber
about cur dogs in his sheep and what an unlucky chance
it was that Sam and Vinie picked up fox scent and threw
the other hounds off any cur-dog scent around.

There was no chance to any of it; it was planned, all
planned. King Devil had waited years for this, careful to
kill his sheep and leave those of the other men.

Once in a hard snowy winter when he was a boy, he
and Preacher Jim had found a half-eaten ewe with fox
tracks all around; and more than once John had found a
ewe or a lamb dead with fox sign all around. Everybody
knew that foxes could kill full-grown sheep; King Devil
could kill better than any other fox; he could kill like a
cur dog, and smarter than a cur dog, he would know to
pick the first warm nights in May before the sheep were
sheared and when the ewes, weak from giving milk, could
die easy with overmuch running.

He went on after Maude. He didn't want to see his
neighbors; he didn't want their advice about selling his
sheep; he wouldn't sell his sheep; he wouldn't crawl in the
dirt for King Devil; he'd mortgage his land and lose it
first.

Chapter Twenty-five

═•═

NUNN NEVER SPOKE of his dead sheep again unless forced to by some neighbor's conversation, and often he avoided his neighbors because of their much talking and many sighs and headshakings, not alone for the lost sheep, but also for Sourvine Tucker, who never came home. Many nights Lister listened on the Pilot Rock for him, and Lister's oldest children, helped by Lee Roy and the Tiller boys, scoured the woods for miles around. But soon Sourvine was a memory with other hounds like Zing and Del and Bonnie Mae, but even such lovers of Zing as Jaw Buster and Lee Roy agreed that Sourvine was the prettiest mouthed of them all, living or dead.

There were headshakes, too, over Nunn Ballew when he went to town and came home with near a truckload of wire fencing, some barbed, but most of it stout, high, woven, that had cost a mint of money, Blare said. Neither Blare nor any of his neighbors had ever bought woven wire, but Blare had looked up the price in Samuel's Montgomery Ward catalogue, and such wire was only for the rich kind of farmers who lived around Town, not for the likes of Nunn Ballew; maybe his credit was good, but with no wool and lambs to sell, how would he pay his debt? He couldn't moonshine again till his new corn crop was in, for in the dry year before he, like a lot of other people, had hardly raised enough corn for bread, let alone moonshine.

But nobody asked Nunn about his plans, not even Milly, who on many twilights, while they sat in silence taking their after-supper chews of tobacco, would study his flat-cheeked, big-eyed face turned toward the sunset and wish he'd never bought fence to work himself to death

on putting up, and sigh because he'd taken the loss of his
sheep so much to heart.

It was God's will that all His children have some bad
luck, and it was a sin to fight against it, especially so in a
time like this when God had sent the finest growing season ever known in the valley and crops grew like crops in
the Promised Land. And Milly, thinking on the season
and sleepy-headed even before the last red light had
faded, would forget her worry over Nunn and fall into her
big worry, the long worry of the summer—that some cul-
tivated plant would smother in the weeds, or some
bite of food would waste before she could feed it to her
family or can or dry or pickle it against the winter.

And though Suse kept house and minded Bill Dan while
her mother worked, Milly could not put all her time on
saving food, for weeds as well as crops flourished in the
good growing weather, and on days when the soil was dry,
Nunn had all his family in the cornfield by daylight, and
after a long rest through the hottest part of the day, they
worked on until the hill shadow had climbed past Sue
Annie's cabin and the whippoorwills were calling. Lucy
was a big girl now, going on eight years old, and though
not yet as tall as her hoe handle, hoed her row with the
rest, and Deb and Bill Dan alone were left to stay in the
shade with the hounds.

This year more so than on other years, Milly and the
children worked the fields alone, and often Lee Roy
plowed while Nunn hunted the pups or worked on the
wove-wire and cedar-post fence going up around the storehouse field and farther spring.

Milly hated the fieldwork but never complained, though
after the first ripening wild strawberry, life for her was
one unending race against the seasons, for the times of
harvest were early like the spring, and wild-strawberry-
picking time in June was hardly finished before it was
cabbage-krauting time and the first of the white horse
apples were falling, begging to be canned or dried or made
into vinegar, and high on the ridges the huckleberries
were ripening, thousands of the little bushes blue-purple
with the fruit.

In spite of all the work, Milly on many days found a
freedom and a peace she had never known, the first vaca-
tion from housekeeping and baby tending that she had

had since marriage, for Suse, who had suddenly shot up and now promised to be of a size of Aunt Marthie Jane, was a shade taller than her mother, a great grown girl going on fifteen; and though she had always hated housework and had ever been an impatient baby tender, more and more as the summer lengthened she was the keeper of the house and Bill Dan.

In huckleberry-picking time Milly liked to get away from the house before full dawn. Lucy and Lee Roy and Sam and Vinie would be at her heels, hunks of cold corn bread smeared thick with butter from the just freshened Betsey in her tucked-up apron, and all the empty lard buckets in the house jangling on her arms. She would climb up and up until she could look down and see, not houses or barns or fields, but a lake of fog, blue-looking and still in the shadows of the hills; while above her the Pilot Rock changed from gray rock to red-gold. Soon, on the steep ridge shoulders where, among old crooked pines, the finest berries grew, the sun struck hot and bright and the piney woods smell mingled with the odors of drying dew and wintergreen and ripened huckleberries; and Milly, sniffing, picking with both hands, watching Lee Roy and Lucy to make certain they picked their bushes clean, would think on a fat winter with full jars and feel a great contentment.

By midmorning, and before Bill Dan had cried overmuch for the breast, she and the children would be home with lard buckets full. Most of the time Suse would have jars clean and waiting and a good fire going in the cookstove. But sometimes the fire was out, the stove cold, and the iron pot of green beans, that with boiled potatoes and corn bread was the chief fare of the daily noonday meal half cooked or burned. Milly would begin a shrill angry calling of Suse, and Suse would answer, maybe from no farther away than the garden, where she had gone on the excuse of hunting cucumbers; but often she was gone to the woods, and would come running, Bill Dan jouncing on her hip, her ragged dress tail showing fresh tears and with briar scratches, red-lined with blood but unheeded, on her bare feet and legs.

Milly would shame her and scold her for neglecting her work and trolloping through the woods like a no-good whore, and even at times threatened to whip her, but mostly she was patient; it just seemed like poor Suse wasn't able to get it into her head that she was through school and mighty nigh a woman now, instead of a child to go running through the woods, and that people, especially Sue Annie, would talk about her if she didn't stay home and work like other girls her age. But one day when Milly was reminding her that it mightn't be so long before she had a house and youngens of her own to tend and that she ought to be thankful—when she was Suse's age she hadn't had a good home of her own but had to work in other people's houses—Suse had got real sassy.

"You got paid an you had clothes an shoes," she had said, her eyes sparking up.

"Honor thy father an thy mother," Milly had said, and remembering the bitterness of cooking other people's bread, had slapped her hard across the mouth and added, "If you hadn't loped all over th hills at school last term, your shoes would ha lasted."

Suse had turned away with clenched hands and tears sliding down her face, but never again had she complained or asked for shoes.

Early in July, Nunn sold three lambs and his little store of wool and bought dog feed and Milly's list of patent medicines, but there was little money left for clothing, except what must be bought for Lee Roy and Lucy to keep them decent in school, and he dared add nothing more to the great debt he had made for fence.

Suse with the others came flying down the path to meet him, but stopped still when she saw the smallness of the bundle. Nunn looked at her with troubled apologetic eyes as he held out a package wrapped in green paper. "These is work shoes," he said. "Th man guaranteed 'em to last," and added after an instant's hesitation, "Come fall, I'll git you some Sunday shoes when I sell Betsey's calf."

Suse shifted Bill Dan to her other hip and stood swallowing hard and made no move to open the package.

It was Milly who opened the shoes and nodded over them in satisfaction, for they were of ankle height, hobnailed, heavy, sturdily built as a boy's. "You won't be a wearen these out fore spring," she said. "An it ain't like you had to have somethen fitten to wear to school; them little old oxfords he's been a gitten you ain't hardly worth carryen home." She glanced almost pityingly at Suse's shoulders, slumped above the baby. "He'll manage to git you some Sunday shoes that you can wear thout bean afeard Sue Annie'll make fun of em," and added in all sincerity: "I wish your feet hadn't growed so—you could wear my Sunday patent-leather slippers."

Nunn walked quickly away, answering none of the eager questions of Milly and the younger ones about his trip to the valley. He knew that for the first time Suse understood how poor he was, too poor to keep her in Sunday shoes, much less send her to high school.

Nunn thought again of Suse as he worked on the fence next morning. He remembered the stricken look in her eyes and that she had eaten none of the candy, and he thought of how she had sat hour after hour pulling burs from the wool, and the way she had vomited and vomited but never complained when she had to stand straddled over a half-rotten sheep in the hot spring sun and jerk the wool from the stinking flesh and so save a little from King Devil's destruction.

He cursed, rubbed the sweat from his eyes with the back of one hand, and threw down the heavy iron spud post-hole digger with the other. His shoulders ached and his legs were all a tremble from the long jabbing at the stone.

As he stood silent, frowning down into the half-finished hole, Willie Cooksey spoke from behind him.

Nunn looked around and saw him, friendly enough, but smiling, or so it seemed to him, the same smile of pity and ridicule that had come into his face the night they had fought at J. D. Duffey's, and though that was over long ago, both men agreeing it went against their grain to hold a liquor quarrel between them, Nunn felt now the same old anger and wished the man had not come.

"Nunn, you look peaked and wore out as a widder woman with colicky twins. It'll take a mine drill er dinnimite to dig thet hole," Willie said as he pulled out his jackknife and squatted in a shady spot. "If'n I was you, I'd quit this fencen anyhow fer a spell—your river-bottom corn is a hurten in th weeds."

"It ain't been planted hardly three weeks," Nunn said, trying hard to show no anger, no concern over his corn in the weeds, and none of the fear, touching him now as in other moments, that the rolls of woven wire for which he had signed the lien on his land would never be strung on posts and holding his sheep.

Sweat was in his eyes and he wiped it away and stood, breathing heavily, staring down into the hole but thinking now of liens and mortgages. The storekeeper for all his friendly ways was a sly one now—Nunn had offered him a mortgage on Maude and Jude, Betsey and all his remaining sheep but the man had suggested a lien on his land—it was less trouble—only a bit of paper, the man had said. Milly's name ought to be on it, but it didn't matter. And Nunn had signed a note promising to pay his old debt of $78 and his new debt of $233 for fence and corn and lard and flour to take him through crop-making time.

He remembered he had had a drink or so and wondered as he had signed just what was a lien, and had wondered on at times until he asked John two weeks ago. John had shaken his head dourly—liens were contraptions of the devil that a man ought never to put his hand to—a man had to go to law to collect on a mortgage, but a lien now, the holder didn't have to bother; he could take the land as he willed. And the old man had talked on of liens and mortgages in his quarrelsome grumbling way, then stopped suddenly and asked with a stern but pitying glance from his gray eyes, "You ain't signed a lien on your work mare an everthing else fer fence to keep them little bit a sheep in? That wove-wire fence must ha cost a sight a money."

Nunn had shaken his head and looked quickly away, trying to hide the guilt in his eyes. Lying he was. John no more than Samuel or Milly would think he had signed away his land.

It seemed he had been thinking a long time, but Willie was talking again as if his last words had just been finished. "But you got your river bottom in so late th weeds ull fair take it in this good growen weather. I don't like river-bottom corn," he went on with the satisfied air of a man whose corn, planted in early May, was now laid by in early July. "They's allus th danger they'll come a early tide to th river an wash it all away fore it's hardly ready to cut."

"Yeah," Nunn said sullenly. "Yours all got washed

away onct, I recollect—in th shock. I've allus saved my corn and I figger I allus will."

Willie smiled and disregarded his sullen tone. "They's allus a first time fer everything," he said, and added with a touch of pride: "I'm aimen to do somethen fer th first time this summer. I'm aimen to take my four oldest up to Indianer at tumater-picken time an pick tumaters; a man with a family can do right good, I've heared say. They're already signen up people in Town at that employment place, beggen fer em. They pay you by th basket an my youngens works fast."

Nunn grunted. "They won't let youngens work under fifteen er sixteen I've heared it said."

Willie shook his head. "When school ain't a goen on they will, an anyhow, so long as th youngens don't live there they'd let em work if they was ten years old." He folded his knife and got up and stood a moment hesitant and humble, like a man hunting words to beg a favor. "Whyn't you an your two oldest come along with we'uns. Th picken don't begin good fore early August, an by then your corn, late as it is, ud be laid by. It's all new to me, this worken on public works," he went on hurriedly, flushing. "I'd feel better with a neighbor man along, an you—you've been around."

"Git Blare er Joe C.," Nunn answered shortly. "They both worked up in Indianee back when times was good."

"An have em git drunk an mebbe th law—I've heared say it's bad up in them parts. They'll put a man in jail just fer carryen a pistol; they might put us all in a strange jailhouse an me not knowen a soul to git me out."

"Blare don't drink," Nunn said.

"No, but he cain't read or write no better'n me an th youngens." Willie flushed and went on hurriedly: "You know none a us ever went past th second grade cept Sureenie, an she's plumb fergot all her letters. Up there, you need somebody to do readen an writen."

"You'll git along," Nunn said. "I couldn't leave Milly an th little youngens, an they'll be th hay to git in. I'm goen to have more'n th barn an th storehouse ull hold."

"Aw, Nunn, come on. Lee Roy's a good plowhand, better'n some men. Leave him with Milly. John and his boys ull have to cut yer hay anyhow, like they done last year. You an Suse come—they say a quick-worken gal can pick more'n a man. Why, I bet you all could save $300 or $400. We could all batch together."

Nunn shook his head. "I got plenty to do at home."

"Aw, hell, man; sell them few sheep you've got left; they won't do no good this summer hemmed up in John's pasture, an they'll all die with worms in th fields you're a fixen; you know you cain't raise sheep less'n you put em on a range. Leave Lee Roy an Milly to manage an go with us an come back home fer lasses-maken time with money enough to buy back th sheep you've lost. I tell you, man, you'll make money. That war acrost th waters is a maken times good, an a taken men off to them trainen camps is a maken help kinda scarce so's th pay'ull be good."

Nunn pushed his hat back and looked at him but said nothing.

"Aw, come on; if'n it's King Devil you're a waiten to git, you've skeered him out a th country an that ought tu be enough."

Nunn grunted. "That ole fox ain't a maken me do nothen."

"Them hounds a your'n, they'll hunt by theirselves; t'other evenen I heared em a singen away so sweet, some-where's back toward Brush Creek bout dusty dark, an I could hear you still a plowen an a payen em no mind. Milly an Lee Roy could manage an you and Suse—"

"I've got to get this fence finished, I tell you," Nunn interrupted with a fierceness he hadn't meant to show. It hurt to know his family could manage without him, but worse for Willie to know why he wouldn't leave the valley.

Willie disregarded his anger. "Then let Suse go. She could do our readen an writen. Sureenie—she's twelve a goen on thirteen—she's a goen. You know I'd never let em git into any kind a meanness."

Nunn straightened his hat, dusted the dirt from his knees. "I ain't so hard up yet that I've got to send my youngens off to public works. Well," he added with a last despairing glance at the half-finished hole, "I recken you're right; it'll take dinnimite an I'll have to be a gitten up th hill to borrow a charge a minen powder off'n Joe C. an Blare."

Willie, too, got up. "You think it over, Nunn, an mebbe

you'll change yer mind. It's a goen to be money-maken times if'n that trouble acrost th waters keeps up; Sue Annie was a tellen me that Blare an Joe C. was a maken good money since they opened th coal mines."

"I've had enough a minen," Nunn said, and he turned away, eager to be rid of Willie and the thought like a hammer beating over and over in his brain that he could maybe make enough this summer to pay off his debt. Willie spoke the truth; times were good; all things were getting higher, even the little farm stuff a man had to sell. Samuel was paying twenty-four cents a dozen for eggs. But he would build the fence; he wouldn't let King Devil put him out of the sheep business and off at public works in Indiana.

After a polite "Better come and go home with me," Willie, on his way home from taking a letter for the next day's mail, got up and walked away through the brush toward the Cow's Horn road.

A brushy little thick-limbed cedar tree not ten feet away swooshed as from a plunging wild thing and Suse darted out, the jug of fresh spring water, which was her errand, forgotten in her hands.

"Please, Pop. Couldn't we go—we'd make a sight a money—why, I'd make more'n enough to start me out to high school. An to go riden on a train all th way to Indianee; if them Cookseys can do it, we could. Lee Roy could manage like he said." She was looking straight into his eyes, seeing Indiana cities and people and strange fine country glimpsed from a flying train, with high school and new dresses and a real winter coat at the end.

He jerked the water jug from her. "Shut up an quit tellen me what to do. What a you mean, anyhow, sneaken around an eaves-droppen in th brush? Git on back to th house where you belong." And his voice, snarling and animal-like, seemed to come from that part of him that lived past his will and his reason, the part that hunted King Devil and left all manhood behind until he was but one beast hunting another.

Suse did not flinch or drop her eyes in meek acceptance as Milly would have done, but stood a moment straight-shouldered and high-headed and looked at him, and her eyes were older than her dangling braids and small pointed breasts pushing in sharp outline against the outgrown ragged, faded dress. Her face, too, was unchild-like, hard with scorn and anger as she said, "I hid in th bushes because I wasn't decent fer a body to see in these rags, an I ain't got no better—but one ole dress I been saven to wear to meeten if'n I got some shoes." And she turned and walked away—stepping proudly on her bare, calloused, briar-scratched feet.

Nunn lifted the jug to his lips and over it watched her go, and it wasn't like watching one of the children going back to the house from some errand but a part of his life being taken—King Devil took Suse as he had taken the sheep and his money—and his life's strength and his hopes and his plans and the peace that was the right of every man who worked and did no wrong. At least he wouldn't lie to himself; it was the big red fox that kept him home, not his bit of farming.

He put the jug in the shade, squinted at the sun—about mid-morning high it was—then started back along the widely cut fence row, pausing at times to push against one of the peeled red-cedar posts so new that under the hot sun it smelled still like fresh-cut cedar boughs. A faint look of pleasure lighted his gaunt big-eyed face each time he put his weight against a post and found it unyielding. And setting the posts here above the creek bank along the rocky wooded hillside was about the hardest part of the fence building. He'd finished this much; he'd finish the rest and somehow, some way he'd pay the debt.

He followed the fence until he came to the big corner post by the post-office path, then took the path down and across the creek and up the hill. It was bad enough to borrow post-hole diggers and sledge hammers from John, but he hated to borrow from the Tillers and stand respectfully silent while they advised him on fence building and sheep raising. You couldn't raise sheep under fence, they'd say; they'd all die of worms; they who'd never raised a sheep or built a foot of fence.

The day was sticky hot and sultry and he wanted to stop in the shade by the path an rest, but would not; used to be he had never noticed this hill or any other. He sighed; he wasn't the man who had at many times stood a twelve-hour shift in the mines as car loader, or even the man, young and full of plans and dreams, who had come to the valley five—no, seven years ago now. He stopped, the seven striking him, not in his head or his reason where he knew it, but in his heart. Seven years—that was a long time. None of the things planned were done—and he was getting old. He was thirty-five. No, thirty-five was young. Preacher Will had been old as that or older when he got religion. Religion! If he had religion he could leave King Devil to go his way, but before a man could get religion he had to give his heart and soul to God and get God's grace to forgive his sins. How could a man be certain God would forgive? How could he know God wanted his soul? How could a man know he hadn't committed the unpardonable sin? What was the unpardonable sin? Why did he think of all that now? Suse? If he lived to be a hundred and caught King Devil and died a millionaire, that wouldn't help Suse now—unpardonable, unforgivable. *It were better for him that a millstone were hanged about his neck, and that he were drowned in the depth of the sea.* Preacher Jim had preached on that when Othnel Dugger left his wife and child to starve and went away with a stranger woman.

Chapter Twenty-six

THE FALL THAT YEAR was damp and warm and still, so that the river-bottom corn was slow to ripen up for cutting, and it was October and near molasses-making time before Nunn started work on it. Milly pitied him because he had to cut the corn alone, but he wouldn't keep Lee Roy from school, and she couldn't help because her jaw teeth were bothering her again, her jaw swollen so she could hardly see from one eye; Suse couldn't help either —Bill Dan had a teething diarrhea and kept her busy washing diapers.

Nunn, however, felt no pity for himself; Milly had helped in all the other work of the fall and he was glad to work alone for a change, though he wished, as he broke four hills down for the beginning of a shock, that he could have brought Suse along. She needed a change from the whining baby and her quarrelsome mother and the endless housework. Then he forgot Suse and most of his troubles as he cut the great tall stalks, each with two heavy, down-hanging ears of yellow corn—corn as fine as any Preacher Jim had ever raised. He'd have plenty of corn this year to carry him through till corn-cutting time again; he might even keep Lee Roy's Jude till spring; there'd be plenty to fatten Rosie's eight pigs and maybe Rosie, too; some said hogs yould maybe go high as ten cents a pound, and if they did, the hay money and the hog money and the money from Jude would just about pay off his debt—if they could live without meat, almost no clothes, and hardly any store-bought grub.

He frowned, remembering Lee Roy's eyes when he'd learned that most of the hay was sold, sold uncut in the

358

field—something no Ballew had ever done—to Ansel Anderson for $75 so that Nunn could pay off some of his debt to the storekeeper in Town. He imagined Milly when she learned there'd be another winter with no meat, thought of Suse waiting for Sunday shoes—he'd make crossties, he might even moonshine again—no, he wouldn't do that, but he'd make some money some way. Pretty soon he'd be through fencing. His eyes lightened as he thought on the fence. King Devil might lead him to hell and past but it was a fine feeling to have the sheep all safe in the storehouse field and room for Betsey at night so that she never had to be hunted of mornings and when finally found, sucked dry by her half-weaned calf.

The sun rose higher and took away the chill of early morning fog, the sandy soil, from being damp, grew pleasantly warm through his shoes, and from the steep wooded bluff and hillside above came the smell of wild grapes, overripe now and drying in the sun, of horsemint dried and gone to seed, and the odor of damp, freshly fallen leaves beginning their slow change into earth, a smell that always made Nunn think of fox fire on rainy nights and rotten moss-covered logs.

All these and the smell of the freshly cut corn fodder were pleasant things, like the sight of the wild sunflowers glowing in the sun along the river, the river itself, blue and sprinkled with red and yellow leaves; and the red-and-white-striped morning-glories that bloomed among the corn, only now the flowers were beginning to wilt, each with a pearl of dew caught in its throat, it seemed a sin on this blue-and-gold morning to kill the pretty things as he cut the dead corn they grew by.

The river, higher than on most falls, gurgled softly over the shoals; and in the little space of time between carrying an armload of fodder to the shock and walking back to cut more, when the rustling of the corn was silent, all the little sounds lost on a windy day, but loud now in the stillness, came to him: a peckerwood working on a dead beech limb in the bluff above; the *plop, plop* of his shoes in the sandy soil; the twittering of the wild canaries as they bounced among the sunflowers; the rustling whisper of a sycamore leaf as it settled after a slow sliding fall against the earth; the buzz of a few late-hunting wild bees among the wild asters; and on the bluff side above him now and again the chattering of a squirrel—on some still damp morning he ought to go squirrel-hunting. Back in the mines when he came dirty at dawn from the night shift, he'd think of the fog-wetted woods in the valley and of how he had squirrel-hunted as a boy and how he would again when he bought the Old Place—the years had gone now and he never had.

He frowned, listening. Sam and Vinie had been home with Milly when he left and hadn't been gone on a long fox hunt in more than a month, except for the regular Saturday night hunts with Jaw Buster and the Tillers that had started early this fall because of the damp still nights. But over in Tuckerville King Devil was stealing chickens by the dozen: three different people had seen him in broad daylight; twice Sam and Vinie had been on his scent within the last month, but for all the good they'd done they might as well have stayed home, and any day now he expected them to saunter off to Tuckerville to hunt King Devil scent.

Aye, Lord, it was too fine a day to waste worrying over King Devil: it was good to be a man cutting corn on his own land, not working for somebody else on somebody else's land; unless some uncommon bad luck overtook him, he'd never lose his land.

Not long after, he heard Willie Cooksey at the top of his boat-landing path, singing a song he must have heard in Indiana: "A tisket, a teskit, a little yeller baskit," and Willie sang it as if he held the basket with the world inside it.

The Cookseys had been home a week; he'd heard their songs at twilight but had never seen them nor had any of the post-office crowd. They'd come to the end of the gravel at Samuel's in a rented car—some said it was a taxicab that Willie had hired all the way from Town, but that was only gossip. They came in the dark and walked the rest of the way home and only Lister Tucker's wife, up with a colicky baby, had heard the strange car on the highway in the dead of night.

Rumor had it they'd brought back fistfuls of money and a hound dog. Nobody had seen either, but Sue Annie had found their tracks in the road and their shoes were all new. Nunn and the Tillers, too, had heard sometimes the sad howling and sometimes for the last few nights the angry yapping snarl of a chained hound, but whether the hound came from Indiana or no farther away than the end of the Cow's Horn nobody knew. Willie had had no hound since Bogle and had at times sworn to give up fox hunting and buy a white feist dog, but now Nunn heard him break off his song and call, "Come on now, Springer, foller me. They ain't been no fox scent in th Cow's Horn since man kin recollect—an you're no rabbit hound but a guaranteed foxhound—er, by God, you'd better be."

But Nunn, listening, thought Willie's last words held something of doubt, for the song was not picked up again, and instead Willie's curses, oaths new-brought from Indiana, came clearly down across the water, and a moment later the joyful bay of a pretty-mouthed hound on a well-loved scent, be it possum or razorback range hog.

Willie's oaths came in a thick black flood, but the hound sang on somewhere in the river bluff upriver from the Cooksey path about halfway down, and in a place so brushless, steep, and craggy that Nunn wondered what the scent could be—only a wildcat or a screech owl would live in such a place.

But whatever the scent, he admired the hound. In spite of Willie's cursed commands, he came slowly on around the bluff, losing the scent at times and whimpering now and again with fright at finding himself on a crag so narrow there was hardly room to set one foot ahead of the other, rocks and river water one hundred feet below, sheer rock above and no way of turning back; in spite of it all he came on, and the trail, whatever it was, was sweet under his nose and he would now and again sing out in a long crying bay.

Nunn heard no more of Willie, but by the time he had finished his shock, the hound had worked his way along the bluff almost opposite him on the other side of the river, but high on the bluff, hardly twenty feet below the top, running behind a fringe of cedar brush on the narrow crag. He sang out again and a moment later Nunn saw him as he came out of the brush onto a narrow sloping crag. She was big, black and tan, and a bitch, and from the way her hide glistened in the sun when she stood, head lifted, looking at a narrow jagged shelf of stone six feet away to which the scent she was following must have gone, Nunn thought she was as likely a looking hound as he had ever seen, too good for Willie Cooksey to own.

Nunn left off his work to watch, wondering if she would take the tricky dangerous leap, a jump Vinie, for all her stout heart, would not have taken unless Sam took it first.

The hound whined and looked uneasily around her, sniffing the stone her body pressed against—plainly the scent could have gone in the one direction only and that ahead—but she seemed to ponder the question that troubled Nunn: How could a bitch as big as she gather her body on the narrow sloping stone for such a long and dangerous leap? The thing she followed must have been much smaller and lighter-footed than she. She knew the danger and what she was up against—plainly she was no fool bred by fat farmers in the flatlands of Indiana, but a hound of the hills, never seen and heard in these parts because she had lived somewhere in Alcorn on the other side of the river.

The bright black and tan of the bitch's body flashed against the gray stone and her feet came solidly on the crag she had leaped to, but it was so narrow she swayed an instant and looked ready to fall, then she was belly down, foot dangling for lack of room, but safe and inching slowly forward.

Nunn in his excitement took off his hat, clapped it on again, and wanted to yell. He heard Willie again, more clearly now, for he, like the hound, was opposite Nunn, running along the bluff edge; the going for him had been easier and quicker than for the bitch, so that he had been able to run back up the hill and around and come above her at almost the precise moment she made her jump.

Willie saw only the end of it, and all out of breath with rage and running, screamed, "Fall—fall an break yer God-damned neck, you—you rabbit-chasen varmint—" But he hadn't breath enough for talking and running, so he ran.

Willie, unlike the hound, had known the bluff since childhood, every craggy path by which a venturesome boy could climb even part way down. Just ahead of both him and the hound there was a little stout-trunked twisted cedar tree clinging to a crevice in the rock two or three feet below the top and a little above the narrow ledge the hound followed.

It was no trick at all for a nimble boy to climb down the cedar tree and onto the ledge the hound followed, but Nunn wondered if Willie could do it—climb down, then dangle from the cedar tree with one hand, and get the hound up with the other, for big as she was, the ledge was too narrow for her to turn around. It was as tricky a bit of business as he had gone through the time he got Vinie off the face of Brush Creek Canyon.

He watched Willie as he climbed down the tree, then hung a moment, his new, well-greased Indiana shoes gleaming in the sun as they waved above nothingness, hunting for the ledge, and when at last they found it they seemed, from Nunn's distance, to be on nothing, like a fly's feet on a wall. Willie stood, his body pressed against the rock, one hand still reaching high and holding to a root of the cedar, then slowly, still holding, he turned sideways, facing the way the hound would come.

The hound had not yet seen Willie, for she was still belly downward, inching herself along; but once, hard as it was to do all pressed against the rock the way she was, she bayed as if to tell some listening master she still held the scent and would hold it no matter how hard the going. "Leave her be," Nunn called, curious to see where she would go.

"They's no foxes in this Cow's Horn, an I ain't a wanten no damned rabbit-chasen bitch," Willie answered in the sullen, chip-on-the-shoulder tone that came into his voice when he had had only just enough liquor to darken the complexion of the world, but not enough to change Willie and the world together into a gay place where men sang and danced for joy an fought for fun.

"It could be a fox she's a trailen," Nunn called back, ashamed of meddling with any man when he was going about his own business on his own land, but hoping somehow that the hound, she was so happy-sounding, could go on to the end of the trail, whatever it was.

The ledge widened, and she stood up and bayed, pausing as she opened her mouth to look around her, down at the river and up at the blue October sky, as if she knew in her hound's way that freedom in the fine fall weather, after being chained up and maybe teased by Willie's wild boys, was good.

After a few more cautious steps she saw Willie and stopped and studied him and tried to wag her tail and could not because of the stone her body pressed against.

Willie's voice as he spoke to her was mealy mouthed kind. "Come on, Springer, don't be afeared, my pretty bitch— come on a few steps furder an you'll be at th end a th trail an safe ferever after, ferever after safe."

The hound was still, studying him with lifted head and uncringing tail, more curious than afraid, as if to say, "Is this a man or some new kind of beast?"

"Please don't, Willie," Nunn called again, for the first time understanding what was in the man's mind.

His words and the puzzlement and wonder in the hound's body were familiar. Sometime back before Zing died, the Sextons had come to a Saturday-night hunt on Schoolhouse Point and brought a pretty brindled hound, new-bought in town for $20. They'd made their brags and sure enough, when Zing picked up King Devil's scent the hound had for a time stayed up with Zing and Speed—as sweetly singing a bit of flesh as Nunn had ever heard. But when King Devil tried to kill the hounds and lose the scent with a dozen tricks up and down the craggy bluffs below Sue Annie's house, the hound had fallen silent; and, too honest to wait and cut like Drum and Blunder, he had, after a while, during which the Sextons cursed him bitterly, come whining back to the hunting fire. Bred in the rolling farm lands around town, the rough going over the crags had been too much for both his untoughened feet and untrained wind.

Josh Sexton, when he heard its whining, had stood calling as Willie called now; it, too, had stood half curious, half afraid, its eyes big in the firelight; then slowly, while all the hunters watched in silence, it had walked up to Josh, its puzzled eyes full on his face, but with no tail wagging or belly dropping. There'd been a big hunting fire, for the night was cold, burned down when the hound came in to a red-hot bed of blue-tongued embers.

The hound had walked the last few steps to his master and then hesitantly, for he knew he should have stayed with the scent, licked Josh's hand. Josh had grabbed him; Nunn for the first time and alone of all the others knew what the Sexton was about and had run up crying, "Don't, Josh. Please don't," but already the hound's body was flying in a high arc toward the fire.

He landed in the flaming coals with a howling scream, and still howling had tried to leap out with his hair all flaming about him, but Josh must have jerked a leg out of place as he flung him in or maybe broken his back; he couldn't get out; his screams and his struggles sent him deeper into the coals while all his hair flamed up like a cotton rag. Nobody had a gun to shoot him and end his misery: Jaw Buster threatened to throw Josh after him but only stood and watched him die, and as Jaw Buster watched, great drops of sweat came to his forehead.

There was cold sweat on Nunn's hands now as he watched this hound sniff the stone again and then go on, but once more she stopped and looked at Willie and listened to his, "Come on now, doggie, come on jist a few steps furder."

Willie held with one hand to the cedar tree above, and when she stopped by his shoes, puzzled by the man who barred her way, Willie kicked out hard with his right foot, and the hound, too surprised to seize Willie's overall leg as Nunn wished she would do, struggled an instant for footing on the narrow ledge, whining, swaying, clawing at the stone. Willie kicked again, and the bright black and tan body flashed in the sun as it dropped with a howling cry to the rocks below. Nunn ran to the river's edge and looked across for sign of life, determined to wade the shoals and put it out of its misery, but he saw no movement, heard nothing; and after a moment's staring, he went back to his work in the corn.

Chapter Twenty-seven

ALL FALL there'd been such a flood of babies that Sue Annie was almost afraid to get out of hearing of the house for fear someone would send for her. Then, when the baby storm quieted a little, she was behind in all her work, even the washing; she'd had to finish digging her sweet potatoes and tie a broom and make a mess of hominy, or so she apologetically explained to Milly when she finally did come. And last week, on the very day she'd promised herself a day-long visit with Milly, Flonnie and Hattie came with all their youngens below school-age size for her to mind while they took Ruby and rode Jaw Buster's truck to town and stayed the day so that all three could get permanents and spend what was left of their men's money on fancy grub and clothes; Joe C. and Blare were talking about pulling out for Indiana soon as the roads got so bad Jaw Buster couldn't haul their coal —times were good again like they had used to be when any man that wanted one could get a factory job—and anyhow the WPA was dead.

Milly nodded and never let on but what she believed every word Sue Annie said. She knew the old soul hadn't come to tell her the news of the settlement but to find out how many walnut kernels she and Suse had got out and what she meant to buy with the money they would bring, and, sure enough, the first thing she saw when she got to the fireplace room was Suse as she sat in restless weariness over a pan of cracked walnuts.

"I'll bet you're finally aimen to git you some Sunday shoes in time fer th revival," she greeted Suse. "Ruby come home frum school one day an said Lucy said you all was a saven ever walnut you could find, but ain't it awful tedjus?"

Milly flushed but Suse only nodded and went back to her work, while Sue Annie took a chair by the fire, pulled up her dress the better to warm her shins, for the day was brisk, then spat quid and juice into the ashes and hurried into the latest news, which was that Lureenie Cramer was coming back pretty soon—she'd written special to Sue Annie to ask if Joe C. could borrow Sue Annie's mule to bring down her stuff on the sled. She had a radio, she wrote—

Sue Annie paused to let the news of Lureenie's return sink in, caught Suse's surprised and pleased glance. Well, that was about all Lureenie wrote—she'd learned the rest from Keg Head—and God, oh, God, that was plenty. Lureenie was in the family way again—way, way gone, expecting maybe before Christmas. Rans had been getting drunk off and on, was making barely enough to get by on, Keg Head had said; and even if Rans was his boy, he was a walking pile of sin and wanted everybody to pray for him when the revival started. "Pears to me," Sue Annie said, with a hitching up of her chair, "he could use some prayen fore the revival begins."

"Them Cramers," Milly said, "ain't nothen but trash."

Sue Annie shook her head. "Rans, now, he ain't worth th salt it ud take to cure him onct he's hung, but th Cramers now—take ole Keg Head, he's most too full a religion to have much a th milk a human kindness, but he's allus been a good provider; his wife's never had to be ashamed uv th table she set er her house plunder neither. An Mark can't be more'n nineteen, but he's a doen plumb good maken ninety-five cents a hour."

"That's all a lie," Milly said. "I aint never heared a nobody a maken that much money."

"They pay good in Deetroit," Sue Annie said.

"Deetroit," Suse gasped. "Did he go, honest?"

Sue Annie nodded and shifted disgustedly in her chair. "Lord God, I'm fergitten everything; so many a goen an a comen these days. Mark went off to Deetroit more'n three weeks back—that's why Lureenie had to come home. In Cincinnati, Mark was already a maken more than Rans, an he never was no hand much to drink, so's it was him Rans was allus a fallen back on—a borrowen

money an a knowen if'n he got so biled in beer he fergot
he had a wife an youngens—I've heared say a beer
drunk is th worstest kind a drunk uv eny—why, Mark
wuz there to take him home."

"I wonder now how it ud be to go so far away," Suse
said, her hands wandering like her mind and dropping
a kernel into the pan of hulls.

"Shit-fire," Sue Annie said, "why Deetroit ain't sich a
fer piece, not like where Olen Anderson's a goen now—
days on days a blue water they'ull be tween him an
home."

"Old Ansel shorely didn't sign them papers fer him to
go away an take that soldier trainen an him not much
past seventeen," Milly said.

Sue Annie sighed as she poked at a stubborn walnut
kernel. "Yeah, he signed. Olen's been a beggen to go an
take th trainen ever since they started th business—he
wants to see th world, he says, an it ain't like he was a
goen off to war like Uncle Ansel done in th Spanish-
American." She then went on to tell how Ansel got to
thinking the boy might get into some meanness, for he
had seemed wilder than Jaw Buster and the other boys,
so Ansel had finally signed—Olen had been gone better
than a week and last mail he'd written a letter and told
Ansel he was going where he'd hoped to go—they were
going to train him in Hawaii.

"I've fergot what little schoolen I ever had, so I don't
jist rightly recollect, but Miz Hull said it was a fer, fer
piece away," Sue Annie said. "Old Ansel now, I seed
him read th letter—a standen there in the post office full
a people like they wasn't a soul around—an I'm tellen
you, he walked slow when he went to take it to Hannah.
She'd never give in fer the boy to go."

"Olen, he'll be halfway around th world frum us," Suse
said in an awed hushed voice, then, looking down into
the walnuts, she could see the map in the eighth-grade
geography—a square of blue bounded by the United
States on one side, and halfway across, little dots in the
blue—the Hawaiians, and further still, the Philippines
and then Japan. Her mind tried to see Olen Anderson,
who had smiled at her from a load of hay, dressed in a
soldier's uniform in the strange hot country, but the dots
were too small and too far away, and Olen, smiling only,

never talking to her alone, was unreal, too; and it seemed like a story she'd read in the paper—but Mark and Detroit were real—it was funny to think a body could take the start in the post-office path and keep right on, past the end of the gravel and into the highway and end up in Detroit. She tried to think of some way she could bring Sue Annie to talk more of him without giving her any suspicion of the kiss or that they had walked together.

"Shit-fire, Suse," Milly was crying, "you're a droppen kernels in th hulls. What ails you enyhow? It's all fer you. Why, Lucy wouldn't have made such a gome." And Milly looked ready to slap Suse.

Sue Annie stopped in the middle of a description of Flonnie's new rayon dress, took the pan of cracked walnuts from Suse, pulled a hairpin from under her head rag, and went to work. "These walnuts ain't hurt, Milly, but Suse is a goen to be, if'n the pore child has to set by th fire thisaway all th time like a old woman. Bottlen her up thisaway, she'll bile over on you an bust like a full keg a sweet cider set to sour with a tight-stoppered bunghole."

"But I allus worked when I was her age," Milly said.

"Now, Milly, you was a liven in a minen town a worken an a sparken th boys—a thinken already on a marryen Nunn. You're like Ann Liz Cooksey—she was a sayen th other day when I went to see her big range cookstove an new linoleum—"

"Range cookstove in Ann Liz Cooksey's cabin?" Milly cried, and it was her turn to drop a hull into the kernels.

"Lord, God, ain't you heared nothen, Milly?" And Sue Annie was off on the Cookseys, their money, their fine new clothes, their life in Indiana, but mostly about the great stove, finer even than Uncle Ansel's, with white doors and a hot-water reservoir.

She told of its trip by Vinie Sexton's wagon from the railroad in the valley to the ferry at Sexton Crossing; Willie took off the warming oven and the hot-water reservoir and the doors and the feet and wrapped the stove in layers and layers of pine brush for the wagon ride, then he and eight of his children came behind, each carrying one or more pieces, all walking carefully and stepping high so as not to stumble on the rocky road to the ferry, like they'd had baskets of eggs on their heads and no hands to hold them.

She mimicked Willie in the quarrel he had with the Sexton because he wouldn't drive carefully enough, and told how Willie with his family and the great stove almost sank the ferryboat so that old Crawley Foxton had to make two trips. There was the trip on Willie's side of the river with his mule staggering under the weight of the stove on the sled and all the youngens staggering and stumbling with their loads up the steep river road into the Cow's Horn. Willie nearly killed his mule and then he almost killed himself and all his famiy getting the stove through the kitchen door and under the stovepipe hole in the wall; Sureenie dropped a cap on her toe and Claude Jean got his hand caught between door and stove. Willie himself buckled at the knees when he tried to lift one side, and Ann Liz, with her side a good fifteen inches from the floor, sang out, "Jesus God, Willie, what ails you enyhow? You left your strength behind in Indianiee?" Then, when it was up, the youngens all got scared and thought it was alive when the thermometer in the over door moved; and Ann Liz went around on tiptoe for fear the hot-water reservoir would blow up like she'd heard said that in the olden times the steamboat boilers blew.

Suse joined in the laughter less heartily than Milly; she wanted to hear more of Mark and Lureenie, but it was dusty dark with a drizzle of rain before Sue Annie finished with the stove, and Suse was left to count the days until Lureenie's coming, when she could see and hear the radio and Lureenie would tell her of life in Cincinnati.

And every time the guineas squawked she went running to the door to see if it wasn't Lureenie.

But one afternoon early in November, while she helped Nunn unroll a length of woven wire at the far end of the line of posts he had set above the creek bluff for his big field, Milly came with Bill Dan on her hip and a half-bushel split basket swinging heavy on her free arm.

"I seed Lureenie pass," she called to Suse excitedly, sliding the basket to the ground, "an I want you to run around quick an take her this grub—it ain't much but it's all I had cooked—an kind a help her git straightened up —pore soul, she looked plumb tuckered."

Much to Nunn's disgust, Suse, when Milly called, had
dropped her end of the roll of wire and run up to her
mother. She grabbed the basket, then stopped, frowning
at her clothes first and then at the basket, "I hate to go so
raggedlike—an this grub, Mom, it looks so—so common."
Milly had sent Lureenie only what she had ready-cooked
at home, which happened to be the afternoon's baking of
the sweet potatoes for the family snack when they all
came hungry home at chore-doing time, a few shiny
rounds of molasses bread left from yesterday, about a
peck of yellow, mellow late pears, the whole topped by a
huge cabbage that had happened to be on the kitchen table.

"That's plenty good enough fer Lureenie er anybody
else," Nunn said shortly, then asked of Milly as he came
up and helped himself to a sweet potato from the basket,
"How'd her highness like Cincinnati?"

"We never talked none," Milly said in disappointment.
"I was out barefoot a hullen walnuts when I heard Joe
C. a comen around th road with th sled. I was all raggedy
an my hair all tore up, an I hated fer him to see me—I
knowed he'd start a tale, but while I was in th house a
hunten my shoes an a kind a readyen myself, why Lureenie an her youngens went by; she'd took th corner a th
path an beat Joe C. an was mighty nigh to th corner a th
garden fore I seed her—I recken she was too wore out to
stop."

"Too biggity," Nunn said.

"Aw, Nunn, you jist don't like Lureenie," Milly answered. "Th pore soul looked most too wore out to do
anything but drag in home—a carryen one little youngen
an th next un a whindlen an a draggen to her dress tail—
run on now, Suse, an help her git settled. Sweep that old
hole up a little an carry her up some night water an hunt
some wood—her biggest ain't hardly as old as Deb."

Suse was complaining again. "I wisht I could a took her
something nicer." She felt that Lureenie, fresh from Cincinnati, with sugar-baked cakes and fresh meat every day,
mightn't like such coarse fare.

"Aw, git on," Milly insisted. "She looked most too wore
out to cook. If'n she's got a heap a fine city grub, I ain't
seen it. There weren't hardly nothen on th sled, an to my
mind no money to buy none. Now git on, so's you can git

back before full dark, else them Tillers 'ull be a tellen
tales on you." Milly hesitated and wished Nunn were
some place else. "Try to find out, Suse, has she got eny
new house plunder a comen."

"Aw, Milly, you're worse'n th Tillers," Nunn said angrily, "A nosen an a asken pryen questions."

"If'n I don't find out she ain't got no new furniture, Sue
Annie will," Milly answered, and Suse hurried away, eager to see Lureenie but eager to be out of hearing, too.
Used to be Nunn and Milly never quarreled, but lately,
seemed like Nunn was so ill-turned he quarreled at them
all, even Milly.

Suse felt better about her offering of coarse country food
when, after running most of the way around to Lureenie's,
she smelled before she could see the cabin, hidden over as
it was with a year's growth of brush and weeds, the odor
of dried beans just beginning to boil, the rank rough smell
of beans softened by no boiling bacon smell.

She shifted the basket to her other arm and came on
more slowly until she saw the cabin set high on the hillside above the road. She stopped and pulled a handful of
beggar-lice from her skirt, disappointed not only by the too
familiar odor, but also by the silence, when she'd hoped
to hear the radio playing.

Though it was a long time till dark, already the shadow
of Pilot Rock Hill lay over the cabin, and Suse, looking up
at it, shivered; it was so little and so old, the moss-covered
clapboards of its roof curled until some stood out against
the sky like the dead broken limbs of trees. The rotten
porch posts, which had stood crookedly when Lureenie
went away, were even more rotten and crooked now, and
horse weeds and cockleburs growing where the porch floor
used to be touched the sagging porch ceiling.

And all the paths Lureenie had made—to the river, to
the spring under the hill, the path Suse walked, all were
grown up until at times it was like going through a tunnel
of weeds. She walked slowly on up the path and paused
at the open door, and stood a moment blinking, trying to
see into the shadowed spaces of the windowless, log-walled
room which with its emptiness and shadowy corners
seemed surprisingly big for a cabin looking so little on the
outside.

The fire was low, like the fire of a woman forced to get

her own wood, and the one little window in the back of the cabin had long since lost its glass and was boarded up to keep out the rain. Cluttered in a little heap by the door were the few bundles that must have come on the sled; these and the two old beds, each in a corner of the room, and a bottomless chair with missing rungs by the hearth, were the only furnishings.

In a moment Suse could make out the children all piled on one of the beds, sleeping on the same shuck tick that had been there when Lureenie went away, and covered by an old tattered quilt Milly had given her when she first came to the valley. And on the other bed, covered by the new cheap coat she had worn away, lay Lureenie, still and soundlessly asleep like one dead; but when Suse called softly, so as not to awaken the sleeping children, she stirred, then lifted on one elbow, looking; and Suse, staring at her sleep-sealed face, wondered, for Lureenie looked old and tired, ugly tired, with her skin yellow and her eyes red with pouchy rings under them, as if from overmuch weeping or too little sleep.

She smiled, and Suse saw that her front teeth were beginning to yellow and snaggle like Milly's and Flonnie's, and when she said, awakening more fully, "Why, it's Suse. God, I'm glad to see you Suse—you've growed so I didn't know you fer a minnit," Suse realized that her talk, instead of being sharply bitten off and citified as Sue Annie had said it would be, was as if she had never been away.

Suse set the basket on the floor and Lureenie got out of bed, not jumping straight up but rolling onto her side and putting her hands on the bed to steady herself as she swung her feet down, the way Milly had to do for a few weeks before Billy Dan was born. She came to the hearth, smiling at Suse, but looking mostly at the basket.

"Mom thought you might be too tired to cook an th youngens ud be hungry, so she sent you this—it don't amount to much—jist what we had ready cooked in th house," Suse explained somewhat apologetically, and feeling suddenly a stranger; the year Lureenie was away seemed a long, long time.

Lureenie took a sweet potato, a big one, broke it in two and took a large bite, skin and all, before she answered. "That was real good a your mom. She must a knowed I couldn't make that little old step stove work. Th pipe's plumb rusted out." She swallowed the rest of the sweet potato and reached for another. "But I recken me an th youngens can git along with the cooken on th hearth; that little lean-to shed of a kitchen's colder than th outdoor's anyhow." And still chewing and swallowing in quick hungry gulps, she went on to ask after Milly and Nunn and the children.

And Susie hated herself and kept trying to look away, but some contrary part of her kept watching Lureenie eat the sweet potatoes, counting, noticing how each went down in three bites only, and how Lureenie talked with her mouth full, and how it was only after she had eaten four that she took time to peel one, and that after she had peeled it she held the peelings a moment in her hand, as if unable to make up her mind to throw them into the fire.

And Suse never asked, "How was Cincinnati, Lureenie?" or some such as she had meant to do.

"I must a been starved," Lureenie said, when she had eaten nine. "We ain't eat nothen since we left on th eleven o'clock bus last night. An," she went on, "I've been awful hungry fer somethen baked fer a long time. In that furnished room they was nothen but what they called a gas plate—two burners—all a body could do was boil an fry, two things at onct." She glanced through the open door, which gave on a sweep of rolling brush-covered hillside and more hills across the river. "It's good to look out," she said. "That furnished room now, it was in a house on a hill, a real steep hill, but th house was low down on th side, not high, an they'd made a wall tween th upstairs uv th house an th hill, an my winder looked agin this wall."

"I didn't know Cincinnati was so hilly like that," Suse said.

Lureenie nodded and talked on in her soft voice, speaking quickly, like a person who didn't want to be asked questions, but, too, like a lonesome woman who hadn't talked to anybody in a long time and was greedy for talk. "It seemed to me, th best I could tell, that it was a kind of low deep valley, set on a river, but always it was so smoky-like an foggy I couldn't see acrost th town. I recollect a bean out one day—a windy day in April; I was hurryen to the store—most a th time Rans brought in th groceries. I couldn't handy take all th youngens outside at onct: after bean inside so long they'd start a runnen ever whichway, like little diddles in a thunderstorm, an run right into th street an git killed, an I dasn't leave em by theirselves in that furnished room; they was liable to fiddle with them gas burners or fall out a that high winder, so mostly I stayed to home; but, anyhow, I recollect a bean out one pretty day a runnen to th store an I looked up an right acrost frum me I seed a hill, green it was with grass, so close it looked I could see th trees was swellen out to bud, fer it was a day like here when th wild plum's in bloom an everbody's hurryen to git corn ground ready; an all winter I never knowed that hill was there.

"I asked Rans about it that night an he said it was a park where youngens could run an play; he said he'd take us there some pretty Sunday." She swallowed the last of a chunk of gingerbread. "But he never did."

And Suse, looking into her eyes as they stared out the door, wanted to go away, but could think of no excuse for leaving so soon, and instead asked about the radio, and then she wished she hadn't, for it was plain Lureenie didn't want to talk about the radio. "I don't have no batteries yet," she said, "an I dasn't take it out of its box; th youngens might tear it to pieces," and she nodded toward a disappointingly small box that looked old, as if the radio were secondhand, and then rushed into a quick telling of the pretty music in Cincinnati; gay, loud, marching music from the parades with their many bands in the streets, and though no marchers came Lureenie's way, the music they made was so loud than even she and the children could hear it in their back furnished room; the Decoration Day parade had been the best. "It come so clost I could make out what I knowed was drums an horsn—th youngens cried to go, an I might nigh did; but Rans, he was afeared to take us, th youngens could a got lost in th crowd; an a sight big crowd it was, he said." She stopped with difficulty and took a bundle from the floor. "I'd better start putten this stuff away fore th youngens wake up—they'd be a messen an a gomen into everthing."

Suse watched as she undid the bundle, but with disappointment saw only familiar medicines like Milly kept at home—castor oil and turpentine and croup medicine, but there was a tiny bottle of darkish liquid that Lureenie held out for her to see. "Cake coloren," she said. "I've allus wanted me a bottle. Mom used to bake fifth-Sunday

meeten cakes—they'd be in layers, yaller an pink mostly
—she'd allus buy some when enybody come around taken
up an order from Larken. This's red an I got it in a ten-
cents store; they was one on the corner clost to me; Rans
said th ten-cents stores down in th town where th big
buildens was was th biggest things a body ever seed—an
right in the middle there was a fountain spouten water in
a square a ground with grass, an bands played there a
sight, he said."

"Mebbe we can fix up th stove so's you can bake a
cake," Suse said, as Lureenie set the little bottle on the
mantel.

"I doubt it," Lureenie said.

The baby began whimpering and crying. Suse wanted
to be out of the house; she didn't want to watch the children tumble out of bed and swarm over the basket of
food like—like pigs at a trough; she glanced quickly
around the room before she remembered that Milly had
told her to bring water for Lureenie. "Where's the water
bucket, Lureenie?" she asked. "I'll bring you up a bucket
—I—I cain't stay so long; I've got to help Mom git supper."

Lureenie brought the rusty water bucket. "I guess th
leak's got bigger while I was gone," she said.

"I'll plug it," Suse said, and hurried out the door, hating
herself for lying like a Tiller and always imagining things.
Lureenie was only hungry from the long bus ride, but why
hadn't she bought something on the way? Rans wasn't like
Nunn; he was working and making money every day.

She was halfway up the path to the spring when Lureenie called to her and came walking in clumsy haste,
waving a letter. "I don't know what's got into me," she
said, when Suse had run back to meet her. "It's a letter
Mark sent you by me," she explained, handing Suse a letter with her name on it in strange writing. "But don't tell
Nunn I give it to you—I—I don't think he'd like it so
well."

Suse took the letter, too surprised and embarrassed to
say anything; the first letter in all her fifteen years she had
ever had, and from Detroit and a boy at that. "I recken,"
Lureenie said, glancing back toward the house, where another one of the children was now crying along with the

baby, "you knowed what I sent you last Christmas. Mark bought it."

Suse nodded, her cheeks red. "I thought maybe it was, leastways th bracelet."

"He bought it all, after asken me what I thought you'd like—he wanted to send you somethen finer—he makes good money—but I knowed your folks ud suspicion it wasn't me if I let him send you too much."

"They never acted like they thought anything about it," Suse said in a low voice.

Lureenie glanced worriedly at the letter. "It's none a my business, but I wouldn't let Nunn know if I was you," and added with a kind of warning in her voice, "He thinks a heap a you."

"I ought to thank him," Suse said.

"Maybe you can," Lureenie said, and hurried back toward the house; all the children seemed to be awake and fighting over the food.

Suse ran on to the spring under the hill, then dropped the bucket by the leaf-choked pool and opened the letter, remembering the kiss, flushing as if it were Mark himself she looked at instead of his writing only—two pages of small neat angular writing, and an envelope, stamped—and addressed to him.

She hoped it wasn't a silly love letter but told something about Detroit. She hoped he could write and spell enough so that she could read it but Mark, she'd heard, had been through the eighth grade; Keg Head's place was close to the church and the school over the river.

She unfolded the closely written pages and her eager heart would not let her eyes read it sentence by sentence as they read ordinary things, but they must go leaping here and there: "I think you're pretty, Suse—I hope you have not got stylush and cut your hair—I like Detroit. The factories at night they make you think of Hell, Suse.—People say we'll go to war—ugly women—funny sounding people—fat—called me hill billy—mashed his mouth—place where they make the machines that make the machines—a union—big lake—cold and ugly—drive their cars like they was running from the devil."

The flame in her cheeks had spread to her ears by the time she reached the last:

I love you, Suse. Write to me; put it in this envelope
and give it to Lureenie. She can send it with her letter to
Rans in Cincinnati, and he will send it on to me. He
couldn't tell on you if he wanted to, for he can't go back
home.

Brush slithered softly behind her, and after a moment's
panic, she shoved the letter down under her outing-flannel
petticoat, between her breasts; but when she looked behind
her it was only Vinie, white in the deep shadow, hunting,
as ever, for fox scent.

Chapter Twenty-eight

THE GRAYNESS OF NOVEMBER deepened, and almost every night the cold thin rain sounded on the roof like sad whisperings; Milly, who could hardly see to work on the walnut kernels, was weary of the dank dark fall and complained that she had counted eighteen days in a row when there was never a sunset or a sunrise. But when Milly complained of the weather or of anything else, even the impropriety of a grown young woman like Suse helping outside in the fencing or the crosstie making, there was no real scolding in her tone, for in spite of the dull gray weather and an aching jaw tooth, life to Milly was good.

The fall work was done. The house was so crammed with food against the winter that the old floors in the loft room sagged, and it would have been hard to find room even for another peanut. Milly liked to climb the outside stair and stand in the middle room and feast her eyes, especially late on a sunny afternoon, when long bars of golden dusty light seeped through the boarded-up western windows and seemed to lay a touch of gold on all things there; even the piles of black waiting-to-be-hulled walnuts were gilded with the autumn light. Almost half of the big room was taken up with the chewing tobacco, its great leaves cured to shades of rich deep coffee-colored brown and red-shot coppery bronze, still on the stalks waiting limply soft and ready for stripping.

The rest of the room was filled with the things cold couldn't hurt: crocks and lard cans of molasses and honey in the comb, jugs of vinegar and jugs of strained honey, more lard cans of peanuts and hulled black walnuts and hickory nuts, and butternuts; buckets and cans and crocks

of shelled cowpeas with a few dried beans, though since
the bean bugs got so bad they'd had to eat more cowpeas
than beans.

Hanging on the walls and from the rafters were strings
and strings of dried green beans, dried pumpkin, dried
okra, dried peppers both sweet and hot, meal sacks plump
with dried apples or peaches, clusters of little yellow ears
of popcorn with their shucks stripped back and braided
together. Scattered through everything were bunches of
dried herbs; many from beds set by Aunt Marthie Jane
—horehound and catnip and peppermint and sage and
tansy—and from the woods and fields were feverweed and
dog fennel and sweet fennel and goldenrod and life everlasting and seneca snakeroot and yellowroot and mayap-
ple root, most of these for medicine, with a few things like
heads of flowering dill saved for their smell or flavor.

The long room over the kitchen, less cold than the middle room, seemed at first glance given up completely to
onions; piles of big and little and red and white and yellow were scattered on the floor, while the walls were
draped with what looked to be one endless string of
onions big as saucers. But here and yonder on the floor
would be a big warty cushaw or a pile of little red-gold
pie pumpkins, and a little of the canned stuff, ten or
twelve cardboard boxes, each holding one dozen half-
gallon jars, of canned green beans and pickled cucumbers.

Milly sighed often when she glanced at the canned
goods; she did wish she had a smokehouse with a cellar
under it with rows and rows of shelves where she could
have all her six hundred half gallons of canned stuff and
see it all at once, and where there would be no worries
about its freezing. When she wanted a jar in a hurry, it
was hard to recollect just where it was—the blackberries
and apples in the cubbyhole under the stairs; the peaches
on the high shelf and under Deb's bed; and also in the
middle downstairs room the tomato and cucumber and
onion pickles; the honey-and-molasses-sweetened apple
butter and peach butter and apple and peach and pear
and quince and strawberry preserves scattered all over the
place because they wouldn't freeze any more than the
blackberry jam or the plum butter; and the huckleberries
and wild strawberries and kraut stacked along three sides
of the fireplac room, and the soup mixture, jars and jars

of corn and tomatoes and okra, and the mushrooms—the mushrooms would make her think of the sweet potatoes, for a corner of the warm room above the fireplace room was given over almost entirely to a mammoth pile of huge sweet potatoes, the biggest and the reddest, Sue Annie once declared, that mortal woman had ever raised.

Milly liked to look at the great heap, curing now into dry unblemished roots that when baked were soft and smooth and sweet as honey spread on velvet. She liked to stand by a broken-out window with the sweet potatoes behind her and look down at the four big mounds of cornstalk-topped earth that marked the four big holes filled with Irish potatoes, cabbage, and turnips; and she would wish again that she could see it all together, their winter's food: the storehouse, the big barn and the little barn stuffed with corn fodder and cane fodder and hay and gathered corn, the two big stacks of oats beyond the garden, the river-bottom corn which still stood unfathered in the shock; Betsey, her calf, the sheep, and Rosie and her pigs, almost as big as their mother now, and fat as butterballs.

She wished sometimes that Nunn would kill a pig; but when she pointed out that it was past the middle of November and still no fresh-killed meat, he always said that the weather was too warm and then changed the subject quickly, and at times she had an uneasy suspicion that he meant to sell the pigs, maybe most of them, to pay off his debt, for she was pretty certain he was in debt for the fence; then she would forget her imagined prospect of another meatless year in gloating over the way Betsey was holding up in her milk in the late fall like this.

She rather pitied Betsey in a way, since Nunn had finished fencing the side of the big field next the house and garden so that Betsey, try as she would, could not get into the garden or to her calf in the storehouse field. Maude and Jude grazed peacefully enough in the last summer's corn and hayfields, and showed no mind to run away past the two unfinished sides that lay toward Lureenie's and the Brush Creek country; Betsey didn't care to go in that direction either, but often she came to the fence and bawled dolorously, with many wistful glances toward the oat stacks and the good picking left in the garden.

One misty afternoon early in November, while Suse helped Nunn in the crosstie timber on the river hill and the other children were in school, Milly, hearing Betsey's sad bawling, took pity on her while Bill Dan was asleep and took her an apronful of little late short-core apples as a kind of comfort gift. As Betsey reached for the apples with her long curling tongue, Milly talked to her, scratching her forehead, reminding her what a sinful cow she had been. "Fer seven long years, Miss Betsey, I've planted me a late patch a seven-top turnips fer greens, an everfall, Betsey, fer seven falls you've been patient to wait till them turnips got big enough fer winter greens, an then you've et th whole patch, pulled it up turnip by turnip, so th tops couldn't grow agin—an me a starven all winter fer turnip greens. An what allus made me so mad, Betsey, you ain't no hand fer turnips—recollect when we've run short on fodder I've tried to feed you good big turnips saved in a hole, an you've never tetched em cept one winter when you was starven."

Betsey batted her white-lashed eyes and reached for another apple. "Your traipsen days are ended—"

The young guineas, grazing in a band in the storehouse field, screamed and flew as high as the storehouse; Milly dumped the rest of her apples on the ground in front of Betsey and raced back to the house to get into her clean apron and Sunday shoes in case some of John's folks were coming to see her or visit Lureenie. But after much peeping while she combed her hair, she saw that it was Samuel and Andy walking through the storehouse field, looking at the sheep, the fence, and all things in a way that made her proud. Andy stopped by the pigpen which Nunn had moved below the little barn last summer when the flies got so bad, but Samuel went on walking the row of new fence that led to the top of the river hill, close to the place in the woods where Nunn was making ties.

Milly wished Suse wasn't out working with Nunn, maybe acting wild and tomboyish as Sureenie on the very day Andy came—Suse was getting old, awful old never to have a beau—she wished Andy would come more often or Suse could go to the post office—she'd better get back to the walnut kernels, else the poor child would never get her Sunday shoes. Over the kernels she remembered Lureenie again; she'd been meaning to go visit with her all day; poor thing, she was getting so big she could hardly get around. Lately she sent her letters by Nunn and he brought what little mail came for her—she wondered if she was hard run; there hadn't looked to be much grub on that sled—in a day or so she'd go with a big basket full of jars of honey and molasses and some peanuts and popcorn for the children. These walnut kernels were tying her down worse than a baby, and Sam and Vinie too—they'd been gone all night; if they weren't back when she heard the school children at afternoon recess, she was going to blow the horn and make Nunn go on the hunt—most likely they were visiting Tuckerville again, but something bad could have happened.

She peeped out again to see if Andy had gone on. He was now among the sheep, scratching a tame old ewe on the top of her head; she sighed and guessed that he and his father were not on their way to see Nunn in the crosstie timber after all; maybe Andy thought that Suse was in the house and was too bashful to come knocking; it was a funny time of day to come courting and why wasn't he in school?

But almost at that moment Suse was looking up from the crosstie she sawed to meet Preacher Samuel's admiring glance. Her hand was for a moment lifeless on the saw handle as she flushed, thinking of him not as the preacher, but as Andy's father. Then Nunn, with his back to the preacher, was saying, "What th hell, Suse—you gone to sleep? You're a draggen down on th saw."

Preacher Samuel smiled at her and said to Nunn's back, "Maybe you're a holden up your end fer easy sawen, Nunn."

Nunn looked around in surprise, saw the preacher, and smiled with genuine gladness as he stopped work and turned around to shake hands, for it had been a long time since Samuel had been down to visit him.

Samuel praised the wove-wire fence and Nunn's fine pigs and pretty sheep, and opined that a lot of people who swore Nunn's sheep would all sicken if taken off the range might get surprised. He commented also on the big stack of crossties Nunn already had on the edge of the sand-field; white oak and all number ones they looked to be. "I notice they've got good straight cuts on both ends," he

said. "You must have a good saw hand," and he smiled
again at Suse.

Suse smiled back while Nunn praised her. Best hand
in the family, he said; she never pulled too little or too
much, nor lifted up, nor bore down, nor twisted sideways.

And Samuel nodded as if making straight saw cuts were
an important thing, and Suse was suddenly bashful, wishing they would talk of something else and that it was
Andy who had come instead of his father. She had never
been able to understand the stern-eyed preacher; he'd
never paid her much mind that she could recollect, for
with so many of his own, he'd never been any hand to go
around patting little children on the head or telling mothers their babies were gifts from heaven.

The only time he'd ever been known to say a word
about little children was once to Ann Liz Cooksey when
after a sermon she was walking past him in the door with
the suckling baby in her arms, another holding to her
dress tail, Willie with the one not walking good in his
arms, with Sureenie and five others of diaper-carrying
size strung out along behind. And the preacher as he
shook her hand had said, "Miz Cooksey, I feel that God
has a special place in heaven for you. Your babies are
the onliest ones that knows how to keep quiet. An your
hound dog never comes in an sniffs around like the rest."

And Ann Liz had laughed with a flashing of her big
horseteeth as she wrung the peacher's hand. "It's easy.
I allus fill th ones a cryen size full a catnip tea fore we
start an cut a big peach tree limb fer th ones uv wigglen
and gigglen size an lay it on the mantel where they all
can see it—an they know I'll use it."

But lately, on their few chance mettings—for she had
gone but seldom to the store and not always to church
and not at all since her shoes wore out—he had always
smiled on her; and once, back last winter, Milly declared
Suse had got more for three dozen eggs than Nunn could
get for five dozen, and Suse had not mentioned that
Samuel had given her two candy bars with sternest admonitions to eat them. For a little while during the long
walk down the hill, she had thought of carrying them
home, but divided among them all it would have been so
little; so she had eaten them both, feeling guilty, the first
time she had ever had a candy bar all her own.

Now he smiled at her, and before settling down to talk with Nunn, remarked that they'd missed her in th choir but he hoped she would come to the revival—old Battle John Brand was to conduct—sometime before Christmas.

Suse nodded, feeling shy and strange because he talked to her as if she were a woman, and was glad when he turned again to Nunn and remarked that a wove-wire fence was well worth the time and trouble. Times were changing and it took a lot of good timber that could maybe be sold and a lot of work to make the old-fashioned split-rail fence with stakes and riders, or posts with bored holes and rails set in, the kind John's sons and Ansel's older boys had made twenty years ago. He thought he might get wove wire enough for his yard and big garden; the old fence of white oak slats he had rived the first winter he was married was falling down and he had to have something, he said. In spite of the fog-dripping trees all around, he and Nunn squatted with their backs against a big sound beech near by and fell into a lazy long, easy talk of many things: Nunn's fattening pigs that were doing uncommon well, the good harvest, the weather, a letter Uncle Ansel had had from Olen in Hawaii—and at that Suse, sitting on a white oak stump, lifted her head, listening, her face eager and alive.

"Looks like everybody is goen away," Nunn said, pushing his hat back and looking up through the trees after Samuel had told of how Lister Tucker was now working full time on the railroad section gang, living with the crew and thinking of moving his family to the valley.

"They'll all be back soon's th good times is over," Samuel said. "There's Lureenie Cramer already back— I recken," he continued somewhat worriedly, "I must a made her mad; she ain't been around th store in three, four mail days. Th first day she got back she bought a little jag a beans an lard an meal on credit, an you know I don't hardly ever give credit; then pretty soon she was back an asken fer credit agin. I didn't let her have it; it was none a my business in a way, but I knowed she had th money; that same mail day Ruth cashed a money order Rans had sent her, then made a money order for Lureenie to send off to pay on that radio." He stopped as if ashamed of talking about his neighbors.

"I don't blame you," Nunn said. "I've heared it said

that when Rans cleared out he left owen you a great big
bill."

"Not so big," Samuel said. "He always come to me with
his WPA check to cash, already owen most of it; but he
cashed his last one across th river th day he left so quick.
I never did ask Lureenie fer th debt, but seemed like she
could a said somethen fore she started another bill—but
I'm thinken now maybe I've done wrong."

"She shorely wasn't fool enough to send ever cent
she had off on that radio," Nunn said, and added somewhat dourly, ashamed of seeming stingy, but it wasn't
fair that Lureenie had a radio while Suse and Milly had
nothing, "Don't worry, she won't starve. She borrows
somethen off'n Milly mighty nigh evertime she comes to
see if I got any mail fer her to send a letter, an I bet
mebbe Keg Head's come visiten with a mule load a grub;
he's not th man to let his grandchildren starve." Nunn got
up and invited Samuel to come see the fence.

But Samuel remained an instant, drawing a pattern
through a clump of moss with his finger and frowning. "Th
river's pretty high. I bet Keg Head is so busy haulen in
corn from his river bottoms he ain't give her no mind. I
mebbe ought to go around there, but she ain't hardly ever
been to th church an she might think I was a tryen to git
her trade or meddle in her business."

The men seemed to have forgotten Suse, while she
sat a few feet away on the log, silent, listening because
there was nothing else to do. She, too, felt guilty and uncertain. Though Milly had told her she could go, she'd
been only once to see Lureenie since she came home
more than two weeks ago. They'd been busy and the
weather had been wet, but mostly she guessed it was because visiting Lureenie now seemed no more fun than
visiting Flonnie Tiller or any other old married woman.
And Lureenie seemed ashamed, like she didn't want her
or anybody else around. Maybe she was hard run, real
hard run, and wouldn't let on; Suse remembered the
despairing look that had come to her face last mail day
when she had come at dark to see if Nunn had brought
her mail and there was nothing.

Then she forgot Lureenie; Samuel was looking up the
hillside and saying, "I was beginnen to think you was
lost." Andy was coming down the hill, swinging his legs

in long easy strides—her heart tripped and fluttered like a captured bird—he looked so tall, almost as tall as Preacher Samuel, and handsome in a red-checked shirt— a funny shirt with the tail out—and overall pants, dark blue with copper rivets. "I stopped to look at th sheep," he said, and looked at her with the same pleasant glance he gave her father.

Suse flushed, remembering the heavy work shoes that made her feet look big below her thin, briarscratched legs; the too-small faded, tattered dress and the too-big jumper, Nunn's old jumper that Milly wore sometimes when she was in the family way; her hands, brown and calloused and chapped; her braided hair tied in a blue bandanna; and the memory of her face when she looked at it in Nunn's shaving mirror, brown and thin, with the cheekbones standing out like a boy's and a spattering of freckles across her nose, not soft-cheeked and palely white and pink like those of the girls in the magazines Mark had sent her.

Samuel smiled on him and jerked his shirttail. "Ain't this somethen. It's all th style in high school, he says. He would have me buy him one in Town, but I never thought he'd wear it a courten."

"Who's courten?" he asked, blushing furiously, careful not to look at Suse.

Samuel laughed his rare laugh of gladness and gaiety, usually reserved for some sinner with a just-saved soul. "Who's courten? Now that is somethen. I'll bet I've heared you wish fifty times Suse could ha gone to high school."

"Sure," Andy said, and to Suse, watching greedily, he seemed less bashful, with an easier turn of speech than he had used to have. "I wanted her to go because I knew she'd like to." He turned to Nunn and his eyes glowed. "You've got pretty pigs, pretty as any I've seen."

The others talked for a moment then of hogs and sheep, but Suse hardly heard for the hurt that came when she realized that Andy had rather look at hogs and sheep than talk to her.

Preacher Samuel was explaining the real reason for his visit: he'd wanted to see Nunn's wove-wire fence stretcher he'd made from an old block and tackle fastened to a contraption of bolts and two-by-fours put together by a pattern laid out in a government bulletin.

Andy glanced wistfully up toward the fence row, then back at Suse sitting motionless on the stump. "Me an Suse'll keep the saw a goen," he said, and came over and picked up Nunn's end.

"How come you didn't go to school today, Andy?" Suse asked as she took hold of the saw.

"Teachers' meeten," Andy said, squinting at the cut.

They began the sawing—and after a moment or so the log seemed big, terribly thick and slow to saw through, for it was plain Andy had no mind to stop until the cut was done. She wished he would stop and talk with her about high school; now and then she glanced quickly at his brown bare head, curly-haired in the damp mist, but he seemed interested only in the wet sawdust that leaped from the saw rakers.

And when they were done at long last and the crosstie length lay ready for hewing, he straightened, but his frowning gaze was fixed on the finished cut. "I hope it's straight like the other," he said, and added somewhat apologetically, for he was slightly winded, "I ain't sawed much wood lately."

"You couldn't do much work a any kind an go to high school—I've heared"—she stopped, realizing with an embarrassed confusion strange to all her other times with Andy that he would say "heard," not "heared";—but after an instant she went on without correcting herself—"that you leave mighty early on th school bus an git—get in real late."

"Since th days got short I don't hardly see daylight at home," he said. "But in pretty weather th bus ride's nice; we sing an talk an kid one another."

"Kid?" she asked.

"You know—tease er torment."

"Oh! What kind a songs do you sing?"

"Oh, all kinds; school songs an pep songs they'ull sing at th basketball games, an songs we hear on the juke boxes."

"Juke boxes?"

"They're things like a phonograph, only bigger an louder—an they take th records on an off theirselves when you put a nickel in. They're all around th town."

She tried to see a juke box—see it take the records off

and lay them on, and failing, asked, "Is high school hard, Andy?"

He shook his head and smiled at her. "It ud be easy as pie for you, Suse. Th kids all fuss about th algebra an some don't make their marks, but to me it don't seem hard as our arithmetic last year—recollect that silo problem that Miss Burdine couldn't work an you could?"

She nodded, and asked as Andy picked up Nunn's ruler and prepared to measure out a second tie length, "What else do you study, Andy?"

"I'm taken th agriculture course—algebra, English, general science, history, and agriculture," he said, reaching for his pocket knife to notch the mark.

She wished he would sit on the log and tell her about everything: what was general science and did he write themes in English or diagram sentences the way old Andrew had made them do when they were getting ready for their eighth-grade examination. She watched while he measured all over again, to make certain he was right the first time, and made no move to help him when, satisfied at last that his mark was correct, he picked up the long crosscut saw and tried to put it into place—he was awkward with the saw, she thought. Nunn, now, could with one light quick motion, all unhelped by her, lift it from the ground and put it on the log, the middle teeth exactly where he wanted them, her handle ready to her hand.

Andy fiddled so that at last she took her handle and helped him set it on the mark, but stood stubborn, her end held firmly, when he started to saw. "Andy, what does 'agriculture course' mean—you goen to high school just to learn to farm?"

"Not exactly—it would help, but mostly I took the agriculture course so that if I go to college I can learn to be a forester or a soil-conservation man—or maybe a county agent."

It was like a dream—a boy she had known all her life talking of going to college—not just to little piddling teachers' college like they said where Miss Burdine went, but the real university at Lexington.

Andy pulled on the saw but still she would not let it go. "Do you honestly recken you'll go to college, Andy?"

He stooped to make certain the saw teeth were exactly on the cut before answering. "I'm plannen on it, and

Pop wants me to. He's forever wishen he'd been to school an college like th town preachers. I could work most of my way like my general science teacher said he an lots of others did—you're a holden a little to th right, ain't you, Suse?"

She sighed and loosened her tight grip on the saw and went to work with the light but strong swift hand Nunn praised so. The sawdust flew, the sharp clean smell of fresh-sawed oak wood grew stronger, and from somewhere above, a fog-drenched leaf dripped now and then onto her head. And the saw's song was the only sound between them. Inside her there was a mounting loneliness, and she thought with pleasure of the letter she would write to Mark—he had told her more in a letter about Detroit than Andy would tell her in even a whole day's visit of high school, but Andy had never had any turn for talk. Mark wasn't so talky either. He told her things to please her. Mark maybe thought magazines were silly, just as he had thought Miss Burdine silly, but he had sent her some—she wished she could see one of the books Andy studied in high school. She thought of Mark's letter, as yet unanswered, because it didn't seem just right to send him a letter in secret, and anyway she'd never had a chance to do more than steal out some sheets from the narrow slick paper tablet Milly saved for the rare letters of the family—hidden with Mark's envelope and a stub of pencil in a crevice in a stone on Pilot Rock Hill.

The tie length fell with a little crash and she straightened up from the sawing just as Andy did; their eyes met and he smiled, the same warm friendly smile he had used to give her in school. "Let's saw down a tie tree," he said. "I've not sawed down a tree in a long while."

The tree was just fallen, exactly where Andy had wanted it to fall, when Samuel called from somewhere up by the fence that they'd have to be getting on.

Susie watched Andy go up the hill, and she stood for a long time, her arms lax at her sides, staring up the hillside.

A few minutes later, when Milly's quick, exasperated horn calls came, saying the hounds had not yet come home, she looked eagerly at Nunn, and he saw that she wanted to wander in the woods alone. "Go to th Pilot Rock an listen awhile," he suggested. "But hounds er no,

you'd best be home by supper-gitten time er your mom'll
have a fit."

Suse hurried first to the sandfield spring, where Milly
after blowing the horn had left it in the crotch of a little
hickory for Nunn, then across the graveyard field and up
Pilot Rock Hill, running up all but the steeper slopes,
worried that some prowling animal or person might have
found Mark's envelope and her writing materials.

But they were safe and dry in their crevice in the rock.

She put them in her jumper pocket and climbed the
craggy trail to the top of the Pilot Rock, up and up until
the tops of the high-growing poplars were below her and
she and the steep face of the rock she climbed were alone
together; and at last she was on the narrow wind-beaten
top hardly bigger than the fireplace room at home, bare
save for three wind-crippled stunted pines and a slab of
stone like a table or a coffin on the western side.

Of all places she knew, she loved the Pilot Rock best;
on clear days the hills rolled in blue waves into infinity,
and her thoughts could go rolling with them, farther and
farther away, free as birds flying.

Nunn said that the farthest line of hills she could see
southward was Tennessee and that on a clear day a body
could, by looking east, see peaks that were Virginia; but
mostly her dreams and her eyes turned northward, where
often she could see the smoke of trains and sometimes
on a still, clear day a grayish smoky blob low down against
the sky that people said was Town.

Today, past the smoky blue where her eyes could not
go, her thoughts went; straight north was Detroit with
Mark there, thinking sometimes of her as Andy never
thought; and the bright, ever calling North seemed closer
than on other days, even though the nearer valleys, and
all the farther hills were hidden in the gray November
mist and she seemed alone in the sky with a life beyond
the hills as close as the old gray house in the valley. And
out there in the mist was Mark, close, closer than anyone
she knew, and yet so far away.

She was staring northward into the murky mist when
low down against the hills she saw a black speck moving,
and her heart leaped a little. Maybe an airplane would
come over, fly low, and circle the Pilot Rock as one had
once done a year or so ago; but in a moment she heard

the high wild honking, faint now, but with a wildness that
always made a tingling in her hair and a coldness in her
hands, the sound of wild geese going over.

Soon she could make out three V-shaped bands moving
high and effortlessly across the sky, flying toward the
Pilot Rock as if it were a milestone in their path. One
band flew straight over her head, so low she could see
the beating wings of the leader who held together the
two long lines behind, meeting in him, then spreading
outward into the sky, weaving, bending like grass-blades
blow in the wind, waving far outward at times, like the
slowly opening wings of some fantastically shaped bird,
then closing until the birds seemed a line of black dots in
the sky, the lines never still, never breaking, with each
goose keeping his proper place and proper distance behind the other.

She watched, craning her head, turning slowly, her eyes
never ceasing to follow them in their flight. The honking
grew fainter and fainter, until she could not have told
when the sound of it ended and the memory began; the
flowing lines grew thinner, smaller, blacker as they
moved southwestward. One instant she could see three
thin black strings blowing against the gray sky, then only
the gray sky; but she looked still into the empty grayness,
something inside her, like the spirit of God that came on
Milly at church, rising and flying with the birds, straining
after them, crying and calling fit to burst her heart, but
soundless and wordless, because there were no words that
could tell the thing, only the knowing deep inside her that
she, Suse, would go away into new fine country, as the
wild geese were going now.

Only, the wild geese would come back with the
spring, and they went together; but when she went, she'd
go alone and she'd never come back.

She pulled pencil and paper from her jumper pocket:
she would tell Mark about the wild geese going over. She
sighed suddenly and pulled her jumper more closely about
her; up on the Pilot Rock the air was cold. More fun
than anything, maybe, would be to have a long winter coat
with fur on the collar and sit in the school bus next to
Andy and sing as they went down the graded gravel.

Chapter Twenty-nine

—⚬—⚬—⚬—⚬—⚬—⚬—⚬—⚬—⚬—⚬—⚬—⚬—⚬—⚬—⚬—⚬—⚬—

SUSE LAY STOMACH DOWNWARD on the stone table and wrote to Mark, mostly little things: about the neighbors, Nunn's new fence, the big harvests, the coming revival, the wild geese; and crept in here and there were wishes, wantings she never mentioned to those around her; she wished she could hear a band, see Detroit, go inside a factory, go to high school, get away from the Little Smokey Creek country; for writing to Mark was a little like praying to God—he would hear and understand maybe, but most likely never answer, and certain he would never come around to plague her with memories of her wishes or tell them to the neighbors. He was gone and he wouldn't be dragging back home like Lureenie.

She glanced up, thinking, and saw that the hills rolling gray under the mist were grayer still with twilight, and that far below, white night fog had covered the river. She sprang up. Milly would be in a fine fit of quarreling and so would Nunn; he'd told her not to stay. She'd have to end the letter. What did it matter what she said—but another letter from Mark, slipped to her in secret by Lureenie, would be fun and exciting, too. Hastily she wrote, the paper fluttering on the stone: "Write to me again, Mark. It's so lonesome here I wish I could see you," She hesitated an instant, then wrote, "I like you Mark, Good-bye."

She thrust the letter into her pocket, leaped down the crags of the Pilot Rock path, and ran on around the hill and down through the woods to Lureenie's house, where Lureenie, with the baby on her lap, and the three other small children sat in a quiet row on the doorsill and looked down the path and across the valley, like people waiting for something, Suse thought, running around the house corner. Then she thought no more of Lureenie, for it came over her all in an instant what she was doing, and she hestitated, blushing, remembering Mark.

Lureenie turned her head, saw her, and smiled. "God, I'm glad to see you, Suse. I've got a letter writ to Rans, an I was a wonderen if I could ever git around to your place to git somebody to take it to th post office. Seems like I'm awful short a breath this time."

"I hope it ain't all sealed," Suse said, and held out her letter to Mark.

Lureenie took the letter, but held it a moment, as if uncertain what to do, "Oh, Suse, are you certain you want to send it? I—I courted Rans secret like this, an pretty soon we run away—an now I cain't go back ever— an—" She stopped, as if ashamed of showing overmuch of what she felt.

"Pshaw, I ain't crazy over Mark. It's all in fun," Suse said, and waited impatiently while Lureenie, slow and heavy in all her movements now, went into the house and addressed an envelope to Rans and put the two letters into it. She was halfway home, the letter in her jumper pocket, before she remembered guilitily she'd ought to have stayed at Lureenie's long enough to make certain she was all right and not in need of anything.

Then she forgot Lureenie in thinking with more disgust than guilt that not once on the Pilot Rock had she recollected to listen for the pups; Nunn and Milly would both be down on her, and she stopped stock-still in the early dark when, as she came running down the path across the upper garden, she heard Nunn's curses from the little barn and Milly's quarreling talk from the fireplace room.

She stopped and pulled an armload of little Georgia onions, grown in the warm misty fall like onions in spring, and went on and stood cleaning them by the kitchen door, listening with head bowed over the onions, wondering worriedly, though against her reason, if Nunn and Milly could know about the letter.

Then Milly was lifting her voice and calling in sharp scolding, "Suse, ain't you got supper set up yit? Your pore tired pop'ull be in pretty soon."

"I'm cleanen onions. Did you know we had green Georgia onions big enough to eat?" Suse called back.

"You don't say," Milly said, pleased, then her voice changed and she was off on her quarreling again, and Suse, setting dishes onto the table with unaccustomed softness so as to listen, learned that Sump Tucker from Tuckerville had ridden by on his way to John's and stopped to tell Milly that Jeremiah Tucker had sent word by him to tell Nunn that his hounds had stopped in at his place and that Jeremiah promised to take good care of them until he himself could bring them home or Nunn could come for them.

Milly was more than a little riled. King Devil was eating the Tuckers out of house and home—they'd do anything to get Sam and Vinie to stop with them and run themselves to death on a scent their own fool hounds couldn't hold. Milly bet Nance Tucker—she had such a God's plenty of everything—was right now frying pork-shoulder meat for Sam and Vinie; no wonder Sam and Vinie wouldn't come home; and poor Nunn killing himself from daylight till dark in the crosstie timber and mad as a hornet because somebody had left the gates open and six ewes had gone off and now he would have to take time out to get Sam and Vinie, and it was all Nance Tucker's fault.

Then her voice was rising again, "Suse, honey, recken you could find some pickled gherkins? I think they's a can down in behind them boxes a canned tumaters in under Lee Roy's bed; they'd go good in th beans with th green onions; an Nunn, he's a feelen so bad over his sheep a gitten out. He blames Lureenie for leaven a gate open—but to my mind it was some a th Tillers. I told him—"

Suse took a handful of matches and hurried away to hunt pickled gherkins, humming a little. Nunn did love gherkins pickled sweet in honey and sour in vinegar. It was good to know why Nunn cursed so; he might quarrel and rave and cave all through supper, but at least it wouldn't be for her.

However, much to everybody's surprise, supper was a pleasant meal. Nunn saw first the pickled gherkins and then the green onions, and Milly, remarking his glance, said wasn't it fine to have fence so the hogs couldn't root in the Georgia onions the way they had done on every other fall; and this made Nunn remember all the fine things Samuel had said about his fence and his farming, and as he told them to Milly her nods and her smiles made them seem finer still, and she was emboldened to wonder how other people managed without woven-wire fences.

Suse, careful not to mention the Pilot Rock in front of Milly, told of seeing the wild geese go over; Nunn predicted a change in the weather, maybe an early snow; and he tilted back his chair with a glass of buttermilk in his hand and said, aye, Lord, let there come a foot-deep snow and stay there, for soon as he got these six fool ewes back home, this would be one winter when he wouldn't have to sheep hunt; he'd put a chain on every gate in the storehouse field and keep them there.

Milly had thought that at milking there was a smell of snow in the air, and Lee Roy hoped there'd come one three feet deep. They had grub and feed enough to last till spring, so what did they care? And all of them, even Deb, felt a pleasant security, a closeness not of kinship only, but also as a group of workers who after working long and hard together were now able to rest and enjoy the things they had earned.

The feeling of general pleasantness was further increased when, just as Milly and Suse were settling themselves to the walnut-kernel picking, Vinie pushed open the kitchen door and she and Sam came rushing in, whining and barking, licking the children's faces, springing on Milly, sniffing over the house as if to make certain it was home, until Milly cried, "Hypocrites, acten like you loved us, when you're allus a runnen away to take up with them fine Tuckerses."

Nunn opined that after resting the day, Sam and Vinie had got restless and gone hunting, but finding no scent worth their trouble had come home. Milly complained that it wasn't Sam and Vinie's fault they'd stayed away; Nance Tucker had tolled them in with the smell of fresh pork, she knew, for they weren't hungry. The pan of walnut kernels was on the floor by the hearth when the hounds rushed in, and Vinie had only stuck her nose in and nibbled at one, not grabbed a whole mouthful the way she had once when she'd run in hungry. Nunn said they'd have to charge Vinie for all the walnut kernels she'd eaten, and everybody laughed, even Bill Dan.

And Suse, ever on the lookout for a good speaking moment, said, glancing toward the mantel and trying to act all unconcerned and easy in her mind, "They's a letter Lureenie hopes some a us can take up to the post office fore mail time Friday mornen."

"Why don't she mail her own letters?" Nunn stormed. "Don't she think I've got nothen to do but fetch an tote fer her?" He turned to Milly. "I recken she come with a empty basket, a empty belly, an a empty bucket, an left with em all full, th way she allus does."

"I ain't seen hide er hair uv her," Milly said, and the children's eyes opened wide at her sassy way with Nunn, "but I think it's a pore business when a neighbor woman in th shape she's in cain't ask a little favor; an as fer th little she's borrered, I ain't so pore I'd begrudge her one bit of it, even if she never pays a lick uv it back—an her mebbe hungry."

"If'n she's hungry it's her own fault. Rans is a senden her money, Samuel said, an she's a spenden it fast as she gets it on money orders fer that fool radio an batteries—who brung th letter, enyhow, if'n she didn't?"

"I brung it," Suse said, and added quickly, "I run around to her place fer a minnit—I thought I heared sheep bells over that way an went so clost I went on in."

"Why in hell didn't you go on after them yoes? An quit a runnen off to her house. I'll whale you if'n—"

"Was she all right, Suse?" Milly interrupted with the complacency of a woman who knows she's in the right. "Did she act mad er enything? Nunn's rared so about her borrern things, she might a heared him, er one a th little youngens—it ud be about like Lucy—could ha said—"

"Hell-fire, woman, I'll talk th way I please," Nunn roared. "Th good-fer-nothen trollop ain't starven, her with her radio an her new clothes an her painted fingernails—an you quit a letten Suse go runnen off to her house: she'll be a huggen up to one a Rans's brothers, an you'll have a Cramer son-in-law or more like a Cramer bastard on your hands. Now th next time that redheaded beggar comes a beggen you tell her—"

"Mark's gone," Milly said in a tight hard voice, and

Suse said, "You must think I'm a fine girl," and Lee Roy spat into the fire and said, "Hell, I'll take th pore woman's letter up th hill to th mail, come mornen. Why, you wouldn't make Maude go up th hill in the shape she's in." And Suse said, "It ud be awful to go hungry an sleep cold."

"You sound like you thought we was rich," Nunn said with a mixture of disgust and pity. He glanced about the room, bare-looking and ugly and cold in the flickering firelight, and thought of the room as he remembered it when it had been Aunt Marthie Jane's parlor. There had been a carpet all stretched tight from wall to wall, red wool it had been and warm, too, on a Sunday's winter night when the whole family was allowed to sit in the parlor after supper.

There had been furniture of dark polished wood to glimmer and smile in the light of the bright wood fires. Aunt Marthie Jane had a cherry corner cupboard old Uncle Eli Cramer had made, a walnut center table with a long fancy cloth and the album and the Bible and a telescope in the middle, a big four-poster bed with a blue coverlet she had woven as a girl, rocking chairs, and finest of all, the parlor organ Aunt Marthie Jane had bought for her girls with years' savings of egg money, for Preacher Jim had always held music, like tobacco and whisky and powder on a woman's face, to be a sin.

Aye, Lord, there were good days then, before people forgot God and the land wore out and the big timber was all cut and sold. Everybody had plenty, and if they did run low on something, they would borrow a side of meat until hog-killing time or a few gallons of molasses to run until the next sorghum making. Nunn spat out his quid and strode to the bed in the back corner, disgusted with Milly and Suse too. He wanted to tell Milly to hurry on to bed, for his back was cold, but he did not. He settled more deeply into the featherbed, pulled the wool quilt up above his chin, and was for a moment conscious that it was warm, warmer maybe than anything Lureenie had.

Maybe the woman was hungry, he rose on one elbow and spoke sharply to the kernel pickers by the hearth. "I'm sick an tired a hearen about Lureenie. Milly, th very first day you can find th time, take a basket a grub around to her, nothen like cabbage or taters, but somethen like honey er canned goods, so she won't think you think she's a starven, an find out is she or ain' she, an I'll bet you'll find one a Keg Head's young boys with her an a lot a his grub, an plenty a stuff from th store over th river—an I don't want to hear no more about her."

Suse opened her mouth to tell him that Lureenie might have grub but she was certain she had no company, when Lee Roy nudged her and Milly gave her a sh-sh-ing look. "I'll go see her pretty soon," Milly whispered, "an don't go gitten him riled up no worse," she added, glancing toward the bed where Nunn lay as if asleep.

Milly, as she picked the kernels in the firelight, worried a time over Lureenie then her thoughts turned to Nunn, and she wondered if it could be wanting a drink real bad was what made him so cross. Sue Annie on her last visit had told her that Flossie Anderson had told her that Lanie Tucker had told her that Lanie's cousin Reuben Mclellan from away on the other side of Tuckerville was starting out with a mule load of sorghum whisky every Saturday night and that Milly ought to keep Nunn at home—but wanting a drink and knowing there was one in the country oughtn't to make him ill as a copperhead in dog days.

But next morning Nunn was in fine fettle, for there was an inch of snow on the kitchen floor where it had blown in through the never shut door, and more snow coming down. The ewes, fat as they were, wouldn't poison themselves eating mountain ivy bush for a day or two; King Devil wouldn't chase them in the snow, and so he would snake up the rest of his cedar fence posts while the good snow was on; and it was a fine day for Milly and the youngens all to stay inside and shell a turn of corn. Milly frowned on the early snow; November snow was the worst snow for croup of any, and anyway she'd had her heart set on visiting with Lureenie, but she couldn't wear her patent leathers out in such weather and now she'd have to wait a day or so; a November snow never stayed long.

At twilight the air seemed soft and warm as that of a rainy night in spring, and Nunn predicted a flooded creek by morning; but instead of rain more snow fell, big straight-dropping flakes damp enough to cling to the thinnest of beech twigs, yet firm enough to bear their weight on the ground until the sagegrass fields seemed no longer washed with red, but lay solid white.

The weather continued cloudy and cold, and two days later, when the snow still lay deep, Nunn declared that next morning he must hunt the sheep; with all sagegrass and fern and even river cane so long under the snow, they might eat ivy and die.

It was hardly daylight when he took down the powder horn that had belonged to Old Ned, Preacher Jim's father, filled it with salt and slung it over his shoulder, filled an old saddle-bag with corn for the yoes and a corn pone for himself, and after Milly had greased his brogans well with mutton tallow she had been saving from the winter before to doctor Deb's croupy breathing, he set out.

Lee Roy had begged to go, for the snow was so deep old Andrew could never get through it, even with his little mule, but Nunn made him stay home and help Milly make a kettle of hominy. He liked to sheep-hunt alone, especially on a still snowy day when the world seemed new and scarred by nothing worse than flocks of twittering snowbirds or an occasional rabbit.

He walked up past the old graveyard and on up the shoulder of Pilot Rock Hill, pausing at times to listen for sheep bells. He crossed a long low crooked mound of snow that marked the rotted rail boundary fence between his land and the Ledbetter place. The Ledbetters were all gone now, had been for years; old Pru and Sam had bought the land from Preacher Jim's father and cleared it and built their house and raised a big family, and some of their married children had lived there until the land wore out. It was nothing but scrub pine and gullies now around the rotted cabin where Lureenie lived. Once this hillside had been a cornfield; it was scrub white oak now, some getting close to tie-making size, but mostly no-good, crooked overgrown brush—no matter how big a sprout might grow, it was still brush and could never be an honest-to-God tree growing clean and straight from seed.

He crossed the ridge and plowed down through soft snow piled high on soft unrotted leaves that let his feet down and made the snow seem deeper than it was, until he came to the narrow deep-walled gorge of Brush Creek. He stopped and looked down; far below a thin stream of water, blue-black against the snow, slipped silently along a smooth stone bed; hemlock and ivy and laurel grew in the scant bits of earth on either side of the stream, and they, too, like the water, were black and silent, strange and wild somehow, as if they were a long way from his home and his land, instead of just across the hill.

And somehow since King Devil had killed his sheep all along Brush Creek, the place had seemed like part of another country, a wicked hateful country into which the red fox led him, more and more against his will.

He walked slowly down the canyon rim but saw and heard nothing except that once from under the tentlike shelter of a snow-weighted hemlock a pheasant sprang into the air with a troubled uproar of beating wings. He reached the mouth of the creek where a great flight of stone ledges, like giant steps, dropped into the Big South Fork.

The river, not risen yet by the new-fallen snow, lay still and soundless as a river of some unshining gray-green metal under the snowy sky. Nunn went along the edge of the low bluff above it, following a narrow slippery path made of large flat rocks laid side by side in a leveled-off strip in the steep earth bank above the bluff.

The steep rock-strewn hillside above seemed determined to force the path over the bluff into the river, but had never succeeded through all the hundred and fifty years or more the path had been there. Nunn knew the path from childhood; he had followed it many times at Preacher Jim's heels or riding behind him on a sure-footed mule in snowy times like this. Preacher Jim it was who had told him about the path: how long, long before the Civil War, not long after the Revolution, Preacher Jim's great-great-grandfather had had his hired men make the path. That Ballew could sheep-hunt for days and never be off his land, for he had owned it all from what was now Samuel's boundary, past Nunn, on across the three creeks, including their headwaters, to what was now Tuckerville on the other side of Bear Creek.

That was a long time ago, but even Preacher Jim could remember back to the days when there was no railroad closer than Cincinnati, and most everything brought on then came up the Big South Fork in winter, when the water was above the shoals. The old man used to tell a story of riding up the river path when he was a boy, carrying a load of dried ginseng root and goose feathers to a store somewhere above the mouth of Bear Creek.

Now and then Nunn stopped and studied briefly a cluster of the green cane that grew denser and thicker as he walked up the river, until at times the path seemed a tunnel under the snow-weighted cane. But there was no sign that sheep had browsed. As he went on, the river bluff grew higher, sheer walls of stone dropping down to the water, and the path was constantly forced higher into the steep hill above.

He came to the mouth of Bear Creek and stopped there, as he always did, and looked down into the great bowl-shaped valley that the little creek, lying still and black, had made for itself by the river. The bottom of the creek lay almost as low as the river, so that in flood times the river water made a mile-long lake, yet the sides of its steep-walled valley rose as high as the highest ridge in the country. Looking up, Nunn could see the black trunks of giant lightning-scarred pines; below these, in the steep but rich, never plowed soil of the sides, grew some of the few big poplar left in the country, never taken because they couldn't be floated out in the sluggish backwater of the creek. But sooner or later they would be cut; the government owned the land now and the government could do things simple mortal man could not do.

In the bottom of the valley, close by the still creek water, grew the great hemlocks, their wide lower limbs bowed down into the water with their weight of snow, He walked down the steep path to the creek, and as he walked the walls of the valley rose up about him and made the sky and all the world seem far away.

He listened a time, then stooping like a man going into a cave, he went into the green-and-white-ceilinged tents of some of the snow-weighted hemlocks, but found no sign of where sheep had been before the snow fell. He took a fresh chew of tobacco and stood, trying with his mind's eye to follow the wanderings of his ewes.

Used to be they had liked to graze in the old Taylor fields on the south fork of Bear Creek, a favorite grazing ground of the Tucker sheep, for in spite of losing some sheep in the spring, the Tuckers had never put their flocks under fence as had John and Nunn. Now, if the

Tuckers had brought their sheep in a few days ago when it looked like snow, his would have followed and be now somewhere up around Tuckerville. But Jeremiah was such a cautious, careful kind of farmer, he might have brought his sheep in so long ago that Nunn's had never seen them, and in that case they would most likely be in the old Taylor fields.

He debated a time whether to follow the road on around to Tuckerville and inquire of the Tuckers or go up Bear Creek, climb out the top, and cut across to the Taylor fields and into Licklog Valley, where there was a good chance of their having gone if alone.

He didn't much want to see the Tuckers: they would be after him to come hunt with Sam and Vinie, and worse yet, they would most likely want to buy them. They couldn't offer as much as Elias Higginbottom, but they would offer plenty—not because they were hunters and loved hounds, but because they were good sober farmers and wanted King Devil out of their settlement at any price. He didn't want their dickering and he didn't want to see their fine farms. Sump and Jeremiah had inherited some pretty good land and had added to it, and now that the WPA had built a gravel road from the highway to Tuckerville, the Tuckers were seeing good times, trucking out timber and coal and crossties from their rough hill lands, building new barns and even chicken houses, and improving the fields of their almost level farm lands.

He would go up the creek, climb out by the rock house behind the fallover, and cut across country to the Taylor fields. And so he worked his way slowly up the valley, stopping now and then to listen for bells, but often only to look at something, long and intently, with the pleasant light that was the beginning of a smile in his solemn eyes.

Once he looked up at a wide-leafed laurel bush, big almost as a tree, that grew all alone in a little cove below a low curving edge of sandstone, and the pleased look faded as he thought of Milly once, looking at the laurel and commenting on its size and wishing she could see it in full bloom; and he had promised her she could, and she had laughed and didn't guess she ever would; it was such a job to mind the youngens in the woods come spring.

He remembered he had said he would stay home and

cook dinner some fine spring Sunday and she had giggled at the notion. And now Suse was big enough to stay home and mind the little youngest, and Milly had never seen the laurel bush in bloom, and it was their first fall on the place that she had seen it and he had promised her; Lucy was a baby about big enough to walk good on level ground, and Angie Mime was on the way. Milly hadn't climbed the rocks so well, he recollected, and Tom had eaten a lot of winter huckleberries, but they hadn't hurt him a bit.

He turned abruptly away from the bush and stalked up the creek. Some day he'd buy rolls of tight-woven wire and fix Milly a yard, a place just for grass and flowers, and he'd give her a seed catalogue and ten whole dollars and tell her just to spend it all on garden seed and flowers and roots and shoots of pretty blooming things like the town women had in their yards—like Pinkney Deegan's wife had.

As the creek valley gradually narrowed, with its sides rising more abruptly, walking grew more and more difficult, and Nunn was often forced to grab a bush or overhanging branch to keep from slipping into the water. He looked hopefully into every ivy-curtained rock house. The walls of the canyon grew so close that the boughs of the hemlocks crossed and recrossed above the creek to make at times a snow-covered tunnel floored with running water and walled with twisted ivy bush. The snow came on more thickly. Nunn began to wish he had gone the road to Tuckerville. He couldn't climb out now until he got to the fallover, and that, he guessed, was two or three miles away. There was nothing to do but try to get on; if he turned back now, the day would be half gone by the time he got to the river, too late to do anything but go home. He'd never walked up the creek to the falls; some said it couldn't be done except in real dry weather, and then there was a copperhead under every rock and a rattler on every ledge.

After bringing on a miniature snowslide and landing in water above the tops of his shoes, he gave up trying to walk any place except in the creek itself, wading little frothy eddies that rose above his knees, and up rocky ledges where the water boiled cold and swift about his shoe tops. The stream was littered with the debris of old

storms and forgotten floods; uprooted saplings caught on
the rough hunk of rock fallen from the bluffs above, tops
and twisted trunks of hemlocks and water maples uprooted by floods and landslides; half-fallen trees bridged
the stream, breast-high fern; green as the cane above the
snow, and twisted, matted ivy bush, its slippery treacher-
ous roots hidden by snow and water, laid traps for his
water-soaked brogans. Once he caught his toe in an up-
looped root and went sprawling face down into the water.

He cursed the sheep and the snow, but mostly the
hounds; without them he would have dared face his
neighbors and gone by Tuckerville. Sometimes he had to
crawl, but he kept on pushing up the stream bed that
now rose rapidly but smoothly like some giant millrace
cut in stone. He was standing on the thick trunk of a
hemlock fallen across the creek when he heard it; the
sound seemed to drop down from the same great but in-
determinate height as the snow, the warming tinkle of a
sheep bell—the old Bossie Jean bell. The other Bossie
Jean who'd borne twin lambs every year and had had
two stolen by King Devil the spring before she herself
was killed by him was by now only another memory in
a long list of remembered Bossie Jean Ballews, each of
whom had worn the little copper bell with the flat clapper
that Old Ned Ballew had made in his blacksmith shop
about the time of the Civil War.

Nunn crashed on, followed an abrupt turning of the
narrow creek bed, and sounds and smells swarmed over
him: the bleating of ewes, men's voices, the smell of
wood and tobacco smoke, and farther away and muffled
a wood chopper on dead wood it sounded.

He knew now that only a few feet away, hidden behind the curtain of brush and snow, was Tucker Fallover,
and that deep back in the wide warm room behind the
water curtain the Tuckers had taken shelter with their
sheep and at least one of his own.

The ledge of stone over which the creek water fell was
like a board pressed high up in the V of the valley,
pressed so hard that it had pressed back the sheer bluffs
and given the sides a more gentle slope, so that a man
could, by holding onto the ivy bush, walk up and around

the waterfall and go into the deep, high-ceilinged rock house behind the water.

Before Nunn could accustom his eyes to the dim light or make out which of the Tuckers it was who squatted in the smoky red glow of a low fire, somebody said, with no show of surprise, "You're late, Nunn. You missed all th fun a driven down your sheep, an now we'll have to charge you hotel fare fer these six heads. Say, did them hounds a your'n git in?"

"Way atter dark, th triflen things," Nunn said, and took off his jumper and hat and shook the snow from them, and flailed more snow from his overall legs, meanwhile explaining that fox-hunting, especially hunting for King Devil, would be no good in all the snow, and that Sam and Vinie wouldn't be worth a pinch of salt a month for sheep-hunting.

"That big old red fox is a doen us dirty over this way," Jeremiah said with a little headshake, and threw two more thick slices of fresh pork shoulder on the coals, where it began a slow sweet-odored sizzling along with a row of other slices; and young Clem Tucker spilled more coffee into the pot from a paper sack and ran to hold it under the water curtain and then set it on the coals.

Nunn took a chew of tobacco and squatted with his back to the good steady heat of the dead-chestnut-wood fire and listened while Jeremiah told of the time they had had on the long sheep-hunt. He and his brother Sump and Sump's married son—they were out getting wood and feed now—and the boy here and two more at home had started out yesterday morning soon as it was light enough to see. His old daddy, Enoch, had smelled more snow in the air the day before, and all night the fire had tramped snow, and sure enough it had started snowing before they'd gone five mile, and they must have walked forty before the day was over; and he went on telling in his slow, almost caressing voice all the hard rough walk and the coaxing and the running and the driving as if it all had been a pleasure, even the stampede of the half-wild sheep into Tucker Fallover cave here when home and a hay-filled barn were not half a mile away.

Nunn glanced up at mention of the word "hay," and thought of the half of his he had sold and the rest cut with a borrowed mowing machine. "You an all them boys saved a sight a hay, I bet," he said.

Jeremiah smiled, "We got a new mowen machine. Nothen ud do that next to oldest boy a mine that's a goen to high school an a studyen agriculture but what I must git me a new mowen machine an save more hay, like the county agent said."

"You've joined the AAA business?" Nunn wanted to know.

Jeremiah nodded, speared a hunk of pork shoulder, and laid it on a freshly reddened bed of coals, watching it as he explained that since they'd finished that new graveled road out from the county seat about two years back, the county agent and the AAA men had started coming out and all the Tuckers had joined. He had held out longest, for his old dad was dead set against it from the beginning, but the boys now—they'd wanted everything from a registered bull to a field of alfalfa.

While Jeremiah talked, his brother Sump, the same deep-chested, big-featured kind of man as Jeremiah, came in loaded with bundles of cane-blade fodder, and not long after the married son with more dry chestnut wood for the fire, and behind him came the grandfather, Enoch, with a half-gallon jar of pickled beets and a stack of still warm corn pone, yellow with eggs; behind old Enoch came a little yellow-headed boy with a foot-high, thin-layered jelly cake, a bowl of butter, and jars of quince preserve and honey in the comb.

All greeted Nunn with cordial handshakes, then old Enoch, after a study of the doneness of the meat, spread his hands and said grace. Gradually, as the first sharp edges were taken from their appetites, the men talked again, mostly now of King Devil and the damage he had done through the fall. Jeremiah helped himself to another slice of pork shoulder, sandwiched it into a corn pone and helped himself to a pickled beet. "Is it th truth now, Nunn, that a man offered you a team a mules, a full-growed registered black Aberdeen Angus bull, an a mowen machine for them hounds when you had em runnen up in th north end a your county last winter?"

Nunn smiled and shook his head. "Not that much," he said, and added—for he wanted to end all plans they might have for a trade—"but I wouldn't ha tuck it if I'd been offered twice that much."

He thought he saw a flicker of puzzled wonder in Jeremiah's dark blue eyes and maybe disappointment in Sump's, but the married son, more talkative than his elders, said, "Them hounds has rid your part a th country a this big fox—King Devil? We was hopen we could git em to chase him fer us."

"I mean to git him, not chase him ferever," Nunn said, and something in his sober voice made the Tuckers talk of other things, and for a time they all talked after the fashion of men of neighboring communities who have always known each other but seldom meet more than once every six months. There was more talk to the season's farming just past, and Nunn, listening more than he talked, was uncomfortably conscious of the same feeling, too close to shame, that had kept him silent while the strange farmers in the stockyards talked. Or was it that these men, his neighbors, thought of him as more hunter than farmer?

They had mowing machines, barns full of hay, and maybe money in the bank and checkbooks in their pockets like Samuel; they had sowed rye in the fall, and except for flour and coffee and sugar and some bit of fancy foolishness their womenfolk might buy for the table, they hardly knew the taste of store-bought grub. Their smoke-houses no more than their corn cribs were ever empty; they had molasses and honey by the lard can full; they never graveled for new potatoes because they never ran out of old; hog-killing time for them was from November to March—and now the county agent was making them better off than they had been.

He swallowed the last of a piece of juicy pork shoulder, picked up a round of the yellow corn pone, intending to slit it open with his pocket knife and lay in another thick slice of sizzling meat. But instead he smeared the bread with butter and dropped in chunks of honey in the comb. He had just remembered that only the other day Milly had been wishing for fresh meat to cook when Deb came whindling around her for some more fried sausage meat like that Sue Annie had sent as a present when she killed her fattening hog. And unless he killed Rosie, the brood sow, there wouldn't be any meat—he'd have to sell the fattened pigs to pay on his debt. Unless she went visiting, Milly would hardly know the taste of any meat but a little chicken, maybe a little mutton, before next fall.

There was a pleasant coziness about the place, warm and dry and full of the smell of good food and wood smoke and sheep's wool, the last a smell Nunn had liked since childhood, and the men were friendly, more than glad to have been able to do him a little turn of kindness in the matter of looking after his sheep. Three winters ago, in a wild snowy time in March, Nunn had driven in and kept twelve of their ewes for almost a week. Still, Nunn was glad when after sitting for a decent interval after eating he could say he had better be getting on or dark would overtake him halfway home.

The men, understanding how it was to get a band of sheep through thick black woods, did not urge him to stay longer in the cave, though they did beg him in sincere heartiness to leave his sheep with their own and come spend the night with them. Nunn explained that Milly would be bad worried if he stayed away all night, and the men understood; and Enoch said his old wife had been talking of riding over to see Milly and Lureenie Cramer—they had been hearing things about Lureenie and were kind of worried, but he reckoned they were just tales. Somebody had told that Lureenie and her man had had a kind of falling out in Cincinnati, and she had come home and he wasn't sending her any money and she was out of anything to run on and about to starve and not even able to get her own wood, for she was expecting along about Christmas.

Nunn said he reckoned she was all right; Preacher Samuel said she had been getting money, and he guessed her father-in-law, Keg Head Cramer, was helping her, maybe had one of his boys staying with her; but he didn't rightly know, maybe he ought to stop in and see her on the way home. A twinge of uneasiness about Lureenie pricked Nunn for an instant, then died as he listened to old Enoch talk about his old woman with a warm indulgent smile: she would be sure to go see Lureenie in a few days; she had to have some kind of excuse for a ride on her old mare that she had ridden to church for almost twenty years, but now that the new graveled road was finished and she had a son-in-law mighty good to take her in his care, she never got to ride the old mare.

They all helped Nunn break out his ewes and head them home. Well-salted and full of feed, they refused to be tolled and kept shying away from the cave mouth when he tried to drive them out, and once out and up the steep slippery path to the top of the creek canyon, they kept scattering and circling through the brush in every direction except the road home.

Then Enoch sent one of his grandsons racing home for Blue, the one old hound he had, a fat, half-blind beast that hadn't lost sleep over a fox in ten years. At last Blue came, yawning and barking hoarsely at intervals, enough to scare the sheep into a submissive huddle eager to trot after Nunn had taken first a sniff and then a taste of the shelled corn he poured on a flat rock brushed clean of snow. After that it was easy; he walked slowly on, now and then pausing to scrape snow from a rock and drop a few grains of corn, calling "Coo-sheepie" in a soft unhurried voice as he walked away from the corn; the new ewe in the old Bossie Jean bell always came first to the corn, and the others followed her.

Aye, Lord, give him another year with a halfway good season and he'd be out of debt with a fenced farm to boot; he had plenty of corn fodder and hay to run him till crops came in again, and there was a God's plenty of everything to eat but meat and sugar and flour; another winter on cowpeas and cornbread and canned goods wouldn't kill them all; by late March Milly would be selling lots of eggs, and with the war across the waters things would be high come spring; he'd get a whole lot of crossties made and have a little wool to sell and a few lambs.

He walked on, less than half his mind taken up with the docile sheep, the rest full of pleasant dreams and plans and the sense of security and peace that was often his, and Milly's too, on a snowy winter day like this when the animals were all safe at home with promise of feed till spring and there was no bad sickness among the children and the snow put a stop to fox-hunting.

Compared to the route he had come in the morning, the ridge road down to the mouth of the creek, though longer, was easy walking. As the day lengthened and the sheep came on more steadily, Tuckerville and its prosperity gradually fell to the back of his mind, to be fished up and thought over at odd times. He felt carefree and gay almost, as he had used to feel when he was a boy bringing in his grandfather's sheep in a snowy time like this, and now and again running away from the sheep to track rabbits in the snow.

Past Brush Creek he followed the old wagon road that once men had followed all the way from Tuckerville up and around the headwaters of Bear and Brush creeks, on down past his place and on to the valley. At intervals near the road were smooth open patches of snow bordered by old twisted-limbed and black-trunked apple trees half smothered in young forest growth and briars. Sometimes in the middle of the plot, looking much like a big tombstone in the snow, would be a chimney where in summer the chimney swifts still came. Around them tangles of honeysuckle and rose of Sharon bloomed in early summer, and in spring the fiery red of a lush burning bush in full flower would startle the passerby, though sheep hunters were almost the only travelers along the road now.

Nunn, walking slowly after his sheep, pondered with a mixture of wonder and sadness on the lost people. Where were they and their children and grandchildren? When he was a little boy only thirty years ago, people had lived in these houses, mostly two-room log and a lean-to they had been, each with a little white feist dog yapping at a horse's heels and a timid woman with a baby on her arm and a knee-high child clinging to her skirt and a huddle of bigger ones, all coming to the door to see the preacher pass on his big gray horse with his little orphan grandson behind. Where had they gone, those lost people? What were they doing? They hadn't left the country because they wanted to. They had starved out when the land washed away and wouldn't grow corn.

He shivered for no reason at all and hurried; gray daylight was merging into gray moonlight with no moon visible, but a dim diffused light that seemed to rise more from the white earth than fall from the gray sky. The road climbed a hill, passed by a crookedly leaning gatepost with no gate, climbed higher through a scrubby stand of young white oaks, then out across the upper edge of a tilted rolling field where even the snow could not completely hide the sheer walls of great steep gullies, their clay sides black in the deepening gloom, not black like dirt or rocks, but black like holes or the mouths of caves.

Not fifteen years ago the hillside had been a cornfield; now wildcats came out of the tall timber and screamed in the gullies. Aye, Lord, gullies and scrub pine and saw briars were taking the world.

The road turned over the hill, and the Bossie Jean ewe's bell began a quick light jangle as she trotted down the road; she and her followers were just beginning to know, the fools, that their last year's children, their lady friends, and their husband were all just ahead in a warm dry place full of shelled corn and corn fodder. Nunn hurried after them, and as the road wound lower on the hill, he could soon make out Lureenie's house, a crooked block of blackness against the snowy brush-covered hillside above.

He wondered if she were home, it was so still up there; and if smoke came from the chimney, he couldn't see it in the dusty dark; a lazy woman, a low fire, he'd heard tell, and certainly from the looks of her fire Lureenie was lazy; not like Milly. His mind's eye saw her now: about this time of day she'd be churning by the fire, or maybe just finished straining the night's milk and pouring the warm foam down on the hearth for Flonnie the cat in front of a good clean bright-burning fire. Her slack-coal fire, topped with a bit of hickory wood, would be throwing long red tongues of light through the windows and across the snow until even the very snow seemed warmed.

He came to the place where Lureenie's path went up from the road, and he stopped and looked up at the house a moment; he didn't want to go visiting Lureenie, but maybe he ought to make certain if she were home; Milly would be asking if he'd seen Lureenie; most likely, though, she was gone over the river to Keg Head's; he saw no wood on the porch, and the whole place looked bare and ugly and dead.

He'd hate to be married to a woman like that, one that didn't half keep house. In the big fireplace room at home now, Milly almost always had something cooking in a black iron kettle hung over the fire that smelled good when a man came in out of the cold; and the youngens were always roasting peanuts or potatoes in the ashes, and on one corner of the hearth would be the yellow crock with cream set to clabber, and all around there'd be signs of Milly's work: a pile of walnuts waiting to be cracked, a half-tied broom, or a big pumpkin she'd laid

out to cut up or a sack of corn on the cob she'd picked out
to shell for hominy, or a quilt on a quilting frame—always
something. He'd cursed more than once when in the dark
he'd waded through a quiltful of unshelled cowpeas, but
a man got to like such—

He had reached the house and stopped before the open
door into the fireplace room; for an instant he was certain
they were gone from home: the fire was only a handful
of smoking embers; there was nothing cooking, no sign of
food, or woman's work, or children's play. Then, from a
far-back corner, he heard the quick, rasping breath of
what sounded to be a bad sick child.

He started toward the bed, then whirled and ran across
the porch, calling Lureenie. He stopped, listening for her
answer, looking up the hillside, but everything was gray
and indistinct, blurred in snow and twilight until it was
hard to tell which was a rock and which a snow-covered
tangle of briars. He took another step, debating whether
he should run home for Milly or carry the sick child home
with him, when a little sound, familiar, but hard to place,
came to him: from under a little white oak on the edge of
the woods it sounded.

He heard it again and this time he knew it, and wondered how such a sound came to this dead place. Off in
the brush under the white oak he heard plainly a cow or
a hog crunching, chewing an apple or a sweet potato, more
like a pig, a hungry pig, too quick for a cow, but not loud
enough somehow for a hog. Rosie and her big pigs were
the closest hogs; maybe they'd got out, but they wouldn't
come away out here; and it wasn't sweet potato—it was
acorns, and what animal would be hungry enough now in
the plentiful fall to hunt acorns under the snow?

He walked nearer the tree; the crunching stopped, but
he heard a faint rustle, a smothered secretive sort of sound
like a man might make caught stealing. He glanced down
toward the sheep, but they were already lost in the deepening gloom, and the leader's bell marched steadily home.

He went into the snowy brush under the oak tree, then
struck a match and looked around; a child's eyes stared
up at him, big eyes, the biggest eyes he thought he'd ever
seen; he saw wisps of tangled hair and streaks of black
earth on the thin upturned face, but mostly he just saw
the eyes, for clamped across the lower part of the face,

just under the nose and hard on the mouth, was a long
thin brownish hand; there was black dirt on the hand and
under the fingernails and a stain of blood on one knuckle,
as if the hand had been digging in the dirt and in its haste
had struck against a stone.

He felt the burn of the match on his fingers and it fell
and made a little hissing sound in the snow. The quick low
crunching began again, and then what he had thought was
a gray rock or a bush lengthened to the height of a woman
and Lureenie spoke in a low faltering voice, as if she were
trying hard to speak and think at the same time. "I—we
didn't know who you was a comen along an striken a light
right in our eyes—I come out to git some wood an they
follered me."

The children had not moved but squatted motionless in
the snow like frightened quail in grass. One of them, a
little one it sounded like, began a loud heartbroken sobbing, "You've spilt em, Mommie—I can't find em."

There was a little scuffle, silent almost except for the
children's hard excited breathing and then an angry
outburst of slaps and cries. "That's mine. He's got my
acorn, Mommie. Give it to me. She's got a whole handful." Nunn saw the black shapes crawling around in the
dirt and snow, felt them crawling across his shoes, and
anxious fingers groped in the snow about the toe of one
shoe and pulled at it and then let it go.

Lureenie bent and flailed her hands about; he heard
the slaps, and one—the boy, Nunn thought—she seized
by the hair and shook until he turned on her and struck
her wrists. The children made no outcry, only moved out
of reach, and the quick hungry crunching began again,
except for one that pulled at Lureenie's dress and sobbed,
"I didn't git any, Mom."

Lureenie drew a long sobbing breath, and for a moment, while the child clung crying, she stood perfectly still,
until in the dark she seemed more like a black rock than a
living woman. She turned suddenly and with one hard
animallike cuff knocked the child from her.

Nunn saw that she had an ax and took a step backward.
Somebody needed to stop and see about Lureenie, but he
wished to God it hadn't been him. She was crazy. Living
out here by herself in the hard winter when she was so
far gone in the family way had run her crazy. He stared

at her dark shape with a mixture of revulsion and pity, not untouched by anger. No woman had the right to treat her youngens so.

He went over and picked up the little one, still sobbing face downward in the snow. He was surprised by its lightness; it didn't seem half as heavy as Deb, and when it struggled like a frightened rabbit in his hands, it seemed its thin bones, sharp under the soft flabby skin, would pierce his own flesh. He held the child and spoke to Lureenie in the same low kind voice he used with the half-wild ewes. "Come on in now, Lureenie; you an them youngens'll git your death a cold."

He thought she started to say something, but there was only another long sobbing sigh. He reached for the ax, at the same time holding the child out of her reach. She didn't try to hang on to the ax. It was an old dull poleax.

He stood there feeling the ax in the dark, thinking of Milly, suddenly trying both to remember and not remember what she had said about Lureenie; whatever she had said, it hadn't been enough; if she had said enough, he would have come. There was no harm in the ax, he realized. Lureenie wasn't crazy: she was starving. Everybody had been like himself; they thought she had money and grub, and she wouldn't beg.

He dropped the ax and let the child slide to the ground. "I'm sorry, Lureenie. You go to th house. I'll run home an bring—some things—an Milly."

And after him her voice came. "I—I hate tu beg, but could she bring some castor oil an turpentine? Th baby, he's awful sick."

"Don't fret. Sue Annie an Milly, they'll pull him through."

Chapter Thirty

BUT DOWN AT THE HOUSE that night Sue Annie and Milly were less certain that little Doddie, even though a Cramer, would pull through. He was nothing but skin and bones to begin with, and from the looks of his cracked and swollen lips and black hollowed eyes he'd been sick, bad sick for maybe a week. Lureenie had doctored him the best she could, but she didn't know much about doctoring anyhow; and she'd run out of medicine and everything else, even wood, in the deep snow, Lureenie explained in a tired voice between gulps of coffee yellow with Betsey's cream and bites of gingerbread Suse had baked that morning.

Milly listened as she roasted onions over a little bed of coals drawn to one corner of the hearth.

Sue Annie shredded wormseed down into a quart fruit jar full of warmed molasses and sulphur. "It ain't your fault. That Rans an Keg Head, they both ought a be beat with hick'ry poles an salt on th lashes till they beg to die—I lowed he'd a been over with grub an his boys to git some wood."

Lureenie smiled a slow wan smile and stared into the fire with her big, black-circled, shiny eyes. "Don't carry on so, Sue Annie. You know—" She paused, searching for words. "You know, when a body goes through enough trouble, all that seems to matter is haven a good fire an a bite to eat. I don't hate nobody—Rans, he sent me some money, but I spent it."

Sue Annie stirred the sulphur round and round and studied its thickness as it dripped from the spoon and in between times looked at Lureenie, a worriment in her

416

eyes that almost never came there. This woman smiling at the fire was no more than the ghost of that old Lureenie who had laughed and cried and loved and hated, cursed Rans every time a child was born, then laughed at her pains when she heard the first cry of her child.

Sue Annie put a little more wormseed in the sulphur and molasses. "You'll be all right—you'll git along. You'll hear frum Rans an you'll last a long time yit."

Lureenie smiled, almost gaily. "Me, I don't want to last a long time. I think I'd ruther go out like a cedar bush in a brush fire than wear out slow like a doorsill."

Sue Annie sighed. "Child, th world cain't git along without doorsills to walk on; that's why th good God made women; but it's allus seemed to me that all women, when they die, they ought to go to heaven; they never have nothen much down here but hell."

"Aw, Sue Annie," Milly said, "men has their troubles, too."

Sue Annie spat into the fire. "Nothen hurts a man much; if it does, it kills him."

The wood fire made a dancing light in the room, and Sue Annie's chin and nose and shoulders, bent above the worm medicine, made a black picture like a witch's likeness on the farther wall, and Lureenie was a redheaded ghost looking at things in the fire. Milly drew closer to her roasting onions and wished she were home; the women oughtn't to talk so; life was a wilderness of woe and vale of tears like in the songs, but there was a life everlasting with sweet Jesus.

But in a minute Lureenie seemed more like herself and got up and went to the kitchen and quieted the youngens fighting and quarreling over the food Sue Annie and Milly had brought, and for the first time showed shame for the rags and dirt on herself and the children; she had been out of store-bought soap and had been ashamed to borrow any more homemade from Milly, she explained as she began scrubbing up Bill, the oldest one.

Doddie's medicines were all ready by now, but Milly, as she picked him up to carry him to the fire, wondered if they'd do him any good. He made a little groaning grunt with each short hard breath and kept pulling his head back like a dying lamb, while under his ribs there was a crackling tearing sound like starched cloth ripping, only

not so loud unless you put your ear to it, and then it was
loud, louder than anything.

Sue Annie, though, didn't seem bad worried, not about
Doddie anyway. "We'll pull him through," she said.
"Nothen much ails him but cold in his lungs, maybe a
touch a th fever an worms, mostly worms eaten it up—an
starvation," she added bitterly, after glancing up to see if
Lureenie had come in from the kitchen. "Why in hell
didn't th fool come to me when Samuel wouldn't give her
no credit an Keg Head didn't come? I ain't religious like
them."

"I recken she kept on loven Rans an a hopen an a
prayen an—"

"Loven," Sue Annie said, and added a string to her
particularly black oaths as she pulled up Doddie's ragged
dirty cotton shirt and tied a bit of cotton oozing with
turpentine around his navel to make the worms start
down. She then warmed a good-sized flannel cloth, dipped
it in a mixture of melted lard, turpentine, and coal oil,
warmed it again, then wrapped it around his chest.

Milly moved nearer the fire for the baking while Sue
Annie rolled two rosin pills from the hunk in her pocket
and laid them on Doddie's tongue. "If'n they go th wrong
way an he kind a strangles, grab him quick by th heels,"
she instructed Milly, and wiped the turpentine and grease
from her hands and wondered if she ought to begin on the
onion poultices and tea or give the worm medicine time to
sink in a little.

Milly advised her to wait long enough for the rosin pills
to kind of settle, as strong feverweed tea generally made
a little youngen like this puke the first three or four times,
and he might lose all the rosin and turpentine. Sue Annie
studied him and shook her head. To her mind he was
most too far gone to puke, but she'd wait awhile, and anyhow, she wanted to give all the others a round of molasses
and wormseed and sulphur now, and then, just before
they went to bed, some good strong tea made with life-
everlasting, sweet fennel, ratbane, and feverweed, for
every last one of them was wormy as could be and full
of cold and they'd all get down about the time Lureenie
did, and it would be a pretty mess if they didn't get doctored up beforehand, but this first round of medicine
might'n do any good; worms wouldn't get much of the

medicine when a body's stomach was full, for they would
eat the grub instead, but the youngens, poor things, would
have full stomachs from now on if she had to spend every
cent of her old-age pension and Dave's, too, for meal and
lard, and she went kitchenward, carrying the quart jar of
molasses and sulphur and wormseed.

Milly sat and tried not to listen to Doddie's breathing or
watch a place on his neck flutter and beat like a dying
sparrow's wing. She wished Sue Annie would hurry back.
Tom had died on her knees like this and so had Angie
Mime; only, for a long time before Tom had died, his
head was pulled way back and his breath hadn't seemed
to go deeper than the top of his throat. Sue Annie's laughter and encouraging talk as she dosed the three older
children came from the kitchen. It seemed that Florie
Dell, the middle one, didn't want to take her dose of
medicine, for she heard the urging of Sue Annie, "It ain't
bad, Florie—tastes a lot like candy. Better swallow it
down, honey, or them ole worms'ull eat holes clean
through yer belly an come crawlen out yer nose an git in
yer ears while you're sleepen." And Lureenie's halfhearted
threats of a good whipping if Florie Dell didn't take her
medicine, and a child's frightened, hiccoughing sobs and
Sue Annie's voice coaxing for a while, more threats from
Lureenie, then Sue Annie, out of patience and determined:

"You bigger youngens hold her, this stuff's gitten cold
an I've got to git back to Doddie. Delphie, you grab one
shoulder an hand; Bill, you take the other'n. Lureenie,
you'll have to hold her head an nose er she'll strangle like
a drenched sheep."

A scuffle and Florie Dell's screams, the excited tittering
of the other children, the sound of a slap and the screams
smothered down into a choked gurgling, then the sound
of old cloth tearing and Sue Annie's angry cry, "Shit-fire
down my asshole, she's a spillen it all." And Florie Dell,
wormseeded molasses rolling down her chin, dashed
screaming into the yard.

The others came shrieking behind her. Bill grabbed at
her just as she sprang through the door, but she went on
with another wild scream, and Bill stood a second staring
at a handful of yellow hairs, then, with an oath of Sue
Annie's, rushed after her They rested, half dressed as they

were, followed. Sue Annie cursed the black oaths she
ordinarily reserved for a father who fainted or vomited
while witnessing the birth of his child, while Lureenie
stood in the door and screamed commands for them to
come back before they caught their deaths of cold or tore
their feet up in the dark.

The screams and loud talk penetrated to some bit of
consciousness left to Doddie; he moved his hands with
quick aimless motions and rolled up his eyeballs, while his
leg and shoulder muscles quivered so that Milly jumped
up and hurried to Sue Annie, her arms weak and shaking.
Sue Annie was standing by the door, yelling into the darkness, telling the children that if they didn't come inside the
black witches and one-eyed women and red devils who
lived in the sinkholes would come out and eat them up.

"Take him quick, Sue Annie. He's a dyen," Milly
begged, and Lureenie, who had gone to the edge of the
porch calling after the children, heard and whirled about,
seized Doddie roughly in her arms and ran to the fire
screaming, "He's a dyen. He's a dyen. Oh, Jesus, I didn't
mean I wanted him to die, not now."

Doddie seemed to have no breath, but the tremors in
his arms and legs increased in violence, spreading through
his whole body; his eyeballs rolled up and back until only
the bloodstained whites showed.

Sue Annie jerked him from his screaming mother in
some anger. "It's all this screamen an carryen on that's a
doen it, an th turpentine's a setten them worms crazy an
a maken em bite. It's nothen but a worm fit. Now shut up
an be quiet."

Doddie stiffened suddenly, thrust out his arms and legs
and lay rigid like one long dead. Lureenie ran through the
door, crying and calling for Nunn and Blare cutting wood
on the hillside.

Milly dashed into the kitchen, and unable to find water
in the dark, scooped up a handful of snow by the door
and ran and rubbed it over Doddie's face. Sue Annie
brushed off the snow, turned the child stomach downward,
spat out a stream of tobacco juice, and glared at Milly.
"God Almighty, woman, I allus thought you had some
sense. A hot wet rag to his head an feet's what he needs,
nothen cold, an a spoon to keep him from swalleren his
tongue. Git me a spoon now, quick!"

Milly dashed into the kitchen, remembered that the pine torch they had used earlier in the evening was burned out and she would have to get another, dashed back in time to hear Sue Annie's calm but disgusted command: "Well, git me a hot wet rag, if they's any rag to wet. Here, untie my apron."

She knelt and untied Sue Annie's apron band, one of her big white baby-catching aprons, then dipped it into an iron kettle of water hanging on one end of the fire crane, and following Sue Annie's instructions, wrapped it around Doddie's stiff, dirty, chapped feet and legs.

It seemed useless. He lay like a dead child, stiff, with his eyes frozen open and bloody froth from his chewed tongue seeping from the corners of his mouth, his teeth clamped tight on the piece of wood Sue Annie had grabbed from the fireplace when Milly did not bring a spoon.

Lureenie's cries and screams came faintly from high up on the hill where the men were cutting wood. Milly shivered, listening, then pushed the burned-out chunks of the foresticks together and laid on another log. "Pore thing, seemed like when Tom was in his dyen sickness—a cold slick rainy time—seemed like I'd a give my soul to a run sometimes."

"But you didn't though," Sue Annie said. "You set right there an held him till he died, an that's what a woman's got to learn to do."

Bare feet thudded over the floor and Florie Dell came in and stood hesitantly by the chimney corner and glanced timorously at them.

"Look what you've done," Sue Annie said, "screamen an carryen on; you've sent your little brother into a fit, an your mommy's run off into th cold."

"Is he dead?"

"No, he ain't dead, an he ain't goen to be if'n you behave an take your medicine. Milly, git that worm medicine an give her two great big spoonfuls."

The child followed Milly's motions with big apprehensive eyes, gagging as she watched with hard quiverings of her stomach and stiffening of her chin, but she opened her mouth and swallowed two spoonfuls of the stuff. She gagged and shivered, bent suddenly double, her stricken, water-filled eyes gazing beseechingly at Sue Annie. Sue

Annie shook her head fiercely. "You better not puke that
up. Put your hand over your mouth an swaller it back.
Hold it now. I'm about out a wormseed; keep a swalleren
it back if'n it keeps comen up."

Florie Dell crouched, gagging and shivering and swallowing; the two others crept softly in to watch, Bill with his
hard blue white-lashed eyes bright with laughter.

"Now they're all here," Sue Annie said to Milly, "start
em on the feverweed an life-everlasten. An you, Bill,
you're big enough to run up on th hill an tell your mom
Doddie's all right. Take this good strong tea now; don't
stand there a batten your eyes at me like a frog in a thunderstorm; drink it down an maybe it'll brile some a th
meanness out a you."

Sue Annie took a fresh chew of tobacco, then directed
Milly to get the mutton tallow and the hog's jawbone she
had brought, break the bone and take the marrow out and
mix in with a little tallow and they would grease the soles
of Doddie's feet and the palms of his hands and bake them
to the fire.

Not long after, Lureenie came back and stopped at the
door and peeped timorously in like some half-wild stranger. "Is—is—" she began, holding onto the doorjamb.

"He's a lot better'n you're a goen to be if'n you don't
behave. He's a limberen up fine," Sue Annie said with
more kindness than she usually showed to chickenhearted
women.

After a long look at Doddie, Lureenie dropped to the
woodpile and leaned her shoulders against the chimney
wall and sat, her chin fallen forward on her breast, breathing hard and shivering. Milly brought her a cup of catnip
tea, and she held it a while in her long lax-fingered hands
and drank a few careless sips, then set it on the floor and
seemed to lapse into a long dreaming doze.

She roused somewhat when men's feet came crunching
heavily through the snow and Nunn and Blare came in
with armloads of sweet-smelling oak wood. Milly asked
Lureenie twice to move so that the men could lay their
load of wood on the pile.

"Shit-fire, Milly, you'd make a corpse git up an carry
its own coffin. Take th wood out an lay it on th porch," Sue
Annie commanded in some exasperation.

Milly sighed but said nothing. It was hard on Nunn to

hunt sheep all day and then cut wood in the snow half the night and nothing but hard words. But Sue Annie had one of her man-hating fits coming on, and any man who came around would catch it, because Rans wasn't handy.

The onions were roasted soft now and Milly mashed them with a fork, spread them thickly on a piece of meal sack, and following Sue Annie's directions, laid the poultice under Doddie's armpit, hurriedly fixed another and laid it under the other arm, then dipped Sue Annie's apron in hot water and wrapped it firmly around him while Sue Annie drew yet nearer the fire to drive the heat in.

By now Doddie had limbered up enough so that Sue Annie thought he could swallow the wormseed and sulphur. She held his nose while Milly poured it in, and as he swallowed, she smiled her peculiarly joyful smile that wrinkled her cheeks back to her ears and made her old eyes young as a girl's. "This youngen's a goen to pull through—if'n he'd a been anywhere near dead he'd a strangled to death a tryen to swaller this thick stuff."

She then made the other children wash their feet and legs in hot water and some strong lye soap she had brought, let Milly hold Doddie while she made another pot of tea strong with feverweed, black seneca, yellowroot, horse mint, golden seal, and life-everlasting, and then as each child dried itself on a feed-sack towel Milly had brought, it swallowed a cupful of the strong stuff and, watery-eyed and gagging, went to bed.

In between times she doctored Doddie, pouring spoonful after spoonful of an especially strong mixture of feverweed and black seneca down him, reheated the onion poultices, and laid a fresh turpentine-soaked rag on his navel.

Lureenie still half lay and half sat on the woodpile, her hands hanging loosely at her sides, her legs outspread in a vulgar, shameless, not-caring kind of way, Milly thought. Her mouth was open like a drunk man's and her tangled, matted red-gold hair had come unpinned and fell about her face and shoulders. At times the firelight picked it out and it flamed alive and red and sometimes the firelight picked up the struggles of the unborn child, and Sue Annie would now and then glance at it in a worried kind of way. Milly looked at it, too, and glanced around for something to throw over the woman, but finding nothing, for the scanty wraps of the family were piled on the sleeping children, took off her own apron and laid it over her.

"She ain't cold," Sue Annie said.

Milly took a chew of tobacco. "What if one a th men was to come in sudden an see her setten thataway an th youngen a kicken like a mule colt tangled in bob wire?"

Sue Annie made a gentle shushing sound. "Don't be a botheren her now. Let her sleep; to my mind it's the first she's had since this youngen took sick and she run out a everything." She shook her head. "She's lost heart and she's full a cold, maybe comen down with th fever." She tilted her head and studied Lureenie's abdomen. "An that youngen don't seem to hang right somehow; runnen up an down that slick river hill to her fish basket ain't done her no good."

After a while Milly's apron slipped from Lureenie, but neither Sue Annie nor Milly noticed. Doddie had another convulsion, and in spite of Sue Annie's encouraging talk, Milly thought he was going to die. Death was like some light-footed beast out there in the snow, light-footed and trackless as King Devil, but there, ready to slip in when nobody was looking.

She looked at Doddie lying stiff across Sue Annie's knees, a blue look on his face and his eyes rolled back like they were rolling away from things they didn't want to see. Maybe he could see death coming, and death, right at first, wasn't angels at all. Tom hadn't smiled when he died— he'd looked afraid and little and pale and pitiful, like a hungry whipped dog gone into a corner.

She quickly crossed the room and pushed the door to and came back and stood with her hands outspread to the fire while Sue Annie watched Doddie struggle with a breath, give it up, then try again and make it. "I think they's a worm somewheres around his windpipe," she said, paying no attention to Milly's terror. "This turpentine's a setten em crazy," she added with satisfaction. She wiped sweat from her forehead, then turned and looked back at the door. "Aw, Milly, you've shut th door. We'll smother to death, me a setten right on top a th fire with this youngen. A body needs air. You know I never shut th door at home."

Milly hesitated. "Couldn't I hold him, Sue Annie, an you move back from th fire?"

"What's th matter, child? You cold? Then build up th fire."

Milly pulled the door ajar and tiptoed back to the fire. Sue Annie poured four more tablespoonfuls of tea into Doddie, and as Milly knelt, holding the cup, she glanced into her face with its wide frightened eyes. She stopped, the fifth spoonful poised above Doddie. "What th hell, Milly—you look skeered. You ain't silly enough to think he's a goen to die?"

Milly shook her head and dropped her eyes. "No—I wish we had more people, though—Ruth Hull or Hattie or somebody."

Sue Annie spat into the fire, poured in the fifth spoonful, watched Doddie with satisfaction as he swallowed. "A whole houseful couldn't do no more'n we're a doen."

"But if somethen—somethen bad was to happen, it would seem easier to have more people."

"Shit-fire, child, a houseful a people can"t keep death out th door—if'n it wants to git in. Is that why you shut th door, thinken it was out there a wanten to come in?"

Milly looked up at her, her eyes big. "How—how did you know?"

"If'n it hadn't a been for Aunt Marthie Jane, I'd never a got through, but back when th flu first come around, an all Little Smokey an all Deer Lick come down at onct—"

And Sue Annie went on to tell about the night her Beulah, the next to the least one, took so bad sick. Aunt Marthie Jane was sick, not real bad sick, they said, able to be up and down and wait on the others, but too sick to cross the creek and come up the hill to see her Beulah, and Sue Annie herself was too far gone in the family way to get down there and help her. It was with Marthie, and she was forty-four years old then and the change was already working on her; and between it all she was half crazy most of the time and felt so bad she couldn't always get down to do Aunt Marthie's washing, for with Dave off always drunk and seeing to nothing and the cow dry, she needed the money bad.

But anyhow they all got sick. Nobody but Sue Annie thought Beulah was much bad—she didn't act right somehow. Still, she didn't seem much hot and she didn't breathe hard, like a child with the fever, and she got up out of bed that day and played outside, and before suppertime Dave went off to get some chewing tobacco at the post office, he said, but she was pretty well certain he was going off to a still on the other side of Deer Lick, and begged him not to go. But he went on.

Along about dusty dark she saw Beulah sitting on the porch, just sitting, not hardly breathing seemed like, and that blue look—the old people called it the bloom of death —in her face. Then she sent after Dave by the two biggest boys, hoping maybe he'd get a little whisky, for back then all whisky was safe for babies. But seemed like Beulah kept getting worse, and she sent the two biggest girls down the hill after Nancy Ballew, for it still wasn't full dark on the ridges. But nobody came, not even her own children.

Dave was down drunk and the boys had done right by him and stayed and built a fire; and the girls had met Nancy Ballew in the road and she was hurrying up to Aunt Marthie Jane's; she didn't know that Beulah was so bad and begged the girls to come with her. And so she sat by herself with Beulah on her knees; it was a long night; like a month of black December nights all put together; she kept the doors open—she could look out and see some stars, and she watched them, for seemed like they made some company. And when they began to get pale, Beulah died; she died easylike, just kind of slipping out like the stars.

And after a while she carried her to the kitchen and laid her on the table—funny how death hits you all at once: you know and you don't know at first. She didn't know it somehow, know it hard, until when she was building up the fire, all at once she looked back sudden at Beulah, scared she'd fall off the table, for Beulah had been an awful one to climb. And Beulah was just like she'd left her, with one arm up over her eyes. And she stood a long time with a handful of red-cedar-root kindling—she'd never been able to abide the smell of dried cedar root since—and looked at her all still there on the table and never going to fall off any more—and she knew she was dead.

Then she knew she couldn't stand there forever or she'd never get that arm down straight like it ought to be, so she hurried with the fire and got warm water quick and washed her all good and combed her hair.

When she stepped to the door to fling out Beulah's wash

water, she heard a coffin ringing in the valley—nobody could make a coffin now that could ring like the ones old Eli Cramer made—and she knew Aunt Marthie Jane was dead; dead with a houseful of people around her. And she wasn't sorry somehow that she'd had Beulah all to herself before she died. Death would get in no matter how many people came, and Milly mustn't be afraid—seemed sometimes that people got borned just so they could die.

Milly pulled out fresh coals to roast more onions. Doddie stirred and coughed a little, but Lureenie still slept; sometimes she was restless, moving about on the woodpile and talking; once she was back in Cincinnati and cried to come home, and another time she was telling Rans to hurry on with the potato seed or a thunderstorm would come before they could be planted. The children, too, were full of dreams and sleep talk, snoring and crying and coughing, continually throwing off their covers and asking for a drink, then falling asleep again before Milly got back with a dipper of water.

"They've eat too much, pore things," Sue Annie said, "an that medicine's a maken th worms act up."

Milly hoped Deb had not kicked off the covers at home and wondered if Nunn was still cutting wood up on the hillside. Sometimes she went to the door and looked out; it was clearing, and through the scud of snow cloud some stars shone, but by the few she saw she couldn't tell the time.

Doddie had two more convulsions before the night was out, and Milly rubbed his feet and hands, heated tea, mashed onions, got little Florie Dell out of bed when she awoke crying and vomiting, for she couldn't hold the worm medicine after all. The night moved slowly on, though to Milly the stars in the crack of sky seemed frozen there, unmoving, unblinking.

A screech owl came up from the river bluff and laughed and shrieked and cried not far away. Sue Annie said it was a sign of a change in the weather, but to Milly the sound seemed not to belong to some warm living bird, but was the voice of death and trouble and worry and pain, a cry from that gray trackless beast that waited out there in the snow.

After a while the owl hushed, and Milly must have drowsed a little as she squatted by the fire, warming a pot of tea. Something brought her suddenly awake, and she looked up to find Sue Annie's eyes searching her own. She listened, her eyes on Sue Annie, her ears hunting the sound that had broken through her sleep, and in a moment heard the soft creak-creaking of someone—a bare-footed child or a light-footed woman, walking in the snow behind the house.

"Somebody's out there sounds like," Sue Annie whispered.

Milly got up and stood listening, her ear against the house wall. Her mouth felt dry. "Why—why don't they come in?"

Sue Annie looked back at the open door. "I don't recken one a them youngens has slipped outside an is walken around in its sleep."

Milly went to the bed, but the children were all there. The gentle walking sound began again, and Milly hurried back to the fire and stood by Sue Annie with her hand on the chair back, her wide eyes searching the house wall as if she would look through it. Sue Annie spat into the hearth. "Let me lay this youngen down an we'll go peep around th house corner."

Groping and stumbling, they catwalked along a log sill in the floorless porch, stepped out into the snow at the end, and looked along the house wall by the chimney from where the sound had seemed to come. Outside, under a wide sweep of stars, Milly felt bolder and walked on to see if anything was on the other side of the chimney.

Nothing was there, but as she turned back and glanced out into the dark, something large and white and roundish, whiter than the snow on the ground, stood not many feet away. A coldness like cold water dripping through her hair and trickling down her shoulders came over her; her knees were weak and her feet heavy and it seemed they would never get her back to Sue Annie.

She seized the older woman and pulled her toward the house. In the firelight Sue Annie looked into her fright-widened eyes and said, "I recken you think you've seen a haint; it was just snow on a bush er somethen."

Milly rolled her tobacco across her dry tongue. "It was Aunt Marthie Jane."

"You jist think it was," Sue Annie said without much conviction. She took Doddie from the bed and sat down again with the child, who was now breathing with a curious gasping strangled breath.

Milly looked down at Doddie. "She's come fer him."

Sue Annie shook her head with an angry gesture of denial. "Well, she'll go back emptyhanded, fer she ain't a goen to git him. If'n I can git this worm out a his neck, he'll be all right."

"She's come fer somebody," Milly said. "She walked around outside all night fore Tom died."

"Aw, Milly—" The snow-walking sound began again, and Sue Annie dropped her voice, as if she did not want her remarks heard on the other side of the house wall. "Somethen else could maybe make that noise; lots a times when it's turnen colder they's funny noises in trees an rocks; mebbe it's th fire trampen snow in a new kind a way we don't know about. Or she's jist restless an walk sometimes—you know that—she's maybe mad about all a us letten pore Lureenie an her youngens starve, an I don't blame her one bit; but I wish to God she'd take off her head an hold it in her arms an go to th Cincinnati jailhouse er wherever that Rans is an set all night on his bed, all night an ever night fer a—"

Doddie struggled and retched, and water smelling strongly of turpentine and feverweed spurted from his mouth and nose. Sue Annie turned his stomach downward, held his head over the hearth, ran her finger far back into his throat, and after a moment's exploratory probing pulled out two large round yellowish-pink worms, twined and twisted like unwound wool. She watched the worms wriggling on the hot hearth with satisfaction. "Marthie's mebbe come fer somebody, but not this youngen."

Aunt Marthie Jane went away, then came back again, but after what seemed a long time, the stars paled, and with the blue dawn came Samuel, walking slowly, with a great load on his back. "I didn't—" he said, and meeting Sue Annie's angry glance, he stopped in the doorway and let the sack slide from his shoulders. "I figgered," he went on, speaking slowly in a troubled kind of way, "she had money when she sent off payments on th radio, an was mad when I didn't give her credit."

Lureenie was still sleeping, and Sue Annie took his load of food with scant show of gratitude. "Next time don't figger so hard; jist read yer Bible—him that hath two coats give to him that hath none—an don't ask what yer neighbor done with his or why he ain't got any fore you give."

Samuel opened his mouth, glanced in pity at the sleeping Lureenie, then turned away.

By noon there was a beaten path to Lureenie's door, and no one came who did not carry a heavy grass sack or split basket, and all brought their food with shamefaced guilty airs and often brief worded apologies for not having known. John, whose rheumatism was bad in the wet snowy weather, came limping behind a sledload; the Tuckers came on muleback with legs of mutton and hog meat, sacks of new-ground meal, and lard buckets of molasses and honey; the Cookseys, the Sextons, the Tillers, and many others came bringing any number of things—dried apples, fodder beans, butter, home-made soap, hominy, peanuts, and sweet potatoes; even old J. D., who hadn't walked any place except to his still in years, brought half a bushel of potatoes and a square of fresh-killed shoulder meat.

Last came Keg Head Cramer with a fresh-killed chicken, but "bowed down with sorrow," or so he said, to hear of his daughter-in-law's affliction.

Chapter Thirty-one

MILLY WAS TYING a broom one morning early in December when Ruby, who had been staying with Lureenie, came running with Doddie bouncing on her hip and the other children squalling behind. Ruby was so out of breath and excited she could hardly speak, but Milly knew what her business was and told her to leave Lureenie's children with Suse and go quick for Sue Annie.

Milly quickly got into her Sunday shoes and a large stiffly starched feed-sack apron she had kept in readiness just for this, hunted the scissors, a clean boiled flour sack, and all the black pepper left in a box she had bought at Samuel's not long before.

Suse went on tying the broom but watched her mother's preparations and wondered what each thing was for—she knew the pepper was for tea to drink and make the pains come right or something, but why the scissors? If the woman wasn't big enough—she'd heard talk of small-made women—would they cut her with the scissors? Her hands were sweaty on the broom handle, but still she wished she knew. She'd never so much as seen Betsey have a calf; her mother had watched them both too closely when Betsey's time was near—and it was only a few years back she'd learned from Ruby Ballew, amid much giggling and shaming because of her ignorance, that babies did not sprout from toenails planted, as Milly had said when Tom was born, and grow until a granny woman found them and carried them to some woman sick in bed.

Milly soon set out, after many threats and warnings to Lureenie's children and Deb, who hadn't gone to school, of what would happen if they played in the fire, touched

431

matches or coal oil, and admonitions to Suse to take good care of the babies, get her dad a good dinner when he came in from post-hole digging, and keep the house readied in case somebody happened in.

In spite of the two whindling, diaper-dirtying toddlers, the mischievous older children, a new hole rusted in the stovepipe, and all the work to be done, the day dragged for Suse. Hattie and Sue Annie passed; and not long after, Hattie came back, apparently on her way to John's, for soon she and Nancy came hurrying by—trouble on old Nancy's face, worry and excitement on Hattie's.

And after they had passed on the short-cut path by the kitchen door, with only brief preoccupied "Howdies" for Suse standing with a baby on each hip, Suse turned away, wondering, between her problem of rocking two babies to sleep at once, how things were coming with Lureenie and why Sue Annie sent for Nancy. When Doddie was born Milly had gone with Sue Annie and they had brought the baby alone and everything was over before dinnertime.

Nunn came in to dinner, ate quickly and in silence; and Suse, watching him, thought there was a worriment in his face too, but asked no questions and made no comments on Lureenie, for she knew it was not decent for a girl to talk about such things to any man person, even her father.

Not long after dinner Mrs. Hull and old Aunt Hannah Anderson came up through the yard, but unlike the others, they paused a moment by the kitchen door to rest after the steep climb up from the creek. Suse invited them in, for three of the children were now asleep and she'd had a chance to wash the coal smoke off her face, but the women said they must get on.

"I hope it's all over when we git there," Aunt Hannah said. She was a thin little sprig of a woman with a thin little birdlike voice and today, in spite of her errand, she seemed particularly joyful, ready to break into giggling laughter. "I ain't fitten to go to a place of pain and trouble," she said to Suse with a gay smile, and while Mrs. Hull listened with a kindly indulgent air as if she had already heard the story several times, Aunt Hannah explained how she had in that day's mail got a card from Olen saying he was on land again, and a letter telling

about Hawaii and the army; it wasn't so bad, he said, but
sometimes a lot of work—the day he wrote, he'd been
stacking lumber at a place. She pondered a moment. "I let
Ansel take th letter home, but I wish I hadn't; I disremem-
ber so, but seems like this lumber stacken was on a place
called Hickum Field, an his post-office address—it wasn't
Hawaii?" She pondered a moment, then after explaining
that now that she knew Olen was safe across the waters
she wouldn't worry any more, for he'd be safe in Hawaii
as at home she and Mrs. Hull went on.

While the children slept, Suse made a thick flour paste,
wetted a brown paper sack with it and pasted the sack
over the fresh-rusted hole in the stovepipe. The stove
smoked less and the supper corn bread and sweet potatoes baked more quickly than they had for days, and
Suse hummed a little and wished Milly would get on
home so that she could show her how fine she'd fixed the
stovepipe; she knew she'd be pleased; but Lucy and Lee
Roy came in from school and Nunn from his work on the
fence and went about their chores, and still Milly had
not come. Twenty times Suse must have run to the western door to look across the graveyard field before she saw
Milly coming home.

She started to run through the garden, calling to know if
it were girl or boy, then stopped, knowing from Milly's
walk and the set of her head that she was only a tired
woman coming home and not the bringer of good news.

Suse shut the door, for the evening air was cold, and
tramped restlessly about the house; Bill Dan was hungry
for the breast, bawling on her hip, but Milly was so long in
coming that Suse peeped out a window, wondering what
could stay her so. After much searching she saw at last the
top of her brown head and her clasped hands lifted as if
in prayer, the rest of her hidden in the weeds by the fence
row. Nunn was sober and the children well; it must be Lureenie for whom Millie prayed.

Suse remembered she'd left the corn bread keeping
warm in the too hot stove, rushed back to the kitchen,
smelled the burning bread, and wondered if she ought to
run and give that to the pigs and bake more in a hurry or
take a good scolding from Milly; while she wondered,
Milly came in through the kitchen door. She never noticed
the smell of burning bread, but took Bill Dan and went to

sit and nurse him by the fire. Suse followed her there and
stood with her hand on the mantel and wanted to ask a lot
of questions and asked none at all. Milly looked so tired,
her shoulders humped above the baby. What made her
tired? And when she looked on Lureenie's half-wild children, noisy, sassy, and forever messing and goming, her
eyes were not scolding but sad.

Milly looked up, found Suse's troubled, questioning
eyes, and told her to go up to the little garden and see if
she couldn't find some Georgia onions big enough to eat,
and hurry on before it got too dark to see. Suse suspected
that Milly wanted her out of the way; when Nunn came in
from the barn chores, she maybe wanted to tell him something about Lureenie.

And when she came back down the garden path, she
heard their low-toned troubled talk through the open
kitchen door. She caught the words "elbow foemost," from
Milly, and then, "Sue Annie tried three times to straighten
it an hurt th pore soul somethen terrible; 'twas all we
could do to hold her." Milly's voice went lower still and
Suse heard "doctor," and with much straining of her ears
gathered that Sue Annie wanted a man doctor from Town,
but that Keg Head, Lureenie's father-in-law, had said it
was against the Bible, and that Sue Annie had cursed him
something awful and said that, Bible or no, Lureenie
needed a doctor, for she was sick to begin with, and that it
was the $30 or $40 a Town doctor's trip would cost that
worried Keg Head more than the Bible.

Nunn's voice came loudly, as if in anger. "Mebbe Sue
Annie is right; mebbe th woman needs a doctor. We—me
mostly—has let th woman starve. Are we goen tu let her
die?"

"God's will is God's will," Milly said in a slow solemn
voice. "I knowed Lureenie was hard run, but she didn't
have to starve; she could a asked, an enyhow—I think
Sue Annie's mostly wore out an skeered. Lureenie's been
a carryen on so, a screamen an a beggen us tu kill her,
acten like a young girl with her first un. She's pulled on
my hands till it seems like my arms is loose."

They argued a little in words so low Suse could not
hear, but in a moment Milly's voice came, kind as if she
comforted a child, "An enyhow, who ever heard uv haven
a man doctor all th way out frum Town jist to bring a

baby? He couldn't do no more'n Sue Annie's a doen now, an her goen hungry an eaten acorns has got nothen to do with th hard time she's a haven now."

"Mebbe women is different frum sheep," Nunn said, "but you let a yoe about to lamb git lost off in a snowy time an starve down in th woods, an she'll have trouble, mebbe die tryen to drop her lamb."

Suse stood thinking in the dark until Milly called her sharply to come with the onions; and when her mother saw her face, she asked, "What makes you so big-eyed an skeered-looken, girl—you seen a ghost?"

"Nothen," Suse said, and was glad Nunn asked her to hold the lamp so that he could see to shave; she knew by his shaving in the middle of the week that he would go watch the night at Lureenie's in Milly's stead.

Nunn went away immediately after supper; the children went to bed soon after, and Milly, too tired to work on the walnut kernels, lay down to let Bill Dan nurse and fell asleep as soon as he. Suse cracked a few walnuts but was fidgety and restless, thinking of Lureenie. She had seen her several times since Doddie's sickness, for Nunn had insisted that she or Milly go see the woman every day, but Suse had never much enjoyed the visits; Lureenie had always seemed so still and sad and tired somehow, more like a woman waiting for the day's end than a woman living through a day, never talking much, not even of Rans, though the mail days passed into weeks and still he sent no letter. But for all the strangeness of Lureenie since coming back from Cincinnati, Suse felt that Lureenie would rather have her around than any of the women gathered there, few of whom had ever been about her until now; many, like the Tillers, had made fun of her flighty notions and bemeaned her every chance they had. And now she was sick, bad sick, and there was no one of her kind or a close friend around her.

Suse stood a time with her back to the low fire, looking in the direction of Milly's bed. After her mother's breathing had been a long time regular and she had roused once —Suse never knew if she were sleeping or waking at such times—and straightened Bill Dan and pulled the covers around his shoulders, Suse took off her shoes and tiptoed through the middle room and out the kitchen door.

Outside, she sat on the doorsill and put on her shoes,

frowning a moment at the half-grown moon that seemed no more than six feet above the Cow's Horn and dimmed by fog and broken snow cloud, then sprang up and ran along the short-cut path through the garden and across the graveyard field; she didn't mind coming back in the dark, but Milly might be awake.

The clouds slipped from the moon and she saw again its lowness in the west and ran on. She had reached the strip of rocky scrub woodland that began on the boundary of Nunn's land when a sound different from any night sound she had ever heard came directionless in the fog. Suse stopped, her nostrils lifted a little, more curious than afraid, but unpleasantly conscious it could make her afraid. After a moment she walked on and soon saw the lights from Lureenie's cabin. She stopped, wondering what she would say if Nunn saw her first and told her to go home; Sue Annie, she was certain, wouldn't mind her being there at least long enough to say a few words to Lureenie.

A sobbing, yet animallike shriek came down from the cabin; Suse stopped and stood trembling. The long shriek ended and after a moment Suse walked on, understanding now that the other noise she'd heard had been Lureenie, too. Another scream stopped her at the porch steps; she waited until it was past, and then went in.

Nobody noticed as she went in; she saw the backs of people sitting by the fire, Keg Head and some of the Tuckers and two of the Sexton women. The people by the fire seemed not to want to see or hear what was going on in Lureenie's bed in a back corner of the room.

Sue Annie sat sideways on the foot of the bed; Lureenie half lay and half sat in front of her. There were other people there, but between Sue Annie's bent, tired sagging shoulders and the broad back to a Tucker man she saw Lureenie's face, fallen backward against a pile of pillows and folded bedclothes. Suse had seen sick people and dead people and people in pain, but never a face like Lureenie's; it no more than the scream seemed to belong to Lureenie or have anything to do with the mounded belly under the dirty quilt or the blood on Sue Annie's apron or with anything that had ever been or would be again; among all the big people and framed in the masses of red-gold tangled hair, it seemed little, no bigger than a child's face, but the eyes staring straight up were not a child's eyes nor Lureenie's eyes as she remembered them.

Against the tight-drawn skin of her face that had the dead bleached look of sun-scorched brick-colored clay, her eyes were shiny blue in the lamplight, a soft blue, like blue-green water in the spring, and looking up through the smoke-blackened ceiling and the fog and the stars behind the fog, they hunted for something, looked up at once with an immeasurable desire and a knowledge born of many failures that there was no finding the thing they wanted.

Sue Annie lifted the covers on Lureenie's drawn-up knees and shut away Lureenie's face, but Suse still saw those helpless ever-searching eyes. She watched while Lureenie had another labor pain. Her head came forward from the pillow; Hattie took one hand in both her own, the Tucker man the other; Mrs. Hull put a hand on each quivering knee, big Ann Liz Cooksey held her head, and big Jane Tucker laid her hands on her sides, just below and forward of her hip bones and pressed hard.

Lureenie pushed with her feet and pulled with her hands, the Tucker man throwing all his weight against her one thin arm, and Hattie the other, while Lureenie, her stomach arching upward, her shoulders forward and her head, in spite of Ann Liz Cooksey's hands, going backward and backward until it seemed that her eyes, pushed out of their sockets by the pain, were searching for something in the back of the bed. In the pitying, wincing silence of those about the bed, Suse heard the breath suck in through Lureenie's open mouth and out again in that gurgling, inhuman grunt of agony.

When it seemed that the sound was something that had begun at the beginning of the world and would go on into eternity, and Suse stood waiting, her body tensed like the bodies of the others around the bed and by the fire, and like those others, hoping against her reason that this one pain would do some good, might even be the end, it stopped. All the strength went from Lureenie's body, her hands slipped from the loosened grasp of the hands holding them, and she seemed to grow smaller and shrink away, and her eyes once more looked into things on the other side of the ceiling.

Mrs. Hull bent and wiped the sweat from her face,

while Sue Annie took her hands away from under the bedclothes, wiped dark blood on her apron, lifted one arm and wiped sweat from her forehead and chin on her sleeve, still looking down at the two thin humps made by Lureenie's widespread knees under the bedclothes, her glance tired and despairing.

Suse walked off kitchenward. From force of habit, she built up the fire in the cookstove and set a pot of coffee to boil. She watched it boil over, and it might have boiled away had not Mrs. Hull come for a cup for Sue Annie, who, though the others might take their turns about Lureenie, never left her place.

The cup was full and Mrs. Hull was looking for cream, and Suse had said, "Sue Annie never takes cream or sugar," before Mrs. Hull gave her full notice, and then only smiled pityingly when Suse protested that she was big enough and old enough to help. "Why, you're not as old as my Andy," she said. "Get your father to take you on home an don't think about it." She sighed. "You'll be in Lureenie's place soon enough—if you're like th rest of us."

Suse went outside. She found a dark spot on a sill in the old porch corner, just behind the oblong of light from the door. She sat stiff and still, as if she were in church at Communion, and listened. She heard Lureenie's grunts and moans. Sometimes she cried out and Sue Annie would chide her, "You're wasten your pains, child." And the next time it would be only a grunt. Sometimes she heard her talk in disconnected scant hoarse words, as if her very tongue was tired and full of pain; she would ask to get up and walk, or ask to sit up or turn over on her side, or beg for water, and Sue Annie would always say, "Child, you know there ain't nothen you can do but lay flat an take it," or "You know you cain't have water; you'll jest waste your pains a puken it up."

At other times Lureenie would beg to be killed, beg for a doctor like the Cincinnati women had, and sometimes, seeming to forget there were no batteries, beg for the radio to be turned on; she wanted to hear pretty music, she said. Sometimes she talked like a woman in her sleep— she was cooking a big chicken dinner and calling Rans in out of the hayfields.

And in and out through Suse's head would go the old

brags and boasts and plans and wishes Lureenie had made to her. "I always thought I'd like to live on a neat little farm with a fenced-up garden and a pretty yard with grass and a painted picket fence and two big flower beds by the door, and never run out of good things to cook." Sometimes the things Lureenie had said were so strong in her head she hardly noticed what Lureenie said now, and nothing at all of what the others said—except Sue Annie, who came once to the group by the fire, and speaking particularly to Keg Head, and with more pleading in her voice than Suse had ever heard said, "That woman's got to have a doctor." But no one spoke, and after a moment Sue Annie went back to the bed.

Nunn and the other men came in with armloads of wood and took their turns by the bed and drank coffee in the kitchen where Mrs. Hull in that kind patient way she had, chided Nunn for letting Suse come to a place like this and get scared half to death—she'd never marry now.

Nunn left his coffee half drunk and went out the door and home to find Suse's bed empty and Milly rousing as he entered. But after he assured her that he was not hungry, that Lureenie was about like usual, that all the children were sound asleep and covered well, and that he wouldn't stop in on his way back from looking at the ewes —that was why he had come, he said—he hurried outside and back to Lureenie's.

Lureenie now seemed to have lost most of her reason— she screamed and cried and begged to die in a voice hoarse and dry. She wouldn't bear down to her pains any more, or maybe it was just one long pain—Sue Annie couldn't tell. The listeners by the hearth were restless and Keg Head went outside to pray.

Lureenie fought to get out of bed; she had to get down to the river to see if there was any fish in the fish basket. The children were hungry and she had to pick wild greens, and she was in Cincinnati, crying to get out of the furnished room and see the sunshine on the hill. At other times she would lie spent and silent, smiling with tender eyes. Rans was home and they were sitting by the fire and the radio was playing and she would listen with a pleased, childishly happy look on her face, and the men holding her in bed would listen too, with lax fingers and hands, and Keg Head's prayers from outside in the tumble-down root house came loudly:

"Dear kind Heavenly Father, look down—"

Nunn, searching through the house, wished, as he had wished dozens of times, that somebody had tried to get a doctor and that Keg Head wouldn't pray so loud. He found Suse at last; she was sitting stiff and still in the dark porch corner, shivering a little, her hands clenched in her lap. Nunn took her roughly by the shoulder and with no words pushed her across the porch, careful to keep her away from the oblong of light. He didn't want the Hulls and Tuckers talking about how he couldn't make his own children mind.

Suse walked meekly before him across the porch and down the path. They came opposite the old root house just as Keg Head chanted:

"Oh-h, Thou all-wise God, in Thy mighty wisdom and mercy—"

Suse, with the quickness of a darting bird, bent and picked up a rock glimmering faintly in the path. Nunn heard the whing of it and a crunching clunk against rotten wood. Keg Head's prayers stopped and Suse said, not loudly, yet with no attempt at whispering:

"God damn th ole stingy son of a bitch—"

Nunn tried to find her mouth in the darkness to stop it up; it seemed somehow that everything she was doing was not a sin against herself, but a black, black sin on him.

Her head twisted away from his hands.

"God damn him, an you too, Nunnely Ballew. You let her starve. An God damn th God-damned God for setten around an letten you do it." She ran from him into the dark brush and cursed Nunn and God and Jesus Christ and the world with the same oaths he had so often used and a few of Sue Annie's dirtier ones. They hit him like stones, and he flinched into himself like a man being beaten.

It seemed a long time before she stopped, and then it must have been only for lack of breath. He could hear her hard breathing and the crackling of brush and saw briars as she crashed through them.

"Come on now, Suse," he begged, and added, with an attempt at authority, "Come on and git home. I won't lay a hand on you. I ought to beat you half to death, trollopen around in th dark."

"You couldn't do no more harm than you've already done me, couldn't hurt me no worse—th meanest thing you've done fer me was bringen me into th world. It's too bad Mom couldn't a had a pair of sheep shears that'd cut my head off when I was borned."

"Shut up, Suse. Talken Sue Annie's dirty talk. You'll end up a bad woman."

"In a Cincinnati whorehouse, you mean. Well, it's a pity Mom couldn't a gone to one when she was my age; she'd a had a sight easier time."

"Aw, Suse," he spoke slowly. He had the sickish feeling that he lied and she spoke the truth. "You know I've done th best I could by your mom an I'll do th best I can by you—"

She forgot the short-cut path and strode on down through the corn swag toward the Cow's Horn gate. "Aw, hell. You've always done th best you could to keep her in th family way. An you do get worried when she ain't able to work an wait on you." She went on striding down the road. "As fer me, you'll marry me off to some little shaved-tail son of a bitch when th rest gets big enough to work. You've not got money to keep me in shoes now."

He spoke in desperation, with no time to think. "Aw, Suse, honey, I'm aimen to send you to high school next—"

"High school, hell! You'll never have enough to send me in decent clothes to th post office, let alone high school. You're always aimen; never finishen nothen—"

A mule shoe struck a rock in the field and Blare Tiller spoke from out th darkness, excitement in his voice. "Nunn, what does th United States own that ain't in th United States an it begins with a P?" And he went on to tell how word had come in over Uncle Ansel's radio that someplace had been bombed, but all that he could recollect about the business was that it had been done by some funny slant-eyed kind of people who lived in a place where we sent missionaries.

"Aw, you're all mixed up," Nunn said as he walked on; "if'n they's any truth to it atall, it's th Germans has bombed th Panama Canal—we own that an it begins with a P. They've all been a jarren an a fussen around a sight."

"It warn't th Germans, I'm pretty certain," Blare said,

puzzled, and added as he kicked his mule into motion again, "but whoever it is, an if'n it is th beginnen a war like they said th radio said, we'll have em licked in a week er two."

Suse was silent during the rest of the walk to the house, her mind continually jumping between Lureenie and the news Blare brought. God, God, why had she been borned in such a place? Why couldn't she have gone to high school and learned things with Andy? Out in the world women were having their babies in hospitals and people were reading newspapers and listening to the radio.

Nunn stopped at the kitchen door, and after sternly whispered commands to go inside and go to bed and never tell Milly how she had disgraced herself, he went away. Back to Lureenie's, Suse guessed.

And all night long, in her half-dreaming, half-waking sleep, it seemed that people passed to and fro on the short-cut path by the kitchen door or along the Cow's Horn road.

Then it was muggy daylight, and Milly, with her hair freshcombed and nursing Bill Dan by the fire, was calling her to get her lazy self out of bed and get breakfast. The step stove was roaring red and biscuit-baking hot when Suse got to the kitchen. Nunn sat by the eating table sipping coffee; his face wore the gray, drained-away look that came to it after a two-day drunk; but she knew without sniffing that he hadn't been drinking. He glanced up at her, smiled a tired sad smile, and put his arm around her waist. "You must take your time about marryen, Suse."

She swallowed and felt like crying; it had been so long since Nunn or Milly had hugged or kissed her the way they had used to do when she was a little girl. "How's Lureenie?" she asked.

"Worse," he said, and bowed his head over the coffee, as if he didn't want to look at her or anyone.

Milly came in in a clean apron and her visiting clothes and drank coffee, but seemed less downhearted than Nunn. Suse gathered from their talk that Mrs. Hull and Nancy Ballew had guaranteed money for a doctor, and that Blare had gone to get Jaw Buster to go with his truck to Town and hunt one; Milly thought they would have done better to send Samuel, but he was gone with his truck and wouldn't be back till tomorrow morning. Nunn agreed; Jaw Buster's tires were bad, and he'd be half a day getting there in that old truck, and once there he mightn't find a doctor that would come late in the day.

"You go on an stay," Nunn said to Milly as he got up from the table, and added with an angry bitterness, "if you can. I come away—I couldn't stand it no more—when she took them—convulsions, Sue Annie said."

"Chickenhearted," Milly said, and went away.

Nunn went off toward the sheepfold after telling her not to bother cooking for him, she'd have her hands full with the youngens. Suse tried to work and watch the children, but often she found herself standing in the kitchen door or looking out the western windows to see what people passed across the graveyard field. Many passed both going and coming, even old John and J. D. Duffey's young wife, with a baby on her arm; but none stopped to talk with Suse and she saw no man doctor in a long-tailed overcoat and with a black satchel in his hand go hurrying by, as she had seen in pictures.

Near sundown Jaw Buster passed, red-faced and tired-looking; and seeing him alone, Suse felt a great emptiness, like a hole in her heart.

She milked Betsey; Lee Roy did the barn work, but at dusty dark Nunn came by with Jaw Buster. The big man would not stop, and when he had gone, Nunn, seeing the questions in Suse's troubled face, told her that Jaw Buster had got late to Town and had tried four doctors; two were too old to walk so far from the end of the gravel, they said; one never went out on baby cases, he said; and the other was too busy getting ready to examine men for soldiers; but they had sent some pills.

"Pills," Nunn said, and cursed and went away again.

Suse got the children to bed, and when she'd burned away two sets of foresticks, she got in bed with Bill Dan and Doddie and Florie Dell.

It seemed a long time later that she was awakened by a strange sound; she lifted on one elbow and saw, in the light of the freshly built up brightly blazing fire, Nunn mending the band on the sewing machine; Milly had been quarreling at him for days to mend the frayed band with a bit of leather. He must be drunk or crazy to do such work now in the dead of night. "Pop," she called in a frightened whisper.

"Don't be a waken th little youngens," he said. "Your mom's got some sewen to do come mornen."

In a moment she got out of bed and started toward the kitchen. Milly would need coffee as she sewed Lureenie's shroud.

Some, Keg Head hurried him so.

Chapter Thirty-two

LUREENIE HAD NO FUNERAL. Keg Head and several of the others thought it would be better to have the funeral in the spring. Maybe Rans would be back by then, and in any case the weather would be more settled and more people could come.

At daylight word was sent to old Nopen Creecy over the river to come and make the coffin, and Keg Head himself went down to John's, where there was always a little stock of seasoned coffin wood. John had enough black walnut, dressed and seasoned to a rich nut brown. Keg Head hesitated over it a moment and then went on to the cheaper poplar; a man could only do so much, he said; all he'd ever get out of it was the partly paid-for radio, and that was little enough for burying the woman and raising her children, though the children wouldn't be so bad, especially the oldest girl; his wife had never had a girl child and she needed help about the house.

Keg Head had stopped at Nunn's to rest and have a cup of coffee, when he happened to look out toward the graveyard. "Tarnation all tarnation," he said, and could hardly be persuaded to stay long enough to finish his coffee; for somebody—it looked to be the Tiller men, though in the early-morning fog it was hard to tell—had already started on Lureenie's grave.

There was bad luck enough already in the world, so Keg Head said: his own born son gone and unheard of for weeks, maybe dead or penned in a Cincinnati jail for some little fight that didn't amount to a thing; and his boy's wife dead through no fault of his, but the neighbors would say, at least with their eyes, that starvation had hurried her on,

445

and that fool Sue Annie claiming a doctor could have saved her, but God's will was God's will. Now there was no use to ask for more bad luck by letting the sun go down on an empty grave, and everybody knew there was nothing that would bring bad luck quicker than by letting the sun set on an empty grave.

So Keg Head rushed away to hurry things on; John's mules couldn't bring the coffin lumber fast enough, and all morning, while he worked, old Nopen mumbled and grumbled, declaring it was the roughest job he'd ever done, Keg Head hurried him so.

Twice the old man sent to see if Lureenie's shroud was ready, and the first time Milly had to send back word that Mrs. Hull had not yet come down the hill with the cloth Samuel was to get in Town. Mrs. Hull came at last, taking her time, not yet knowing that Lureenie was to be buried that day, and complaining that Samuel, manlike, had forgotten to get any lace or white ribbon for trimming, but would go again in the afternoon, when she was home to stay with the younger children; then Lee Roy had to run up the hill with word for Samuel that the burying was to be in the late afternoon and that Samuel couldn't go again to Town.

The shroud was almost finished when Suse came hesitantly up to her mother with a full-skirted yellowish petticoat spread wide in her hands, showing rows and rows of lace halfway up to the waist. "I know it's great-granma's wedden petticoat; I took it out a that old trunk upstairs, but I think—she wouldn't mind—just one little row, Mom—Lureenie—she liked lace an pretty things, an—" She choked and stood staring beseechingly at Milly.

Milly frowned. The most she'd ever touched of Aunt Marthie Jane's things stored in two big trunks was a quilt when she needed one bad, but Mrs. Hull, with her mild eyes so much like Andy's, smiled and nodded. "It would be nice," she said.

So Lureenie had lace at her throat and her wrists, too; and Flonnie, who was good at making flowers, made tissue-paper roses for her hair.

But everything went slowly. When the shroud was finally finished, Hattie and Ann Liz Cooksey, who had laid her out, tore up her hair trying to get her into it, and that had to be fixed again; and then she must have swelled a little or something, or maybe Keg Head had measured in too big a hurry or not measured at all, but, anyhow, the coffin wasn't quite wide enough and they had to turn her a little sideways; and by then she was too stiff to do much with and her head kept turning with her thin wide shoulders and stuck up in the air, and they had to squeeze to get the coffin lid down.

Sue Annie frowned over it and shook her head, and Mrs. Hull said openly that it was a shame; but Keg Head, with a handful of nails in his mouth, glanced through the open door and saw the house shadow long in the pale wintry sun and said to Blare, through the nails in his mouth, "Set a little harder on this corner," and hurried, driving the nails down with short sharp blows.

Suse, after watching them put her away, ran up on the hillside and stood behind a little cedar tree and cried, a shivering, soundless kind of crying, while eight men, her father among them, carried the coffin out the door, then over into the path. While four men held the burden in their hands, the other four squatted and put their shoulders under it. They rose slowly, and Jaw Buster's corner went higher than the others, for he was tallest.

Willie Cooksey walked ahead and with quick strokes of an ax cut brush from the narrow path. Behind came a little knot of men and lastly a few women, Hattie and others, with babies in their arms, and Nancy Ballew with a split basket in which she had brought food for the coffin makers in the early afternoon.

The men carrying the coffin hurried, those in front almost stepping on Willie's heels, so that he soon gave up trying to clear anything except the bigger brush, and the men went on, heedless of the branches that slapped at their faces and arms and the coffin.

More than once, Milly and others of the crowd glanced back at the sun. Already it was just above the hill. And in the little rocky pine-woods swag at the edge of Nunn's farm, the shadow of the hill lay blue across the path.

They reached a high, unrotted freshly cut pine stump, and Keg Head bade the coffin bearers rest one end of the coffin on it and let four others take their places. They would save time that way, he said.

Nunn and three other men dropped behind and slung the sweat from their foreheads with their hands and twisted their tired shoulders while four others took up the load.

The four new bearers walked even faster than the others, so that the women carrying young babies were hard pressed to keep up, and walked heedless of their Sunday shoes, splattering and splashing through the half-frozen mud.

The path came out of the pine woods into a cleared bit of low level land where Nunn had corn each year, and here the tips of the sagging fodder shocks were tipped with gold, but even as they looked the gold faded, like some bright powder dissolved in water. The path wound up a low clayey hill that led to the top of the graveyard field. And the four men under the coffin, dripping sweat and breathing hard, made slow time, their feet slipping and stumbling in the slick clay mud, until Jess Cramer and Blare Tiller and a Tucker man stepped up and put their shoulders under. Nunn's place alone remained empty, for he, unlike the others, seemed in no mood to hurry.

The seven men went with quick short doglike steps, so that the coffin on the seven uneven shoulders bounced and jiggled and at times threatened to slide backward when they went up the steeper places. Behind them the younger women with babies, who had gradually fallen behind, began a clumsy running, and Lureenie's next to the last one began a shrill crying of "Wait, wait."

But with all their hurry, blue shadow lay along the level sweep of dried grass and clover in the graveyard field, and even as the coffin bearers went running toward the graveyard, the coffin bouncing on their shoulders, the shadows rose to the men's knees and the mound of red clay among the white tombstones that had glowed golden red when the coffin topped the hill was a black mound now, silhouetted against the farther hills.

One of the Cramer boys ran ahead and let down the bars, and Paul and Silas Ballew ran up with plowlines, uncoiling them as they ran, and laid them by the grave. The bearers hurried on, but by the time they came to the angel head on Aunt Marthie's tombstone, it was touched with only a thin halo of gold; and when the men had got the coffin down and on the ropes, after letting it tip so far on its side they heard Lureenie thud against it, the graveyard lay all blue in the shadow, though across the valley the sun still shone on Sue Annie's cabin, and above it the pines, rising on up to the ridge crest, were red-black and shining in the dying light, and further up the valley the western windows of the schoolhouse were plated with golden fire.

The crowd stood breathless, and more than one glanced uneasily about at the blue twilight and down into the deeper dusk of the open grave.

Samuel pulled out the small Bible he always carried in his back hip pocket, walked to the edge of the grave, and stood with it open in his hand. He had not brought his big Sunday Bible with Christ's words in red and the edges brushed with gold, nor had he worn the fine new suit Mrs. Hull had made him buy last Eastertime, and now he wished, with a heavy yearning sorrow unusual for him, that he had worn the suit and carried the big Bible.

There was some trouble with the plowlines; in their haste the bearers had left one end too short. First they tried pulling it under the coffin, but the line stuck in the mud and the coffin had to be lifted. The men, especially Keg Head and Blare, worked clumsily and too hurriedly, with many apprehensive glances at the ever-narrowing band of gold on the hills. Across the valley the schoolhouse windows had faded and the dark wood of Sue Annie's cabin had merged into the darkness of the pines.

There was a murmur of whispers in the crowd and a muted argument between Hattie and Milly; Hattie contended that it was foolish to hurry further, the sun had already set on the grave and that was all that mattered, while Milly, thinking ahead fearfully of all the bad luck such a thing could bring, insisted that as long as the sun shone on the high hills it had not set.

At last the plowlines were evened and the coffin lowered into the grave. But the last ray of light had faded from the ridge crest and there was nothing but the angry blood-red sunset light that lingered on the snow and dyed the pines.

Blare and Keg Head seized shovels and flung in each a shovelful of rocks and earth before Samuel, staring into the sunset, noticed and lifted his head in a short angry gesture.

"Brethern, we can take time for a bit of Scripture, I hope."

He held the Bible open in his hand, but he looked into the sunset and talked, not in his loud preacher's voice, but softly, like a man speaking to himself or to the sunset.

"Charity suffereth long, and is kind—" And he went on with the thirteenth chapter of First Corinthians, Paul's words he had tried so hard to live by—at times. He finished, and old Nancy, who was always first to shout in church, said "Amen."

Samuel looked around the crowd. "Let us kneel and pray," he said.

Hattie, who was holding her baby, and Flonnie Tiller, who had on a new coat, glanced warily down at the muddy snow and remained standing, while others who had grown overly warm in the long rush to the graveyard were beginning to feel the twilight cold and were eager to go home and had no wish to add further to the burden of bad luck brought by the setting sun to risk getting chilled after being wet with sweat.

Samuel dropped his knees flat in the mud, lifting his two arms in a commanding gesture, and said again, "Let us kneel."

Then the crowd knelt, and with his eyes fixed on the angry flush of light overhead, Samuel beseeched God:

"O Lord, this woman has died in sin. Her last words were black oaths. She screamed to die an be out of her misery; she hungered for death as a bridegroom hungereth for his bride. She sinned, O God, and her sin was black.

"Her sin was black, God, but my sin was blacker, God. We left her in want an misery. She knocked; we did not open th door. She asked, and we did not give.

"She suffered and it was not Thy will, O God, but man's greed, O God."

Keg Head lifted his head and looked fixedly at Samuel. "God's will was done," he intoned in a loud argumentative tone. "Sweet Jesus seeth th sparrow fall," Ann Liz chanted, while Milly and Flonnie intoned, "Amen, Sister."

"Th woman died because we stood by an watched her die fore we'd try to get a doctor," Samuel groaned. "Visit Thy wrath upon us, O God. But spare her. Scourge us, O God—we are the sinners—"

"Amen," Nunn said in a low fervent voice, and Milly for a moment forgot Samuel's terrible request for God's wrath in a foreboding that Nunn was going to take to preaching like Preacher Jim.

But Nunn's thoughts were far from God. He knelt—he had never been known to kneel in church or say Amen like the others—but held his head up, his wide-open eyes in his unbowed head were looking out into the troubled sunset, black bars of cloud across yellowish walls of light.

There'd be another tumble-down house on the road to Tuckerville now, and after a few years there'd be only a chimney where grew the little star flowers Aunt Marthie Jane had carried in her apron on a visit to old Prue and set behind the chimney sometime in the faraway golden years of his childhood.

The little star flower would bloom in the spring and the honeysuckle and trumpet flower and myrtle go climbing up the chimney—and after a while the government would buy the land and his house would be the last in this country. Would it go, too, and his children scatter and leave their graves to grow up in sumac brush and briars, the way the Ledbetter children left the graves of their parents and their brothers and sisters? His place could go, even in his own lifetime. His children could go, go out like half-feathered birds too weak to fight the world, like Lureenie—like Suse: if the thought struck her, she could go away and be married tomorrow to anything, a Cramer, or worse, one of the watery-eyed Gibsons from Barnett's Bend, born with the bad disease, and Suse's senses were all there were between her and the world. He couldn't give and he couldn't protect.

The sunset was the flushed face of an angry God glaring at him. The thoughts that tormented him, crazed him at moments when he was half drunken or half asleep, struck him like new pains from old wounds; he could have saved his two dead children. Angie Mime was dead almost before he knew. He remembered the fine fall nights, warm and still, when night after night it had seemed Zing would have King Devil before dawn. Before Tom died, he'd hunted all fall and left his corn too late in the river bottom; and there'd come a five-day rain to bring a November tide to the Big South Fork, and he and Milly had left the children and worked all day and part of the night getting out the corn, for it was all he had that year. Tom was already full of cold and croup, and while they were gone he had played in the rain. Nunn remembered Milly, tired and muddy, smacking Suse in the middle of the night, because when they came home they found Tom asleep in his wet clothes, and he remembered Suse, little and crying, all swagged-back from carrying Lucy in her arms. And Tom had got up next day, burning hot with something like the fever, Sue Annie said, but even then he could have gone for a doctor. He hadn't thought much about it then; he hadn't any money. Then King Devil had barked in the hills and his mind and his body and his heart had gone out after him.

King Devil had caused his children to die and his farm to stay in the brush and briars. King Devil had made Zing die, and he, Nunn, had got drunk that night and fought with the Cramers; and because he was mad at the Cramers, he had let Lureenie starve, and she was dead now. And that Red Devil of a fox that had ruined him was alive in the hills.

Milly touched him on the shoulder. He looked away from the sunset, darkening now, and saw that Samuel had finished and the crowd was going home. He helped fill up Lureenie's grave, and while they worked, fiddle music drifted down in a thin wail of sadness from Sue Annie's cabin on the hill—some hymn, he guessed it was; no dance tune, he was sure.

Keg Head said that it was a sin for that drunken old renegade Dave to play for a funeral, but Samuel said Lureenie had always liked music, and since old Dave was the only one who'd thought to give her any, he was glad and meant to go by and tell him so.

A silence lay on the men as they worked, and when the grave was mounded they went away quickly, with few words, each to his separate path, like men ashamed of themselves and of each other.

Nunn put up the bars, and when he started home he realized he was alone and the last to leave. He smiled a little, wondering were the others only forgetful or were they cowards. When a man was the last to leave an unlucky gathering like thirteen at table or a burying after sunset like this, the whole of the bad luck fell on the last man, but if several stayed and left together; it would be shared. Milly might worry but he wouldn't; he'd never in his life had any bad luck but what he'd brought on himself.

Chapter Thirty-three

AFTER LUREENIE'S DEATH and word the war had come to
Hawaii, where Olen Anderson trained, the people, like
children who, wading through ever deepening mud, feel
with their bare feet in eagerness for a stone, turned their
thoughts toward God and eternity, and from miles around
they flocked to both the morning and evening services of
Deer Lick Revival, where Battle John Brand told them in
many sermons and many prayers that God and God alone
could lead them through the seas of blood and pain and
sorrow that lay ahead.

Though it was known that Battle John and Samuel dif-
fered on many points of Scripture, some even hinting that
Battle John's beliefs were tinged somewhat by a sympathy
for a religious sect much like that Milly had joined in her
girlhood, most people, and particularly Milly, admired
the big, white-bearded, black-browed, blue-eyed man, and
looked upon a two-week revival conducted almost wholly
by him as a rare glory.

Back in the fall before Lureenie died, Milly, as soon
as she heard that Battle John was coming, had hurried
the walnut-kernel picking so that Suse could have decent
clothes to wear; and when she learned that Nunn meant to
sell all eight of the fattened pigs as well as Betsey's calf,
she put away her sorrow for the meatless winter and secretly hoped that he would supply what the walnut-kernel
money lacked and buy Suse a long coat with fur on the
collar, like Sureenie Cooksey's.

But when he came back from his day-long trip in Town,
she could have cried when she saw what he brought: a
little cheap, blue woolen jacket, so skimpy that when Suse

tried it on her wrists hung out red and raw-looking as a half-feathered chicken's wings, with the shoulder seams looking ready to split and her big bosoms pushing off the buttons. Suse jerked it off quick and then tried on the shoes, but she didn't like them either, and sassed her daddy. Didn't he know that all the girls, high-school girls, wore low-heeled shoes now, not patent leather like an old woman's, like Sue Annie's?

"But I couldn't git what you wanted in your size," Nunn said, meek as a lamb, so meek to a sassy child it riled Milly; and anyway, it seemed like she was the one ought to be quarreling; here she'd picked out walnut kernels all fall, hoping to get some pretty clothes for Suse; and he'd sold all the pigs and the calf, and all winter she'd have nothing to cook but beans, with chicken only for company, and hogs were sky-high—eleven cents a pound, he said he'd got—and then bought barely enough dry goods to keep them decent; only one length of piece goods, and that all of a pattern, cotton and cheap it looked to be, barely enough for her and the girls. She'd hoped he'd get her rayon stockings like Hattie and Flonnie Tiller had, and something for Bill Dan—he'd never had a thing but hand-me-downs since he was born. But instead of Nunn, her vexing disappointment turned on Suse. "Shut up, sassy big-mouth, you ain't no high-school girl; an your pop cain't help it cause you're so over-growed an your feet so big you cain't git em in a common-size shoe."

"Aw, Milly," Nunn said, handing her a square of sweet chewing tobacco, "don't be a haven th girl ashamed; why, her feet ain't so big, and she's a goen to be a fine big upstanden woman like Aunt Marthie Jane—Aunt Marthie wore a number seven shoe." He frowned over the too tight jacket. "Th clerk—she was a woman, young an mighty flippity—she ast me what your size an I said I didn't know—then she ast me your age an I said fourteen, an she said take size fourteen."

"Lord ha mercy, Nunn, honey; why, Suse'll be fifteen come February, an big to her age; enybody ud know fourteen was too little," Milly cried.

"Lord, Lord," Nunn said, and wished they'd all be quiet; after the trip to town his head felt all a-rattle. He was sorry in a way he'd been so stingy; but it was good to feel the debt was gone—all but $40; and Jude would pay that when he sold her in the spring.

Vinie came sniffing at his strange town smell, and he shooed her roughly away. If he could sell her and Sam as Elias Higginbottom was always plaguing him to do, he'd buy everything his womenfolks wanted and most of what he needed. As usual on a winter Saturday, he'd run into the county board member and they had talked awhile of hounds and hunting, and he'd promised the man that after the revival was over and the worst of the winter weather, he'd let him know when a big race was on so that he and Pinkney could come and bring their hounds; Elias had long wanted a chase after the big red fox he'd heard so much about.

Nunn felt better about Suse's revival outfit when two or three days later Milly called him into the fireplace room to see Suse in her new blue dress. She looked pretty as a picture with her straight proud back and high head with the long red-brown braids would round it like a queen's crown, but little wisps escaping to make curls about her neck and ears; he didn't want to tell her she was pretty for fear of making her vain, but he did tell her he bet she looked the way Aunt Marthie Jane had when she was a girl.

Suse patiently turned this way and that while Milly admired her handiwork and studied the hang of the hem with tilted head. She didn't want to hurt her mother's feelings when she'd put so much of the new blue cloth into her dress that there was only enough left for a dress for Lucy and an apron for Milly, but she guessed she did look the way Aunt Marthie Jane had looked not long after the Civil War, and she knew she wouldn't wear dress, jacket, or shoes to church. The dress was too long, long as an old woman's, for it didn't show her knees the way Ruby's and Sureenie's clothes did, and it seemed like Milly knew only one way to make a dress, long sleeves, full skirt gathered into a tight band; maybe, as Milly said, the style was becoming, for her waist was small; but the other girls were wearing skirts and sweaters or rayon dresses, and this thing was cotton—cheap cotton. She'd die before she'd have Andy see her so.

During the first few days of the revival, Milly quarreled at her continually because she wouldn't go, though Nunn,

as if suspecting what the trouble was, told her she ought
to go, but never insisted, and when Milly quarreled too
much, reminded her it was a handy thing to have Suse
stay home of nights with the three least ones. Sometimes
when Milly had gone, Suse would take out the blue jacket
and try it on, then quickly take it off again, her eyes
bright with angry tears. The revival was getting more and
more exciting; Milly was always bringing home stories of
how this one shouted or that one talked in the unknown
tongue, but more than that, Suse liked the bits of news
she brought, mostly stories of the German spies in the
county that she'd heard from the Tillers and the Sextons,
and of men going away to work or to war.

Suse wondered at times about Mark, but never asked;
nobody had heard from Rans, and it was pretty well
agreed that he had either left Cincinnati and forgotten his
wife and children or got into some bad meanness and
landed in jail. Keg Head's wife, people said, was almost
as bad worried over her Rans as old Aunt Hannah Anderson was over Olen. Then one morning, three or four
days after the opening of the revival, Suse stirred the gravy
round and round in careful unconcern while Milly told
that Ann Liz Cooksey had told her that Keg Head had
persuaded Mark to go from Detroit to Cincinnati and try
to find his brother; Mark hadn't said exactly when he
would do it, but from the sound of his letter they thought
he'd be in home by Christmas.

That morning Suse hummed as she washed the dishes;
it was nice to think Mark might be in any time; she
wouldn't be in church, but he might come by the house
and she could see him; she hoped he wouldn't try to kiss
her but would tell her all about Detroit; most like he
would—he was kind. If he had been in the country, Lureenie wouldn't have died; Mark wouldn't say she had
died because she was proud-turned and mean—he'd hate
the others who'd let Lureenie die the way she hated them
at times. Maybe he would come sometime while she and
Nunn sawed ties; with him she never thought about her
old clothes and how she looked; seemed like it was only
with Andy she was so bashful.

The next news Milly brought couldn't wait till morning;
Suse awakened to hear her mother telling it to Nunn as
they sat by the fire, warming after the long cold trip

down from Deer Lick Meeting House. "I think it's a sin,
a black, black sin in a preacher an his wife," Milly was
saying; and Suse lay still under the covers to learn about
the sin, and heard soon that the sinner was Samuel, who
wasn't making all his children come to hear Battle John;
Andy hadn't been once, and when Hattie Tiller asked
Mrs. Hull why he didn't come, she'd said that Andy didn't
want to miss school for the morning service and
wanted to study in the evening, and that it was a big help
to her to have him willing to stay home with the little
youngens. Milly sighed and wished she could persuade
Suse to go; people would be saying she made the girl stay
home.

Next morning, when Milly began her usual begging of
Suse to go, Suse surprised everybody by getting into her
new clothes and making the long trip with the rest of the
family up and around to Deer Lick, though when they
had reached the gravel, Suse began to wish she hadn't
come, and tried to think of some excuse for turning
back, or at least lingering behind the rest of her family.
She knew they all looked like something she had seen a
few times in a chance daily paper; squares of pictures with
a little reading, funny reading, and funny back-hill people to make you laugh. Milly, as always when she took
the little youngens, rode ahead on big slow-footed Maude;
that was bad enough, but she rode an old sidesaddle
that had belonged to Aunt Marthie Jane, and instead of
putting Bill Dan in front and Deb behind, she'd rigged up
a set of old mail saddlebags that had been in the storehouse and put a child into each, with enough baked sweet
potatoes and late pears on Bill Dan's side to make the
bags balance. On either side of the pacing mare trailed a
hound, behind came Lucy in Suse's old coat cut down to
her skimpy size; Nunn and Lee Roy came next, with Suse
as far behind as possible.

Though the day was chill with a northeast wind, Suse,
when they neared the churchyard, took off her jacket
and carried it on her arm like one warm from overmuch
walking. In the churchyard she walked more slowly still,
lingering as long as it was decent for a grown girl to stay
outside the church house, in order to listen to the men
gathered in little knots and groups as they talked, not, as
in other years, of crops, neighbors, politics, and religion,

but of the war and the wild excitement in the outside world.

Even the older and more religious, including John, Andrew, who had dismissed school for the revival, and Keg Head, all gathered about Battle John and some stranger visiting deacons, were touched by the war; and Suse shivered in a kind of joyful excitement as Battle John lifted his voice and intoned: *"And I looked, and behold a pale horse: and his name that sat on him was Death, and Hell followed with him. And power was given unto them over the fourth part of the earth, to kill with sword, and with hunger, and with death, and with the beasts of the earth."*

But Keg Head contended that the fourth seal was not yet broken, but only the second seal as yet, the red horse with a sword that was to take peace from the earth. Old John, listening in the absentminded way of a man who has heard Revelation quoted through three wars, smiled at her, and she went on, but paused again near a group listening in some excitement to Blare Tiller.

She gathered there'd been another wreck on the railroad; two box cars went off the track about midway of Rattlesnake Curve yon side of the valley tunnel. Blare was certain it was the work of a German spy, there was one who lived not ten miles away. "I've allus said he'd bear watchen," Blare said. "What ud he come to these parts fer in th first place—claimed him an his wife was wore out with city liven—an they come here frum a way off fer their heatlh. Weak lungs he claims he's got—"

But Blare was cut short by a excited Sexton who declared the FBI had found another German spy in Town; for thirty years or more he'd lived in Town and pretended to be a doctor, but truth will out, and he was the own born son of a man whose father came over from Germany. "He had a cellar full a bombs an—"

Suse heard no more. Ann Liz Cooksey, with a white handkerchief fluttering in one big brown hand, was bearing down upon her; behind her came Sureenie with the baby, Cureetie close behind with the diapers; little Dovie followed with the Bible, and young Willie next, with a jar of pickles to go with the family dinner, which was carried in split baskets and buckets of various sizes by Willie and the five oldest boys. Ann Liz smiled and clapped her on the shoulder and declared she was pretty as a picture, and why hadn't she been to church, and was Milly inside; she'd been meaning to ask her for a quilt pattern.

Suse smiled and tried to talk, but all the while she was trying to make the blue woolen jacket small under her arm, and at the same time trying not to look at Sureenie's fur-collared coat as if she wished she had one like it.

The church house was filled with the murmuring of women's voices as they sat in quiet decorum, many with babies on their laps, waiting for the services to begin. Suse followed Ann Liz to the bench near the stove on which Milly sat with the Tiller women, and listened while Hattie Tiller told of the dream she'd had last night: she had seen a red cedar coffin—bright it was, like gold in a low-setting sun—by a green, green grave, like a grave in spring. Strange, now, wasn't it, like a token or a sign, to dream of a casket by a green-mounded grave?

Milly told of how she dreamed one night of Angie Mime, her face and part of her body all floating, like out of a mist, and glad she had looked and smiling, like a child gazing on a thing well loved. And Hattie said the dream meant that someone Angie Mime loved was to join her soon in heaven; and Milly, listening, clutched Bill Dan tightly to her breast, then asked aloud the forgiveness of God. God's will was God's will; if he wanted to take another one to the graveyard and then to heaven to meet the ones already there, His will be done.

Little, still-turned Flonnie Tiller, who seldom spoke at home but often shouted in church, told in a low hesitant voice of how she had dreamed of a blooming pear tree in which sang a flaming bird; and the bird sang with a sweet sad calling that made her want to follow; but when she tried to get up and follow the calling, she awoke, and seemed like for a long time she was lonesome there in the dark for the bird, even with Blare and the youngens sleeping around her.

Suse, too, had had a dream, but she never told it. She'd dreamed one night that she was with Lureenie somewhere in a kitchen with a big cookstove range like Ann Liz Cooksey's, and Lureenie looked the way Suse remembered her when she moved into the valley and Suse was a little girl, curls down her shoulders and pretty even teeth flashing below her laughing eyes. The two of them were looking at a cake they'd baked, all colored with Lureenie's cake coloring, the bottom layer palely pink, growing pinker through three more layers until the topmost was almost red; it was the prettiest cake, baked just right in a big bake oven; she was smearing on the frosting, real sugar frosting, when Milly had awakened her.

"What are you a laughen at?" Milly had wanted to know, and had come to the bed and felt her forehead to see if she was feverish with fransied dreams. And Suse had lain a long time crying, with her pillow pulled over her head so that none could hear.

Mrs. Hull came in and asked her to sit in the choir. Suse flushed, thinking of her clothes, and would have refused; but Rachel, who wore the same clothes she would have worn to school, came laughing and pulling at her hand and bade her go.

Once on the platform behind the pulpit, she was glad she had come; singing with the others helped pass the time away, and only a few feet away was a window through which her bored glance often passed during Battle John's sermon and the long, long prayers of Keg Head and the shorter ones of John and Samuel and the visiting deacons. And the old wish that had come often, with sharp hopeless longing, the last few months, the wish she'd been a boy, came back again as she watched Lee Roy go by toward the back of the graveyard where the bigger boys and the unsaved of the men, such as Nunn and the Andersons, pitched horseshoes on the sunny mornings.

They pitched at a decent distance from the churchhouse door, but often the thundering voice of Battle John would sweep their way, rising above the clink of the horseshoes, and the men would pause, horseshoes in hand, and hush their low-toned talk and listen, though often, as in the case of Nunn, it was against their will.

And as the revival meetings mounted in heat and fervor, and every night and almost every morning another sinner came sobbing to the mourners' bench, seeking God's grace and eternal salvation, the crowd of horseshoe pitchers thinned by days; at night, all, even the wildest of the boys, stood listening in the darkness past the open door. God's wrath seemed in the thunderous fire of Battle John's voice, and when he called with a mighty but musical bellowing for sinners to come to the mourner's bench and cry for their souls lost in sin and wasted in immorality, even as Rachel wept in the wilderness for her lost children, reminding his hearers always that tomorrow might be too late, everlastingly too late, many thought of Gabriel's horn on the judgment day, calling men to justice before a stern-eyed God from whom there'd be no turning away.

And on the night Battle John preached from the text *The harvest is passed, the summer is ended, and still we are not saved,* the unsaved men and boys pressed ever nearer the open door, then began a silent, almost furtive slipping into the house, as if God pulled them against their will, and soon they overflowed the backmost benches and stood in the open spaces about the door and by the walls.

Nunn had listened from the beginning, drawn by childhood memories of Preacher Jim preaching from the same worn black walnut pulpit and the same text, his voice less loud than Battle John's but filled with an inexpressible sorrow and foreboding as he cried out to his people: *"The harvest is passed, the summer is ended, and still we are not saved."*

Like Preacher Jim, Battle John began by picturing the joys of the year's good harvest, speaking in a joyous chant as he enumerated the various crops of the countryside and how, now that the season was ended, they were stored for the winter, and that God in his mercy had given an abundance so that there need be no hunger for man or beast.

And he pictured God's harvest of souls in heaven: the greeting by the heavenly choir with golden harps and many songs, and the gentle kindness of God and of Christ as the weary, the hungry, the sick and the old, the persecuted, the crippled, the poor and the sorrowful, the afflicted who had known life on earth only as one long road of pain, traveled only with the help of God—but at last the long rocky uphill path, beset by thorns for aching feet and rain and heat and cold and darkness, was ended, and the soul came at last to heaven and the throne of God.

Then, from gazing upward toward God's throne, Battle John lowerel his head and smiled upon the people, whispering: *"And I saw the dead, small and great, stand*

*before God, having the harps of God—and God shall wipe
away all tears from their eyes; and there shall be no
more death, neither sorrow, nor crying, neither shall there
be any more pain, for the former things are passed
away.*

"*They shall hunger no more, neither thirst any more;
neither shall the sun light on them, nor any heat*—" His
voice rose a little as he looked at the women, gathered
mostly in the center of the house near the stove. "Your
time of weepen an of pain, dear sistern, will soon be
ended here on earth; but, oh good sistern," and he looked
at Milly and then at Jaw Buster's wife, "will you weep in
heaven? Will you be lonesome in heaven—will your family circle be unbroken? Your little ones has gone afore
ye; your fathers an your mothers, they dwell in the Promised Land an sing th song of Moses an the Lamb, but
what about your husbands? Ah-h-h, will you see them in
heaven—drinken, carousen, fox-hunten, liven in sin? An
your grown sons an pretty daughters. Ah-h-h, women, will
they come to you in heaven, or will you be lonesome in
the Promised Land? You'll play a golden harp an wear a
jeweled crown an sing around th throne of God, but,
oh sistern, will there be tears in your eyes as you sing?

"Will your men an your sons an your daughters, will
they be a part of God's harvest? Will they meet you on
th banks of th river Jordan? Or will you be alone, dear
sistern—alone—everlastenly alone, while them you love
are cast into outer darkness an cry to you frum th flames
of hell?"

Bill Dan and others of the babies stirred in their sleep
as their mothers' tears fell on their faces; and all over
the house the saved, both young and old, sought with their
eyes the unsaved of their kin. Some half rose in their
seats to go and search out the sinning loved ones, but
Battle John stayed the movement with an uplifted hand
as his voice rose above the sobs of the women and the
cries of "Glory," and "Amen, brother," from the deacons
and visiting preachers.

"There is another harvest, dear brethern, dear sistern
—th reaper is never aweary; ever day to him is as a day
of victory; he gits your sons, he gits your daughters, he
gits your men. An how does he git em, dear sistern? How
does he git em? Ah-h-h, he leads em to put off till tomor-

row what ought to be done today. 'I'll have my fun,' th
sinner says, 'an when I'm old an wore out an my time
comes to die, I'll repent."—Repent, th sinner says.
Ah-h-h-, th devil never tells him that some day, some
hour, some minute, it may be too late, everlastenly too
late, too late, too late."

He lifted his arms and looked up through the roof to
where God seemed to have stopped work in heaven to
listen with downbent head, as Battle John's voice rose into
a crying wail of sorrow and foreboding of doom. "Too late
—too late, th sinner learns th devil's got him; night an day
he mourns, but God don't hear him when he screams, '*O
Lord, how long shall I cry, and thou wilt not hear! even
cry unto thee of violence, and thou wilt not save*'—not
save—not save. Do you hear that, you sinners by th
door? You're a standen there a thinken God is like to a
fisherman patient to stand all day an take ever fish that'ull
bite, but God ain't like that—no—," and he groaned,
remembering the dark mysterious ways of God.

"Brethren, if you leave your corn in th shock through
a warm wet winter, do you harvest it come spring when
it's sprouted en rotted? No—no. God don't want a rotten
soul in his harvest neither.

"If you leave your sweet taters undug till there comes
a hard killen frost, will you harvest th sweet taters? No
—no. Their harvest time is past; they're left to rot, worthless to you even as your soul may be worthless to God.
You sinners, a standen back there a thinken God will
save you when you take th notion—it's th devil a maken
you think that. Recollect Jesus said, *Not every one that
saith unto me, Lord, Lord, shall enter into the kingdom
of heaven.*

"How do you know you've not committed th unpardonable sin? How do you know less'n you see if'n you can
git th grace of God? They's many a one prayed an cried
an cried an prayed an never got it; they cried, 'Lord,
Lord,' but it was too late. Maybe th young mother who
went from your midst so short a time ago, maybe as she
lay a dyen she cried, 'Lord, Lord,' but was she saved? Did
she repent? Ah-h-h, brethren, she put it off. An now it's
too late, everlastenly too late—too late."

The women, remembering Lureenie, cried afresh, and
Keg Head, after a loud "Amen, Brother," began a sob-

bing chant as tears rolled down his face, "Pray fer her man, my son; pray fer her little children I've took to raise; pray, brethern an sistern, pray."

Battle John paused for a drink and went on, now in the hushed tone men use around the dead. "Ah, think of th woman, young—in th yers to come her little children will visit her grave an they'll whisper, 'Mommy, will we see you in paradise?' An frum th flames uv hell that mother will look upward an try to whisper 'No.' Her man is young, of a God-fearen family; he may knock and God may answer, but he'll never see that wife in heaven —no—no—too late, everlastenly too late."

And he sobbed, while great tears, shining like pearls in the yellow light, fell from his face.

"Aye, Lord, brethern, fear not death. Death is a little thing. *The day of trouble is near;* death is all around us. *The sword is without, and the pestilence and the famine within. The vine of the earth is gathered and cast into the great winepress of the wrath of God.* No, no, fear not death. *Fear not them which kill the body . . . but rather fear him which is able to destroy both soul and body.*"

He paused and asked in a low conversational tone, pointing his finger toward the men in the door, directly at Nunn it seemed, though he was almost completely hidden among the big Anderson men: "Now, what, brother, can destroy both soul an body, destroy your soul so's there'll never be a harvest for God? Strong drink? No. Whoring women? No—no. A breaken all th Ten Commandments? No. It's th devil, brother, th devil a worken in you. How do you know he's not a worken in you now, Did Judas know, long, long afore he betrayed th Son a God? Did Peter know? Maybe God has turned you over to be tempted of the devil even as he turned Job an his own born Son. Are youen strong in th armor of righteousness an th sword and buckler of th Lord to withstand that temptation? Ah-h-h, th devil is strong, mighty strong; weak souls are to him as corn is to hungry swine. He laughs an rubs his hands and smacketh his lips with th joyful gloating of a hungry man sitting down to a well filled table. Ah, brethern, th devil enjoys his harvest."

And then Battle John laughed; he threw back his great white-haired head and laughed, a long shrill wild laugh that made the padding hound dogs pause and study him with lifted heads in perplexity; he threw his head back and under his white upstanding beard the laughter gurgled down his hairy throat and in his belly made a loud ho-ho-ing; his hairy chest showing beneath his unbuttoned sweat-stained shirt heaved; his eyes from being softly filmed with tears were hard with the satanic laughter, glittering as the serpent's eyes doubtlessly glittered in the Garden, and his brows, thick with tufts of long up-curving hairs in the center, were black above the blue glittering eyes.

Satan's laughter rang through the house and out the door, and the thumping ho-ho-ho's roused the hitched mules drowsing under the white oak trees until they stood ears a-twitch and heads lifted. When it seemed the laugh would never end, Battle John dropped his chin, smoothed down his flustered beard, and smiled gently on the congregation and said in a choked tearful voice, as one crushed down with an infinite sorrow, "Ah, yes, my friends, th devil laughs to find you in his harvest, an God weeps. He hates to see you cast into hell an outer darkness. Ah, good sistern, think how it ud be to have a loved one burn up afore your eyes, an you could see th flames —fire an dark—fire an dark—that's hell. All things are possible with God; only God could make a hell.

"You'll cry, 'Oh, woe. Woe is me—woe, everlasten woe.'" And he descibed hell, described it until even Lee Roy shuddered and Lucy went all a tremble, never hearing Milly's thrice-repeated hiss to let go her neck for she was choking the life out of her; and then as he went on describing the flaming serpents with red-hot scales and smoking breath that wrapped themselves about the sinful sons of men, Milly forgot Lucy was choking her windpipe and never noticed that Bill Dan had pulled his head from the fresh breast she had given him and that her milk went in a fine spray over her dress and as far as Sue Annie sitting in front of her.

Instead of God, the devil now sat on the roof, and the snakes and the flames of hell pushed against the windows, and the darkness of night now became the outer darkness peopled with tormented souls.

Even the men and boys standing in the back where Nunn stood were motionless, their eyes unblinking and fixed in terror, like the eyes of fresh-caught fish. Nunn's eyes alone moved, jumping first this way and then that, like hunted squirrels in a treeless field; now and then some word of Battle John's came to him or Keg Head's sobbing cries of "Woe—woe. Spare us, Lord," and Flonnie Tiller's echoing, "Yeah—spare us, Lord."

Nunn was hearing still Battle John's cry, "Did Peter know—did Judas know?" Preacher Jim had asked the question when he was a boy and he had known the answers, but the answers hadn't mattered. Peter had never known he would deny Christ, and after knowing, he had gone out and wept bitterly. Did he, Nunn, know he would chase a fox the rest of his days—would he moonshine again come spring? What would he do? Did God know? Did the devil know? Could he right now walk up to the mourners' bench and get the grace of God and leave the fox and the hounds and the whisky all behind? Would God give him peace and grace and save his soul? It seemed his only chance. He licked his dry lips and thought of his children dead and Lureenie dead—dead maybe partly because of him. He saw Suse in the choir—she looked now the way she often did at home, angry and sullen and sad; in her whole life she'd hardly ever had a thing she wanted—this last batch of canned dog feed had cost more than her clothes. She was standing there now, ashamed of her cheap skimpy clothes.

Suse, however, wasn't thinking of her clothes; though only that morning she had complained of having but the new dress to wear, and that everybody knew she'd missed the day before because she'd had to wash and starch and iron her dress. She stood now and looked at Battle John and hated him, and felt herself an outcast and a sinner, knowing that if he spoke the truth and Lureenie was in hell, she hated God also, hated Him almost as much as she did some of the people around her who during the revival talked about Lureenie, with her soul lost to perdition, in sly tiptoeing voices, the pitying but self-satisfied voices of women bound for heaven while Lureenie screamed in hell.

At school, when there was nothing else to do and nothing else to read, Suse had read much in old Andrew's big Bible and had at times puzzled over many things, but until tonight the puzzles and the mysteries of the Bible had seemed far away from her troubles as a human being here on earth. And much of what she read had seemed kind and clear and comforting, like the words of someone very old and very wise and kind—kinder than Nunn and Milly. But since Lureenie's death and the tears of the righteous like Keg Head, not for the cruelty here on earth that made Lureenie want to die or maybe even killed her, but for her soul, though she had been a good and righteous woman, Suse had wondered at times about the whole pattern of sin and immortality.

She stood staring with clenched hands, hardly noticing that Battle John had reached the gasping state where every third sound was an exaggerated "Ah" of breathing, and every second gesture was that of wiping sweat from his face and neck. He had finished with hell and was now the voice in the wilderness, crying with lifted arms, "Repent—*repent ye: for the kingdom of heaven is at hand.*" He gave a mighty strangling "Ah," and lifted his arms, crying, "Pray, sistern, pray; pray, brethren, pray; pray for these a weepen on th mourners' bench ah; pray fer the stiff-necked sinners back by th door ah; go seek them out an soften their hard hearts with your prayers ah, an your tears ah; pray, sistern, pray."

And he collapsed in the pulpit chair while the women and the older of the saved men, who for the last few minutes had been craning their heads to search out sinning neighbors and relatives, now arose with solemn tearful faces and began their work of praying by those on the mourners' bench or urging the stiff-necked and stubborn to come to the mourners' bench or at least walk up and give a hand to the preacher as a token they wished the prayers of the righteous.

The choir under the leadership of Blare Tiller, who had been saved since childhood, began, "Are you Washed in the Blood of the Lamb,"

Suse roused a little from her denial of God as set forth by Battle John and sang wih the others and watched to see if Milly would start in her direction to fall on her shoulder and weep, wetting her neck with hot tears as she prayed in a loud sobbing voice for the sins of her daughter. Milly had done that for three nights now, much to Suse's anger and embarrassment; it seemed to Suse that she had little sin compared to Ruby Tiller, who was

saved and so was never bothered. But she, like Ann Liz
Cooksey's Sureenie who sat beside her, had blushed and
sweated but borne it all with meekly downcast eyes; and
now Suse saw Ann Liz start as usual for her Sureenie, but
as she came up the platform steps, Ann Liz turned and
glanced despairingly toward the door through which unsaved Willie had always slipped at the end of every sermon, and often before the end, like Nunn.

But tonight Willie, in common with the rest of the men,
and even the boys, had stayed, some held still in the long
wonder of the road to hell, others afraid to venture out
into the devil-ridden dark, but most, like Lee Roy, stood
waiting in expectation of some rare good shouting after
such a hot sermon. Shouting and hysterical babbling from
an overflow of the spirit were uncommon in Deer Lick
Church, for Preacher Samuel frowned upon such and was
fond of quoting: *Let all things be done decently and in
order,* and: *For they think that they shall be heard for
their much speaking.* But since the coming of Battle John,
more than one had shouted, and Flonnie Tiller spoke
every night in unknown tongues, too carried away in
sanctification to notice Samuel's dark frowning glance,
just as tonight Sue Annie alone remarked how he frowned
each time Battle John quoted a verse of Scripture from
which he left out a word or so the better to drive his point
home, or ran verses of two different books of the Bible
into one, or quoted half a verse as a whole, and Sue
Annie had noticed, too, that when Battle John spoke of
Lureenie, Samuel's frowns were blacker still, though all
evening he, as well as John, had not been overly sparing
with words of condonation, such as "Amen" and "God
bless you, Brother."

Suse saw Ann Liz look once at Willie, then whirl and
start in his direction, and the quick hope came that tonight Milly would leave her alone and go pray over Nunn,
who stood near Willie, his face pale, his big eyes, bigger
and sadder than common, fixed on Preacher Samuel.

Suse craned her head to see if Milly went to Nunn, but
the Sexton women on their way to their men behind her,
unsaved, but forced into the choir because of their bass
voices, were all around her; then Millie was upon her,
crying in the sobbing chant that came to her only in the
church, "Oh, my daughter, think on your sins, come up

an mourn fer your sins, pray that God in his mercy can look down an give you grace an peace everlasten."

Suse sang on, staring straight before her, anger brimming in her red flushed face, her shoulders stiff and unyielding under Milly's encumbering arm. Milly kissed her cheeks repeatedly with weeping slobbering kisses, and Suse struggled against the rising anger and repulsion. At home it was, "Do this, do that—shit-fire, Suse, you'll have all th neighbors talken." But here it was all love and kisses. She couldn't recollect when anybody had kissed her at home.

"Recollect your sins, oh-h-h, recollect your sins, my daughter," Milly chanted as Suse sang on, her hands clenched at her sides.

Sureenie Cooksey, on seeing that Willie had stopped to be prayed for, fell all awash with tears and scuttled to the mourners' bench. This left a gap on Suse's other side that Hattie quickly filled; her head was now on Suse's other shoulder and she was sobbing, "Oh, young woman, go an pray fer your sins—pray, pray, fore it's too late, everlastenly too late."

"Yes," Milly chanted, her tears rolling down Suse's neck, "don't stand stiff-necked an stubborn—th Lord's a watchen."

Hattie's snuff-smelling mouth was near Suse's as she chanted, "He's a waiten, a waiten with outspread arms—someday it'll be too late—don't be like Lureenie."

Suse's clenched hands moved suddenly outward and her bent elbows struck both her mother and Hattie, for it seemed like a ball of fire shot through her head when Hattie Tiller—the lying gossip—the dirty-mouthed mother of Ruby—spoke in slobbery pity of Lureenie. "Lureenie," Suse said, and she knew the words ought to stop, but they wouldn't, "was a God damn sight better'n a lot a th sanctified sinners that let her starve an can't quit talken about her even when she's dead."

"Woman, you're fergitten you're in the Lord's house," Hattie said. "You ain't out in a field like th time you cussed out yer pap an Blare heared you."

"An Ruby can still cuss like a mule driver, if Sue Annie's to be believed," Milly said, her voice hard with anger, and her angry glance fixed on Hattie instead of Suse.

"Believe th words a th infidels like Sue Annie if you want to," Hattie said and smiled as she turned away.

" 'Are you washed' "— Suse sang, and would not look at Milly, who stood a moment breathing hard, before she said with a chaotic mingling of anger and sorrow and pity, too: "Suse, this is a black disgrace you've put on yerself an them that raised you. You—you'll never live it down."

" 'In th blood a th Lamb?' " Suse sang, and didn't care; she didn't have to live it down—she'd be an outcast all right—she'd go away.

After a moment Milly went away and a growing loneliness laid hold of Suse, and from being brash and bold, she wanted to cry—and for a moment was afraid she would and that someone would see and think she was weeping for her sins, so that soon all the women in the house would come weeping over her to pray.

But from the growing commotion in the back of the house, she realized with much relief that tonight the women were occupied chiefly with the unsaved of their men. She wondered if Nunn would get religion; he'd looked so pale and strange a while ago, but most likely he'd only been drinking—J. D. Duffey, she'd heard it said, had gone back to stilling again and had peddled out a mule load of moonshine every night of the meeting— she hoped it was whisky instead of religion working in him. If he got religion and acted like Milly, he'd never let her out if the house after this night's doings. She tried to see him, but he was lost in the press of the bigger people all about him—a chunk of the group broke away and started down the aisle toward the mourners' bench— Willie Cooksey, surrounded by his womenfolk, walking stiff-legged and glassy-eyed, with Ann Liz shouting and weeping, "Two a my family's a tryen to find th road to glory, Lord. Hear their prayers, O God—Pray, brethern, pray—"

Battle John was striding down the aisle to grasp Willie's hand, and Keg Head, praying by the shivering weeping Sureenie, lifted his arms on seeing Willie and cried, "Glory be to God, brethern—another lost sheep a hunten th fold."

Suse now could see her father. Milly was kneeling on the floor, her arms twined around his knees; Hattie Tiller had one arm across his shoulder and her upturned face

was aflood with tears as she prayed, while Flonnie and
J. D. Duffey's wife, their babies in their arms, and Nancy
Ballew stood facing him, their voices in prayerful, sobbing
supplication mingled in a babbling chant so mixed and
twisted that to Nunn it seemed wordless, and he thought
of the Tower of Babel. Preacher Jim had preached on
that long ago when he was young and before he had
known sin. He wished they would go away and wondered
why he had stayed—maybe this night he could give his
heart to God and God would save his soul. He took one
step forward, and Milly, kneeling by his shoes, sprang up
with a joyful smile. He never saw her; he never saw anything around him. He was thinking of another night two
falls back, about this time of year—the night King
Devil's eyes had for an instant glowed in the dark and he
had thought he would kill him—why hadn't he known he
couldn't kill him? He knew now he could never let him
go; if he didn't know it, God did, and would never give
him grace. He turned and went toward the door—as he
walked, he felt a hard strong hand on his shoulder, and
Samuel was saying in the quiet everyday voice with
which he sold groceries, *"It is good that a man should
both hope and quietly wait for the salvation of the Lord."*

It was cold outside, and he stood a moment on the
church steps, shivering, his body damp with sweat. A cigarette glowed in the darkness and a voice he recognized as
Jaw Buster's called in a hissing whisper, "Nunn. Nunn
—I thought you never was a comen. They's a good race
on. Listen." And far away, crossing Kelly's Point it
sounded, he heard Vinie following a fox, and from the
wild anger of her singing cry, it was a close race and the
fox was red.

"I waited for you," said Jaw Buster, after he had listened for and heard his Speed. "Seems like we're about
all that's left to hunt. Th rest has either gone er got
religion—an I've been thinken lately that when somethen
happens to Speed—he's gitten purty old—I'll quit the
business like Lister done."

"We'll go to Schoolhouse Point an listen," Nunn said.

Milly had watched Nunn out the door, then turned to
the mourners' bench to help in the prayers. She envied
Ann Liz Cooksey with two of her family repentant. She,
Milly, had led a godly life, yet none of her own would so

much as let themselves be prayed for; now that lying,
long-tongued Hattie would smear it all over the country
that Suse had cussed a blue streak in church and hit her
mother. The word, she knew, had slipped out—Suse
hadn't meant it any more than she'd meant to hit her with
her elbow, but Hattie wouldn't tell it that way. Oh, Lord,
she did wish Suse could get some sense. She saw Deb and
Bill Dan and Lucy asleep on the bench and wished they
were home—in spite of the growth of his tizic tree, Deb
still had tizic and the croup, and from the looks of things
—eight on the mourners' bench now—they'd all be
praying here till midnight. And Nunn striding around
outside, waiting for her in the cold; it was hard on him
to wait so. She roused Lucy from her nodding half-sleep
and told her to go tell Suse that as soon as she'd finished
this song to take Bill Dan and Deb to the door. Nunn
would be close by the door; he was every night; Suse was
to take Deb and Bill Dan and go home with him. Lucy
and Lee Roy would stay and come home with Milly when
the prayers were over.

Suse tossed her head defiantly on learning Milly's commands—Milly could have told her herself, without having
Lucy coming so biggity and bossylike to tell her what to
do—but Milly, she guessed, was too mad to speak to her;
most likely she'd get a whipping tomorrow and Milly
wouldn't let her come to another meeting of the revival.
She hated Milly for sending her home now—Lee Roy
would get to hear the shouting and the unknown-tongue
talk while she had to take the babies home like an old
married woman.

Battle John called on the choir to sing "Jesus Is Calling," sing it with their hearts and try to get at least one
penitent through to God; and Suse was trilling, "Come
home, come home," not thinking of the words or Milly's
anger, but listening to Keg Head's sobbing chanted
prayers, and feeling alone, almost afraid in her loneliness,
for it seemed to her she hated God. She could never love
God, not after Battle John's sermon tonight—Lureenie
would go to hell. Was that right, now? And God seemed
unjust and cruel, more cruel and unjust than Milly or
that lying Hattie could ever be. They, at least, wouldn't
stand by and let a woman starve, and had they sat at the
Last Supper in the place of Christ, knowing what He

knew, they would have told Judas and he would have
gone away and so saved his soul from hell.

She shivered at the sinfulness of her thoughts and
looked about the church, her eyes searching from point
to point, hunting she knew not what, anything to take her
mind from God. Sue Annie, dignified in a black hat and
her black-silk Sunday dress, all bought with baby-catching
money, smiled at her as she relieved Flonnie Tiller of her
baby, so that Flonnie might be unencumbered when
time for shouting came. Sue Annie had never been on a
mourners' bench or made a profession of faith. Some
hinted that she was an infidel, but when questioned by
the few bold enough to risk her tongue, she had always
answered that if she ever did happen to get religion, she'd
be certain to lose it on the next baby case; but she always
came to church and watched the goings-on and tended
the babies and warned women far gone in pregnancy
against over-much shouting and excitement. Suse wondered now if Sue Annie knew what she had done; she
wondered if when Sue Annie was a girl she had ever
quarreled with God as she quarreled now.

Then back by the door, his uplifted face clear in the
lamplight, she saw Mark Cramer. Her tongue stumbled
over the words of the song, then stopped altogether, and
she stood looking at him—one moment remembering with
blushes the letter she'd sent him telling him she missed
him and wished she could see him—and the next all in
a happy confusion of gladness that he had come. She no
longer felt an outcast in a lonely world; Jesus and God
couldn't understand how she felt about this hateful place
and the hateful people, but Mark would. He stood still
with his hat in his hand and watched his father pray with
the same air with which he had watched Miss Burdine
that night in Sue Annie's cabin—and then he looked at
her, hunting her out with one movement of his head, as if
he had looked at her so many times he knew exactly
where to find her. She gave him one quick warm smile,
then dropped her eyes, shamed, for in all her inward tur-
moil of anger and loneliness and shame and gladness at
seeing him, she thought again she was going to cry—for
Mark would understand why she cried.

The song was finished and Suse sat down with the rest
of the choir, determined now to stay until everybody
should go home, but Milly lifted her head from praying

over Sureenie and shot a hard commanding glance in her direction; and Suse, in reluctant slowness, put on the blue woolen jacket and went to the sleeping babies, embarrassedly aware that Mark was watching her.

When she picked him up and wrapped him in his blanket, Bill Dan began a lusty squalling, and Deb, holding to her dress tail, whimpered to be carried, too. And as she went down the aisle past Mark, who smiled at her, she could not keep back hot angry despairing tears. She had wanted so to speak with him, to hear him tell about Detroit.

She pushed her way through the crowd in the back, most all of whom were too taken up with the goings-on around the mourner's bench to notice her passing.

She stood on the porch and called Nunn softly three times, but Maude's nickering from the white oak grove was her only answer, and no one outside to ask where he might be. She tossed her head, squared her shoulders, h'isted Deb to her other hip and went on toward Maude; she could, if she had to, take the youngens home by herself. Oh, to be carrying babies through the dark on a potbellied old mare when all the other girls stayed for the singing and shouting and then walked home with their beaus in good new clothes—good girls whom other people loved and who didn't hate God and Christ.

She began crying again as she stood facing Maude with the two babies on her hip, both sound asleep by now; she'd have to lay one on the ground while she put the other into Milly's saddlebag contraption—but how?

"Suse?" It was Mark's voice, soft, questioning, as if to make certain she was alone.

"Oh, Mark," and because his voice was kind, concerned for her, all her anger and her loneliness were dissolved in a burst of weak helpless crying; heartbroken and helpless tears took complete hold of her so that she was neither embarrassed nor angered, as she had always been at other times when someone watched her cry.

"Aw, Suse," he said. "This place an that crazy preacher ud make anybody cry," and he took Deb with one arm and put the other about her waist and pulled her, all weak and willing, against him, and her tears dampened the shoulder of his jacket, while he whispered over and over, "Don't cry, Suse. Th whole world ain't like this place."

"I'll never git away," she moaned. "An they'll be recollecten what I've done as long as I live." And she told
him all in broken sobbing how she had cursed in the
church house and Hattie Tiller had heard her. And how,
worse yet, she hated God—the things He had done, like
sending Lureenie to hell.

But he only laughed. "My brother ought to be alongside
her," he said. "He's in that Cincinnati jailhouse. He
thought I was joken when I told him through th bars his
woman was dead an his youngens starven. He knowed
he hadn't sent her much money, but he thought Samuel
would give her credit or she'd go to Pop."

"Th river was high," Suse said, shivering, remembering
Lureenie's hopeless ever-searching eyes.

"So th good people let her die," Mark said, glancing
toward the church house from which there came a great
burst of shouting. "They'll put her in hell so they'll never
have to come face to face with her in heaven. But no use
in your carryen on over it, Suse; you nor me neither
can't change th world. Let's get these youngens home an
we'll set by th fire an talk; I'll tell you about Detroit." And
he took his arm away and turned to put Deb in one of the
saddlebags.

They rode around the ridge and down the hill through
the frosty starlight on the big sure-footed mare; Suse sat in
the saddle and Mark sat behind her, arm about her waist.

At the house he helped her put the children to bed and
built up the fire. And something about his hot insistent
hands, touching as they worked together and his body
against her own in the saddle told her it was wrong for
them to stay so late in the empty house together. And she
told him so, reminding him that Nunn would tear the
country up if he knew, and the neighbors would talk. He
laughed and pulled her against him. "Aw, Suse, don't be
afraid of me—nobody'ull know. An anyhow," he added,
teasing, "if you've already gone to hell, ruined your repu-
tation, what difference does this make anyhow?"

Chapter Thirty-four

PEOPLE SAID THAT YEAR the winter came all in a lump;
the revival closed in a six-inch snow, and all through January, in lamb-dropping time, more snows came, wet as
March snows, melting continually, but always freezing
again before another fell, so that the crags and cliffs were
sheathed in ice, and on northern slopes the ground lay
under a deep blanket of rough ice-filled snow.

Sam and Vinie drowsed by the fire, for all things came
out but little in the ice and snow, not even King Devil,
who had left his scent only once in Tuckerville and that
around Christmas time, when Sam and Vinie were gone
three days and then had to be hunted and brought home
from Jeremiah Tucker's, where they had been treated like
high-born guests and fed on broiled unsalted mutton
steaks. Jeremiah had tried again to dicker with Nunn for
them, but had received such scant encouragement that old
Andrew Mclellan, that day visiting the Tuckers and re-
puted to be the stingiest man in the country, suggested
that Nunn breed Vinie to Sam and sell her pups to him
and the Tuckers—he would pay $30 for two. Nunn only
grunted at that; he had no wish to breed Vinie, and each
time she was in heat, he went to no end of trouble to keep
her from getting in the family way.

At times he hated the hounds, who seemed as happy
with strangers as with him, and was thankful for the
snowy weather that kept them home, for no matter what
the weather, he was always busy either making crossties
or, when the ground was thawed enough, digging post
holes and setting posts on the other two sides of the big

477

pasture field that took in the new graveyard, went to the river bluff, and to the lower boundary of the old Ledbetter place. Soon he was so nearly through that he knew that by full spring he could have the field finished and ready for his sheep. He'd got eighteen lambs from the ewes King Devil had left, and men like John and Keg Head, who had once shook their heads and declared he could never raise sheep under fence for they'd all die of worms, now praised the thriftiness of his little flock, and admitted times were changing and sheep with the times, but opined that drenching them so much with the worm medicine he'd learned about in town must take a lot of time. Nunn would always point out that the drenching of them took less time than the hunting had used to do.

When the pretty weather came in early February, he had to leave the fencing for plowing, but he turned only enough ground for the early garden patch; then, with all his family and Maude, and even Jude in a patched-up harness John had given Lee Roy for his help last fall in the molasses making, worked from daylight till dark at brush cutting, rock piling, and gully filling in the new pasture field. It was hard, back-breaking, skin-tearing work, but Nunn in particular worked with the old joy he had always felt when winter was almost over and he could start farming, good farming like this, that would leave his land richer instead of poorer.

But pretty weather brought hunting again, and one morning at daylight Nunn heard the yapping of Sam and Vinie in the river bluff below the old Ledbetter place; he guessed it was the young gray fox they'd been chasing the night before, a son, he supposed, of the old three-toed vixen they had caught before they were a year old. He was harnessing Maude when he heard them; Lee Roy had already gone to the field with Jude to snake up the little brushy pines cut the day before; Suse and Milly were busy in the house; and he'd be the one who would have to go dig out whatever the hounds had holed. He looked toward the sunrise, where high massive grayish clouds predicted bad weather, maybe rain, or even snow by tomorrow, and cursed and begrudged the lost work hours.

He was disgusted still more when, after the long walk down the river hill, he found that the holed fox was in a solid limestone ledge. The hide would have been worth something, but be damned if he'd waste half a day to see if the fox would smoke out. But Sam and Vinie yapped so frantically that he built a low fire in front of the small-mouthed den and hurried away, leaving smoke and fox and hounds to work things out together.

He glanced back once, knowing it was against all law and reason to leave a fire untended in the woods on a fairly dry day, but it was built on a shelf of stone, and the sunrise promised a still cloudy day; but just to be on the safe side, he'd send a youngen about midmorning to make certain it was out.

The work went well that morning, and Nunn thought no more of the fire. With the others, he ate a hasty lunch in the field and hurried back to work, urged on by an increasing cloudiness and a light wind from the southwest that smelled like rain. Nunn figured that if they hurried and neither set of old harness broke they could get all the brush they had down dragged and piled by dark, and so it was with some disgust that he heard Milly say to Suse, "Here comes Sue Annie, an us all ragged as half-picked chickens an dirty to th bargain. You've tore your skirt agin till you're plumb indecent, an that old jumper; you'd better stay out a sight."

But Sue Annie, out of breath and excited, stopped about a hundred feet away and made violent motions for them to come to her, and from her exaggerated frowns and arm wavings they gathered that something untoward was taking place in the graveyard which they must come and see.

Thy were working in the far end of the pasture above the creek-mouth bluff, and all except Suse, who with Bill Dan on her hip lingered behind the others, ran up the field to a low knoll within sight and sound of the graveyard.

And there they saw Rans kneeling by Lureenie's yellow grave. And they heard his voice: "O Lord, God of Heaven, Thou who ledst th children of Israel unto th promised land an dried th widow's tears an saw th sparrow fall—O Lord, O Lord, O kind heavenly Father, look down; my cup runneth over, darkness compasseth me, sorrow blackens my days; too late, too late; O Jesus, God on high, look down; look down, I beseech thee; have pity, dry my eyes. She died in sin. My wife, my own wedded wife, O God, she died in sin, in iniquity, unforgiven, un-repentant, unregenerate, and unrecon—"

"Well—is he or ain't he?" Sue Annie asked.

Nunn shook his head in puzzlement, without taking his eyes from Rans, outlined against the valley walls across from the graveyard knoll. "Drunk?"

Sue Annie blew her breath up her nose with angry vigor. "I say he is. Dave says he ain't. An Rans says he's got religion."

Lee Roy nodded his head thoughtfully. "It would be hard to tell. He allus prayed so good when he was drunk, better'n Samuel in a revival. Recollect, Pop, that time you all got down in Cedar Thicket Holler, an Rans started a prayen on a carryen on; an Mom thought it was a honest-to-goodness preacher a prayen an mebbe a comen on to th house, an she put on a clean dress an her Sunday shoes."

"I never did hear him pray, though, like he's a prayen now: mebbe th spirit has fell on him fer true," Milly said.

"Spirit of th devil," Sue Annie said and dropped to rest on a little pole.

"If God's got any pity, Lureenie's th one ought to have it stead a Rans," Suse, standing a few feet behind the others, said in a low voice, and for a moment forgot some of her terrified wonderings of how much Rans knew about her and Mark in thinking on Lureenie, quiet and at peace down under the ground—maybe she was in hell, but life above the ground could be hell, too, and unlike hell below, you were lonesome and all alone.

Sue Annie was pulling Milly's dress tail. "Set down. I cain't stay but a minute. Lemme tell you—" she begged with another eager twitch of the dress tail.

Milly sat down somewhat reluctantly; there was a little pine thicket in the swag between her and the graveyard field and unless a body stood up they couldn't see Rans so well. But it was plain that Sue Annie would burst if she couldn't tell her tale.

This morning she had been coming from the spring with a bucket of water when Rans came through the yard gate. At first she hadn't known him, all dressed up in a store-bought suit with vest and long-tailed overcoat. She had not seen any man in a long-tailed overcoat but Samuel since three years back last Christmas when she went to Town, and she didn't know what to think for a minute, then she saw it was Rans with the stiff-legged Cramer walk and she nearly dropped the bucket and said —here she giggled—"God Almighty, Rans, I thought you was in jail."

And he stopped and lifted his hand, and said in a prayerful kind of way, "Sister, like Enoch of old, I have walked with God. I forgive you."

And Sue Annie was certain he was drunk then. His big pale-blue eyes were bulging out and red-looking and his jaw was all stuck out like he was ready to fight something, but she wasn't afraid and said, "Well, God or devil or whatever you've walked with, it's too bad you couldn't a come in this direction a little sooner an mebbe kept your wife frum starven or leastways a been with her when she died."

But he didn't bat an eye. "It was God's will," he said an pulled a plush-covered box lettered in gold from his overcoat pocket, and she could tell by the fine outside and red plush lining that whatever was in it had cost a lot of money, more than Lureenie had ever had. There was a Bible in the box; the crinkles in the leather back all stamped in gold flashed like jewels in the sun, and when he opened it, the wind riffled through pages all edged with gold, and with Christ's words in red. "God has shown me th light," he said and thumbed through the Bible.

Sue Annie said she asked him straight out, "How much it cost, Rans?"

"Thirty-one dollars and ninety-five cents, box an all," he said.

She cursed him then; the blackest, dirtiest oaths the devil ever brewed flew in her head and out her mouth; she couldn't help it. The thought came to her that $31.95 would have got a doctor for Lureenie, and that the fine store-bought suit and the long-tailed overcoat would have kept her in grub half the winter.

Rans just stood with his Bible in his hand and batted his long-lashed eyes, like a frog in a hailstorm, while she cursed him. Dave walked up behind her and grabbed the bucket of water; he thought for sure she was going to throw it on Rans, overcoat and all—and maybe she would have. When she got out of breath, he went off as far as

the road gate and prayed. That drunk prayed for her, Sue
Annie said bitterly.

"But he could be sober an just took hard with religion,"
Milly insisted.

Sue Annie spat hard at a quartz pebble.

"You women gabble on so I cain't hear him," Nunn
said chidingly.

Suse stood with the baby on her hip and listened sometimes to Sue Annie, but heard little of what she said—she
was wondering when the night trains stopped at the valley.
Some night, after the others were asleep, she would start
walking—and take a night train from the valley; it didn't
matter where the train went—just so it didn't go to Detroit. Some way, somehow, when it was all over she would
pay back Mark's money—it was a sin to have taken it,
even though he had shoved it into her jumper pocket, two
$20 bills, more money than she had ever seen. He'd stood
a moment, his arm about her shoulders, frowning down
into her face. "Maybe," he had said slowly, as if he hadn't
wanted to say it, "we'd ought to git married, Suse—
you—"

She had jerked from his arm, and something in her face
had made him look at her in surprised anger. "My God,
Suse, do you think I'm not good enough for you after—
after what you've done?"

"Oh, no. No." She had forced herself to put her hand,
all shaking, on his shoulder, but she couldn't tell him;
there were no words to make him understand. What she
had done was done—it was over—sin it was, but for one
sin only she wouldn't pay with her whole life—all her life;
a woman didn't love a man when she lay lonesome in his
arms, her thoughts like birds flying past the man—all her
life to be Mark Cramer's wife and live in the Cow's Horn
while he worked away or went to war.

He had kissed her again, his eyes more troubled and
wanting than angry. "If—if everything ain't all right, Suse,
take th money an come to me. We couldn't live together;
they ain't houses in Detroit now fer them that's there, but
we'd git married an you could come back an stay with Pa
an Ma."

He'd said that, and it seemed a lifetime since. She'd
hidden the money under a flat rock in a pine thicket on
the edge of the river hill and counted the days—until now

she knew that what was done was done—but it wasn't over. If she were a woman married, Sue Annie would already have known.

The hissing snap and crackle of a burning pine caused her to look around. She stared an instant in stupefied surprise: at the farther end of the sandfield the pine thickets leading up to the graveyard field were walls of flame crowned with rolling clouds of thick white smoke, while more smoke billowed up from the river bluff.

None of the others had noticed the fire; they were in front of her, watching Rans, and the wind blew straight across the valley so that none of the watchers smelled smoke. The money that was to take her away was down on the river hill—it looked to be all on fire. She ought to tell Nunn; he'd set the fire, and if it got to the government land it meant a big fine and maybe jail—she'd get away before the others saw and get the money. She slid Bill Dan from her hip and ran, with no looking back, straight toward the walls of fire below the fence row.

Flames snatched at her as she jumped between two burning pines onto an island of green fern, scorched but not in flames; she heard the others on the knoll, Milly screaming "Fire," and Nunn's cursing and Lee Roy's calling to Jude. She ran over a patch of smoldering hillside, and from the other side of the burning wall of brush she heard Milly's screams—she'd never heard her mother scream like that, pure terror in her voice as she cried, "Suse! Suse! Oh, Suse!"

Suse hesitated, licked her dry lips, glanced up at the fire, then around the hillside; the money was still a good piece away; she ran a few steps farther, glanced once over her shoulder—if Milly saw her she might think—Milly screamed again, a sobbing, breathless calling. Maybe Deb was lost or Milly on fire and running in circles. She ran up the hill and then along the edge of the fire, trying to find an opening. The fire was traveling fast up the valley; if they didn't hurry and put it out, it would go through the brush above the creek bluff to the garden fence. She ran along a smoldering pine trunk, jumped over clumps of flaming sagegrass, and found herself at last in a safely burned out but still smoking briar patch. She remembered that she would burn her shoes, remembered again that if she pulled them off, her feet would blister, and ran on, trying to find a cool spot.

She heard Milly's screams again and ran through the smoke in her direction and came to a higher open space where she could see: all the valley fields except the meadows, and even the brushy outer edges of these, seemed either to be on fire or about to be; and the big pine woods below the new graveyard was a roaring, hissing mass of smoky flame. A little pine would go up in one explosive flash of flame, then through the smoke other flames would leap high above the pines and twist and writhe like fiery birds struggling to be free.

Then she saw Milly and the youngens and Milly turned and saw her, and for an instant there was glad relief in Milly's voice as she said, "Suse. Oh, Suse, I thought you was burned up alive"; then quickly it changed to harassed scolding. "What in th devil do you mean goen off like that? I thought you was fighten fire by yourself, an you're off to th river, I recken. Now listen—"

"But, Mom—" She stopped, unable to think of any excuse.

Milly handed the squalling Bill Dan into her arms, jerked Deb and Lucy from behind her, shoved one of Deb's hands into Suse's, the other into Lucy's. "Now listen, Suse, mind me once an mind me true or you'll let one a these youngens git burned up alive. You take these youngens—Lucy, don't you er Deb let go—straight to th house hard as you can. Hurry; they ain't safe here. Take em, an when you git there, git th hunten horn an blow. Blow like hell—everthing we've got's a goen—everthing." Her eyes flashed up out of her smoke-blackened face. "Now mind; git there; blow that horn; then mind these youngens; never let em out a yer sight." She shivered with some imagined terror. "Stay in th house less'n it gits too close, then go to th spring, an set, jist set an hold on to them youngens. Now git." A piteous, helpless look came into her face. "Dear Jesus," she said, and went running away, grabbing a green pine brush as she ran.

Suse started out with the children at a clumsy jogging run. At first there was plenty of room for walking, for the middle of the field had been fairly free of brush and sagegrass, but as she neared the Cow's Horn road the walls of fire drew closer. Lucy snuggled up against her and began to cry and scream as a cloud of pine smoke closed over them. Suse threatened to throw her down to the one-eyed woman in the Blue Hole and hurried on; somehow she'd go around the fire and get to the money. She didn't know how she'd do it, but she had to.

She reached a spot where a burning brush pile on the lower side and a flaming cedar thicket on the upper almost met. Flames leaped at each other, and smoke made a blind wall. Lucy squealed and hung back. Suse threw her arm around her waist, caught Deb with her other hand, held Bill Dan against her body with her elbow, and half dragging, half carrying, got them through.

The house was in sight now and Lucy broke free and ran toward it, but Suse, badly winded, stood a moment staring, sick at heart and unbelieving. Smoke was already boiling up from around the old sugar trees not far from the main barn where Preacher Jim's road crossed the creek.

The breeze had freshened and shifted, coming more west than south. Fire, already halfway up the shoulder of the hill to the Pilot Rock, was now sweeping up the valley toward John's place; and if the fire in the hill came on above the house, it would quickly get into the pine woods and brush above the spring, and from there to the house. It wouldn't be just her money, but the house and the little barn with all the corn—a crazy hope that she knew was sinful came to her as she ran on to blow the horn: maybe everything Nunn had would get burned up and he would have to go away to work and she with him.

She had hardly taken ten steps before she heard Nunn's horn, blown by somebody strange to it. She reached the garden fence, lifted Bill Dan over it, and with Bill Dan laughing with joy at the wild ride and Deb squalling behind because he couldn't keep up, she tore through the garden and around the house corner to see if the little barn was on fire. Smoke drew up the little valley of the spring branch and curled around it and hung in a thick cloud over the spring, but down in the cedar thicket by the barn she heard above the crackling of fire in cedar boughs the ring of an ax. She ran on and saw soon in the eddies of blue cedar smoke a strange man in familiar overalls slicing down little cedar trees with Nunn's good double-bladed ax. She put Deb and Bill Dan on a flat rock

in the middle of the Cow's Horn road. "Set," she said
fiercely, and dragging Lucy with her, ran on until she saw
the man was Rans. He must have seen from the graveyard, and knowing they were all gone, he had run to the
house, blown the horn, and changed his long-tailed overcoat and store-bought suit for Nunn's overalls.

She stared at him a moment as he cleared a lane in the
cedar thicket so that the fire could not cross to the barn;
he glanced up, recognized her, and smiling slyly under his
lifted ax, asked, "You feel able to fight fire?"

"An why mightn't I be able?" she said as she pulled out
of reach of the flames a big cedar that he had cut. She
was almost blind for breath, and the green cedars were
heavy and her back ached, but she'd die before she'd let
on.

Then from the direction of the creek she heard other ax
blows and then the flail of a pine brush on burning leaves.
In a few minutes Blare came leaping between two burning
cedars. He stopped only long enough to see if his singed
head was in flames and beat out a smoking spot on an
overall leg, then he pitched in and helped Rans save the
barn.

In a few minutes after the cedar trees had flamed up
and gone down, fat Ruby Tiller pushed through the
smoke, giving at every slow step a hearty flail to the
ground fires with a big pine brush. Urging her from behind came her mother, Hattie, with her bonnet crown
singed but fat Rowena safe on her left arm, leaving her
right hand free to beat with a bough. Three-year-old Oval
walked with one hand on her dress tail; behind him came
Bernice Dean, Dewey, and John Robison, each using a
pine brush suitable to his size.

Hattie and Blare had not waited for the horn. They had
seen the fire from their houses on the hill. "God, I'm glad
to see you, Suse," Hattie said, and stood Rowena on the
rock by Deb and Lucy with the two next to the least ones,
and after giving Bernice Dean an expressive poke with
her pine brush and telling her to mind Suse, started on.

Rans smiled at Ruby, who smiled back in pleased surprise, as Suse caught Hattie's arm. "Please, Hattie, let
Ruby mind th little youngens so's I can go fight fire on th
river bluff."

Hattie looked at her bloody, smoke-blackened face and

singed hair, the bleeding briar scratches on her arms and legs. "You've about killed yourself already," she said. "Better rest awhile an let Ruby fight fire; they's never no danger a her a goen too fast," and she hurried away to the flaming garden fence.

Suse stood on the flat rock, her arms lax at her sides, and watched the fire race closer to the house with the unconcerned air of a stranger. If she could only leave the youngens, there was a path cut out to the creek now, and she could walk in the creek water down to the Blue Hole, crawl around it, and be there in just a little while.

Lucy gave a shrill screech and Suse looked at her. Bernice Dean had grabbed a flaming cedar bough and was teasing Lucy by waving it over her head and threatening to set her on fire. Lucy jumped in a direction unexpected by Bernice Dean and her hair did catch fire. Bernice Dean screamed louder than Lucy. Suse slapped the fire out of Lucy's hair, took the still smoking bough, and in spite of Milly's teaching that it was bad manners to whip a visiting child no matter how it acted, laid the limb about Bernice Dean's shoulders and bottom a few times, shook it hard at the others, then ordered them all to sit in a row on the rock.

In spite of everything Hattie and her older children could do, the lower garden fence above the Cow's Horn road began to flare up with fire racing through the dried crab grass in the garden. Suse looked on with dry despairing eyes; if a rail fence burned so, everything in the woods would be cleaned out.

"God, Suse, I'm glad to see you. I was wonderen how I'd fight fire with all these youngens." And Flonnie, Blare's wife, came with Opal on her hip, and Ollie, Onie, Olean, and Alben W. Barkley walking in closed formation behind, followed by Lead and Drive with Joe C.'s Drum and Blunder, who had been out possum-hunting when Hattie left home.

"Don't look so down in th mouth, honey," Flonnie said. "We'll save th house enyhow." She pushed Onie down onto the flat rock, put Opal in his lap, told Ollie to be a good girl and keep the hounds out of the fire, took one last chew of tobacco from her apron pocket, laid her bonnet on the flat rock with Hattie's bonnet, tied her apron tight around her head and shoulders, grabbed a heavy

little cedar tree in both hands, and ran up to the thicket
above the spring. Fire had come around the hill and
down; there was nothing now to keep it out of the tangles
of honeysuckle and black locust that almost touched the
house, and the pit of the old root cellar hardly ten feet
from the house wall was a ready-made bonfire, filled as it
was with years' accumulations of leaves and overgrown
with masses of honeysuckle and roses.

Not long after, Sue heard above the snap and hiss of
the fire in the brush behind the house the rattle of trace
chains and clink of mule shoes on the rocks in the post-
office path. They were coming on at a smart clip with the
quick light step that Samuel's off mule used when Andy
rode him—it was a Saturday, and of course Andy and
Samuel, too, would come.

She strained to see through the smoke and soon saw
Andy riding up the path by the little barn. He sat sideways
and saddleless on the mule; it was plain he had broken
out from the plowing, and without taking time to undo the
hames and collar, he had hooked up the trace chains and
hurried to the horn call.

She wanted to run away, but instead stood waiting,
straight-shouldered and high-headed in spite of Bill Dan
on one hip and Flonnie's baby on the other. He looked so
handsome, not so much as touching the hames, not even
when the mule went down and up the steep sides of the
spring branch.

He came on, looking straight ahead, smiling a little, but
not at her; he hadn't seen her any more than he seemed
to have noticed the smoke or the fire leaping at the house
or the people up in the brush above the spring, some
chopping out a fire lane, others flailing with pine boughs,
children darting to the spring with buckets, pots, lard
buckets, anything that would hold water to throw on the
fire by the house.

Blare yelled at him to rustle up and start dragging brush
from the sides of the house. He looked up, saw her, and
checked his mule, and leaning low so that his face was
just above her own, said in a quick excited whisper, "Suse,
I've got good news; soon as school is out, Pop's goen to
let me go away to work with some other high-school boys;
th pay's good, an Pop says I can save my money an make
a start toward goen to college—he never made up his

mind to let me go till a few minutes back, when I was turnen potato ground."

Suse stood perfectly still with the babies on her arms and looked straight into his eyes. "I know you'll do good," she whispered, "awful good; you'll go on through high school—an then through college—I know."

"What's th matter, Suse? You—you look strange somehow."

"How do you think she ought to look, an her house an everthing she's got a burnen up while you stand an gabble —git a move on." It was Samuel, passing Andy at a fast walk on the other mule, not even taking time for his accustomed smile at Suse. He glanced an instant about him, then started barnward. "Come on; they's maybe enough hands to save th house, but th big barn over yonder's a goner less'n somebody gits there quick."

Andy looked toward the big barn, where flames from the brush and weeds in the back reached for the dry plank wall, then kicked his mule in the flank and trotted away like a boy riding on clouds to a vision.

Flonnie's Opal was tearing at her dress collar and saying over and over, "Titty, titty, give Opa; titty," but Suse saw only Andy as he checked his loping mule, leaped off, and ran around the barn to disappear in the smoke. The fire in the pine thicket between the house and garden made so much noise she couldn't hear what went on at the big barn. She waited a moment to see if the barn would burst into flame: the hay and fodder there would make a mighty fire. But when no flame leaped above the smoke, she turned back to the children. She didn't look at the barn again; it was so far away and hidden in smoke. It didn't matter that Andy was there; it didn't matter how close Andy was or how far; he was a world away; maybe he had cared a little; but now she hoped he never had. She wished she could quit seeing him—his eyes so kind and the way his hair—

Lucy was screaming again like a child possessed of a devil. Suse whirled to see if one of the others had set her on fire, but Lucy was jumping up and down and pointing toward the house. Flames licked around from the corner where the smokehouse had used to be, and smoke poured out of the broken upstairs windows. "What'll we do?" Lucy sobbed, her terror changing suddenly to heartbreak.

"Nothen," Suse said. "Mom said not to fight fire with you youngens."

Lucy sobbed and shivered, Deb screamed, and so did all the others. Suse watched Flonnie and Hattie run with buckets to the barrel of water that always stood by the kitchen door, then picked up a switch. "Now shut up, you youngens. Lucy, hush your screamen—we've still got our corn, an they's plenty a caves— Caves; maybe," she went on as if speaking to herself, "people like us belongs in caves."

"Recken we'll go to th one under th Pilot Rock?" Lucy asked.

Suse nodded. "It'll be as much fun as bean an Indian. You'll sleep on beds made out a pine boughs an roast everthing in th ashes, an Pop'ull go away an git a job, an then we'll all go."

"Goody," Lucy said, and like Suse, watched the feverish, excited work of the men and women and children with little fear. The women were running to the spring for water now, while the two men rolled the half-emptied barrel around to the end of the house. Fat Ruby, whom few had ever seen run, dashed out the kitchen door with an eight-pound lard bucket of what Suse took to be the churning, and ran around the house with it.

Lucy cried again as she watched flames from the honeysuckle over the old smokehouse pit lick around the corner of the house wall, but after a few minutes Hattie called down to them through clouds of smoke, "You'uns can come up now; th danger's over."

Suse turned to the children. "Come on, youngens; th damned thing ain't goen to burn down after all: I recken th smoke we seed a comen out th upstairs winders jist blowed in one side an out th other."

Once inside the house all eight of them set up a whining squalling clamor for bread, milk, molasses, honey, beans, butter, and apple butter. There wasn't any milk and not enough bread for them all, but there was a freshly opened half-gallon jar of Milly's good cucumber pickles on the eating table. Suse gave them each a pickle and they worked on these with only a little quarreling and fighting while Suse built a fire, set a pot of coffee to boil, and baked a skillet of corn pone.

Hope that some woman would come and relieve her of

the children had long since died—she could only hope
now that fire had not gone under the thin flat stone—if
only she'd buried the money and not rolled it in moss and
slanted the stone like a roof to keep it dry.

Now and then she glanced out the door or a window.
The buildings all seemed to be safe, and though the valley
was too filled with smoky murk for her to see much, there
didn't seem to be much fire any more on Nunn's land,
nor had it traveled far across the creek; she could hear
Sue Annie's shrill tongue as she walked along what must
have been a fire line on the other side of the creek. But
on the hillside above the farther spring, the old rail fence
that was the boundary between Nunn and John was a long
snake of flame flashing out through the smoke; the loss of
the fence wouldn't matter; it was the poplar timber, and
that was maybe saved. She wondered where all the people
were; gone to fight the fire on the other side of Pilot Rock
where the government forest began, she guessed.

The gloom deepened. The children took their fill of hot
corn bread and molasses and grew quiet and drowsy. Bill
Dan and Deb went to sleep, and after a time of crying for
the titty, Opal and Rowena did, too. Suse got a pan of hot
soapy water and began to scrub up Lucy and the others—
she did hate a dirty youngen—maybe they'd all go to
sleep and she could run to see about the money—no, she
couldn't do that. Nobody but a low-down trashy woman
ever left a little youngen asleep by itself in the house.

An early smoky heavy twilight came like a gray fog into
the valley, and Suse, because there was hardly any coal
oil, built up the fire in the fireplace for a little light. She
was out by the root-house hole, picking up some half-
burned limbs and twists of honeysuckle for the fire, when
she felt the first drops of a fine slow rain, more like a fog
in her face than a rain. She remembered that after dinner
Nunn had hurried them all at the work because it looked
like rain—but that seemed a lifetime ago. By the time the
fire was going good, and she had sung Hattie's next to the
least one to sleep, she could hear it on the roof.

It had begun to drip from the eaves when Flonnie
came, covered with grime, her skin and clothing torn by
brush and briars and out of breath from running down the
hill. Soon as that fine misty rain had started, she knew
they could do without her at the fire—they never did let

it get a head start over on the government land, but for awhile it looked like all Brush Creek country was a goner and Nunn would go to the penitentiary for true, but the Cookseys had come just in the nick of time—the rain would help and the fire could do without her easier, she figured, than her baby could do without titty.

Wakened by her mother, Opal began squalling, "Titty, Mom, titty," as if she were starved, and the others, becoming suddenly awake and lonesome for their mothers, all began crying at once. Flonnie called for Suse to come see if she could do anything with them; it was enough to drive a body crazy.

Suse never answered; she was already running bareheaded through the rain. Flonnie might curse and quarrel and slap all the youngens till their ears rang, but she wouldn't go off and leave them.

She topped the river hill and stopped, staring down. Below her the steep river hill, its mosses and thick layers of leaves smoldering still, lay black and strange, like a place she had never seen. The flat tilted rock had been between two little cedar trees upriver from the path and about halfway down the hill. Where had they been exactly? Some part of them was surely left, enough so that she could find at least the stone. She walked slowly down the path, pausing every step or so to look for a familiar landmark; the rain came on more heavily, and all around the murky twilight was thickening into darkness. Halfway down the path she stopped and stood a long while staring through the fire-blackened woods; full dark was falling over the valley fields before she turned about and came slowly home.

Chapter Thirty-five

THE RAIN SLACKENED during the night and Nunn and Lee Roy were out at daylight, walking the fence rows to see what damage the fire had done; but save for some old rail boundary fence that Nunn had never used, and the odds and ends of brush and fence above the hillside pasture and a few crossties, the fire had done but little hurt. Nunn's widely cut fence rows had saved the new fence posts in the brushy places and none of the closely grazed land in grass and lespedeza had held enough dried stuff to carry the fire. John, when he came up about midmorning to look things over, reckoned that it was a God's blessing the fire hadn't happened a couple of years back before Nunn got the storehouse field grazed down, or else, brushgrown and weedy as it had been, the big barn and the storehouse would have burned.

And Keg Head, when he came with Rans, opined the fire had saved Nunn and all his family at least a year's hard work of grubbing and brush cutting, for practically all of the brush and briars in all of Nunn's fields were burned into white ashes, so that Nunn, standing in Milly's upper garden, looked over a farm that held the new strange look of a familiar bearded face seen shaven for the first time. He could see his new fences going straight and even over the rolling fields; gullies heretofore hidden in brush showed themselves, but Lee Roy, going about with a swagger, for he had proven himself a real fire fighter, said that, come full summer, he and Jude would have them filled with rocks and the burned trunks of the little pines.

Milly in particular was pleased with the way the fire

had cleaned out the scrub pine and brush in the yard and
around her gardens; but better yet was Preacher Jim's root
house. Completely covered with honeysuckle and wild
rose, as it had been for years, it had looked more like a
little hillock than a hole in the ground, and had been a
breeding ground for snakes, and once a family of skunks
had lived in it, safely out of reach even from Lee Roy.
Grubbing out the thickly growing, many-rooted honeysuckle had seemed like a hopeless job, but the pit was
clean now, with no work at all; two sides walled with the
big hand-hewn blocks of stone still stood; the others were
fallen from their proper places, pushed by the slowly but
forever prying roots of the honeysuckle and cabbage roses
Aunt Marthie Jane had set there when the smokehouse
was new. But the rocks were all there and could be put
back with hardly any trouble; and Nunn ought to do it
right away before the pit grew up again, or so Sue Annie
said.

She had come down early, mostly, she said, to see how
Suse was; she'd thought she looked so peaked last night
when the fire was over, but then she hadn't been looking
a bit well lately; she'd brought her some dog-fennel tea
flavored with honey and peppermint so that it wouldn't
taste so bad. Milly giggled when she sniffed the still warm
tea. "You shore you ain't a bringen that to me? When I
was in th family way with Deb, you brung me a pot a that
—I recollect it made me mad—I felt awful sick to my
stomach an my back a hurten, but I didn't think a soul
knowed, not even Nunn."

"Law," Sue Annie said, setting the tea far back on the
table, beyond reach of Vinie's pushing nose, "it's good fer
most any ailment, specially young girls when they git—
peaked, porely-looken spells." She looked at Milly, then
at Suse, building up the cookstove fire with Bill Dan on
her hip. "Milly, ain't you noticed how porely she's a
looken here lately? She ain't looked real well since back in
th winter; along toward th end a th revival I noticed her a
looken bad. Ain't you noticed, Milly?" she repeated, her
voice rising a little with the insistency of the questions.

Milly pushed Vinie's nose out of the lapful of fodder
beans she was looking over, frowned over a length that
had blackened in the drying, gave Suse a careless, good-
humored glance, then went on with the beans.

"Aw, Sue Annie, you'll have th girl hypoed like Daradie Sexton. She's been sick to her stomach off an on here lately; sick headache she's maybe a goen to have—Nunn said Preacher Jim had it off an on all his life—but it's readen so much; she got some a them books."

"Magazines you mean, Milly; Meale Anderson said that was what Nunn got in th mail. Sample copies they was. Leastways," she went on with a little smile, "they was marked that away, an Meale, she ought to know. She goes to high school."

"An, well, anyway," Milly said, "whatever they are and wherever they come frum, she's been a setten half th night a readen by th fire, an it's a given her th sick headache. If'n she don't quit it, I'm aimen to burn em, ever one—if she has to read, she can read th Bible."

Sue Annie smiled. "Now, Milly, I'd say she's read her Bible more'n a heap a people I could name. Th night Battle John put Lureenie in hell, she was th onliest one spoke out agin him. Mebbe she give Preacher Samuel th guts to stand up an preach on 'Judge not that you be not judged,' an remind us all that Jesus saved th thief on th cross."

"Samuel," Milly said, "ull be a causen a schism in th church. He made some I could name mad by his preachen agin speaken in th unknown tongues."

"Looks to me like they's a schism already," Sue Annie said, going to the door to spit. "One bunch a you has got pore Lureenie's soul in hell an one bunch has got her in heaven. You'd all ought to git together an put her someplace fer good; she had too hard a time on earth, pore soul, to be treated this away after she's dead. If I was God, I'd give her a seat right by my side an give her everthing she wanted." She sighed and looked out across the fields. "But I recken, sean how Rans has got th call, she'll have to go to hell—he'd never have th nerve to meet her face to face in heaven—him with Ruby on his arm."

"Ruby?" Milly cried, and even Suse roused a little from her misery and looked around.

"Sparken right along," Sue Annie said, and after taking Bill Dan from Suse, she settled herself and told of their courtship, her tongue edged with disgust and ridicule, and described how last night, after the fire, he'd walked Ruby home and stayed to supper and asked a blessing so long the biscuits went cold. And after supper Joe C.—he was

thickheaded and didn't catch on—he kept staying around
by the fire in the big house, trying to talk politics and religion, but couldn't get anything better out of Rans than a
grunt or two; he'd tried telling about the last big race the
hounds had run on King Devil but had been cut off quick
when Rans said, "I've give up all such sinful ways,
Brother," and Hattie had to whisper to him twice, so loud
Rans maybe heard, "He's come a sparken Ruby—come
git to bed with me, you fool."

"An when Joe C. finally did git to bed, he laid there in
th back corner a looken at them two by th fire, an after a
while, he said, 'But we ain't that old, Hattie—not old
enough to have grandchildren.' "

Sue Annie laughed. "I've brung fourteen grandchildren
a my own an I ain't through yit, an I'll be a starten on
great-grandchildren if that fool Hattie has her way." She
sighed and went again to the door to spit. "Mebbe it's like
she says though. Better to marry Ruby off young than
have a bastard on her hands—like some—er mebbe an
old maid—" She looked toward the Cow's Horn road as
she spat, then lifted her voice in loud greeting.

"Lord, God, Amos, don't tell me you're a needen me
agin—why, it ain't been nine months since th last time."

Suse looked out the kitchen window and saw Amos
Tucker, son of Jeremiah, riding up through the yard toward the house. His mule was sweat-streaked and mud-
splashed and breathing hard when he stopped by the
kitchen door; but Amos looked a little foolish and his
smile was somewhat sheepish as he explained that at daylight he had got the news—it had come around somehow
by the valley that Nunn Ballew was burned out of house
and home, had lost a child and his white she hound, and
that he, himself, was burned so bad and in such pain that
he screamed one minute for people to kill him and the
next was out of his head and thought he was in hell.

He would not accept Milly's invitation to dismount; and
in answer to Sue Annie's questions concerning things over
in the Tuckerville country, he complained that King Devil
was killing all the chickens in the country and some young
lambs, but that everybody was about as well as common;
measles had got into the neighborhood—one of the Widow
Martin's little chaps had come near dying—he wouldn't

break out; they'd used chicken manure and sheep droppings and all kinds of teas for days.

"You all well?" the man asked Milly, but looking past
her toward Suse, who stood a little behind and to one side
of the women, as if even with all her curiosity to see a man
almost a stranger, she herself did not wish to be seen.

But he bent forward in the saddle and gave her body a
quick prying glance until even Milly noticed the curiosity
in his gaze and said, "That's Suse, my biggest un—she's
so bruised an scratched and swinged up by th fire a body
cain't tell what she does look like."

"Gitten to be a woman," Amos said, and shaking his
head to all Milly's invitations to light and stay for dinner,
rode out into the burned-over fields in search of Nunn.

Nunn was glad enough to see him, but frowned when he
heard of the doings of King Devil and that the man
wanted him to come with his hounds the following Saturday night.

"I ain't asken you fer fun," Amos said. "I've tried everthing—traps, watchen, hounds—looks like he's a goen to
steal us out a house an home. It makes a body so mad
they fergit they've got religion."

Nunn kicked a charred persimmon bush over with the
toe of his shoe. "He ain't never give me no chance even to
git religion. Th first year I come back to this country he
treated me like he's a treaten you, an he drove pore old
John mighty nigh crazy. It's jist in th last year or so that
Sam an Vinie kept him clear out a this settlement—old
Zing, he never could."

"But you'll come," the Tucker insisted. "Th old woman
cried an carried on night a fore last when she counted her
hens an found three more gone since th last counten no
more'n a week ago. 'He'll be our ruination,' she says, 'an
you'll have to go off an work in one a them factories.'
Funny to think a damned fox could run me out a th
country where I was borned an raised."

"I figger in some ways he's been my ruination already,"
Nunn said.

Amos glanced over the rolling fields, following the fence
rows with his eyes. "Less'n you be mighty bad in debt,
you're in good shape. You done good to buy that fence
last year; this war's a goen to make fencen sky-high an
hard to come by. I figger it's th onliest way to keep brush

out a farms like our'n thout cornen em to death; keep em
fenced an keep yer cattle an sheep on em stid uv in th
woods—then a body don't have to keep grubben out a field
if'n they leave it out a corn a few year. Well, are you a
comen?"

Nunn considered while Amos begged and urged and
prophesied: maybe one more good race and Sam and Vinie
would chase King Devil out of the country; maybe, if they
had a real big hunt with a lot of hounds, they'd get him.
Someday somebody would be bound to get him; soon, it
ought to be, for he was getting old.

Nunn shook his head. "I ain't been chasen him but
seven, an most foxes run enyhow fer twelve, fourteen
years. I figger King Devil's mebbe good fer sixteen." He
smiled a little sadly. "That leaves nine more to go. But I
tell you what I'll do this once," he said, "then I've got to
be through with hunten till my crops is laid by." And
somewhat reluctantly he went on explaining his plan: the
Tiller men were going to Indiana in two or three weeks
and wanted a rousing good hunt before they went—Jaw
Buster would come with Speed, the Sextons would all
come with their hounds, and there were two men up around
Town, both with pretty good hounds, who'd been plaguing him to invite them down for a race on King Devil;
they had a car and could come out on that new Tuckerville
WPA road that went almost to Amos's place, and from
there walk to Tucker Point above the mouth of Brush
Creek.

Amos was more than pleased with the plan and agreed
to go himself and wait on Tuckerville Road and greet the
strangers and direct them to the meeting place; he would
spread the word of a big hunt coming up two weeks from
this coming Saturday night, and Nunn could do the same
in his part of the country; together they'd make the loudest hound-dog music King Devil had ever heard.

"But I'm a warnen you," Nunn said as Amos rode
away, "King Devil, I've took note, don't hardly ever run
frum about th middle a February till mebbe April, an two
years back he never came out at all in February—an by
th time this hunt comes up, it'll be gitten deep into February an he mayn't come out."

"He'll come," Amos said, "if'n he hears a heap a hounds

—it's like him," he added bitterly, "to like a lot a fuss an worriment."

When Amos had gone, Nunn wished he hadn't come; he had taken much of the goodness from the morning. Nunn had been walking his fields and thinking how much work the fire had saved him; in only a day or so he and Milly and the children could with Maude and Jude get the burned-over pasture field in pretty good shape for sowing grass and clover seed, so that by the time it was dry enough he could be ready to turn corn ground. But now it was King Devil—King Devil, King Devil, always King Devil, but give the devil his dues, if he hadn't started the fire to smoke out a fox, he'd never have got his farm burned off—but if Rans hadn't been there and Sue Annie and the rain hadn't come along, he'd maybe be burned out and facing a government trial into the bargain.

He started to heave a pine pole into a gully, and remembered it was Sunday. He would shave and write to Elias Higginbottom; Elias and Pinkney, too, would be pleased. It was nice to know such men; he wished he had a decent house where they could come and spend the night as he had spent the night at Pinkney's. He glanced up at the sky. It was clearing; the sun would be out by noon; maybe by Saturday night two weeks it would be raining again or snowing, and the big hunt would be off; he didn't like big hunts.

But when the night set for the hunt came, the weather was perfect: still and damp and not too cold, with layers of cloud like many layers of thin silk over a moon gone only two nights into the waning, so that even in the deep valleys there was a thin shadowless light, so dim and so broken with cloud and fog and mist that it seemed seeping sometimes from the earth, sometimes from the sky, more akin to the crawling fog that rose slowly out of the river valley and the creek valleys than light coming from one source only.

Early in the afternoon the Tiller men and the Sextons went by with their hounds on their way to gossip and visit and take supper with the Tuckers before the hunt began. Jaw Buster had already sent Nunn word that he would be late on a lumber-trucking trip and for Nunn not to wait as he would come with Lister, who, though he still swore he would never own another hound, came now and again to the Saturday-night hunts, though some said he came mostly in the hope of hearing the lost Sourvine.

So it was that Nunn came alone over the old wagon road with his hounds through the early dark. Sam quarreled and complained at being brought through the woods on collar and chain when all around there might be fox scent, and Vinie unchained, but following Sam against her will, whined and pretended at times to run away. Nunn encouraged them on, trying to put an enthusiasm in his voice that he did not feel. He wished the night was over and wondered what hounds would never come back and what men would be drunken at sunrise and who would be fighting and who would spend all of God's Sunday dog-drunk in some rock house; himself, maybe, for all he knew. He had left the wagon road and turned into the path along the river before he heard the many-voiced crying of the gathered hounds on Tucker Point, and when the path had climbed the river bluff, he saw the hunting fire, a red radiance in the white mist. At the high point where the path turned down to cross Brush Creek mouth, he stopped and drew a deep breath, then blew his horn as a signal that he was within hearing and the hunt could begin. Sam and Vinie, who had hunted with all the other hounds and so had no need to get acquainted, could range on this side of the creek while the others hunted on their side, for when any one hound cried that he had found fox scent, every other worth his salt would go to him.

He unchained Sam, and the two hounds began an eager sniffing circling hunt of the woods above the path. Maybe, he reflected, as he walked on, they remembered that almost a year ago they had found King Devil's scent among the dead sheep by this same path, at almost the exact spot where he had stood to blow his horn.

He went on across the creek and up the hill, but heard no hunting bay from the chaotic medley of woofs and barks and snarls and yips that came from Tucker Point on the other side, and no sound at all from Sam and Vinie.

He had exchanged news of his farm and his family and told about the fire to Elias and Pinkney and passed the time of day with several of the Tuckers and others gathered there, before Old Spring, one of the Tucker hounds, let out a full-throated hunting call not a hundred feet from the hunting fire.

Elias looked around in disgust. "Why, that damned pot-licker a mine was a sniffen an a snoozlen right about there not five minutes ago."

Sump Tucker spat into the fire. "Man, don't curse yer hound," he said. "To my mind that scent warn't there five minutes ago. This fox we're all a hunten"—and in the firelight his eyes were big with puzzlement and wonder—"why, pears like he loves to be hunted." He listened to Spring, an eager angry hound on a hot scent. "He's heared our horns an our hounds an he's come." He glanced at Nunn. "Would you say that was him, Nunn? Listen—"

Spring's voice was like a war cry, and from all around the ridge top the other hounds were running toward the sound. Nunn listened, pondering, but in the end shook his head. "I couldn't rightly say," he said. "It must be red fox enyhow from th way they're bunchen in—but there ain't no hound there I know right well. If it was Speed, now, er one a mine, I soon could tell."

"It's our King Devil," Amos Tucker said, his voice eager-angry, like the hounds. "My old Bloom had scent a somethen low down on th creek road. I heared him sing out once; then he left it when Spring called him to come—he ain't a leaven one fox fer anothern less'n t'othern is King Devil."

The hounds ran up the ridge toward the head of Brush Creek, and soon the woods were silent save for the talk and laughter of the men, many of whom, much to Nunn's disgust, were ill hunting companions, too talkative to listen or let anyone else listen. He moved out of the circle of fire-light and stood with his hat in his hand but could hear nothing except Brush Creek far below. He stood so for a long while, wishing he were alone; he saw the glint of a fruit jar in the firelight and a man silhouetted black against the red glow as he tilted his head drinking, then Willie Cooksey, who had come, so he said, to strike a bargain for a hound, was calling, "Nunn. Nunn. Where's my ole pale, Nunn Ballew? I want him to have a drink too."

"Save it fer me," Nunn said, trying to sound as good-natured as possible. "I'll mebbe be needen it fore this night's over."

"You're a thinken King Devil ull take your gold-headed

white she hound into the Promised Land, I recken," Willie
called back.

Nunn never answered. In a minute he would go and
have a drink—he felt old and cold and tired inside; someday Vinie would die and so would Sam, but King Devil
would run on and on and on.

He had turned away from the firelight and was staring
out into the gray-white faintly luminous fog that had risen
now above Brush Creek Canyon when a twig snapped
softly behind him. He looked around and saw a small man
not much bigger than he and recognized Pinkney Deegan,
and between him and the firelight, the great black bulk of
Elias Higginbottom.

"We want to listen," Elias said, "and that Cooksey man's
a mocken his wife a tryen to save him in church, an it goes
against Pinkney's grain. He's a religious man."

"My religion ain't a hurten," Pinkney said. "It's my
hound. I wish we could hear him an I can't back there."

They all squatted, listening, but no hound's voice came
except that of Wildrose Tucker when she came whining
home on three legs.

Elias was getting restless. "I come to hear some runnen
—an all that pack a hounds would make some pretty
music," he complained, and wondered of Nunn if there
was no better place for listening.

Nunn explained how until eighteen months or so ago
they had always used the Pilot Rock, particularly when
King Devil ran, but since Sam and Vinie had come into
their stride he'd left Little Smokey Creek Valley pretty
much alone, going through it once, maybe, in the course of
a night's running, but never up and down it and round and
round the Pilot Rock as he had used to do. The trouble
with both Bear and Brush Creek canyons was that they
were so deep and narrow that twenty running hounds
couldn't be heard unless a man was almost on the edge,
as they were now. On the last race King Devil had run,
and the one before that too, he had spent the night and a
part of the day running up and down the canyons—a
tricky, exciting business, Nun explained, for it was hard
even for King Devil to climb out of them. One was
blocked by a waterfall coming straight down between
stone sides, the other headed at a spring gushing from
under a high straight bluff, and both were bounded by

steep craggy banks leading up to sheer walls of stone; it was only near the mouths that the sharp bluffs were broken into crags a fox could travel, though few hound dogs save Sam and Vinie could follow.

Lately King Devil would run up one side of the creek, sometimes in the creek water, sometimes on the steep brushy banks where running, even for him, was slow, but slower still for the hounds. Twice, that Nunn knew about, he had gone clean to the headwater, crossed the creek, and come down the other side—Sam and Vinie would never cross the creek until he crossed—they wouldn't leave his scent and try to trap him; but some night, he figured, the Tiller hounds would get onto his trick, and instead of following him to the head, would cross the creek and wait on the other side till he came down with Sam and Vinie behind him—then they'd have him.

Elias slapped his knee. "Now that ud be a pretty thing to hear. When do you recken it'll happen?"

Nunn smiled ruefully into the fog. "Never, most like—but it's th onliest way, I figger, he'll ever be took. Sometimes," he went on in a low despairing tone, "I think Sam an Vinie's too damned good ever to git him. They've trailed him so much they'll foller him up an down places on th river bluff where a body ud think a catamount couldn't go, but them Tiller hounds—Drum specially, he's lazy; he'll never go down a bluff no more—he'll just walk along th edge a sniffen here an yonder—if'n King Devil's scent comes under his nose he'll take out after it, an if it don't he'll quit er possum-hunt. He ain't ambitious. Th damn trouble is he's so damned slow King Devil ull be down an back up agin, if'n he's a comen up, fore Drum can find where he went over."

"Aye, Lord," Elias said in disappointment. "Mebbe somethen like that's a goen on somewheres an we're a setten here a hearen nothen. Let's git to thet Pilot Rock or somewhere," he said and got up.

Nunn continued to squat frowning into the misty moonlight. "I wisht I knowed whichaway to go. We might set on any knob an hear never a sound, an him a runnen all th while—people in th valley has seen Sam and Vinie an heared em lots a times along about daylight."

"Why, them hounds a Nunn's, they've been clean to Tennessee twice. A man stopped once at th store in th val-

ley an asked whos'ens that white she hound with th gold
on her head might be—an him frum way down in Tennessee, a hunnert miles er more." Blare, unnoticed, had
come up out of the darkness and now stood a few feet behind Elias.

"All a tale," Nunn said and got up. "It ud be a far piece
fer you to walk—six miles there an back, but I'm a thinken
we'll hear on th Pilot Rock at home. He never does what
a body think's he'll do. If'n that scent Spring picked up
was his'n, he knows they's a great parcel a men all a
wanten to hear him run—why, contrary like as he is, he'll
run where they can't hear him."

"That's right," Blare said, and added, "Nunn, you've
hunted that fox so much you know him like he was your
own born brother—"

"Maybe he is," Nunn said, and went to tell the Tuckers
what he planned to do.

The Tuckers, too, were getting restless at the soundless
race, but as Hiram's wife, Gertrude, was far gone in the
family way and nervous while he was long from home,
they decided to go to a high point only about two miles
away and on their side of Bear Creek. Somebody, then, as
Jeremiah pointed out, would be pretty certain to hear
something, split into three groups as they would be, for
Willie, though he was already most too drunk to tell a
hound's bay from a screech owl's cry, declared he would
stay where he was, and many of the others, mostly
younger men and boys out for a Saturday night's fun, decided to stay with him.

Nunn and his party of the two Tillers, Elias, and
Pinkney had just climbed out of Brush Creek Canyon,
with Blare complaining because they had heard nothing,
when Nunn pointed to a red glow, faint and dull in the
fog and seeming high enough in the sky to be a red star
or a wandering airplane. "We'll mebbe be a hearen pretty
soon," he said. "That's Jaw Buster's an Lister's fire on th
Pilot Rock: they've mebbe run smack into th race, or
leastways they've heared somethen or they'd never a
stopped." And all unknowing, he hurried faster until
Pinkney, striding behind him, said, "We'll wind Elias."

Nunn went more slowly until they came to a place on
his own land on the shoulder of Pilot Rock Hill, not far
from Lureenie's cabin, a spot good for listening; and

above them the red glow on the Pilot Rock dimmed and brightened with the shifting fog.

In the still damp air all the sounds of the night came clearly: the drip, drip of leaves, the roar of Little Smokey Creek dulled and muffled between its stone walls as it leaped the three falls above the river, the cry of a screech owl somewhere in the Cow's Horn bluff, the clink of the bell on Betsey as she chewed her cud in Nunn's new pasture field that cornered not far from where they stood, and once the clink of steel on stone as Maude shifted in her standing sleep—now down near the wove-wire fence above the creek, almost half a mile away, but coming clearly through the fog like a sound through water.

Nunn could hear the ticking of the big old watch Elias carried and his short excited breathing, and at times he thought he could hear Jaw Buster on the Pilot Rock, whistling a snatch of tune, but of a hound's voice he could hear nothing.

Blare, whom he heartily wished had gone with the Tuckers or stayed with Willie Cooksey, was telling Elias that they were getting close to Nunn's place, then telling him, as if it were a wonder the like of which had never been seen, of the rods and rods of wove-wire fence Nunn had put up—wove wire with two strands of barbed wire across the top, fence that would hold sheep or goats or anything, Nunn wished the fool would hush—Elias would think his neighbors ignorant, foolish-turned men, for Elias in all his born days had most likely never farmed behind anything but wove-wire fence.

"It's dogproof an foxproof, mighty nigh rabbitproof," Blare was saying.

Elias grunted. "Hunten won't be so good anymore when all th country's hemmed up in wire. It's mighty nigh ruint it around my place; hounds allus a lamen theirselves on th danged wire."

"Oh, th hounds all knows it's there," Blare said. "Ole Drum, he hemmed a rabbit in th finished corner not two weeks back; rabbit got skeered an lost its head—didn't know to jump—Nunn hogproofed th bottom; he couldn't go under."

Nunn's mind swung back to the rabbit; he hadn't seen it happen really, only a squeak between Blare's talking; they'd looked around and Drum was crunching its back.

"I wonder now," Elias was saying in a low talking-to-himself voice, "does this King Devil fox we're a chasen, does he know this fence is here?" He nodded toward a clump of black skeletons of sumac brush showing white in the fog. "An does he know they's been a fire,"

"He knows everthing," Blare said. "He's mebbe come an watched the day we fit th fire, an many's th time, I bet, he's come an watched Nunn work on th fence."

Elias shook his head. "Them hounds a his'n would a picked up th scent, wouldn't they, Nunn? You've said they go a hunten by theirselves a lot."

Nunn never answered; he never heard: he was thinking of his fence. The big field—wire stretched on two sides— only posts on the two sides away from the farm; the rabbit hadn't known about the wire on the two sides. Did King Devil know? Did he know about the fire? Even a man found fresh burned-over woods strange walking. How would a fox find running in burned-over ground—ground with a thin layer of damp ashes that would hold his scent easy as mud? And try as he would, he could not keep down the old, too familiar pounding of his heart and tingling in his hair.

Blare caught his arm, held to it as if afraid. "Lissen. Somethen—somebody's in th bush up yonder."

"It's a haint fer true," Nunn said and raised his voice in a loud "Yaa-hoo."

Elias, who breathed almost too hard to hear well, jumped and looked nervously around, but in an instant Lister Tucker's answering "Yaa-hoo" came singing down through the fog. They waited and the sounds in the brush on the hillside grew louder and Blare said, "Sounds like they was runnen."

Nunn said nothing. He was thinking of the creek bluff above the Blue Hole; many times King Devil had tried to lead hounds to death there, but now there was wire above the bluff. Did King Devil know about the wire?

Blare, listening to the men come down the hill, was saying worriedly, looking all around him in the thickening fog, "Sounds like they was runnen fer sure. Recken— recken they're skeered?"

"Be still," Nunn said.

"A hound?" Pinkney whispered.

"Sam runnen th other side a Schoolhouse Point—I recken."

"Sounds more like th left fork a th holler," Blare said, whispering too.

Lister called again from the woods above, but softly, as if afraid of being heard by something other than the men, and in a moment the black shapeless bulks of him and Jaw Buster came rushing through the fog. Both men were breathing hard, less from running downhill, it seemed, than from some overpowering excitement that quickened their hearts and thickened their tongues.

"What th hell," Blare asked. "We'uns was figgeren on comen up an you all come down a runnen. Is they a den a wildcats that—"

"Fer Christ's sake, be still," Jaw Buster begged when he was close enough that Blare could hear his urgent almost moaning whisper.

Lister came on more slowly. "They're runnen on yon side a Schoolhouse Ridge, side-hill runnen—dippen low down—we cain't hear em fer a little spell. Oh, Nunn," he went on, "you'd ought to ha been with us on th Pilot Rock. This is one time Sam an Vinie an Speed are a chasen King Devil. Honest to God, he's skeered an a runnen fer all he's worth," and Lister drew a deep excited breath and rushed on. "Ain't you never thought about this fire an your fence? If'n he tries to lead em to the Blue Hole, he's ruint—ruint—ruint. God, I wish old Sourvine could come back frum th dead for one hour tonight."

Nunn tried to show none of the excitement that made a hammering in his ears and his breath come short, but made a formal little business of introducing Elias and Pinkney to Jaw Buster and Lister, but Lister could not be quiet and babbled out the story of the race, hysterical, almost like a woman who has seen a vision. "King Devil got tricked this night, I figger," he said. "Me an Jaw Buster was a walken along, jist had climbed on up around th hill road past Lureenie's old place when we heard th Tucker hounds. Old Speed cried to go like his heart was broke, but Jaw Buster held him, knowen he'd never git a thinken maybe th fox ud swing back around this away."

"Well, he swung around th head a th creek all right; he must a gone over th divide an then come back on this

side, then right clost to th .... , it sounded like—we
wasn't high enough to hear real good—peared like he run
smack into Sam an Vinie; he swung back some, it
sounded, but he kept on a comen thisaway. We figgered
he heared them other hounds all through th woods behind
him, some yon side a th divide, some this side, an we
figgered he'd keep a comen thisaway, so we turned an
headed quick fer th Pilot Rock—but we heared him afore
we got there, a swingen around th mountain like he done
that night he killed that pretty pup a Rans's at th roll-
over."

Nunn nodded and Lister laughed. "Well, he swung onct
an he didn't swing no more. We was a standen straight
up frum here, right clost to th Pilot Rock path, when Sam
an Vinie come a singen down through John's piney-woods
gap. Jaw Buster lets Speed go an he sings out fit to wake
the dead an starts toward Sam and Vinie on this side a th
mountain; an King Devil, stead a swingen back he took
up th valley into John's poplar timber then across an
around Schoolhouse Ridge where he is now—a runnen
hard—a taken no time fer nothen." He pulled a half-
emptied pint bottle from his pocket, held it on his palm
as he added, trying to search out Nunn's eyes in the
murky light, "An, man, I figger if'n he comes back thisaway an tries to swing low on this side a th mountain,
they'll git him on the fence. He won't make fer th head a
Brush Creek; they's hounds thataway—listen."

Nunn pushed his hat back and glanced at the bottle and
understood why Lister rattled on so. He stared up through
the fog and wished Lister would hush and wished he could
see the stars. They would maybe quiet the crazy wildness
of his thoughts. Still, it was true, King Devil was a fox
like other foxes. He could be taken, so why not tonight,
when the woods were full of hounds? He found no stars,
only fog in his face, so thick now it was like a fine mist of
rain, and his voice was flat and weary as he said, "You're
kind a liquored up, Lister. Recollect th night he killed
Zing. He run then like he was chased—but he warn't."

"Mebbe not," Lister said, "but Zing wasn't Sam an
Vinie. Listen."

Nunn sighed and took a drink when Lister offered it
and heard the Tucker hounds and the hounds of Elias
and Pinkney and others he did not know, first faint be-

hind the Pilot Rock, then louder as they topped the hill.
Sam and Vinie had, by the grace of God, run into him—
but only after he'd been able to tangle the scent up so for
the hounds behind him that they'd had to spend half the
night unraveling it. Spring and a sweet-singing bitch Elias
said belonged to Pinkney were in the lead as they came
down through John's pine woods and swung with no hesitation on to the cold trail back around the Pilot Rock.
Elias groaned. "I was hopen they'd find th fresh scent
an go off th way Sam an Vinie went."

"King Devil's smart," Blare said. "He'll run mighty
nigh th same way half a dozen times, but he's allus keer-
ful to spread his trails wide apart to keep th hounds a
runnen. You hear Sam an Vinie yit, Nunn?"

"I thought I mebbe did, but with you an them other
hounds together I cain't hear nothen."

Then Sam let out his singing yodeling cry from the far
side of Schoolhouse Point, and excitement lay over Nunn
like a hard steel spring, winding harder and tighter and
tighter, until his hands and feet were cold with it and his
breath came short and gasping. King Devil was coming
back this way; he couldn't turn and go over Deer Lick
Ridge—no fox had ever crossed over it—he wouldn't
swing back around Pilot Rock Hill: hounds were baying
and bogling every hundred feet or so all around the mountain. He could take to the river bluff below Sue Annie's
place or go up the valley past John's to the head of Little
Smokey Creek and out—but would he?

Sam and Vinie crossed Schoolhouse Point, were over
the hill, down through Nunn's land, and by the creek.
Nunn held his breath for Sam's next calling. Would he
be going up the valley or down? It was too much to hope
he would come straight across. A screech owl screamed,
restless and angry at being unable to see in the thick
white fog. The laggard hounds on Pilot Rock Mountain
followed the trail above him in the woods, and far down
in the field below, Maude nickered softly to her unweaned
colt. The sounds were big, like thunder crashing by his
head, and he cursed them, even though he could hear his
own short hard breathing, and wondered with a part of
his mind if Elias wouldn't burst with holding his breath
so and pondered Pinkney's still turn that lay on his

breath as well as on his tongue, for he had never heard
him breathe.

Then Sam was singing out at the creek crossing. King
Devil must have jumped from stone to stone where the
creek was narrow; he hadn't fooled any time away trying
to get the hounds off the scent. He couldn't take the time.
God, he was hard pressed—Lister was right: whichever
way he went he was being chased—chased. Nunn gripped
his arms about his drawn-up knees and rocked on his
heels and never noticed the cold sweat trickling down his
nose as Sam and Vinie cried from up the hillside toward
the gap. He hadn't gone up the valley and he hadn't gone
down; once through the gap he had one chance, and that
was to swing back above John's place instead of around
the Pilot Rock—the woods behind the Rock were too full
of laggard hounds for him to risk it.

Sam and Vinie sang out almost to the gap, working fast
and steadily up the hill; seconds later Spring and the fore-
most of the other hounds that had swung once around the
mountain were in the pine woods, pouring down the hill
in a flood of sound. Elias was shaking his fist into the fog
and bellowing, "Cut, you fools—cut to that white bitch."

They must have cut, or maybe the fresh trail ran under
their noses, for a moment later twenty hound voices
seemed raised in Nunn's hillside pasture field around from
the old graveyard where Zing was buried. Only one lone
hound, a laggard, but honest and hard-working, bayed
evenly as he was wont to do on a none too hot trail, for
just now he was following King Devil's first swing around
the mountain—cold now. The lone hound never seemed
to hear the other hounds close behind him on the hillside
but lower down—King Devil must have heard the hound
ahead and the hounds behind, or maybe he'd planned to
come down the mountain and run sharp to the creek bluff
edge as of old.

Instants later Sam and Vinie had made a sharp turn
downward and bayed near the upper corner of Nunn's
new pasture field not two hundred feet away; loud and
wild and triumphant and happy, close on King Devil—
closer than they had ever been. And as Nunn realized
that soon, soon King Devil could be in a fence corner
with Sam and Vinie and a dozen others behind, the spring
that seemed wound around his body was broken and he

leaped to his feet crying, "Sic him, Sam. Sic em—" He stopped and was ashamed to show such childish excitement, for in all his years of hunting he had never cried out to a hound.

"They'll git him," Lister was crying. "He don't know that fence is there."

"He could run alongside it," Nunn said, and tried to put a calmness in his voice, and then for the first time realized he was running down toward the lower edge of his field, and that all around him ran the other men, some before and some behind him in the fog, but louder than their trampling feet came the crying of the hounds from low down, almost to the fence above the Blue Hole they would be now.

"He's—" Blare began, and a sound like the twanging of some giant untuned banjo came up through the fog that, as they ran lower down the hill, had thickened and stretched now like a lake, shoreless and dimly seen.

"He's run into th fence," Elias gasped, several feet behind the others.

"Not him," Nunn said, and stopped. "It was some hound; he's run straight to th fence an turned sharp along it like he does on a bluff edge—Sam an Vinie are still a folleren—listen."

"Jesus God, he'll git away," Lister said, disbelieving.

Blare was waving his arms and crying into the fog, "Cut, Drum, you damn fool. Cut, Blunder, cut like you done on th rabbit."

The men, like sheep stampeded for no cause, started running again for no cause, swinging now around the graveyard knoll, then down through the field toward the end of the wire on the river hill, and like sheep, they stopped again when Blunder's possum-hunting bark came echoing through the fog; at the end of the fence he was, somewhere ahead of Sam and Vinie. What with the sounds striking straight and sharp through the fog and the echoes of twenty different hound voices ringing back from the Cow's Horn bluff, the men, running again, seemed in the middle of the hunt themselves and could tell little of what was happening until above the plop of their feet in the ashy earth they heard the mad, insistent clamor of hounds that have brought a fox on bay; their yips, barks, snarls, and crying curses were centering in a little swaggy place where trees grew and in wet times there was a spring.

"They cain't miss him now," Lister gasped. "Oh, Lord, I wisht Sourvine could ha come back fer this night."

"I wouldn't lay money on it," Nunn said. "He can still git away—he don't fergit nothen—he's run up a little leanen tree—a black gum by th spring; I recollect it now —Maude an Jude they scratch their—"

"I'll lay money—five to one," Elias called from behind. "Nothen flesh an blood could git away frum all them hounds. Take me up, Nunn?"

"Took," Nunn said, jumping over a charred pine pole, "but all I've got in my pocket's $5." He ought to say $5 was all he had in the world—money kept back against trouble—but let King Devil have it; when he was gone, trouble would go, too; but it was like him, the black-hearted beast, to let himself be trapped by a fool Tiller hound and run into a tree like a coon, not in fair running through the woods to his—

A piercing shrieking scream, no human sound, no animal, but filled with terror more than speech, rose from among the clamoring hounds; it rose above their many-tongued crying and for an instant stilled them until the night was the mad shriek only, echoing through the fog. The men, like the hounds, were stilled by the strange wild cry and stood gaping, fixed in their tracks like wooden men, hardly noticing that when the skriek ended there was after it another, a strangling, howling, gasping cry, like the wail of a child, Nunn thought, hurt to its death and scared.

Blare was the first to move; he came in a long running stumble to stand quivering by Nunn and saw Buster, who had been a few steps ahead of the others. Then Pinkney was speaking, his voice low and level as always. "That noise we're hearen right now is a hound done to its death —I heared one scalded onct."

Blare remembered that he wore, as usual when hunting, a miner's cap with its ready-to-light carbide, and reached and after some fumbling took it from his head, but he stood all ashake, unable to fix the water or strike the flint, and Nunn jerked it roughly from him, listening with a cold heaviness in his heart: the dying hound could be Sam or Vinie and he wouldn't know; the voice that came from it was the voice of death and not its own.

The light leaped out with a little hissing that made Blare jump, and while Nunn regulated and returned the cap to Blare's head, the lone voice of the dying hound hushed, and he grew conscious of the other hounds, whining, scattering with puzzled yaps and snarls, and one, a friend maybe of that one dead, was howling, but through it all no glad wild hunting bay. He thought of the first wild cry, tried not to think, and said to Blare, "Come on, man, git a move on wit that light. I've told you lots a times that sooner er later King Devil would lead me an them hounds a mine to hell—this is jist a little a th beginnen—th devil hollered, that's all."

Blare tried to speak, but the words disconnected and stuttering, seemed sounds falling from the mouth of an idiot, "Wh-wh-at wuz it?"

"What was what?" Nunn asked, careful to match his stride to Elias's clumsier, slower gait. Maybe they'd all break and run before the night was out. Lister and Jaw Buster stood and waited for the light; the two big men stood shoulder to shoulder, and Joe C. stood shivering, trying to wedge himself between the two, like a calf caught in a cold rain nuzzling up against a cow. In the blue light Nunn caught quick glimpses of the faces about him, and all, even Pinkney's, seemed gray as the ashes under their shoes.

He was walking on, half supporting the tottering, trembling Blare, when a dark shape loomed for an instant in the fog, then leaped on Elias with a glad whimper at meeting humankind. Elias gave two quick steps backward before he recognized the thing for a hound, but not his own. It was old Blunder, who knowing that lights and men and his master Blare went together, had come to the light.

Blare spoke to him and he came with a glad whimpering, sniffing at his shoes and his hand, but as Blare walked on with the others, Blunder, though he had helped in the killing of more than one wildcat and could handle a razorback boar, half wild from being on the range all fall, whimpered and slunk behind, his tail between his legs, then broke into a long howl.

Lead and Drive and many other hounds, even Spring,

came to the light, all with the slinking, ashamed air of
brave dogs for the first time run into something they
could not fight.

They had walked a few minutes in silence when close
by in the fog Nunn heard Vinie sniffing and snuffing with
the little eager whine she often gave when she knew the
scent was nearby but could not find it. Seconds later Sam,
not fifty feet away on his other side, sang out that he had
found what Vinie hunted. Spring and one of Pinkney's
hounds ran after, but most continued to slink whining
along with the men.

Nunn heard the gurgle of the spring and in the long
shaft of carbide light could see the charred trunks and
limb of trees and knew they were close to the leaning
black gum, for since the fire had cleaned out familiar
thickets and ancient rock piles grown up in saw briars,
he found himself lost in the fog on his own land. The light
confused him only more, and Blare kept pressing against
him, jumping continually at every blackened skeleton of
bush and tree.

And Nunn in his heart cursed him and the fog
together. He wanted to get on and see—he wouldn't see
Sam and Vinie and he wouldn't see King Devil dead, but
there must be something close by the black gum where
the scream had been.

Lister let out a terrified "Jesus God," and jumped as if
he had stepped in fire. Blare bent his head in that direction, and shining up into the carbide were a hound's eyes,
wide open but expressionless in death. "Jesus God,"
Lister said again. "I thought I'd tromped on a little dead
younген—his paw felt like a hand."

But Jaw Buster was silent, swallowing hard, for the
hound was Speed. The men crouched down and looked
at him, all except Blare, who stood up and kept glancing
behind him in the fog that lay even thicker by the spring,
so that the men huddled over Speed could hardly see
each other.

There was no mark on his body, but something had
crushed in the back of his head so that blood trickled
from his ears and his mouth.

"Leastways he never suffered none," Jaw Buster said.
"Whatever killed him killed him quick."

"Looks like he's been clubbed to death—one blow," Elias said.

And Nunn said, "They're anothern somewheres. He ain't th one we heard—he didn't have no chance to do no howlen."

"Anybody bring a gun?" Blare stammered. And added, when no answer came, "I brung my old single-shot pistol along; I didn't like thet lonesome road down th river to Bear Creek. But I ain't so much as got her loaded," he added, ashamed through all his fear to let them know he carried a gun.

He knelt then by Nunn and loaded the old pistol. It wavered so in his trembling hands that Nunn cried, "Fer God's sakes, either hold it still er give it to somebody that can. I'm glad you brung it; somebody's got to get that pore hound out of its misery."

Below them on the hillside the fence squeaked softly once and then no more. They all looked around and Blare, with his wavering pistol, crouched closer to Nunn, his fear-crazed eyes rolling as he tried to see in all direction at once and kill the unseen thing that would surely spring on him from out the fog.

Nunn happened to glance down at the pistol and saw that it now pointed directly at Pinkney, who had sprung to his feet when the fence squeaked and now stood with his back to the others, staring down into the fog.

Nunn cursed and seized Blare's hand, and after pointing the pistol firmly toward the ground, h'isted the shivering man to his feet. "You're a goen to kill somebody. I know that old gun. Joe C.'s filed th trigger till a flea jump could fire it. Now, by gum, you've got th light an th gun; me an you're a goen to walk down there an take a look —nobody's goen to walk in front an take a chanct on gitten shot."

"Yeah," Jaw Buster said, seizing Blare's other arm. "If nothen else, you'll kill Nunn's stock. I seed a horse's sign by Speed."

"Unshod—but plenty big," Elias said.

"It's my full-grown filly," Nunn said, swinging on to Blare as Jaw Buster, sick with grief at the loss of Speed and boiling with rage at a man who'd carry a pistol among friends, pulled Blare through burned brush and over rock piles until the man moaned that he was being killed.

They were only a few feet from the fence when Blare screamed and struggled against Nunn's hard hand on the pistol handle.

Nunn, too, saw what he saw, a whiteness like a thicker blob of fog moving noiselessly down along the fence row. He spat out his tobacco to get spit enough to speak. He had no white cow, no white horse—a sheep would run.

Blare's pistol cracked, and Lee Roy's voice, troubled but unafraid, called out, "Don't shoot me too, Pop. in all this commotion you've mebbe already killed Jude."

"Jude?"

"Yeah. Me an Mom an Suse was up a listenen an we heared her scream—I run out in my underwear. Is she hurt?"

Elias swore and said, "I'd ought to ha knowed. I recollect onct I run to help a neighbor save a burnen barn an heared a mare scream somethin like that."

And Lee Roy repeated, "Have you seed her, Pop? I thought I heared somethen on th river hill an climbed th fence to go see."

Nunn cleared his throat. "You git on back to bed where you belong to be. If'n Jude's hurt, I don't know it —somethen skeered her."

"What? She ain't afeared a hounds. She's mighty skittish though, if somethen comes on her suddenlike," Lee Roy said, "but she would a heared th hounds a comen." Then he asked, as if only remembering a trivial matter: "What happened to King Devil, Pop? We thought fer a minnit you had him."

"How in th hell would I know? Now git on back to bed," Nunn roared, disgusted with his hunting companions but more with himself. He'd been so excited he'd loosened his grip on that fool Blare's hand, and it was only luck Lee Roy wasn't dead.

The whitish blob of underwear moved away, and Elias leaned against a tree and roared with laughter. "We are th damnedest fools," he said. "Seven men skeered to death, with a pistol an a light, an a little scrap of a boy puts us all to shame. Your filly's went crazy an struck out at th hounds. We was all skeered too bad to think about th horse sign."

"We'd a heared her a runnen," Blare said, wiping the sweat from his face.

"She wasn't shod, an they's no brush left much to make a noise," Nunn said.

"But how'd King Devil git away?" Lister, who had been somewhat tipsy half an hour ago but was now cold sober, asked.

"I figger," Nunn said, "that if'n we go look agin around that leanen black gum we'll see. I figger King Devil was hard pressed fer onct in his life—an he run up the leanen tree—but too late fer th hounds not to find. Then Jude was a standen under it er clost, an he jumped on her back. That set her crazy—she's pawed out an killed Speed an that other hound, not meanen to, an in all th fracas King Devil jumped a big jump an got away, er mebbe he's rode her a piece."

Blare shook his head uneasily. "I never heard uv a fox a riden a mare."

"I seed one onct ride a band a sheep acrost a field," Elias said, and added admiringly, "Lord, man, that Sam and Vinie—they're worth any six hounds I ever seed. People say th war'll ruin th price a houns an race-horses, but I'll give you $350 fer em right now—cash—er swap some pretty cattle er some mules er tools."

Nunn sighed and shook his head. "When I git King Devil."

Elias laughed and reached for his billfold. "You'll never get that fox. Anything that had th luck he had to-night wuz borned to be chased, not took."

"I figure that myself sometimes, but I'll keep a chasen him," Nunn said.

Elias took a long leather purse that bulged with what, when he opened it, appeared to be bills wadded into little balls. He uncrumpled one, held it under the light, and seeing it was a twenty, handed it to Nunn.

Nunn shook his head. "I ain't a sellen."

"Hell, man, this is th bet," Elias said, uncrumpling other wads that also turned out to be twenties. "I don't even know if'n I got $350 on me. I sold a little passel a hawgs at th yards today, and know I've got a five somers." He found it at last and handed it to Nunn, who took the money somewhat reluctantly.

"It don't seem right," he said in embarrassment. "I ain't never bet before."

"You been a betten yourself against a fox fer God knows how long," Elias said, and added wistfully: "I wish to God you'd sell me them hounds. I'd breed that Vinie right away."

"Yeah," Blare said. "Why don't you, Nunn? Old Speed's dead, Zing's dead, an my old Drum—I'm pretty certain that was him frum th way Blunder's howlen— pretty soon Sam er Vinie, one ull go—er both. An anyhow, they ain't nobody left to hunt in these parts."

Lister nodded. "They're a sayen this war's a goen to take ever man out a these hills; them that can't fight has to go to factories—less'n they're big rich farmers."

"I'd ruther be in th fighten than shut up in a factory," Nunn said. "An I figger I'll hunt King Devil till they come fer me. I had no hand in starten all th damn war an I don't figger on goen out an a tryen to stop it—less'n I have to."

A strayed hound laid a cold nose on Blare's hand, and he jumped and gave a little squeak, then smiled ashamedly and looked around. "Well, boys, if'n me an Joe C. gits ole number eleven at the valley come mornen, we'd better be a gitten on. Can you'uns do thout th light?"

"Sure, sure," Nunn said, and added his good-byes and well wishes and warnings to stay out of jail to those of Lister and Jaw Buster. He dropped to his heels and watched Blare's light grow dim and more dim in the fog. He wished he could walk away from King Devil like that —just walk away and never think of him again, the way Blare would; yet Blare had almost as much reason to hate him as he—one spring, four or five years back, King Devil had in three weeks' time killed every hen, upward of fifty, Blare owned—and tonight he had lost a hound.

"Got another drink, Lister?" he asked, and added when Lister handed him the bottle: "Th liquor, it helps to keep me frum thinken on how old I'm a gitten when I feel like I was already laid six feet underground." He emptied the bottle and searched for man shapes in the fog as he said, "Well, we'd all better be gitten on; I'm afeared fer some uv these stranger hounds—King Devil ull most like lead em over a cliff, sean as how he's already tried it onct tonight."

But he continued to squat a moment, the empty bottle in one hand, his head drooped low, with his chin on his chest, like the head of a tired child.

Chapter Thirty-six

WHEN LEE ROY came back to the house and told Milly
that Nunn was sober and with Pinkney Deegan and the
big fat rich farmer out from Town, she went to bed and
slept the light but unworried sleep that was her habit
when Nunn was gone but sober and in good company.
She'd stayed up so late listening to the hunt that Suse had
a fire going in the cookstove when Bill Dan roused her
by his screaming and clawing for the breast, and by the
time he was finished, the fragrant smell of boiling coffee
seeped into the fireplace room, and Milly called to Suse
to keep the coffee hot, that Nunn might be in at any time.

But the coffee boiled away, the bread baked, then got
cold while Milly waited breakfast for Nunn, though the
younger children were whimpering with hunger, and Lee
Roy, back from hastily doing the barn chores and finding
no breakfast on the table, grabbed a hunk of last night's
corn bread and ran away up through the garden, Jude's
patched bridle dangling on his arm, his pockets stuffed
with corn.

"Come back an eat," Milly called after him. "Your
pop'ull—"

"My pop'ull lay drunk till he gits sober," he called
back, sassy anger in his voice. "If'n he was sober, he'd
already a been here." He turned and looked at her, not
like a child but like a hard-working man to a silly woman.
"I've got to see about Jude. She got skeered so last night
she could a lamed herself." And he ran on, his red head
rising for an instant out of the fog, then lost again in the
thick whiteness.

Milly turned wearily back to the kitchen; maybe Lee

520

Roy was wrong. Nunn could be late and sober still. She found Suse's eyes slipping past her face and out the door, and as she watched her all unnoticed, she realized it had been a long time since she'd looked at Suse, really studied her. Sue Annie was right—she didn't look well. She had a yellowish look like her liver was out of fix—and she looked so troubled; Milly had never seen such trouble and despair as Suse stared at nothing out the door.

Milly's heart turned over for Nunn. Maybe Suse had heard something—somebody had brought bad news while she was at the milking. "Suse," she asked, her tongue thick with fright, "has anybody been by? Has anybody told you anything?"

Suse jumped and looked at her in a quick scared sort of way, like she'd been caught in some meanness. "What a you mean, Mom? Nobody's been by."

"You was a standen there a looken so down in th mouth," Milly said relievedly. "I thought mebbe some-then awful had happened to yer pop er one a th hounds had come home thout th other."

Suse began a quick hunt for the dishrag. "I wasn't thinken on a thing," she said.

"Suse, if'n it's th dishrag you're a looken fer, you're holden it," Milly said, suddenly lighthearted, giggling almost, at Suse's wool-gathering ways. "What ails you anyhow? What's a troublen you? You've been a punyen around an a pinen away, sour an sullen as a ole woman. Nunn was a sayen th other day he hadn't heared you sing or hardly seed you smile fer weeks on end. What ails you anyhow?" she repeated to Suse's back.

Suse stopped, a half-washed dish in her hand, her head lifted as if she searched for an answer in the wall behind the stove. "I guess, Mom," she said slowly, "that th older a girl gits th less there is to sing about in th world."

Milly laughed. "Shit-fire, Suse. You've got liver trouble; a young woman like you a talken thet away. If'n you start out thisaway by th time you've lived as long as I have there won't be any singen left atall. What you need is a good mess a sassafras tea, an sean as how it's Sunday an I caint work at nothen else, I'm a goen up on th hillside to that tree clost to th old graveyard an grub out enough roots fer us all to have a round a tea—if'n I can find th grubben hoe."

"Oh, Mom—" Suse began, and Milly saw with something close to terror that she was crying, soundlessly, but crying, her tears falling into the dishwater—she had hardly ever seen Suse cry since Suse was as old as Lucy.

She started to say something but could think of nothing except, "What ails you, Suse?" and after a moment's staring turned away and with some relief left to hunt the grubbing hoe and dig the sassafras root. Young girls like Suse were often notionate and touchy, and in a way poor Suse had plenty to cry over.

Here she was, going on sixteen and had hardly had a beau, and her so overgrown and big-footed she'd maybe never get one now, with the war and good times taking every man out of the country; but big or no, she needed better clothes; that was mostly what ailed her—no fitten clothes and no beau and her so big, with her hair more red than brown, and freckles into the bargain—not many, but enough on her nose to notice less'n a body looked first at her hair and her eyes; and Milly, while she hunted the grubbing hoe and climbed the hill and dug into the earth under the sassafras tree, fell into a long musing over the kind of dress she would make for Suse to wear to church on summer Sundays—she wouldn't wait for lamb or wool money but would sell eggs and buy the cloth.

She leaned an instant, resting on the grubbing hoe, looking down as she had already looked so many times at the Cow's Horn road and then at all the paths meeting at the kitchen door, but the road, like the paths, was empty, and she sighed, thinking on Nunn. Where was he and what was he doing?

She pulled at the long red root, savoring the strong sweet odor of sassafras that came from the bruised wood; with it there was the smell of the fresh-dug clayey earth, and Milly sniffed with pleasure, for the earth smell made her think of spring; she squeezed a handful of earth, let her fingers spring away, and saw the earth fall slowly apart in her hands. Lord, Lord, it was dry enough again to plow; if it wasn't Sunday, she'd dig up a lettuce bed and sow a pan of cabbage seed.

She had a goodly length of sassafras root grubbed out when from across the creek she heard a funny jingling. She stopped her work to listen, grubbing hoe in hand, but in an instant understood. Sue Annie was on her way to that big rotted sugar tree log in Cedar Thicket Holler below the screech owl's nest. That was on Nunn's land, and Sue Annie would get that good log dirt and have cabbage plants to set before anybody else in the country, even Nancy Ballew.

Sue Annie always beat everybody on pepper plants and sweet-potato slips, even the Cookseys, but she never bragged about it, for she had been born with heat in her hands and she never could raise a decent radish; they were always fiery as pickling peppers, and her onions, even green ones, always strong enough to make a body's hind end smoke. Milly, though, ran more to cool things: she most generally had the earliest and finest lettuce of anybody in the country, and it grew on, sweet and tender till July, when Sue Annie's was bitter and stringy; and her cabbages always grew so fast that worms never had a chance—but this year Sue Annie would beat her even on cabbage; it looked like rain and it wasn't right—she was a church member and couldn't work on Sundays, but Sue Annie wasn't and could do anything she pleased.

She searched the sky, the sun already weakly red under thickening cloud; the Lord said, save the ox on a Sunday—maybe he would forgive a lettuce bed when it looked like rain by Monday.

She was hurrying down the hill, loaded with sassafras root, grubbing hoe, and a charred pine pole she'd found still standing and dry and good for kindling in this time of wet wood, when Sam and Vinie came running up to her. Vinie leaped to her shoulders and licked her face and Sam ran round and round her, now and again snatching her wind-lifted apron in his teeth. Silly they were, like young lambs with the spring, and plainly they hadn't run all night; from their unswollen eyes and lively ways, the race must have ended not long after Jude screamed. When Vinie leaped on her for the third time, she flung down her load and stood a moment, her arm about the milk-white neck, the big hound's paws on her shoulders. "God love it —it's glad I am to see you home again an all in a piece after that awful run on King Devil last night."

And Vinie, as Zing had used to do, lifted her head and whimpered at mention of King Devil, and Sam, standing with his nose by her knee, threw up his head and laughed. "God love it," she whispered again, smoothing the golden

specks on Vinie's head, "seems like you're th onliest ones
on this place that ain't allus a fretten an a pinen fer
somethen they ain't got, an is happy. Where's Nunn?"

The hounds studied her an instant with wide mute eyes,
as if they were familiar with the question but never knew
the answer.

Milly sighed and gathered up her load; the hounds
hadn't run since midnight, and where was Nunn since now
and midnight—sober, he would have been home. Oh,
Lord, oh, Lord; she'd go spade her up a lettuce bed and
it would make her quit worrying so over Nunn; God
would forgive, and she'd put it under the apple tree and
load it with chicken manure the way she always did;
nothing made better lettuce than hen manure and apple-
tree shade.

She was spading up the lettuce bed when Lee Roy came
home, singing as he rode bareback on Jude, and when
they chanced to be alone he smiled and told her she'd
burn in hell for true, planting a lettuce bed on Sunday,
then gave her, with the half-ashamed showing of love for
his mother that came to him rarely now and never when
others were around, one spray of arbutus, the palely pink
buds half open and the leaves still weathered from the
winter. She thanked him, but wished it could have been
Nunn who brought her the first flower of the spring—
like it used to be—but used to be was gone; and someday,
when Lee Roy carried other flowers on other springs to
some woman not his mother, this now would be the used
to be, and she would sit and recollect the apple tree where
always she had made a lettuce bed, and Lee Roy with
the flower.

Oh, Lord, her head was all gone wool gathering; she
was worse than Suse, she'd dug into the horehound bed—
if she didn't hurry, Sue Annie would be bringing her a
mess of lettuce before hers had its second leaves—the
clouds were thickening and there'd be rain by dark maybe.

But Milly had her lettuce sowed and covered with brush
to keep the scratching hens away in plenty of time to milk
and then eat supper before heavy dark fell in the valley.
And as she went down through the yard with the milk
bucket in her hand, she was tired with what ought to have
been the good sleepy tiredness that comes from the first
garden work of the spring, but mostly she thought with

dread of the long night ahead, when she couldn't sleep till Nunn came home; and maybe he wouldn't come home. She was wondering what she'd do if he wasn't home by next day's dawning when she heard Ann Liz Cooksey calling across the river in the direction of Sue Annie's.

She was too low down by the little barn to make out the talking that passed back and forth across the river bluffs, but caught Ann Liz's shrilling "Come," then more talking, like an argument back and forth, and Ann Liz's further screaming, "But she cain't come."

Milly listened all atremble. Nunn could have gone with the Cookseys across the river and be bad hurt from some kind of fight and they'd sent for Sue Annie. Old Mother Creecy brought the babies and did the doctoring on the other side; Sue Annie hadn't gone over there on a case in years: too many babies flooded her side of the river, she always said.

The milk bucket jingled in her trembling hand. Lord, Lord, she wished Nunn were home and over in the storehouse feeding his ewes and their young lambs—the lambs had baaed a lot she'd thought today—it was a bad sign, old people had used to say, when lambs cried at noon, and today their crying had made her lonesome, thinking on Nunn—maybe he'd never feed his lambs again; and she began to cry, and cried on as she milked, her forehead pressed against Betsey's flank, soundless tears sliding down into the foaming milk.

"Well, Milly, ain't you done milken? Git a move on— this night you've got to go with me to Cordovie Foley's at th fur end a th Cow's Horn."

Milly turned away from Betsey and stared up at Sue Annie in surprise while Betsey hastily swallowed the nubbin she chewed, picked up the last one, and started through the door. "Go on, cow," Sue Annie said, stepping aside. "Milly's got more pressen work than strippin away on you. Git a move on, woman," Sue Annie begged, "it'll be dark fore Nunn can git us over th river, an frum up in my cow pasture it looked vigrus wild—they's come a quick tide from a big rain up toward th head."

Milly got up from the milking. "But Nunn, he ain't home."

"God almighty, th devil must be a chasen me er mebbe th Lord's mistook me fer Job. But devil er God,

nothen's a goen to keep me frum that girl," Sue Annie
cried, and as she hurried Milly up to the house and into
her Sunday clothes, her troubles poured out in one long
spit-punctuated stream. Ann Liz had called across and
said Cordovie's time had come but that old Mother Creecy
was sudden taken sick with her heart spells and couldn't
come.

Sue Annie knew different: old lady Creecy had lost
her nerve, for the last time the Foley woman—didn't
Milly know where she lived—on a rocky little scrap of a
farm right where the Cow's Horn ended on the other side
of Keg Head's place, but because they traded and went
to church on yon side hardly anybody on this side knew
the Foleys—well, anyhow, this Foley woman had nearly
flooded to death last time, flooded till she went blind and
old Mother Creecy figured she'd die for true this time, so
she took to her bed and told them to send for Sue Annie—
and Sue Annie could have the name of letting the woman
died on her hands.

Lord, God, didn't Milly know that Blare and Joe C.
had lit out early for the 10.22 at the valley, and ought to
be halfway to Indianie by now. No, Flonnie couldn't
come along: didn't Milly know her baby had the thrash;
had it so bad she meant to send at daylight for Lulu Sexton to come blow in its mouth? Hattie come? Didn't Milly
know—there was her other Sunday shoe behind that row
of blackberry jars under the bed—Hattie was too busy
killing chickens and baking sugar-sweetened cakes an
helping Ruby primp and priss to help her old mother-in-
law? Rans was there again today—stopped in on his way
home from Sunday school at Deer Lick. She'd hoped and
Joe C. had hoped the law would land him in jail for dynamiting the river, but last Saturday somehow he'd made
peace with the law, leastways he'd gone to Town and
showed himself and got back home—they said Preacher
Samuel told him—no, no, never mind hunting the comb,
Milly didn't have time to comb her hair anyhow—that if
he wanted to do any praying in Deer Lick Church, he'd
have to make his peace with the law same as with the
Lord. Now it looked like he'd be loose anyhow long
enough to spark Ruby enough to get married while Joe
C. was out of the country and Hattie egging him on.

"Shorely Ruby wouldn't git married an her so young,"

Milly said, grabbing half a hand of long dark red for the night's chewing and kissing Bill Dan on Suse's hip.

"She's mighty nigh a year older'n Suse," Sue Annie said as they went out the kitchen door.

"But Suse ain't so much as walked with th boys yit," Milly said.

"Well, maybe she ain't walked—exactly," Sue Annie said, and hurried down toward the Cow's Horn road.

Milly glanced back once at the house: all in a fluster as she was from hurrying so, she knew she had forgotten something. She'd never left Suse and the little youngens alone in the house at night before, but they ought to be all right; many a woman no older than Suse was keeping house for a man and a baby. She hurried after Sue Annie, but hurry as they would, the early dark of a cloudy night before moon rise came down so thickly that even the white limestone rocks gave no glimmering on the path down the river hill, and Sue Annie stopped to light her big, windproof lantern.

Milly stiffened suddenly as Sue Annie held the flame to the wick. "Lord God, we fergot to call across to Ann Liz, while we was on top a th bluff, fer th boys or Willie to come with their boat."

"Fergitten, th devil," Sue Annie said. "When Ann Liz called she said I'd have to git Nunn to row me in th boat Rans come over in this mornen. Willie's down drunk somewhere's like Nunn, an Ann Liz has sent her three biggest uns on th hunt uv him."

Milly drew a sharp breath of relief: Ann Liz's big boys would take care of Nunn along with Willie; everything would be all right. She felt almost gay as she watched Sue Annie's thin, black-stockinged legs swing back and forth across the little yellow pool of lantern light. She wondered, but unworriedly, which of them would do the rowing; sometimes when she and Nunn took the children to the river on a summer Sunday afternoon, she had rowed for fun, and that in daylight when the river was low; but most likely Sue Annie's talk of a high flash tide was only one of her tales and the river wouldn't be so very high.

But when they had crossed Nunn's riverbottom cornfield and come to the place where the path crossed the low, rock-strewn creek mouth, yellow backwater, ugly with dirty yellow foam and debris from the river banks, showed in the lantern light.

Milly stopped and noted the silence of the shoals: when the water didn't rattle at all, the river was high, too high for two lone women to cross in the fog and the dark; but Sue Annie only said, "We'd best walk around—lessen we want to ruin our clothes; it must ha been a big rain not so fer away—the way she's come a rollen down," and quickened her pace a little and swore at the time lost in walking up the creek and around the backwater.

It was while they were stumbling and groping over the steep pathless creek banks that first Vinie and then Sam came leaping on Milly with glad barkings, plainly determined to follow her wherever she went. Milly was vexed; she knew she'd forgotten something, and that was to tell Lee Roy to fasten the hounds in the house until she had been a good time gone; but Sue Annie only laughed and said that seeing as how they had no man, Sam could be one, and that anyhow they'd turn back when they saw the skiff, and then she fell into a long remembering of a hound Dave had once had—a big black bitch that had followed her to every birthing she'd attended while it lived —and a sight of company it had been on a wild dark night, even when people were along.

Milly's wonder of how they would cross the river changed to worry when she saw the skiff. Willie's little old flat-bottomed straight-sided thing that nobody used any more except the boys who went fishing seemed a puny handful of planks to ride the wild river as she looked at it in the lantern light, all pressed against the bank as if hunting shelter from the rising water.

Sue Annie was jerking off shoes and stockings and directing Milly to hold the lantern while she waded into the water and undid the boat chain, fastened to the washed-out root of a red river birch already a foot or more under water. Sue Annie, after some groping, found the chain and untied it, then gave the end to Milly to hold while she put the lantern into the boat, got herself into the rower's seat, and slipped the oars into their locks.

The hounds had been running back and forth, sniffing at the water, barking at the boat, and watching the women with lolling tongues and excited eyes. They had never ridden in a boat, but when Milly sprang in they followed.

Sue Annie cursed and Milly cried "Shoo," but Sam and Vinie stayed, whining, shivering, crouched with dragging tails on the muddy bottom between the two seats, for when they and Milly jumped, almost together, they'd pushed the boat from the rim of quiet water by the bank, and instantly the current was like an invisible hand, pulling the skiff through the foggy dark.

"Th current comes clost to shore right here," Sue Annie said, and took two fumbling, uncertain strokes that made the old boat jiggle and rock. All around the unseen water made a gentle hissing, and though the wind was still and there were no waves, Milly heard water lap over one side, then felt it on her legs. She moved a little on the seat and felt for the water, leaning out and reaching down, but instead of touching it with her fingers only, her whole hand went in, and she realized that the water moving swiftly through her fingers was only two or three inches below the top of the boat. When she had rowed for fun on a low river in daylight, the boat had always been high in the water.

She spat out her tobacco; it didn't taste good anyway, and in a moment said, "Sue Annie, ain't we a goen down-river—th Cooksey landen, it's might nigh straight across."

Sue Annie nodded as she leaned resting on her oars. "We'll never make it straight acrost—we'll go down sidlenlike, I figger, an land where th current comes clost to shore on th other side."

"We'll mebbe go clean to th end a th Cow's Horn, where th river bends out—an it gits swift tween here an yonder," Milly said.

Sue Annie said nothing, did nothing but feather the oars, and the skiff was like a log bobbing in the current. Milly thought of logs—the river in this sudden rising would be full of logs and trees and brush, and a body couldn't see them in the dark. Sue Annie pulled gently on one oar, but gentle as she was, Milly, still crouching with her hands in the water, felt the river rise like a hungry mouth sucking at the boat; Sue Annie let the boat slide back from the unseen yawning mouth, and once more the water gurgled through Milly's fingers as they flew downstream. "Sue Annie," she asked, "ain't th boat a leaken? They's water all around my feet—an seems like we are a riden mighty low in th water."

Sue Annie heaved on the oars before she answered. "Th river, it's vigrus swift tonight, an a little straight flat skiff like this ain't no good fer crossen swift water. When she comes down hard like this below th shoals, th middle uv th river rares up like a runnen boar's back—you've seen in flood times how a log in th middle'ull bob under."

"Yeah."

"Well—this damned Cooksey boat's more kin to a log then a canoe," Sue Annie said, and Milly, studying her dark seamed face in the pale glow of the lantern, saw the same grim anger that had been there when Lureenie was in her death convulsions and Sue Annie had sat with no talk and no tobacco chewing, only oaths, sometimes, that nobody had started in time for a doctor. Milly watched the thin muscles under her wrinkled old woman's neck stand out as she bent low over the oars, forcing the boat slowly but steadily into the ever-quickening current. She felt the water rise in leaps and little gurglings on her fingers and tried to see past Sue Annie's face, but behind her there was nothing but the same thick darkness that lay all around the fog-thickened circle of lantern light. She wished, oh, Lord, how she wished she could see the river or the stars. How far away was the shore? She turned her head, slowly searching up and down and all around, but in the foggy dark she could not even see a rim of the river bluff against the sky.

"Pears like we've been on th water a long while," she said after a time.

"Yeah," Sue Annie said, riding once more with the current. "That baby'ull be out a th bones an into th flesh," and added after an instant's silence, during which Vinie let out a troubled whimper, "I wisht to God we didn't have these damned hounds."

Milly swallowed. "Mebbe I'd better try to throw em out. They could swim to shore—I recken."

Sue Annie shook her head. "They might claw at th sides an turn over th boat," and as she spoke in a slow flat voice, so different from her usual shrill chattering, there was mixed in with all Milly's other thoughts an instant's crazy feeling that she rode the black river to her black death with some mad wild witch. "Turn back, fer God's sake! Turn back," she cried, rising a little in her seat and jerking her hand from the water.

Sue Annie heaved on the oars, her eyes in the darkness above, and said in a breath, short-winded, "Wiggle or scream, woman—an this plank box, it'll mebbe go under." She feathered the oars and leaned forward, looking at Milly. "I ain't a turnen back; they ain't nobody to take us over. All my life I've had to kill my own rattlesnakes—nobody to run to an scream fer help." -

Milly's thoughts came up like pictures, brightening the dark: the black look of the fresh-turned earth of the lettuce bed; Bill Dan's little red-gold curls in the early sun this morning, or was it yesterday morning when the sun had come out for a little while? Suse's face—in memory it looked yellow and her eyes big and sad—no, scared, more scared than sad. Why was Suse scared? Water lapped over the knuckles of the hand that clenched the skiff rim. She wished she hadn't made a lettuce bed on Sunday. Sue Annie's head was bowed low over the lantern—the oar handles across her breast, gathering herself for the next pull, the pull that would send them under.

But Sue Annie did nothing but hold the boat steady with the oars as they flew down the river, and Milly realized that she was tired—she could hear her short hard gasping breaths above the hiss and gurgle of the water and Vinie's low moaning whine. "Lemme me at th rowen, now," she begged. She'd rather row, or try it, than sit so still.

Sue Annie shook her head, and without loosening her grip on the oars, bent over and wiped her sweaty forehead on her coat sleeve. "They won't be much more rowen," she gasped. "We're gitten clost to th bottom uv th Cow's Horn whefe th current crosses over when th river makes a sharp bend to straighten out. Listen!"

Milly had heard but thought it was only some sound of the boat. She realized now that it was a sound ahead in the darkness to which the current carried them—the whining, sobbing, creaking splash, splash of bending trees and sapling fighting the full current of the river as it bit into the big bend at the end of the Cow's Horn. Milly swallowed and gripped the boat with both hands, but Sue Annie whispered calmly, "They's pure rock there straight up above a little bank, an th river there in flood, it runs vigrus wild, if'n we let it take us there we're goners—we've got to git acrost—now," and she was heaving on the

oars again, all her body pulling with her arms, her face
slipping back past the lantern light.

The skiff, like a thing afraid, tried constantly to slip
back from the crest of the rolling water; it creaked as the
current quickened, and the masses of rushing water seemed
ready to bury it in their hurry and roll over it instead of
under. Milly felt water crawl upward toward her ankles
and through the thin boards of the boat she felt with the
soles of her feet the pushing, pushing of the water and
bumps that at times seemed like waves, though the night
was still. She tried not to think how the river would look
by day in a flash flood like this, boiling yellow below the
shoals, racing yellow foam down the length of the Cow's
Horn Narrows, and at the end the swift whirl around the
big bend. The moaning water-weighted trees cried out
with a louder sobbing and Sue Annie gave a mighty pull;
the boat creaked and quivered as it bucked and bounced
by what seemed a foam-flecked wall of water of the lantern light—and the wall was toppling, coming in, coming
over, but the skiff was sliding past, though Milly's lap
was full of water.

Sue Annie's head was low once more above the oar-
locks, and a great drop of sweat, yellow in the lantern
light, slid down her nose. She gave a gasping grunt and
pulled again, her body lengthening out and stiffening with
the pull until she seemed a woman laid across the seat instead of sitting. Vinie whined and sprang to her feet, shaking herself. Milly felt the river knock the skiff like one
great fist and water sloshing all around her; she tried to
pray, but heard herself whimpering like Vinie. Poor Nunn,
how would he ever manage alone?

Sue Annie was forward again, her oars above the water,
and their handles, almost meeting in the boat, seemed
holding up her drooping figure. She leaned a moment, resting, before Milly realized that they were across the hump
of the current and the skiff sliding back from the crest into
ever calmer waters. She had been a fool; why, the boat
wasn't half full of water—no more than covering the bottom of the lantern.

Sue Annie was rowing again with slow exhausted sweeps
when she gave an angry gasping, "Shit-fire, there goes my
head rag."

Milly looked and saw dimly on the upper rim of lantern

light a whitish something that looked to be Sue Annie's head rag standing in mid-air. "Git it," Sue Annie begged; "I never did bring a baby thout a head rag."

Milly held up the lantern, and standing on her seat, reached and pulled the head rag from an overhanging sycamore limb, but had hardly got settled again before Sue Annie was swearing again and declaring they must be on top of a brushy bank; brush caught at the oars so that she couldn't row, but when she felt for bottom it was still an oar length away, so there was nothing for it but to pull themselves to shore; she would hold the lantern and Milly could do the pulling; she must be getting old; the little row on the river had about white-eyed her.

The swinging lantern showed sycamore limbs and the tops of river birch and maple brush, while the skiff bobbed gently in a still backwater littered with foam and debris, though only a little piece away through the darkness the brush of a steep riverbank swished and splashed as it wrestled with the current.

Sue Annie listened to the sound with satisfaction. "They was a little while I thought we'd end up there," she said, and revived somewhat and took a fresh chew of tobacco. "I wonder where we're at," she said. "It don't matter so long as we're on yon side a th river, but we'll mebbe have a heap a walken to do."

Chapter Thirty-seven

THE TWO WOMEN began the slow hard climb up the river hill, heaving themselves up the steep slippery banks by holding to the trunks of brush and trees, crawling at times along narrow ledges where Milly was hard put to hold the lantern, and other times pushing their way through banks of briars that scratched their hands and faces and tore at their clothing.

Sue Annie, hurrying, more worried with each passing moment over the waiting woman, caught her dress tail in a clump of giant blackberry briars and in her hasty efforts to untangle herself got more and more entangled and in the end climbed on, leaving the most of her skirt. She was certain that somewhere in the hillside not far from where they had landed was a path—that is, if they had landed at the end of the Cow's Horn—but she couldn't take time hunting the path, for, as she had told Milly, all she was really certain of was that they were at the foot of a hill; the thing to do was to get to the top, and try to do it before the lantern used up all its coal oil.

Sam and Vinie, after their first joy and surprise at finding themselves alive and on land, had, as was their custom, begun a sniffing and a searching for fox scent. The sound of their zigzagging back and forth, hunting a way up the ledges, guided the women away from crags too steep and high to climb and told them in which direction they should crawl on a ledge to find a way off and up.

They had been crawling for what seemed a long while along a narrow limestone ledge, made almost impassable in places by jagged hunks of rock fallen from some bluff above, and in other places so narrow and with its edge so down-sloping that Milly worried for Sam and Vinie hunting their way ahead; worse yet, she could hear almost directly below her, it seemed, the moaning swish of the brush in the current—they were, it was plain, going downriver as they worked their way up, and now they were directly over the wildest part of the river where there would be no swimming out for a hound.

She was crawling, inching forward on her stomach, when Sue Annie, following behind, pulled her foot. "Can you git thet lantern back tu me thout fallen off? I think I feel a way up here. We dasn't foller them fool hounds no further—that river sounds mighty clost; we could be a goen down stead a up—an whatever we're a doen we're a goen downriver, away frum th Cow's Horn, an if I recollect right, they's a straight-up bluff down thataway a gnat couldn't climb."

Milly was rising slowly to her knees, steadying herself with one palm outspread on the stone, trying with the other hand to get the lantern back to Sue Annie, when below her in the bluff, yet some few feet ahead, she heard Sam give a hunting call. She stopped, listening in surprise; Sue Annie listened too, and nodded, "I told you this ledge was a goen down." She stood up then, and took the lantern, swung it over the nothingness in front of her: rising out of the foggy dark below, they could see the twigs of what might have been brush growing in some steep hillside a few feet below, or trees that stood with their roots in the risen river; above there at first seemed nothing but gray stone, then, right by Sue Annie, Milly saw a narrow crack, sloping steeply upward, but so narrow it didn't seem that even Sue Annie could get her thin old body into it edgewise.

Sue Annie explored it with her hands. "I'll try it," she said, "but if'n it peters out fore I git to th top er runs into th hillside, I'll have a time a gitten out." She inserted herself into it, pulled herself upward for a little space, then called down to the waiting Milly, "Now, if'n I start a fallen—why, don't try to ketch me—we'd both land in the river."

Milly could not turn around, but crawled backward until she lay with her face by the bottom of the crack, the lantern in it. She could see nothing of Sue Annie but could hear her grunts, the scrape of her shoes on the stone, and once the tearing of cloth, but no word, not even an oath.

It seemed a long while that she waited, peering up into the darkness, hearing the river—reaching up for her, it sounded—listening always for Sue Annie, but some part of her mind noticing now and again that she was hearing Sam and Vinie filling the night with their hot wild hunting cries—mad and glad they sounded, as when King Devil ran—then Sue Annie was crying in a gasping but jubilant voice, "Praise God, Milly, I'm at th top an I see a light pretty close by. I do believe we've come smack to where we want to go. You can start now; it's a powerful hard pull, an you'll have to leave th lantern."

Milly pressed her palms hard against the stone and rose on her knees, trembling a little; the empty darkness and the crying river seemed pulling at her hair as she moved up to the crack, then slowly, and with a feeling of having found refuge, she edged herself into it and felt hard stone under all her body and more stone so close to her back that when she drew up her knees her hips came hard against it.

The lantern was just below her in the bottom of the crevice, safe from any wind, and for a little space some light seeped past her, then the angle of the crack, from being gently sloping, steepened, and she could see nothing, not even her hands, pressing, clawing, pulling in front of her. She felt the skin scrape from her hands and knees and knew her Sunday coat was ruined along with the already ruined shoes; but she grunted and groaned as little as possible, for Sue Annie, with more breath to spare than at any time since they had reached the river, was continually calling down encouragement and advice, as if she thought Milly couldn't do what she had done; and Milly wondered, somewhat enviously, if, come forty years from now, when she was as old as Sue Annie, she could make this climb, or if even now she would have had the nerve to be the one to go ahead. For if she hadn't known that Sue Annie had got through, she would have stayed stuck in some of the tighter places or never got up some of the steeper ones where the wall was smooth, offering no handhold, and it was only by pressing a hand and a foot on each side, like a woman climbing a well, that she was able to go on.

Sue Annie grew impatient and kept telling her to hurry

—the baby would be borned and the woman flooded to death if she didn't get on; and Milly gritted her teeth and scraped with her knees and pushed with her toes and wondered whether, if she fell, she would bounce from the ledge and land in the river or would she hang on the treetops. Then Sue Annie was calling down in great excitement, "Milly, when Nunn sobers up you can tell him Sam and Vinie are th best rabbit-chasen foxhounds in th country —can you hear em?"

Milly could hear nothing but her pounding heart and her breathing, yet gasping she answered, "It's a fox they're a chasen."

"There ain't no foxes in th Cow's Horn. It's bound tu be a rabbit."

Milly could not then answer but in a moment gasped, "Then you got turned around in the river a it's your own river bluff we're a climben an your own light on th top a th hill you're a looken at."

"Jesus, God," Sue Annie said, and the thought held her silent while Milly climbed and at last felt with one high-reaching hand the top of the bluff.

Sue Annie heard her, hunted her hand in the dark, found it, and heaved.

"Don't lean back," she warned, "er you'll go right over. We're right on th edge. I'm a holden to a little tree."

She pulled and Milly pushed and heaved until instead of Sue Annie's hand she felt the rough bark of a little tree and stood clinging, gasping. Sue Annie was right; they were at the top, clean above the river fog—she could tell where the black hills across the river ended and the sky began— and turning around she could see a light high in the sky, like a house on one of the rolling hills in the Cow's Horn or the way Sue Annie's light would look if a body climbed up to the edge of Sue Annie's old cow pasture—for wherever they were, it was fox country. Sam and Vinie had chased him out of the bluff onto a hillside, it sounded from the way they ran, and it sounded too as if they almost had him. She'd never heard them sound so gay and glad, so vigrus mean.

Sue Annie was crashing up through the brush on the gently sloping hillside. In a moment Milly stumbled after her, toward the light. It wasn't Sue Annie's cabin, most likely Hattie's—she lived downriver from Sue Annie, and

King Devil had used to run a lot in the river hill there. Lord, Lord, Cordovie or no, she'd be glad to get home into some clean dry clothes—maybe Nunn had come—she hadn't thought of him since she'd learned about Willie's boys.

"Praise God, praise God," Sue Annie was gasping. "We did git acrost. There ain't no good sound stake an rider fence like this anywhere's close to my place."

Milly stopped and listened. Sam and Vinie were working up the river bluff, and it sounded like King Devil and he wasn't taking much time to throw them off the scent—maybe couldn't.

"Where are you, Milly?" Sue Annie was calling. "A listenen to them hounds chase rabbits? That younguen 'ull be a walken fore we git there."

Milly followed her voice and came soon to a rail fence and after that they walked across a rolling cornfield where, in the fog-free dark, fodder shocks stood out against the sky, and Sue Annie's petticoat tail was a bobbing band of whiteness below her coat.

They neared the square of light falling through an open door that showed a porch post and a gourd dipper hanging from a nail. "I wonder where we're at," Sue Annie whispered, then cleared her throat and called from the porch steps, "Is anybody home?"

"Saints alive," a booming voice came that they both recognized as Ann Liz Cooksey's, and then the big woman was rushing out the door. "Saints alive, you must a flew. An here me an Keg Head's woman was a thinken you mightn't git here atall."

"Why?" Sue Annie asked, and wrapping her coat around her to cover up her lack of a skirt, strode into the house, not even answering Keg Head's wife, who cried in admiration, "You two crossed that rush-tide river in th dark!"

Milly followed and found herself in a clean bare one-room log cabin furnished with two beds and some split-bottomed chairs near the fireplace, and with a door opening into the lean-to kitchen with a little step stove smaller than her own.

A pale, plainly frightened woman looked up at Sue Annie from the bed in the further corner. "I'm shore glad to see you," the woman said with glad, beaming eyes, "an I shore thank you for comen so quick an all—already I feel better." Her drawn-up knees began a violent quivering. She glanced at them with a forced, apologetic smile. "I don't know why they act thataway," she said. "I ain't to say skeered."

"Lord God." Sue Annie rested with a hand on each quivering knee and spoke with her widest and kindest smile. "You ain't got a thing to be afeared of, woman. Everything's a goen to be all right—a little childbed shakes you've got, that's all."

Cordovie tried to smile again, but only swallowed. "Mebbe it won't be like th last time. I flooded so—I couldn't hardly git my strength back to do my work fer th longest time, an I didn't have no milk fer th baby, and it just got punier an punier till it—"

"But I ain't a goen to let you flood," Sue Annie said, still leaning on the woman's knees and smiling. "You an th baby are both goen to be all right—it's a goen to be a boy an be a President. First time I ever brung a baby in my petticoat tail—we got off th path a little an got tangled in th briars—an it's th first time I ever borned a baby with no man person around an two foxhounds fer company."

"But Keg Head's here," Keg Head's wife said; she was a tall, thin, whey-faced, big-eyed woman, spoken of always, on the rare times someone chanced to mention her, as Keg Head Cramer's wife. And though Milly had known Keg Head since she had come to the valley, this was the first time she had seen his wife, and never had she heard him call her by name, but always as "my woman" or "th old woman."

Sue Annie turned around and looked at her, then smiled at Cordovie. "I said 'a man,'" she said.

Fear lifted a little from Cordovie; she giggled almost gaily, but a pain caught her in the giggle as she lay grunting and straining.

Ann Liz and Keg Head's woman hurried forward each to take a hand, but Sue Annie, watching Cordovie critically, waved them away.

The pain was short and Cordovie managed to smile. "They're a comen along good," she said. "I wisht Silas— that's my man—was home; he's gone away to work in Muncie, Indianie, an don't—"

"Evenen, Miz Tiller. Evenen, Miz Ballew," Keg Head said, coming through the door.

"I thought you was a prayen," Sue Annie said, straightening up from Cordovie.

"I was out by th barn," he said in his Sunday voice. "Maybe God heard me an helped you over that wild river on this dark night. It was shorely Him who guided your footsteps so's you could come so soon."

Sue Annie frowned and glanced about for a clock, and finding none, looked at Keg Head and smiled. "It ain't so soon, but we'd a been here a sight sooner if'n we'd a had a decent boat an th lantern hadn't run out a coal oil so's we lost th path on that pitch-black river hill—but it's soon enough fer Cordovie."

Keg Head pulled out his watch. "By railroad time it's ten minutes an two seconds after eight o'clock—not much more'n two hours since Ann Liz called you—an it's mighty nigh an hour's walk frum Ann Liz's place to here after you git up th river hill."

"Lord God, man," Sue Annie said, taking the cup of coffee Ann Liz brought from the kitchen, "you didn't think I'd walk when I had that good swift river to bring me along. We rid th current till we was jist acrost frum Cordovie's landen an above th big bend, then all we had to do was climb th hill."

Keg Head shook his head and looked at her in grudging admiration. "They's many a man forty years younger than you that wouldn't risk that swift water in th dark in nothen but that little skiff—an many's th man couldn't do it," he said with another shake of his head.

"I bet I'm a looken at one now," Sue Annie said with a pleasant smile.

Milly smiled when the others smiled and nodded over their talk and wondered if her face was full of blood and mud. She knew her hair was all torn up like Sue Annie's —that was what made Ann Liz stare at her so. And Keg Head's woman didn't act a bit friendly—uppity somehow —maybe she was a distant-turned woman with an uppity way for everybody; but even Cordovie had given her what had seemed a strange swift pitying look when Sue Annie told her who she was. She was glad when Keg Head said he'd go back to watch and pray some more;

he was always looking at her like he wanted to say something.

Cordovie had another pain. Sue Annie finished her coffee hastily, then declared it was time she got scrubbed up with good strong soap and Lysol. She and Milly went to the kitchen, where Sue Annie nodded in approval at what she saw: white outing-flannel baby things warming on a chair by the stove; the open oven full of clean scorching rags; melted lard on the oilcloth-covered table to clean the baby; scissors and twine boiling in a pan.

Sue Annie and Milly washed themselves and combed their hair, put their wet Sunday shoes and coats and sadly torn hose by the hearth to dry, and soon Sue Annie, in the fresh big white baby-catching apron she had carried in her bosom, took her place at the foot of Cordovie's bed. Her small quick hands went exploring under the bedclothes while her eyes, staring down upon the patchwork quilt, were narrowed with concentration like eyes seeing what her hands felt. Now and then she nodded with approval of what she found; at other times she frowned, searching still with her hands, but there never came into her face the secretive, clamped-jaw look that came when a baby was coming breech first or the waters had been gone three days, when she sweated and never chewed her tobacco for hours on end. Finished, she smiled at Cordovie. "You're a comen along fine—everthing's goen to be over pretty soon, less'n your pains stop."

"Then we'll give her black-pepper tea an quinine to hurry em on," said Ann Liz, who, what with her own eleven children and the help she had given Mother Creecy at times, considered herself something of an expert in midwifery.

Sue Annie spat vehemently into the fire. "We ain't a given Cordovie nothen to rile her blood all up an make it run. She don't need nothen." She considered a moment, then turned to Milly. "You're th least un an not much good fer a woman to pull to, an you're tired enyhow; whyn't you git a old grass sack an try to find some ice er snow—they ought to be some on th north side a th house; we stumbled over plenty a comen up that river hill."

"They's ice in—" Cordovie began, but another pain caught her, and she whimpered, glancing apprehensively

at the bed in the other corner to see if her noise was
awakening her four-year-old daughter who slept there.
Soon, however, she was smiling again and able to tell
about the ice in the rain barrel.

Milly lighted Ann Liz's lantern and went in search of
it, glad to be away from the women; they made her feel
strange somehow, with their eyes full of whisperings behind her back. She had found the rain barrel and was
holding the lantern and looking down to see the thickness
of the ice when she heard Vinie's scent-hunting yip in the
field she and Sue Annie had walked through.

She stopped listening; she forgot the ice, the borning
baby, the lantern in her hand, everything except that Sam
and Vinie had worked the fox out of the river hill into
an open field—and the fox, from the sound of the
hounds, could be King Devil. Hope swelled in her heart
until it fairly choked her breath away—King Devil, as
usual, had laid a trap of backtracks and crisscrosses, but
Sam and Vinie might unravel it. All life would be different if they did; King Devil was hard pressed to leave the
bluff for the open field; tired still from last night; the only
time in his life, maybe, when he didn't run for fun.

Sam took up Vinie's eager, angry yapping. They
sounded like starved hounds smelling food behind a
locked door. If only—she wondered how Nunn could sit
so still so many nights and listen—listen all night with this
hope that choked and hurt and made her want to run and
help the troubled hounds. It hurt too much—she couldn't
bear down to it like a woman to a labor pain.

Gropingly, half knowing what she did, she put chunks
of ice into the grass sack Ann Liz had found for her, carried it to the porch, wrapped it in an old sheet as Sue
Annie had directed, then left it handy by the door and
went in. The gathered women, and Cordovie, too,
stopped what she had thought was a hushed tiptoeing
kind of whispering, and all were silent as she went up to
the fire and stood warming her hands and her bare feet.

Sue Annie flashed her a kindly but strangely pitying
glance and smiled. "We was a talken about th war, Milly,
how it an them factories are a mebbe goen to git ever
man out a these hills fore it's over, an us women'ull have
to be th ones to drive the cows to th bulls an git our own
wood an go fer th mail. I figger," she went on, speaking

with a remembering sadness unusual for her, "it'll be like I've heard my granmammy tell, when all th men uv our settlement went off to help General Wayne save Deetroit an was gone all winter, an all th meat the women had was what they shot wild in th woods, deer an turkey, an them thin—an in this war it'll be a lot th same; th women an th youngens left in these hills, they'll have to look out fer theirselves, and they'll have a heap th hardest time than a lot a th men—but they'll git no brass bands an no bonuses. Ah, me," she sighed and looked into the fire.

A silence fell among the women and Milly knew that when she came they had not been speaking of the war, and then forgot to wonder, for clearly in the silence she heard Sam's hunting bay, the same full-throated singing out she'd heard him give one day when he saw an old red fox above the Blue Hole.

An instant later, Keg Head, all forgetful of his deacon's suit and his deacon's behavior, both of which he wore to all weddings, births, and deaths, came hurrying in, big-eyed and excited. "Say, ain't that Nunn Ballew's hounds a—"

"I thought you was a prayen an you're a fox-hunten," Sue Annie interrupted.

"Frum th goens-on, it's a red fox—mebbe that ole King—" He would not say "devil." "Listen—but they ain't no foxes in th Cow's Horn," he remembered, puzzled by his memory and the running hounds.

Sam sang out like a fresh-tuned fiddle. Milly hurried to the door with Ann Liz at her heels, but Sue Annie smiled knowingly and spat into the fire. "Sure, it's Nunn Ballew's hounds. What a you all think I rowed em over that wild river fer—fun? They've hunted King Devil everplace else cepten in th Cow's Horn, an I figgered it was time they tried th Cow's Horn. Milly said a comen up th hill they'd got scent a King Devil." She nodded over the hounds' crying, but turned and watched Cordovie gather herself for a pain. "King Devil's smart; he's kept all th other foxes run out an stays hisself an runs in th river bluff where no hound never goes, an does all his mean-ness on our side—here, Keg Head, grab holt a this wom-an's hand—Ann Liz, come away frum that door an git th other. What in th hell are we all a doen, fox-hunten er granny-wifen?"

Cordovie's pain was long and hard, but above her moaning grunts and heavy breathing, Sam's and Vinie's triumphant crying came ever louder from the field.

Cordovie fell back exhausted, moaning: Sue Annie smiled and patted her knees trembling under the bed-clothes. "About two more like that, woman, an you'll be through."

Keg Head, the instant Cordovie's grip slackened, had dropped her hand and rushed to the door. Milly was just behind him, peering out into the darkness.

Vinie cried with a gay swèet singing, not two hundred yards away. Milly grabbed Ann Liz's lighted lantern, and careless of her bare feet, ran down into the field. She heard Keg Head coming behind her and Sue Annie's calling, her voice angry-shrill, "You two'll git turned out a th church fer fox-hunten on a Sunday night an at a birthen into th bargain."

But Milly ran on toward the singing hounds, the lantern swinging in her hand. Something like a leaping shadow was an instant in the lantern light, then, whirling, was out again. Keg Head was shouting, "That's him—it's King Devil. We've turned him with th lantern."

Then Sam's wild cry, more a vicious snarling bark than a hunting bay, was rising above Keg Head's voice and then the thud of animal bodies in the soft earth of the cornfield; Vinie yipped once, as if in pain, but Sam was snarling—he'd snarled like that when he was a pup and tore up Deb's rag doll; Milly heard her own voice crying, "Don't tear him up, Sam. Don't tear him up—Nunn's got to see."

She jerked a cornstalk from a shock to beat away the hounds, but when she reached them, both stood motion-less, sniffing at the still form on the muddy earth.

Keg Head grabbed the lantern and swung it jerkily to and fro, trying in his excitement to see all parts of the fox at once. Milly saw the long red hair, stained in spots with new-shed blood, but gleaming still. She pushed Vinie's hard-breathing nose away and ran her hand along the fox's belly—something moved feebly under the skin—one jerk and then it was still, like the first and last struggle for life in a baby chicken too feeble for the hatching. Milly jerked her hand away, shaken by disappointment as from a blow.

"It ain't King Devil." she whispered. "It's a vixen—ready to have her litter."

"But it is King Devil," Keg Head said, studying the long-nosed, pointed-eared face in the lantern light. "Look, there's a cropped ear; an, anyhow, King Devil, I allus figgered he was a vixen, he was so sly an smart."

"Pore thing," Milly said, and again, "Pore thing, if'n she hadn't a been a vixen they'd never a caught her. That race last night tired her down—an swimmen that wild river."

"She's come home last night fore it got so high," Keg Head said. "They's lots a places higher up where she could cross with hardly any swimmen—an in summer when it's low she could wade the shoals."

"Pore thing," Milly said again, and touched the belly with its distended teats, but it was still now.

Keg Head laughed. "What a you a pitying her fer! Better pity Nunn—look at all th time an money he's spent a chasen a fox an it a vixen."

"Millee-e-e!" It was Sue Annie's voice, sharp and angry and shrill.

Milly sprang up and raced toward the house light, but in the darkness past the porch steps she heard the sound, sad and scared and lonesome-sounding, the way all her own and all others she'd known had cried, the first wail of a fresh soul in a wicked world.

She ran on across the porch, grabbing up the sack of ice as she ran.

Keg Head's wife held the lamp while Sue Annie held the purply red, squalling baby across her knees and finished the second tie on the navel cord. She glanced up at Milly's coming, nodded over the ice. "Lay it on, under the bedclothes, right acrost her belly, low down," she directed.

Cordovie was giggling hysterically, saying, "I cain't think it's all over so quick an easy."

Sue Annie looked up with an exaggerated frown on her mouth that went strangely with the gaiety in her eyes. "Lay still, woman. I ain't aimen to have no flooden here —if'n I have to prop th foot a yer bed up on sticks an make Keg Head set on yer belly. She watched while Milly put the ice in place, then glanced into her face, "King Devil?"

"Queen Devil—but leastways it was that big ole fox with th cropped ear Nunn has hunted all these years an that we'uns all has seen; he—she was ready to find pups."

Sue Annie sighed and pulled a little bottle of nitrate of silver from her apron pocket, unscrewed the cap, and screwing up her eyes in sympathy with the screaming baby, dropped a few drops in each of his eyes. "Sam an Vinie tonight has come on her unbeknowinest like—an th river riz so sudden she couldn't wade away. Git on here with that lard, Ann Liz."

Ann Liz hurried in from the kitchen with a mound of softened lard on a lard-bucket lid. "Looks like she'd a holed up somewhere on th river hill."

"I guess she figgered she's ruther die a runnen than be smoked to death er dug out," Sue Annie said, turning the baby stomach downward and slapping a great gob of the warm soft lard on the back of his head. "My notion is that onct, when she was little, she had a taste a bean penned up; mebbe took frum a den when she was little by somebody that cropped her ear an tried to make a pet uv her—that's why she was so smart an mean an a haten people so—er mebbe she liked us, specially Nunn, and she stayed around in this country an let herself be chased. She's mebbe lost half a dozen mates since Nunn got scent a her, but allus she stayed clost to him."

"Mebbe," Milly said, and turned her drying shoes by the fire and wondered why she felt so little gladness, only tired and dead inside—but the vixen had run so free: not many things could be so free. It was sad it had to die, though she was glad, of course, very glad that it was dead. She thought of the lantern left burning in the stone: maybe that crack she and Sue Annie had climbed had been her trail, and when she saw the lantern burning there, she went a new way, strange to her, and so lost time.

Sue Annie, whose spirits ballooned with every moment that passed and so lessened Cordovie's danger of flooding, told Milly that everybody who'd ever suffered from the big red fox ought to meet at the schoolhouse and set a big dinner on the ground, like a fifth-Sunday meeting, and invite Nunn and Milly and pay up the bounty money they'd all said they'd give sometime or other to see King Devil dead.

Milly nodded and tried to smile, then moved her chair a little way so that each time she looked through the door she would not see the red-gold gleam on the porch floor where Keg Head had laid King Devil by Ann Liz's lantern.

"Jesus God," Ann Liz cried and came near dropping the lard and showed neither fear nor shame when Sue Annie interrupted to remind her that she'd get turned out of the church for swearing, but went right on to say that the night's business would kill Willie, for it must have been King Devil's trail his hound was on when he kicked her over the cliff. "Oh, Lord, he'll go right back an git drunk all over again," she said.

"Mebbe he ain't sober yit," Keg Head's wife said.

"Yes, he is," and it was Ann Liz's oldest boy, standing in the door, staring at Milly and Sue Annie with big eyes.

Ann Liz sprang up, sharp scoldings rolling from her tongue; didn't he know he hadn't any business around a place like this—he'd be a disgrace to the country.

Lotho meekly turned his back and stared out into the night and said above his mother's scolding yell that everybody on yon side of the river thought Milly and Sue Annie were drowned. Ann Liz quieted her scolding, and while the women listened, he stood on the porch with his back to the door and told how he and his two brothers had started down the river with Nunn and Willie, both limber drunk and vomiting. But by the time they got to Nunn's landing, they'd both sobered up some, mostly from the rough ride in the bottom of the boat and being splashed with water all the way—the night was so black and they hadn't any light and the river was coming down like forty wild horses, so they'd gone to Nunn's—and learned that Milly and Sue Annie were gone on the wild black waters.

Nunn and Willie both had sobered up like spring-bladed jackknives and come across the river—he finished the last of his story as he ran across the porch, just remembering he'd beat them all and run home and found his mother gone and run on to Cordovie's to see if she was all right and bring them the news. They hadn't made Willie's boat landing but climbed out on the river bluff: he'd got up first and Willie had told him to run get the

lantern, and for all he knew, Willie was still lost in the
bluff, yelling for a lantern.

Milly called after him to run quick and tell Nunn that
King Devil was dead, but she never knew if the boy
heard or when Nunn knew. Not long after, she and the
other women saw lights across the field. Milly knew it
was Nunn and the Cooksey men: it seemed like a month
since she'd seen him. She wanted to run herself and tell
the news, but Sue Annie kept her busy brewing tea for
the baby, so that it was Keg Head who walked out to
meet the men.

She heard their feet on the porch while she stoked the
fire in the little stove, and by the time she reached the big
house door, Nunn stood with the other men and stared
down at the brightness on the porch floor. In a moment
he squatted down and ran his hands gently back and forth
across the red-brown flanks. He looked up at Milly and
the others gathered around, and Milly saw that his hands
were shaking; and there was a pulled wonder in his
voice, like a disappointed child's, when he said, "But he's
so little—so little," and he picked up the lantern and set
it by King Devil's head and looked into the green-eyed,
pointed face, repeating, "So little."

"Why, Nunn, she's uncommon big fer a fox—puts me
in mind a little a that cur dog that woman teacher had.
What'ud you think she'd be like—big as a yearlen calf?"
Sue Annie asked.

Nunn looked up at her, and with the lantern on the
floor and the strange shadows falling upward, his face
seemed all gray-shadowed eyes as he said in a low,
absentminded voice, "He allus seemed big somehow—
bigger lots a times than anything else in th world."

Chapter Thirty-eight

NUNN SMILED AND SHOOK his head at the grocery clerk. "It's mighty nice a you to save me back a batch a that canned dog feed like I allus use, sean as how there ain't goen to be no more till the war is over, but, man," and he leaned forward on the counter and his brown eyes bloomed with smiles like a laughing baby's, "I ain't never buyen no more grub fer hound dogs. I'm through with fox-hunten—got nothen on my mind but farmen—them hounds a mine, they caught th fox."

The grocery clerk gave a low whistle, leaned one elbow on the counter and his chin on that, and said, "How was it?"

And Nunn told the story of King Devil's last race as he had already told it that day, first to Elias Higginbottom, then to a man at the AAA who inquired after his hounds, the sheriff's wife in the courthouse to whom he paid his taxes, the owner of the farm and feed store when he went to pay his debt, and now to the clerk who had sold him flour and lard and beans, and as a special treat for Milly and the children, a jar of peanut butter and two cans of salmon. The grocery clerk whistled again when he asked what Nunn had done with Sam and Vinie and heard that he had sold them to Elias Higginbottom for what Elias said was $350 in cash and goods: $150 in cash and a whole truckload of goods. "Th awfullest lot a goods I ever seed," Nunn finished.

The clerk clapped Nunn on the shoulder. "You done good, real good—an with this war a comen on an all, it won't be cheap to feed two hounds, lessen you are a man like Elias Higginbottom. He's got so much all he has to do is set an watch it make more."

"He don't set much," Nunn said, and added, still marveling, "He's a mighty openhearted man in a trade, though," and started away, then turned back, remembering. "Lord, Lord. I've talked so much I've lost my mind. I'm plumb fergitten candy fer th youngens. Gimme fifty cents worth all mixed up, an one, no, two a them yaller an white sticks fer th baby."

And while the grocery clerk picked out the candy, Nunn asked with a hesitant clearing of his throat, "Can you tell me where I could git my oldest girl a dress—a kind a Sunday dress, not jist a dress pattern er a piece a goods, but a dress all ready made. Somethen pretty—but I don't want no uppity clerk—an nothen over $20."

The clerk directed him to a woman's clothing store just off the square, but when he went up to it, he hesitated, looking through the wide plate-glass windows at high-heeled shoes that had no toes and a dress, or maybe it was a long-tailed petticoat that had no top. He glanced down at his worn shoes and the overalls, clean and starched, but with thrice-patched knees, and hesitated, his hands damp, but he felt the four $5 bills in his pocket—the bet money he had got from Elias not two weeks back. Five dollars he'd spent on liquor that night, but the rest he'd saved for a dress, a nice dress Suse could wear to church and then to high school in the fall—for she would go to high school in the fall.

He opened the door, a revolving thing like the bank doors he had walked past but never through, and instantly his feet were soundless, as if sunk in mud, and he stopped, flushing, and with a quick guilty downward glance, thinking he had stepped on some fine soft stuff fallen on the floor, but he saw that he stood on a soft deep carpet, not thin like Aunt Marthie Jane's Turkey-red, not stopping a few feet from the door like Samuel's so a man could see what he was getting into, but right up to the doorsill, a soft pale green like leaves in the spring, too fine for his dirty shoes, and offering no island of bare wood where a man could stand in peace. While he stood uncertain of whether to risk another step or no, a soft voice said, "Can I help you, please?"

He glanced up, startled, for he had heard no sound,

and saw a woman and felt a great flood of relief: she did not look to be young and uppity and she was big, with bosoms like Aunt Marthie Jane. "I hope so," he said, remembering he had, like a heathen, forgotten to take off his hat, and flushing again and at last taking it off. "I don't know much about what I'm doen. I want to buy a dress, a nice dress but nothen flashy fancy, fer my little girl, but I just cain't rightly name th size. Somethen I bought late in th fall like, was too little."

The woman smiled. "They grow so fast. Now can you think about how tall she is on you."

Nunn flushed again. "I don't know what in tarnation ails me. I didn't mean to call her little. In her shoes she's tall as I am—a big fine upstanding girl with bosom"—he choked and in a moment went on, "of about your size an build, but just a little girl, jist turned fifteen, a goen to high school come fall."

"I think I can fit you up," the woman said. "Come this way." And she never looked at his dusty shoes. It wasn't so hard then to tell her how much he wanted to pay and that he wanted nothing skimpy in the shoulders, for she had high proud wide shoulders like his grandmother had.

But when she held the dress up for him to see, his head grew all in a whirl and tobacco juice was gathering in his mouth and no place to spit. "To tell you th truth, lady," he said and pulled the money from his pocket, "you know more about this business than I do; somethen pretty but enduren an becomen."

The clerk asked about Suse's hair and eyes, and he felt more flustered still. "Her hair—it don't allus look th same, an her eyes don't neither—they ain't so brown as mine, my wife says, but no pure gray neither. An her hair—it's mighty pretty, long and braided—in th sun it's like th copper bands on our cedar chair when Milly scrubs em fresh with ashes."

"Oh, she'd look pretty in this dress, green wool crepe, with a white collar. High shoulders are getting to be all the style now—it's the war and uniforms." She smiled. "Skinny round-shouldered women are out; they want big straight-shouldered women that can do things."

"My wife's skinny an round-shouldered an she can turn out a heap a work a day." He nodded over the dress she held up on a hanger. "Wrap it up," he said, wondering if he would have to swallow his tobacco juice. However, he made it to the street, hardly noticing in his relief that she'd only taken three of the fives and then given him back a little store of silver.

He stood a moment, breathing deeply, smiling down at the wide box of gray cardboard. A lot of money for such a little thing—more than one of his ewes with twin lambs by her side would bring—but Suse ought to have it. It was King Devil money—she'd suffered more than the others from King Devil—kept out of high school and tied down at home.

A little wind warm as a wind in spring ran up the street and flapped his old black felt hat, still held in his hand. He put it on, but in spite of all the press of people hurrying by, he stood a moment considering, sniffing at the wind, warm, blowing up for a rain, like a wind in spring —but it was spring, the second day of March. Milly and the children would be carrying chicken manure, hurrying to get the onions set before another rain came. He wished he were home plowing, turning ground with Maude and Jude and the big double-turning plow that Elias had thrown in with the hayrake and mowing machine. Almost new the plow was, for Elias's last boy left at home was going off to war and Elias would have time for horse-tended stuff no more. What he couldn't tractor, by God, he wouldn't grow, the big man had said, and that was everything but tobacco; and he had talked on about tobacco, how now, with a war coming on, it would pay a man to grow it, for it would go sky-high.

What was Nunn's quota, anyhow? Hell's bells, didn't he have any quota at all? The AAA must be crazy, and him getting most of his land in grass. They ought to give him at least an acre-and-a-half quota—that much fairly good land ought to bring in at least $800 or $900 in even a middling-good season. Nunn, when he could get a word in edgewise, had explained that he'd never asked for a quota because he had no tobacco barn, for he'd never raised any white burley—just dark for chewing.

Elias had laughed and said he could use his house for a tobacco barn; he had done that when he'd started in the tobacco business, and in two years' time he'd cleared enough money to build a tobacco barn. Now, Nunn must grow some tobacco. He, Elias, was a committeeman on the AAA and he'd see about getting him a base; if he couldn't, Nunn could grow it anyway, pay the tax for the first year, and still make money, for he was certain tobacco would be high. It was getting a little late to burn a tobacco bed, but Nunn could try it, and then, if he had to, buy his own plants. And so a part of the $150 cash had gone for tobacco canvas and seed.

The clock in the courthouse steeple struck two, and Nunn roused and hurried across the square. He wanted to be home; he wanted to see Milly's eyes when she saw the pretty black cow, her sides already bulging with her second calf, due sometime in May, Elias thought. He hadn't been certain; she was only one of more than a hundred grade Aberdeen Angus he owned; he'd been meaning for over a year to get shet of her, for though she was big and black and pretty, her beef conformation was poor, and even for her first calf she'd given so much milk it took the scours, and the herd hand had to milk her—and Elias had no time for such foolishness now, with the war. He didn't want a cow on his place that was neither beef nor dairy, but she would be nice for Nunn.

In the shadow of the courthouse Nunn saw the seller of onion sets, and the man looked up at him and smiled and pointed to the lone red onion in the pile of white. Nunn smiled back but he walked on; he didn't want any liquor on this good day: he didn't think he'd want liquor ever again.

When he reached the truck, Jaw Buster was patching a spare tire, and John, who had come, too, on some business he had not mentioned—serious business with the bank, Nunn guessed, for he had worn his Sunday clothes, or maybe he had come to a lawyer to make his will—stood and scratched the black cow tied forward in the truck and smiled at the way her black hair glinted in the sun.

"You all done?" Jaw Buster asked, looking at his bundles and packages.

"Yeah," Nunn said, stowing his parcels here and yonder in the cab. "An some doen it was," he added, and looked up at both men and smiled. "I'd ruther a fit two rattlesnakes with both arms broke than do what I've just done."

"Parten with them hounds, I bet, went hard," Jaw

Buster said in a moment, as if he'd first had to think up something to say.

"No. I was damned glad to be shet a them—ever since they caught King Devil I've hardly slept fer thinken they'd git lamed er kilt fore I could deliver em to Elias. I bought a dress fer Suse—a fancy go-to-meetin dress frum a fancy store." And as Jaw Buster drove out of town, he chattered on about the fine figure he'd cut in the store and how he'd come near swallowing his tobacco, and on and on; it was like he'd had liquor enough to make him happy drunk, and he hadn't had a drop. He stopped, realizing that neither man had answered him. Each sat looking straight ahead; seemingly they paid no more heed to his prattle than if he'd been a child.

Because he was smaller than most of his neighbors, he always sat in the middle when three rode in the cab, and now he glanced first at Jaw Buster and then at John—it seemed to him that both faces held the look not of men too full of their own thoughts to pay attention, but of men who hear and do not want to speak. He was for an instant lonesome in his joy. He wanted to sing; he wished Jaw Buster would sing, something loud and wild and gay— seemed like the damn fox had been a witch and laid a spell on his head, and the spell was gone now and he was riding home with no debts and farm machinery he had always wanted and a cow; and he would grow tobacco and make money—not much money; he'd never wanted money; just a good decent living, education more than he had had and a little piece of the world for his youngens.

He was glad Lee Roy wasn't old enough to go to war —war, that was why Jaw Buster and John were so still now, had been so still and distant-turned like on the ride out. Two mail days back there'd come another letter from Jaw Buster's brother, Olen. Mrs. Hull had taken it from the mailbag with a glad smile; her smile faded when she saw the postmark, December 3—he was still working and drilling on Hickum Field. Most of John's boys were too young or married, but he had one who'd gone west into the timber country six or seven years ago and never married and was somewhere in his middle twenties. Nunn wondered an instant if the old man worried much. But it was like some said in Town—the USA could lick the whole shebang in a little more time: the country was still addled from the surprise, but in a month or two the USA would really lay them low.

He looked up at John and the old man smiled at him, something kindly, almost pitying in his smile, a familiar smile, bringing back things long gone and dead—the night Aunt Marthie Jane had died and he, a big boy older than Lee Roy, had gone blubbering with his head on Old John's knees, and the old man had stroked his hair and smiled the same smile he smiled now. Then it had seemed to say, "Be ye good or bad, boy, drunk or sober—I'm still your kin an friend."

John was getting old; Nunn was a man with a farm and family, but John had forgotten and so smiled on him still as if he were in need of help and pity. He looked old and tired, terribly tired, but strangely peaceful, the uncaring peace of a man in his coffin; and his voice, too, was tired and peaceful when he said, as Jaw Buster coasted down the hill to the Cumberland River Bridge and the truck made little noise, "Well—I've sold my poplar timber."

Jaw Buster whistled in surprise and Nunn looked at him in wonderment, but he noticed neither. He sighed and looked away toward the river valley, and his eyes came away from the brown plowed fields as if finding nothing there they wanted, and they were empty, like his voice, as he went on: "I recken it's like Nancy says—this war's made timber high, so sell it an make my will so's there'll be no fighten an no lawyer bills mongst my youngens when I'm dead."

"Aw, you'll live to be a hundred, Uncle John," Nunn said, and tried to make his voice hearty and gay.

John shook his head. "I'm gitten on; you're th one that'll have to see about th school an take my place as election officer, an git to be a deacon an help in th church, an carry on th name. I ain't got no youngens that'll stay Paul, he's already a plaguen me to go away to work fer day's wages in a factory—he's a goen on fifteen an tall fer his age—but mebbe now he'll stay when he hears men are a comen to cut my poplar timber."

"Mebbe so," Jaw Buster said, and as if to get the old man away from his troubled thoughts, he talked to Nunn of his old slack-coal pile on the hill. They must do what the Sextons were doing—get the railroad to leave a coal car on the siding at the valley, and he would haul Nunn's slack and they'd ship it away to Chattanooga. They wouldn't get rich but they'd make something.

Nunn nodded; the elation he'd first felt on hearing how much his slack coal was worth was gone now. He wouldn't be fencing or hunting this year. He'd work on the house and the root house and use the slack-coal money for repairs, or maybe he'd put a new roof on the old barn and paint the tin on the house and storehouse. He'd like to talk about such things but did not, the men were so silent; he wished he were home, showing Suse her dress and answering the million questions Milly and the children would ask.

He was glad when they hit the ridge road and he knew Samuel's store and the end of the gravel were near. It was Friday, a mail day, and there would be people about as always; and some would laugh and joke with him and admire his pretty cow, and ask how much his farm machinery had cost and show disbelief when he told them it all came from Sam and Vinie—the same disbelief they had shown when they saw the hounds as pups, little and half weaned, and he told how much money had gone into them.

But though it was a fine day of white spring sunshine and warm south wind, Samuel's store was locked, and only Samuel's little white feist dog came yapping as the truck ground to a stop by the porch steps. "Everbody out a worken?" Nunn asked, looking around at the empty silence.

"It's th war," John said as he opened the truck door. "Be like th last time; things'ull git stiller an stiller when th men goes away."

Samuel, in his working clothes, came at last to the barking of his white feist dog; he and his family were all working to get a patch of early potatoes planted, he said. He admired the cow an instant with his eyes, and said, sure, Nunn could leave her in a field until she quieted down and he and Lee Roy could come to take her home, and leave the farm machinery by the store until he could haul it home.

They all helped unload the farm machinery and then the cow, and when the cow was safely in Samuel's barn lot, Samuel glanced again at her and then away toward the farm machinery and said, though his voice was still sounding and empty as he said it, "You've done good, real good—in your fox-hunten an hound-dog traden," and turned away to unlock the store door so that Nunn could put inside all the groceries and dry goods he could not carry home.

Nunn took only the candy, Suse's dress, some of the cloth he had bought for Milly, and lastly a lantern, a great shining thing he had bought for Sue Annie. He and the Cookseys had hunted up and down the Foley path and found the boat only a few feet above the foot of it, but had never found the lantern, though Sue Annie had insisted she left it in the path, or at least close by. It was a strange business and Keg Head had shaken his head over it—somebody was bound to have taken Sue Annie's lantern—a disgrace to the country it was, for there'd never been a thief in the Cow's Horn. The lantern couldn't have been any place else but in the path, Keg Head had insisted, for the path came up a steep and narrow bit of sloping hillside with overhanging bluffs on either side that nobody, and certainly not two women in the dead of night, could ever climb. Nunn's mind, as it had gone back many times, went back to that last race, the happenchance of it all—it almost made a man believe in things laid out and foreordained, like rows in a cornfield waiting for their seed.

"Samuel," he asked suddenly without meaning to, "do you believe in what's goen to be will be?"

Samuel smiled. "Not so much as Battle John." He laid his hand on Nunn's shoulder and said, still smiling, "I used to think you was foreordained for hell—but now I ain't so certain." He hesitated, as if his head told him what his heart would say were better left unsaid. "I figger you've still got a chance. When you've done th decent thing—then try to make your peace with God. I recken He will still save your soul."

"I feel now," Nunn said solemnly, for he had thought of it before, "that I can live a righteous life; no more drinken an carousen around. That's all over."

"I hope so," Samuel said.

Nunn wanted to talk more, but Samuel stood with the keys in his hand like a man eager to be back to his work—and he gathered up his load and came away. Jaw

Buster had already turned around and was gone with
his truck, and John's back was growing smaller as he
took the path across Samuel's ridge field down to the
valley and home.

Nunn hurried, eager to be home but glad to stop at
Sue Annie's: she'd be pleased with his gift of a fine new
lantern and she'd want to hear all about what he'd got
for the hounds, and most likely he'd never get away
without showing her Suse's new dress.

But no one came to his knocking, and the bucket of
water on the porch was warm and flat, as if Sue Annie had
been long gone from home.

He walked around the cabin and found old Dave in a
spot sunny but sheltered from the wind, drowsing with his
cane between his knees. He roused somewhat at Nunn's
coming and stared at him a moment with his faded blue,
farsighted-seeing eyes, and knew him then and said,
"Howdy, Nunnie, boy. I thought you was home."

And Nunn could not tell whether under his lowered
lids he slept or stared away past the river and into the
Cow's Horn, but when he asked, "Where's Sue Annie?"
the old man answered, without looking at him, "Down
at your place."

Nunn started to speak of the lantern but did not. Dave
was so old, past eighty, and had grown feeble through
the winter, and with his deafness and his stillness was
so shut into his world, so far away, that talking to him
was like walking a long way to get into a house and finding
it locked.

He came around the house, but at the porch corner he
stopped as he had stopped at other times when the
trees were bare, for standing there, he could look down
and see his house and most of the rolling valley fields
and much of the hillside pasture fields above. And he
saw more clearly than before how much the fire
had cleared away, and he saw for the first time how clean
and new and fine his fences looked, all shining in the
sun, and that his pasture fields where the tame grass and
clover grew were turning green, greening before any of
the other fields around. The maples by the storehouse
were reddening up with bloom, and under them, like
white dots on the grass, he saw his sheep, with Maude
and Jude and Betsey grazing not far away. Before many

springs had passed, all his valley fields would be green with grass in the early spring, and where less than twenty ewes with lambs grazed now, he'd have a hundred big black-faced ewes.

The memory of his first winter on his own land came back to him, the winter before the spring when King Devil first came to steal all Milly's hens. That first winter had been cold, but it was good to be out of the hot stinking mines and work always above ground and feel the cold or the rain or the snow as he worked. He saw himself again on a cold snowy twilight when the frozen hills lay around the valley like blue iron, and he walked home from the big barn and saw ahead, fainter even than the early stars, the yellow light of the kitchen window, while just behind him there was the rustle of fodder being lifted from the manger by Betsey's hungry lips and the crunching sound of Maude eating corn, and across the frozen storehouse field the northwest wind came bitterly through the blue twilight. But warmer than the wind was cold was the thought that all things—the animals behind him in the barn, the woman and children behind the yellow light ahead—were safe and warm and fed, secure behind the land and his own two hands, just as the valley lay walled from the bitterest winds by the hills—then King Devil came, and he had forgotten maybe what his two hands were for.

A gust of wind rocked the plum trees by Sue Annie's kitchen windows and whirled a brown winter-weathered oak leaf past his face. Aye, Lord, the new oak buds were pushing off the old. Spring it was, and he'd better git a move on if he meant to pile brush and burn a tobacco bed by sundown—he'd have to do it today; the wind was blowing up for a rain.

He ran down the short-cut path but stopped at the foot-log and listened, hoping Milly and the children had heard his feet on the rocks and would come running to meet him, but he heard nothing but Bill Dan crying in the yard—a lonesome, tired kind of crying, as if he had cried a long time alone.

Nunn hurried on up the steep path from the crossing, sweating a little under his many-packaged load. Milly and all the bigger ones were hurrying to get the onions in the ground, and nobody had time for little Bill Dan,

Then he was out of the creek bluff on the rolling hillside below the little barn, and looking down, he smiled, for even in the washed red clay between the limestone rocks in the path, he saw the tiny, round-leafed plants of just sprouted lespedeza. Aye, Lord, some day he'd have grass and clover, some kind of clover on every foot of his cleared land except a little bit for garden truck and tobacco and corn; and sometime between crop making and haymaking he'd burn a limekiln and spread the lime in some of the sandfield swags where the land was sourish and up in the hillside pastures where the limestone petered out and the sandstone began.

Three ewes were drinking from the water trough, and when he came around the little barn they lifted their heads and looked at him, recognition as their provider of hay and corn in their mild eyes, and one, more gentle than the others, came sniffing at his hands. He glanced at her, then looked up toward the upper garden, but Milly's onion rows were empty—maybe they were all done. They must be, for now, above Bill Dan's crying, he heard Lucy on the big road gate singing some kind of little song, something old Andrew must have tried to teach her at school and she'd misunderstood the words, for over and over she sang in a sad little humming voice: "O cobweb, come an dance for me beneath the shining sea."

She never noticed his coming, but stared out along Preacher Jim's road as if looking for someone; he saw that her dress was torn and dirty and her pale straight hair tangled about her face—Milly oughtn't to let the youngen go so; she didn't look like she'd had a dab of water or felt a comb since she went to bed last night. "Why ain't you a hepen yer mom, Lucy Mae?" he asked.

She jounced a little on the gate and broke off her humming song and smiled, and he saw that her face was dirty streaked, as if from many dried-up tears. .

"Mom told me to stay on th gate," she said, and leaning from the topmost bar, she reached her skinny dirty arms and caught his neck and gave him a hard tight squeeze. "Oh, Pop," she whispered, "why is it Mom'ud ruther see Suse dead in her coffin like Lureenie—and buried in the graveyard like Tom an Angie Mime?"

"You're a thinken things. Th one-eyed woman in th

Blue Hole'ull git you fer handlen sich talk. Yer mom ain't said nothen a th kind."

He spoke to the top of her head, snuggled now into his shoulder like a blind wet kitten, snuggling into the first warm thing it found that offered refuge from the cold. He saw a red switch mark on her arm and said, still stroking her hair, "You've been up to some meanness—an yer mom's had to whip you. Ain't you ashamed?"

Lucy shivered and clutched his neck the harder. "She told me not to listen an sent me away—I went back was why she whipped me."

"Listen?"

"Hello, Pop." It was Lee Roy in the doorway of the little barn where the corn was stored. "Th meal is runnen low," he said, "so I thought me an Deb ud shuck out a turn a corn." He never looked to see what Nunn carried or asked about the hounds—and Nunn remembered now that when he left with Sam and Vinie at daylight he'd told Milly and the children a lie—a little white lie. He'd said that since he had to go to Town for seed and such, he'd take the hounds along and have them shot against rabies as Elias had been plaguing him to do since they were pups. He hadn't wanted Milly's carrying on and telling them good-bye like they'd been humans and the children blubbering on the gate—and now he recollected how Lucy had cried and hoped the mad-dog needle wouldn't hurt them the way the county-health needles hurt her. But Lucy didn't recollect.

Lee Roy would ask in a minute now about the hounds, and Milly would come running down the path to meet him. He pulled Lucy's arms from his neck, went through the gate, and smiled at Lee Roy. "I've brung you a heap of things you've allus wanted, boy—a mower—" Lee Roy's eyes in his tear-smudged face were like Lucy's arms, reaching out to him, clinging, never noticing the bundles in his arms. He took a step forward as if he, too, would fling himself on his father, but stopped, as if remembering his father was only Nunn, a man, and held no ease for pain or refuge from all-embracing trouble. His jaw quivered and he angrily pushed back the long red hair he'd been trying to train into a pompadour and turned back to the corn.

Nunn strode up through the yard, his arms still burdened with the forgotten bundles. He found the kitchen empty, with the cookstove cold, and it seemed to him his feet rang hollowly across the kitchen and through the middle room in the still house, as on the day when he had unlocked the door to move in from the mines.

But the fireplace room seemed full of people; they sat stiff and still by the low fire, as if they watched about the dead. He saw Keg Head Cramer and the newly sanctified Rans and Sue Annie and Milly and Suse—and that was all; it had seemed like a lot because at his coming all the eyes had turned on him, and for a moment the eyes were like the hands of men strong beyond mortals, all pulling him to pieces. Then he was looking into Milly's eyes alone; he saw sign of sorrow and much weeping, not the quiet resignation of unembittered sorrow that had fallen on her when the babies died, but all flamed about with shame and anger.

He understood something of what must have happened and glanced quickly at Suse, and it was hard to think that she was so big and a woman grown, for her eyes looking into his were his child's eyes, scared, but more hopeful than scared, the way they'd used to look when Milly told him of some little meanness she had done, fighting the Tillers maybe, or loping Maude bareback across the field.

Keg Head and Rans—the bundles slid all unnoticed from his arms and he was leaping across the hearth, crying "Rans!"

Sue Annie and Milly and Keg Head were all upon him, and Rans was backing away, holding out his empty hands.

"It was Mark, you fool," Sue Annie shrilled, but there was kindness in her hand on his arm.

He looked down and saw clamped in his hand his old long-bladed knife; all unknowing he'd opened it in his pocket, the instant he shoved his hand in. It was a trick he'd learned in the rough wild years in the coal mines, opening his knife with one hand and the hand in his pocket, but never had he done it since coming to the valley.

Milly pushed him gently into the chair in which she had sat. "A knife won't do no good—now," she said, and then spoke on in a low voice, choking now and again on the words. "It was a pretty day this mornen—she hadn't been feelen so good—so's I told her that while th rest of us was setten out onions she could take th eggs up to Samuel's an git all th worth a them in cloth fer herself—mebbe enough fer a dress. I thought it uncommon strange she didn't want to go, but I kept her till she started gitten ready."

Milly dropped her head and spoke to the hearthstones in a still lower voice. "I jist happened to run back to th kitchen to remind her to recollect thread when I seed her, all a pullen an a heaven—to make that new blue dress I made with a tight band fer th revival—fasten on her middle.

"She looked at me—an me at her; an she knowed I knowed. I asked her an I begged her who it was, but she wouldn't tell. I recollected then that tea Sue Annie had brung her th mornen after th fire—and then I recollected Keg—people acten kind a quair t'other night when me an Sue Annie went over th river. So I sent fer Sue Annie—she knowed; she seed em meet in church thet night we thought she rid home by herself."

Nunn got up, walked close to Sue Annie. "I recken you smeared it all over the country. You—you could ha come to me."

"I didn't know nothen to smear," Sue Annie said, "an I wasn't th only one seed em meet in th church house an then leave close apart an then learned Nunn had gone fox-hunten that night, but nobody said anything—they dasn't; they knowed nothen to say, till he come back," and she turned her black scorching glance on Rans. "That night after th fire, he come to Joe C.'s. a asken an a hinten an a prayen fer her, an a sayen Mark, when he went back to Deetroit, had stopped to see him in the jailhouse an said he loved Suse mighty well—an he kept on a hinten around till we all knowed, an pore Suse showed somethen was wrong—but people stood up fer her. Samuel got wind uv it an sent word down by me to tell Rans to read his Bible where it says: *A wicked man walketh with a froward mouth. He winketh with his eyes, he speaketh with his feet, he teacheth with his fingers; he deviseth mischief continually—*"

Nunn looked at Rans and then at the knife in his hand. Milly tried to pull it away. He let her take it and turned to Keg Head. "A knife's no good—talk's no good—but

that boy a your'n has got to come home from Deetroit—
an marry Suse—he's a comen if'n I have to go git him."

Suse sprang up and stood and stared at Nunn in unbelieving terror.

"Amen, Brother," Keg Head said, with something of
the same gleeful smacking of his lips with which he ended
a grace. He talked on then, smiling a little, looking first
at Nunn, and then at Suse's pale, twitching face. "When
I first got wind a th matter, I said a marryen we'll have
to have—an that's why I've come. Nobody sent fer me."
And he explained how Rans had gone early to Hattie's
to cut her some wood because Joe C. was gone, and while
Rans was there Ruby had gone to Sue Annie's to borrow
lard, and Dave had told her Milly had sent Lee Roy for
Sue Annie with word that it was something about Suse.
Rans had known what the something was and left his
woodcutting and come back home to fetch his father.

"An he come," Sue Annie said, "fer to take Suse home
with him."

"It would stop the evil tongues," Keg Head said, "an
show th world that me an Nunn Ballew both wants to do
th right thing. In th old days when preachers was scarce
in th country, if'n th girl an th man set up housekeepen
an give notice to th neighbors, nobody thought hard a
them fer not waiten till a preacher passed by—but if'n he
didn't have no house, th girl moved in with his folks an
they was man an wife in th sight a th neighbors an God."

Nunn said nothing, never glanced at Suse when she let
out a shivering "No."

Keg Head gave her a smiling yet somehow spiteful
glance, and turned again to Nunn. "It ain't our fault th
girl—an my boy, too, has done wrong; but it'll be our
fault if we don't try to set it right. Let Suse come home
with me. My old woman's big in fer it, too; it ain't the
end a th world, she says." He gave Sue Annie a smiling
look. "Sue Annie here knows they's many a first baby
born fore its full time's up; Suse won't be th first un it's
happened to. My old woman won't hold it agin her; 'bring
her on and leave her stay till we can git Mark home,'
she says." He took a step nearer Nunn, looked down at
him while he said, "Man, do you know what folks are a
sayen? Why, they're a sayen you cain't make Mark marry

Suse—it's a disgrace; but leave her come with me an it'll stop th evil tongues."

Nunn stood with clenched hands, looking up first at Keg Head and then at Rans, both tall men—hitting them, killing them would do no good—but Mark, he was the one. "How do I know he'll come? But if'n he don't, I'll—"

Keg Head smiled. "Oh, he'll come—sooner er later. Th way I heared it, he's wanted to marry her all along; but th young lady here, she wasn't in th notion."

"Is that right, Suse?" Nunn asked in a low dry voice. Suse nodded slowly above her twisting hands.

"Did he say anything about marryen after—after—"

She nodded again, without looking at him, then whispered, "Fore he was leaven he said he mebbe ought to marry me—but like he didn't—didn't want to."

"An what did you say?" he went on.

She lifted her head with the old familiar quick proud gesture. "I said I didn't want to."

Milly's face flushed red with shame, and Keg Head said to Nunn in a good-humored chuckling tone, "I've heared say they's many a gal gits cold feet an wants to back out on her wedden day. Suse's all riled up now; her an her pore mammy, too; an Mark's a feelen hurt—but soon as I write him I've brung her home with me, he'll know she means business now an he'll come."

"Oh, Nunn," Milly burst out. "I've tried all day to git her to go quietlike home with Keg Head an spare you this an let me a told you when we was by ourselves together—an all this talken an th other youngens a hearen th talk an mebbe a knowen—but all Suse ud say was, 'Wait till Pop gits home.' An me a tellen her that you an nobody, not even God, can undo what she has done."

Nunn felt the rough chimney rock with his hand and leaned against it; it was good to feel the rock, so hard and old and firm— Samuel had said to do the decent thing—and Lucy hanging on the gate, crying every day from the gibes of the children at school, "'Lucy's sister Suse is a witch, witch; she can have a baby thout a man.'" And the AAA boys or Pinkney Deegan or Elias visiting, "That your least un, Nunn?" "No—that's my oldest girl's." And Milly, crying, praying, quarreling. And the child—"come-by-chance; come-by-chance; your long-tailed mammy lost her pants." And Lee Roy, sullen and silent and knowing. But Suse—Suse, who'd never lived by God and the neighbors no more than he, to go as Keg Head's hired girl into the never done work of raising Lureenie's children along with her own and waiting on Keg Head and his wife in their old age; Suse, the proud one, to be tolerated and shamed and prayed over.

He never noticed the breath-held silence and the waiting eyes. Suse's eyes, he knew, were on him, coming to him like Lucy's arms—funny she could hold her head up enough to look at him, hold it proud and high. He couldn't hold his head up: all these years he'd held his head down in a way, drinking and fox-hunting and carousing around, but that was over now. He felt the hand-hewn stone pressing into his palm—but that was over now. The chimney rocks were very old; long before Preacher Jim was born there'd been a cabin here, and Preacher Jim's father had torn it down and built a new log cabin around the old chimney, and Preacher Jim had built onto it and—the stone was very hard and very old—it would maybe outlive this house and Lee Roy some day would build a new house, another new house, around the old chimney. Suse's eyes looking into his were young and soft and hopeful.

"Suse," he said, leaning now with both hands behind him, palms pressed against the stone, "I ain't a holden th wrong you've done agin you—but this fire—it's never warmed a bastard."

He heard Milly's low moaning "Oh," but Suse was silent, standing still with her head lifted, looking into his eyes; she was addled like a person listening for thunder when the lightning comes so close they never hear the thunder. She kept her head up and looked at him until Sue Annie spat quid and juice into the fire with a loud angry splat. The little sound brought her back to the world and she understood what he had spoken, and slowly her bright head drooped lower and lower, like a rain-drenched sunflower at twilight. She never looked at him or anyone, but walked away from the fire and through the middle door.

He heard her slow feet across the middle room and out the kitchen door, and Keg Head was saying, "I'll go with her now; you bring her things, Rans."

What were her things, he wondered—nothing but the clothes on her back. He wished Sue Annie and Rans would go away—but they were whispering in the kitchen; he'd never heard them go. Only Milly was left, Milly with her hands reaching up to the mantel and her face on her upstretched arms—Suse's head had almost touched the mantel. Milly was crying. He hated the ugly sniveling sound she made; he hated everything. "What are you a cryen about?" he asked in hot anger. "I've done what you wanted."

"But I never thought you'd do it," she said. "You—you've never seemed to mind before what God thought an th neighbors said."

"It's different now," he said.

He wanted to go away. If he stayed, he might hit Milly. Where was it he'd meant to go—someplace, to do something. He turned his back on Milly and looked into the fire, but it was low, all gray ashes and black embers; somewhere there was a brightness, a shining thing like fire. It was the fox hide on the farther wall, King Devil's hide; he'd stretched it on a board and Suse had hung it there. It made a bit of brightness, she had said, and when the sun was low, near sundown in the winter, it would touch the hide and make it red—and so it did.

Milly was speaking, trying to make her voice sound as if nothing had happened—as if she'd never borned and raised a child named Suse. "Where's the hounds, Nunn?"

"I sold em."

"Sold em." She stood a moment, openmouthed, and then began crying again, a pent-up, drenching flood of tears.

He knew his voice was loud and wild, but he couldn't stop it. "You cry like that over two damned hounds, an your own child worse'n dead."

She looked at him, and there was a hard anger in her face and a disgust for him as a man he had never seen, not even after a long drunk. "Th hounds was th onliest real fine things we've ever had an—oh, Lord, Lord," and she went away.

Not long after, he heard the jingling of her milk bucket as she went down through the yard—it was too soon for milking time—mostly, he guessed, she wanted to squat and cry, with her face in the cow's flank, where nobody could see.

He was still staring at the red shining hide when Rans

came in from the kitchen, and Rans, like Milly, tried to put an everydayness in his voice as he said, looking at the bit of fur, "That shore is a pretty thing, now; you'd ought to hand it down to your grandchildren fer a keep-sake."

"I figger it'll be handed down," Nunn said.

Rans glanced curiously at Nunn, then turned away toward the fire, taking a Bible from his pocket as he did so. "While I'm a waiten fer Milly to git back an git Suse's plunder together, I think I'll read th Bible awhile. I'm a readen it straight through like Samuel advised, all th way, a skippen nothen."

Nunn said "Yeah," without turning his head.

Rans nodded, settling himself in a chair. "It's mighty hard readen in places, an I git along slow, but I figger it's worth it—but right now seems like I been a folleren th children of Israel into th Promised Land ferever—an what a time they're a haven—what a time—but, praise God, th most a them got there."

"I wonder," Nunn said, still staring at the hide, "if'n th ones that got there ever thought about them that died on th way."